EARLENE FOWLER

Author of
*Arkansas
Traveler*

"Engrossing...
a compelling story
of families torn
apart by divided
loyalties."
—*Publishers Weekly*

SEVEN SISTERS

A Benni Harper Mystery

BERKLEY
PRIME
CRIME

$6.50 U.S.
$9.99 CAN

DON'T MISS THE OTHER
BENNI HARPER MYSTERIES

Fool's Puzzle

Irish Chain

Kansas Troubles

Goose in the Pond

Dove in the Window

Mariner's Compass

Arkansas Traveler

ISBN 0-425-17917-6

9 780425 179178

50650

EAN

Seven Sisters, *a challenging pattern that features a single six-pointed star surrounded by six identical stars, was most likely inspired by an observation of nature—the Seven Sisters is a loose grouping of stars in the constellation Taurus. Although the stars in the cluster appear to be close together, they are, in fact, quite far apart.*

Praise for Earlene Fowler's
BENNI HARPER MYSTERIES

SEVEN SISTERS

"Fowler's regular characters all show significant growth; the mystery itself is satisfying both as a puzzle . . . and as a story about secrets buried in a family's past."   —*Booklist*

"As in all of Earlene's previous books, in addition to the mystery there are numerous other threads cleverly interwoven in the plot . . . enjoyable . . . well-written."
—*San Luis Obispo Magazine* (California)

"Benni is feisty, caring, loving, and one heck of a part-time sleuth . . . a not-to-be-missed view into the worlds of crime and the elite."   —*Rendezvous*

MARINER'S COMPASS
Winner of the Agatha Award for Best Novel

"Captivating . . . [an] excellent addition to a notable series."
—*Publishers Weekly* (starred review)

"Fowler's plots can be as outrageous as Ellery Queen's, her turf is Ross Macdonald's, and her tone is heir to Grafton and Paretsky . . . [She is] an up-and-comer worth watching."
—*Nashville Scene*

"Fowler's best work to date . . . *Mariner's Compass* points the way to quality reading for the heart, mind, and soul."
—*Ventura County Star* (California)

continued on next page . . .

IRISH CHAIN

"A terrific whodunit! The dialogue is intelligent and witty, the characters intensely human, and the tantalizing puzzle keeps the pages turning."

—Jean Hager,
author of *The Redbird's Cry* and *Blooming Murder*

"A blue-ribbon cozy . . . This well-textured sequel to *Fool's Puzzle* . . . intricately blends social history and modern mystery." —*Publishers Weekly*

FOOL'S PUZZLE
Nominated for an Agatha Award for Best First Mystery

"Characters come to full three-dimensional life, and her plot is satisfyingly complex."
—*The Clarion-Ledger* (Jackson, Mississippi)

"Breezy, humorous dialogue of the first order."
. —*Chicago Sun-Times*

"I loved *Fool's Puzzle*. . . . [Earlene Fowler] made me laugh out loud on one page and brought tears to my eyes the next. . . . I can't wait to read more."

—Edgar Award–winning author Margaret Maron

Berkley Prime Crime Books by Earlene Fowler

FOOL'S PUZZLE
IRISH CHAIN
KANSAS TROUBLES
GOOSE IN THE POND
DOVE IN THE WINDOW
MARINER'S COMPASS
SEVEN SISTERS
ARKANSAS TRAVELER

SEVEN SISTERS

EARLENE FOWLER

BERKLEY PRIME CRIME, NEW YORK

This is a work of fiction. Names, characters, places, and incidents either
are the product of the author's imagination or are used fictitiously, and
any resemblance to actual persons, living or dead, business
establishments, events, or locales is entirely coincidental.

SEVEN SISTERS

A Berkley Prime Crime Book / published by arrangement with
the author

PRINTING HISTORY
Berkley Prime Crime hardcover edition / April 2000
Berkley Prime Crime mass-market edition / April 2001

The Penguin Putnam Inc. World Wide Web site address is
http://www.penguinputnam.com

ISBN: 0-425-17917-6

Berkley Prime Crime Books are published
by The Berkley Publishing Group,
a division of Penguin Putnam Inc.,
375 Hudson Street, New York, New York 10014.
The name BERKLEY PRIME CRIME and the BERKLEY PRIME CRIME
design are trademarks belonging to Penguin Putnam Inc.

PRINTED IN THE UNITED STATES OF AMERICA

10 9 8 7 6 5 4 3 2 1

For

*Debra Jackson, my wonderful baby sister
and the real quilter in the family*

and

*Helen May,
dear friend and one of the most
courageous women I know*

ACKNOWLEDGMENTS

I never forget that books and lives are not written completely alone. Some of the people below have helped me with gifts of information and technical advice, some with personal support and friendship, many with touches of both. To each of them I extend my gratitude and also confess that any mistakes in the manuscript are mine alone:

O, Lord, our Lord, how majestic is your name in all the earth!

Clare Bazley—for your precious friendship, insightful comments and for the great information on quarter horses, and

Tom Bazley—for giving me one of the best lines in this book.

Tina Davis—for your special friendship and cheerful, giving spirit.

Karen Gray, deputy district attorney, San Luis Obispo—for sound legal advice, and research help above and beyond the call of duty (with an extra thanks for being such a tremendous friend).

Jo Ellen Heil—for your Spirit-filled friendship, your graceful suppport, and your prayers, I truly give thanks.

Christine "Nini" Hill, the Queen of everything—for a friendship that defies description: No one makes me laugh like you do.

Steve Himmelrich, detective, San Luis Obispo Sheriff's department.

Robert A. Jakucs, retired LAPD detective, Pacific Division.

Lynda Kay, M.D.—for expert medical advice.

Dean James and Donna Houston Murray—much treasured writing buddies.

Jo-Ann Mapson—beloved friend, writer, and shopping partner.

Mike and Magaline Messina and Lisa Marrone, fire captain, Department of Forestry—for showing me the Carrizo Plains.

Pam Munns, officer, California Highway Patrol, and Janice Mangan, officer, San Luis Obispo Police Department—for generously sharing your life and experiences.

Judith Palais, my ever remarkable editor, and Deborah Schneider, my wonderful agent.

My husband, Allen—who proves to me every day that love isn't only someplace that you fall, but something that you do.

SEVEN SISTERS

The Seven Sisters quilt pattern, like many others, was most likely designed from an observation of nature. The Seven Sisters, or Pleiades, is a fairly loose grouping of stars in the constellation Taurus. Although seven stars can be seen with the naked eye, binoculars or telescopes reveal it actually consists of several hundred more. The quilt pattern itself, a single six-pointed star surrounded by six identical stars, has been seen as early as 1845. It became popular again during the Depression era, when hand-piecing difficult and challenging patterns was popular. It is also known as Seven Stars, Evening Star, and Seven Stars in a Cluster. An interesting phenomenon of the Seven Sisters star cluster is though they appear to be close together, they are, in fact, quite far apart.

THE BROWN FAMILY

First generation:

JOHN MADISON BROWN—judge, father, and husband (deceased)

ROSE JEWEL BROWN—96 years old—wife of John Madison Brown, mother of seven daughters

Second generation:

CAPITOLA "CAPPY" JEWEL BROWN MATTHEWS—75 years old—oldest Brown sister (took back her maiden name when she divorced her husband)

WILLOW JEWEL BROWN D'AMBROSIO—74 years old—second Brown sister

ETTA JEWEL BROWN—73 years old—third Brown sister

DAISY JEWEL AND DAHLIA JEWEL BROWN (first set of twins—deceased)

BEULAH JEWEL AND BETHANY JEWEL BROWN (second set of twins—deceased)

Third generation:

SUSANNA "SUSA" JEWEL MATTHEWS GIRARD—47 years old—Cappy's daughter

CHASE MADISON BROWN—48 years old—Cappy's son

PHOEBE JEWEL BROWN D'AMBROSIO—Willow's daughter (deceased)

Fourth generation:

BLISS JEWEL GIRARD—22 years old—Susa's daughter

JOY JEWEL GIRARD—22 years old—Susa's daughter

ARCADIA JEWEL D'AMBROSIO NORTON—29 years old—Phoebe's daughter and Willow's granddaughter

GILES NORTON—35 years old—Arcadia's husband

1

"BUT WE'RE IN love," my stepson said, his dark chocolate eyes burning bright with the passionate angst of a nineteen-year-old male in full-blown heat.

"Oh, Sam," I said, trying to choose my words carefully. "You're still so young." I reached down and scratched behind my dog's soft brown ears. Scout was a part Labrador, part German shepherd mix with a suspected itinerant coyote grandparent. He gazed up at me with adoring ocher eyes.

"You were nineteen when you married Jack," Sam replied.

There was no way I could argue that point with any sort of genuine conviction. I had indeed married my first husband when we were barely nineteen, and it had been a warm, loving relationship working together on our ranch for fifteen years until he was killed in an auto accident two and a half years ago. Since then, I'd moved to town, married Sam's father, Gabriel Ortiz, San Celina's police chief, and acquired a new life. A life that included being, or attempting to be, a proper police chief's wife, curator of San

Celina's folk art museum, still occasionally wrangling cattle on my family's ranch, and often acting as the buffer between my volcanic husband and his equally explosive son.

Now it appeared love was in the air. Or a reasonable facsimile. And it wasn't even spring. Like the haunches of old mountain lions, the hills around San Celina were spotted with early September golds and tans, adhering to the old Central California Coast joke that this region possessed only two actual seasons, green and brown. Downtown streets were equally covered with new Cal Poly University students flush with excitement, hope, and abundant checking accounts. It was a natural fact that the hills would retain their dusty colors a good deal longer than the students did either their excitement or their bank balances.

"So who is this mystery woman?" I asked, leaning back against the sofa in the Spanish-style bungalow Gabe and I had called home for the year and a half we'd been married. We'd recently begun the frustrating task of house hunting because though this house was fine for one five-foot-one-inch widow lady with minimal luggage, it was spatially challenged for the burgeoning possessions of a married couple. Unfortunately we'd discovered in the twenty houses we'd viewed so far that our individual opinions as to the perfect house were as different as his silver-streaked black hair was to my strawberry blond. Yet another mid-life relationship challenge.

"She's so great," Sam said, flopping down on the sofa next to me. "You'll love her. Actually you two have met." The wide, gorgeous grin on his gingersnap-colored face made me instantly suspicious.

"We have?" I racked my brain trying to remember who I knew around his age who might be in the running. The redheaded girl with the pierced eyebrow who worked weekends at Blind Harry's Bookstore where Sam also worked?

The cute waitress with the wide blue eyes at Liddie's Cafe? The vegetarian girl in hemp clothing at Kinko's I'd seen him flirting with when I'd picked up orders for the museum? Sam, like his father, was a very attractive man, so the possibilities were endless.

"Yep."

I frowned slightly at him, gripping to my chest a suede pillow decorated with a bucking bronco. "I hate guessing games. Just tell me."

He ran his long fingers against the hair on Scout's neck, making it stand up. Scout's tail thumped agreeably on the tan carpet. "It's kind of complicated."

Apprehension rippled down my spine. "How complicated?"

"She's kind of pregnant."

I groaned loudly and threw the pillow at him. "Sam, how could you?"

He dodged it and went back to playing with Scout's hair, refusing to meet my eyes. "Dad's gonna kill me."

I didn't dispute his statement because I couldn't guarantee his dad's reaction. If not death, then tar and feathering was a distinct possibility. My place in this scenario, as it had been before, was to see if I could convince these two stubborn, emotional men to sit down and discuss the problem rationally. A headache, the first of many I was certain, started tapping on my skull's inner walls. I touched my temples with my fingertips and started rubbing small circles.

"Well," I finally said. "What are your plans?" Since he had just started his sophomore year at Cal Poly, worked part-time at my best friend Elvia's bookstore, and lived in the bunkhouse at my family's ranch, his ability to care for a wife and child was, to say the least, skimpy.

"Guess I'll just take each day as it comes."

Resisting the urge to strangle his tanned, muscular neck, I said, "Sam, you're pretty much past taking each day as it comes. You have a child on the way who will need bottles and diapers and health care and a car seat and . . ."

"Geeze, Benni, I know all that. I was hoping for a little more support from you. Lectures I can get from my dad."

And you will, I promised silently. "This girl you're in love with, how does she feel about being pregnant? Has she told her parents yet?"

"She told her mom. Her mom's kind of a hippie-type and thinks it's totally cool. Her dad's living up north in a commune or something. He's a carpenter and grows stuff in his garden to sell on the side."

I didn't dare ask what kind of stuff. What kind of family was he marrying into? "Her mom lives here in San Celina?"

"Yeah, on a ranch over in Amelia Valley. It's a winery, too."

Amelia Valley was south of San Celina about fifteen miles, on the eastern side of Interstate 101 across from Eola and Pismo beaches and Port San Patricio. Famous for its temperate climate and excellent soil, it was some of the most beautiful and valuable land in San Celina County.

If they were ranchers, then they were possibly people I knew, if only casually. Our county's ranch community was a tight, small group. "So, who is her family? Who is she?"

He stopped playing with Scout's hair and looked directly into my eyes. "Promise you won't get weird or anything."

"Sam, I'm not getting weird, I'm getting annoyed. Just tell me."

He dropped his head and mumbled a name.

I ducked my head lower to hear him. "What did you say?"

"Bliss Girard."

"What! Please tell me you're pulling my leg." If I had

another pillow within reach, I would have held it down over his face.

The absolute fear in his eyes was real. As well it should be. "I'm sorry," he whispered. "But we love each other. Really, we do. We want to get married."

"Sam, how in the world am I going to tell your father that you got one of his best rookie cops pregnant? You want to answer me that?"

"Not really," he said.

2

SAM LEFT, WITH the promise that he'd be back about five p.m., so we could share the joyful task of telling his father that he was going to be a grandfather. I hoped Gabe would be in a congenial mood since this was the first time in weeks he'd managed to steal a day to work on his master's thesis in philosophy. Sam was smart about one thing—Sunday was definitely the best day to drop this bomb on his father. Hopefully some of the sermon Gabe and I heard at church this morning on forgiveness and tolerance was still resonating in his brain. But just to be safe, I started baking M & M cookies. Gabe adored M & M cookies, and I figured after his favorite dinner of chiles rellenos and smoky pinto beans topped off by a beloved dessert, he'd be in a mellow, cholesterol- and sugar-sated stupor before we broke Sam's news. As I mixed the stiff cookie dough, I thought about Bliss Girard and her family.

Though they were an important presence in San Celina's agricultural society, I didn't know them well since they had never been cattle ranchers. Their combination quarter horse breeding ranch and winery was called Seven Sisters because, I assumed, of its location. From their magnificent Julia Morgan–designed house, which I'd visited once years ago during a holiday homes tour, there was a breathtaking view of the ancient Seven Sisters volcanic peaks that stretched down to Morro Bay, the last peak being Morro Rock.

It was only recently that I'd connected Gabe's youngest and newest officer with the Seven Sisters clan. At a departmental picnic last June she and I had a short conversation about the best way to treat shin splints in horses. She had overheard me talking to Gabe's assistant, Maggie, who owned a cattle ranch with her sister in North County, and offered an opinion about the overuse of anti-inflammatory drugs without regard to the serious consequences down the road. That worked into an interesting conversation about the burgeoning popularity and controversy of a more holistic approach to horse and cattle health. It was during our conversation she revealed her relation to the Seven Sisters dynasty, as it was known in San Celina County. In fact, her maternal grandmother was the renowned Capitola "Cappy" Brown, former rodeo star and respected quarter horse breeder.

"You didn't grow up around here, did you?" I'd asked. She was much younger than me, twenty-two to my thirty-six, but the agricultural community in San Celina isn't that big, and I was sure I'd have heard her name or seen her somewhere through 4-H, the Cattlewomen's Association, at a Farm Bureau function, or in connection with one of my gramma Dove's eclectic groups of which Cappy Brown or one of her two sisters were often members.

Bliss shook her head no. She was a small, muscular woman with thick blond hair pulled back in a neat French braid. Delicate features and large gray eyes gave her a fragile, sheltered look, and I wondered if that was a difficult persona for her to overcome as a cop. "I grew up on a commune outside of Garberville. That's north of San Francisco." Looking at the ground, she relayed the information with a wry, slightly embarrassed tone, her pale skin flushing pink to the edge of her downy hairline.

"I heard it's real pretty up around there," Maggie said.

"It is. My dad still lives there," Bliss continued, "but my mother moved back to Seven Sisters when Grandma Cappy fell off a horse and broke her arm six months ago. Mom's a nurse-midwife. I left the commune when I turned eighteen and worked as a groom for my grandma while I went to Alan Hancock College in Santa Maria. I've wanted to be a cop ever since I can remember. One time when I was eight I was out with my dad, and he was pulled over and busted for possessing some marijuana. I was really scared, but this old cop, he was really nice to me. He told me that they wouldn't hurt my dad and waited with me until my mom came to pick me up. He didn't look at me as if I were a piece of trash, and, well, I decided I wanted to be just like him. His name was Lyle, that's all I remember." Then, as if realizing she'd revealed too much personal history to her boss's wife, she tightened her lips. Her face remained rosy-colored, and a forced scowl only made her look more vulnerable.

I kept my face serious, hoping to reassure her that her revelations wouldn't affect my respect for her. "We all have people in our lives who we can say influenced us. Actually, your grandmother was a real inspiration to me as a girl."

"Why's that?" Maggie asked.

"Cappy Brown was a trick rider in the rodeo during the forties and fifties, and for a while taught a barrel-racing school out at her ranch. That's how I really came to know her. She used to take her students around the state to compete in amateur rodeos. The best show I ever saw was one she put on for four of us girls in an empty arena one morning in Bishop. She did things on her horse I'd never try, and she was in her fifties. She used to tell us that anything we wanted to do was possible, that there were no 'boy' jobs or 'girl' jobs, only jobs."

Maggie's head nodded in approval. "Sounds like my kind of woman."

Talking about her grandmother softened Bliss's expression. "She'd tell us grandkids to always ride tall in the saddle. I bet I've heard that a million times."

"And, girl, you've sure as shootin' had to heed that piece of advice a few times at work," Maggie said.

The frown reappeared on Bliss's face. "They've learned not to mess with me."

"They?" I inquired.

Maggie chuckled. "This poor little child has been hit on more times than those old mission bells. You can't blame those besotted fools at the station. Just look at her."

Bliss's frown deepened. "All I want is to be a good cop. I don't have time for a boyfriend."

Well, I thought, as I mixed the M & M's into the cookie dough, *apparently she found a little time.*

Gabe, bless his experienced little cop's heart, was immediately suspicious when he sat down for dinner at our pine kitchen table.

"So, what's up?" he asked, digging into the steaming chiles rellenos. "Did you find a house you know I'll hate?"

"Nope."

"Seriously, you're buttering me up. Why?"

I wouldn't tell him, changing the subject every time he brought the conversation back around to it. When he was almost through eating, when I was in the middle of describing the latest house the realtor had shown me, Sam knocked on the front screen door.

"In the kitchen," I called out, smiling widely at my husband.

Gabe's wary, blue-gray eyes traveled from my face to his son's, then back to mine. A small groan rumbled in his chest. "I should have known. Just what are you two plotting?"

"I'm starved," Sam said, opening the cupboard and taking out a blue-and-white stoneware plate.

"Let's finish eating," I said, patting the top of Gabe's hand.

Gabe shook his head and took another bite, his expression stern. "You'd better not be quitting school again or tell me you're on drugs or in trouble with the law."

"It's not any of those things," Sam said quickly, taking a seat across from Gabe. "I swear."

Gabe's face relaxed as he pushed aside his empty plate. "Then anything else is a piece of cake."

I unwrapped the foil-covered plate and held it out to him. "Have a cookie."

His eyes lit up at the sight of his favorite dessert.

"Better make it two," Sam encouraged.

3

"I'M WHAT?" GABE bellowed.

Sam yelled back, the timbre of his voice an eerie, younger version of his father's. "I said you're going to be a grandfather. Get over it."

I pushed my way between the two glowering Ortiz men, resting my hands firmly on Gabe's chest. "Gabe, we can work this out. It's a little inconvenient maybe, but . . ."

"I should have expected as much from you," Gabe said over my head. "And just who is this girl you got in trouble?"

"She's not *in trouble*," Sam snapped. "She's pregnant, and we're going to get married. No big deal."

"Married! And what do you plan to do then? Where are you going to live? What are you going to eat? How are you going to support this girl and her baby?"

"Dad," Sam said, his voice lower. "I love her, and it's my baby, too."

I moved from between them and watched as the realization of what Sam said hit Gabe. His Adam's apple moved once in a convulsive swallow. He cleared his throat and asked in a less harsh voice, "Who is she?"

Sam looked at me in desperation. I nodded in encouragement but kept a hand on Gabe's forearm.

Sam straightened his spine and said in a composed voice, "Bliss Girard."

Gabe's left eye gave a single twitch, then not a muscle moved on his face. I knew he was shocked, but I also knew he was drawing on every ounce of his cop's experience not to react.

Sam shifted from one sandaled foot to the other, his face flushed under his deep surfer tan. "I'm not going to ask you for money. Bliss and I will work this out."

Gabe gazed back at his son for a long minute, then turned and walked out of the room.

Sam wiped a bead of sweat from his upper lip, his brow wrinkled in confusion. "I thought he'd go ballistic when he found out who she was."

I shrugged one shoulder, unable to explain his father. "He's tired, Sam. Things have been busy at the station these last few weeks with school just starting and that homicide over near the train station. He's under a lot of pressure."

"He's really mad, isn't he?" Sam's face became sad. Then, as rapidly as a summer rainstorm, it turned angry. "I don't care if he is. It's not his life. Bliss works for him, but he doesn't own her."

I gave his waist a quick hug. "The worst is over, stepson. It'll take some time, but Gabe will get used to it. Then mark my words, he'll be the most doting grandpa you've ever seen."

"Thanks, *madrastra*," he said, using the affectionate Spanish term for stepmother. He ran his fingers through his black, cropped hair. "One parent down, one to go."

"You haven't told your mother yet?"

Gabe's ex-wife, Lydia, was a prominent defense attorney who, after a recent divorce, had moved from Newport Beach and taken a position at a Santa Barbara law firm specifically to be closer to Sam. Because of her busy schedule, we still hadn't met. Sam went down to Santa Barbara to visit her a couple of times a month. The only picture I'd ever seen of her was one of Sam and her when he graduated high school two years ago. If I'd been given twenty-five words or less to describe her I would have said: black hair, black eyes, thin, tall, gorgeous, and Saks-Fifth-Ave–classy. It was easy to see how her and Gabe's combined genetics produced a parade-stopper like Sam.

"How do you think she'll react?" I asked.

"She'll be irritated, but not as much as Dad. She was always more into damage control than Dad. Prevention is more his thing."

I raised my eyebrows, but didn't reply. Prevention, in this case, would certainly have been the more prudent action, but I wasn't about to get into a discussion about birth control or abstinence with my nineteen-year-old stepson. That was definitely in the realm of biological parental privilege. "When are you going to tell her?"

"Tomorrow. Me and Bliss are having lunch with her in Santa Barbara. Then I guess Dad and her will have a pow-wow."

The first of many, no doubt. My stomach churned slightly at the thought. "Well, good luck. And, Sam . . ."

He sighed extravagantly, resigned to hearing one more piece of advice.

"Everything will work out. You and Bliss will make great parents. That's gonna be one lucky baby."

A slow smile spread across his face. "Thanks, Benni. I really needed to hear that."

In the bedroom, Gabe was sitting on our bed staring at

the floor. I sat down next to him and rubbed small circles on his solid back. "Friday, it's a baby. It's not the end of the world."

"He's so young and irresponsible. And one of my own officers! It's just too much of a coincidence. What was he thinking? What was she thinking? What . . ."

I laughed out loud, grabbed the back of his neck, and squeezed it. "Thinking? Friday, they weren't *thinking*, any- more than we were when we were so *in lust* a year and a half ago. Remember how many people whispered about us when we got married so quickly? Did we care? Not one bit because all we could see was each other. We were in blind love, just like Sam and Bliss. It's just a fluke that she works for you. I haven't heard how they met, but I'm guessing the first time was last year when he and I tried to stop those jerks from wrecking your dad's truck. I also bet they've really worried about how to tell you about their relation- ship. I've talked to Bliss a few times, and she doesn't strike me as being a frivolous woman."

"She isn't," Gabe said, his face thoughtful. "I imagine this has been difficult for her. She must care a great deal for Sam to risk it."

"Not hard to do. You Ortiz men do tend to be irresisti- ble."

He turned and pushed me down on the bed, covering me with his heavy, warm body. "By the way, what do you mean *were* in lust? What's with the past tense?" He bent down and kissed me deeply, his tongue hard and sweet and tantalizing.

"Okay, okay, *are* in lust," I murmured, as his lips moved down my throat, setting a line of electric sparks on my skin.

"And don't you forget it," he said, unbuttoning my shirt.

"Hmm, this will be something new. I've never made love with a grandfather before."

He undid the last button and pulled my shirt back, his blue eyes bright against his mahogany skin. "That, *niña*," he said, "is something you won't be able to say an hour from now."

4

AT THE MUSEUM the next morning, before tackling my accumulating paperwork, I called the ranch.

"Did Sam finally tell you?" I asked Dove. I'd called her last night and after swearing her to secrecy, told her about the baby.

"Yes, he told me and your daddy at breakfast," she said. "I pretended to be surprised, but I suspected something was going on. He'd been off his feed for about a week. When he turned down a second helping of my banana-cinnamon rolls morning last, I knew something fishy was up. I'm already looking through my patterns for a crib quilt. What do you think of Tumbling Blocks?"

"Can't think of a more appropriate pattern, but maybe you should think about a marriage quilt first." I doodled interlocking circles on the scratch pad in front of me. "Maybe the Wedding Ring pattern."

"That's too predictable. The Broken Dishes pattern is nice, and I could make one a lot quicker."

I laughed and started coloring in one of the circles. "Not

to mention it could be a prediction of what's in their future. Are you coming into town today? Want to have lunch?"

"Wish I could, honeybun, but I'm brainstorming down at the senior citizen center all day trying to figure out a way we can earn the seven thousand dollars we need to replace our kitchen."

"Didn't the insurance company cover the fire?" One of the members (a *man*, Dove and the ladies immediately pointed out to anyone who asked) had attempted to fry some tacos and started a grease fire that gutted the kitchen.

"They covered it, but they're wanting to do it the cheapest way possible. We need the money to upgrade and enlarge our capacity."

"So, any great money-making ideas yet?"

"This is the most pathetic, unimaginative group of busybodies I've ever laid eyes on. Can't think beyond bake sales and quilt raffles. We need big money fast. Like I said, we're brainstorming today. I told them that this dang committee has six hundred years of experience between them. Land's sake, we should be able to come up with something more clever than selling cupcakes."

"Well, good luck."

"Luck is for the birds. We need cold, hard cash."

"Put me down for twenty bucks."

"Huh, big spender," she said, hanging up on my laughter.

Next I called Elvia at the bookstore and told her about Sam and Bliss.

"Did you take Gabe's gun away before telling him?" she asked, not entirely kidding.

"Tell him what?" I heard my cousin Emory's voice in the background.

"What's that low-life journalist doing there so early in the morning?" I asked. She'd been dating my cousin,

Emory, a writer for the *San Celina Telegram-Tribune*, for almost a year now. He'd moved to California last year from Sugartree, Arkansas, to wine and dine her, and apparently that's all that has taken place. We'd certainly been counting on attending a wedding soon, but we'd hoped it would be Emory and Elvia's. Emory was crazy in love with my best friend, and I was pretty sure she loved him, too. It was getting her to admit it that was the horsefly in the liniment.

"He's trying to tempt me with almond scones," she said.

"Is it working?" I asked hopefully.

"We'll see. So, how about lunch?"

"Noon at Liddie's. Bring the journalist if you want."

"So he can pay?" Elvia asked, laughing.

"Of course, what else is he good for?"

Emory's voice came on the line. "What's going on, ladies? My ears are positively flaming."

"You fill him in, Elvia," I said. "I'll see you both at noon."

I'd finally settled down to my paperwork and was composing yet another grant request when JJ Brown, one of the newest additions to our artists' co-op, knocked on my door frame.

"Got a minute, Benni?"

I glanced up from my new laptop computer, grateful for the interruption. "Sure," I said, gesturing to the black vinyl and metal visitor's chair across from my desk. "I've been fiddling with the line spacing on this blasted thing for fifteen minutes and am about ready to toss it in the trash and sharpen a pencil. Any interesting diversion is definitely appreciated."

She grimaced at the gray plastic machine on my desk. "I am the original technophobe. I'm determined to be the only person in my age group who never learns to use a computer."

"Right now I know how you feel. So, what can I do for you?"

She settled back in the chair and gazed at me thoughtfully. JJ was a welcome, though sometimes controversial addition to the group of forty or so rotating artists who belonged to the co-op sponsored by the folk art museum. In the three months she'd belonged to the co-op, her hair color had changed no less than four times. She was fond of East Indian–style skirts, sixties' bell-bottoms, and belted, rayon dresses that I vaguely remember my elementary schoolteachers wearing. Of course, on JJ they looked decidedly funkier when you added her spiky, fluctuating hair, her blue, green, or black nail polish, and the fake rhinestone beauty marks she placed in surprising spots on her body. Some of the more conservative co-op members found her off-putting at first, but her gentle sense of humor, her generosity and willingness to work, not to mention the beautiful and exacting details of her hand-sewn storytelling crazy quilts quickly changed people's minds. Her true gratitude for being included as a co-op member touched me and immediately made me like her.

"Can I close the door?" she asked.

I nodded and settled back in my chair. This sounded serious. I hoped that someone hadn't really hurt her feelings and she was going to leave the co-op. We needed our younger artists to keep the co-op from becoming too set in its ways. Her unusual crazy quilts had caused quite a controversy in craft circles. Rejecting the traditional silks and velveteens of most crazy quilts, she used a combination of vintage and modern fabrics, conversation prints, leather, bones, and antique buttons to create a modern crazy quilt that defied even the controversial pattern itself. Each of her creations carried a theme celebrating life's most important moments—birth, first day of school, marriage, divorce, death—and were starting to get noticed by certain parts of professional craft circles. All it took for an artist was to be "discovered" by a respected, well-connected folk art collector, and her career was on its way. I hoped that happened for her not only because she deserved it but, selfishly, so our folk art museum would benefit from the publicity, making it slightly easier to obtain those ever-elusive grant funds.

She sat down and twisted her legs together under her thin, flowing skirt. "Guess I'll just spit it out. I wasn't exactly truthful to you on my co-op application."

"Oh?" I said, sitting forward and lacing my fingers together.

She looked down at her hands, her face tinted rose. Her stiff, olive green, spiky hair reminded me that I'd promised Gabe I'd make asparagus this week for dinner. "I'm so embarrassed," she said.

"What did you lie about?" I prompted, feeling slightly alarmed.

"Nothing about my art," she said quickly, looking up at me with clear pewter eyes.

"So, what was it, your age? Are you really sixty-five?" I laughed, trying to set her and myself at ease. She couldn't be more than twenty-two or twenty-three. Whatever she lied about couldn't possibly be that serious.

She laughed with me. "No, I really am twenty-two. I . . . It's that . . . Actually, the person I put as my next of kin, my dad up north . . . He is, well, sort of . . . but not the nearest next of kin . . ." Finally she blurted out, "Bliss Girard is my twin sister."

"Oh." I sat back in my chair. Not a serious lie, but definitely a surprising one. Her twin? I'd never have guessed it. They couldn't look more different. "So, I assume you've heard the news."

She straightened her spine. "Bliss and Sam came by last night. They said they told you and his father yesterday, so I figured I'd better come clean."

"Why the big secret? You're not ashamed of your family, are you? Cappy's a great lady."

She nodded vigorously. "Don't get me wrong, I love my family and I'm very proud of them. That's why I use Brown as my professional name. They're just so overwhelming at times. I think that's why my mom took off with my dad when she was seventeen and lived up north while me and Bliss were growing up. She'd always felt overpowered by Grandma Cappy and her two sisters and especially Great-Grandma Rose."

I nodded in understanding. Rose Jewel Brown was more than just the matriarch of one of our county's richest and most influential families, she was practically an icon. Without her years and years of hosting charity events, General Hospital's children's wing would have never been built or sustained. Even now, the Harvest Ball she started back in the forties was still one of the premier charity events in San Celina County. I'd only attended it once, last year, since before that not only were the society people who supported it out of my social league, the ticket price, two hundred and fifty dollars per person, was way beyond my financial range.

"How is your great-grandma?" I asked.

"She just moved to a retirement home outside San Celina. You know, the one on the way to Morro Bay."

I nodded. I'd taught quilting classes at Oak Terrace Retirement Home over two years ago. Or at least I threaded needles for the already talented quilters. Before I married Gabe, I'd also stumbled across a homicide among the residents, an incident the ladies in my quilting circle there still loved to discuss.

"Why did she leave the ranch?" I asked. The Browns were extremely wealthy people who could afford to hire full-time home care for Rose Jewel.

JJ shrugged. "It's what Great-Grandma Rose wanted. Says she doesn't want to die at the ranch. She didn't even want to visit anymore. All the sisters, Grandma Cappy, Great-Aunt Etta and Great-Aunt Willow weren't thrilled, but Great-Grandma Rose always gets her way."

"That's odd. Most people *want* to die in their own homes. How old is she now?"

"Ninety-six." JJ's dainty young face looked amazed at anyone being that old. "Anyway, between the perfect Rose Jewel, Cappy and her horses, Willow and her politics, and Etta and her winery, I think my mother just wanted to escape to someplace where she could breathe. Not to mention the ever-present Silent Sisters, as Bliss and I used to call them."

"The Silent Sisters?"

"The sisters who died. Two sets of twins. Add them up and you get the seven sisters the ranch was named for."

"I thought it was named for the volcanic peaks."

"Well, I'm sure that had something to do with the name, too. When my great-grandfather came here from Virginia right after WWI, he just called it the Brown Ranch. The two sets of twins died after they moved here. Cappy was about eight at the time, my great-aunts a few years younger. Great-Grandpa Brown changed the name to honor them. They died really young—right after they were born. No one had twins in the family again until Bliss and I were born."

"That's right," I said, an old memory coming back to me—when I first met Bliss I asked her about her name. "Bliss said she had a twin sister named Joy."

JJ grinned. "That's me. My full name is Joy Jewel. She's Bliss Jewel. All of the Brown women have the middle name

Jewel in honor of Great-Grandmother. I like JJ better. It's what my dad calls me."

"So that's where Seven Bars Jewel came from," I said. The stallion they had standing stud was well known and in demand because of his ability to produce not only winning racehorses, but also superior cutting horses. Daddy had considered breeding his quarter horse mare, Reba, to Seven B, as they called him, but the five-thousand-dollar stud fee the stallion commanded was definitely more than we could afford. "He's a beauty."

"Yeah, he's the cornerstone of Grandma Cappy's breeding operation. He has direct lineage to Three Bars."

Though I didn't know much about quarter horse breeding, even I'd heard of Three Bars, one of the most famous quarter horses that ever lived. He'd produced extraordinary offspring in racing, halter, and cutting events.

I searched her dainty features for a resemblance to Bliss. "Are you fraternal twins?"

She laughed and untwisted her legs, relaxing again. "Actually, we're identical, but we've done everything to avoid looking alike. Our parents always encouraged our individuality."

I peered closer at her face, decorated with bold, bright makeup and was surprised to see that underneath she and Bliss did indeed have the same bone structure, eye color, the same arch of eyebrow.

"I fit right in with our parents' hippie lifestyle," JJ continued, "but Bliss has rebelled since she was a kid. She would alphabetize our canned goods and use her birthday money from Cappy to buy file folders to organize her school papers. She drove Susa and Moonie insane trying to turn the commune into her version of *The Brady Bunch*."

"Susa and Moonie?"

JJ colored slightly again. "My mom and dad. Their con-

ventional names are Susanna and Brad. Anyway, Bliss
moved in with Cappy the minute she turned eighteen.
Frankly, I think they should have let her live with Grandma
earlier. She probably would have been a lot happier, but
my parents believed in keeping the family together. It's not
what people think. We didn't grow up without morals. My
mom took us to the evening folk mass every week at a little
Mexican church near the commune, and she and my dad
really loved each other. Even their split-up wasn't vindictive. I had a wonderful, if slightly irregular, childhood."
The last sentence was said with a hint of defiance. She'd
obviously been forced to defend her parents' lifestyle before.

"Are you and Bliss close?" I asked, curious. There were
no two identical twins who could look and act more different, so I couldn't imagine how they'd relate.

"We've always gotten along great. What annoys her to
no end in our parents doesn't seem to bother her with me.
We've seen each other once a week since I moved back
down here when Susa did. Bliss and Susa live out·at the
ranch, but that's just a little too much family for me, so I
rent a house downtown. Sometimes Bliss stays with me if
she has to work a double shift and is too tired to drive
home."

"How's your family taking the news about the baby?"

"Susa's excited, of course. She's been looking for something to focus on since she left Moonie. Cappy's in the
middle of racing season and is always training some horse
or another, so she's distracted. She just said she trusts that
Bliss will do the right thing and handle it fine. She and
Bliss are just alike. I can imagine Grandma Cappy having
a baby in the morning and breaking a green filly that afternoon without batting an eyelash. Great-Aunt Willow and
her granddaughter, my cousin Arcadia, are scandalized, be-

ing the conservative society branch of the family, and Great-Aunt Etta's too busy with grape harvest and the crush to pay attention to anything unless it has to do with wine."

"How's that working out, having both a winery and a horse-breeding operation?" The struggle between cattle ranchers and wineries for available land was a hot topic these days in San Celina County.

"It's been nine years now, and Seven Sisters Winery is rapidly taking over the family, which is causing a lot of problems between my grandma and her sisters." She shifted in her chair, scratching around a red, paste-on jewel on her neck. "The ranch is run by a trust left by my great-grandfather, and there never was a source of conflict until Great-Aunt Etta started the winery. My mom's brother, my uncle Chase, is involved with the winery, too, and has voted at times against Grandma Cappy. They begrudge her every penny she spends on the horses."

Chase Brown, Cappy's son, was a local lawyer, former city council member, and a regular at the political shindigs I was often forced to attend these days with Gabe. He was in his late forties, never married, and handsome in that alcohol-flushed, decadent, aging-movie-star sort of way that appeals to some women.

"Didn't your great-grandfather intend it to be only a horse-breeding farm?"

"Yes, but even though Cappy's got a great reputation, I guess quarterhorse racing took a big plunge in the early eighties, and that hurt her as a breeder. She's slowly built the business back up, but it's never been the same. The winery has its ups and downs, too, apparently. Both need a lot of money to operate, but it seems like the winery is slowly becoming the family's main business."

"Wine is certainly taking over the county, that's for sure," I said. It was a sore spot among ranchers, and I heard about it constantly from Daddy, more so, it seemed, in the last year or so. Daddy and his friends called the wine people "those grape assholes" whenever Dove wasn't around to reprimand them.

She stood up and smoothed down her thin skirt. "Well, times change. We can either float with the current or drown as Great-Aunt Willow loves to say. I don't necessarily like it, but she's got a point."

I shrugged, not willing to delve any further into something I felt so conflicted about. I'd had enough changes in the last two years to last me a lifetime. Things staying status quo for a few months looked pretty appealing.

"So," she said. "What I actually came in to do besides confess was invite you and Gabe to dinner at the ranch tonight. Grandma Cappy thought it wise that we all get together and meet each other since we'll be related soon. I know it's short notice, but she figured we'd better start making plans."

"Have Bliss and Sam set a date? He didn't say anything to us."

"I think that's what's on the agenda tonight. Will you come? Oh, and ask Dove and your father, too."

"We wouldn't miss it for the world. I'll call Dove right now."

I caught Dove just as she was leaving and told her quickly about the invitation. "Are you and Daddy busy?"

"We'll be there with bells on. I haven't seen Cappy in a month of Sundays. Now we're going to be kin. That just tickles me."

"It'll be interesting, that's for sure," I replied.

I finished up the grant application and watered my scraggly fern before going out to the central co-op room. The co-op studios, once the Sinclair hacienda's stables, were separated into small storage and workrooms that accommodated the woodworkers, painters, potters, and other folk artisans. The main studio was usually filled with quilters, since it was the only room big enough to hold our two quilt frames, which could extend from crib to king-size with the adjustments of a few screws. We'd taken to renting out the room and quilt frames for a small hourly fee to various quilting groups. It was one of the small ways the museum could supplement our always fluctuating sources of revenue. I loved it when the local quilt groups rented time, because they always showed up with some wonderful snacks—quilters are often award-winning cooks. Sure enough, the room had filled with quilters since I entered my tiny back office three hours earlier, but I resisted the lemon bars on the counter, telling myself that lunch was just minutes away. Maybe there would be some left for my three o'clock sugar fix.

The San Celina Cotton Patch Quilters were working on a huge quilt in the dominant colors of purple, burgundy, white, gold, and green. Each square was an appliquéd scene of vines, grapes, and leaves representing a different variety of grape grown in San Celina County. The exotic, romantic-sounding names of the grapes were embroidered at the bottom of each square—zinfandel, cabernet sauvignon, chardonnay, pinot noir, grenache, viognier, merlot, syrah.

"It's beautiful," I said. "Who's it for?"

"It's a raffle quilt," a silver-haired woman in a Hopi storyteller quilt vest said, looking up from her work. "The Harvest Wine Festival in Mission Plaza is this weekend, and the money goes toward the free clinics in Paso Robles and San Celina. The winner will be announced on Saturday at the Zin and Zydeco event."

"Gabe and I have tickets," I said. "He loves zydeco music. Not to mention wine."

"You'd better buy some raffle tickets, then," the woman said. "A dollar a piece or five for five dollars."

"Gee, what a deal," I said, pulling a five out of my faded Wranglers.

She took my money and handed me five numbered tickets. "We thought about making it five for six dollars to see if anyone fell for it, but Edna there is making us toe the line. Still thinks she's a guard at the county jail."

Edna, a titian-haired lady in her late sixties, raised matching red eyebrows. "You gotta watch these ladies. They'll do anything to get good health care for needy kids."

"What a lawless bunch," I said, laughing.

At Liddie's Cafe downtown I wiggled through a group of tourists perusing the specials written on the blackboard in the cramped 1950s' lobby. Liddie's "25-Hour" Cafe had been the locals' favorite eating place since before my family even came to San Celina in the early sixties. Fancy restaurants and trendy cafes have come and gone, and still Liddie's survived. With its taped red vinyl booths, Formica tables, faded pictures of 4-H lambs on the wall, and country classics on the jukebox, it was more than a tradition; it was almost a shrine to the way things were. Buck, the eighty-year-old owner, didn't believe anyone worthwhile recorded songs after Tammy Wynette and George Jones in their prime, though he consented, when a few of us younger regulars complained, to allow Dwight Yoakam, Emmylou Harris, and Dale Watson a place on the roll.

And then there was Nadine.

Standing behind the counter, she eyed me over her pointy pink eyeglasses. Her matching pink uniform was crisp and clean and had one of those handkerchief name tags that no one ever sees waitresses wear anymore except on television. Or at Liddie's.

"They're in your usual booth," she said, nodding toward

the back. "You ask Emory how long he's gonna put up with that girl a-teasin' him, like a kitten with a broken-legged grasshopper."

"No, thanks," I said cheerfully. "I'll leave that fine and nosy question to you." Everyone, especially Nadine, was dying to find out when Emory and Elvia would tie the knot. Little did she know that another wedding was on the horizon before theirs. I relished having information before her.

"I'll fine and nosy you," she called after me. "What will you be wanting today, Miss Priss? They've already ordered."

"The chili any good today?"

"It won't give you ptomaine poisoning, if that's what you're asking."

"Extra cheese and onions, Miss Nadine. I surely thank you." I turned and blew her a kiss.

She grumbled under her breath, then snapped at the tourists. "For cryin' out loud, people, you've got two choices— take it or leave it." Then she yelled my order to the cook.

In the booth, Emory and Elvia were sitting side by side, not speaking.

"Everything okay?" I asked, sliding across from them. Nadine had already brought my water and large Coke. I sipped at my water and looked from Emory's face to Elvia's—her face was neutral, his troubled.

"Fine," Elvia said, but the tone of her voice told me otherwise. Her full red mouth turned downward.

Emory's green eyes were miserable and a little resigned. I wondered just how long my blond, urbane, Arkansas Razorback–obsessed, and very rich cousin would continue to pursue my beautiful but reluctant friend. It had been eleven months of one step forward, five steps back, and though he was a patient and optimistic man, his fuel gauge seemed to be moving precariously close to empty. I knew the reason she was so wary of men, a devastating relationship with a sabbatical replacement professor when she was twenty-three—one who'd told her he was single, but she later found out was married with five kids and no intentions of leaving his family. There'd been a couple of relationships since then, but none that had any power over her emotions. Until Emory. He was different, she knew it, and that scared her to death. There were so many things I could explain to him about her, but didn't. Her history . . . and her feelings for him were something she had to tell him.

Oh well, the road to love was a bumpy one—I certainly knew that. Thank goodness things had smoothed out for me and Gabe in the last few months. Maybe some gossip would take their minds off their personal problems. "You'll never guess what I found out only minutes ago about Bliss."

Elvia put a phony, interested expression on her face and straightened the collar of her forest green wool suit. "Tell us."

Emory sipped his black coffee and remained silent.

"She's an identical twin. Her sister is a member of our co-op, and I never knew they were related."

"If she's an identical twin . . ." Emory started.

I held up my hand. "I'm telling you, Emory, they're like a German shepherd and a poodle. I noticed the resemblance after JJ told me, but honestly, it was a surprise to me. JJ's a quilt artist. You might have seen some of her work around town. She makes very untraditional crazy quilts that kind of tell stories."

"You mean JJ Brown?" Elvia said. "I bought one of her quilts to hang in the children's department at the store. It portrayed some of the original Grimms' and Hans Christian Andersen fairy tales. I liked it because she stayed true to the stories—they weren't all Disneyed up. Cinderella's stepsisters go blind in the end."

"Never heard of her," Emory said. "What does she think of Sam's dilemma?"

Before I could answer, our food arrived. Elvia had a salad and vegetable soup, Emory, his favorite Western omelette with a side of avocado. Nadine beamed at Emory. "Anything else, sweetie?" she asked him.

"No, ma'am," he said, giving her his best Karo syrup smile. "It all looks so delicious I swear I don't know where to begin."

"Saved that avocado for you 'cause it was the best of the bunch."

"My dear Nadine, you are a queen among women, and I gratefully offer you my heart."

I snorted at his words.

Nadine whacked me in the shoulder with the back of her hand. "Missy, you could take a lesson in manners from your cousin here. And it wouldn't hurt you to remember that *tipping* is not a country in China." With that, she turned and marched away, her thick-soled shoes squeaking across the old linoleum floor.

Elvia laughed out loud, causing Emory to beam. The tension between them eased a bit.

"So, find out anything else?" Emory asked, digging into his omelette.

"Not much. I'll probably find out more tonight, though, since Gabe, Dove, Daddy, and I are invited to the Seven Sisters ranch for a get-acquainted dinner."

"Don't you know the family already?" Elvia asked.

"Dove and Cappy—that's Bliss and JJ's grandma—belong to some of the same clubs. I've seen Bliss's uncle around, but he's in his late forties, so we never ran in the same crowd. Bliss, JJ, and their cousin, Arcadia, are in their twenties, so they're quite a bit younger than me. Except for

Dove and Cappy, our families have never had any reason to connect."

"Until now," Emory said.

"Until now," I agreed.

"That name Arcadia sounds familiar," Elvia said.

"She and her new husband, Giles Norton, are frequently pictured in the *Tribune*'s society section," Emory supplied. "Cappy's younger sister, Willow, had a daughter named Phoebe who died in a plane accident with her husband about twenty years ago. They had one child, a daughter named Arcadia, who was nine at the time. She went to live with her grandmother Willow. A few years back, Arcadia married Giles Norton of the ultra-snobby Napa Valley Nortons. Demands to be called a 'vintner' rather than wine-maker, which is the more favored term among wine people in this easygoing little county. His father is William Giles Norton of Napa Valley fame. The family has owned wineries in Napa Valley for a hundred years. Giles is currently running the Norton Winery over the grade in Paso Robles. The winery's not very old, but everything in it is the best. Word on the grapevine, so to speak, is that he's itching to become a large presence down here in San Celina County, and he doesn't care how he does it."

I looked at my cousin, amazed. He'd only been living here eleven months and he already knew more about most of the inhabitants than I did. "Well, I'll be meeting the whole clan tonight. I'll give you both the full report to-morrow."

Elvia left first since she had a sales rep due at the store. Emory and I stayed longer, sharing a cherry cobbler à la mode.

"So, what's going on with you two?" I asked.

He shrugged his shoulders under his tailored Hugo Boss sports jacket. "We're at an impasse. I want more commitment. She's happy with things the way they are."

I didn't answer because I didn't know what to say. I loved both of these people so much, and though a part of me was thrilled they were together, I also knew it could spell disaster. Already things had become a little awkward between me and Elvia since we couldn't dissect this relationship-in-progress like we had with other men she'd dated. I didn't want her hurt, but I also didn't want my cousin, who was more like a brother to me, to be hurt either. I sighed and patted his hand.

"Enough about me," he said, setting his spoon down. "How's this unexpected pregnancy affecting you and the chief?"

It was my turn to shrug. "He's upset, of course. Thinks they're too young and too irresponsible. He'll cool down. They both have very concerned families, so I'm guessing too much help will be more their problem than not enough."

He looked at me steadily. "No, I mean how is this affecting you and Gabe personally?"

I knew what he was talking about and wanted to ignore it. But Emory, who'd been my bosom buddy since our pre-teen summer together at the ranch the year his mom died, knew better than anyone the mixed feelings I had every time someone I knew became pregnant.

"More to the point, are you okay?" he asked.

Another sigh escaped my chest. "Emory, you know how it is. We had the tests, and they say there's nothing wrong with either of us. Obviously it isn't him. He has a son. The next step is all that fertility stuff, and I'm not sure I want to do any of that."

"Why?"

I carefully folded and unfolded my paper napkin, not looking at him. "All that poking and prodding. The drugs. You know how I hate going to doctors. Maybe I don't want it bad enough to go through all that. If it happens, then great, but if it doesn't . . ." I ran my hand over the napkin, smoothing it. "Maybe that's just how things are supposed to be."

"You'd make a great mom."

I continued to play with my napkin, reluctant to confess, even to this man who had been my closest confidante since childhood, the sadness inside of me at the thought of having a child. How my mother's death so early in my life left me terrified about repeating that with my own child, how a part of me was secretly glad the decision had been taken out of my hands.

"Do you and Gabe ever talk about it?"

"Some. He's mostly concerned that I'm happy, and right now I am happier than I've been, so I'm just going to deal with what's on my plate right this moment and leave the rest to God."

"Wish I could be that wise," he said, crumpling his own napkin and tossing it into our empty dessert bowl. "I just want to grab Elvia by the hair and haul her down to the justice of the peace."

The image made me laugh out loud. "You'd better hope these tables aren't bugged, 'cause if my feminist friend ever heard you say that, you'd be seeing her taillights fifty miles down the highway before you could blink those gorgeous green Southern eyes of yours."

THAT EVENING I performed a scenario familiar to every woman on earth—standing in front of the closet an hour before the big event, moaning I had nothing to wear.

"You should go shopping more," Gabe said practically, tying a patterned silk tie in front of our long mirror. He always had the appropriate clothes for everything. Tonight it was gray wool slacks, a blue-gray tweedy jacket, and a dark gray shirt.

"I hate to shop," I said, but knowing he was right.

With Elvia's voice in my head giving me directions, I finally decided on a pair of black wool Anne Klein pants she'd made me buy, a lapis-colored silk shirt, my good Lucchese boots, and a pair of silver, turquoise, and lapis earrings by Ray Tracey, a Navajo jeweller from New Mexico whose clean lines and unusual combinations of stones appealed to me. They were a gift from Emory, who'd once interviewed the artist for an article he did for *Southwest Indian Arts and Crafts* magazine.

On the drive to Amelia Valley, Gabe casually mentioned that he had talked to Lydia earlier that afternoon.

"Oh?" I murmured.

"She's upset about Sam, of course, but I calmed her down. She doesn't know Bliss, thought she was some young girl trying to trap him. I set her straight." He glanced over at me.

"Oh," I repeated noncommittally. There was no way I was being pulled into commenting on anything to do with his ex-wife.

"She's coming up this weekend. She's staying at the San Celina Inn."

"An article in the *Tribune* said they've just redecorated. I'm sure she'll like it."

He gave a low laugh and said, "If she doesn't, they'll hear about it."

At least I had a few more days before I met this assertive and gorgeous woman. I'm not a particularly jealous person, but I had to admit it would have made me a lot happier if she didn't look quite so much like a *Vogue* model or wasn't so incredibly successful, not to mention having a child in common with my husband. I picked at a piece of white lint on my knee. In some ways I envied Sam and Bliss. It was so much easier when you're young and have minimal history to cloud a relationship.

"So," I said, changing the subject, "tell me everything you know about wine so I don't appear unsophisticated around these people." I had a problem. Not only did I not particularly like wine, I didn't like grapes—grape any-thing—the fruit itself, grape juice, grape jelly, not even that horrible grape soda pop Gabe and Sam loved so much. "There's red and white, that much I know. Now, quick, tell me the rest so I can fake it."

Gabe laughed and maneuvered his sky blue '68 Corvette down the interstate off ramp and headed down a long, twist-ing country highway. "That's one of the things I love about you, *querida*. Your complete confidence in your ability to pull one over on people even though your confidence is significantly greater than your ability."

I whacked his biceps with the back of my hand. "Do what the lady says or you'll be sleeping in the doghouse with Scout."

"He sleeps in the kitchen," Gabe said amicably. "At least I won't have far to go to the coffeepot in the morning."

"Wine, Friday. Tell me about wine. I don't want to insult Sam's in-laws-to-be. Tell me what I should do."

"Be yourself, sweetheart, with a few alterations. Drink what they put in front of you and say it's marvelous. Smile a lot. Try not to make your cauliflower face when you drink it."

My cauliflower face was what he called my expression when I taste something I can't stand. Faking it has never been one of my strong points.

"I can do that," I said.

The sky had faded to a lavender dusk when we came to Seven Sisters Road. Two-hundred-year-old oaks, leafy ash,

and a few scattered maple trees canopied the narrow, twisting road and formed long, jagged evening shadows. Though
it was still only the latter part of September, there had
been a slight frost a week ago, and some of the maples
had turned reddish-yellow, adding an unexpected color to
the dusty green of the oaks. After five miles of winding
road, we came to the entrance of the ranch. A white
wrought-iron arch was topped by the Seven Sisters brand—
two back-to-back interlocked S's. Underneath the arch,
swinging from two chains, was a simple wooden sign:
SEVEN SISTERS RANCH—EST. 1922. Underneath that sign dangled a slightly larger one carved with the outline of seven
peaks: SEVEN SISTERS WINERY—EST. 1985. We drove
through the open gates, passing still-green pastures with a
few horses contentedly browsing the ground. Farther down
the road, the pastures turned into rows of grapevines. Set
among the rows were two gray-and-white farmhouses with
window boxes filled with bright red flowers, too far away
for me to name. One of the houses had tiny, blinking white
Christmas lights scattered throughout the small bushes in
front of the wraparound porch and a Volkswagen van
painted with a colorful mural parked in front.

"California fireflies," I said, pointing at the lights.

We went by a row of stables and then drove up a slight
incline, passing the tasting room—once the original land-
owner's residence. Its whitewashed adobe walls and red tile
roof were a twin to the folk art museum. We turned a corner
where the "new" ranch house perched on top of a hill overlooking the valley. The Craftsman-style house was painted
shades of tan and brown, blending in with the oaks and
pines growing tall and lush around it. A sprawling three
stories, and lit up bright as a ballpark, it looked large
enough to house three or four families. In the circular driveway were parked a half dozen cars, including one of

Daddy's blue Ramsey Ranch trucks. We pulled in behind a gleaming maroon Jaguar.

Gabe eyed the Jag and whistled under his breath. "The gang really *is* all here."

"What do you mean?" I asked.

"That's Lydia's car. She said she wouldn't be able to reschedule the trial she was working on, but apparently she did."

I looked through the windshield at the sleek, expensive car, my heart sinking, my armpits growing damp, thankful that it was almost dark so Gabe couldn't see what was, no doubt, the cauliflower look on my face.

5

THE DEEP-SET front porch was comfortably crowded with some bent willow tables and chairs, a long porch swing, and three Adirondack benches. All were covered with identical green plaid cushions. A large, triangular dinner bell, the kind Dove used to call Daddy and the hands in from the barn, hung next to the porch steps.

"This is some place," Gabe said in a low voice.

"Eighteen thousand square feet," I said, for some reason remembering that fact from the long-ago home tour. "Designed by Julia Morgan herself. She and the judge were personal friends, I heard."

"Who's Julia Morgan?"

"You've never heard of Julia Morgan?"

His face was blank.

"She only designed the Hearst Castle, a ton of YWCAs, some big conference center up in Pacific Grove that's supposed to be the biggest arts and crafts–style complex in the country, and a good deal of the houses in Berkeley. Never got the credit she deserved, probably because she was a woman."

He groaned under his breath. "Don't tell that to Lydia, or we'll be hearing a lecture half the night on how men keep women down."

"Which might do you some good, *el patrón*," I said, my voice slightly mocking as I knocked on the carved front door. *Maybe I'd like this Lydia after all.*

Cappy herself answered. She was dressed in neat black Wranglers, a black cowboy shirt with yellow roses embroidered on the yoke, and shiny black round-toed riding boots. Except for the occasional newspaper photo, I hadn't seen her for probably ten years, but she hadn't changed much with her cropped, iron gray hair, wide, strong jaw, and tanned skin, whose real beauty was found in the deep lines radiating from her clear, gray eyes and faintly overbitten smile.

"Benni Louise Harper, I swear you don't look a day over eighteen," she said, putting a wiry arm around my shoulders, giving me a hearty squeeze. "You still riding every day? Still practicing your rope tricks?" She looked up at Gabe. "You would be surprised what this one can do with ropes."

Gabe grinned at me and winked. "Is that right? We'll have to talk about that."

Cappy held out a short-nailed, age-spotted hand. "Cappy Brown here. You must be her police chief."

"That would be me," he said, taking her hand. "Gabe Ortiz."

"Pleased to make your acquaintance, Gabe. I've heard through the grapevine you're doing a bang-up job policing San Celina. Come on back to the big room and we'll get you a glass of wine." She nodded over at me. "Let me tell you, Chief, you're darn lucky to have corralled this one. She comes from good stock."

Gabe laughed and took my hand. "My grandfather was the best horse trader east of Dodge City, Kansas. He taught me if they had strong legs and good teeth, you can't go wrong."

"Sounds like a man I'd be proud to trade with. Come along now."

"Good teeth?" I said under my breath, elbowing him in the side. "You're going to pay for that remark, Friday."

We followed her down a long hall past a dark wooden staircase toward some open double doors.

The room was large and airy with an open-beam ceiling, reminding me of the sitting room of an expensive Montana hunting lodge. The sounds of people laughing and the tinkle of glassware washed over us the minute we stepped over the threshold. The deep brown leather sofas and wingback chairs were well used and comfortable-looking with bright, geometric Pendleton pillows tucked in the corners. Old, probably priceless, Navajo rugs were tossed casually over the backs of straight-back mission oak chairs. An antler chandelier, the lightbulbs cleverly hidden among the horns, lit the room with a warm glow. Behind a dark oak bar, a picture window stretched from one end of the room to the other, framing a breathtaking view of the Amelia Valley, its orderly seams of grape rows, and the Seven Sisters volcanic peaks, shadowed blue and gray in the waning evening light.

"Wine at the bar, and appetizers are over on the sideboard," Cappy said, pointing to the south side of the room where a small group of people gathered. "Help yourself. It's some of our 1988 vintage. A good year for the pinot noir, Etta tells me, though I've always preferred the '91 estate chardonnay. We're barbecuing a top block of beef and chicken and, for those with more exotic tastes, some wild boar my son, Chase, and our ranch manager, Jose, shot a few days ago. We have wines to match anything you care to eat, of course." She glanced at an antique grandfather clock next to us. Tiny carved racehorses, necks stretched for the finish line, ran around the clock face. "We'll probably be eating in another half hour or so. Chase will pour you whatever you want." She gestured to the man behind the bar.

Chase was dressed casually in an expensive sports jacket and white golf shirt. His blotchy face and loud laugh made me guess he'd been sampling the wine long before the first guest arrived. He stood in front of seven or eight wine bottles, each bearing a version of the silver-and-white Seven Sisters label—the seven volcanic hills with three horses connected tail to nose, running in front. "If you're not a wine drinker," she continued, "we have a full liquor cabinet, and Chase once worked as a bartender on a cruise ship. So if you drink it, he should be able to make it." She rolled her eyes. "One of his many unsuccessful forays into the world of real work. The rest of the time he practices law. I keep telling him if he practices enough, he might get halfway decent at it. My two sisters are late, as usual, but they'll eventually slither in." She looked up at Gabe, her mouth twisting into a sly, scheming grin. "You and my baby sister have tangled, I'll venture to guess."

"Who's your sister?" Gabe asked.

"Willow Brown D'Ambrosio. She was one of the city council members who voted against the budget initiative that would provide the city with more money for additional police. I can give you the license plate of her Lexus if you like. She's always parking in handicapped spots using our mother's sign even when Mother's not with her."

"Well, as to the voting, it's a free country," Gabe murmured, letting his voice drift off, not addressing the illegal use of the handicapped placard.

She winked at me and gave a deep belly laugh. "He's being a politician now, isn't he? I bet he wants to string her up by her diamond-studded ears. Probably would do her good. Shoot, she might even enjoy it."

I laughed at the somewhat shocked look on his face. I'd known there was no love lost between the sisters, since I could remember Cappy talking this way when I was a teenager. Old age and maturity obviously hadn't softened their attitudes toward one another.

"I think I'll go see how Jose's coming with the meat. Let me know if you two need anything and don't let Giles, Willow's no good grandson-in-law, talk you into buying stock in the company. No matter what he says, we're not selling out to his daddy's corporation."

"She's certainly something," Gabe said, watching Cappy stride across the room.

"That's mellow for Cappy," I said. "You ought to see her when she's really aggravated." I stared after her curiously. "Wonder what that remark about selling out was about."

Gabe shrugged. "Family squabbles. What would you like to drink?"

"Anything. I just need something to hold." I never could eat or drink comfortably at parties where I didn't know the people, especially when gorgeous ex-wives lurked in the bushes.

I spotted Dove and Daddy over by the natural stone fireplace gazing up at an original William Matthews watercolor of cowboys herding cattle through a pebble-strewn creek. Daddy held a glass of wine, gesturing up at the painting, nodding his head at something Dove said. I quickly scanned the rest of the room, looking for other people I knew and, if truth be told, for Lydia. I wanted to catch a glimpse of her before she saw me. There didn't seem to be anyone resembling the woman in Sam's picture, but I did see Sam and Bliss over by the picture window. He looked unusually subdued and even surprised me with his appearance. I don't know who helped him pick out the clothes—Gabe certainly hadn't—but he wore dressy dark slacks, a slate blue linen shirt, and black leather loafers. It was hard to believe this handsome, neat young man was the kid whose normal attire was either baggy surf shorts or faded Wranglers. Bliss wore dark green tailored pants and a thin, off-white shirt, her pale hair hanging loose and wavy around her shoulders. Sam dipped his dark head a moment, listening to something she said, his eyes drinking her in. They were a physically striking couple, no doubt about it— not just because of their youth, but also because of the stark difference in their coloring. I studied them a moment, contemplating what their child might look like.

Behind me Gabe said, "You look wonderful, as always." His voice was low and pleasant, his practiced public voice. Through the thin silk of my shirt, I felt his large hand on my elbow. "Benni, I want you to meet Lydia."

I turned and faced her, licking my suddenly dry lips. She was even more striking in person than in Sam's photo, though, I was happy to see, not as beautiful. Taller than my five feet two by about five inches, her black hair was cut in a straight, shoulder-sweeping style, making the most of its glossy ebony shine. Perfect makeup softened her sharp features, her face dominated by the deep brown luminous eyes she'd passed on to her son. Her red designer suit— Armani, Anne Klein, Chanel, Elvia would know—fit her frame without a bulge. Though she was eight years older than me with skin that, I gleefully noted, showed it, I still felt like a mixed breed ranch horse standing next to a champion Kentucky Thoroughbred.

She held out a French-manicured hand. "I'm happy to finally meet you," she said. Her handshake was firm, dry, and assured, befitting a successful professional woman. "I've heard so many wonderful things about you."

I paused for a moment. "Me, too," I finally said, thinking, *Oh, very clever reply*. That should send her running to the hills in intellectual terror and intimidation.

Gabe said, "I'm on the way to the bar to get Benni a drink. Would you like something?"

"That would be wonderful. Just bring me my usual."

"Chardonnay is apparently one of Seven Sisters' specialties," he said.

Her deep-throated laugh caused a glimmer of recollection on his face, obviously bringing back an intimate memory. That and the fact that he actually remembered what she liked to drink intensified my feelings of not exactly jealousy . . . More like anxiety.

She laughed again, teasing him with the memory. His nervous returning laugh tempted me to smack him.

Oh, geeze, forget anxiety. Jealousy is exactly what it was.

After he left, attempting to be mature, I said, "Cappy says their '91 estate chardonnay is very good."

Her lips curved in a half smile. "Are you a wine aficionado?"

Don't even try to compete in that arena, a small voice inside me warned. "No," I said, for once heeding the sensible voice. "Cappy just told us that. Actually, I know next to nothing about wine. Don't even like it. Don't even like grape juice."

She laughed again, heartier this time, a there's-no-male-to-impress female laugh. "You're honest, I'll give you that.

If you want to know the truth, Benni Harper, if I wasn't a more secure person, I'd hate you. Not only did you manage to snag Mr. Evade-All-Emotional-Entanglements over there"—she nodded at Gabe's broad back—"but my son practically worships you. I do appreciate you taking care of my two men so well."

Her two men? I cleared my throat, stuck for a comeback. Gabe hadn't been *her man* for almost nine years now. Before I could think of a retort, Gabe returned with a glass of wheat-colored wine for Lydia and a club soda for me.

"The appetizers are really something," he said. "You ladies should check them out."

"Thank you," Lydia said, taking the glass from Gabe, her hand lightly brushing his. "I think I will after I reconnect with my son and future daughter-in-law." She sipped the wine. "Umm, this *is* very good. Ms. Brown certainly does know how to make wine." She looked up at Gabe, her expression serious and worried. "We need to talk about Sam."

"Call me at work tomorrow. We'll compare schedules and get together."

"I'll do that." She turned back to me. "It was so nice finally meeting you, Benni. We'll see each other again soon, I'm sure."

"I'm sure we will." I took a huge gulp of my club soda, annoyed at myself for acting like a tongue-tied junior high school girl.

"She's very worried about Sam and Bliss," Gabe said, watching her walk toward their son. "I think she's going to try to talk them out of getting married."

"And what do you think?" I asked, trying to be calm and mature about everything, attempting to ignore the explicit and very appealing mental picture of her falling off

San Patricio pier and being eaten by a passing great white shark.

"She should be worried. They are young and naive. Then again, I'm proud he wants to take responsibility for this baby. Makes me think that we did some things right as parents."

I tucked my arm through his. "You did a lot right in raising him. Sam's a wonderful person, and so is Bliss. Everything's going to work out just fine."

"Your optimism is appreciated, though not necessarily shared. I spent too many years in a patrol car going to family disputes caused, in part, by the stress of immature children trying raise their own children. Not to mention that he's marrying into a family that appears to already have its share of animosity."

"Oh, go chow down on the appetizers, you cynical old cop. And drink some sweet wine while you're there to brighten your outlook."

He kissed the top of my head and headed back toward the oak bar. I walked over to Dove and Daddy, who were now comfortably situated on a long leather sofa next to an open window.

"Hey, honeybun! I swear, isn't this place just like out of a magazine?" Dove said, patting the sofa next to her.

"Hey back." I gave each a quick hug and sat next to her. Daddy stood next to the window, eating some barbecued Portuguese sausage. "I think it was in a decorating magazine once on California ranch estates. Maybe it was *Country Living* or *Sunset*."

"I think it was *Sunset*," Dove said. "I remember Willow a-braggin' about it at some historical meeting. She used to attend real regular, but I hear she spends most of her time either doing city council stuff or taking care of her mama. I guess Rose Jewel is a real handful over at Oak Terrace."

"Really, why?"

"Apparently nothing is ever right to suit her. Willow's over there almost every day. Would've been a lot easier if they'd just kept her here."

"She didn't want that," I said, tucking my arm through hers. "JJ, Bliss's sister, told me that she didn't want to die on the ranch. She won't even visit anymore. I guess that's why she's not here tonight."

"Well, that's odd," Dove said.

"I know."

"How do you know Bliss's sister?" Dove asked.

"I thought I told you. She's one of the artists in the co-op. I just found out today that she and Bliss are twins, though you'd never guess it by looking at them."

Another couple had arrived, so I said, "Okay, tell me who everyone is." Dove's memory for faces and names, even of people she'd only met once or twice, was phenomenal.

"I'll start with the two who just walked in," she said in a low voice. "Now pay attention, 'cause I'm not going to repeat myself."

Daddy let out a chuckle, the whole situation amusing him to no end. The one thing you had to say about my father was society or money didn't impress him in the least. If you took care of your family, weren't cruel to animals or children or people weaker than you, worshiped God, worked hard, respected the land and paid your bills on time, you were okay by his book no matter how much money or status you had. If you didn't, you were plain white trash, no matter what color your skin happened to be.

"The woman in that flowy pink dress is Willow's granddaughter, Arcadia Norton. Handsome fella with her is her husband, Giles Norton."

"Snooty old Napa Valley wine family, I heard," I com-

mented. Arcadia had an all-American, shampoo-model prettiness with long, light brown hair and ivory skin. Giles was
dressed in a pair of pressed khaki pants, a starched button-
down shirt, and suede tassel loafers. Very Ivy League–looking. Thanks to Emory, I knew Arcadia was twenty-nine.
Giles looked to be in his late thirties.

"Rumor has it among the grape assholes . . ." Daddy
started.

Dove shot him a severe look. He grinned and gave me
a broad wink. "Word among the grape *growers* is that he's
trying to merge Seven Sisters with Norton Wine Group.
Wants to go national within two years and international
within five and that Willow is for it and Cappy is fighting
tooth and nail against it. Don't know where Etta stands.
They've got some real fine pasture land up in the foothills
they're clearing to plant more grapes. Gonna take down
about two hundred oak trees I heard, though the greenie-
beans are fighting it with some of their fancy lawyers."
Greenie-beans is what Daddy calls the most rabid environmentalists. He shook his head, amazed at the whole thing.
"We ranchers are lookin' pretty good to the greenie-beans
these days. At least they can't accuse us of killing oaks."

"That explains a comment Cappy made to me and Gabe
about Giles," I said. "Which one is Etta?" She was the third
and youngest sister, the unmarried one. The one who had
taught home economics for years at Amelia Valley High
School until she retired back in the early eighties and
started making wine as a hobby, learning as she went along
from articles and mail-order wine books. I remembered seeing bottles of her homemade wine at the MidState Fair back
when I was a 4-H kid showing my lambs and calves. Her
wine always won blue ribbons.

Dove pointed across the room. "Etta's over there, talking

to Sam and Bliss and that pretty Spanish lady."

I grabbed her finger and pushed it down. "Very funny, Dove."

"Did you meet her?" Dove asked.

"Yes, and she's very nice."

"You best watch her. I don't cotton to how she's a-lookin' at your husband."

"I told you, she's very nice. We had a nice talk."

"Heed my words, honeybun. She looks like one who could surely nice you to death."

"Enough about her," I said, trying not to let my irritation show. "Etta's the one in the black velvet blouse and skirt, I'm assuming." Her outfit was plain except for her fist-sized Navajo squash blossom necklace.

"That's her," Daddy said. "They say she's a genius with wine, that the winery would be nothing without her. Drives the other wine fellas crazy, Bob down at the Farm Supply says. A lot of them old boys have fancy degrees in some kind of wine culture or something, and she runs circles around them. Wins all the big awards. And to add flies to the manure, she's a woman."

Dove and I glared at him simultaneously.

He held up his hands in apology. "I was just reporting what the boys at the Farm Supply say."

"Viticulture," I said, remembering the chapter I'd read on it years ago when I was taking classes for my minor in agriculture. "The study of cultivating and growing grapes is called viticulture."

"Whatever," Daddy said, eating his last sausage, then using the toothpick on his teeth. "Whatever that degree is, she ain't got it, and they do, and she still makes better wine than any of 'em. Apparently that woman can make wine out of raisins. I say more power to her."

"Here, here," Dove agreed.

Etta looked like a protégé of Georgia O'Keeffe. I guessed that Bliss, with her pioneer spirit, was probably Cappy's favorite and that maybe JJ, being an artist, might be her great-aunt Etta's favorite relative, especially since Etta had never married and had any children or grandchildren of her own.

My assumption proved correct when JJ came in from the back patio and Etta rushed across the spacious room and took JJ's face in her large hands. Following JJ was an earthy, fortyish woman with lush graying blond hair flowing down her back. She watched Etta's enthusiastic greeting with an uneasy expression. The earthy woman looked enough like Bliss and JJ that she had to be their mother, Susa—the ex-hippie nurse-midwife. Tonight she looked like any slightly artsy, upper-middle-class San Celina matron with a preference for autumn-toned gauzy dresses and handmade bead jewelry. She stood quietly watching her daughter chatter with her aunt, as much a part of the exchange as if she'd been a stranger at a bus stop.

Behind us, Cappy started tapping the side of her wineglass with a silver knife, continuing until the noisy voices quieted down. Dove and I stood up and faced her.

"Everyone's here but Willow, and she said she'd be here as soon as the city council meeting is over, so I think we'd best get on with the toast and go eat that delicious barbecue Jose has been slaving over. As the oldest member of the Brown family here, I welcome you all to Seven Sisters Ranch. We are—"

"And winery," Giles broke in, causing a few titters in the group.

Cappy stared at him a long, uncomfortable moment, her eyes boring holes in his forehead. Then she smiled. "Of course, Giles. Seven Sisters Ranch and Winery." She said the last word slowly, deliberately. "We are here to celebrate the engagement of our own sweet Bliss to a fine young man, Sam Ortiz." She held up her glass, and we all followed suit. "Long life, easy trails, and much happiness. Now, let's eat."

I searched the crowd, looking for Gabe, wanting to catch his eye. He was standing next to Lydia, Etta, and JJ. I watched as he clinked glasses with Etta and JJ, then turned and did the same with Lydia. She smiled at him, and he smiled back. Then they walked over to their son, whose face was flushed with excitement and embarrassment. Gabe hugged Bliss, and Lydia hugged Sam. Then Sam and Gabe hugged. At that moment, Giles passed next to Bliss and whispered something in her ear. Her face flushed pink and she gave him a look that, had she been wearing her gun, might have proven dangerous. Then Sam turned back to her, and in an instant her smile returned. Giles moved over to the bar and poured a glass of wine, then leaned against the bar watching Bliss and Sam with narrowed eyes.

"Why don't you go over and stand with your husband?" Dove whispered in my ear.

"He's busy right now," I said, determined not to appear the paranoid second wife.

"And going to get a might busier if'n you don't get over there and guard the rooster roost."

"I trust him," I said firmly. "This situation is something he and Lydia have to work out. Sam is their son."

Dove made a disbelieving sound deep in her throat. "All I have to say is you'd better keep your eyes open on this one."

"Nothing to watch, Dove. They just want to work out what's best for Sam."

"Let's eat," Dove said. "I do believe you're getting light-headed."

"Daddy!" I turned to him, exasperated. "Would you please talk to your mother?"

"Don't look at me, pumpkin," he said, setting his empty plate and glass down on the arts and crafts–style coffee table. "Your gramma gets something in her craw, may as well try to wrestle a bobcat as change her mind."

"Just be nice to her," I grumbled in Dove's ear as I took her arm and we walked out to the patio.

"Me?" Dove feigned shock and hurt. "Honeybun, I'm always nice to everyone."

I scanned the sky.

"What are you looking for?" Dove asked.

"The cloud holding the lightning bolt that God will strike you dead with for lying."

She smacked my hand. "You are more stubborn than a roomful of Baptists. And that's all you know. If God wanted to strike me dead, He wouldn't need a cloud."

Laughing, we walked out to a brick patio overlooking the neat vineyards with the Santa Lucia mountains in the distance. It was almost dark, but the patio, thick with clay pots filled with flowers and ferns, was cleverly lit by recessed lighting and electric lamps made from old mining lanterns. Part of the patio was glassed in, facing west with a clear view of the Seven Sisters peaks. The rest of the patio was tiered with steps leading down to deep second and third levels, plush with emerald grass. The second level had long tables covered with white tablecloths and set with china plates, silverware, and linen napkins embroidered with the Seven Sisters brand and huge bowls of green salad, coleslaw, wild rice salad, San Celina sourdough bread, spicy pink pinquito beans, sliced avocados, tomatoes, and ripe strawberries the size of small apples. In the middle of it was a cake inscribed with Bliss's and Sam's names and a detailed picture of two horses nuzzling—one a deep, dark brown, the other a palomino. At the bottom level, with only a white rail fence separating the grass from the grapevines, a traditional Santa Maria–style cast-iron barbecue was being manned by a thin Latino man in his sixties and a younger man who looked like his son. We helped ourselves to the food and made our way back up to the top level where round tables were set up.

"I'll go eat with my husband if it will make you happy," I told Dove.

"Doesn't make no nevermind to me. It's your life," she said, shrugging.

I found Gabe at a table inside the glassed-in porch where he was sitting with Bliss and Sam. We were joined shortly by Lydia, Cappy, and Willow, the third sister, who'd left the city council meeting early. She was dressed elegantly in a navy tailored pantsuit with a maroon blouse. An antique watch hung from a thin gold chain around her neck. Her hair was the same iron gray as Cappy's but cut in a soft wavy halo around her head.

"I'm going to sit right here next to the chief," she said, smiling mischievously. "See if I can convince him to loan me some of his officers for a charity fashion show the Monday Club is putting on."

Gabe smiled his politician smile, but I knew he'd rant about her nerve to me later on that night.

The conversation wasn't as awkward as I feared it might be. Lydia was subdued and pleasant and didn't hog the conversation or make any more veiled references to her former relationship with Gabe. Sam clearly loved his mother and was excited to have both his parents in the same place, even under the strained circumstances.

After we'd eaten once and people were milling around contemplating seconds, I excused myself to find a bathroom. I found a guest bathroom right off the front hall and

was coming out when I heard an argument on the porch.
The front door was partially open so only a screen door
separated me and the people arguing. Nosiness getting the
better of me, I paused to listen.

"Don't think I won't," a man's voice said, low and
mean.

An older female voice answered in a tone so low I
couldn't make out the words. I edged a little closer, telling
myself it wasn't being rude, that I was looking out for my
stepson and that any conflict in this family would eventually concern him.

". . . not by you," the man answered, his voice louder. It
was then I recognized it was Giles's voice. "I'll do it tonight if I have to."

"You won't," the female voice answered. Cappy's?
Etta's? Their voices sounded enough alike I couldn't tell.
Then there was silence.

I ducked back into the bathroom, afraid they would
come through the partially open door and find me behaving
so tacky. I combed my hair and inspected my makeup for
a good five minutes before emerging. I glanced out to the
porch. It was empty except for a fat calico cat licking one
paw. One thing for sure, I didn't envy Sam's entry into this
turbulent family.

When I got back, Chase offered to open the tasting room
for a private tasting and Dove, Daddy, Gabe, Lydia, Susa,
and Sam accepted. Willow, Arcadia, and Etta went upstairs,
and I decided to take Cappy up on her offer to show me
the horses. With Bliss riding in the backseat, Cappy drove
down to the stables in her faded blue Jeep Wagoneer.

"I've had this baby since 1972, and she's never broke
down on me once," Cappy bragged, dodging a pothole in
the dirt road leading to the stables. She gave a cheerful

honk to the group walking down the long driveway toward the winery and tasting room.

"Sam's mother is quite a looker," she said, glancing over at me, a mischievous glint in her eyes. "No doubt Sam got the best of both parents. I can see why my granddaughter would fall back on her heels for him. Just like you did for his father."

"Grandma!" Bliss said in an aggrieved voice.

I stuck my tongue out at Cappy. Bliss gave an uncharacteristic giggle.

"Benni Harper, you haven't changed a bit since you were sixteen," Cappy said good-naturedly.

"That's not true," I said, turning to grin at Bliss. "I know way more cuss words now."

She and Bliss laughed, and for the first time this evening, it seemed as if Bliss relaxed a little. About a half mile from the house, we reached the stables. Cappy had built a beautiful setup—a row of freshly painted double stalls, enough for forty horses, two hot walkers, an outside wash rack, three corrals, a separate tack room, a graded half-mile training track, and plenty of shade trees.

"Are you full up?" I asked as we walked through the first stall row. A black-and-white long-haired barn cat followed us, darting between our legs, mewing loudly.

"Almost," she said. "We've got six free stalls, but they'll be filled soon." She bent down and picked up the complaining cat. "Figaro, you're almost as big a nag as Giles. You don't need one more saucer of cream." The cat purred as she stroked his black head.

I reached over and scratched under his chin. "He looks like he's wearing a hood."

"He's a criminal, all right," Cappy said. "Stole our hearts a long time ago." The cat purred a reply.

"Grandma's been taking in boarders this year," Bliss explained, stopping to fondle the nose of a strawberry roan filly with a pencil-thin blaze. She put her face close to the filly's and blew softly in the horse's nostrils.

"Quarter horse breeding isn't what it was," Cappy said. "Not since the early eighties when they took away the tax benefits for racehorse owners."

"JJ mentioned that this morning. How would that affect you?" I asked.

Bliss jumped in with the answer. "It affects everyone involved with racing or breeding. If rich people can't use racehorses as tax write-offs for their other businesses, then they don't buy them anymore, and people lose jobs all the way down the line—trainers, grooms, pony girls, breeders, feed brokers, people who work at the racetrack, farriers and tack suppliers. I could go on and on. A lot of people are involved with the business of horse racing and breeding who don't work directly with it and usually they don't have the education or means to find jobs anywhere else so they end up on welfare or robbing liquor stores." She smiled. "Which, of course, gives *me* job security. One thing about being a cop, there's always bad guys."

Cappy smiled and passed me a handful of carrots. "Got her trained pretty good, don't I?"

"You sure do." I took the carrots, breaking them in half as I followed her down the center aisle of the stalls. "I understand what she's saying. It's like when beef consumption goes down. It affects more than just the ranchers who raise cattle. And most of the jobs involving cattle are the same as with your industry, people who can't get jobs in other industries. Not everyone can be a computer programmer."

"Exactly," Cappy said. "I wish a few politicians understood that."

We walked from stall to stall, feeding carrots to the

horses as she relayed their histories, showing me the ones she had high hopes for and the ones she intended to run in claiming races.

"Claiming races?" I said. I'd been to a few horse races in my life, but didn't know much about the intricacies or terminology of the industry.

"That's when the horse is basically up for sale in a race," she explained. "People can make a bid for the horse by filing a claiming form and leaving a certified check on deposit before post time. The purse"—she paused and looked at me—". . . that's the money awarded to the winners of the race, goes to the owner who entered the horse, but the horse will legally belong to the successful claimant so even if the horse gets injured during the race, it's the responsibility of the new owner. It's a gamble, though. But if you know your stuff and have a good working crystal ball, you can pick up some great deals in claiming races. We've bought two claimers that went on to become stakes horses and bred them into our line."

"What's a stakes horse?" This was a whole new world to me. Good ranch horses only needed three qualities— excellent health, no fear of cattle, and a willingness to learn. Some of our best ranch horses were uglier than a bucket of mud, but they had a magic sense when it came to working cattle.

"In simple terms, a stakes horse is one that, after it's shown exceptional talent by winning races and clocking some fast times, can run at the big money. Stakes horses are the best of the best." Cappy stroked the nose of a muscular bay with friendly "people" eyes.

"This business sounds about as predictable and profitable as cattle ranching," I said, stroking the neck of a young mahogany-colored horse who had finished his carrot and was tossing his head for more. "Young man, that's all you get tonight." I held out my empty hand. "See, all gone."

"That's Churn Dash, a two-year-old we're planning on running in a few races this year. He foaled out late so we've waited on entering him. His mama was Seven Sisters Dash. She wasn't a great runner herself, but she sure can produce them."

"He's beautiful," I said, rubbing my fingers along the star and stripe on his face. "What a great name. Did you know it's a quilt pattern?"

"Actually, I did," Cappy said. "In my office I have a quilt made by Mother in that pattern. We named him in honor of her."

"I never got to know Great-Grandma Rose that well," Bliss said, coming over and running her hand down Churn Dash's neck, scratching his withers. "I wish Susa hadn't moved us away when we were so little." Her tone was slightly bitter.

"Your mother always was one who had trouble taking the bit," Cappy said. "Guess she wanted her own life."

"Your great-grandma is certainly a famous person in this county," I said to Bliss. "They practically have a shrine to her down in General Hospital's children's wing."

"She raised most of the money that built that wing," Cappy said. "And she started both the candy striper volunteer group and the home nurse program. Health care in this county, especially for children, owes a lot to Mother."

We went into the tack room and working office, and I couldn't help but admire the rich assortment of shiny, well-cared-for tack. As Cappy listened to her answering machine messages, I walked past the long row of photos of winning horses on the panelled wall. In the center was a large, expensively framed photograph of Seven B winning a race by a length. A photo underneath showed a younger Cappy and a bunch of other people posing in the winner's circle with the horse and his trainer, a strong-looking blond man with a thick, reddish mustache. Everyone wore wide smiles.

"That was taken fifteen years ago," Bliss said. "When Seven B won the All-American Futurity. That's the biggest quarter horse competition in the world. It's a million-dollar purse."

"How exciting that must have been," I commented.

Cappy came and stood next to us. "Yes, but like anything else this competitive, you're only as good as your last win. Seven B hasn't even produced a stakes winner in a few years. We're hoping that will change soon. Believe me, when you aren't winning at the track, only the feed man knows your name." She checked her watch. "We'd better get back and see to our guests. They're probably ready for dessert about now." At the Jeep Bliss hung back.

"I think I'll walk," she said. "I need the exercise."

Cappy, her face aggravated, started to say something, but I broke in.

"Want some company? I could use a walk, too, after that fabulous spread."

Bliss shrugged. "I don't mind."

"Okay," Cappy said. "I'll see you two in a few minutes." She reached into the glove compartment of the Jeep and took out a small flashlight. "Take this. There's lots of holes in the road."

"Oh, Grandma . . ." Bliss started.

"Don't you, 'Oh, Grandma' me," Cappy countered. "I'm only—"

"Thanks," I said, breaking into her sentence and taking the flashlight. "We'll be careful."

"She's already driving me nuts," Bliss complained as we watched her grandmother drive up the road, a small cloud of dust trailing after her. "She's the last person I expected to be treating me like I was a piece of expensive crystal."

"She's just concerned," I said, falling in with her irritated strides.

"She was breaking green horses when she was pregnant with my mom. Great-Aunt Willow said they considered locking her in her room the last three months."

"Maybe that's why she's so concerned about you. 'Do as I say and not as I do. If your friends wanted to jump off a cliff, would you? Don't make that face, young lady, or someday it will freeze that way.' All the things mothers and grandmothers say to us to try and keep us from being hurt. What they're actually saying is—'I'm afraid the world will hurt you the way it did me and I don't want that to happen.' Of course, they can't stop it and they know it, so they tell us dumb things and for the moment they're saying it, they feel better."

She was silent, and I thought I'd gone too far in my mini-lecture. "Then again," I added, bumping her shoulder with mine, "they could be just trying to keep us from having any fun at all."

She laughed and bumped me back. "I think that's it."

We continued walking up the gravel road toward the house. The flashlight illuminated the path as we looked up to the September sky, wild with stars, trying to remember constellations we'd learned in science class.

"Too many years ago for me," I said, after only being able to find the Big and Little Dippers and Orion and the planet Venus. Bliss picked out Aries the Ram and Aquarius the Waterbearer.

"Did you know that there is a cluster of stars called the Seven Sisters?" she asked.

"No, I didn't."

"My dad showed them to me." She pointed up to a spot in the sky where a faint grouping of stars was visible. "It's in the Taurus constellation. It's also known as Pleiades.

Seven stars can be seen with the naked eye, but with a telescope or really good binoculars you can see that there's actually a couple of hundred. Look, they appear to be close together, but actually they're really far apart." She gave me a slight smile. "As my dad says, just like Cappy and her sisters."

"Seems like the name of your ranch has all sorts of hidden meanings."

"No kidding," she said.

The hint of sharpness in her voice caused me to glance at her in surprise, but she kept walking and didn't elaborate.

Sam, I thought, *what have you gotten yourself into?*

"Let's stop here for a moment," she said when we reached a weathered wooden bench in front of a large metal building. A small security light bathed the area in a stark white glow. "I'm feeling a little sick."

I sat down next to her. "Want me to go get the Jeep?"

"No, it's not that much farther. It's just that I seem to be getting my morning sickness at night. Lucky for me, I'm on day shift for the next three months."

We sat silently for a moment, uncomfortable with the mention of her pregnancy. The fact that I was married not only to her future father-in-law, but also her boss caused an awkwardness between us that was hard to breach.

"So, what building is this?" I asked, turning to look.

"It's part of the winery. We store barrels of fermenting wine here. My uncle Chase has his office here." She put a fist up to her mouth, her face grayish-green in the harsh light.

"Should I go get Sam?"

She swallowed hard, and her coloring came back. "No, it's just a spell. Really, I don't do this very often. I've found a good doctor, and he says I shouldn't have any problems, that this feeling sick is perfectly normal and should pass in another month. I'm going to be able to work until the baby's born." She turned pink, which looked a whole lot better than green. "I'll tell the chief that myself. I'm not trying to, like, pull strings or anything. I've made an appointment with him next week to talk about my schedule."

I touched her hand. "Bliss, you don't have to explain anything to me. What happens between you and Gabe on a professional level is not my business. Gabe is adamant about keeping his personal and work life separate."

"I guess Sam and I have screwed that up, haven't we?"

I gave her an encouraging smile. "I doubt it's the first time this has happened in a family and I also doubt it'll be the last."

Not answering, she looked over at the dark vineyards. In the cool darkness, we watched a partial moon rise over the vineyards, the Santa Lucia mountains craggy and black behind them. The heavy scent of ripe grapes sugared the air, giving it a flavor you could almost taste. In the distance, a horse whinnied, the sound causing a nervous echo from another horse, then another and another. Like cattle, horses were such group animals. When one of them was afraid or agitated, it passed through the herd like fire in parched rye grass.

"The hills remind me of a quilt pattern called Moon Over Mountain," I said, just to break the uneasy silence. "It's a simple one, with clean lines and not a lot of pieces. But it doesn't really capture the beauty of mountains. Mountains have such wonderful three-dimensional peaks and valleys that are impossible to capture in a flat pattern. Like the difference between a cartoon character and a real person. We get the bare essence, but nothing else."

"I'm scared, Benni," she whispered so softly I wasn't sure I heard her right. She didn't look over at me, but continued to stare at the dark hills.

I reached over and took her hand, squeezing it gently. "I know." What else could I say to her at this moment? Take heart? Things will work out? You're stronger than you realize? *I know.* The only thing we can truly tell another person who is afraid or in pain. I know the unknown is terrifying. I know what fear is. I know what pain feels like. *I know.*

What I didn't realize until much later was she wasn't talking about Sam or the baby.

6

WE WERE STILL sitting on the bench when the urgent clanging of the dinner bell reverberated through the valley. I didn't think anything about it, assuming Cappy was calling everyone back up to the house for dessert, until Bliss jumped up, her face twisted with panic.

"What's wrong?" I asked.

Without answering, she took off running up the gravel road toward the house.

I caught up with her, my heart pounding, and asked again, "Bliss, what's going on?"

"She only rings the bell in an emergency. I know a shortcut through the fields." She took off running through the rows of grapes. I followed her, keeping my eyes on her blonde hair bobbing through the lush green vines. Prickly branches caught at my silk blouse, snagging it in places that would irritate me later, but at that moment my only mission was to keep up with Bliss.

My side felt splintered when we reached the front porch. Bliss dashed in ahead of me, calling out for Cappy. Her grandmother appeared, followed by Etta and Willow from behind the closed doors of the living room we'd occupied a few hours before. She closed the doors behind her and said calmly to me, "You'd better find your husband."

Her serious tone caused Bliss and me to glance at each other in apprehension.

"Why?" I asked.

"There's been an accident."

"Who?" Bliss asked.

Her grandmother's face was sober. "It's Giles. He's dead."

Before she could elaborate, we heard a mixture of voices out on the porch—Gabe, Dove, Lydia, Sam, Daddy. They were laughing at something, obviously unaware of the dinner bell's ominous purpose. They entered the hallway, and Gabe's smiling face turned instantly serious when he saw us.

"What's wrong?" he asked. Sam went over to Bliss, who was standing motionless as a trapped fawn, her hand grasping her side as if searching for the weapon that wasn't there.

"It's my grandson-in-law, Giles," Willow said. "We need to find my granddaughter, Arcadia, and—"

"She was down at the tasting room with us," Dove said. "Until about a half hour ago. She said she was coming back up to the house."

Cappy's face looked troubled. "Gabe, you'd better handle this." She opened the door, and Gabe entered the room. We all pushed forward, stopping only when Gabe commanded us to stay where we were.

Lying on the floor in front of the fireplace was Giles in a rapidly spreading pool of blood. A .38 revolver lay a small distance from his body. He lay on his back, the gun above his outstretched hand, as if he were reaching for it. The entry point of the bullet could barely be seen, but I knew the force of a .38 bullet. If we turned him over, half his back would be splayed open, his insides a tangled mess. Gabe bent down and pressed his fingers to Giles's neck. I watched my husband's face, trying to gauge by his reaction whether Giles was actually dead. Behind us we heard Susa's soft exclamation.

"Let me by," she said. "He might be alive." She pushed past us and ran over to Giles. She kneeled down next to him, her eyes rapidly surveying his chest wound.

"He's dead," Gabe said quietly, pulling his hand back and standing up.

She ignored his words and gently pressed her fingers in the same spot Gabe had. Moments later, she said in a choked voice, "Oh, no."

Gabe looked over at Cappy. "Where's the nearest phone besides this one?" He nodded at the phone on a side table.

"My study," she said, pointing down the hall. "Last door on your right."

He looked over at the rest of us, which now included Chase, Jose, and Jose's son, who seemed to have appeared from nowhere. "I need all of you to go out on the front porch and stay there." He walked over to me and said in a low voice, "Benni, I left my cell phone in the car. Go into Cappy's study and call nine-one-one. I don't want to leave the scene."

Arcadia picked that moment to walk up to the crowd. Her soprano voice rang out. "I was upstairs powdering my nose when I thought I heard the dinner bell. What's going on?" When she moved around the crowd and saw Giles lying on the blood-soaked carpet, a strangled cry came from her throat. We all stared at her, morbidly compelled to watch her reaction. She started toward Giles's body, but Gabe gently blocked her way. "I'm sorry, but you'll have to stay back." He nodded over at Willow, who took his cue and rushed over to her granddaughter.

"Grandmother?" Arcadia said, her voice strangled. "What happened? Who did this?" Willow put her arm around Arcadia's shoulders and murmured softly in her ear. Arcadia started sobbing, her slight body convulsing.

"Benni, nine-one-one," Gabe reminded me. He turned and looked at everyone and said firmly, "Everyone out on the porch, now. And no talking, please."

As everyone started slowly moving toward the porch, I went to the study and made the phone call. The dispatcher replied that sheriff's deputies would be there in a few minutes, that an officer was only a few miles away. When I came back into the hallway, the hallway was empty, and Gabe had closed the living room's double doors.

Gabe walked over to me. "What's the deputies' ETA?"

"The dispatcher said a few minutes. I told them you were here."

He nodded his approval.

"So, what do you think?" I asked in a low voice.

The skin around his prominent cheekbones tightened. "I think my son has picked one heck of a family to marry into." He put his hand on my shoulder and massaged it gently, more, it seemed, to comfort himself than me. "Why don't you join them outside? I'll be out after I talk to the sheriff's deputy."

Out on the porch, I went over to Dove, who was sitting at the far end in one of the Adirondack chairs. Daddy stood next to her, his face subdued, holding his white dress Stetson in his hands. "Are you all right?" I asked.

"Just fine, honeybun. What's Gabe got to say about this?"

"All he said was he wasn't thrilled about Sam marrying into this clan."

On the other end of the porch, on a padded bench, Willow sat next to her granddaughter, Arcadia, who was quietly sobbing into a small lacy handkerchief. She rubbed Arcadia's back, whispering into her ear. Bliss stood next to Arcadia, her face ashen. Sam, his face fighting panic, bent down, murmured something in Bliss's ear, then lay his hand tentatively on her back. Her face relaxed slightly, and a small shudder ran through her. Lydia stood on the top porch step, her expression uncertain.

"Bliss, honey," her mother said. "Why don't you sit down?"

"I'm just fine," Bliss replied, her face going stiff again.

The sharpness in her tone surprised me, but Susa's genial expression didn't change. She just patted her daughter's arm and went over to where her mother, Cappy, sat on the other side of Arcadia.

A few seconds later two sheriff's patrol cars pulled up behind Gabe's Corvette. A uniformed officer stepped out of each and, after a brief talk, strode up to the porch, heading toward Lydia, who would be the first one they'd encounter. I moved around her and met them, informing them I made the 911 call and that Chief Ortiz of the San Celina Police Department was inside.

We silently watched them enter the house. A few minutes later Gabe came out and said, "The detectives and the investigative team are on their way. They'll need a statement from everyone. Please refrain from talking to each other until they've had a chance to question you." He went back inside the house.

In about fifteen minutes, another vehicle arrived. A truck, actually. A big red Dodge. The man who stepped out appeared to be in his late thirties and wore a tan cowboy hat, sharp-pressed Wranglers, a Western-style sports jacket, and golden brown ostrich cowboy boots. When he came up the porch steps, he nodded at us genially, then walked into the house without a word. About a minute later, one of the uniformed deputies came back outside, probably assigned to keep an eye on us and discourage talking. I leaned my head against a wooden post and sighed, knowing we were in for a long night.

Ignoring the deputy's presence, Lydia walked over to me and asked in a low voice, "You seem to understand my son. Should I go over to him?"

I stared at her, surprised. Asking my advice about her son was the last thing I expected. *Oh, geeze, don't turn out to be nice*, I thought.

"He'd probably deny it with all his Latin machismo," I whispered back, "but I'd say having his mom stand next to him right now would definitely make him feel better."

The sheriff's deputy frowned at me and Lydia, shaking his head. I felt like a school kid caught passing a note.

"Thanks," she murmured. Pointedly ignoring the deputy in a way I couldn't help admiring, she walked across the porch, said something in Sam's ear, then lay her hand on his shoulder. Sam's tense face eased at her touch.

By the time Gabe and the cowboy detective came back out on the porch, more cars had arrived, and soon the yard and house were full of crime scene personnel. Gabe came over and stood next to me while the detective cleared his throat to get our attention.

"Excuse me, folks." His voice had a soft Texas twang, like an electric guitar slightly out of tune—not enough to be unpleasant, but enough to notice. "I'm Detective Hudson. I know this has been a hard night on all y'all, but please bear with us a little longer. Since we don't really know what happened yet, we're going to have to question each of you on an individual basis. Just some standard questions so we can try and figure out what happened.

There's three of us, so it shouldn't take too much of your time."

His voice was so friendly and easygoing it was almost easy to forget that this wasn't an accident, but was most likely homicide, and there was a good chance that someone standing on this porch had committed the crime.

After a quick consultation with Gabe, the two other detectives asked Dove and Daddy to step into the house. The rest of us waited, a deputy still watching us. About a half hour later, Dove and Daddy were given permission to leave, and they came over to me to say a quick good-bye.

"Call me tomorrow first thing," Dove said, hugging me hard.

"I will."

"See you soon, pipsqueak," Daddy said, kissing my cheek.

Probably because they knew I was with Gabe, I was one of the last to be questioned. My interview, almost three hours later, took place in Cappy's office off the front hallway. The Texas detective had placed two deep-green leather visitor chairs side by side in front of Cappy's large oak executive desk, slightly turned toward each other in a nonintimidating way, as if he and the witness were just having a pleasant chat.

"I'm Detective Hudson, Mrs. Ortiz," he said, reaching out to shake my hand. His palm was smooth, warm, and a little damp. "I'm sorry this has taken so long."

"It's okay. You can call me Benni," I said, not wanting to go into the fact that although I was officially married, I wasn't officially an Ortiz.

"Great, Benni, then. Please have a seat." He gestured to one of the green chairs. After sitting down, I tried to get my bearings, by glancing around Cappy's office. It was a mixture of funky cowgirl kitsch, Native American elegance, and colorful Mexican folk art, organized in a way that looked straight out of a magazine spread. A brown-toned framed poster of a Pendleton cowgirl riding a bucking bronco shared wall space with a bright acrylic painting of an Indian warrior and a folk art cross painted with happy scenes from a Mexican wedding. A loveseat upholstered in a tan, brown, deep green, and red Pendleton blanket fabric sat between floor-to-ceiling oak bookcases. In a corner, a burnished mahogany-colored tooled sidesaddle rested on a fancy oak saddle rack. Above it was a gallery of framed win pictures, Cappy smiling proudly in each one, and an oil painting of Seven Bars Jewel. Behind the desk hung the Churn Dash quilt—made of brown and gold calicos and pale muslin—that Rose Jewel Brown had created and was the inspiration for the name of the two-year-old colt I'd seen earlier.

The detective cleared his throat to get my attention. "Excuse me, ma'am. Can we get started now?"

I jumped slightly, felt myself flush. "Oh, I'm sorry. The room distracted me."

He nodded and glanced around the office. "It is somethin' else. My mama would love it. She's an interior decorator in Dallas." He looked down at the palm-sized wire-ring notebook in his hand. The front was decorated with the characters from *Beauty and the Beast*. When he looked back up, he caught me staring at it and smiling.

He turned it over and scrutinized the cover, laughing himself. "It was all I could find," he said, sitting back in his chair and crossing his legs, ankle to knee. His golden brown ostrich boots had deep brown shafts. "I think it was left over from my daughter's last visit. I reckon I should have just torn the cover off, but as my dear old daddy would say, if a man can't act like a girl sometimes, then he ain't a real man."

I thought about his comment for a moment, trying to decide if it was insulting to women.

He grinned at me, an amused twinkle in his dark brown eyes. "Now, why don't you tell me everything you saw and heard and what you were doing, say, the half hour before y'all heard the dinner bell callin' you to the house."

While I talked, he made notes in his cartoon notebook, his smooth-shaved, country-boy face screwed up in a concentrated frown. He reminded me of the type of boy in school the teacher always picked for Tom Sawyer's part in the class play. The kind who would pull your braids, then look so cute and wide-eyed innocent when accused that the teacher glanced back at *you* with suspicion.

"Then we ran through the wine fields because Bliss knew a shortcut and we found Cappy, Willow, and Etta standing in front of the double doors," I finished.

Nodding, he made a few more notes, then looked up at me, his boyish face thoughtful. "Now, if you don't mind, I'd like to pick your brain for a moment. Off the record."

I became instantly wary. He apparently forgot I was married to a cop. There was no such thing as "off the record." Especially in a homicide investigation. I waited for his question, nervously jiggling my foot.

"You're pretty connected in the agriculture community here in San Celina County, right?"

"I guess. I've lived here most of my life, and my gramma and daddy have owned a ranch here since the early sixties."

He grinned again. "That Dove, she's a real kick in the pants. You know, she got me to commit to a donation for their senior citizen center's new kitchen before I even asked two questions. That's the first time anyone has finagled a charity donation out of me during a homicide investigation. I was tempted to swear her in as an honorary deputy and set her to questioning folks. We'd have this wrapped up in time for biscuits and gravy."

"She's one of a kind," I agreed, laughing. "How much did she shake you down for?"

"A hundred bucks!" He shook his head. "My own dear grandma Hudson, the Lord rest her soul, would have loved her."

I smiled, then involuntarily yawned. "Sorry, it's been a long night. Are you through?"

"One last question. Take some time thinking about it and answer it now if you want or call me at the office." He pulled a business card out of the inside of his jacket and handed it to me. "I just want your input on what is going on in this family."

I thought for a moment, torn between the loyalty I felt toward Cappy because of our past association, not to mention the general loyalty among the agricultural community who'd, with good reason, often viewed government officials with more than a little suspicion.

"Well," I said, "there was probably some friction between Giles and Cappy, because the two things they do are so different, and there might be some disagreement as to how to utilize the resources on their land."

"Such as?"

"Whether pasture land should be used to raise horses or be covered with wine grapes."

"Can't a big place like this do both? Ms. Brown said . . ." He flipped back through some pages in his notebook. "This property is about eleven hundred acres. Isn't that enough for everybody? Forgive my agricultural ignorance, but I'm a Houston city boy. My father was an accountant. The only agriculture I'm familiar with was my mama's prize-winning roses."

"A good part of their land is probably not productive,"

I said. "And often the best pasture and feed-growing land
is also the best land to grow grapes. Not to mention the
problems with the property being reassessed once they
grow grapes on it, which puts it in a higher tax bracket.
Keeping Seven Sisters a horse-breeding ranch would definitely keep the property taxes down. That's about all I
know about it. Doesn't seem like much of a motive for
murder. They seem to be working it out okay, from what
I've heard." There was that little jibe that Giles made during Cappy's toast, but that didn't seem important enough
to mention. And there was the comment JJ had made in my
office about the winery causing a problem among the sisters, but no doubt he'd found that out when he questioned
JJ.

"What about Etta and Giles? How did they get along?"

"I have no idea, Detective. I don't really know the family well. I mean, our families have known each other for
years, but we're not intimate friends. We don't run in the
same social circle, if you know what I mean."

He nodded. "I understand this Giles Norton comes from
a pretty famous wine family up in Napa Valley."

"I heard the same thing," I said, leaving it at that.

He gazed over my shoulder to the saddle behind me,
staring at it until I thought he would bore a hole in the
thick leather. "Something's not right with this whole scenario."

"Oh?"

He turned his attention back from the saddle to me.
"Don't you find it all just a little too . . . neat and organized?"

I sat back in my chair, a bit confused. "Organized? I
don't know what you mean."

He gave his head a small shake, reminding me of
Cappy's horses. "Never mind, just some ramblings of a

suspicious old Texan. Anything else significant you think I should know?"

I hesitated, then said, "I did overhear an argument, but I'm sure it's nothing."

He nodded at me to continue, and I told him what I'd heard outside the bathroom.

He asked, "You're sure you couldn't recognize the female voice?"

"I told you, it could have been Cappy or either of her sisters. Have you heard their voices? They all sound alike. Besides, I was just passing by and only caught a bit of their conversation. I didn't actually stop and . . ." I paused, realizing I'd just begun a lie.

He grinned, as if he could see the moral struggle inside my head. "So maybe you had to tie your shoe or something," he said, looking down at my pull-on boots. "Happens to me all the time. Then you just happened to overhear a little more . . ."

"That's all I heard," I snapped, embarrassed.

He uncrossed his legs, his face suddenly serious. "I'll be in touch if I need to ask you anything else."

"One more thing," he said when I reached the office door.

I turned around, waiting.

"If you hear anything or someone inadvertently drops a remark about this situation . . . or you remember something else about that *accidently* overheard conversation, you will give me a call."

His face was open and friendly, but his voice had taken on a definite authoritarian tone I recognized. Cops. When they're sworn in I think they're given a transfusion of dictators' blood.

"I always cooperate with the authorities," I answered.

I waited for Gabe on the porch with Lydia and Sam,

who'd already been questioned. While we were waiting, a man with a leather medical bag arrived. The family doctor had come to see Arcadia, who was understandably in bad shape. I guess when you were high up enough on society's ladder, doctors still made house calls.

"Why don't you call in sick tomorrow?" Gabe said to Bliss as we walked down the gravel driveway to our cars.

She stood a little straighter. "I'm fine, sir. I'll be at work as usual."

"Maybe it would be better . . ." Gabe started.

"He's right," Sam said. "You should stay home and rest."

"I said I'm fine." Her voice had an edge to it.

"Bliss," Gabe said, his voice taking on his no compromising *el patrón* tone. "I really think . . ."

"Hey, guys," I said, interrupting. "She knows how she feels."

Gabe and Sam shot me an almost identical frown.

"Benni's right," Lydia said. "And so is Bliss. Let her decide if she feels well enough to work."

They turned and frowned at Lydia, whose black eyes remained unmoved by their irritation. "Boys, how many times do I have to remind you that most women do have the mental capabilities to make quite complex decisions? Especially when it concerns their own bodies."

To my consternation, I was beginning to warm up to Lydia.

She turned and held out a hand to me. "Not quite the best circumstances to meet, Benni, but I'm glad we did. We should have a nice long lunch and get to know each other better."

"Certainly," I said, taking her hand and thinking, *I'm not that warm yet, sweetheart.* I turned back to Gabe. "Let's go home. I'm tired."

On the drive back home, he was silent, and I knew he was worrying about Giles's murder, Sam and Bliss, and how it would affect their lives. He was already in the process of moving her in his emotions from being an employee to being his daughter-in-law, the mother of his future grandchild, part of *la familia*. I sighed, worrying about Bliss, too, wondering how she would manage juggling the two. I wanted to bring up the question of whether she should even be working for the San Celina Police Department if her father-in-law was chief, but figured this wasn't the time to ask. To take my mind off our escalating domestic issues, I turned it to something even more disturbing—Giles's murder. I had a feeling Detective Hudson didn't understand how little the Brown family and mine saw each other socially. Being a city boy, he obviously didn't know that within the ag community there was just as much social hierarchy and class distinction as anywhere. And the Brown family was way above my family socially, even if we did occasionally cross paths during common charity and agricultural events. Then again, now that Bliss and Sam were going to be married and with Gabe's political status as a police chief, the Ramseys were moving on up the social scale. I rested my chin in my hand and stared out at the dark hills slipping by. As much as I liked Cappy and Bliss, the thought of my family being connected with the Browns, even in the most peripheral way, troubled me. Detective Hudson was on the right track. Something in that family wasn't right, and whatever it was, it was bad enough for someone to commit murder. And I didn't want any part of it.

At home, after taking Scout out for a quick walk and giving him a dog biscuit to make up for his lonely evening, Gabe and I settled into our own bed.

"What's going to happen next?" I asked, turning on my side to face him, too agitated to sleep.

"The detectives will go over the statements to see if anything doesn't match up. Most likely that's what they're doing right now." He settled deeper into his pillow. "It'll be a real pain-in-the-ass investigation, what with the prestige of the people involved. Glad it's the sheriff's baby, not mine. And I'm especially glad I don't work a homicide detective's hours anymore."

"Who do you think killed Giles? Except for us, there was no one but family members there. Most homicides are committed by family members; I've heard you say that. Who would you put your money on?"

"I'd put my money on it's not our problem."

"It *is* our problem in a way. Sam's marrying into this family. We need to find out which one of them is a murderer before he does." Gabe's breath, slowing down as his body neared sleep, smelled like spearmint.

"So, what did Detective Hudson ask you?" I prodded.

"The normal questions."

"Like what?"

"He probably asked me the same things he did you."

"Detective Hudson seemed to think I had some sort of insider view of the ag community and of this family."

"What did you tell him?"

"That the Browns ran in a different social circle. That I didn't really know them that well. Well, I know Cappy pretty good. And JJ somewhat. But what I know about the rest of the family is just stuff I've read in the papers. He asked me to let him know if I hear anything."

Gabe's head shifted on the pillow. I could feel his intense blue gaze in the dark. "And you said?"

I laughed softly in the darkness. "That I *always* com-

pletely cooperate with law enforcement whenever it's requested."

His hand reached over and tickled my side. "Sure you
do. Just like the first time we met."

"I do," I protested, wiggling away from his hand. "I
cooperate with you at least three times a week."

"Benni, you know it's extremely important for you to
tell Detective Hudson everything you know."

"I *did*."

"And whatever you find out."

I was silent.

"Benni." All his don't-interfere, this-is-none-of-your-
business, leave-it-to-the-professionals, you're-going-to-
really-get-hurt-someday lectures were summed up in that
one word. Marriage shorthand. You gotta love it.

"Benni," he repeated.

"All right, all right," I promised, laughing.

He grabbed my waist, pulling me toward him. "Ms. Harper, what am I going to do with you?"

"I seem to remember you asking that very same thing
the first time I was called into your office."

"So I'll do now what I was thinking about then."

Some time later I said in a groggy voice, "That, Chief
Ortiz, was highly unprofessional of you. It might even be
against the law."

"So report me to Internal Affairs."

7

THE NEXT DAY at the folk art museum, before I'd even taken off my Levi's jacket, the phone started ringing. Though the murder happened too late to make the *Tribune*, it had been carried on the local morning news. Naturally my first phone call was from Emory.

"I'm goin' to take your name out of my will," he said, his Arkansas drawl thicker than normal this morning, probably because he hadn't had his requisite three cups of espresso. "Why didn't you call me when all this was happening last night? I could have come down and gotten a scoop."

"For one thing, Gabe would have killed me. He loves you to pieces, Emory, but he hates your career choice. Two, you aren't even the paper's crime reporter, so what do you care? Three, you wouldn't have gotten your lazy butt out of bed to do it anyway, so why are you bellyaching?" I chewed on the tip of my pen, unperturbed by the dramatic noises sputtering through the receiver.

"Since when has what the chief thinks about your escapades ever stopped you? I may not be the crime reporter, but I could have clued her in and garnered a favor of the gargantuan variety, and for your information, I wasn't in bed, but you are right, I was doing my best to get there."

"So how did your date with Elvia go?"

"We went to the melodrama down in Oceano. Dastardly deeds and damsels in distress. Reminded me of a day in the life of Benni Harper."

"Very funny. Actually, last night did remind me of a crazy melodrama. People all over the ranch when the shooting took place, a rich, crazy family, and a detective straight out of central casting. A Texan, no less, wearing honey-colored ostrich cowboy boots and writing in a *Beauty and the Beast* notebook. I tell you, Emory, it felt like a TV episode penned by a sleep-deprived, schizophrenic script writer."

"Now I'm even more perturbed. I would have surely enjoyed the spectacle. Why wasn't I invited? I'm family."

"Don't blame me. I didn't make up the guest list. Though we recognize the fact that your father and my grandfather were first cousins by marriage and that your father also married my mother's first cousin qualifies you as immediate family, I'm not sure they would. Believe me, you'll be meeting the Brown dynasty at some point in the future since our families are now loosely, soon to be tightly, connected. I'm not sure how Giles's death is going to affect the marriage plans of Sam and Bliss. It's no surprise that no one got around to talking dates or anything."

"What a nasty little bed of cottonmouths your stepson has stumbled into. So, who do you think did it?"

"Is that my cousin asking or a reporter?"

"Depends on the answer. Seriously, one of our reporters got a weird call about the Brown family shindig yesterday evening. Seems something was going down at the Brown estate that night, and this person wanted a reporter to be there to record it."

"Something going down? That sounds like bad movie dialogue. Who called?"

"That famous fella Anonymous. Anyway, the reporter who took the call brushed it off as a prank, then could have kicked himself when he heard what happened."

"Do you think Giles's murder was planned? No, that couldn't be it. Who would plan a murder, then call the press to come cover it?"

"Good question. Let me know if you find out the answer."

"Seven Sisters is scheduled for a full slate of wine activities starting this weekend. I wonder how Giles's death will affect that."

"It'll triple the amount of people who go," Emory said. "I have only my column to write, which I was thinking might have something to do with the inconsideration of family members who have inside tracks to breaking stories that could help the careers of their loved ones—"

"I have no inside track," I interrupted. "You're as bad as that detective. Believe me, no one knows less about this situation than me, and I plan on keeping it that way. I have enough on my plate with Sam and Gabe circling each other like deranged coyotes, not to mention Mama Coyote herself slinking about."

"Was she there? I thought you said she wasn't coming up until next weekend."

"Apparently she pulled some strings and got her pending cases continued so she could check on her son. For that I have a begrudging respect for her. At least she's putting her son before her job."

"Tell me," Emory said, his voice settling into that intimate, confidential tone that said he was ready to hear some dirt. "What is the dragon lady like? Did you spill a drink on her Armani suit? Grind your boot heel on her Ferragamo pumps? Tell me everything."

"There's nothing to tell, you old gossip. She's a very nice woman. We had a nice talk. She was very supportive of her son. She's very—"

"Yeah, yeah, nice. Don't forget who you're talking to, sweetcakes. I know the Southern definition for nice. Any Southern lady worth her crystal egg plate would rather eat dark meat chicken salad made with storebought mayonnaise than be called *nice*. Were her insults very clever?"

"Not so very," I said, allowing him that much. "A couple of gibes reminding me of her connection to, as she put it, her 'two men.' "

"You'd better watch out, my gullible little pullet. If she's just coming off a divorce, she might be feeling unsettled enough to want to renew old ties with something familiar, namely your handsome Latino husband."

"Give me a break. They were divorced over nine years ago. Gabe said they wanted completely different things in life. She hated what he did for a living."

"Which was?"

"He was working undercover narcotics then. She wanted someone more conventional, someone who wore a suit and went to work every day like a normal person. She liked parties and social stuff. She didn't want to be married to someone who stumbled in at all hours all stressed out because of some drug bust, smelling like a sewer. She wanted someone—"

"Someone who is, say, the highly respected and socially prominent chief of police of a pleasant little town like San Celina?"

I froze, silent for a moment, his words articulating thoughts I'd been denying. "Okay, you're right, he's probably more now like the man she wanted then, but anything between them was over long before Gabe and I started our relationship. Don't do this to me, Emory. I don't need it right now. Things are finally running smooth between me and Gabe."

Emory sighed over the phone. "Sweetcakes, I'm not trying to cause problems between you and the chief. I just don't want anyone to rustle your husband when you're not paying attention."

"He's not a prize bull, Emory. No one can steal him from me. He's with me because he wants to be." I said the words with conviction. I didn't fool my cousin one second.

"Better buy yourself some new lingerie," he advised. "And start cooking his favorite meals more often."

I growled at him over the phone. "You are such a man!"

"Yes, I am," he said calmly. "And if you're smart, you'll listen to me."

"I'm hanging up now."

"Benni—"

"I repeat, I'm—"

"Lunch?"

"Only if you promise this subject is closed."

He was silent a moment.

"I mean it, Emory."

"Okay, okay, closed for the day. But not forever. How about Thai on the Run?"

"You know I hate Thai food. McClintock's."

"You and your hamburgers. Noon."

"And it's your treat since you're being such a jerk."

"Since when do you ever pay for a meal when we dine together?"

After almost three hours of diligent paper-pushing and phone work trying to get our next exhibit arranged, I wandered into the main room of the co-op studios to watch the finishing touches being put on the wine quilt that would be auctioned off at the Zin and Zydeco gathering Saturday night. I half expected to see JJ today, but certainly understood why she probably wouldn't come in. The co-op group was a pleasant one, but they loved gossip, and I was sure she didn't want to face the curious looks and questions.

After a quick foray through the museum, which was showing a display of original wine label art created for Central Coast wineries, I went out the heavy Spanish front doors and headed across the parking lot to Gabe's old 1950 Chevy truck parked under a graffiti-scarred oak that was probably older than the hacienda. I was unlocking the front door when a red Dodge Ram 1500 V8 Magnum truck pulled into the lot. Since I knew the vehicles of just about everyone who volunteered at the museum or belonged to the co-op, and Tuesday morning was rarely a time for casual visitors, I watched it curiously as it pulled next to my truck. There was something that was vaguely familiar about it, but the windows were tinted, so I couldn't see who was driving until the door opened and a foot wearing a forest green lizard skin cowboy boot appeared. Detective Hudson's brown head and the rest of him followed seconds afterward.

"Hey, glad I caught you," he said, smiling widely. He wore a pale green tailored Arrow shirt and another neatly pressed pair of Wranglers.

I walked around and met him at the tailgate of my truck. "What's up?"

"Just wanted to update you. They're sending the recovered bullet and the gun down to the crime lab right now. Well, actually I'm taking them there myself."

I waited for a moment, not sure why he was telling me this.

"Bein' used to a big city, it seems weird not having a crime lab right close. I have to go to some town down south . . . Golatta, I think it's called. And I have to wait for it since the Browns are such famous and respected people in this town. I'm pretty sure there's more to this than anyone realizes, but the sheriff wants it cleared up ASAP. And, he said, he'd prefer the killer not be a family member. I'm guessin' they're a big financial supporter of his, and he doesn't want the till dried up. What do you think?"

"The town's name is Goleta," I said, not answering his question. "It's a little north of Santa Barbara."

"Santa Barbara. Isn't that where that singer Michael Jackson has that weird ranch of his? With carnival rides and circus animals?"

"I don't imagine the city fathers would prefer that to be *the* thing they are internationally known for, but, yes, his estate is in the general area. Actually it's closer to Santa Ynez." I glanced at my watch. I had exactly fifteen minutes to get to McClintock's. "Was there something specific you needed to ask me, Detective Hudson?"

"You want to tell me about this argument you heard between Mr. Norton and that woman again?"

"I told you everything I heard last night."

He looked at the ground, gave a good ole boy kick at the dirt, then looked back up and grinned at me. "Please, bear with me, ma'am, but I'd just like to hear it one more time. For my own clarification."

"Okay," I said with an exaggerated sigh, thinking how much alike cops are. It was the same thing Gabe would have done. "But there's nothing different today than what I told you last night."

He nodded as I talked, watching my body language in that way I'd grown used to since being married to a cop. He took out his *Beauty and the Beast* notebook, flipped through the pages, and wrote something down.

"Is that it?" I asked, jiggling my keys with impatience.

"For the time bein'. Just one more thing. Since you're

kind of on the fringe of this family and I'm takin' it you'll be seein' more of them, I was wondering if you'd just kind of keep your ears open and let me know if you hear anything that doesn't sit right with you. You know what I mean." His friendly brown eyes smiled at me.

"You're asking me to snoop around my stepson's future in-laws." This guy was starting to get on my nerves.

"Well . . ." He gave an apologetic but hopeful look. "You do it so well."

I glared at him, completely annoyed now. "What?"

His country-gravy grin spread across his face again. "Your reputation precedes you. I've only been with the department about five months, but I wasn't here but a few weeks when I heard the stories about you."

I felt my face grow warm. "First piece of advice about San Celina: Don't believe everything you hear."

"Now I do apologize from the bottom of my heart. I never meant it as anything but a compliment. Why, I admire the tenacity and vivacity with which you solved your many homicide cases here in San Celina. You're a legend, you know."

I narrowed my eyes at him. "The molasses is running a bit thick here, Detective Hudson."

"Since we're working together on this case, please call me Hud."

I raised my eyebrows and scratched my neck. "Hud?"

"Yes, ma'am. Like the movie."

"What movie?"

"What movie? How can you say that? *The* movie. One of the greatest movies ever filmed. *Hud*. With Paul Newman. It's a *Western*, for cryin' out loud. I can't believe you never heard of it."

"I thought Hud had something to do with low-cost housing." I really had seen the movie. It was just fun teasing him. Besides, I hated that movie. It was depressing. Paul Newman plays a bad guy who is never brought to justice.

He gave me a disparaging look.

"Hud's a dumb nickname. What's your real name? And for the record, I never agreed to snoop for you."

"My first name's Ford. But I've always been called Hud."

"Ford? Like the car?"

He nodded.

"Ford Hudson? Were your mom and dad nuts?"

"Now, that is something we could discuss at length sometime over a big ole cup of strong coffee. My mama is the finest lady to walk the Texas earth. My old man was unique, no doubt about that. And, yeah, they were both a tad nuts. It could have been worse. If I'd've been a girl, they were going to name me Cadillac."

I grimaced. "Cadillac Hudson?"

"Yeah, good thing the little guy sperm won the race, huh?" He faked a sympathetic expression. "And I understand about the snooping. Chief Ortiz would most likely take away your allowance if he found out."

I frowned at him. "Gabe and I don't have that kind of relationship."

"So, you don't do whatever he says?"

"Of course not!"

"So, if you hear anything, you'll call me?"

I wanted to strangle him. He'd managed to maneuver it so if I didn't, it looked like I was under Gabe's thumb. "I told you, I *always* cooperate with law enforcement. Why are you singling me out, Detective Hudson?"

"Hud. Like the movie."

"Detective."

"Well, me bein' new here on the Central Coast and to the sheriff's department and this bein' my first homicide case, I figured I'd need someone in the know. You seemed like a friendly, intelligent face." The expression on his face was so open and earnest I couldn't help but relent a little. Men who were secure enough to admit they needed help held a certain type of power over women. Then again, the guy was a player, no doubt about it, and his aren't-I-cute Tom Sawyer act probably fooled a lot of people . . . likely most of them women.

"No one would ever believe it if I told them you asked me to help you. Not to mention my husband would have your head."

"You're right on both counts, which is why I'll deny to my dyin' day this conversation ever took place."

"Let me get this straight. You're asking me to help you on this case by snooping around, which, if my husband found out, would give him the conniption fit of the century, and never get any credit for it if anything comes of it because you'll deny you ever asked me to help you."

He nodded. "That's about it in a nutshell."

"You want to tell me why you think I'd even consider it?"

He thought for a moment. "Personal satisfaction for a job well done?"

"I don't think so."

"Justice for a man killed in his prime?"

I just raised my eyebrows and didn't answer.

"How about I'm guessin' you won't be able to help yourself, and you're gonna get involved anyway, no matter what your hubby thinks?"

"Thanks, anyway, Hud-like-the-movie, but my detecting days are over."

"Yes, ma'am." His voice was so smug and disbelieving I wanted to smack him.

"I mean it."

"In that case," he said complacently, "do you know of a good place to eat lunch and kill some time in Goleta?"

8

"YOU'RE LATE," EMORY complained. "I ordered for you already."

"I was detained by the authorities," I said and told him the whole story. By the time I finished, my hamburger and fries and his turkey sandwich had arrived.

"Hud?" Emory said. "You mean, like the Paul Newman movie?"

"Believe me, he's no Paul Newman. And there was a book first. It's ten times better than the movie. *Horseman, Pass By.* Larry McMurtry wrote it."

"You don't say?"

I rolled my eyes. "If you want to marry Elvia, you'd better bone up on your literature, my friend. Cliff's Notes don't count. Apparently, this cop's given name is Ford Hudson."

"Oh, lordy, and I thought being named after a school and a woman's nail care product was bad."

"I can think of worse nicknames for a Texan."

"Like what?"

"Bubba, for one. Joe Bob. Tex."

"You've got a point." He reached over and snatched one of my steak fries. "Are you going to tell Gabe that this sheriff's detective, this Hud"—he shook his head and laughed again—"is putting you on his payroll?"

"I never agreed to anything and since I don't plan on *doing* anything, I don't think it even warrants repeating to Gabe. Especially when he has so much to worry about with Sam and Bliss."

Emory chewed thoughtfully. "Whatever you say."

"Let's forget about this problem that isn't really ours and concentrate on the ones that are. Has Dove approached you about any money-making ideas for the senior citizen center?"

"She was askin' about a walkathon, but I told her that the paper's already sponsored three this year, and though a new stove, refrigerator, and Martha Stewart wallpaper might be important to them, it would have a hard time competing with muscular dystrophy, diabetes, and breast cancer. She made me ask anyway, and our editor-in-chief nixed it."

"I told her I'd try to come up with an idea. The problem is there are so many fundraisers that it's hard to think of one that hasn't been done. Are you going to the Harvest Wine Festival this weekend?"

He pushed his lunch plate aside. "Yep, I've got a full week with the crush activities starting Friday. Seems like every winery in San Celina County has something going on, and my esteemed editor-in-chief wants as many of them covered as possible for a special insert. I'm suspecting the powers that be in the local government are pressuring him to play up the wine aspect of our fair county to better compete with big brother Napa up north."

"That's all we need, something to bring even more tourists into the county," I grumbled.

He patted my hand. "The times they are a-changin', sweetcakes. Cows are out, grapes are in."

"I know, but I don't have to pretend to be happy about it."

We were on our way out when we ran into Bliss and Miguel, one of Elvia's younger brothers and a four-year veteran of the San Celina PD. They were waiting at McClintock's long wooden bar under the TAKE OUT sign. Seeing him in his dark blue uniform carrying a loaded gun and steel handcuffs never failed to amaze me since the memory of cuddling him in my thirteen-year-old lap and singing him to sleep when he was three was still so strong in my mind.

"Hey, Miguel, Bliss," I said. "Who's protecting the streets of San Celina while you two are goofing off?"

"How's it going?" Miguel said, pulling out his wallet when the waitress walked up with two brown paper sacks. Bliss handed him a ten-dollar bill. She nodded at me without saying a word.

"Okay, I guess." I turned to Bliss. "How are you?"

"Just fine," she said, her voice tight. "Have you seen JJ today?"

I shook my head no.

"We had breakfast this morning in town, and she said she was going into the museum to talk to you. Something about giving you tickets to a reception she's going to."

"Oh, yeah, the barrel tasting and artist's reception at the San Patricio Resort in Eola Beach. She was supposed to get me a couple of tickets."

"I'm covering that for the paper," Emory said. "Sunday afternoon, right? Seven Sisters and a bunch of other wineries are hosting a tasting from some vintages that will come out in a couple of years and showing some of the label art being produced by local artists."

"JJ's designing some new labels for the syrah and pinot noir vintages," Bliss said. "One's named after Churn Dash. She's been watching me train him for months, taking pictures and making sketches."

"Who's Churn Dash?" Miguel said, counting out her change.

"A two-year-old quarter horse they'll be running at the track soon," I said. "He's a real beauty."

"I'm working him every evening and the weekends," Bliss said. She lifted her chin slightly and looked into my eyes, as if to say, "we've got nothing to hide." "Whenever you're free, come on out and watch."

I smiled at her. "I'd love to. Is it all right to bring my dog with me?"

"As long as he doesn't go crazy around horses."

"No problem, he's extremely well trained. I'll surprise you one day and take you up on it."

"Ready to split?" Miguel said.

She nodded, taking her paper sack from him. "See you at the ranch," she said to me.

"Count on it," I said.

Outside, Emory clapped me lightly on the back. "Very good, Detective Harper. Now you have free access. Hud will be right proud."

"I'm not going out there to snoop," I said, pulling on my leather barn jacket. "I'm just trying to establish a relationship with the girl who's marrying my stepson. That's all. And the horses do interest me."

"Take a notebook," Emory advised. "Believe me, at our age relying on our memory is death." He laughed. "Whoops, bad choice of words."

"Oh, go find a grocery store opening to cover," I said.

"Now, now, as dear Aunt Garnet would say, let's not let the nasty bird land in our apple tree. Where are you headed?"

"I'm dropping by the Historical Museum to pick up some research one of the ladies there has done for me on early California Chinese folk art and Hmong quilting. We're thinking about having an Asian exhibit next spring."

He kissed me on the cheek. "Be careful in your investigating, sweetcakes."

"I'm *not* doing any investigating," I called after him. His laughter was drowned out by two Ford Ranger pickups dragging down Lopez.

In front of the old brick Carnegie Library building, which Dove and her historical society friends had managed last spring by somewhat radical means to lease from the city for the next twenty years, I ran into JJ coming down the stone steps.

"Benni! What a lucky break for me. Now I don't have to go out to the museum. I have your tickets right here." She opened her small crocheted purse.

"Thanks," I said, taking the tickets. "It's Sunday, right?"

She touched her hair, the green slightly less bright today. "I'm so nervous about it. I'm showing my designs for the new labels and I'm always apprehensive about people's reactions. This is the first time Aunt Etta's let me design the labels, so I want to do a good job. I'm going to actually be working on one there—a watercolor of Churn Dash running, with Great-Grandma's quilt in the background."

"I'm sure they'll be great. How are things at home?" JJ was much easier to ask than Bliss, and for a split second I couldn't help but wish it was JJ Sam was in love with, not Bliss. On the surface, it seemed as if they would be better matched. Then again, I knew better than anyone else that love never paid attention to who matched and who didn't.

"Everyone's in a tizzy, of course. That weird detective left a message for me on my answering machine. Said he wants to talk to me again. Is that normal? I told him everything I knew the night it happened." She rubbed her lips together, slightly smearing her burgundy lipstick.

I stuck my hand deep into the pockets of my coat. "It's not just you. He dropped by the museum this morning to talk to me, too. I couldn't tell him anything else either. I think he's just fishing."

"Giles's family is having a fit about it, as you can imagine. His father is a very powerful man. He flew down in a private jet as soon as he was told. I wasn't at the ranch when he arrived, but I called Jose, and he said there was quite a shouting match between him and Cappy. He claimed we were harboring a murderer."

She was understandably upset by the accusation, obviously not wanting to face the fact that he was probably right. I couldn't help asking, "Who do you think might have wanted Giles dead?"

JJ's face twisted in thought. "I have no idea. He was a jerk, but exactly the type of guy I'd expect Arcadia to marry. Bliss would probably know more than me. She's lived here since she was eighteen. I've only been here a few months."

"I just saw her and Miguel at McClintock's buying lunch. We didn't talk about Giles, but then, Miguel was there and so was my cousin Emory. Emory writes for the newspaper, so that would tend to keep her from saying anything."

"I'm worried about her."

"We all are, but she'll be okay. Pregnancy isn't a disease. She and Sam will work things out."

She reached up and fiddled with the four silver dangly earrings trailing down her left ear. "It's not just the baby.

She's been upset about something else, and she won't tell me what. That's not like her. She usually tells me everything."

"Have you asked her about it?"

Her dark lips turned up in a wry smile. "Get Miss Closed-Mouth Cop to talk when she doesn't want to? I figured it had something to do with work. I knew about her and Sam, so it wasn't that. And she told me when she first suspected she was pregnant, even before she told Sam. Like I said, we usually tell each other everything."

I gave a deep, dramatic sigh. "If it has to do with her work, welcome to the wonderful world of law enforcement relatives. We should start a group. Cop-Anon."

She giggled. "I forgot, you know all about that."

"Trying to get them to talk to you when they don't want to is, as my gramma Dove would say, like trying to milk a two-thousand-pound bull. Ain't possible. Also, don't forget, she's got Sam now, so that might be where some of her confidences are going."

"He's her first boyfriend, you know. I always knew when she fell it would be hard."

"If it makes you feel any better, even though he's young, he's a really decent human being. And I'm not just saying that 'cause he's my stepson and I happen to be crazy in love with his dad."

She touched my forearm lightly. "I know, Benni. It just seems like so much has changed so fast."

"I hate to break the news to you, but as you get older, it only gets worse."

She shook her head, her earrings making a soft, tinkling sound. "What a depressing thought."

* * * * *

I WALKED THE three blocks to the Historical Museum where I interrupted a meeting of the San Celina Senior Citizen Kitchen-Raising Committee, the honorable Dove Ramsey presiding.

"Sit down, honeybun," she said, pointing her gavel at an empty chair in front. "We're almost done."

After an excruciating half hour of listening to the seven people on the committee carp and pick at each other's suggestions, Dove brought the gavel down with an angry slam. "People, the bottom line is we need twenty thousand, we've got three, and the insurance will pay ten. We need seven thousand dollars and we need it fast."

"What's the hurry?" I asked.

"The kitchen has to be rebuilt soon," Sissy Brownmiller said. "There's lots of seniors who depend on the hot meal they get there. It's sometimes their only good meal of the day. It's already been shut down a month. We've borrowed the kitchen at First Baptist, but they're getting kinda restless about us going back to our own place."

"I'm telling you," Dove said, "we need something that no one's ever done here before. I'm sick of bake sales and quilt raffles. We need something that'll stand out. Something people really want. Something they're willing to shell out lots of their hard-earned money for."

"Like what?" Sissy countered. "Bake sales and quilt raffles are all we know how to do."

Dove smacked the gavel down again. "Ten-minute break! Get something to eat and drink, and we'll study on this some more."

At the dessert table, filled with apple turnovers, oatmeal cookies, cream puffs, and Sissy's blue-ribbon–winning black walnut–chocolate chip coffee cake, I grabbed a cream puff, a slice of coffee cake, and a cup of Folger's coffee. Though this group was high class in their home-baked goodies, they'd never bought into the baby boomers' addiction to gourmet coffee. Theirs was hot, black, and strong. I put an extra dollop of milk in it to cut the stoutness.

Dove pulled me aside. "Have you heard how things are doing at Seven Sisters?"

"I just talked to JJ. She's pretty agitated, with good reason. She doesn't want to admit it, but everyone knows the killer had to be someone in the family. I don't think she's ready to face that yet."

"It's hard thinking one of your kinfolk would have that kind of meanness in them, but it wouldn't be the first time. That little Texas boy working on the case is a sharp one. I fathom he'll ferret out the bad apple in the bunch right quick. His mama raised a good boy. He donated a hundred dollars to our new kitchen."

"With a little arm twisting from you, I heard."

She opened her eyes wide in mock innocence. "Why, honeybun, a person can't make another person do something they don't want to do. It was purely voluntary."

"Right, kind of like the military draft. Anyway, if you'll tell me where the information Mrs. Shandon left for me is, I'm outta here."

"There's an envelope with your name on it near the cash register."

"Thanks."

BY FRIDAY, GILES'S murder had been relegated to second-page news since there was nothing new to report. It was still on people's minds and lips, though, according to Elvia. Her mystery reading group at the bookstore had spent more time talking about San Celina's real-life mystery than their fictional English one. Gabe and I didn't even discuss it since his department wasn't handling it. We did, however, talk at length about Sam and Bliss, their impending marriage and parenthood.

"At least she'll be covered by insurance," Gabe said. "Lydia and I are relieved about that." We'd sat down for a rare breakfast together. Usually he jogged with Scout and ate before I got out of bed since I rarely had to be at the folk art museum before nine o'clock, but the telephone had jarred me awake at six-thirty this morning while he was still out jogging. My grouchy hello had been answered by Lydia's sensuous contralto voice.

"Benni? Did I wake you up?"

"Uh, no, I was . . . just . . . taking a sip of coffee." I sat up in bed and ran a hand through my tangled curls, smoothing them down, as if she could see their wildness. "Gabe's not here."

Her laughter grated in my ear. "Out jogging for five miles before his two cups of coffee, bagel with grape jelly, glass of juice, and a quick glance at the front page and sports section."

It irritated me slightly that she knew his morning routine that well. "I guess some things never change."

"Actually, the jogging is new in the last few years, but everything else is the same. If nothing else, our Gabe is predictable in his unpredictable way."

Our Gabe. Yikes. Someone lock the knife drawer. "Want me to have him call you?" I said as sweetly as I could manage without any caffeine in my system. "It's Lydia, right?"

"Right. Lydia Ortiz. Tell him I'll be at home for the next hour, then at the office. He has both numbers."

"Ortiz?" I said without thinking. "I thought you got remarried."

The sexy laugh again. "His surname was Dembrowski.

I figured Ortiz suited me better. Besides, it's been my professional name since I was twenty-two. Gabe and I parted on amicable terms. I don't have any animosity about his name."

"Oh," I said, the irony not lost on me. My husband's ex-wife had his last name, not her second husband's, and I, his current wife, still had the name of my late husband. "I'll tell him you called."

"Thanks, Benni. I'll let you get back to sleep now. Sorry to wake you. Good-bye."

"You didn't wake . . ." But she'd hung up before I could finish my protest.

Gabe found me fifteen minutes later, standing in the kitchen wearing one of his old blue LAPD T-shirts and watching coffee drip into the pot.

He came over, lifted my hair, and nuzzled the back of my neck. "No woman has ever looked better in my T-shirts than you." His warm tongue licked a cool, wet circle on my neck.

I turned and snapped, "And just how many women have you seen in your T-shirts?"

He jerked back, surprise widening his eyes. "Whoa, let's start over. You are the most beautiful woman I've ever seen not"—he held up his hands—"that I *ever* look at other women to compare, because I don't, but *if* I did, you would be the most beautiful, I'm absolutely sure."

Glaring at him, I poured a cup of coffee. His dark face was glossy with sweat, his damp cotton shorts clinging in a way that was not unattractive. The sincerity in his blue-gray eyes was real, and his white, slightly crooked smile seduced me, as it first had in Liddie's parking lot that cold November night a few years ago. I held out the mug of coffee to him. "You're lucky I'm in love with you, Friday."

He took the coffee, then kissed me on the cheek. "PMS,

sweetheart?" he whispered. "Shall I fetch the Godiva chocolate?"

"Oh, man, you're asking for it now," I said, swatting at his stomach. "Bad cop, no doughnut."

He laughed, and Scout, who had been watching our exchange with his one German shepherd ear straight up in worry, barked. I took a dog biscuit out of the jar on the counter and tossed it to him. "Good Scout. I wasn't talking to you. You are the one male in this house who knows how to keep his mouth shut."

"And why are we so cranky this morning?"

"We are *not cranky*. Do you want some toast?"

"No, I'll have a bagel." He opened the refrigerator door. "Are we out of grape jelly?"

I growled inwardly, then said in an even voice, "By the way, Lydia called while you were jogging. She said she'd like you to call her back. She'll be at home for the next hour, then at the office." I poured myself some coffee and pushed my way around him to get the milk, taking it over to the kitchen table.

"So that's what's wrong," he said, his voice amused. He faced me, the jelly jar in his hand, his expression searching. "Was she rude to you?"

I sat down, propping my elbows on the table. The wooden chair was cold against my bare thighs. "No, Gabe, she was perfectly gracious. I just need a cup of coffee. Call her."

When he came back from calling her, he sat down at the table across from me. I was well into my second cup of coffee and feeling a bit more genial toward the world, even one that held perfect first wives. "So, what did she want?" I asked.

"She's coming back up here to spend the weekend. Says she wants to get to know Bliss better, that last weekend was not a good way to start an in-law relationship. She wants us all to go to dinner tonight."

"I agree that it was a rough start to a relationship. Do you think Sam and Bliss will go?"

"I called Sam already, and he's not working at the bookstore. I know it's Bliss's day off. He says he's sure she'll want to come. Lydia'll be staying at the San Celina Inn, so we're just going to eat there."

"Their pot roast is great. It's usually crowded on a Friday night though. You might want to make reservations."

"So, are you free?"

"Me?"

He nodded. "Lydia specifically told me to tell you that you were included."

"How thoughtful of her," I said, thinking, *Bland face, Benni, bland face.* "But this doesn't really have anything to do with me, so I'll pass."

"What do you mean it doesn't have anything to do with you? You're my wife. You're Sam's stepmother. Of course it has to do with you." A tinge of irritation crept into his voice.

I went over and pushed my way onto his lap. "Let me attempt to be a mature human being about this. You go to dinner with your son and his fiancée and your gorgeous ex-wife and let me just trust you, okay? I'll grab a sandwich and harass Elvia at the bookstore if she's not on a date with Emory."

He buried his face in my neck. "I'd rather have you come with us, but it's up to you. Lydia may be gorgeous, but don't forget she dumped me a long time ago."

I laid my cheek on his damp, black hair, my heart troubled, thinking, *that's my problem, Friday. I'd feel a heap better if you'd dumped her.*

• • • •

LATER AT THE museum, in the early afternoon when I'd
finally caught up on all my paperwork, I decided to take
Bliss up on her offer to watch her work the horses. Since
I knew it was her day off, I called the ranch, hoping she
was there.

"Come on down," she said. "You're welcome anytime.
I'll be exercising Churn Dash in about an hour," she said.
"We'll be down at the training track."

I went by the house, picked up Scout, and arrived at
Seven Sisters stables a little before two-thirty. Scout, his
nose quivering with new, tantalizing smells, reluctantly
obeyed my command to heel as we walked behind the stables and down the short path to the training track. Bliss was
jogging Churn Dash around the freshly graded black dirt. I
waved to her, and when she waved back, he took the opportunity to crow-hop and dance around, generally behaving squirrelly. She scolded him verbally and gently brought
him back under control with firm, experienced hands.

I climbed up on the metal rail and watched her start
around the track at a lope. With the cool, early-afternoon
ocean breeze sweeping over me, I felt myself relax and
really enjoy the pure, incredible beauty of a young horse's
muscles at work. He fought her, aching to break into a run.
You could see the pleasure in his neck and ears as she rode
him around the half-mile track. I knew enough about horses
to see this one had something special—that unpredictable,
unknowable thing you couldn't breed into an animal, the
thing that made them go the extra mile, make the extra
effort, the thing that made you suspect they'd keep going
until they collapsed. That thing some people called heart.

After two times around the track she walked him for a
while, cooling him down. Then she rode him over to my

perch on the railing. She pulled off her jockey helmet and shook out her blond hair.

"Glad you could make it," she said, reaching down and patting his neck. "What do you think?"

"He's something special, no doubt about it."

She nodded, her hair blowing wild around her head. "We sure think so. Like Grandma Cappy said, we haven't had a stakes horse in a few years. We're hoping Dash will change that."

She climbed down and led him toward the gate, which I'd already opened. I followed her to the tie stall where she untacked him and slipped on a baby blue halter. She stopped briefly, touching her hand to her stomach, her face tightening for a moment.

I hesitated before saying, "Are you okay?"

"Fine," she said. "Just a little sick spell."

Knowing it was none of my business, I didn't say anything about the safety of riding a racehorse so early in her pregnancy, but I couldn't help wondering if it was a wise choice.

"Can I clean him up?" I asked, thinking she could at least rest while I did that. "I kinda miss doing that on a regular basis now that I'm a city girl."

Her eyes were disbelieving, but she said, "Sure, if you want."

We led Dash over to the wash racks, and she leaned up against an oak tree as I hosed him off.

"Why aren't you coming to dinner tonight?" she asked, scratching behind Scout's ears.

I ran the slow-flowing water over Churn Dash's brown back. "I thought it might be easier for you to get to know Lydia without me there."

She wrinkled her nose as if she smelled something bad. "Designer suits and those perfect nails. And she's a defense lawyer. I can't believe she and the chief produced Sam. Frankly, she scares me spitless."

I laughed in recognition and camaraderie. "I know the feeling. I still feel that way about Gabe's mother. But we get along okay. Of course, there are two thousand miles between us."

"I'd feel a lot better if you were going."

"Sorry, but I have a dinner date with Scout tonight."

"I'm jealous."

She watched me silently for a moment, then said, "Can I ask you something? Just between us?"

Thinking it was another mother-in-law question, I said, "Sure."

"What do you think is more important, your family or your job?"

I answered without hesitation, "Why, your family, of course." Then I instantly regretted my quick response. "Unless . . ." I started, thinking *Unless your job is to uphold the law*. She looked like she might dissolve into tears at any moment. There was no doubt she knew or suspected something about Giles's murder, and it was clearly upsetting her.

"Unless what?"

I turned off the hose and reached for the scraper hanging on one of the metal posts. "Bliss, I'm not sure I'm the person you should be asking about this. Maybe you should talk to Gabe."

"No! No way!"

Her emotional response surprised me. "Bliss, I know it's your family, but if you know something about Giles's murder . . ."

"Forget it," she said, pushing herself away from the tree trunk. "It's not your problem. Put Dash on the hot walker when you're finished cleaning him up and let Luis know.

I have to go take a shower and get ready for tonight. Thanks for your help." Her tone was clipped and businesslike, but her expression belied her voice. Her gray eyes were full of fear.

"No problem." I turned back to Dash, trying to hold back my anger and embarrassment, and started scraping water off his back and flanks. I was irritated at her giving me just enough information to get me involved and curious, but not enough to do anything about. When I was through, I led the horse over to the hot walker, clipped his halter to it, and turned it on. Luis was in the second barn shoveling clean shavings into a stall. After informing him of Dash's whereabouts, I whistled for Scout and headed for my truck.

Glancing in my rearview mirror at the house on the hill, I had to agree with Gabe. Sam had picked himself one heck of a family to marry into. There were times I really liked Bliss and times I felt like smacking her upside the head. I smiled to myself. In general, I tended to feel that way about most cops, including my own husband.

After dropping by the museum to pick up my laptop computer with the vague thought of working tonight, I took Scout home and fed him. After puttering around the house for a few hours, trying not to worry about what Bliss had told me, I finally decided to walk the five long blocks downtown, grab that sandwich, then visit Elvia at the bookstore. Scout gave me a baleful look when I hooked the leash to his leather collar.

"Sorry, Scooby-doo," I said, giving him a quick belly rub, which made him happy. "But this town has leash laws, and we're a law enforcement family. We have to set a good example."

At six o'clock, downtown was busy with tourists just arriving for the wine activity weekend, Cal Poly students already hitting the bars, and families out for a stroll and an ice-cream cone. The city had declared the crush an official city celebration with flags hung from the wrought-iron lampposts depicting grape clusters and wineglasses. Even Blind Harry's had gotten into the spirit with their display window filled with wine books, crystal and pewter wine-glasses, decanters, antique wine bags, and carafes, and huge piles of artificial grapes.

The San Celina Inn, a restored old hotel with a mission-style theme and one of the most popular restaurants in the county, was a little over a mile north, up near the train station, so I walked with Scout down Lopez with no fear of running into Gabe and his ex-wife. I was proud of the mature way I was handling her presence in our life. I bought a roast beef and Swiss cheese sandwich, planning to take it to one of the many benches lining San Celina Creek, which meandered through the center of town, past the mission, and eventually ending at the ocean. Luckily I was across the street when I spotted them at Geppetto's, a new Italian restaurant next to the ice-cream parlor. Gabe, Lydia, Sam, and Bliss were sitting next to the window, laughing at something Sam was describing with exagger-ated hand gestures. I froze, staring at them, people weaving their way around me. They looked so . . . right. Unaware of the tight grip I had on Scout's leash, his low whine brought me back to reality.

"Oh, I'm sorry, boy," I said, loosening my hold. I stooped down and rubbed behind his floppy Labrador ear in apology. He licked my hand in forgiveness. "Let's go before they see us."

I ducked into Gum Alley, a local artistic landmark cre-ated and maintained by generations of gum-chewing col-lege kids, to Blind Harry's back door and punched in the security code. Leaving Scout in the stockroom on a rug that Elvia had provided especially for his visits, I walked through the children's department to the wooden stairway leading down to the basement coffeehouse. All the way downstairs, while waiting for my coffee order, and winding my way through the Friday night crowd to a table in the back corner, I talked to myself about the picture I'd just seen—there was nothing to worry about, Gabe loved me, I *was* invited and chose not to go, and, yes, they looked great together, but looks weren't everything, were they? Okay, so they had history, too, but that was a long time ago. A long, long time ago. Okay, they had a son together. One child. *One*. He was grown now. And *he* liked me, too. I was so involved in my silent pep talk between bites of my sandwich I didn't notice anyone around me until a chair next to me scraped across the wooden floor. I glanced up into Detective Hudson's smiling face.

"Is this chair taken?" he asked, sitting down before I could answer. In the background, the folk singer started crooning "Blue Moon." Detective Hudson cocked his head and listened for a moment. "My mother's favorite song. She's a music teacher in Abilene."

"I thought you said she was an interior decorator in Dallas."

He rubbed his chin and grinned. "You've got a good memory. Where's your husband?"

My jaw tightened, and I looked away, pretending interest in the folk singer's performance. "Out to dinner with his son."

"And his ex-wife?" he inquired, his voice softly mocking.

I turned and stared at him, unblinking. "Are you following me?"

He shifted in the tall wooden library chair. "You're right, it's none of my business. Just hate seein' such a pretty woman look so sad."

"Would you cut the bull and tell me what you want?"

"Just wanted to know if you'd heard anything new on our case."

" 'Our' case? I told you, I'm not involved." I picked up my sandwich and took a small bite.

He unzipped his black leather jacket, leaned back in his chair, and crossed his legs. Tonight he was wearing bright red bullhide boots. Black shafts stitched with rainbow-colored swirls peeked out from under his Wranglers. No Arrow shirt, only a pure white T-shirt.

"Those are the ugliest boots I've ever seen," I said. "They look like something a pimp would wear."

He grinned at me. "Thank you." Then he leaned forward, placing both boots flat on the floor. The folk singer finished her song and started another, an Emmylou Harris song, "Even Cowgirls Get the Blues."

"You went out to Seven Sisters ranch today."

"You *are* following me!"

"Did you find out anything?"

"I wasn't trying to find out anything."

"Sure."

"Detective Hudson, listen up, because I don't plan on repeating myself. I am not going to snoop for you. Not now, not ever. Got it?"

His face turned serious, and I caught a glimpse of an intensity that startled me. "Benni, I have something important to share with you and I'm telling you because your husband probably already knows or will shortly, and you need to know it, too, whether he thinks so or not. We aren't dealing with a heat-of-the-moment homicide like it first appeared."

"We aren't?" I said, before realizing he'd won and pulled me into thinking of this as something we were doing together.

"I suspected as much Tuesday when I was taking the gun and bullet down to the lab in Goleta."

"Why?"

He said slowly, "The bullet didn't match the gun. The gun found at the scene was a .38 revolver. The bullet came from a 9mm semi-automatic pistol. They cause similar wounds, which is why no one questioned it at first. I'm kind of a gun nut so I knew when the bullet was recovered that it was a FMJ pistol bullet and not a lead round nose or partially jacketed revolver bullet."

"What?"

"A full metal jacket. Also, we didn't find a casing at the crime scene, so they must have taken it with them. Add that together with the switching of the guns and you have a premeditated murder, darlin'. Unless you or one of your family members had a grudge against Mr. Norton, it appears one of *his* family members most definitely had this planned all neat and pretty or was a pretty quick thinker." He couldn't resist adding, "Just like I told you that night."

"But it doesn't make sense," I said. "Why would someone take that chance when all of us are there? They could have killed him when he was out in the fields or in his office alone or any number of better times than when a party is going on. I think you're stretching the facts to fit your theory."

His face stayed genial. "You don't want to face the fact that someone in one of your most prominent families, a family your stepson is marrying into, is nothing but a cold-blooded killer."

I stood up. "I think this conversation is over."

He caught me again upstairs in the art section where I was glancing through a new book on Outsider artists from the South.

"Anything worth reading?" he commented from behind me.

I didn't turn around. "Don't you think you'd be serving our county better harassing someone who had some genuine involvement in this case?"

"Just one more thing before I take your subtle hint and leave. Aren't you wondering even just a little who called the paper *hours* before Mr. Norton was shot to say that there was something going down at Seven Sisters?"

I didn't answer and in a few minutes I could tell he was gone. I took the Outsider artist book to the front counter where Elvia stood leafing through a book catalog.

"Put this on my account," I told the clerk working the cash register.

"What's up with the rhinestone cowboy?" Elvia asked. "You two were really going at it over there."

"Let's go outside," I said.

We sat on the bench in front of her store, and I told her what he said and how I didn't want to get pulled into this whole mess.

"Looks like you already are, *amiga*. And what else is wrong?"

"What do you mean?"

Her look could have withered a hundred-year-old rosebush. "This is your *hermana*, you dope. I've known you since second grade. I know when things aren't right with you."

I described the happy little scene in the Italian restaurant.

She clucked under her breath, causing me to laugh because she sounded so much like her mother, though I wasn't stupid enough to say that out loud.

"She wants him back," she said.

"Dove thinks so, too."

"Listen to your grandmama, then."

"And do what?"

"Don't let her have him."

"Are you, of all people, telling me to fight for my man? Elvia, that's the most unliberated thing I've ever heard you say. I'm going to report you to the feminist police. They'll revoke your NOW card."

She laughed, poking me with one of her red nails. "Benni Harper, feminist or not, if and when I ever decide a man is *mine*, you can bet *mucho dinero* that I'll never let any other woman have him until *I'm* through with him. If you need it, I have a great book on poisons at the store."

"Maybe I'd better warn Emory."

Her smile turned into a tiny frown. "He's not even close to being important enough for me to poison, so don't worry about it."

We made plans to have lunch at her mother's next week, then I went back inside and reclaimed Scout from his bed in the storeroom. The walk home went quicker than usual since my mind was reluctantly worrying over the case. Who had called the paper hours before the murder, claiming something was going to happen at the Brown estate that night? Did someone know Giles was in danger? Why not warn him directly, then? Had the killer called? No, it didn't make sense that anyone planning to kill Giles would want a newspaper reporter there. Unless there was some other announcement that was going to take place. Certainly it wasn't Sam and Bliss's engagement that would bring a re-porter out to Seven Sisters. Maybe the announcement that the company was going to merge with Norton Winery? As earth-shattering to the Brown family as that might be, to the rest of the world it was merely another family business being eaten up by a corporation. In this case, a corporation owned by one of their in-laws. That information might make the financial page, but it certainly didn't warrant a reporter being sent out after regular business hours. Then there was that conversation I had overheard—"I'll do it tonight if I have to," Giles had said. Do what?

I was settled into bed reading my new book when Gabe came in at a little before eleven o'clock.

"How was dinner?" I asked, watching him pull off his leather jacket.

"It went really well. I'm feeling a little better about things, though Sam still doesn't have a clue as to how difficult his life is going to be."

"Neither did we at that age."

He smiled. "No, I suppose not."

After he was in bed, he asked, "What did you do this evening? I missed you, by the way." He nuzzled my neck.

"Walked downtown with Scout. Went to the bookstore and listened to some music. That folk singer I like who sounds like Emmylou plays on Fridays, and I need to tell you about . . ." He kissed me long and deep, cutting off my words before I could tell him about talking to Detective Hudson. That was my excuse anyway.

As we made love, though I fought it, my mind flitted over images of him and Lydia, how beautiful they looked together, how they had made love just as we were doing now.

"Querida," he whispered, his shadowed eyes watching my face as his wide, calloused hands cupped my waist. I wondered what he had called Lydia in bed.

Looking down into the strong, familiar planes of his face, an image of Jack came to me, the only other man I'd made love with. Our fifteen years together went so fast. I barely remembered what his lips felt like on my skin.

Gabe closed his eyes, and I wondered if he was thinking of Lydia, of the other women he'd been with, of me. Life with this man was so much more complex than I'd ever imagined it could be, not just because of the complicated adult life he brought with him, but also because of our very different histories.

Then I gave myself over to him, something I never found hard to do with this frustrating, often unfathomable man who made me feel safer than anyone ever had, and for that moment, lost to the hands and lips that had come to know my body so intimately, I told myself the lie all lovers tell themselves, that I was special, that no one had ever made him feel the way I did and no one ever would.

9

"I'M GOING TO the office to catch up on some paperwork," Gabe said at breakfast the next morning. "What time is that wine thing? What's it called?"

"Zin and Zydeco. It starts at six-thirty. I'll give you your ticket now, and we can meet there." I slid the white ticket across the table. "I'll save a dance for you."

He put it in his wallet, took one last swallow of coffee, and kissed me on the lips. "No way."

"For your next birthday, I'm buying you dancing lessons," I said.

"Oh, by the way, I ran into Detective Hudson last night. He told me something interesting."

"What?"

I told him what the detective had found out about the bullets. Gabe's face sobered as he slipped on his jacket. "That's not good."

"So I assumed."

He looked at me intently. "Why did he tell you this information? Were you questioning him about his case?"

"No, he offered the information without me putting bamboo shoots under his nails."

Gabe didn't look convinced. "Please stay out of this."

"I am!" *Tell him about Detective Hudson*, a little voice inside me encouraged. But the expression on his face told me that it was doubtful he'd believe me. Not with my past record. "I swear I'm avoiding this like poison ivy."

Still looking skeptical, he left for work.

Frustrated, I picked up his breakfast plate, throwing a bagel piece to Scout, then stacking the dishes in the dishwasher. That was enough chores for me today. I hadn't been out to the ranch for a couple of weeks so I pulled on jeans and a pink cotton tank top, since the news said it would be in the upper eighties, and called for Scout.

We dropped by the folk art museum first to check on things. Saturday was usually a big day for both tourists and the artists. Many of our co-op artists worked full-time at other jobs during the week and tried to catch up on their inventory over the weekend. True to form, the gravel parking lot was almost full, and I was forced to park in a space near the empty back field. Out front, D-Daddy, my loyal and very inexpensive assistant, was hosing out two oak half barrels once used to age wine, preparing them for plants. He was a seventy-five-year-old Cajun man who'd spent forty years captaining a fishing boat off the coast of Louisiana and was the most dependable assistant I'd ever hired. His daughter, Evangeline, was a member of our co-op.

"I been thinkin' maybe some nice red geraniums," he said, turning one barrel over to drain. "Maybe some impatiens. What do you say, boss lady?" He gifted me with one of his dazzling smiles. With a thick head of white hair he babied with every sort of potion you could imagine, a lean, fit body from years of hauling up fishnets, and the stamina to dance all night, he was, according to Dove, quite in demand down at the Senior Citizen Friday Night Dance Socials.

"Whatever you want, D-Daddy. I know who the *real* boss is around here."

"The real boss is the boss who bosses the boss."

"Ha, he doesn't boss me. Only thinks he does."

"I was talking about Dove," he said with a cackle.

"Okay, you got me there. Are you going to the Zin and Zydeco event at the mission?"

"Wouldn't miss it, *chèr*. Save me a dance."

"You can have 'em all, D-Daddy. *El patrón*'s got two left feet."

Inside, all three pottery wheels were churning away with clay artists waiting, a tan snowstorm of wood dust thickened the air in the woodworking room, and two quilts were set up in the large room, a double and a queen size. The double was a log cabin made with retro western prints from the thirties—little buckaroos lassoing cattle that reminded me of the pajamas I wore as a girl. The queen was another wine quilt—this one was an appliquéd silk and taffeta Dresden plate pattern featuring the signatures of local winemakers. In the middle of each Dresden plate a cluster of grapes was embroidered. The colors were vibrant reds, greens, yellows, blues and burgundies, salmons and pinks. With a black background, the effect had the stark simplicity of an Amish quilt combined with the richness of a Victorian crazy quilt. I stood over the quilt admiring it, looking for names I recognized. I spotted Etta Brown's neat, small signature in one circle. Two circles away, next to his father's was Giles's bold scrawl.

"Quite a tragedy out at Seven Sisters," a quilter wearing trifocal glasses commented. "Heard you were there." The women surrounding the quilt all looked at me expectantly.

"It is a tragedy," I agreed, then turned and walked down

the hall to my office, closing the door behind me. I sat down in my chair, resting my chin in my palm, wondering what was going to happen in the Brown family when one of them was charged with murder.

Though I hated admitting it, it appeared that Detective Hudson was right. One of the Brown family had probably killed Giles. And if that was true, there would be repercussions that would follow Sam and Bliss their whole lives. What a way to start a marriage . . . or a family.

A rap on my door interrupted my philosophical thoughts.

"Benni?" JJ's voice called from the other side.

I jumped up and opened the door. "Come on in."

She closed the door behind her and shoved an envelope at me. "Read this." Her voice was high and agitated.

I opened the crumpled envelope and took out a sheet of thick ivory stationery with the Seven Sisters logo printed on top. It read:

I'll use it if I have to. Tell Cappy.

"It's Giles's handwriting," she said. "There's more."

I looked back inside the envelope and pulled out a sheet of cheap white typing paper. It was a crude crayon gravestone rubbing showing a single lily of the valley.

"Where did you get these?" I asked.

She ducked her head. Her hair lay flat and soft today, a deep red/brown merlot color. Without her spikes, she appeared younger, more vulnerable. Her kohl-lined gray eyes glowed with fear. "It was in Bliss's suitcase. I admit I was snooping, and she'll never forgive me if she finds out, but she's been so upset, and I've been worried sick. She won't talk to me, and so I went to Sam, and he says he feels like she's holding something back from him, too. I have to put it back before she gets off duty at three, but I had to show it to somebody. I'm so afraid this somehow will make the police think Cappy had a reason to kill Giles."

I studied the note, then the gravestone rubbing. "Do you have any idea of the significance of these flowers?," I asked.

"No," she said, rubbing her eyes, smearing her makeup.

This would not look good for Cappy if the sheriff's detectives saw it. Bliss's question about the importance of job versus family made sense now. "Did you show it to Sam?"

She shook her head no.

"Good, don't. He doesn't need to be pulled deeper into this." I chewed on my bottom lip. To be honest, I wish she hadn't shown it to me.

Tears welled up in her pale eyes. "Oh, Benni, I'm so sorry to drag you into this. It puts you in an awkward position, but I didn't know where else to turn. I thought about going to my mom, but she and Cappy have such a prickly relationship that I don't know what this would set off. I swear, everyone in my family hates each other." She put her face in her hands and started crying softly. I led her to a chair and sat down next to her, rubbing her back like you would comfort a small child.

"It's okay," I lied. "We'll figure something out."

I went over to my desk and ran both sheets through my fax machine, making myself passable copies, then handed the originals back to her. I stuck my copies in the pocket of my jeans. "But, JJ, the reality is that someone did kill Giles, and sooner or later the sheriff's department will figure out who."

She raised her tear-stained face and looked at me with such trust that I felt like crying myself. "What should we do?"

I sat back down beside her. "Let's take it one step at a time. It appears from Giles's note that he knew something about your grandmother that he thought he could use to blackmail her. We need to find out what that is."

She settled back in the office chair, folding her hands in her lap like a child trying to behave. "I know a few things, Benni, but Susa and Moonie left Seven Sisters before Bliss and I were even a year old. We came back for occasional visits, maybe three in my whole childhood, so there's a lot that's happened in the family that Bliss and I don't know about."

"Tell me what you do know."

"Great-Aunt Cappy and Great-Aunt Etta have been fighting over the trust fund since Etta started the winery. Cappy didn't mind it when Etta's wine was a hobby. She even seemed proud of Etta's blue ribbons, but when Etta started wanting money for the winery and it came at the cost of Cappy's horses, there were fireworks."

"When did Giles come into the picture?"

"Arcadia met Giles at some wine dinner up in Napa Valley. It was apparently love at first sight for my cousin, and they got married three months later at a huge affair at his father's estate. About a year or so later I started hearing through Susa's conversations with Cappy that Giles was making noise about merging the wineries."

"How did Etta feel about that?"

"I think she was all right with it. All Etta wants is to be left alone to make her wine. It's more than a job for her. It's like a calling or something. She's obsessed with making the perfect bottle of wine."

"Sort of like producing a champion race horse," I commented, thinking how much alike the two sisters were. "So where does your great-aunt Willow fit into this?"

"Ever since Arcadia's parents died when she was nine, Great-Aunt Willow has tried to compensate by treating Arcadia like a little princess. Whatever Arcadia wants is whatever Willow wants, providing it doesn't hurt her image in San Celina society."

"So Arcadia marrying into a Napa Valley wine dynasty was definitely something that made Willow happy. That might eliminate her as a suspect. Killing Giles would be like killing the proverbial goose with the golden egg. Besides, I honestly can't imagine Willow shooting someone."

"That's how much you *don't* know about the Brown women," JJ said grimly. "All of them were taught to use guns early in their lives by my great-grandfather. That's one of the reasons my mother moved away so young, I think. She's always hated guns and anything to do with hunting. Willow and Etta are just as capable of shooting someone as Cappy, believe me."

I looked at her in surprise, struck dumb for a moment. Then I asked, "What about Chase? Did he and Giles get along?"

"They liked to drink together. And they were hunting buddies. I never saw them argue, if that's what you're asking."

"How did Chase feel about this merger with Giles's family's winery?"

"I think that Uncle Chase would be fine as long as no one cut off his allowance." She said the words without rancor or bitterness, just stating a fact. Then she thought for a moment. "Cappy was counting on him to vote her way at the next family meeting. From what Susa said, the executor of the trust fund said that someone was going to have to start cutting back, that the trust can't afford to support two unprofitable businesses."

"So the winery isn't doing well either?"

"It's up and down, I guess. They had a bad year a couple of years ago, lost sixty percent of their grapes to an early frost. It's a business that's always on the edge."

"Like horsebreeding and racing."

She nodded, her hands still grasped tightly in her lap. Her skin was pale under its bright makeup. A sheen of tears brightened her eyes.

I thought for a moment. "Okay, what about Arcadia? How were things between her and Giles?"

"They had their fights from what Bliss told me. He wasn't exactly faithful."

"Anyone in particular?"

"From what I hear, he wasn't particular. Bliss once said that he and Chase hunted more than just wild boar together, but she never went into detail. The only thing I ever heard about was she caught him a few months back with one of the tasting room girls. Grandma Cappy and my aunts put a stop to that, though I heard they didn't fire the girl. That surprised me, actually. I guess Giles had more power in the family than I realized 'cause Arcadia is Willow's little darling. Bliss said Cappy wouldn't let them fire her. I have no idea what *that* was about."

"So, Arcadia certainly had a motive and as much opportunity as anyone at the party. Can she shoot? Do you think she'd have the nerve to do it?"

"I have no idea. It seems like I remember Susa saying Arcadia's father fit into the Brown family perfectly, that he was a gun nut like everyone else in the family. But she was nine when he died, so I don't know if he ever taught her to shoot."

"Just out of curiosity, what's the story on the men in this family?"

She held out a hand and started counting them off on her blue-tipped fingernails. "My dad's up north. Cappy's husband, Stephen . . ."

"You mean your grandfather."

"Right. I never met him, so he's only a name to me.

Anyway, he ran off to Taos in the late fifties to be a painter. My mom was just a little girl. He died in the sixties, I think. Aunt Willow's husband . . ."

"Arcadia's grandfather."

"Right. He was a rodeo rider. The story is he was gored to death by a bull in Reno, but the truth is he was shot by a jealous husband in Barstow."

"Prim and proper Willow Brown was married to a rodeo rider?" I couldn't help laughing at that incongruous picture.

JJ joined my laughter. "I guess we all have our weak moments, and he was Great-Aunt Willow's. Cappy apparently teased her unmercifully about it until Willow flew to Taos and seduced my grandfather and made sure Cappy heard all the details. There's a family rumor that there's a nude painting of Willow painted by my grandfather somewhere, but I've never seen it."

"So there's no love lost between Cappy and Willow."

"Not much, though they mostly stay out of each other's lives. Aunt Etta is the peacemaker, but Giles moving in on her territory caused some friction between her and Willow at times. He must have been really obnoxious about the merger, because Etta's not someone who gets mad easily. But nothing's ever meant as much to her as the winery."

I looked into her eyes. "How much of this did you tell the sheriff's detectives?"

She gazed squarely back at me, unflinching. "Why, none of it. It's personal. I couldn't tell family problems to one of those detectives. Cappy and the rest would kill me." She swallowed hard, her face blanching when she realized the double entendre in her words.

I was beginning to see just how difficult investigating a crime within a family could be. As Detective Hudson suspected, there was much more to this situation than met the eye, and this family was expert at covering up and making things look good on the surface.

"You realize I have to tell Gabe what you told me, and he'll probably tell Detective Hudson. I can't hide anything from my husband."

She scrubbed at her eyes, causing her mascara to smear. "I wouldn't expect you to. I just feel better that someone knows. But can you at least not tell them where you heard it? I don't think I could face talking to that detective about all this stuff."

I contemplated her for a moment, wanting to reach over and stroke her nervous hands quiet. "I'll do my best. That's all I can promise."

She nodded and stood up to leave. "Thanks."

On the drive out to the ranch, I tried to sort out all the information she'd given me. I'd heard the saying that the rich were different, and there was no doubt that the Seven Sisters clan had their problems involving money, but I also knew that families had squabbled and killed over two hundred dollars just as much as twenty million. The amount of money didn't seem to matter; the power struggle was the same, and that was formed when the family members were children, scripts written and parts assigned often before people were even born.

At the ranch it appeared that Dove was entertaining. A half dozen cars were parked in the circle driveway behind Dove's new little red Ford Ranger pickup with a vanity license plate: DOVESTRK. The house was empty, but her red-and-white country kitchen showed evidence that supported my theory with the long breakfast counter covered with plastic-wrapped sandwich platters, casseroles, pies, and cakes. After picking through them and nabbing a miniature pecan pie, I went through the back screen door and across the yard to the barn. Crackly music poured out of the open double doors. Inside I found Dove sitting on a kitchen stool shouting through one of my old San Celina High Stallions cheerleading megaphones.

"Step, step, pause, step . . . Emmett, it's step, step, not step, shuffle! Lift up those feet, old man! You're supposed to be a teenage gang member! Dang it, Melva, how many times do I have to tell you? You're a Jet, not a Shark. Get over to your own side."

"What's going on?" I asked, coming up behind her.

She turned and frowned at me, her pale peach face disgusted. "Land's sakes, I swear I'm going to sell myself on the street corner. I'd make more money than we'll bring in trying to put on a play."

"First, I think Mac might disapprove just a little of the president of the Women's Missionary Union hawking her wares down on Lopez Street, good intentions and Mary Magdalene notwithstanding, and second, what possessed you to put on a play, and am I guessing right that it's *West Side Story*?"

"Ten-minute break, kids. Don't go too far—we've got hours of rehearsing still to go," she yelled through the megaphone. Emmett Penshaw, apparently the head Shark, made a disparaging gesture with his liver-spotted hand and mumbled something to the snowy-haired Jet next to him.

"I saw that, Emmett," she called through the megaphone. "Give me ten push-ups."

He ignored her and shuffled out of the barn toward the house.

Trying not to laugh since I didn't want her irritation turned on me, I asked calmly, "*West Side Story*, Dove? Are you sure this is the easiest way to make money?"

"No," she said, setting down the red-and-black megaphone painted with my high school mascot—a fire-breathing stallion. "But I've about come to the end of my tether, honeybun. Everyone's counting on me to think of something, but whenever I do, they fight me the whole way. All these people want to do is eat coffee cake and complain about their bunions. We have to make some money fast or we'll just have to settle for what the insurance company will pay us, and end up having to turn folks away who need a hot meal. I need to light a fire under their sorry old butts."

I put my arm around her shoulders and hugged her. "Dove, you know I'll do anything to help, and so will my friends. Maybe having some younger people involved will help your friends get more excited about it."

Her mouth turned up slowly into a big, crafty smile. "Out of the mouths of babes. Honeybun, you have just given me an answer to my prayer. I asked the good Lord for a sign, and your suggestion is it."

"What?"

"I wasn't sure if it was okay with God, but I've got the green light now. Mac told me he thought it was all right, but now, after what you just said, I know it is."

"What are you talking about?"

Her smile grew wider. "You'll find out soon enough." She leaned over and kissed my cheek. "Thanks."

I followed her back to the house where her friends were indeed already halfway through the refreshments and comparing knee and hip surgeries. I was pleased that I'd helped her, though I had no idea how. After eating a tuna sandwich and a brownie, I went out to the porch and called for Scout. He came bounding down the driveway where he'd gone to mark some of the towering oak trees. Lydia's shiny Jaguar slowly followed him. I stood on the front porch and watched Gabe step out of the driver's side and Lydia climb out of the passenger's side.

"Hi," Gabe said, coming up the porch and kissing me

on the cheek. "Lydia came by the office and wanted to know how to get out to the ranch, and I thought it would be just as easy for me to drive out here with her."

She smiled at me. "I wanted to see where my son's been living so happily for the last year." She wore plum-colored slacks, matching linen top, and black, thin-strap sandals. Her hair was pulled back with large Hopi silver barrettes.

I smiled back, determined to stamp down the jealous feelings of seeing them together *again* with positive thoughts and the assertion that she had always been a part of Gabe's and Sam's lives and always would be. I'd better get used to it. It would have helped, though, if my husband hadn't looked quite so happy.

"I can't guarantee the cleanliness of the bunkhouse," I said. "Dove stays on them, but between him and the other hands, it can get pretty grungy."

She laughed, touching her smooth throat with her hand. A large diamond dinner ring flashed in the sunlight. "Benni, you don't have to tell *me* that. I lived with his grime for eighteen years."

That made me feel really stupid. Of course she knew what it was like to have a boy around. Better than me. The obvious fact that she was a mother and I wasn't reared its head again.

"I have to get back to the museum," I said to Gabe. "Do you need a ride back?"

"No, I'll drive back with Lydia so she doesn't get lost. You go on to work."

I tried to quell the slow boil inside me. "Guess I'll see you this evening at the wine thing."

"Wine thing?" Lydia asked.

Gabe turned to her, his face animated. "It's one of the harvest events. Zin and Zydeco. You might still be able to get a ticket. What do you think, Benni?"

"I have no idea. I suppose you can try."

"Don't worry," he said to Lydia. "I am not without influence in this town. I'll get you in."

"Wonderful," she said, beaming at him.

Oh, yes, wonderful, I thought.

"I am not without influence in this town. I'll get you in," I mocked Gabe to Scout while driving back to town. "What a pompous thing to say." I growled and made a face at my dog. Scout whined and loyally licked my hand. I ruffled his head and blew him a noisy kiss. "You're the guy for me, Scout. Always and forever."

I drove past the museum, not feeling like facing either paperwork or the million and one questions and requests that always dogged me at work. Before I realized it, I found myself turning off on the road that led to the Seven Sisters ranch.

You're not snooping, I told myself. *You're just going out to visit Bliss, see the horses, maybe tour the wine-tasting room that you missed the night of the engagement party.*

It was almost three o'clock when I stopped at the stables where things were pretty quiet. A Mexican groom was preparing to wrap the legs of a bay mare with a swollen fetlock. Figaro, the masked barn cat, greeted me by weaving around my legs. I bent down and stroked the long black stripe on his back.

"*Donde* Señorita Bliss?" I asked the groom.

He shrugged his answer—I don't know.

"Señora Cappy?"

He jerked a thumb up the road. "*En la casa grande.*"

In the big house. "*Gracias.*"

I wandered around, petting the horses, then decided to walk the quarter mile to the wine-tasting room and the rose garden, which was quite famous among San Celina's flower set. It was a warm, pleasant afternoon, the temperature hovering around eighty. Walking through the garden might give me the time and solitude I needed to think about what I should do with this new information I'd acquired. The one person I was definitely going to avoid was Detective Hudson, who seemed to have an uncanny ability to sense when I was holding something back. I'd give this information to Gabe and let him talk to the sheriff's detective.

It was a smart move leaving my car at the stable, because the parking lot was completely full and the winetasting bar as crowded as an airport at Christmas. Tourists were well into their wine weekend on this Saturday afternoon. There were two dark red limousines from Will's Winetasting Tours parked in front of the rugged adobe tasting room. Chase, Etta, and two female employees were all pouring wine and chatting with customers. It appeared Emory was right. The murder had only caused business to pick up. Either that or a lot of these obviously out-of-town customers hadn't heard about it yet. I left Scout comfortably situated under the shade of an ash tree with the command to stay and stepped inside the cool, spicy-scented tasting room.

Though the outside was adobe, the gift shop and winetasting room duplicated the Montana lodge theme of the big house. The gift items ran the gamut of pewter wine corks shaped like horse heads to glassware etched with the Seven Sisters logo to local salsas and hand-tinted postcards of the magnificent Brown house and rose gardens. I picked up a brochure that explained the history of the adobe structure and the rose gardens.

The long dark oak tasting bar with a brass foot rail and brown-and-white cowhide barstools must have set the family trust back a pretty penny. Hanging behind the bar, an original Donna Howell-Sickles watercolor of three cowgirls with strong thighs and sky-sized grins also told me no expense had been spared. A built-in fireplace was at one end with a dozen or so padded mission-style chairs surrounding it. Over the carved mantel was a professional portrait of the entire Brown family. I weaved my way through the chattering wine tasters and stared up at the photograph. Everyone's smile was flawless and I couldn't help but wonder how many shots it took the photographer to achieve this polished picture. I stepped closer. The smiles were perfect, but there wasn't a genuine bit of emotion in one of them.

I stared a little longer at Giles's face. What had he done that caused one of these people to murder him? Was it blackmail like his letter implied, or something else? Maybe Arcadia, as dramatic as her reaction had been that night, had, in reality, become fed up with his philandering. The switching of the guns did sound planned, as Detective Hudson said, but it could just as well have been a quick recovery by her grandmother and great-aunts who by no means lacked the nerve to pull it off.

I made a note to call my friend Amanda Landry, who was also the volunteer attorney for the folk art museum, to see if I could finagle her into loaning me her investigator, Leilani, for a day to see what kind of history she could find on Giles Norton, his family, and his extracurricular activities.

"Can I help you with something, Benni?"

The man's voice startled me, and I turned, laughing nervously, to face Chase Brown. His face was already flushed with the explosive red color of a habitual drinker. Like his picture in the portrait above us, his lips smiled, but his eyes remained blank. He held a glass of dark red wine. "Are you here for a tasting?"

I shook my head no. "I came to watch Bliss work with

the horses, but she's not here, or at least the groom doesn't know where she is. I was going to go on up to the house, but I decided to walk over and see the wine-tasting room and garden since I missed it the other night . . ." I paused, suddenly aware that a small group of people were inching closer, listening to us.

"Why don't we go outside?" he said in a low voice, taking my elbow. I tried pulling away politely, having always hated that controlling gesture, especially in men I didn't know well. He let go when we got outside. "People are bottom feeders," he said, taking a big gulp from the wineglass.

"I guess it's been hard on everyone," I said.

"You said it," he said, gesturing toward the tasting room with the wineglass. A bit splashed out, staining his hand. He impatiently wiped it on his dark slacks. "Giles was basically a pain in the ass when he was alive, and he's proving to be even more so now that he's dead."

I didn't answer, hoping he'd continue. It was a well-known fact that Chase was half drunk most of the time, and there was no better place to get information than a partially drunk, irritated person.

"Don't get me wrong," he said, looking down at me out of red-veined eyes. "We had us some good times, me and Giles. The guy could shoot, no doubt about it. And hold his whiskey. He could hold his friggin' whiskey."

I nodded, as if agreeing that it was indeed a legacy to be proud of, the ability of one's liver not to completely collapse while drowning in alcohol.

"But he was pushy," Chase said, "and didn't know when to take no for an answer. The man hated the word no."

"I heard he wanted to take the winery international," I said, trying to make it sound like casual chitchat.

"You heard right. Would've been a real coup for Seven

Sisters. Lots more money. Lots more prestige. I could see the advantages better than some people."

"So," I said, hesitating only for a moment before barging in with my question, knowing this might be the only time I'd ever get a chance to ask. "You were going to vote in favor of the merger?"

He drank from his glass again, emptying it. "Where are my manners? Did you want any wine?"

"Not this early for me, thanks."

He laughed and twirled the stem of the glass in his thick fingers. "There's no cocktail hour for wine, honey. Why, there are places in Europe where people drink it for breakfast."

"Well, I've never claimed to be a sophisticate. About the merger . . ."

"It pissed off the Amazon queen, no doubt about it. But the last few days he had her almost convinced to vote for the merger. Willow and Etta, too. Don't know how he got the queen to even think about changing her mind, but he did."

"The Amazon queen?"

"My dear mother, Capitola, herself. That's what we call her. Not to her face, of course. The queen and her consorts. Giles and I did have our laughs. He was the only man who'd come into this family in a long time who wasn't ball-stripped and beat into compliance by the women in this spider's web. Caused him a good deal of grief, and if I had some wine, I'd toast him." He held up his empty glass.

Before I could answer, a twentyish woman in tight red Wranglers and a silky print blouse walked up to us. "Chase, someone wants a taste of the '92 Merlot, and you said no one's supposed to pour that but you."

"Be right in, honey," he said. "Me and Ms. Harper here are having a little talk. Give us some privacy."

She glanced at me, her pretty, freckled face frowning slightly before turning around and going back into the tasting room. Her irritated walk spoke volumes about their relationship.

I raised my eyebrows in a silent, inquiring gesture.

He twirled the glass by its stem and tried to look chagrined. "She's kinda possessive. Which is ironic considering how free she is with her favors."

I wasn't about to touch that remark. "Who is she?" I asked.

"Just one of the tasting room girls. Giles brought her on. When he was through with her, she and I dated a few times, had a few laughs, a roll or two in the hay—literally." He gave a cynical laugh. "She thinks that constitutes some kind of relationship. But she's a good worker and usually a pretty fun gal. Sure you don't want any wine?"

"No, thanks." I held up the brochure in my hand. "I think I'm going to take a stroll through the rose garden, then go look for Bliss again."

"No problem. You come by any time." He gave me a wet, lopsided smile and moved his face within inches of mine. His breath was sour and stale-smelling. "My casa is always your casa."

I took a step backwards, inhaling a shallow breath. "Uh, thanks."

As I watched him walk back up the steps into the tasting room, I added his information to what JJ had told me. I had been surprised to hear that Cappy interceded for the tasting room girl when she was caught with Giles. Usually it's the weaker person in a relationship, invariably the woman, who ends up losing a job or reputation whenever there's an illicit affair. But I knew Cappy was a fair woman and the least pretentious of the sisters. Maybe she was truly trying to be egalitarian about the situation—assigning blame to both sides where it should be.

Then again, I thought, following a group of khaki-clad wine tasters toward the rose garden, maybe Giles had had something really big on her . . . or the family, giving him the kind of power that would keep his ex-lover employed even under his spoiled wife's aristocratic nose. Did Arcadia perhaps have some knowledge about what Giles had on the family? Why else would she put up with one of her husband's lovers working so closely with him in the winery?

It took me about an hour to see the entire garden, which, according to the shiny brochure, contained ten acres of every type of rose imaginable. Many bushes were in full bloom because of the late summer weather. The sheer number of them was breathtaking. Reading the names of the roses—Apothecary's Rose, Yankee Doodle, Bride's Dream, Secret, Golden Wings, Don Juan, Magic Carrousel—reminded me of the names conceived for wines and quilts. In the center of the garden was a great old queenly rosebush thick with large, heady-smelling blooms—white with red tips. Surrounding it were seven slightly smaller bushes in shades of pink, yellow, and red-orange. The way the flowers were planted almost duplicated the actual Seven Sisters quilt pattern that I'd looked up this morning in my encyclopedia of quilt patterns. I wondered if whoever had planted them had known that. In the quilt pattern there was one star or "sister" in the middle and six surrounding it, similar to the constellation after which it was named.

I glanced at the literature and saw the roses were hybrids named for the seven Brown sisters and their mother. The rose in the center was, naturally, Rose Jewel, the others Capitola Jewel, Willowdeen Jewel, Etta Jewel, Daisy Jewel, Dahlia Jewel, Beulah Jewel, and Bethany Jewel. The last four were obviously the two sets of twins who had died.

What took their lives? Back in the early part of the century, it could have been anything. Many of the cemeteries around San Celina had tiny gravestones erected because of an encounter with influenza or some infectious disease that was incurable before our current medical advances. I wondered if the grandmother, Rose Jewel, thought much about the babies she'd lost so long ago. I sat down on one of the stone benches and listened to the trickling of the four fountains situated in each corner of the center courtyard. Wine tasters wandered up and down the rows, exclaiming over the roses, marveling at their size, abundance, and variety.

"Quite an awesome bush, isn't it?" Susa Girard asked, sitting down next to me.

"It certainly is," I agreed, surprised to see her. "Just how old is the Rose Jewel?"

"At least sixty years old," she said. "It originally was up next to the house in a small rose garden that Great-Grandfather started. When he died, Grandma Rose couldn't bear to look at them, much less care for them, so they were moved down here, and gradually this garden emerged. Jose, our ranch manager, has been the main caretaker since Great-Grandfather died. And with the winery, they've now become quite the attraction. It's one of the biggest private rose gardens in California."

"So it says here," I said, holding up the brochure. We sat for a moment in silence.

"Benni," she finally said. "I just talked to JJ a little while ago, and she told me about the note she found in Bliss's possession. I have a confession to make."

I didn't say anything, but continued studying the slick brochure in my hands. This family had more secrets than a locker room of teenage girls, and it seemed as if I was destined to be a part of their clique.

"I . . ." She stopped, hesitated, then started again. "I was the one Giles sent it to. Bliss found it in my room and insisted on taking it." Her voice faltered, causing me to look up at her. The finely etched lines around her eyes tightened as the sun passed from behind a cloud and brightened the air around us. "She said it would be better if she kept it. That it looked too . . . incriminating for me to have it in my possession."

Keep it or destroy it, I wondered. It's true that it implicated Cappy big-time, and Cappy had a good enough motive just with the conflict between the winery and the ranch.

"When did Giles give it to you?" I asked.

"Monday morning." Her voice stayed low, and I had to move closer to hear her words above the laughing and conversation of other people.

"The day of the party?" Things were looking worse and worse for Cappy.

She nodded, breathing in short, shallow breaths.

"Did you show it to Cappy?"

She gave an ironic laugh. "I was going to wait until after the party so Bliss and Sam's evening wouldn't be ruined." Sitting this close to her, I could see her strong resemblance to Cappy in her firm jaw and proud chin.

"Do you have any idea what he meant by 'it'? What about the lily of the valley? Do you know the significance of that?"

"No."

"Why would he give the note to you and not Cappy?" I asked.

"I have no idea. Maybe he thought I'd be able to talk her into doing what he wanted. Maybe he thought he could scare her by getting me involved. My mother is . . ." She swallowed hard. ". . . very protective of her family. That's not a secret, I'm sure you know."

Maybe he's the one who should have been scared, I

thought. "And what he wanted her to do was vote to merge the Seven Sisters winery with Norton Winery."

"Yes, but she never would have done that. It could possibly harm the breeding operation in a big way because the winery would take—some people would say destroy—all the best grazing land. And more important, we'd be beholden to someone else, to Giles's father, who Cappy's hated from the first minute they met. Nothing would convince her to vote to merge our holdings with theirs."

That's not what Chase had just told me. I kept that to myself. "Why does Cappy hate Giles's father?"

Her natural-colored glossy lips formed a wry smile. "Two peas in a pod is what I'd guess, though she'd throttle me if she ever heard that." She smoothed down her yellow cotton skirt. "Benni, I don't believe Cappy would ever hurt anyone. Not even to save her horses. Really, my mother does have a very high moral code."

I didn't answer. We never want to believe that people we know or care about are capable of terrible and cruel acts. One, it was too frightening to think we wouldn't know evil even when it sat at the breakfast table with us, and two, it was even more frightening to think we'd harbor that same evil within ourselves.

I cleared my throat, feeling awkward and apologetic. "I'll have to tell Detective Hudson, you know."

"I wish JJ would have come to me first." She left it at that, knowing better than to ask me not to. If JJ had gone to her mother first, there's a good chance it would have stopped there.

"He seems like a fair man," I said, folding the brochure over and sticking it in the back pocket of my jeans. "That note doesn't mean Cappy did anything, but Detective Hudson will probably want to talk with you both again." I tried to encourage her. "The fact you didn't show it to her helps, I'm sure."

Her face became still. A soft wind blew tendrils of gray-blond hair around her eyes, but she didn't blink or brush them away. "I know that JJ put you in an awkward position, what with your husband being the chief of police. I apologize for my daughter. Normally she would have come to me first, but these days . . ." Her voice trailed off again. It was a trait I was beginning to see was common for her.

"She just got scared. I was a convenient adult, I think. She was trying to keep you from being involved. Maybe she was afraid it would cause problems between you and Cappy."

"Thank you for listening to her and for being so kind to Bliss."

"You have wonderful daughters."

"Yes, they are." She stood up and used one hand to pull back her long hair. "It seems in spite of Moonie and me."

As she started walking away, a thought occurred to me.

"Susa, there's one thing I wondered."

She turned, her silvery eyes dark and questioning. "Yes?"

"Why did you leave Seven Sisters when the girls were so young? I mean, forgive my curiosity, but I just wondered."

"No great mysterious reason. Moonie just didn't feel comfortable in San Celina County or with my family. You can see why. Cappy and the aunts can be pretty overpowering, and my mother didn't like Moonie much."

An easygoing, hippie-type guy who preferred commune living to building an empire. No, he wouldn't be Cappy's dream husband for her only daughter.

"Is that all?" I asked, hoping for more.

An unreadable expression swept over her face—bewilderment, anger, sadness? I couldn't tell.

"Are you close to your family, Benni?" she asked.

I stuck my hands deep into the pockets of my jeans. "We have our squabbles, but, yes, I'd say we're close."

"No secrets?"

Remembering all that had happened last May concerning my own past and that of my mother and of my father's often frustrating reserve and lack of openness, I answered, "Every family has secrets, I think." I inhaled deeply, the overwhelming sweetness of the hundreds of roses making me slightly sick to my stomach.

"Maybe so, but there were too many unanswerable ones in the Brown family for my taste. Moonie and I wanted to raise our girls in a more open environment. And we did. I don't regret leaving at all. As a matter of fact, if it were possible, I would have never come back to Seven Sisters. But it's JJ's and Bliss's heritage. Good or bad, I couldn't keep it from them forever. I just worry that the malevolence I've always sensed permeated the Brown family will hurt my girls. Especially now that Bliss is going to have a baby. I'll never forgive myself if it does." She turned and walked away before I could question her more.

What secrets? Secrets terrible enough that the family could be blackmailed? Secrets terrible enough to kill to keep hidden?

Those questions churned through my brain when I walked back to my truck. I poured some bottled water into a tin pie plate for Scout. While he gratefully lapped it up, I contemplated my next move. My answer came when Cappy drove up in her old Jeep Wagoneer.

"Benni! One of the grooms told me you were here," she said, climbing out. Her expression appeared congenial and welcoming.

"I thought I'd come out and see if Bliss was working any of the horses. And I hadn't gone through the wine-tasting room and rose garden yet."

She reached down and scratched behind Scout's ears. "So, what did you think of them?" His tail wagged slowly.

"The adobe's been restored wonderfully. And the rose garden is spectacular."

"They should be. They cost enough."

Just the opening I needed. "What's going to happen now? Wasn't the winery mostly Giles's business?"

Her weathered face seemed to lengthen, and her lips and eyes narrowed to a thin line. I remembered the look. Suddenly I felt fifteen again.

"That still hasn't been decided," she said, her voice short. "Is there something I can do for you?"

I felt my face turn red. "No, like I said, I was just coming out to see if Bliss was working the horses . . ."

"She won't be doing that for a while. She's not happy about it, but I won't have her taking any chances with the baby."

I nodded. "Yes, I understand. I guess I'll go, then."

She looked straight into my eyes, a cold steel gray that didn't show a hint of her years. They were the same eyes that gave me no sympathy when, tears in my own hazel eyes, I fell off my barrel-racing pony for the fifth time. *Your own fault*, she'd said at the time. *God gave you thighs for a reason. Use them to stick to your pony the next time.* "That would be best. Give my regards to Dove."

"Yes, ma'am."

Her back stiff as an oak trunk, she strode toward her Jeep, then stopped and faced me. "Benni, no matter what Bliss says, please don't come out to the stables again without my knowledge. We have a strict routine with the horses, and new people make them nervous."

My face was hot enough to fry eggs. "Yes, ma'am."

On the drive back, Gabe's annoyingly smug voice silently reprimanded me for my snooping. *That's what you get*, it said. *Are you embarrassed enough to mind your own business now?*

At home, I took a quick shower and changed into new black jeans, my dressy Tony Lama boots, and a teal-colored silk tank top with a lacy V front. With black and silver Navajo earrings, I didn't look quite as much like I'd just come in from cleaning horse stalls.

And why, pray tell, is that suddenly important to you? I asked myself in the mirror as I fiddled with my curly hair, now past my shoulders, first braiding it, then pulling out the braid and touching it up with a hair pick to show off its thickness. I darkened my eyelashes with mascara and even gave a perfunctory swipe of blush to my cheeks. After staring at myself in the mirror for a truly embarrassing amount of time, I made a face at my reflection.

"You're pathetic. There's no way you can compete with her looks and style." I looked down at Scout's sympathetic gold eyes. "Is there?" His tail thumped twice on the carpet.

I grabbed his muzzle and shook it gently. "You didn't have to agree so quickly, Scooby-doo." After feeding him and giving him a rawhide chew, I headed downtown. It took me fifteen minutes to find a parking space, not unusual for a Saturday evening when there is a downtown event. Two blocks away, the Zydeco band Varise's Red Hot Daddies perched on the steps in front of the mission. The party was already in full swing when I reached the line to enter the roped-off area. After getting my hand stamped and receiving my authentic "Zin and Zydeco—the Only Way to Go" wine-tasting glass, I headed for the food booth set up by Momie Fontenot's Authentic Cajun and Creole Cookin'.

The tantalizing smell of the spicy Cajun sausage per-

suaded me to eat before I attempted to find Gabe. I took
my paper plate of red beans, dirty rice, sausage, blackened
chicken, and hot cornbread to one of the long picnic tables
they'd provided behind the twenty or so wine-tasting
booths. I sat down next to a group of four people dressed
completely in black except for their zebra-patterned vests
trimmed with sequins and matching Mardi Gras masks. One
of the females had a long black feather boa trailing down
her back. But this was a mostly casual affair, and T-shirts
with silly sayings outnumbered the Mardi Gras costumes:
"Forgive Me for I Have Zinned," "It's So Good, It's Zin-
ful," "Zin-sational!" "Zinners Wanted."

Up front the band had announced their next number, a
wild dance song called *Valse a Beausoleil*, and the zebra
clan left to start dancing on the large concrete area in front
of the band. I finished up my food and joined the crowd
wandering from wine booth to wine booth, tasting the different zinfandel wines. All the booths were decorated with
purple and green flags celebrating the Cajun theme and had
bowls of unsalted crackers and bottled water for tasters to
cleanse their palates between tastings. At the Seven Sisters
booth JJ and another young woman poured samples of two
different zinfandels—both named after Cappy's racehorses—Churn Dash Zinfandel and Dashing Rose Zinfandel. JJ's face brightened with a smile when she saw me.

"Do you have a minute?" I asked.

"Sure." She turned to the other girl. "Hold down the fort
for a little while, okay?"

We walked over to the ivy-covered fence overlooking
San Celina Creek. Across the water, people at the cafes
were enjoying the Cajun music from afar. The energetic,
addictive rhythms of the electric fiddle, squeeze box, and
aluminum washboard had me itching to move my feet, too,

and after my conversation with JJ, I was determined to find D-Daddy and claim my dance.

"What's going on?" JJ asked, chewing at a raw red spot on her lip.

"I went out to Seven Sisters today and talked with your uncle Chase. He also told me Giles had been fooling around with one of the tasting room employees. A twentyish red-headed lady with freckles."

Her tongue came out and licked her dry lips. "I think her name is Sheila. She's only worked for us for about six months, but I doubt that she's the first. I told you Giles wasn't faithful, but I never like to know any of the details. He'd come on to both me and Bliss. He was quite impressed with himself, to say the least."

"Do you think Arcadia got fed up and decided he'd fraternized with the help one time too many?"

She shook her head in doubt, her pale cheeks burnished gold by the early evening light. "Now that I've really thought about it . . . somehow I just can't imagine Arcadia doing that, even if she did know how to shoot. She's just not brave enough. What I mean is, she isn't nervy enough. Besides, she'd have cracked in a minute when the police questioned her."

"But her grandmother or her great-aunts wouldn't."

JJ's eyes widened. "No," she whispered. "They wouldn't."

I gave a deep sigh, feeling real empathy for her, one of the few innocent Brown family members. "I had another conversation with your mother. She told me you talked to her this afternoon. I'm glad."

JJ looked ready to burst into tears. "She said she was going to talk to you. I knew if you told the detective, she'd be questioned again, and I didn't want her to think I was sneaking around behind her back. It never occurred to me that Bliss got the note from her. I thought Bliss was only protecting Cappy."

"Your mom's pretty upset that Bliss and you are involved. She said she was sorry she came back and even sorrier you and Bliss are here."

"She's always tried to protect us, but now I think she needs our help. It's her family and, whether she likes it or not, ours, too. So, now that you know who gave Bliss the note, what do we do?"

"I have a problem, JJ. I also ran into Cappy when I was there and foolishly tried to find out what was going on with the winery now that Giles is dead. I think I might have blown it with her. She asked me not to come out to the ranch again without calling first even though she knew that Bliss specifically invited me. She's suspicious, and I don't think I can safely ask any more questions."

"What are we going to do, then?" she asked, tears filling her eyes. "Bliss is the one I'm really worried about. She came over to my house after work this afternoon because she felt too sick to drive to the ranch. I'm afraid something bad's going to happen. She loves Cappy as much as she does me, Susa, and Moonie. I'm not sure how she'll take it if Cappy is the one who killed Giles."

"We don't know that yet. A note that may or may not be blackmail is only circumstantial evidence. That much law I do know. As for Bliss, talk to your mom and see if the two of you can convince her to stay with you in town for a few days. If she's not at the ranch, maybe she'll calm down."

"I'll try, but Bliss feels so darn responsible. Like she has to protect all of us every minute. We have to do something." She watched me expectantly, waiting for me to think of something. I felt like screaming, "Who put me in charge of piecing your family back together?" A slight tremble in her hand when she reached up and touched her blue-veined temple caused pity to well up inside me.

"I still haven't talked to Detective Hudson about all this," I said. "Or Gabe." Below us in a cafe courtyard, a group of people laughed uproariously at something. I was tempted to walk away from JJ and this whole situation and join them. "Once I do, it's out of our hands. Your family's going to come under some tough scrutiny."

"I know, and it's all my fault. I guess I should have gone directly to my mother with that note." She turned and grasped the metal fence, staring down into the bubbling creek.

Except doing that and then destroying it would have dug both her and Bliss deeper into a possible murder coverup, not to mention add another brick to the wall of Brown family secrets. "Do you really think Bliss could have destroyed that note and remained a cop?" I asked softly. "The guilt would have driven her crazy. Frankly, I think you did her a favor by bringing it out in the open. You did something for her that she couldn't do for herself."

Her face softened in relief. "All I really want is the pressure to be off Bliss. Do you think talking to Gabe and this detective will do that?"

"I have no idea, but I also have no choice but to tell them what I know. Maybe you shouldn't be telling me any more if you think it might compromise your family. If you need a lawyer, my friend, Amanda—"

"We have tons of lawyers," she broke in, her voice sharp. "What I need is a friend, Benni. Someone who isn't just out to pin this killing on anyone they can find without regard to who it hurts. As crazy as they all are, they are my family, and I care about them."

"I'm doing the best I can," I said, fed up with the whole business. "I'm not a trained investigator."

She wrapped thin arms around herself in a self-comforting hug. "I'm sorry, Benni. I just don't know where to turn."

"I'll talk to Gabe and Detective Hudson, then get back with you."

"Do you have to tell that detective it's me, Bliss, and Susa who have seen this note? Can't you just say . . ." Her thin nose flared in agitation, like one of her grandmother's racehorses. "I don't know . . . say . . ." A sob escaped from deep in her chest.

"I have to tell him the truth. No matter how Bubba Joe Bob he looks, he's not a stupid man. He knows we have a relationship. He'd figure it out."

She glanced over at the wine booth where the other girl was pouring frantically. The girl gave her a pleading look. "I've got to get back to the booth." She turned abruptly away and headed back to the crowded booth.

Frustrated at being in a situation where I had no idea where to turn, I walked back over to the edge of the crowd to watch the dancers twirl and Cajun two-step to the band's hypnotic beat. I scanned the crowd for my husband, determined to pry him away from his ex-wife long enough to drop all I'd learned today in his very capable lap. His dark head wasn't visible to me even when I hopped up on a small concrete wall and peered over the bobbing heads.

"Señor Jose Friday, where are you?" I muttered, jumping down.

In the next moment, I felt a hand grab my elbow and a low, comically villainous voice whispered in my ear, "Lady, I got your number. Spill the beans before I lock you up."

I twisted around to look up into Detective Hudson's grinning face. Jerking my elbow from his hand, I said, "That dialogue is the most pathetic I've ever heard."

"Almost as bad as my taste in boots?"

I glanced down at his feet. They were clad tonight in a pair of dark brown plain leather ropers with one scuffed toe. "Those actually look like they might have worked a day or two."

"They've seen their share," he said. "Are you looking for the chief? I think I saw him over at the Sierra Robles wine booth. Had the mayor, a couple of city council members, and a very striking Hispanic woman with him."

I ignored his barb. "We need to talk. I've got some information about the Brown family you should know."

"Figured as much. After your talk with Chase, the mother, Susa, and the Girard girl with the crazy hair, I had an inkling we'd need a consultation."

"You'd probably get more accomplished on this case if you'd spend less time following me and more time working on your own leads."

"Didn't have to follow far, Ms. Ortiz. The bench underneath where you and Miss Girard stood has great acoustics. You know, when dealing with a family with this much prominence in the county, I'd be keepin' my voice a li'l bit quieter if'n I was you. That's a little piece of country-fried advice from Bubba Joe Bob himself." His exaggerated Texas drawl mocked me.

A slow blush crept up my neck. "So, I guess I don't need to tell you anything, then. Later." I started to edge my way around a group of people bouncing on the balls of their heels to the music.

"Not so fast," he said, grabbing for my elbow again. But I was quicker and used my small size to weave through the crowd, leaving him in the wake of swaying human bodies. I'd talk to him tomorrow and fill him in on everything he hadn't overheard, but for now I decided to let him stew in his own juices. This continual feint and jab ritual we'd established was beginning to wear on me. Right now, the one person I really wanted to talk to was Gabe.

I finally spotted him across the open-air dance floor, sipping a glass of pinkish wine and talking to the mayor and a deputy district attorney who was running for DA next month. Next to him, looking very comfortable and happy, was Lydia.

He's still *your* husband, I told myself. I took a deep breath and started along the edge of the dancing crowd toward them. Before I could get very far, a hand grabbed mine, and in an instant I was out on the dance floor.

"Hey, *ange*," D-Daddy said, twirling me to the raucous, firecracker beat of a souped-up version of Hank Williams's "Jambalaya." "You ready to shake a leg?"

I laughed and fell in with his rhythm, letting him lead me into steps, twists, and twirls I didn't know were possible while the wild Cajun fiddler pushed the crowd faster and faster with his impossible-to-follow riffs. One song moved into another with only a few seconds for people to catch their breath and start again. Early in our third dance, after D-Daddy had twirled me around three, four, five times, I felt his hand leave mine and another, larger one take its place.

"Hey, Mrs. Ortiz," Detective Hudson said, smiling his Tom Sawyer smile. "Did I forget to tell you these were my dancing boots?"

"What?" I sputtered as he twirled me around three times and spun me around the crowded dance area. It took every bit of concentration I had to keep up with him. Somebody had taught this man how to dance. As we moved around the other couples, I glanced over the crowd, looking for Gabe, hoping with pure petty juvenile revenge that me dancing with another man would seriously annoy him. Naturally he was nowhere to be seen.

At the end of the song, breathing heavily, I jerked my hand out of Detective Hudson's and pushed my way through the milling people. He caught up and fell into step beside me.

"Man, haven't moved like that for months," he said, wiping his forehead with the back of his hand. "It's like riding a bike, though. How about you? Did you enjoy it?"

"Where did . . . ?"

"My mother owns a Cajun restaurant and dance hall in Beaumont, Texas," he said, winking at me. "That's where I was born and spent my delinquently formative years. Did I fail to mention I was half Cajun?"

Another exaggerated mother story. "Good-bye, Detective Hudson," I said, disgusted.

He continued walking beside me, not speaking again until we reached my truck two blocks away.

"What is in those notes you and the Girard girl were discussing?" His face was dead serious now.

"I'll call your office tomorrow and make an appointment," I said, opening my car door. "We can discuss it then."

He grabbed the door from my hand and slammed it closed. His swift and unexpected action caused me to jump.

"I don't think so," he said. Then added, "Ma'am."

I tightened my lips and told myself to breathe deeply. "Fine," I said and in a terse voice told him everything that had happened since JJ first came into my office this morning.

"Add that note with the conversation you *accidentally* overheard at the party, and it sounds an awful lot like blackmail," he said.

"So it appears," I replied, ignoring his gibe.

"Do you think Susa Girard knows what it is Giles Norton had on Cappy?"

"I have no idea."

"Looks like Officer Girard, Miss Girard, and their delightful mother and I need to chat again. And I'd like to take a look at that note and grave rubbing myself. What kind of flower did you say it was?"

"Lily of the valley." A cold breeze . . . or the thought of the grave rubbing . . . caused me to shiver. Goosebumps covered my bare arms. I slipped my hand in the back pocket of my jeans and touched the copies of the note and grave rubbing. I knew I should show them to him right now, but he'd irritated me so much, I decided to keep quiet. Let him get his own copies. "Maybe you should talk to Gabe before you talk to Bliss."

"I don't have to clear anything with Chief Ortiz. He's not *my* boss."

I frowned at him.

"Have you told him any of this?" he pressed.

"I'm on my way home to tell him now. We haven't crossed paths long enough to talk today. He's . . . we've both been busy."

He nodded, his eyes solemn. "Ex-wives have a way of taking up a man's time, that's for sure."

"Is there anything else, Detective Hudson?" I said coolly, not about to discuss Gabe or his ex-wife with him.

"Not right now, but I'll be in touch. You're doin' a bang-up job, Mrs. Ortiz."

"My last name is Harper," I snapped.

His thick eyebrows went up. "You don't say? You're one of them liberated women? Gotta maintain your own identity and all? I'm impressed."

"It's not because . . ." I started, then stopped, annoyed at myself for even bringing it up. "Oh, forget it." I started to climb in the truck, then turned and said, "When you talk to Bliss, please be careful. She's . . . well, she's not feeling too good and this . . ."

"Benni," he said softly. "I'm not going to browbeat a pregnant woman. Give this Texas bubba credit for having some class even if I do wear white-trash boots."

Again I felt my face go hot. It was disconcerting at times how well he read my mind.

He reached over and touched a finger to my cheek. I jerked back, surprised by the tiny jolt of electricity I felt. His knowing chuckle made me want to slap him. He mimed tipping his hat and said smoothly, "Thanks for the dance, darlin'. Most fun I've had since I landed here on the Central Coast."

I watched him walk away, my hand still itching to do something, like throw a rock at the back of his head or slap my own husband upside the head because his preoccupation with his ex-wife was putting me in this awkward position.

Gabe's Corvette was parked in front when I got home, but he wasn't inside the house. They were obviously still cruising around in Lydia's car. I took a quick shower and pulled on a cotton T-shirt and boxer-style shorts and was making myself a vanilla Coke when Lydia's Jag pulled up in front of our house. The clock above the stove read eight o'clock. Through the kitchen window I watched him get out of the driver's seat and walk across the yard, whistling softly.

"Hi," I said, sipping on my drink at the kitchen table. "Guess we missed each other tonight."

"Guess so. I was talking to Larry, that deputy district attorney who's running for DA and Lydia and he discovered they had some people in common. After tasting a couple of wines, we went over to the Thai restaurant for a quick bite. Lydia doesn't care for Cajun food."

"Oh." The ice in my drink cracked, sounding loud in the silence.

He pulled his dark green polo shirt over his head in one swift motion. "It's warm tonight, don't you think?"

"Anything new with Sam?"

He shook his head, throwing the shirt over a chair. "He's worried about Bliss, but other than that, we haven't really formulated a plan yet."

But you and Lydia are sure spending a lot of time discussing it, I wanted to say. Pride and pure-born Ramsey stubbornness kept me from saying it. I was determined not to appear the irrationally jealous second wife. I stirred the ice in my glass with my finger. "I talked to Detective Hudson tonight."

"Again?" A flicker of suspicion came over his face, then was gone. "Well, I'm glad you're cooperating with him. This has to be a tough case to investigate. What did he want?"

Starting with the note JJ found in Bliss's suitcase, I went through everything I discovered today. "Detective Hudson said he's going to have to talk to all of them again."

Gabe nodded, sitting down at the table across from me. "Yes, I can see why." He ran a hand through his thick black hair. "I suspected Bliss knew more than she was telling."

"Gabe, this detective. What do you know about him?"

He leaned back in his chair, his face concerned. "Just another detective, sweetheart. He's new on the force, but apparently has good references from Texas. Why, is he causing you some problems?"

"No, not at all," I said a little too quickly.

His eyes searched my face, but he didn't press for more information. "Just be cooperative, Benni. And try to get Bliss's sister and mother to take their concerns directly to him. I don't like you being that involved."

"Whether we like it or not, we're involved with this up to our eyebrows. And for your information, every time JJ has come to me, I've not only told her to talk to Detective Hudson, but also that anything she tells me I'll have to tell you and the detective."

"*Mi niña muy buena,*" he said, getting up. "Looks like I've finally got you paper-trained."

"Sexist pig." I took an ice cube and threw it at him. He gave a surprised grunt when it bounced off his bare chest.

Later that night, as he lay sleeping next to me, my wide-awake brain hummed like an agitated hive, and I mulled over the events of the day, especially the contents of the envelope Giles gave to Susa.

A grave rubbing of a lily of the valley.

I'll use it if I have to. Tell Cappy.

Was it a real tombstone somewhere? Unfortunately there were lots of cemeteries in San Celina County. It could take weeks to go through all of them looking for a specific tombstone. Narrow it down, that's what I needed to do.

As I drifted closer to sleep, the black crayon rubbing drew itself in my mind, and the refrain *Find the tombstone* reverberated like an echo. Where was this tombstone? And whose was it? And the most pressing question of all: What about it would cause someone to kill Giles?

10

GABE AND I spent the next morning, Sunday, laying around reading the newspaper. No one called or came by, and for a little while I could forget everything that had happened in the last week—Sam's announcement, Lydia's presence, Giles's murder, Detective Hudson's uncomfortable attentions. About noon we met Emory downtown for brunch at a new Mexican restaurant that was getting rave reviews— El Cantina Gallo. Over seafood enchiladas the conversation turned to Elvia's work habits. As usual, she'd been too busy to join us.

"This is her day off, and she insists on going in for a few hours," Emory complained over his empty margarita glass.

"That's just her," I said, scooping up some guacamole with a fresh, hot tortilla chip. The reviews had been right. "If you're serious about her, you'd better get used to it."

"She's driving me nuts," Emory moaned, gesturing to the waitress for another margarita.

My cousin was one of those Southern men who knew

how to wring every ounce of pleasure out of his leisure time. Though deep inside I knew he and Elvia were right for each other, there were definitely some surface issues that needed work.

"Welcome to the real world, Emory," Gabe said, laughing. "It only gets worse."

I elbowed him. "Hey, Friday, we're trying to encourage, not discourage. Remember?"

While we continued to dispense sage and silly advice to Emory, Elvia's brother Miguel walked in. He spotted us and waved. Then he spoke briefly to the man at the take-out counter and came over to our table, adjusting the paraphernalia hooked to his heavy leather police belt.

"How's things going, Miguel?" Gabe asked.

"Fine, Chief. Sunday morning watch is a piece of cake. All the drunks are sleeping it off somewhere. Last night was crazy, though."

Gabe nodded. "I figured when that new bar next to the Chinese buffet started selling beer for seventy-five cents it would be trouble."

"Gum Alley is unwalkable today," Miguel said. "Hope the city gets someone down there to clean it up soon. Puke and piss, that's all those skippies know how to do."

"Skippies?" Emory said.

"College students," Gabe interpreted. "Specifically the drinkers."

"And to think they'll be running the treasury when we're collecting Social Security," Emory said. "Lord have mercy."

"Can we change the subject?" I asked, staring down at my enchilada, which was looking decidedly less appetizing.

"Sure," Miguel said. "Actually, I came over to give you a message, Benni."

"Me?" I said.

"Tell Dove no."

I gave him a confused look. "What?"

"Just what I said. Tell her no. Absolutely not. No way."

"What?"

"Just tell her."

The man at the take-out counter called out his name.

"Gotta go," he said. He nodded at Gabe and Emory. "Later, *amigos*."

"Take it easy," Gabe said.

"Don't work too hard," Emory called after him.

"Ignore that comment," Gabe added.

I cut another piece of my enchilada. "Wonder what his message to Dove means."

"Who knows what our dear Dove has brewing in her box of tricks," Emory said.

"Talk about your mixed metaphors," I said.

"Keep quiet, sweetcakes. I'm suffering this morning. I don't need my English scrutinized."

"Whiny-baby. So are you going to the barrel tasting and artist's reception this afternoon?"

"Have to. I'm covering it for the paper. You two going?"

"Yes," I said.

"No," Gabe said.

I turned to him, surprised. "I thought you were going."

He took a sip of his Corona beer. "Didn't I tell you last night that Sam, Bliss, Lydia, and I were going to visit Lydia's mother in Buellton?"

"No," I said slowly. "You didn't."

"I'm sure I did. Or I must have told you this morning."

"And I'm sure I would have remembered," I said, feeling a slowly rising heat in my chest. "I didn't even know Lydia's mother lived close by."

"Lydia moved her there when she took the job in Santa Barbara. Sam wanted us to come with him and Bliss when they tell her about their engagement and the baby. I'm sure I asked you if you wanted to go."

"No, you're mistaken," I said, really starting to get mad now. "You never mentioned it to me."

Gabe's face set in that stubborn, contrary look that said he was certain he was right and I was wrong.

Emory's amused green eyes darted from my face to Gabe's.

"Well, do you want to go?" Gabe asked, his voice carrying an edge of impatience.

I inhaled deeply, my anger feeling like too much air in a helium balloon. "No, thank you," I said, as sweetly as I could manage. "I promised JJ I'd go to the barrel tasting."

"Fine." He turned to Emory. "Can you give her a ride there and home? I'm late already."

"Certainly," my cousin said serenely. "I'll take good care of your wife, Cousin Gabe."

Gabe wiped his mouth quickly with his linen napkin and slid out of the booth. He leaned over and kissed me on the forehead. "I'll see you tonight, sweetheart."

"Sure," I said.

After he left, Emory studied me silently until I finally blurted out, "Oh, for crying out loud, Emory. What can I do, hog-tie him and sit on his chest?"

He shook his head slowly. "I'm tellin' you, sweetcakes, that woman is plain after your man. You'd best be circling the wagons and filling up the muskets."

"Now you're mixing your historical references."

"So what are you going to do, pray tell?"

"First I'm going to the ladies' room, then I'm going to let you take me to the barrel tasting. The rest, as my famous kinswoman once said, I'll think about tomorrow."

"New lingerie. Many a man has been lured back home with a satin bustier and lacy garter belt."

I tossed my crumpled napkin across the table at him. "Turn blue."

As I was leaving the ladies' room, heading toward the lobby, a voice called my name. A voice I'd heard just a little too often lately.

"Why, Mrs. Ortiz . . . oh, excuse me, *Harper*. What a fine surprise it is running into you on this bright and sunny Sunday afternoon." Detective Hudson, shooting me his stupid grin, threw his arm around a small, buxom brunette wearing a front-laced blouse similar in style to the bustier my cousin was entreating me to buy to save my marriage. She filled it out much more generously than I would have, and Detective Hudson's physical preference in women was painfully obvious. His date, not cracking a smile, scanned me up and down, then discarded what she saw with the flick of an artificial eyelash.

"Hello, Detective Hudson," I said.

"Hud," he said. "We're off the clock."

"And I have someone waiting." I moved past them only to find myself stopped short by his hand grabbing my upper arm.

"I'll need to see you in my office on Monday," he said. "There's some ideas I want to discuss with you about our case."

"Sorry, I work at my real job on Mondays," I said, jerking my arm back.

Emory's Cadillac Seville was waiting for me out front. In exchange for the ride, all the way to Eola Beach I was forced to listen to another lecture on keeping my husband from the clutches of his evil ex-wife.

"That's enough," I declared when we reached the parking lot of the San Patricio Resort and Country Club. "I've heard every argument in your pea-sized, testosterone-fueled brain and I'm still going to do what feels right to me, so why don't you just dry up."

He feigned a hurt expression. "I was only trying to help," he said as we walked across the wide lawn toward the three blue-and-white circus-style tents.

"I think you're trying to ignore your own problems in the love department by becoming obsessed with mine. If Gabe's behavior is bothering you that much, then you say something to him about it."

"I might do that very thing, oh, naive one. But you have to admit it made you mad that he's spending another family-oriented day with the ex–Mrs. Ortiz."

Ignoring him, I handed my ticket to the woman wearing an aqua and black T-shirt with the South Counties Vintners' Association logo—two wineglasses clicking in front of an oak tree—and received my wineglass and tasting guide. Emory flashed his press pass and shook his head when offered a glass.

"I'll use hers," he said.

We entered the first tent where the wineries, twenty-seven according to our literature, had their booths set up. It was similar to the event last night except the booths carried all types of wines—merlots, ports, pinot noirs, chardonnays, syrahs, cabernet sauvignon, and some I'd never heard of—nebbiolo, sigiovese, moscato allegro, gamay beaujolais. The names sounded as romantic as a gondola ride in Venice. The only thing different about these wines was that they were poured from bottles that were hand-labeled since the vintages wouldn't actually be on sale for a year or two. The vintners were hoping wine lovers would take a chance on a young wine and order cases on speculation.

"I wonder if they have anything else to drink," I said, handing him my wineglass. Sure enough, in the middle of the tent were huge aluminum washtubs filled with ice and bottles of fruit juices, Snapple, and sparkling water. I headed toward the drinks, Emory dogging my steps.

"Admit it," he said. "You *were* angry when he told you he was spending another day with Lydia."

I faced my cousin. "Okay, I'm angry. Are you happy now? But what can I do?" He opened his mouth, and I quickly held up my hand. "Wait, let me rephrase that, because you have way too many suggestions. I'm trying desperately to keep this situation from turning into one that will cause a serious problem between me and Gabe. Yes, I agree he's spending a lot of time with her. Maybe too much. But this thing with Sam and Bliss is complicated, and Sam *is* their son. I can't change that. I just have to trust in his love for me, Emory. Please, don't make this harder for me than it already is."

His handsome face softened with a look of genuine contrition. He pulled me to him in a warm, brotherly hug. "You're right. I'm just makin' things harder for both y'all. I'll keep my big mouth shut from now on. But if you need anything, you let me know. Promise, now?"

I kissed his cheek. "Emory Delano Littleton, you know you'd be the first person I'd run to."

"Good. Now I'd better get to work if I'm goin' to have an article to turn in tomorrow. Let's meet back here in two hours."

"Sounds good. I'm going over to the artists' tent and see exactly how a wine label is created."

I grabbed a bottle of sparkling water, twisted off the cap, and walked over to the second tent. Inside were a dozen different platforms where artists, using a variety of media, worked on paintings and drawings destined to be incorporated into wine labels. Some of the artists talked to their

audience as they worked, explaining how they came up
with the idea for each particular wine label.

I wandered through the exhibit of original art displayed
with the finished wine labels framed next to them. Seven
Sisters labels were simple but elegant, with some of the last
year's vintage's labels showing more variety with bold,
brightly colored renderings of the rose garden, the adobe
tasting room, and rows of thick, lush grapevines. Though
I'd only seen her work on quilts, JJ's slightly eccentric,
free-form style was apparent on these labels.

In a corner of the tent, JJ was working on a watercolor
painting of a horse I instantly recognized as Churn Dash. I
mingled with the crowd, watching her add subtle reddish
shading to his brown coat. He was shown at a gallop, and
in the background she'd painted in faint peaches and
browns the pattern of a Churn Dash quilt. A photograph of
the quilt made by her great-grandmother was taped to her
stained easel. In her painting she'd captured the championship bearing of Churn Dash with the arch of his elegant
neck straining toward an imaginary finish line and the subtle, powerful surge of muscles in his strong, solid hindquarters. She glanced up when someone asked her a
question, caught my eye, and nodded at me. I waved and
melted back into the crowd. I wanted to talk to her again
about the grave rubbing, but this wouldn't be the best time
or place to do so.

In the last tent the silent auction items were displayed,
and the line for the gourmet buffet donated by local restaurants was at least a half-hour wait. The food didn't interest me since I'd just eaten, so I headed for the auction
items. There were dozens of things to be auctioned—cases
of wines, bed-and-breakfast packages, limousine wine
tours, and wine dinners for six hosted by celebrity chefs.
Seven Sisters had sponsored a contest and silent auction for
wine bottles decorated by local artists. The entries were

spectacular with each artist vying for the most creatively original bottle. The auction bids were way out of my price range, but the money went for a good cause—the Rose Jewel Brown Children's Wing at General Hospital. The artist won a free case of Seven Sisters' most exclusive handcrafted noble wines, wines that were like a stakes horse, the best of the best. An announcement from the stage informed everyone of the wine bottle design winner. On the stage behind the row of twenty or so decorated bottles sat Cappy Brown, her sister Etta, and dressed in white and sitting in a wheelchair, their mother, Rose Brown. Her face was lightly spotted with age, but her silver hair and soft makeup were perfect. She looked twenty years younger than her ninety-six. The advantages of wealth and good genetics, I supposed. She smiled at the audience with long, pale ivory teeth, giving a palm-out royal wave.

After a long speech of gushing gratitude by the president of the vintner's association to the Brown family for helping to sponsor the event and a retrospective of all the accomplishments and charities instituted by the Brown family and most of all, Rose Brown, Cappy addressed the audience.

"On behalf of my mother and the rest of my family, I thank you for your kind words. Her health being quite fragile, she is unable to speak, but she wanted me to relay to all of you how privileged she's felt to be a part of this county for so many years, how grateful she is for your generosity, and to encourage you to dig deep in your pockets today and support the Rose Jewel Brown Children's Wing. As Mother has always said, without the children we have no future. Thank you."

After the applause, the winner of the bottle contest was brought up to receive his plaque. An artist who'd painted a 16th-century–style Madonna and child scene in exquisite detail won over bottles painted like rocket ships, Marilyn

Monroe, Chumash Indian petroglyphs, peacocks, and the Mission Santa Celine. Starting to get bored, I decided to go back to the wine-tasting tent to see if I could find Emory and convince him to leave early. The lines were five and six deep at each booth as people twirled their glasses, sipped, and pursed their lips, searching for that perfect wine. I looked over the crowd and didn't see my cousin's blond head anywhere. To kill time more than anything else, I sidled close to people and eavesdropped on their comments about wine, which amused me to no end with their pretentiousness. I wished I had a tape recorder so I could replay some of them for Gabe later tonight.

"Stylistically," said a man wearing a baby blue golf shirt and white tennis shorts as he twirled a glass of straw-colored wine, "this would appeal more to the American palate than to the European, don't you think?"

The woman with him, wearing flat gold sandals and a bright pink spaghetti-strap dress nodded and added, "Its aroma is full and pretty, but not quite as multidimensional as I normally prefer."

He took another sip and said, "Yes, it has a ripe flavor. A bit earthy and tart, which is refreshing, but the finish is a little rough."

"There are so many wines like that," she agreed. "More up front than on the finish."

"Many men, too," a deep, familiar voice whispered in my ear. A gentle, bearlike hand slipped under my hair and gripped the back of my neck.

I squealed and swung around.

"Isaac!" I said, giving him a fierce hug. His massive arms lifted me up and swung me around.

"Isn't that Isaac Lyons, the photographer?" the lady in the pink dress exclaimed to her companion. They gazed up at his six-feet-four-inch frame topped with hair as white as a snow owl's, their mouths slack with awe. A diamond earring in his ear caught an overhead light and twinkled. As did his dark raisin eyes when he winked at me.

Isaac set me down and smiled at the woman, his arm still around my shoulders. "Isaac Lyons?" he boomed. "Why, I heard he's bought the farm, that randy old goat. Rumor has it he was caught with another man's wife and took three shots to the belly, but he went down kicking. Hemingway would have been proud." His face grew serious. "Then again, that could have been Gregory Peck. They're often mistaken for each other." Before the woman could speak, he grabbed my hand and pulled me through the murmuring crowd.

"What are you doing here?" I asked as he led me out of the tent.

He pointed to a picnic bench out near the lagoon that flowed into Eola Bay. "Let's talk away from the madding crowd."

We sat down underneath the cool shade of an ash tree. He leaned back on his elbows and I straddled the bench, just looking at him, unable to believe he was really here. Isaac had come into my life and, more important, into Dove's last November, a little less than a year ago when we'd all become involved in a murder that took place on the ranch. Having no family of his own, he'd adopted ours, and we'd welcomed him with open hearts and arms. Well, I eventually did after a rather rough beginning. As famous as Ansel Adams, Isaac Lyons had traveled all over the world, been married five times, taken photographs of kings, popes, cowboys, ranch women, carnival workers, cotton farmers, bar maids and truck drivers. Not to mention five different presidents of the United States. But he was still as down-to-earth as homemade gravy and he was besotted with Dove, which revealed his excellent taste. After our

rocky start, I gave this mountain-sized man my whole heart
and treated him like the grandfather I'd never had. Dove
and I completely agreed on how special he was and also
agreed that it was a good thing he was forty years older
than me, or we'd be cat fighting over his affections. He and
I had kept up a regular correspondence via E-mail.

He was dressed casually, as always, in faded Levi's, a
khaki cowboy shirt with embroidered red arrows on the
yokes, and beaded leather moccasins. His long white hair
was braided in a thick rope, the end tied with a piece of
rawhide. It just touched the top of his hand-tooled belt.

"Do I pass inspection?" he asked, chuckling.

"Your hair's longer than mine," I said, flicking his braid.
"My braid just barely clears my shoulders."

"So your grandma has pointed out. I told her I'm trying
to catch up with her."

"Does she know you're here?"

His broad, wind-weathered face wrinkled in amusement.

"Forget I asked that. Of course she does. Why didn't she
tell me?"

"I flew in last night. She wanted it to be a surprise. She
was supposed to come with me today, but she's busy getting set up for tomorrow at the ranch."

"What's going on at the ranch?"

He shook his head, his little raisin eyes laughing at me.
"Sorry, top secret. She doesn't want to have her idea stolen
by another fund-raising group."

"This has to do with the senior citizen kitchen?" Then I
remembered what she'd said yesterday about her prayers
being answered by something I'd suggested.

"Apparently."

"Are you involved?" I poked his chest. "C'mon, Isaac,
you can tell me. I won't tell anyone."

"Ha," he said, grabbing my finger and shaking it. "Not

a chance, young Harper woman. I'm not procuring the wrath of Dove Ramsey down upon my grizzled old head. You'll find out soon enough."

"Okay," I said, giving in quickly only because I was so excited to see him again. "So, tell me what you're working on now. I'm sorry I haven't answered your E-mail in the last week. It's been insane around here, and I would have needed five single-spaced pages to tell you everything."

He stretched his long legs out and rubbed his knees. "Dove clued me in. I can't believe you're involved in another homicide investigation. Is Gabe ready to lock you in your room?"

I grimaced and picked at some loose paint on the wooden bench. "I'm not involved because I want to be, believe me. She told you everything, right? About Sam and Bliss and . . ."

"And Lydia," he finished.

I made my cauliflower face at him. "Ex-wives. Guess you know about them."

"Do I. Dove says she's quite a looker."

"She is gorgeous, I'll grant you that. And, I'd only admit this to you, actually she's a pretty nice woman from what I can tell."

"And after your husband?"

I made claws at him. "Not you, too. I don't know if she is. Dove and Emory sure are convinced that's the case. Gabe is spending a lot of time with her and Sam, but what with Bliss and the baby . . ." I shrugged.

"Sounds like you're the only one being rational about it."

I looked up into his penetrating, photographer's eyes. "What do you think? Am I being stupid and naive? I've never believed you can force a man . . . or anyone to love you. My cousin thinks I should invest in a closetful of Victoria's Secret underwear. Dove thinks I should stick to his side like glue. My best friend thinks I should spike Lydia's coffee with arsenic."

His thick white eyebrows moved upward.

"She's joking," I said, laughing. "I think. Anyway, I've basically done nothing except sit on the sidelines and watch. You're a man of worldly experience. What do you think I should do?"

He took my hands in his. "Benni, all I know is it takes years for a couple to become a 'we.' Ultimately, some relationships make it, some don't. Who knows why?" He rubbed his big thumbs over the tops of my hands.

"In other words, it's what I suspected. There's nothing I can do."

"He has free will. But then, so do you." He squeezed my hands. "Now let's talk about your murder case. Who do you think did it? Do you need another investigator?"

I slapped the top of his hands gently. "Did Dove ask you to look after me?"

He laughed and shook his head no. "She's so busy with this project, she's barely had time to spoon with me on the porch last night."

"Spoon? Excuse me, you need to clarify to a concerned granddaughter just exactly what that term entails. In detail, please."

"Not on your life. Anyway, I've photographed this Capitola Brown twice, back in the fifties when she was working the rodeo circuit doing trick riding and later in the eighties when I was doing a book on horse racing. Dove says it's pretty certain someone in the family did it. Any ideas who?"

I told him everything I knew so far. "It could be any of them, though that note points strongly at Cappy. To be honest, she's the only one I can picture having the nerve to pull it off. Dove told you the whole thing about the switched guns, right?"

"Yes, so the only lead you have is the grave rubbing. Can I see it?"

"Sure." I pulled it out of my purse and handed it to him.

He took a pair of tortoise-shell glasses from his shirt pocket and studied the rubbing. He handed it back to me. "I'm assuming you're going to look for it."

"How can I? There's too many cemeteries in San Celina County. There are probably some I don't even know about. That would take weeks and even then might be a dead end."

"So you're going to give up? That doesn't sound like you. The Benni Harper I know would be lying in bed at night trying to figure out the puzzle."

"Are you saying I shouldn't? Thank you, but I've already got one man encouraging me to go against my husband's request to stay out of situations like this."

"Who's that? And for the record, I'm not encouraging you, I'm only making an observation concerning your personality."

"You know, you can be real annoying sometimes."

"But I'm right, aren't I?"

"Sometimes I think my cousin Emory was right, and I should have been a detective. I don't want to get involved, but something in me won't rest until Giles's murderer is caught. And it's not because of some great humanitarian motivation, either. From what I understand, he was a real jerk."

"Even jerks don't deserve to be murdered. I think you've got a strong streak of justice running through you, and that's what compels you to get involved."

"You make me sound a lot more noble than I feel. How about you running that speech by Gabe the next time he gets upset at me?"

His hearty laugh made me smile. "Not on your life. He has the power to lock me up, not to mention sic the parking ticket patrol on me. So, who's this other man you say is encouraging you to get involved?"

"A sheriff's detective assigned to the Brown murder. For some reason, he's gotten it into his fuzzy little Texas head that I'll be able to ferret out information from this family that he can't."

Isaac peered out from under his thick, white eyebrows, his mouth turned up into a wide grin.

"Oh, shut up," I said, good-naturedly. "Yes, he's heard about my other experiences. That doesn't mean I'm going to jeopardize my relationship with my husband or my stepson to solve his case."

"So, this detective. Does he wear starched Wranglers, a white cowboy hat, and fancy cowboy boots?"

My eyes widened. "How did you . . . ?"

He pointed behind me. I turned and saw Detective Hudson strolling across the grass toward us.

"Oh, for crying out loud," I said.

"Looks determined," he said.

When Detective Hudson reached us, Isaac stood up. I swung my legs around so I wasn't straddling the bench and leaned back on my elbows.

"What do you want?" I said.

"Isaac Lyons," Isaac said, holding out his big hand.

The detective took his hand. "*The* Isaac Lyons? The photographer?"

Isaac gave his deep laugh. "Depends on who's asking. I think I may have a speeding ticket in Wyoming I haven't paid."

"Ford Hudson. My friends call me Hud. I'm a detective with the San Celina Sheriff's Department, and as far as I'm concerned, your need for speed is Wyoming's problem, not mine. I bought your book on state fairs. Great photos of the carnies. My mother was a photographer with *Life*. She owns a studio now in Odessa. Mostly weddings and babies, bread-and-butter photography."

"Liar," I blurted out.

Isaac gave me a puzzled, then reprimanding look. "Forgive my young friend's rudeness."

I shot Isaac a hard look. Sometimes he could be just a little *too* paternal.

Detective Hudson grinned. "That's okay, I'm gettin' used to it. She's like one of those snarly little terriers. Kinda grows on you after a while."

Isaac gave a small chuckle. "Yes, she does." Then he turned to me. "Dove instructed me to ask you to dinner tonight. She's making pot roast."

"I'll be there."

He kissed me on top of the head and whispered in my ear, "Play nice, Ms. Benni Harper."

Giving him my sweetest smile, I replied, "Suck eggs, Mr. Isaac Lyons."

He gave a great booming laugh and ruffled my hair. "Oh, Lordy, I've missed you."

"Shoot," Detective Hudson said as we watched Isaac stride across the grass. "Didn't know you ran in such fancy circles. Is he a relative or something?"

"What do you want?"

"For you to come to my office at ten o'clock tomorrow."

"Why?"

"Like I said so politely this morning, I have some ideas I need to discuss with you about our case."

"It's . . . not . . . our . . . case," I said. "Shall I say it slower? Write it in lipstick on your forehead? Send a telegram?"

"Do people still send telegrams in this computer age? What with E-mail and all. I've wondered about that."

Not answering, I stood up and brushed past him.

"Tomorrow," he called after me. "Ten o'clock. I'm the third office on the right. Just tell the receptionist I'm expecting you."

Back in the tent, the crowds were still thick and noisy. I waited for Emory at our assigned place, but as usual he was late. He meandered by ten minutes later.

"I have one more person to interview," he said. "Give me another half hour."

"Oh, Emory," I moaned, wishing I'd driven myself so I could leave. Knowing my cousin, it would be more like another hour.

"Go amuse yourself, sweetcakes. Don't be a whiny-baby."

I went back into the artists' tent, hoping to find a chair. Next to some potted trees, near the stage where Cappy had spoken, there were a couple of white folding chairs. I grabbed one and sat down, heaving a big sigh.

"Too much wine?" an older woman's voice inquired.

I turned and looked behind the potted trees and saw Rose Brown sitting alone in her wheelchair.

"Uh, not really," I said, standing up and going over to her. "I don't really like wine."

"Then what are you doing here?"

"I came with my cousin. He's a journalist and he's writing an article for the *Tribune*."

Her eyes opened and closed slowly, like some kind of ancient, slow-moving animal. "I was beautiful once," she said.

"Yes, ma'am," I answered.

"He was a judge and a horseman. His horses were in

demand all over the country. He required perfection in his horses, his law, and his women."

I nodded, thinking, *He sounds like a real prize.*

"Women adored him. Many nights he didn't come home at all."

Suddenly uncomfortable with the awkward personal turn to our conversation, I looked around, trying to find a polite way of escape. "I'm sorry," I said.

"Do you have a husband?" she asked.

I nodded.

"You'd better fix yourself up. He'll leave you for someone prettier."

In deference to her age and, I was assuming, her slight senility, I held back the temptation to tell her to mind her own dang business. "Excuse me, I need to meet my cousin . . ."

The next moment, Cappy walked around the corner and saw me walking away from her mother.

She hurried up to me. "What are you doing?" she snapped.

"Nothing," I stammered. "Your mother . . ."

A panicked look passed over Cappy's face. A few feet away, her mother sat smiling serenely in her wheelchair, her cloudy eyes focused on something behind me. "She's very elderly," Cappy said.

I looked back down at her mother who still wore that spooky, disengaged smile. Was she senile? She certainly didn't sound as if she was when she was insulting my looks. Maybe she was just mean.

"I have to find my cousin," I said, turning and walking quickly out of the tent.

Cappy caught up with me outside. "Benni, wait."

I turned and faced her, shielding my eyes from the bright afternoon sun. "Yes?"

"Sometimes she gets confused. Very confused." Her gray eyes bore into my squinting ones.

"I understand," I said.

She stared at me for a long, searching moment. Both her hands were curled in tight fists. "Do you?"

"I've worked with elderly people, Cappy."

Her lips tightened. "You always did learn quickly, Benni Harper. You knew how to focus. I liked that about you."

"Thank you," I said. She was definitely her mother's daughter. The sudden conversation switch confused me.

"But your one fatal flaw was never knowing when some- . thing was too much for you. You always wanted to ride the horses that were too big or too wild or try some trick beyond your capabilities. Sometimes recognizing your own limitations is the smartest thing a person can do."

"I . . ."

Before I could say any more, she added, "Be smart this time. Ignore whatever my mother said. Don't get in over your head."

I watched her walk back toward the artists' tent, frustrated that she didn't let me speak, didn't let me tell her that all her mother did was insult my looks and, ironically, give me advice on how to keep my husband.

But without realizing it, Cappy had pointed me in another direction. It was obvious by Cappy's overreaction that Rose Brown knew something about the blackmail or Giles's death. The thousand-dollar question was What exactly did Cappy think her mother had told me? And how would I find out what Rose Brown knew?

11

I FOUND EMORY deep in conversation with a new wine maker who was waxing poetic about the quality of grapes this harvest season and the possibilities for San Celina County's growth as a major wine-producing region. I tugged on my cousin's sleeve and demanded his car keys. "I'll wait for you there."

"Fifteen more minutes," Emory said. "I swear."

Inside Emory's luxurious Cadillac Seville, I reclined the cushy leather seat, rolled down the electric windows for a cross breeze, and turned on the CD player, letting the butter-smooth sounds of George Strait soothe my irritated soul. I settled back, closed my eyes, and tried to forget the Brown family, wine, racehorses, my looks, my husband, and his beautiful ex-wife.

I was floating in a soft drowsy state, down a long, slow Southern river, just me and George, when a man's voice growled near my ear, "Dangerous practice . . ." I simultaneously jumped, screamed, and swung my hand out in defense, my heart racing like one of Cappy's horses.

"Dang it all!" Detective Hudson exclaimed, backing up and grabbing his mouth.

"You idiot! You scared the crap out of me!" I screamed. "Don't ever, ever, ever sneak up on me like that! Ever!"

"I was just trying to tell you it's dangerous to nap in an open car where anyone can accost you. Oh, dang, I'm bleeding," he moaned, still holding his mouth.

I climbed out of the car and went over to him. "For Pete's sake, quit your bellyaching. You're lucky it wasn't pepper spray in my hand."

He felt his rapidly swelling lip gingerly, then stared at the blood staining his fingertips. "Criminy, what do you do, sharpen your claws on a whetstone?"

"I don't even have nails." I held up my hands in illustration. Clutched in my right one was the plastic case from George's CD. The sharp plastic edge was obviously what I'd struck him with.

"Assaulted by a CD cover," he said, moaning again. "How will I explain that one at the office?"

"You wouldn't have to if you'd *stop following me*," I said, reaching back into the car and handing him a tissue. "Here, clean up your mouth and shut up."

He brushed away the tissue, pulled a pure white monogrammed handkerchief from inside his jacket, and brought it to his swollen lip.

I stared at it. "A handkerchief? I didn't know men still used those."

He gave a sick smile. "I don't blow my nose with it. I use it to pick up women."

"What?"

"You'd be surprised how many heartbroken women there are in bars. I give them the handkerchief to dry their tears, listen to their sad story, offer a little sympathy, a strong Texas shoulder to lean on, a drink or two, then slip them my card. I always get my handkerchief back clean and ironed and a very grateful first date."

"That pathetic line actually works?"

"Never fails."

"It's despicable."

Unperturbed by my opinion, he dabbed at his mouth again, flinching at the pain.

"What a lightweight. I'd sure hate to have you for a partner."

"The only blood that bothers me is my own," he protested.

I gave him a withering look.

"You know, you are the least maternal woman I've ever met," he said.

His remark hit me straight in the heart, and thanks to my expressive face, he immediately noticed.

"Oh, shoot, I'm sorry, Benni," he said softly. "I didn't mean that how it sounded."

"Forget it," I said curtly.

Emory walked up at that moment and asked, "What's going on?"

"Are you finished with your interviews?" I asked.

"Yes, but—"

"Then let's go."

Emory looked at me, then Detective Hudson, then back at me. "Are you all right? What did he do to you?"

"I said, let's go, Emory." I climbed into the car, buckled my seat belt, and stared straight ahead. We were out of the parking lot and well on the highway back to San Celina before Emory spoke.

"Need to talk about it?" he asked.

I put a hand up to my eyes. "Not right now, Emory. But thanks for asking."

He gave me a worried look, then turned the conversation

to Isaac with whom he'd chatted briefly at the tasting. "He and Dove are cooking something up. He says he'll tell me about it when they need publicity. Couldn't get him to spill a word."

"Me neither. I'm going out there for dinner tonight, though, so I'll give it another try. Why don't you come, too?"

"Can't. I have to get these stories written and dispatched to my editor for final approval. Then I'm going to see if I can pry my ladylove away from her office long enough for a romantic dinner down at the beach." His voice wasn't as chipper and optimistic as usual.

You'd better watch it, I silently told Elvia, *or this one's going to slip right through your fingers, and I know you'll live to regret it.*

We pulled up in front of my house, and it was immediately apparent that Gabe's Corvette wasn't parked in its customary spot in the driveway.

My cousin gave me a sympathetic look. "He'll be home soon, sweetcakes."

I patted his hand, still curled around the steering wheel. "We both got us some kind of troubles, don't we, Cousin?"

"Amen, sister Albenia," he said, leaning over and kissing my cheek. "I'll call you tomorrow and find out the scoop on Dove and Isaac."

Inside the house the answering machine blinked a single message. I hit play, anticipating Gabe's baritone voice. Instead, it was Detective Hudson's.

"Hud, here. Mrs. Harper, in the confused melee of being injured, I failed to inform you that I observed you conversing with the senior Mrs. Brown and I expect you in my office with a full report tomorrow morning."

"Fat chance, Detective," I muttered, pulling on my barn jacket. I left a note for Gabe telling him I'd be at the ranch and to come out if he got home early enough.

I stayed at the ranch until nine o'clock, catching up with Isaac and trying to pry something out of Dove about her fund-raising project.

"In good time, honeybun," she said, "in good time. Now you and Isaac go out on the porch and catch up while I make some phone calls." She stood on tiptoe and planted a kiss on Isaac's lips. "Come get me before you go to bed, sweetie, and I'll heat you up some warm almond milk."

"Yes, ma'am," he said, gazing down at her with pure adoration. She smiled back at him, her own soft peach face matching his glow. Not for the first time I wondered why in the world I ever worried about this sweet, sweet man hurting my gramma.

Out on the porch, we sat on the swing, rocking in companionable silence, watching the evening shadows turn the oaks to black matchsticks against a cobalt blue sky. I tried not to peek at my watch every five minutes and wonder where Gabe was and what he was doing.

"Get things straightened out with that detective?" Isaac asked.

I brought my knees up and rested my chin on them. "I know I sounded like a brat this afternoon, but that business about his mother being a photographer is a flat-out lie."

"And how do you know that?"

"In the few days I've known him, he's claimed his mother lived in four different towns and had as many different occupations. It's either some kind of stupid game he's playing, or he's a pathological liar. I'm leaning toward the latter."

Isaac stretched his arm across the back of the swing. "He seemed nice enough."

"Well, you talked to him for exactly two minutes, so I

wouldn't be trusting him with your life savings if I were you."

With his thumb and forefinger, he thumped the back of my head gently. "Your mouth is getting a tad too sharp for my taste, kiddo."

I sighed and leaned my head against his thick, warm shoulder. In the dark September evening, the crickets echoed the *squeak, squeak* of the porch swing being pushed by Isaac's foot. "I'm sorry. I'm just in a funk tonight."

"I noticed. You've been checking your watch about every ten minutes. Doesn't Gabe have a cell phone? Why don't you just call him and see when he's going to be home?"

"He leaves it in the Corvette, and they probably took Lydia's car to her mother's since Sam and Bliss were going, too." Inside the house, I could hear Dove's cajoling voice on the phone. Whoever she was speaking to wouldn't stand a chance. "Besides, I don't want to seem . . ." I thought for a moment, searching for the right word. "I don't know, possessive. Or paranoid. It's not like this has been going on for months. It's only been a week and a stressful one at that. If our marriage can't withstand a week of weird behavior, then we haven't got much of a marriage."

He patted my shoulder. "He's acting like a self-indulgent adolescent. I think you're showing remarkable patience."

"You don't think I'm being too passive? With what everyone else has been saying, I can't help wondering if I'm being a wimp."

"Wimp is a word I'd never use to describe you, my dear," he said, laughing. "And there's a world of difference between patience and passivity."

"The thing is, even though it irritates me, I think I understand what he's feeling. He's more insecure than people realize. One of the few things he told me about his and Lydia's breakup was her contempt for what he did for a living. He was working undercover, and I guess that's pretty hard on a family—his hours were erratic, he was moody and angry all the time, had trouble reconnecting with the real world when he wasn't working. I don't blame her for pushing him to get out of it. I'm not sure I could have lived with him either. But she said some pretty ugly things about his capabilities of making a living, of supporting his family, about his masculinity. She really hurt his ego, and he's never forgotten it."

"He told you all this?"

"Some of it. Some I pieced together myself."

"So you think he's out to prove she was wrong and in the process rub her nose in it a little."

"Something like that. At least, that's what it seems like to me."

"But you and he haven't actually talked about it."

I stretched out my legs, tingling from being in one position too long, and studied the tips of my boots. "No, with all that's gone on with Sam and Bliss and the murder, we haven't had much time to talk about anything else."

"You'll have to deal with it eventually."

"I know. And we will. I'm just trying to let it happen in its own time. That's one of the biggest lessons I've learned in the last few years. You can't make things happen before they're supposed to or make people do things they don't want to do. Besides, I can't help remembering how understanding and open-minded he was about me staying in my inherited house in Morro Bay last May. He was really there for me when I was acting a little nutso; it only seems fair that I should grant him the same grace." I gave him a half smile. "Providing it doesn't last longer than a week, that is. Then I may just have to get out my trusty bullwhip."

He chuckled. "For her or him?"

"Depends on how I'm feeling that day."

"Well, you're thirty years up on me on that grace thing," he said. "I didn't comprehend that little fact until I was well past qualifying for Medicare."

"I find that hard to believe."

"Believe it. Wisdom has nothing to do with time served on this earth. In my observance, it's learning to let go and let a higher power have the control you foolishly thought was under your puny command. Mr. Gabriel Ortiz is a luckier man than he realizes. Hopefully he'll understand that someday."

"Well, if he doesn't, there is always the bullwhip."

He laughed. "Lordy, I'd never want you mad at me."

I tucked my arm through his. "You are one special gentleman, Mr. Isaac Lyons, and I *was* very wise about one thing. Letting you into my life."

"And next to your gramma, Benni Harper, you are the light of my life."

I hugged his arm to me. "Ha, gratuitous flattery will get you everywhere with a Ramsey woman."

"So I've discovered."

"I'm not touching that comment with a ten-foot cattle prod."

WHEN I ARRIVED home, my lightened mood turned black again when Gabe's car was still gone. That bullwhip was looking better and better. I was in bed cruising the television stations when he came in at ten forty-five. I heard him call out to me, then listen to the message on the answering machine before turning out the living room lights and coming into the bedroom.

"What's that sheriff's detective talking about?" he asked, walking into the bathroom while unbuttoning his shirt. "You are cooperating with him, aren't you?" When I didn't answer, his head popped out of the bathroom door. "Benni, I asked you a question."

"Hello, Gabe. Yes, my day was great. How was yours? Of course I missed you as much as you missed me. I agree, it was such a long day without you. Of course I'll tell you everything, but, please, you go first."

He walked back into the bedroom slowly, his head tilted in wariness. "*Querida*, are you all right? Did something happen today to upset you?" The sight of the dark circles under his tired eyes softened my irritation.

I sighed, climbed out of bed, and went to him, pulling his shirt out of his jeans and running my hands up his warm back. Sarcasm wasn't going to solve this. "No, Friday, I'm just . . . It's nothing. I'm fine. You were later than I expected and I got worried."

"We ended up spending the whole day with Lydia's mother, and then she wanted to take us out to dinner. After we dropped Sam and Bliss off at JJ's house, Lydia and I started talking about Sam, and then one thing led to another. I'm sorry. I should have called."

I pinched his lower back. "Yes, you should have."

He jerked. "Ow! Okay, okay. It won't happen again, I promise."

I laid my cheek on his bare chest, his musky scent so familiar and yet still so mysterious to me.

His hand stroked my hair, and I rubbed my face against his coarse chest hair. "About that message from the detective . . ." he said.

"I'm cooperating with Detective Hudson as much as I can."

He grasped my shoulders and held me away from him, staring down into my face. "What's that mean?"

"Well, I . . ." I didn't know how to explain that the detective was asking me to do exactly what Gabe was asking me not to do.

"Benni, it's one thing when you defy me and get involved in investigations, but please don't embarrass me in front of another agency. I want you to do whatever Detective Hudson requests of you."

"But . . ."

"No buts. I'm too busy right now with Bliss and Sam to be worrying about you. Please, for once, curb your urge to snoop. If you have some information the detective needs, give it to him and then stay out of his way."

"It's not what you think, Gabe. Detective Hudson—"

"Has a job to do and doesn't need you getting in the way. No more discussion. You'll do as he asks, *comprende?*"

"Understood," I said, my voice cool. I pushed away from him and climbed back in bed.

He joined me a few minutes later. "Sweetheart, let's not argue. I know I sound like a drill sergeant sometimes . . ."

"That's putting it mildly."

"I'm really sorry. I'm just so preoccupied with this situation with Sam and this nutty family he's marrying into. I don't want to worry about you being hurt because you've gotten in over your head."

An ominous prickling rippled through me. The last part of his sentence almost word for word mirrored Cappy's statement.

"I know," I said, reaching under the covers, taking his hand and lacing my fingers through his. "I'll stay out of this as much as possible. I promise."

"Good," he said, bringing my hand to his lips and kissing it. "Lydia sends her regards. Said she was sorry you didn't come."

I'll bet, I thought, and the possibility ran through my

mind that I was indeed being naive, that my husband was being stolen right from under my passive little nose.

Then I went to sleep and dreamed fitfully all night of gravestone rubbings and clouds and wine bottles that sprouted legs and became racehorses, and beautiful Mexican women wearing cowboy boots in all the colors of the rainbow.

"IT'S A FULL moon tonight," Gabe said, glancing at the kitchen calendar the next morning. "All the loonies will be out."

"Isn't that an old wives' tale?" I asked. "I saw on one of those magazine shows some statistics that said that there wasn't any more crime on full moon nights than any other."

He stood next to the toaster in his jogging shorts, waiting for a bagel to pop up, his strong thighs still tight and twitching from their morning run. I watched him over my coffee through bleary eyes, feeling like, with all my crazy dreams, I'd only slept two hours instead of eight.

"Let that television reporter take the next seven p.m. to three a.m. shift during a full moon and see if he changes his tune." He grabbed his toasted bagel, juggling it from one hand to the other before dropping it on the plate across from me. As he spread grape jelly over it, he glanced at the morning headlines, then peered at me over wire-rimmed glasses. "Are you going to talk to Detective Hudson today?"

"I guess."

"You guess?"

"Okay, yes, I'll talk to him. I don't really have anything to tell him, though. The conversation with Rose Brown that he's putting so much stock in was nothing that would help him find out who killed Giles Norton."

"What was it about?"

"She rambled about her dead husband, how much he loved beautiful women and good horses."

"That's it?"

My big gulp of coffee burnt my throat. He waited while I waved my hand in front of my mouth. "She also told me I should fix myself up or you'd leave me for someone prettier."

He laughed out loud and took a bite of his bagel. "Lucky thing for her she's elderly and Dove taught you to respect your elders. I take it you didn't smack her."

"No, but I sure wanted to."

"You look fine just the way you are," he murmured, his attention distracted by the newspaper.

And is fine good enough? I wanted to ask, but didn't. I contemplated whether I should tell him about Cappy's reaction to my conversation with her mother. Since we had enough other things creating barriers between us these last few days, I decided to be as open and honest as possible.

"Cappy reacted real strange when she saw me talking to her mother."

His head came up. "How so?"

"She seemed to have the impression that her mother told me something she shouldn't have, that I should ignore what her mother said and to basically mind my own business."

He looked at me over his glasses again, his nonverbal agreement with her obvious.

"I'm no more involved than you," I said petulantly. "She didn't even give me time to say that her mother didn't reveal a thing, only insulted my looks."

He thought about it for a moment. "That bothers me. If Cappy is involved in Giles's murder and she thinks you know something . . ."

"It didn't feel like she was threatening me, Gabe. Besides, I don't think she'd hurt me. Don't forget, I've known her since I was a girl."

"That doesn't make any difference," he said, looking worried for the first time. "If she felt her family was threatened, if she or someone in her family committed that murder and it appears they did, how long she has known you won't matter one bit."

"I can't change what's already happened, but I can stay out of their way. Which I will. If JJ asks me to get involved any more, I'll just say no."

"Good. And don't forget to tell all this to Detective Hudson." He shuffled through the paper and found the sports page. "You know, Benni, I am very happy you're keeping me informed on this."

I opened my mouth to tell him exactly what the situation was with the sheriff's detective, then stopped. I'd never been in such an awkward position. I knew there had always been a slight animosity between the sheriff's department and the city police, though the sheriff and Gabe seemed to like each other personally. Like rival cattlemen and sheepmen, they looked at their professions in different ways and were certain their way was the right one. This situation with Detective Hudson could cause a bigger rift between the two agencies. Maybe I could figure a way to get the detective off my back without running to Gabe.

IT WAS QUIET down at the folk art museum. Monday was our only officially closed day, and D-Daddy used it to do any major work inside the museum itself. Today he was patching up some places in the adobe and replacing a window that broke yesterday.

"Have fun on Saturday, *ange*?" he asked, stopping to

rub Scout's belly. "That boy, Hud, he's real Cajun. He does the dancing, him."

"Only half Cajun, D-Daddy. The other half is pure bullshit."

He threw back his head and gave a rich cackle. "That make him full Cajun, then."

I smiled and said, "Thanks for the dances, but next time don't let another man cut in, okay?"

He went back to slapping on the mixture he'd concocted to match the dusky white adobe walls. "I think he likes you, *ange*. Cajun men, we like the *jolie blondes*. Your police chief, he better be closer watching the chicken coop."

"It's not that he likes me. I just have something he wants."

D-Daddy nodded his head solemnly, his eyes twinkling. "Yes, ma'am, you surely do."

I felt my face warm at his words and gave a nervous laugh. "Not in his wildest dreams, D-Daddy."

I walked outside, passing under the green canopy of honeysuckle and ivy, to my office in the co-op studios. Except for two women in the common area basting a quilt, Scout and I were alone. I grabbed a cup of coffee for me, a dog biscuit for him, and checked through the mail and messages that had accumulated in my box. Then I got down to work, digging into all the letters, reports, and filing I'd gotten behind on, accompanied only by the comforting doggy sounds of my canine companion, the only male in my life I truly understood these days. I didn't even glance at the clock until my phone rang two and a half hours later. Ten-thirty-five and I'd already done a day's work. I was feeling pretty proud of myself when I picked up the phone.

"Josiah Sinclair Folk Art Museum. Benni Harper speaking."

"I'm still waitin'." Detective Hudson's audacious Texas

twang instantly deflated my good feeling. "Did you forget to set your alarm?"

I hung up the phone without answering, knowing I'd regret my impulsive action. It rang again ten seconds later. On the fourth ring, I reluctantly picked it up.

"Josiah Sinclair . . ."

"I know where you work." His voice wasn't amused. "Get over here now."

Ah, the wonderful arrogance of law enforcement officers. What he'd forgotten was that I was married to one. I've been through that be-nice-then-surprise-them-with-force psychological tactic too many times to count. "We both know I can tell you what you need to know over the phone. I don't have time to drive to the sheriff's office."

"I want to see your face when you're talking. That's the only way I can tell if you're trying to pull one over on me."

"Listen up, because though I promised my husband I'd cooperate with you and I try to keep my promises to him, I'm only going to tell you my story once. If that's not good enough, then I suggest you take it up with my husband, *the police chief.* Have you got a pad and pencil?"

There was silence at the other end. Ha, I'd managed to shut him up for one nano-second.

"Rose Brown told me exactly nothing yesterday," I said. "Write that down, detective. *Nothing.* She rambled on like older people do about her dead husband, his fondness for the law, horses, and women, not necessarily in that order. She then proceeded to tell me to fix myself up or my husband would leave me for a prettier woman. That was it. I got away as soon as I could because I've about had it up to my chin with people telling me how to keep my husband from straying and I've had it with you bugging me. Goodbye." I hung up the phone, waiting for it to ring again. When it didn't, I let out a deep sigh and went back to filing, trying to keep my mind off the whole darn Brown family and their internal family dramas.

About a half hour later, I was on my knees, filing in the S–T's, when my office door flew open and a grim-faced Detective Hudson filled my doorway. Scout jumped to his feet, his one German shepherd ear at full mast, a low growl rumbling in his throat.

"Oh, great," I muttered.

Detective Hudson took a step inside the office, and Scout's hindquarters went taut, preparing to spring.

I waited a few seconds before saying, "Scout, friend." Scout sat down and lifted a paw. I reached over and pushed it down. "Don't take that word to heart," I said to the detective. "I have to call you a friend or he'll chew those atrocious-looking boots to leather shreds." Detective Hudson's feet were encased today in navy blue ostrich quill boots. They were ugly, but even I could tell they were expensive.

"I have one more question about what Cappy Brown said to you after you talked to her mama, and since my ear is already half deaf from you slamming the phone in it, I decided I'd probably be more successful and safer continuing this conversation in person."

I turned my back to him and resumed filing.

"Benni, I swear I'll take you down to the station, then call your husband and tell him that though I've repeatedly asked you not to, you've been investigating this on your own."

I turned to gape up at him. "You'll what? Are you saying you'll tell my husband lies about me?"

Any resemblance to Tom Sawyer disappeared when his face hardened. "I'll do whatever it takes to solve this case." The unbending resolve in his voice told me to take that statement seriously.

I stood up, weary of this game. "Detective Hudson, my husband asked me to cooperate with you, and I'm trying to do that. I'm sorry if I was rude, but to be honest, you rub me the wrong way. One minute you're Mr. Texas-cutesy and the next you're Mr. Hard-ass Cop. I'm tired of being manipulated by you and by the Brown family. I'll tell you what Cappy said to me, and then you're on your own."

His dark, serious eyes studied me for a long moment, his hands resting on his hips. Then he said in a solemn voice, "You think I'm cute?"

"Geeze Louise!" I said, throwing up my hands. "That's exactly what I mean."

He grinned. "Just tell me what Cappy said to you."

I told him the same story I told Gabe.

"So obviously she now suspects you know more than you do. I sure don't like that idea."

"Neither did Gabe, but I'll tell you what I told him: I don't think she'll hurt me. I know it appears she is the most likely one to be involved with Giles's death, but I know her better than you and Gabe and I don't think she'd kill someone in cold blood."

His face had the same scornful and superior boy-are-you-naive look I'd seen on Gabe's. It must be a class they take in cop school. Condescension 101.

"Is there anything else you need?" I asked. "I've told you everything I know. Scout's honor."

Scout's ears perked up at the sound of his name.

Detective Hudson searched my face with wary eyes, then concluded, "You're telling the truth."

"You wouldn't know the truth if it bit you in the butt."

"Exactly what does the chief do to shut that smart-ass mouth of yours?"

"Good-bye, Detective Hudson."

He didn't budge.

"What else do you want? I've told you everything I know. Now go do your cop stuff." I waved him away.

He pulled a white sheet of paper from inside his tweed, cowboy-cut jacket. "I have a list of the nineteen cemeteries in San Celina County."

"We have that many cemeteries?"

"Want to go grave hunting?"

I hesitated. To be honest, although the thought of going with him anywhere was not the least bit appealing, the possibility of traipsing through graveyards was. I'd always been fascinated by graveyards, especially the old ones and to actually have a mission, the hunt for this mysterious tombstone with the lily of the valley carving, was tempting.

"Look out, she's weakening," he said, amused.

I glanced over at the phone, causing him to smirk.

"Need to call the chief and ask permission?" he asked.

I glared at him. "No."

"Then let's go."

I thought for a minute, then said, "Why don't we split the list and get back with each other later? That would be the smartest thing to do."

"No way, Detective Harper. With my luck, you'll find what we're looking for and then hold the information for ransom."

"I would not! You make me sound like a criminal or something."

"Outside of her own family, you *are* the only one involved in this case with personal ties to Cappy Brown."

I stood up and faced him. "Look, Detective, if—and I'm saying if—Cappy did kill Giles Norton, I would never protect her from prosecution and I resent you implying I would."

He dangled the sheet of paper in my face. "So, what's keeping you?"

I grabbed the list and scanned it. "I have to be back by six o'clock."

"No problem, I have a date anyway. Say, do you have a camera?"

I gave him an exasperated look while opening the bottom drawer of my desk and pulling out the small telephoto Canon I use around the museum. "For someone who claims to be so good at his job, you sure are unprepared."

"But I always manage to get my man . . . or woman. My conviction rate was the talk of the Houston PD."

"Right, and your mother trains tigers for the circus."

"Actually," he said, switching off the office light as we left, "Mother did work for Barnum and Bailey's once. She was . . ."

I groaned loudly, trying to drown out the latest lie. "I don't want to hear it."

"A clown," he finished.

"How appropriate. How utterly appropriate."

He insisted on driving, reasoning that not only could he deduct mileage whereas I couldn't, his truck was newer, had air-conditioning and a CD player. I didn't like him being in the driver's seat, literally or figuratively, but also couldn't argue his points. The temperature was already in the high eighties, and some of the cemeteries were over the grade in North County where it would most likely reach the nineties. With Scout riding happily in back, we started with the biggest cemetery, San Celina's.

In the cemetery's parking lot, my eyes darted briefly over to the newer section where my mother and Jack were buried. A tinge of sadness struck me, like it always did when I came here. I hadn't brought flowers to their graves for a couple of months. Maybe tomorrow after work . . .

"Everything okay?" Detective Hudson had obviously

caught my glance. You couldn't fault the guy's visual acuity.

"Fine," I said, closing the truck door. "Let's check the Brown family section first. It makes sense that he'd be blackmailing them with something from their own family."

He came around the truck and stood next to me. "Now, that's right smart. Where is this Brown section?"

"I have no idea, but I know who will. And I bet I could show him the rubbing and he'd be able to identify it in two seconds if it's anywhere in San Celina's Cemetery."

"You're not showing that to anyone," Detective Hudson stated flatly. "That's the only lead we have in this case, and the less people who know about it, the better."

"But it would make it so much easier—"

"No."

"Fine, we'll waste time traipsing around graveyards when we don't have to. Makes sense to me."

"Benni, you . . ."

I told Scout to stay in the truck and took off across the green expanse of the cemetery lawn toward the gardener's stone building, not interested in hearing anything he had to say starting with the word "you." Inside, Mr. Foglino was tinkering with an old riding mower.

"Hey, Mr. Foglino."

"Well, hello, Benni Harper," he said, standing up and wiping his greasy hands on the thighs of his gray mechanic's overalls. Mr. Foglino had been the head custodian at San Celina High School for thirty-two years. We'd all loved his wry, gentle sense of humor and the Tootsie Roll pops he passed out with gruff impartiality. When he retired, he went to work for his son who owned two local mortuaries and the San Celina's Cemetery. He'd overseen the digging of Jack's grave and many other San Celinans' graves with the same serious respect he'd exacted over the shiny floors of San Celina High School. Mr. Foglino knew a lot of secrets about the families in this town, including who visited whose graves, how many times, how often, and why. Like a good bartender, he'd probably heard more confessions than Father Mark down at St. Celine's Catholic Church and was just as discreet. He'd caught me a time or two sitting on Jack's grave, my face slick with tears, and wordlessly handed me a package of tissues from his overalls' deep pockets before going back to his mowing.

"How's life treating you?" I asked.

"Can't complain. Got job security and a new recliner. Life's good."

I laughed and gave him a quick hug. "I have a question for you. Where's the Brown section?"

I didn't have to say which Browns. His bushy gray eyebrows raised in question told me he knew who I was talking about.

"That family's sure had its sorrows," he said, scratching his cheek absentmindedly, leaving a thin streak of black oil on a cheek as weathered as barn siding. "Then again, haven't we all?"

"Yes, we have."

"How's that grandma of yours? Tell her I'm sure looking forward to Christmas and some of her delicious fudge. I dole it out to myself a piece a day to try and make it last longer."

"She's feisty as ever. I'll tell her to make you a double batch this year."

"And your daddy?"

"He's good. Been having trouble with some new heifers he bought up north. Prolapsed uterus and some leg problems in one. It's getting better now, though. His arthritis has been acting up a little."

"I hear you there. I tell you, getting old isn't for weaklings. You give him my sympathy."

"Sure will."

"Heard your cousin's back in town."

"Yes, sir. He works for the paper."

"He was a good, respectful boy, I remember."

"Yes, he was. He's grown into a nice man, too."

"Well, that's real fine."

I could hear Detective Hudson shift behind me, then let out an impatient breath. I ignored him. The one thing about Mr. Foglino was you couldn't rush him.

"So," Mr. Foglino said. "Hear you got yourself involved with another family's hullabaloo."

"Not on purpose. I was just there when it happened. I . . ." Then I grinned at him. "Well, yes, I guess I have. But I'm doing my best to stay away from any large falling objects."

He chuckled and wagged a crooked, dirt-stained finger at me. "You're a trial to that husband of yours, missy. You know that?"

"So I've been told a few times."

"How's he doing?"

"Ornery as ever, but I guess I'll keep him."

"He's a good police chief. We're lucky to have him."

"I think so."

I heard Detective Hudson shift behind me again and clear his throat. I turned around and frowned him silent.

Mr. Foglino looked back down at the engine of the rider mower. "Over east of the pyramid, and there's a restroom over there, too, for your ants-in-the-pants friend." He looked up, his pale old eyes amused. "I'm assuming that's why he's dancing around like that."

"Thanks," I said, winking at him. "I'll give Dove and Daddy your regards."

"That was a waste of a good half hour," Detective Hudson grumbled.

I cut across the springy graveyard grass weaving around gravestones. "You know," I said over my shoulder, "you'd get a lot more information out of people around here if you learned how to chitchat a little."

He grunted in reply.

We passed by the famous pyramid mausoleum with the single name WYLIE on the front. Made of concrete and patterned after the real Egyptian pyramids, it was an incongruous monument among the sedate white headstones and moss-covered angels that decorated most of the older graves. It had been there since the forties, and, as usual, there was scattered around the base the remnants of a teenager's late-night visitation, half burnt incense sticks, empty beer and soda cans, candy wrappers, crispy matchsticks. I remember sneaking out here a few times myself when I was in high school, spurred on by giggling friends and the natural attraction of being scared common in most people under twenty. It was regularly patrolled by police officers who calmly shooed its nocturnal visitors away. From the base, you could also see with great clarity the last drive-in theater screen in the county, a mute but irresistible draw to cash-strapped students looking for a cheap date.

"What's the story behind this thing?" Detective Hudson asked.

"From what I was always told, some rich rancher moved here early in the century and built this for his wife and three sons. The youngest son got in a fight with the father and left the ranch to find his fortune in Alaska. The other two stayed home, never married, and worked the ranch. All of them eventually died, leaving no heirs. They were entombed here according to the father's wishes. Everyone except the third son. According to the terms of the will, the monument can't be permanently closed until the last son's body is reunited with the family."

"Which is probably the last thing on earth *he'd* want," Detective Hudson said, his voice suddenly bitter.

I glanced over at him, surprised.

His face stared at the pyramid with a raw, angry look that hardened his farm-boy features. He caught my glance, and just as quickly a smile replaced the angry look. "Time's a-wastin', ranch girl. Which way?"

Puzzled by his swift change of emotion, I pointed to a group of expensive headstones behind the pyramid. He strode away from me, whistling a tuneless melody under his breath. I watched him, wondering what family situation he'd truly left behind in Texas.

We glanced over the fifteen stones that made up the Brown family plot. Inside the square concrete edging around John Madison Brown's and Rose Jewel Brown's large, dark granite headstones were the four tiny headstones of the babies who'd died. Just the baby's names and a small lamb were carved on each one—Daisy Jewel Brown, Dahlia Jewel Brown, Beulah Jewel Brown, Bethany Jewel Brown. I stared at the tiny headstones while Detective Hudson went from headstone to headstone looking for something that resembled the grave rubbing.

"Not a lily to be seen, carved or otherwise," he called.

On Rose Brown's stone her name and birthdate were already chipped into the black shiny granite. The only thing left to fill in was her day of death. I wondered if it bothered her to have a headstone with her name already chiseled in. I knew death was inevitable for all of us, but that was just a little too organized and concrete for me. I'd bought two plots side by side when Jack died, having been encouraged to do so by the mortuary, but buying and carving a headstone—that was a little too obsessively neat and tidy. Look at me now, married to Gabe. Where did I want my earthly remains to rest? Next to Jack or to Gabe? Which was more appropriate? Should Gabe be buried next to the mother of his child to make it easier for Sam and his future children to visit their graves? And really, did it matter? Multiple marriages sure made the business of dying complicated.

Oh, honeybun, Dove's voice sang in my head. *What does it matter where your old bones are when your soul is dancing with Jesus?*

"Nothing even close here," he said, coming back to where I stood. "What're you looking at?"

"Just these tiny headstones. Wondering what it was like for a mother to lose four of her seven children."

"Guess that's how it was back then. Even the rich didn't have access to very good health care."

"No one ever mentioned what they died of."

"With no antibiotics and horrible sanitary conditions, it could have been something as simple as the flu or as complicated as TB or diphtheria. It's a wonder as many people lived as they did. Dangerous times to be a kid . . . or an adult, for that matter."

"On the other hand, we've got drug-resistant bacteria and AIDS now, so who's to say it's any better?"

"Good point." He pushed his cowboy hat back on his head. "So, this didn't tell us much. Let's try the next one."

"Let me see that list," I said when we were situated back in his truck. "We should do this in a methodical way so we're not wasting time running all over creation. Do you have a map of San Celina County?"

He nodded over at the glove compartment, and I pulled out a large, detailed map. In a half hour I had the quickest route planned for sixteen of the nineteen cemeteries.

"Three of these I've never heard of, and they're not on the map," I said.

"Deborah Schlanser, the very kind and gracious public librarian who looked them up for me, said six were inactive. A couple for quite a while."

"That might be why they're not on this map. They're probably old pioneer cemeteries."

"Maybe she could tell us where they are. There must be some record somewhere."

"There probably is, but I say we should check the ones we can today and keep our fingers crossed that what we want is in one of them."

"Sounds like a plan. Hope you like country-western music. That's all my truck plays."

"As long as it's the old stuff."

"My kinda girl," he replied, putting on Bob Wills and His Texas Playboys.

We decided to start with the cemeteries closest to the Seven Sisters ranch then work our way north. By three o'clock we'd only investigated six with no luck. It was beginning to look like this would be more than a one-day undertaking. I had to force myself not to linger over the headstones, reading the inscriptions and wondering about the life of the person who died. The number of children's headstones amazed me, and by the early afternoon the constant reminder of the delicate thread by which our lives dangled started depressing me. Apparently it was starting to show after our seventh cemetery when Detective Hudson found me after going through my assigned section, sitting on the open tailgate of his truck hugging Scout.

"I think we need a break," he said. "You hungry?"

"Kinda." I glanced around the pine-shaded cemetery we'd just traipsed through. It was northeast of Paso Robles, an old cemetery that surrounded the Estrella Adobe, one of the many old adobes scattered around San Celina County. "No McDonald's out here. Guess we'll have to go into Paso

Robles. The Paso cemetery will probably take us a long time. It's pretty big."

"No need for McDonald's. I brought lunch." He went around to the cab and brought out a small cooler from behind the front seat. "Do you want beef or turkey?" He held up two wrapped sandwiches.

"Beef."

He handed me the roast beef sandwich and a can of Coke, then joined me on the tailgate. Though it was in the high eighties, a light breeze blew through the stand of dusky green oaks the truck was parked under, and the air was scented with wildflowers and pines, smelling sugary and slightly burnt, reminding me of the Mexican sweet breads Elvia's mother baked at Christmas.

We ate without talking, occasionally feeding bits of our sandwiches to Scout. It was so quiet we could hear animal life rustling in the cottonwoods and scrub brush around us. When I tossed the last bite of my sandwich to Scout, I started picking burrs off the bottoms of my Wranglers, my thoughts drifting to all the mothers who'd lost so many babies. Was it worse to have one and lose it or never to have one at all? The old poet was convinced that loving and losing was better than never loving at all, and at twenty years old I probably would have agreed with him. There were times now I wasn't so sure.

Detective Hudson stood up, causing the pickup to raise slightly, and dusted his hands off on his thighs. "Ready to get going again?"

"Sure," I said, giving up on the dozens of burrs. It'd been so long since I'd been out hiking this time of year, I'd forgotten about these irritating little things.

I sat inside the cab, staring out the window as Detective Hudson chattered about something to do with a dalmatian he once owned. A thought was niggling at the back of my mind, just beyond my reach, and I couldn't grasp it. Something that wasn't right, about either something we'd just seen or something Mr. Foglino said. Detective Hudson's conversation switched to something about the Thursday-night farmer's market, and I continued to half listen and stare at the passing golden fields. In Paso Robles, we stopped at a mini-mart so I could buy some water for Scout. The detective watched as I poured water in my hand and let Scout drink.

"You've been too quiet. What's going on in that devious mind of yours?" he asked when we got back into the truck and headed up the hill toward the cemetery.

"Nothing." Which wasn't exactly a lie. I was thinking about something, I just didn't know what it was.

Paso Robles's cemetery was the second largest in San Celina County. It overlooked the city and the rest of the valley. In the distance, the mountains you had to drive through to get to Bakersfield and Fresno were sharp-etched against the cloudless sky. We divided up the rows and agreed to meet back in front of the adobe-style restrooms when we finished. There was one small funeral going on down near the entrance, but nothing in the areas we would be concentrating on.

I was walking up and down the rows looking for a carving that resembled a lily of the valley, studying marker after marker, going over each Brown family member in my mind—means, motive, opportunity, then trying to imagine each of them coldly shooting Giles. I hated to admit it, but the only one who had all three and who I thought capable of pulling the trigger was Cappy. But would she kill another human being just to protect her horses or her lifestyle? Then again, what about her sisters? JJ had said all the women knew how to shoot. Was I just being naive by assuming that Willow wouldn't kill for her political career or her granddaughter's reputation or Etta for the winery, or for that matter, Arcadia out of that age-old reason, jealousy? If Giles fooled around on her as much as people implied, she could have just gotten fed up that night and shot him. Happened all the time. Except it didn't fit with the conversation I heard or the fact that someone had called the paper and said there would be something "big" happening at Seven Sisters that night. I ruled out Arcadia. If she'd shot him because of his affairs, it made more sense for it to happen at another time, though I was the first to concede that many homicides weren't planned, but were emotional, spur-of-the-moment acts.

That still left Susa to consider—her peace-loving, hippie persona notwithstanding. What did anyone really know about her? After what JJ said about Giles coming on to her and Bliss, maybe there was something he did that caused their mother to lose her gentle manner for a split second. Though she had spent most of her adult life away living on a commune, she was still raised by Capitola Brown, who would not have allowed shrinking violets to grow on the Seven Sisters ranch. Then there was Chase, certainly capable of pulling the trigger, though, as far as I could see, no reason to. Then again, he was the one left with the cute little tasting room girl in the tight red jeans. Could it have been an argument over something as trivial as who gets her next?

No matter which family member did it, there was no doubt in my mind that Cappy and her sisters were sharp enough and cool enough under pressure to cook up that gun switching scene even with a houseful of guests, including a chief of police. One thing I knew from watching my cousin Emory: Growing up with money often gave you a sense of invincibility, a feeling of entitlement that enabled you to forge ahead when others would hesitate. It could be

an endearing trait, like Emory's pursuit of Elvia, an obnoxious one, like Giles's cavalier affairs, or a deadly one, like
the killing of Giles Norton.

I started down another row, where a monument with a
headless angel was laced with scarlet wild fuchsia. GONE
HOME stated the simple words on the base under the name
CAMPBELL—1902–1958. I leaned against the warm marble
and wondered what had happened to the angel's head and
how one went about replacing something like that. I was
idly looking out over the green cemetery lawns, brightly
splashed with dots of yellow goldenrod, when it hit me.

There were no dates chiseled on the Brown baby's headstones.

I rushed across the smooth grass to Detective Hud, who
was ten rows away, and told him what I'd discovered.

"So?" he said, not nearly as excited as I was.

"So, that means something. Look at all the children's
graves we've seen. They've all had the birth and death
dates."

"Not that graveyard in Estrella," he pointed out.

I impatiently waved his words away. "A lot of those
people couldn't afford expensive headstones. The Browns
could. Why wouldn't they put the dates on the headstones?"

"Maybe because they didn't feel like it. You're reaching
for something that isn't there. I think you've been in the
sun too long."

"You're jealous because I thought of it and you didn't."

"And you're delusional. Go back to the truck and have
a Coke."

"I'm sure I've hit on something, and we're not getting
anywhere trying to chase down a headstone that resembles
this rubbing. We could be looking for days, and I haven't
got that much time. In case you forgot, this isn't *my* real
job. Let's go back to San Celina's Cemetery."

"Even if you have hit on something, and I'm not saying you have, what possible good is going back?"

"We could ask Mr. Foglino. He knows tons of stuff about people buried in the cemetery and he's belonged to the historical society for fifty years. If anyone would know why the tombstones are blank, he would." I started back toward the truck. "Are you coming or not?"

He trotted up beside me. "We really should finish looking through this cemetery. We're just going to have to come back if you're wrong."

"I'm not wrong." Before he could answer, I added, "But even *if* I am wrong, I won't be coming back, you will, so it doesn't matter to me."

"Don't you have a cell phone? Can't we just call him?"

"No phone in the maintenance shed."

He complained under his breath, but kept following me. On the ride back down the grade toward San Celina, I chewed my thumbnail, hoping I wasn't leading us on a wild-goose chase. When we reached the San Celina's Cemetery, I jumped out before he switched off the engine, called out at Scout to stay, and ran over to the maintenance building. Mr. Foglino was just locking the weathered steel door.

"I'm glad I caught you," I said, panting.

"Whoa, slow down there, missy," he said, pocketing his huge set of keys. "What's up?"

Detective Hudson walked up beside me, then stood there with his arms folded and his legs spread, his body language stating his feelings about this extra trip. I ignored him and asked Mr. Foglino, "Why don't the four Brown girls' markers have dates on them?"

An almost indiscernible grunt came from behind me.

"Now, that's a real good question," he said, glancing over at the disparaging expression on Detective Hudson's face. "You've got a sharp eye."

I turned and gave the detective a triumphant look. He rolled his eyes and impatiently shifted from one foot to the other.

"Did he ever find himself a men's room?" Mr. Foglino asked.

"Ignore him," I said. "Tell me the story behind the markers."

"I reckon it's not real common knowledge, having happened so long ago and all, but the reason there's no dates is cause those little babies aren't really buried there."

A tiny jolt of electricity sparked at the base of my neck. "Why not?"

"Story goes that Rose Brown was so distraught over the death of her babies in such a short period, her family didn't want her reminded of them when she visited the family graves. Both her sisters and her mother's buried here. They all died during a flu epidemic, as well as some Brown cousins and John Madison Brown's father and mother, who came to live out here from Virginia after the Depression took everything they owned. Rose Brown used to come once a week with roses for all her kinfolk's graves until she went to live in that retirement home a few years ago."

"But there are markers for the babies now."

"That eldest Brown girl, Cappy, had them made up when her mother stopped coming to the graves."

"But she didn't have the bodies moved back?"

"No, guess she figured to leave well enough alone. Or maybe she's thinking about doing it after her mother passes on. Who knows with that Brown family? They've sure done a lot for our community, but I'm not sure the whole group is wound as tightly as they could be."

"What did the babies die from?"

He stuck his dirt-stained hands in the pockets of his overalls. "Don't recall hearing what happened. I'm sure it's in some old records. Back then—this was about 1926 or '27—babies were dying of all sorts of things that they can cure nowadays—flu, diphtheria, scarlet fever, measles, just plain old infections."

"Excuse me, I need to check in at the office," Detective Hudson broke in. He turned and strode away across the graves toward his truck.

"What's his problem?" Mr. Foglino asked, his dark, thick eyebrows a fuzzy hood over his amused eyes.

"He thinks I'm being silly."

"Don't you have enough problems with one police officer in your life?" he asked.

"Detective Hudson is not *in my life*. We're just working on this case together. So, you wouldn't happen to know where the babies are buried, would you?" I looked at him hopefully. At that point, I was willing to bet that grave rubbing we had would find a match when we found the babies' real graves.

"Sure do, out in Adelaida Cemetery. If I'd known that was who you was looking for, I could've told you earlier. They're up on the hill part of the cemetery, if I recall correctly. Only reason I know that is my mother's best friend's neighbor was the Brown's nanny for a little while. Remember hearing about the babies being buried up there back when I was just a little tyke."

"Was it common knowledge?"

"Don't really know, but I doubt it. It was so long ago, and no one thought overly much about babies dying back then. It happened in almost every family. Probably most people assumed they were buried here, and no one probably ever checked. Like I said, only reason I knew was because my mother and her friend talked about the oddness of them burying the babies so far from the family."

"It is odd. Adelaida Cemetery is pretty far away and over

the pass. It would have been a difficult trip back in the twenties."

"Probably isn't even active anymore. Those old cemeteries are a pain to upkeep. That one's got so many trees and hills and rocks. I haven't been there in years, but I'll bet it's gone completely wild unless someone's taken a notion to keep it up."

"Guess we'll go out and look for them."

"If you can talk your antsy-pants friend into it. He didn't appear to be real enthusiastic."

"If he won't go, I'll go on my own."

Mr. Foglino took his hands out of his pockets and scratched behind a bristly ear, his broad, tanned face troubled. "Be careful out there, missy. It's pretty desolate. Take that dog with you."

"I intend to. Thanks for the information."

He gave a curt nod. "Anytime."

I started to walk away, then turned around and asked one more question. "Your mother's best friend's neighbor. Do you remember her name?"

"Mrs. Knoll. Don't recall hearing her first name. Doubt she'd even be alive, though. I'm guessin' she'd be in her late nineties if she was."

"Thanks." As I walked toward the truck where Detective Hudson leaned against the side, his legs and arms crossed, I wrote Mrs. Knoll's name down on the back of my checkbook register.

"What're you writing down?" Detective Hudson asked.

"Just something I need to pick up at the store," I lied. Something inside told me to keep Mrs. Knoll's name to myself until I figured out how she fit into the picture.

"What did the old man tell you?"

"The babies' real graves are in Adelaida Cemetery. I want to go see them. Bet you fifty bucks we find the lily of the valley carved on them." I gave Scout a quick scratch under the chin, then climbed up in the cab of the truck. Proud of my detecting work, I smirked at Detective Hudson when he climbed behind the wheel.

He pulled out the San Celina County map, scanned it, and immediately started complaining. "This place is in the hills outside of Paso Robles! We just came from there. It's almost five o'clock. We'll never make it out there and back in time for my date at six-thirty."

"Drop me off at the folk art museum, then," I said evenly. "I'll drive out there myself. I'll call you tomorrow and let you know what I find." I turned and smiled at him. "You certainly don't want to keep Bambi waiting."

His face was puzzled. "Huh?"

"Miss Bodice Ripper," I clarified.

He frowned. "Her name's Heidi."

I turned my face to the window, hiding my smile. "Of course."

"Leave my love life out of this."

"You brought it up."

"This Adelaida Cemetery is out in the boonies. I'm not letting you go out there by yourself."

I turned back to him and said, "Excuse me, but you do not have the authority to keep me from going anywhere I please. Besides, I grew up in this county. I'm less likely to get in trouble out in Adelaida than you are."

His face turned a dull red as he started the engine, released the emergency brake, and slammed the truck into reverse. "We could do this tomorrow." Rocks and gravel scattered as he gunned the engine and pulled too quickly out of the cemetery's parking lot.

I swung around and made sure we hadn't lost Scout, who was doing his best to get a toe-grip on the detective's plastic-lined truck bed. "Take it easy, rhinestone cowboy,

I've got a beloved dog in the bed of this city-boy truck. And I'm not waiting until tomorrow to find out if the rubbing is from the Brown sisters' graves, and frankly I'm surprised you want to."

"Heidi hates being kept waiting," he grumbled.

"Then take me back to the museum, and I'll—"

"If I let you go out there alone and you get hurt, your husband will have my head, not to mention other parts of my body to which I've become quite emotionally attached. No way, ranch girl. We're going there together, look for these stupid graves, and then we're through for the day."

"You know, I can't believe you're not more excited about this. It's a break in the case."

"More like a paper cut."

"Who knows what it could lead to? Quit being so close-minded. I swear, those blasted police academies need a creative-thinking class. You cops have thinking skills as narrow as a possum's tail. This will give you a whole new line of questioning for the Brown family."

"What do you know? I have an extraordinary conviction rate so I must be doing something right."

"Dumb luck, most likely."

"And for your information, that Brown clan is one extraordinarily tight-lipped bunch. I've interviewed Cappy Brown and her sisters three times and gotten squat. Half my questions their attorney won't even let them answer. Except for the younger ones, who are not privy to any of the family's secrets, a person would have a better chance finding out the recipe for Coca-Cola than a truthful answer from that group. And for all your bragging, I didn't see you doing any better."

"Then every little *fissure* in this case should thrill you. Shut up and drive."

He tossed the map over at me. "Fine, you shut up and navigate."

I calmly folded the map up and tucked it into his glove compartment. "I don't need a map to tell you where to go." I smiled innocently at him.

His answer was an exasperated, animal-like grunt.

Cops must learn that sound at the academy, too.

It took us almost an hour to get to the cemetery, which was quite a few miles off Interstate 101 on a turnoff out of Paso Robles. We twisted through neatly trimmed walnut groves, past rows of new grapevines thick with emerald leaves, fat, purple fruit hanging heavy and sensual among the lush foliage, under stands of cottonwoods with their bright yellow, heart-shaped leaves and maples just starting their turn from green to yellow to brown. Twisted deciduous oak trees, their trunks massed with poison oak, and white-trunked sycamores shaded the narrow two-lane highway with long fingers of afternoon shadows. The peaceful, empty road caused both Detective Hudson and me to withdraw into ourselves, become quiet and introspective, only startled out of the drowsy monotony of the curvy blacktop when a flock of hen turkeys dashed across the road, causing him to slam on the brakes. I glanced back at Scout, who'd survived the stop fine since he'd wisely laid down in the bed.

"Sorry," Detective Hudson murmured

"Right at the next split in the road," I said.

The cemetery lay on our left with no parking lot, but merely a wide spot in the weeds. We climbed out and walked over to the rusty gate. It was closed, but not locked. I turned and called Scout, since there was no one in this old cemetery who would care if he romped among the gravestones. I left my purse in the locked truck and just took my camera, a pen, and a pocket-sized notebook.

I followed Detective Hudson inside the weed- and wildflower-choked grounds. Except for an old outhouse that was long past its prime, there were only the overgrown graves shaded by oaks that had been here two hundred years or longer.

"Mr. Foglino said he thought their graves might be up on the hill," I said, pointing to a hill in front of us with a sharp, steep embankment covered in brambles.

"Is there a road?" he asked, glancing down at his fancy ostrich boots.

"You should carry a pair of work boots in your truck," I said, pointing to a small, overgrown path behind the outhouse.

"Yes, Mom," he said and took off toward the path.

It was about a quarter mile on a steep path to the upper part of the cemetery. On the hilltop, the trees were thicker; the leaves and brush crackled like tiny firecrackers under our feet. Blue oaks laced with overcoats of Spanish moss gave the deepening forest a spooky, bayou feel.

"Watch out for poison ivy," I said, ducking under a still-leafy oak branch. "It's bad this time of year."

I saw him flinch and subtly pull his arms closer, though in reality I didn't see any near enough to cause us any problems. I laughed silently to myself, recognizing a nature neophyte when I saw one. I stepped over some wild grape vines, stopping a moment to pick some volunteer grapes and squeeze them in my fingers. The sweet smell perfumed the air for a moment.

A rustling sound ahead of us caused Scout to take off into the underbrush, his tail straight out, a low growl deep in his throat.

"What was that?" the detective asked, his voice slightly apprehensive.

I raised my eyebrows. He wasn't lying about one thing; he was definitely a city boy.

"Probably just a mountain lion," I said casually, watching his back stiffen and trying not to laugh. *Yep, that was a definite stiffening.* "But don't worry, most times they don't bother humans. You're not wearing any cologne, by any chance?"

He turned around, his sweating face trying hard not to show panic. "Why?"

I kept my face serious, chewing my lower lip for effect. "Just wondered. They're kind of intrigued by the smell."

"You're shittin' me."

I shook my head solemnly. "Wish I was."

His nostrils flared slightly.

"Aramis is their favorite," I continued, keeping a straight face. "But I've heard the lions around here have been preferring Polo lately."

He narrowed his eyes at me, his lips thin with irritation. "Very funny."

I giggled. "Yeah, I thought so."

He took off ahead of me, obviously angry, and I felt a small twinge of shame for putting him on. A very small tinge.

When we reached the graves, he surveyed the area and gruffly told me to start on the west end and work toward him. "You have your camera?"

"Right here." I held it up.

"Film?"

"Yes, Detective. They tend to work better that way."

"Then let's get to work."

He strode off toward the east side of the cemetery, his anger still apparent in his stride. I whistled for Scout who eventually appeared out of some scrub brush, his nose wet and dirty, his tongue hanging out in obvious pleasure at chasing the rabbit or squirrel that had probably made the sounds prompting my practical joke on the detective.

"Didn't catch it, did you?" I commented, when he sat down and furiously scratched behind his ear. "You guys are all alike, running through the brush, chasing nothing important, but thrilled to your bones you get to chase it."

He sneezed twice in reply.

I started on my end, doing my best not to miss any graves, easy to do in this old, very disorganized graveyard. I was assuming the four sisters would all be buried together, but since the fact they were even buried in this old cemetery wasn't logical, I didn't expect how they were buried to make any more sense.

Once again I was struck emotionally by how many of the dead were infants and small children. So many of these graves hadn't been disturbed or visited in years. One especially touched me, bearing the inscription NATHAN RAY MONROE—AUGUST 10, 1882–DECEMBER 12, 1882, "CROWN'D WITHOUT THE CONFLICT." The baby had been four months old when he died. Walking in and out of the light cast by the thick maples, cottonwoods, and oaks, I felt a chill, as psychological as much as physical, when I read the headstones. One whole family, a father, mother, and six children, surrounded by a rusty Victorian iron fence, had been wiped out by influenza during the same month in 1917. I sat down on a flat rock, overwhelmed for a moment by the tragedy.

"I found them!" Detective Hudson's voice echoed from across the cemetery.

"Scout, come," I called and started running toward the detective's voice, dodging broken markers and uneven sunken spots.

He stood in front of four identical markers, standing in

a row like a just-started fence. On the front of each of them was carved a lily of the valley.

"It *is* about the babies," I whispered.

Then there was a sharp pop, and something whizzed past my ear. With a howl, Scout started toward the trees.

"Scout, down!" I started to run toward him, then found myself flat on my chest, the breath knocked out of me. Detective Hudson's solid, muscular body pinned me to the ground.

"Don't move," he snapped. His thighs instinctively tightened around mine.

Move? I couldn't even get a breath. Gasping, I tried to talk. To tell him I needed oxygen. To tell him it felt like I was dying. I felt his hip bone jab into me as he struggled to pull his gun out of his holster.

Another pop cracked through the silence. Dirt and leaves jumped a few feet from our prone bodies. His thighs tightened again.

I moaned, trying to get a breath, trying to tell him to get off me.

"Hush," he said, pushing my face into the sharp, dry leaves. They scratched my face, and I squirmed, trying to get a hand out to push them away.

"Lie still!" His harsh voice caused me to freeze. My heart *thump-thumped* in my ears, sounding as loud as the ocean.

Though his body grew heavy on mine, gradually my breath came back, and I managed to take short gulps of cool, soil-scented air. As we lay there, the noise of the forest slowly resumed, the chirping of crickets and the chattering of birds telling us our assailant had departed. I could feel Detective Hudson's breath warm and rapid on my neck, then gradually felt the muscles in his arms and legs relax around me.

"Listen," he whispered. In the distance the rumbling sound of a truck's engine moved farther away.

"Good," I mumbled into the dirt and leaves. "You can get off me now." With the immediate threat of danger gone, our position was entirely too personal for my tastes, though I had to admit he had pretty nice thighs.

He laughed softly in my ear, his lips brushing against my hair. His thighs tightened around mine again, voluntarily this time. "I don't know, it was just starting to get fun."

I spit a leaf out of my mouth. "Get off me, you jerk." I shoved my elbow as hard as I could into his chest.

He laughed again, then rolled off me and stood up, reholstering his pistol. He held out his hand. "Someone sure isn't happy with us finding these graves."

Ignoring his offer of help, I scrambled up. "Where's Scout?" I looked around frantically for my dog.

He lay flat on the ground a few feet away, whimpering.

"Scout, come," I said. He jumped up and ran over to me. "What a good, good boy you are." He licked my face as I ran my hands over his body, checking for injuries. "Are you okay, Scooby-doo?" I crooned, hugging his thick body.

"Shoot, he's fine," Detective Hudson said, rubbing his lower back. "I'm the one who just pulled a muscle because of that dimestore Daniel Boone sniper. Bet you a taco dinner it was someone hired by the Browns. They must've been following us all day. Dang it all, I was so busy haggling with you I let them get the slip on me."

"So why didn't you go after them, Mr. Purple Heart, and find out who they were?" Hair at the back of my neck was damp from heat and fear. I lifted it up, letting the small breeze cool my skin.

"My mama might've raised a fool, but my daddy taught me never to get into a fight I didn't have at least a fifty percent chance of winning. No way was I running into those woods. They had the advantage and they knew it. There wasn't a chance this side of Lubbock I would be able to catch them."

"Hmmp," was all I said, tenderly touching a raw place on my cheek.

"Sorry I had to throw you down so hard," he said, tilting his head to look at me. His grin belied his apology. "But you were a perfect target."

"Some excuse."

"I saved your life!"

"Don't deny you enjoyed knocking the air out of me."

"Well, it *was* right peaceful for a few minutes there, what with your mouth not moving and all."

"Eat dirt." I walked back over to the babies' graves, took a notebook out of my back pocket and started writing down the information on the headstones.

Detective Hudson went over and picked up the camera that had flown out of my hands when the sniper shot at us. He turned it over in his hands, inspecting it. "Think this will still work?"

"I don't know. That's why I'm copying down the information."

He came up behind me and took a dozen or so shots of the markers. These did have dates, though nothing else appeared on the plain white marble stones except the lily of the valley.

DAISY JEWEL BROWN—May 1, 1925–November 3, 1925
DAHLIA JEWEL BROWN—May 1, 1925–March 12, 1926
BEULAH JEWEL BROWN—January 25, 1927–June 15, 1927
BETHANY JEWEL BROWN—January 25, 1927–September 9, 1927

"I wonder what they died from?" I asked out loud.
Detective Hudson shrugged. "Does it matter?"

I looked at him, surprised. "Of course it does! It's obvious that whatever Giles was blackmailing the family with has something to do with these babies. How they died might be the key. I mean, maybe someone killed them or something."

He pointed to the lichen-covered markers. "The dates of death don't support that theory. They most likely died of influenza or diphtheria or who knows what else. Look at all the other graves of children here. You're really reaching now."

"If they died innocently, why is someone shooting at us?"

He was silent for a moment, knowing I had him there. Then he said, "I don't know. Might just be that this person wanted to scare us off investigating altogether and after following us all day decided that out here in the boonies was the safest place for him . . ."

"Or her," I said.

He rolled his eyes. "Okay, Miss Feminist, *or her*, to shoot at us. I mean, when else would they? When we were at the folk art museum? Or in the San Celina's Cemetery? This was the best opportunity."

"Except we've been in other isolated graveyards today, like the Estrella one. Nobody shot at us there. They were warning us away from this particular cemetery."

"Benni, if they didn't want us to get here, they would have done something while we were out on the road. There's absolutely no evidence to support your theory."

"You haven't even looked for evidence to support it! You're dismissing it without any serious consideration. That's very poor detective work. I find it hard to believe your success rate is as good as you say with a pessimistic attitude like yours."

"Don't tell *me* how to do my job! Criminy, you can be a pain in the ass."

I ignored his comment and crossed my arms. He knew I was right. Eventually he'd admit it, though not without some whining.

Back at his truck, he searched the ground for tire tracks. The grass had definitely been flattened, but the dirt was too hard to leave any hints as to what kind of vehicle the shooter was driving.

"You know," he said, driving back down the winding country road toward the interstate, "there's a good possibility that all of this is a ruse to distract us from who the real killer is. Did you ever think about that?"

"Okay," I finally conceded. "You could be right. So where does that leave us?"

"Not much of anywhere, but it's something to consider. Do you happen to be carrying your cell phone?"

I dug through my purse and handed him the phone. While trying to ignore his exaggerated excuses to Heidi, I thought about what he said. If it didn't have to do with the babies, then why was Giles killed? His determination to take over the winery was still a possibility, so maybe it was Etta who shot him in a passionate moment, and her sisters helped cover it up. I thought about the Seven Sisters quilt pattern I'd looked up the other day—how it was a pattern of six stars revolving around one in the center, much like the constellation Bliss and I had searched for. Like the pattern and the constellation, there was a center to this, a something or someone all the other events circled around. Was it the grandmother, Rose Brown, and her four dead children? Or was it simpler than that—a moment of anger, a handy loaded gun, a family adept at covering up, showing a good face to the world? After he was finished with his excuses to Heidi, I tried calling Gabe at the office and got his voice mail. Then I called home and got the answering machine, a practice that had been happening a little too frequently this week.

The detective dropped me off at the folk art museum at seven o'clock, and we said a quick good-bye without any more discussion about what we should do next. He was anxious to get to his date, and I was eager to go home and tell Gabe about what had happened, come truly clean about how much I was involved. Then what? Those tiny graves kept reappearing in my head. I wanted to know more about the four babies even if they didn't have anything to do with finding out who killed Giles. I knew someone who worked in the county records department—a girl I went to college with. Tomorrow I'd go downtown and see if she could find their death certificates for me.

The house was dark when I got home. I immediately went into the kitchen and fed Scout, who was two hours past his regular dinner time and was giving me a soulful look telling me so. As I watched him gobble his dinner, I went in and checked the answering machine. There were only two messages—mine and an old one that told me Gabe had most likely been home and gone out again after listening to the message. It better not be Lydia's voice, I thought as I hit replay.

"Chief!" Miguel's voice croaked over the phone. "I'm down at General Hospital. I couldn't find your cell phone number so I hope you get this soon. Bliss took one in the shoulder. I thought you'd want to know." The message time was 5:02 p.m.

I ran for the car, yelling at Scout to stay. On the drive down there, all I could consciously pray over and over was, *Oh, Lord. Make her okay, please, please make her okay.*

12

INSIDE THE EMERGENCY ROOM, there were a few families with sick, cranky children and the requisite medical personnel milling about. There was no sign of Gabe, Sam, or Bliss's family. I asked at the desk, and while the nurse was checking the computer, I spotted Miguel down the hall putting money in a coffee machine.

"Never mind," I told the nurse. "That's her partner over there." I rushed over to him. "Miguel, what happened? Is Bliss all right? What about the baby?"

He watched the liquid splash into the paper cup, not answering me for a moment. His hand shook slightly as he picked up the steaming cup.

"Miguel," I said softly. "Are you okay?"

He looked down at me, his eyes rimmed red, fighting tears with all his Latin-bred masculine resolve. I wanted to put my arms around his broad shoulders and hug him the way I used to when he was three and was startled awake from his nap by a bad dream.

He took a gulp of the hot coffee, then said, "She's upstairs. The asshole got her in the shoulder. She lost a lot of blood and, well, they say it shouldn't affect the baby, but they can't promise . . ." His voice choked.

"What happened?" I asked again.

"A friggin' traffic stop over by the bus station," he said. "She was driving today so she made the approach. He shot her before she could get halfway to the car. I fired two shots, hit his back window, but he got away." He took another gulp of coffee. "They caught him up in Paso about an hour later. He had a half gram of cocaine under his seat. She was almost killed for a stinking half gram of cocaine."

His hand jerked, causing some coffee to slosh onto the shiny hospital floor. He looked down at it, his face a mixture of agony and dismay.

"I'll get it," I said, taking a tissue out of my purse and bending down to wipe it up. "Is her family here yet?"

"They're upstairs. Fourth floor. She's in intensive care, but the doctors say she'll be all right. They just want to keep a close eye on her tonight." He gestured with his cup. Coffee splashed out on his hand. He flinched and said, "Shit."

"Here, give me that." I gently took the cup out of his hand and handed him a dry tissue. "Is there anything I can do for you?"

He wiped his wet hand, then handed me the damp tissue. "No, thanks. My shift's over, so I'm going home. They said there's nothing anyone else can do tonight, and she's got her family up there." His dark eyelashes were shiny with unshed tears. "I shouldn't have let her approach that driver. I should have taken it."

"There was nothing you could do. It's not your fault."

He gripped the butt of his gun and looked down at the floor.

"Bliss didn't like being coddled or treated special. It was

her turn, and she would have fought you to take it. It was just the luck of the draw, Miguelito," I said, using his childhood nickname.

He gave a tremulous smile. "Go on up. I'm sure the chief wants to see you."

I squeezed his upper arm, then walked over to the elevators. Upstairs, I asked the desk clerk which way to the waiting room. Halfway down the hall I could see Bliss's mother, JJ, and Cappy sitting together on a sofa. Gabe's back was to me. Lydia stood next to him, and Sam sat on the wood coffee table, his face in his hands. A doctor walked out of a glass door next to them, and they eagerly gathered around him, blocking him from my view. But even from down the hall, I could hear Sam's agonized cry and watched his mother encircle him with her arms. Susa and JJ clung together, weeping. Gabe stepped over to Lydia and Sam and put his arms around both of them.

I froze, not knowing what to do. Watching Gabe so tenderly hold his son and ex-wife caused a pain in my heart that I couldn't ignore, but to go up to them now seemed like a crass and self-serving invasion of privacy. Trembling, I turned and walked back down the hall and sat down on a chair near the nurses' station, wondering what had happened and what I should do. Was Bliss all right? Was it her or the baby? Or both? Finally I went up to a nurse with a friendly face, trying not to stutter, explained briefly who I was and asked if she could find out.

"Honey, I understand," she said. "I'm a number two myself. It's an awkward place to be at times like this. Let me find out for you."

She came back a few minutes later, her round face regretful. "Your stepson's girlfriend is going to be okay, but she lost the baby. I'm sure sorry."

"Was it the gunshot?" I asked.

She shook her head no. "Most likely not. Pregnant women are tougher than people realize. Unless she'd been shot right in the stomach, her baby, even at two or three months, was capable of surviving quite a lot of trauma. It seems strange, I know, but most likely she would have lost the baby whether or not she'd been shot. Most miscarriages are caused by chromosomal or genetic abnormalities that can't be prevented or treated. There's nothing for anyone to feel guilty about here."

"Thanks," I said.

Back at my car I couldn't help worrying that my decision not to break into the Brown and Ortiz family tragedy would be taken as a sign of not caring. At home, I cleaned up the kitchen and waited for Gabe and prayed for them all, especially Bliss, who would suffer with this the longest—her whole life. And I tried to erase the picture in my head of Gabe with his arms around Lydia and Sam. Jealousy had no place in this situation, but I couldn't get rid of the sad feeling that somehow Gabe had slipped away from me. When I wasn't paying attention, his old life, his old love came back and lured him away. *Fight for your man*, Elvia and Emory had encouraged me. But I knew fancy nightgowns, fierce demands, and pieces of paper that say you're a couple can't buy the human heart.

Finally I called Dove and told her.

"Those poor kids," she said. "Should I come out? Or is there a wagonload of people already seeing to them?"

"I came on home. Sam and Bliss seem to have plenty of emotional support. I'll send flowers and a note tomorrow. I don't know what else to do."

"Not much else we can do. Life's tragedies cóme and go. I don't have to tell you that. We stand up through them or we fall like saplings in a windstorm. All depends on how deep of roots you've grown before they happen. I surely do hurt for them, though. Losing a baby's got to be the hardest thing a woman ever goes through."

"Have you ever? Lost a baby, I mean?"

"Once. Lord, it was so long ago, but there's times it still seems like last week. A little girl in between your daddy and your aunt Kate. I was six months along, and she just came. Back then we didn't have the fancy incubators and such they have now. They let me see her before they took her away. Prettiest shaped head I'd ever seen on a baby. She looked perfect. But God knows best. It wasn't her place to be born to this earth."

"Do you ever think about her?"

Dove was silent for a moment, then said softly, "Every May 3rd."

"Oh, Gramma, I'm so sorry." So many dead babies in the last few days. It was more than my heart could manage.

"It was a long time ago, honeybun. Hurts don't go away, but they gentle."

"Is that a guarantee for all hurts?" I asked, trying not to sound desperate.

"Some take longer than others. And it all depends on the person. A hurt can soften you like a good, wool blanket, or, if you let it, turn you into a pile of dried leaves, ready to crumble at the first footstep. Your choice. Our hurts are what make us human. It's why God had to become a man, to see what it was we were all whining about, see if maybe He'd made things too hard for us."

Thinking of all the little graves in the Adelaida Cemetery, I said, "Sometimes I think He did."

"Well, He also came to rescue us and did a fine job of it, though some might not think so at first. And it's okay to have a doubt now and then. What riles Him is folks not carin' enough to even wonder. Now, come on out to the ranch tomorrow, because me and Isaac got something to show you. I think it'll cheer you up. And besides, I'm going to bake Sam some of his favorite peanut butter cookies, and I need you to fetch them to him."

"Okay. By the way, I have a message I forgot to give you from Miguel. We saw him on Sunday. He said, and I quote, 'No. Absolutely not. No way.' "

She laughed softly under her breath. "No problem. I'll just pull some strings, go over his head to his boss."

"What's Gabe got to do with this?"

She snorted. "I mean his real boss. Now, are you coming out?"

"What time do you want me?"

"Before noon. You can help serve lunch to the crew."

"The crew? The crew for what?"

"Never you mind. Just be here." She was quiet for a moment. "And don't worry. Things'll work out for the best with all this. That's a promise from me to you."

"Yes, ma'am," I said, wanting with all my life to believe her.

I was in bed reading when he came home around eleven.

"You heard?" he asked, his face shadowed with tired lines.

"Yes, I played Miguel's message when I got home at around seven o'clock. Then I went down to the hospital and ran into him outside the emergency room. He told me what happened. I . . ." I stopped and took a deep breath. "I was walking down the hall when the doctor was telling you all about the baby. It didn't seem appropriate for me to break in, so I decided to come home and wait for you." I looked up into his tired face. "Oh, Gabe, I'm so sorry."

He sat down on the edge of the bed. "Sam's over at the hotel with his mom. He wanted to sleep at the hospital, but Lydia talked him into going back with her. Her mother said they gave Bliss some drugs that made her groggy, so I'm not sure how much she's comprehended. Her shoulder's going to be okay, no major damage."

"How's Sam?"

"In shock, I think, but he's handling it pretty well. I'm proud of him."

"When this is all over, maybe you should tell him so."

"I will." His mouth opened in a wide yawn. "I'm exhausted."

"Why don't you sleep in tomorrow?"

"Can't, too many appointments. I'll be okay."

"Then come to bed."

He pulled his suit jacket off and tossed it on a chair. The rest of his clothes he left in a crumpled pile on the floor, telling me how tired he was.

When I turned out the light, he laid on his back and stared at the ceiling. I wanted to say something that would make him feel better, but knew there was nothing I could do but just be here. Under the covers I sought out his hand and held it tight. He cleared his throat in the darkness.

"I . . ." His voice faltered. "You know, I was just beginning to get used to being a grandfather. I never held Sam much when he was a baby. I was thinking that maybe I'd have been a better grandfather than I was a father."

I leaned over and kissed his bare shoulder, then laid my cheek on it. "Sam loves you very much."

"I know," he said, pulling me into his arms, holding tight.

The next morning he skipped his ritual jogging and was subdued over breakfast. I didn't force conversation, knowing one thing about this reticent Latino man I'd married; his grief was a private thing, difficult to share even with me.

"I think I'll send Bliss some flowers. When you see Sam can you tell him why I left last night? Let him know I'm concerned," I said, buttering an English muffin.

He nodded. "Sure, he'll understand. I'll drop by the hospital on my way to work, see how Bliss is doing. What are you doing today?"

"Same old stuff," I said, wondering if I should tell him about the shooting at the cemetery yesterday. His face, craggy with fatigue from a restless night and the anticipation of a day filled with questions and reporters and dealing with Sam's grief decided for me. He couldn't take one more thing to worry about right now.

After dropping by the florist to order Bliss's flowers, I went to the folk art museum more out of habit than any real need since I had caught up on all my paperwork yesterday and the exhibit was doing fine. After chatting with some potters over a cup of coffee, I went to my office and puttered around, sharpening pencils and cleaning out drawers. What I was trying to do was decide whether I should continue looking into Giles's murder. With Bliss engaged to Sam, I felt awkward about trying to prove one of her family members was a killer. What with Bliss's miscarriage and the sniper yesterday, I'd decided that me being involved was too risky . . . for my own life and for the relationships of the people I loved.

I was reduced to washing my small, wavy window when JJ walked in.

"Hey," I said, getting down off my footstool and giving her a quick hug. "How's Bliss?"

"They're letting her come home tomorrow. The wound wasn't very deep and . . ." She swallowed hard, her face contorting in grief.

"Sit down," I said, leading her to a visitor chair. I sat next to her, turning my chair so we were facing each other. "Are you okay, JJ?"

She sniffed and rubbed the back of her long-sleeved chenille sweater under one eye. She was bare-faced today, and her hair was soft and pixielike around her head. "Yes . . . no . . . Oh, I don't know. I'm glad Bliss is okay, but I'm sad about the baby. I just don't know what to do or feel."

"What you're feeling is normal. Just be there for Bliss, that's really all you can do. Let time soften things."

A deep frown narrowed her forehead. "I'm mad, too."

"At who?"

"My grandma. Do you know what she said at the hospital last night to me and my mother after everyone left? That it's probably for the best. That Sam and Bliss were too young to have a baby. How could she say that? Say that Bliss's baby dying is for the best?"

I shook my head, unable to give her an answer. It was a common, if insensitive remark I'm sure many people had said and thought in similar situations.

"How's Bliss's shoulder doing this morning?" I asked, trying to move the subject away from questions about her grandmother that I couldn't answer.

"Much better. Susa's with her right now. I just wanted to come find you."

"Why?"

"To tell you I'm leaving San Celina. When Bliss is healed up, my mother and I are moving back up north. She called my father last night, and they had a long talk. They're going to try to work things out. As for me, I just don't like it here. Seven Sisters and all its problems is something I don't need in my life."

"We'll miss you, JJ. I'll really miss you."

She leaned over and hugged me. "You're one of the few things I will miss." She reached down and petted Scout. "You, too, big boy." Then she stood up and straightened her long cotton skirt. "As for all the stuff about the secrets in my family and who killed Giles, I just don't care anymore. I really understand why my mom left when she was eighteen, why she didn't want us raised around Seven Sisters. Frankly, I'm hoping Bliss and Sam come up north when they get married."

"And I hope they don't," I said, smiling. "But I understand what you're saying."

Her visit helped me decide once and for all that stepping out of the investigation was the right thing. It was Detective Hudson's job, not mine, and right now I was too concerned about my husband and his son to worry about which person in the Brown family was a killer.

I was unlocking my truck, having decided to drop by Elvia's bookstore and catch up on the trials and tribulations of her love life, when Detective Hudson's red pickup pulled up next to me. Scout barked in enthusiastic recognition. The detective stepped out, wearing the plain brown ropers today that he'd worn Saturday night when we'd danced. The sleeves of his blue Arrow shirt were rolled up, revealing a large leather-band Swiss Army watch.

"You should've worn those yesterday for our cemetery tour," I said, glancing down at his feet.

"How's Officer Girard?" he asked.

"They said she'd be going home tomorrow." I looked at him curiously. "How'd you find out about her?"

"It was in the newspaper this morning, but I found out last night. When a cop goes down, believe me, it gets around even if it isn't someone from your agency."

"Did you hear she lost her baby?"

His eyes dropped to the ground. "That stinks. The gunshot?"

"No, the nurse told me that most likely there was something already wrong with the baby, that the gunshot didn't cause the miscarriage. It was just one of those things."

"My ex-wife lost one before Maisie was born. It's hard on a woman."

"That's the first time you've mentioned your daughter's name. Maisie. That's pretty."

He grinned shyly. "Don't get me started, or I'll force you to look at all my pictures. Then after that it's the home videos and refrigerator art. You'll never get free."

For the first time since we met, I almost liked Detective Hudson. "So there's at least one woman who has you under her thumb."

He nodded, laughing. "Benni Harper, you hit it right on the head with that one. Not to change the subject, but what did your husband say about our little wilderness experience yesterday?"

"I didn't tell him and I don't want you to either. He doesn't need any more worries right now. Actually I'm glad you dropped by, because it saves me a phone call. I'm off the case."

"You're chickening out on me when we're getting so close? You can't give up now."

"I'm not giving up, I'm just doing what I should have done from the beginning—let you investigate it alone. I should have never let you talk me into getting involved. We could have been hurt or killed yesterday."

He cracked his knuckles nonchalantly. "They were warning shots. If they'd wanted us dead, we would be."

I threw up my hands in exasperation. "And that doesn't bother you?"

"Not really." He studied the backs of his hands, then checked his watch. Early morning sunlight glinted off the reddish-blond hair on his forearms. His calm expression told me he wasn't kidding.

"You may have a death wish, Detective, but not me."

"It doesn't bother you that an innocent man was killed?"

"We could debate the appropriateness of the word innocent in his case, but, yes, of course, I care. But it's not my job, and I don't want to do it anymore."

He folded his arms across his chest. "I don't believe you."

"You'd better, because it's the truth."

"Okay, one last thing. Look at these and then tell me you still want to quit." He reached into his truck and pulled out a large, manila envelope.

I opened the envelope, pulling out four pages. They were pink with a fancy blue border. Across the top read *County of San Celina*. In the left bottom corner was California's state seal, in the right corner a same-sized circle saying County Recorder, San Celina County, State of California.

The babies' death certificates.

I glanced over them, looking specifically at the cause of death. The first one to die was Daisy. Pneumonia. Dahlia was next. Her cause of death stated simply natural causes. Natural causes was also written on Beulah's and Bethany's certificates. Though they tugged at my heart, they didn't tell us anything we didn't already know.

But . . .

What if someone *had* killed them? What if this person had gotten away with it all this time? I was reacting emotionally, I knew, and that was exactly what the detective was hoping for, that I also knew.

I handed him back the death certificates. "It says here they died of natural causes. Nothing else we can do unless the doctor is still alive."

"Which he isn't," Detective Hudson said. "I already checked. And his records were destroyed a long time ago."

"So that leaves us—no, make that *you*—exactly nowhere. I know I started you down this path, but even I can see when something's a dead end."

He slipped the certificates back into the envelope. "No, you were right. I wasn't thinking creatively enough and I also think you're right about Giles's blackmail attempt being something that involves these kids. Or at least something in the past that the Brown family is trying to hide. Now we just have to think of a clever and sneaky way to find out about this family's past." He smiled at me with encouragement. "Your specialty, Mrs. Harper."

I leaned back against my truck's passenger door. Scout came over and nudged my head, and I reached up and rubbed his chest. Detective Hudson was deliberately manipulating me with his flattery, and I knew it. Yet I was still pulled toward this case. If indeed they'd been murdered, even after all these years, the babies deserved justice. And Giles, whether he was a person I would have liked or not, deserved it, too.

"What would you do now?" he asked, his voice cajoling. "I mean, *if* you were still working on this?"

I closed my eyes briefly, irritated because his plan was working. "Someone should talk to Rose Brown again."

He scratched his cheek, trying to suppress the grin that lurked behind his feigned seriousnss. "My thoughts exactly."

I pushed myself away from the truck. "Guess that would be you since I'm not involved anymore. See ya."

"She'll never talk to me," he said, following me. "That's even if I could get in to see her. I'll bet you fifty-yard-line seats at a Cowboys game that those Brown sisters have already stepped up security around their mama."

"You're probably right, so most likely I couldn't get in to see her either." I opened my door and started to climb in.

"Your friends could, though."

I slowly turned around. "My friends?"

"You teach a quilting class at Oak Terrace Retirement Home, two floors down from Mrs. Brown. There are eight ladies in your class. Four of them have known you since you were six years old. And they've been involved with one investigation with you already, a year ago February during what was referred to as a Senior Prom. Very clever wordplay, by the way." He glanced down at his watch and smiled widely. "Today's Tuesday, and I do believe you have a class with them. Three o'clock. How convenient for everyone."

Surprised, I was speechless for a moment. First, because of his audacity. Second, because I'd completely forgotten that today was the third Tuesday of the month.

He smirked. "What's wrong, did you forget about the class? Come by my office after your meeting, please, and tell me what you find out. Note that I did say *please*." He tipped his Stetson hat.

I opened my mouth to snap back that I wasn't about to involve those ladies in a murder investigation, then closed it again. He knew I'd never be able to resist asking them about Rose Brown now, and I knew he'd eventually track me down anyway, so I said, "Okay."

He stepped back a foot, his hand gripping his chest dramatically, as if shot in the heart. "What? Benni Harper is being cooperative! Lord have mercy on us all, the end of the world is nigh upon us. A miracle has occurred."

"Oh, go milk a bull," I said childishly. I went back to my office to get the museum checkbook. A quilt made by the ladies had sold recently in our small gift shop, and I needed to pay them. When I returned to my truck, the detective was gone.

After a trip to the post office, I stopped by Blind Harry's. Elvia wasn't there, so I left her a note. Downstairs in the coffeehouse, while I was waiting for my mocha, I spotted

Sam at a table. I took my cup and went over to him.

"Hey, bud," I said, sitting down across from him. "How's it going?"

He wrapped his hands around his thick white mug. "Okay, I guess."

"Are you working today?"

He shook his head no. "I just dropped by to pick up my paycheck. I'm going over to see Bliss, but I needed to chill out for a while first."

His voice was so low, the soft buzz of late-morning customers swallowed his last few words.

"How is she doing today? Is she up for visitors?"

He drew in a deep breath, as if getting ready to lift a heavy load. "She's better. She's at her sister's house and doesn't really feel like seeing anyone. I'll tell her you said hi." He looked over at me, his dark brown eyes glossy with pain.

I reached over and put my hand on top of his. "How are you?"

He shrugged and didn't answer, already well trained in the stoic macho tradition of his Latino heritage. But a small portion of the vulnerable young boy he still was leaked out. "I can't sleep that good," he whispered.

I nodded and didn't answer.

Using both hands, he brought his mug up to his lips. After a sip, he said, "Tell Dove and Ben I'll be back out to the ranch tonight. I know I'm behind on my chores. Tell them I'll catch up this week."

"They understand, Sam. You take care now."

He nodded again, and I left him staring into his black coffee.

To relieve the sadness that had crept around my heart, I put Patty Loveless on my portable cassette player as I headed out to the ranch. I was singing along, agreeing with her wearily cynical view of male/female relationships, when I pulled into the long driveway of the ranch.

I slammed my foot on the brakes when I saw the fire truck, the paramedic van, a Highway Patrol car, and a San Celina PD car.

"Oh, no," I said out loud, my heart thumping in my chest, thinking Dove, Daddy, Isaac?

13

I JUMPED OUT of the truck and ran across the lawn to the house. It was empty. On the kitchen counter were casserole dishes covered with tinfoil and a half dozen pies and cakes. Voices came from behind the house, so I dashed out the back door and headed toward the barn. Outside the barn's double doors, a paramedic and a Highway Patrol officer stood shooting the breeze.

"My gramma?" I said, breathing hard.

"You mean Dove?" the paramedic asked.

I nodded.

"In there." He pointed to the barn. "But be careful, she's . . ."

I pushed past them and ran through the barn doors, expecting to see Dove stretched out on a gurney, hooked up to IVs, fighting for her life.

She was fighting all right, but not for her life.

More like for her lights.

"To the left," she yelled through my cheerleading megaphone. "Not that left, your other left. For cryin' out loud,

John, pay attention!" Big John, one of the members of the historical society, rolled his milky eyes at her and patiently moved the tall camera light to where she pointed. Behind her, Isaac sat on a director's chair, fooling around with a large square camera, grinning to himself.

Daddy walked by, carrying a small lamb whose unremitting bleats sounded like a broken car alarm.

"What's going on?" I asked him.

A resigned look on his face told me he'd been roped into this early and perhaps before he'd had his third cup of coffee. He stroked the head of the lamb, whose rhythmic cries didn't skip a beat. "Better ask your gramma, pumpkin. I'm just the hired help."

Behind him, in the middle of the barn, two women I knew from the San Celina Cattlewomen's Association were combing and brushing a white-faced calf who squirmed and called for its mama. Next to the calf, another two women, Edna McClun and Maria Ramirez, members of the Historical Society, were brushing and fiddling with the hair of another hunk of beef. A much bigger one.

And they were giggling like two schoolgirls.

A half naked Miguel, wearing only a pair of faded jeans and his gun belt, stood patiently still, his face slightly flushed, while the much shorter older women, standing on wooden milk stools, touched up his hair and dabbed bits of makeup on his smooth, brown, muscle-defined chest.

"Five minutes," Dove called through the microphone. "We've got February and March waiting in the wings. We ain't got all day."

I walked over to Isaac. "Okay," I said, laughing. "What's going on here?"

He looked up at the sound of my voice, his cracked-adobe face happy to see me. "It was your gramma's idea. I think she's calling it 'Hunks and Babes.'"

"What?"

He pointed at the bawling calf. "She said there's two things women go crazy over—handsome men and baby animals. She got the idea that a calendar showing both would sell like hotcakes. I think she's onto something."

"Not to mention the fact that the famous Isaac Lyons taking the photographs just might help sell a few."

He winked at me. "You know I'd do anything for Dove."

I put my arm around his massive shoulders and hugged him. "And that's one of the reasons you've captured my heart, you old grizzly."

The calf let out another plaintive cry.

"We're going to have to get this show on the road!" Dove yelled. "That baby's getting tired."

I went over to Miguel, who was still getting primped and powder-pouffed by the two ladies. "Miguel, baby," I said, giving him the thumbs-up sign. "Love your new career move. Let's do lunch. Have my people call your people."

He shot me an irritated frown. "My mother's making me do this."

"Ah," I said, nodding. So that was what the mysterious communication between him and Dove was about on Sunday. She had indeed gone over his head to his real boss. Unable to resist, I reached over and ran a hand over his ripply chest muscles.

"Nice and firm, aren't they?" Edna McClun said. She rapped on his left pectoral. "Like a good melon."

"The muscle definition is *muy bueno*," Maria Ramirez. "All natural, too. No steroids."

"He's certainly prime cut," I agreed, nodding solemnly. We all studied his chest closely. "I can't find a flaw anywhere."

"Would you people hurry up," Miguel complained, his

face a deep scarlet. "I've got a shift to work."

We looked at each other and burst out laughing.

"Don't worry about it," Dove said, walking by, the megaphone clutched in one hand. "I have connections with your chief who, by the way, will be Mr. April with chickens."

I turned to her, my mouth open. "Gabe's going to be in the calendar? He never told me!"

"Good," she said, her face pleased. "Then I know I can trust him to keep a secret."

"Mr. April? With chickens?"

"He won't take off his clothes," she said. "Says it ain't dignified. So we decided to go for a sophisticated look. He'll be in his tuxedo surrounded by baby chicks." She elbowed me. "Surrounded by chicks, get it?"

"I get it. Am I right in assuming all the men loitering around outside are today's models?"

She caught Elmo Ritter's arm as he walked by and asked, "Who's on the docket today?"

After adjusting his brown beret, he checked his clipboard. "There's Miguel Aragon, San Celina Police Department, and white-faced calf—Mr. January; then Bill Connor, Arroyo Grande fire fighter, with baby ducks—Mr. March; Ty O'Brien, Highway Patrol officer, with lamb—Mr. August; and Josh Dunbar, county paramedic with shih tzu puppies—Mr. June. We had to reschedule Mr. February, the SWAT team guy, cause the Siamese kittens didn't arrive. The cat lady called and said she couldn't get here until Friday."

"Fine," Dove said. "As long as we get everything wrapped by Friday afternoon so we can get it to the printer's next week." She turned and yelled into the megaphone. "Are we ready for action yet?"

"We're placing the calf now," Edna said, helping the

calf's hairdressers position him in Miguel's arms.

"Oh, shit!" Miguel yelled, holding the bawling calf away from him. "What's this green stuff?"

The ladies jumped back from the splatter, laughing.

"Yes, it is," Edna said.

"Oh, man," Miguel moaned, looking down with dismay at the front of his jeans. "Don't you have any, like, house-trained cows or something?"

"Oh, no," Dove echoed. "Did you bring that extra pair of pants I told you to, Miguel?"

After getting him a new pair of jeans, Isaac cleared the barn set of everyone but him and Miguel.

While Isaac took Miguel's picture and then developed the film in the small darkroom he'd set up inside the house, Dove and I served lunch to the hungry models and helpers.

"Have you seen Sam or Bliss today?" she asked, un-wrapping a huge Pyrex bowl of her famous potato salad.

"I stopped by the bookstore and talked to Sam. He seems to be doing okay, though kind of sad. He says Bliss doesn't want to see anyone right now, including him. He said to tell you he'd be back to the ranch tonight."

"My heart surely goes out to them."

A drop-dead handsome, black-haired man with eyes the color of blue jay feathers parked himself in front of Dove and held out a paper plate. He was dressed in jeans and an Hawaiian shirt.

"I thought you were on tomorrow's list," she said.

"Gotta work tomorrow. I called, and Mr. Lyons said he could fit me in today. Didn't he tell you?"

"Probably, but my brain's been a little full these days. Guess we do have to work around your schedule." She looked him up and down critically before giving him a small scoop of potato salad and one thin slice of ham. His face fell in disappointment. With an apologetic look, I followed her lead and put one roll on his plate.

"You can have more after the shoot," Dove said. "We don't want any paunchy stomachs. The camera lens sees every bulge. Did you bring your uniform?"

"Yes, ma'am," he said, eyeing her bowl of potato salad with longing.

"The shorts?"

"Yes, ma'am."

"Not them baggy ones. The short, tight ones."

"Yes, ma'am. Just like you told me."

"Good, the Doberman puppies will look real nice with the brown."

After he took his food outside, I asked, "What agency . . . ?"

"UPS," she said.

I laughed. "You're kidding."

"You know any woman who isn't half in love with her UPS man?"

Before I left for my quilting class, Isaac showed me the contact sheets of Miguel. "He's gorgeous," I said. He'd managed to make Miguel appear both dangerously sexy and adorably boyish. The calf's dark shiny eyes matched Miguel's, and the delicacy of the animal's fragile pink nose and gangly feet was a brilliant contrast to Miguel's smoldering sexuality. Dove's idea about men and baby animals was right on the mark. Just based on Miguel's photograph, I'd buy this calendar in a heartbeat. And one for each of my friends.

"A photographer's only as good as his subject," Isaac said modestly.

I checked my watch. As fun and distracting as this interval had been, I had to get to my quilting class. My stomach churned, remembering what I had to accomplish there today.

"What's going on, Benni?" Isaac asked. His discerning

photographer's eye had caught the change in my expression. Then again, I never have been the queen of deception.

I explained what Detective Hudson wanted me to do and my mixed feelings about it.

"Maybe you should talk to Gabe," he suggested.

I shook my head no. "He doesn't need that right now. It would just cause a big fuss between him and this detective and maybe some problems between the departments. What can it hurt to just quiz the ladies about the past? Knowing them, they'd bring it up anyway."

"Sounds like you know what you're doing, then." The doubt in his face was evident. "Anything I can do to help?"

"Not really, but you could do me one big favor."

"Name it."

I handed back the contact sheets. "Just don't make my husband look *too* sexy, okay? I've got enough competition as it is."

He leaned down and kissed my cheek. "You don't have a single thing to worry about. I guarantee you've wrestled that man's heart to the ground and hog-tied it for life."

I laughed, hoping what he said was true. "And without a bustier or a garter belt. Thanks, Isaac, you always know just the right thing to say."

"Old age and lots of bad road gives a man a certain cockeyed wisdom, I guess."

"Cockeyed or not, it works for me."

PERCHED HIGH ON a hill overlooking the twisting two-lane highway to Morro Bay, Oak Terrace Retirement Home was a group of salmon-colored buildings where many of San Celina's senior citizens were living the final years of their lives. It had an ambulatory side where the seniors shared rooms and ate in a communal cafeteria, but for all intents and purposes were on their own. Most of the rooms peered out over alfalfa fields and pastures where the seniors watched the cycle of life in the cattle that dotted the scrubby range. Then there was the hospital side. Death Row, the ladies in my quilting group called it without a bit of compunction.

"We're sorry," said Thelma, who at one time owned the largest feed store in the county and had sold me my first pair of spurs when I was seven years old. "We forgot you're a civilian." That's what they called the world outside their exclusive group. Now that I was married to a cop, I was used to their gallow's humor, though I'll admit the first time they called it Death Row, the shocked look on my face caused joyous titters to ripple through my group of eight regulars. Even the term *civilian* reminded me of how Gabe and his colleagues viewed those who didn't carry a badge.

And I guess what these ladies had was a badge of sorts. The badge of time, of making it this far with the ability to still laugh at and enjoy life. So when I proposed we name our group, since we basically functioned as an in-house quilt guild, the fact that they chose Coffin Star Quilt Guild didn't surprise me one bit. We even had black sweatshirts printed with our guild's name in fluorescent pink letters, which each of them was wearing today. The first time I took the ladies to a quilt show wearing the matching sweat-shirts, we caused quite a stir and a whole lot of laughter.

They were all set up in the craft room when I arrived. We were working on baby quilts for Gabe's officers to carry in their police cars to give to kids taken out of violent home situations by Social Services. My function was less of a teacher than a bringer of news, donated quilting sup-plies and fabric, ideas, patterns, magazines, and gossip. There was nothing they enjoyed more than hearing every-thing that was going on at the folk art museum, Elvia's bookstore, the police station, and the Historical Museum. They especially loved it when I was involved in some crime, as I'd been a few times, and were generous with advice on how I should proceed. People's love lives intrigued them to no end, though Elvia and Emory's static romance was frustrating them, and Gabe and I had been getting on too well to suit them. So, just to prime them, the first thing I did was tell them about Bliss and Sam, their secret romance, her unplanned pregnancy, Lydia's arrival on the scene, the engagement party, Giles's murder, and then Bliss getting shot and losing the baby.

"Oh, my," Martha Pickering said, her hand digging in her sweatshirt sleeve for a violet-embroidered handkerchief. She dabbed at her white powdered temple. "That's more than a month of stories on *All My Children*." The others nodded in agreement, their fingers still quilting on the Tumbling Blocks quilt in the frame.

"That Brown family," Juby Daniels said, shaking her head. "They've certainly had their share of baby troubles through the years."

"Starting with Rose herself," Leona Shelton said. Leona was turning ninety-two this year and was our oldest guild member. Though I had to thread her needles for her, she still sewed a straighter, truer quilt stitch than I ever would, using her experienced fingers to guide her as much as her washed-out-denim blue eyes. She'd been San Celina's seamstress of choice for years and years. Her tiny shop downtown across from the courthouse had been the premier place among the rich and powerful for hearing about who was cheating on who, who was having a baby, and often whose baby it *really* was. She still remained a virtual encyclopedia of information of San Celina's citizenry. If you'd put her and Mr. Foglino together, they could have probably blackmailed the whole town.

"Do you remember when her babies died?" I asked casually.

Her pencilled eyebrows moved a notch upwards. "You know about them?"

I stopped stitching and sat back in my chair. "One of her great-granddaughters, JJ, is a quilt artist at the co-op. She told me how the Seven Sisters ranch got its name."

"I surely do remember," Leona said, turning her eyes back to the red and brown quilt. "Rose Brown about went crazy. All them funerals so close together. I made the christening gowns for every one of them babies. Hand-stitched lilies of the valley around the hems. Three hundred–count imported Egyptian cotton with Belgian lace trim. Some nun went blind making that lace, mark my words. Each of those babies was buried in them. I think about that sometimes, my beautiful stitches, that lovely lace, being eaten by worms."

The others nodded, murmuring at the waste. I flinched inwardly at the graphic scene it painted in my imagination. "So, how did they die? JJ didn't know." I looked back down at the quilt. It wasn't exactly a lie. JJ hadn't known how they died.

"Oh, they say it was just natural causes," Leona said, pushing her needle in and out, in and out. "But there was rumors."

"Really?" Martha said. "I was only fifteen at the time, but I don't remember people talking."

"It was kept pretty quiet. Those Browns were prominent folks even back then," Leona said, stopping to cough into a crumpled tissue. She wiped her mouth delicately and continued. "He was a judge, you know. Quite the ladies' man, let me tell you. Good-looking as that husband of yours, Benni, and with none of Gabe's scruples. Rumors were he could have any woman he wanted in their crowd and heard tell he practically did."

"What were the rumors about the babies?" I prompted.

"That somebody killed them, plain and simple," Leona said with a quick nod.

"Oh, my . . . oh, dear . . . oh, Leona, really," the women around the quilt exclaimed.

"Don't shoot the messenger," Leona said, sniffing. "That's what they were saying behind closed doors."

"But who would kill four innocent babies?" asked Mattie Lee Jones, who was the progeny winner of the group with 27 grandchildren and 18 great-grandchildren to her credit. She took great pride in constantly reminding the group of her huge, supposedly close-knit family.

"Mattie Lee," Leona said, "get your head out of that sandbox you call a life. Not many families qualify as the Waltons. Not even your messy group of misfits. Every day of this old world babies are hurt and sometimes killed by their own parents, sisters, brothers, and who knows who else. Why do you think we're makin' these quilts for the police department? And it'll be that way till Jesus comes back."

"Well, I just can't imagine it," Mattie Lee said, her pointy chin jerking up, insulted. "I think you're just spreading vicious old rumors without substance. And as for that remark about my wonderful family, I think—"

"Who cares what you think?" Leona said. "As a matter of fact, why don't you think about kissing my—"

"Leona! Mattie Lee!" Thelma said, her voice sounding the way it did when she caught us kids jumping on the expensive hay bales in back of her store. "Now, let's not set a bad example for Benni here. She's still at an impressionable age, you know. We have a responsibility."

Leona looked over at me and winked. Mattie Lee's chin moved an inch higher. I bit my lip trying not to laugh.

"Okay, just assuming . . ."—I gave Mattie Lee an apologetic look—". . . *pretending* that this horrible rumor had some truth to it, why do you think anyone would do such a terrible thing?"

Leona shook her head. "Who knows, Benni? With what I've seen in my ninety-two years I'm only certain about one thing. Just when you think human beings can't sink any lower, they do. On the other hand, there's more good bein' done out there than bad. So far, anyway."

"Maybe it was for the insurance," Selma Gonzales suggested. She'd been a legal secretary for fifty years and had a kind and intelligently practical view of every situation. "That's always a consideration."

"Did people insure babies back then?" I asked.

"Maybe one of the older sisters did it out of jealousy," Leona said. "Or the judge himself because he thought they weren't his children."

"Rose Brown committing adultery?" Mattie Lee exclaimed. "Why, I can't even imagine that."

Leona gave Mattie Lee a disgusted look.

"Maybe it was Rose's sister," Juby said. "She was an old maid. Heard she had a crush on the judge her whole life. Maybe *she* killed the babies out of jealousy."

"There was the nanny, too," Selma offered.

"Or the butler," Martha added with a giggle.

"Oh, girls," Thelma said. "They didn't have a butler."

I sat back in my chair, my head spinning. These ladies had just handed me even more suspects than I'd started with. That was certainly not my intention when I started questioning them.

"That nanny, Eva something-or-other," Leona said. "I heard she's still living."

Knoll, I filled in silently. The nanny who was Mr. Foglino's mother's best friend's neighbor.

"Still living?" Mattie Lee said. "My goodness, she'd be

ninety-six or -seven. Would she even be able to—"

"To what?" Leona said, narrowing one pale eye in Mattie Lee's direction. "Be *coherent*?"

Mattie Lee's face turned pink, and she leaned back over the quilt, stitching furiously.

"What was her last name?" I asked, just to double-check Mr. Foglino's information.

"Knoll," Leona said, her voice triumphant. "Her name is Eva Knoll. Pretty good for someone in her *nineties*, don't you think?"

"Does anyone know where she lives?" I asked, sitting forward in my seat. Next to talking to Rose Brown again, the nanny who was there when the babies died would be a great source of information.

The women shook their heads no.

"After the last baby died, she was let go," Leona said. "Rumors were she was paid to go away. That tells me there was something fishy going on."

"Did you hear where she went?" I asked, unrolling some white thread and snipping it off.

"Don't reckon she'd go far," Leona said, "if I remember right." She glared at Mattie Lee. "And I do believe I do. Her only family was her father and a child. A boy, I think. Most likely she settled in San Celina County somewhere."

"Do any of you ever see or talk to Rose Brown?" I asked.

"Huh!" Leona snorted. "Miss High-and-Mighty Brown leave her private tower and walk among the heathens? Don't think so."

"Now, Leona," Juby said, shaking her head of poodle hair. "You know Rose is not able to socialize." She gave me a kind look. "Rose Brown has her own suite on the other side of the home, near the offices. She doesn't take her meals with us. But she has good girls. They visit her regularly and hired her private nurses. Tell you the truth, I don't really know why she's here and not at her lovely home, but they say she didn't want to die there. I don't think she's quite all there, poor dear."

The conversation drifted slowly away from the Browns and back to their own lives and the doings of their children, grandchildren and great-grandchildren. I didn't push it, figuring I got what I needed—a confirmation of Eva Knoll's identity.

When our hour session was over, we had a quick business meeting. I showed them the check for the quilt.

"What would you all like done with it?" I asked. Though we had a guild account, they often liked donating it to the Oak Terrace Friendship Fund. It provided bingo and snack money for people in the retirement home who had no families and were barely making ends meet.

"Donate it to the Friendship Fund," Thelma said. "We have plenty in our account." The others nodded in agreement.

After hugging and kissing everyone good-bye, I went upstairs to the offices to take the check to the accounting clerk. After shooting the breeze with her, I walked down the long corridor toward the exit, passing by a large, airy sunroom. Normally crowded, it was empty this early evening. The large clock over the gurgling fountain read five o'clock. Dinner was served at five-thirty, so everyone was probably in their rooms getting ready.

Everyone except Rose Brown. She was, to my surprise, sitting in a wheelchair alone, gazing out the picture window at the English rose garden and beyond at the cars driving by on the highway below. I hesitated for a few seconds, then decided that this might be my only chance to speak to her, so I'd better grab it. She was dressed in expensive-looking camel slacks and a brown cashmere sweater. Good leather shoes covered her small feet. In her lap, on top of a nubby, hand-knitted throw, her hands clutched a neat leather purse that matched her shoes. She didn't turn around or even react when I walked up behind her and softly called her name.

"Mrs. Brown," I said again, a little louder, and walked around so she could see me.

She looked up, her aqua eyes cloudy with age. Really looking at her this time, I realized what a beautiful woman she must have been. And how much Bliss favored her.

"Mrs. Brown, my name is Benni Harper. We talked the other day at the wine tasting."

She nodded mutely. Her face was slack today, traces of spittle pooled in the corners of her pale pink mouth. It was hard to believe she was the same woman I'd talked to only a few days ago, but I knew how, at this age, good days and bad days were as unpredictable as our Central Coast winds.

"Can I ask you some questions? It won't take long, I promise."

She blinked slowly and nodded again.

I hesitated again. Questioning someone this elderly, this helpless, seemed cruel and heartless. And, considering her condition today, so much worse than a few days ago at the wine tasting, maybe even pointless.

And what about those babies? I heard Detective Hudson's voice in my head.

I swallowed and said, "I'm sorry about your babies, Mrs. Brown."

Her eyes looked into mine at the mention of babies. Her mouth started moving, trying to say something. I bent closer, trying to encourage her.

"My babies," she said, her voice low and harsh. "They died."

I knelt down next to her wheelchair. "Yes, I know. I'm sorry."

"Dr. Jacobs was so good to me. We drank tea."

"I'm sure he was." I wracked my brain trying to think of what I could ask her. "Mrs. Brown, do you remember Eva Knoll? She took care of your babies. Do you remember?"

Her eyes teared up upon hearing Eva's name. "The judge sent her away. He said she was a bad woman. She just flew away. Like a bird." A pale, age-spotted hand grabbed mine, pinning it to the cold handle of the wheelchair. "She wasn't bad." She squeezed my hand, then let go and crooked her finger at me to come closer. I bent toward her.

"Rouge," she whispered, her head nodding. "The men love it. They don't even know we have it on."

Great, more grooming tips. I tried to lead her back to the subject of Eva Knoll, maybe find out her whereabouts. "Where did Eva Knoll go?" Before she had a chance to answer, we were interrupted by a sharp voice.

"Excuse me, who are you?"

I stood up and faced the stern-faced woman dressed in a nurse's uniform. Unlike the rest of the employees of Oak Terrace, she wasn't wearing a name tag, so I assumed she was one of the private nurses hired by the family.

"I was just saying hello to Mrs. Brown. We met the other day at the wine tasting in Eola Beach."

The woman peered at me suspiciously and said, "She's not up to visitors today." She'd obviously been warned that people might come by and quiz her charge. She fiddled with the knitted throw in Mrs. Brown's lap, then pushed her out of the room without another word to me.

I stood there for a moment, contemplating what Rose Brown had just told me. Her husband had sent Eva Knoll away. Why? Had she been involved with the death of the babies? If so, why hadn't he turned her over to the authorities? I tried to sort out the things I'd learned. I had to find Eva Knoll, if she was still alive, and talk to her. But how? Then an idea formed.

Before going to the Sheriff's Department to tell the detective what I'd learned, I stopped by my friend Amanda Landry's law office to beg the use of her very capable investigator, Leilani, to locate Eva Knoll.

Amanda's office was above the Ross store downtown. It was located up a set of narrow, steep marble stairs. Inside the small reception room, Muddy Waters played gut-aching blues from a small stereo hidden behind a bushy green fern. Though I'd known Amanda for only a short time and we definitely rooted for different college teams—she was a die-hard 'Bama fan—we'd become good friends. A faithful, dyed-in-the-wool Crimson Tide Alabaman, she'd followed her husband to San Francisco, and when that didn't work out, decided she loved the wild and woolly west enough to make it home. She'd worked for years as a prosecutor for both San Francisco and San Celina, but had sometime back started her own practice with an inheritance she'd acquired from her father, a rich Birmingham judge who wasn't famous for his honesty, integrity, or marital faithfulness.

Luckily Amanda inherited her late blues-singing mother's honesty as well as her weakness for down-and-out musicians.

"He's the best I ever had," she told me as I sat in her office, decorated in deep crimson and dark blue. Leilani was in her adjoining office using her numerous contacts and CD-ROM programs to get a lead on Eva Knoll. "I'm in heaven. I'll never give him up. Never." Her antique oak chair creaked when she leaned back. With the tip of a yellow school pencil, she scratched a spot in her thick head of auburn hair.

"We'll see," I said, having heard this song and dance before.

"I'm serious," she said, giving me her Mississippi-wide smile. The same gorgeous smile that won her almost as many cases as her spur-sharp intelligence. "He's perfect. Doesn't miss a thing. I go to bed happy every night."

"He's a musician. You know how reliable they are."

"He calls me Miss Mandy," she said, her eyes twinkling.

"And you let him live? He must be good."

She sat forward in her seat and pointed the yellow pencil at me. "I'm telling you, cowgirl, my house has never been cleaner. Did you know that place on your stove, where those little round things are?"

"You mean the burners?" Cooking was not one of Amanda's many talents.

"Did you know the thing they sit on, that whole top of the stove, lifts up? You should see what was under there. Disgusting! But, bless his blues-lovin' heart, he's thorough. He cleans *everywhere*," she said, heaving a big sigh. "He's not cheap, but, heavens to Dixie, he's worth it."

"Just don't get romantically involved with him," I warned, "or you'll be out a great housecleaner."

"Never," she declared. "Boyfriends come and go, but a good housecleaner, *that's* hard to find."

Within the hour, Leilani found the information I was seeking.

"She's still alive," Leilani said, her brown, fashion-model face as sober as a prison guard's. "Or at least someone who is signing her name and collecting her Social Security checks is."

"How do you find out things like that, Leilani?" I asked. "I mean, isn't it illegal or something? Privacy laws and stuff?"

"Never ask Leilani *how*," Amanda said, nodding thanks

at her investigator. "Just act like Elvis and say thankyou-verymuch."

"Thank you very much," I said.

"No problem," Leilani replied, her facial muscles not moving a bit. She turned and left the room, shutting the door behind her.

"Does she ever smile?" I asked Amanda. It was hard to imagine the two of them working together, considering how much Amanda liked to laugh.

"I think she cracked a small one when I gave her a Christmas bonus last year. Hey, who needs smiles when you can work the miracles she does. The DA's office still hasn't forgiven me for stealing her."

We both glanced at the address Leilani had found.

"A post office box in Mariposa Valley," I said. "That's out in the Carrizo Plains. I haven't been there in years." The Carrizo Plains was in the far eastern part of San Celina County. Except for a few desert dwellers and sporadic groups of bird-watchers and hikers, the barren Carrizo Plains was pretty much left to its own counsel. Back in the fifties, there was a small flurry of interest by some Los Angeles developers who claimed it would be the next Palm Springs. Some streets were built and lots sold. There was even a motel and gas station constructed for the benefit of prospective buyers. But some kind of complication with water rights doomed the project, and all that was left were some windswept streets, rusty gas pumps, and the shell of the fifties-style motel called the Mariposa Valley Inn.

"I had to interview a witness out there once when I worked as a prosecutor," Amanda said. "The only way to find anyone is to ask at the fire station. It's about a half mile past the old motel."

I folded the piece of paper and slipped it in my back

pocket. "I'll give it to Detective Hudson and let him take care of it."

"Hey, why are you doin' his work for him, might I ask?"

I smiled. "Just to show him I can. He's an arrogant Texan."

"Oh, my, a Texan. I dated an attorney from Fort Worth once. Emphasis on the word once. By all means, use all my resources to put him in his place."

"Thanks, Amanda. Again, I owe you one."

"Who's countin'?"

I used my cell phone to call Detective Hudson. "I'll be there in fifteen minutes tops."

"It's almost seven o'clock," he said. "Where have you been? Your class was over at four-thirty, and it's only a ten-minute drive."

"I'll explain when I get there," I said, hanging up before he could harangue me. I wasn't going to pay cell phone prices to be nagged at by the likes of a twangy-tongued detective. I called Gabe's office where I got his voice mail so I called my house, hoping to find him there. When our answering machine replied, I left a quick message, trying not to project where or with whom he might be.

I sat for a moment staring at Eva Knoll's address. She was a very old woman. Remembering Rose Brown and the guilt I felt about questioning her, I made a quick decision. What I was about to do would make Detective Hudson spit nails and quite possibly strangle me, but morally and humanely, it seemed my only choice. Before I went to his office, I dropped by the electronics store downtown and bought a small hand-sized tape recorder, the kind Emory used for interviews. I took it out of the box, slipped in one of the tiny tapes, and stuck it in my purse.

At the Sheriff's Department, the front desk clerk, a young woman with a painfully sunburnt nose and dressed in a Hawaiian print dress, was hefting her red patent leather backpack over her shoulder, getting ready to leave. The offices appeared to be empty except for the departing receptionist.

"Benni Harper?" the young woman asked. She picked up a green apple from her desk and took a bite.

"Yes."

"He's really pissed," the young woman said, around chews. "I'm a temp. Thank goodness. I'd never work full-time for these nutcases. And they're supposed to be the good guys? *Sheesh.* Third office to your right. See ya."

"Thanks," I called after her, wondering if I should maybe follow her out and phone my information in.

I knew Detective Hudson was going to be annoyed that I didn't run over to his office the minute my quilt class was over, but I hoped he'd be appeased when he heard I had the name and address, or at least the post office box number, of the nanny who cared for Rose Brown's children. Not to mention the information I'd just gotten from Rose Brown herself. Maybe the killer of the babies had been living in San Celina all along, out in the desolate Carrizo Plains. That still didn't explain why Giles would be killed, but I was confident that talking to this Eva Knoll would bring us one step closer to finding out who killed Giles and why.

When I came within his eyesight he bellowed, with a drill sergeant's snappy bark. "Where have you been? Get in here. Now."

"Unless you can the attitude," I snapped back, "I'm outta here." I added in a lower voice, "Jerk."

He came barreling out of his chair. "What?"

Keeping my voice calm, I said, "Quit acting like a Nazi. I got here as soon as I could. What is your problem?"

Without answering, he inhaled deeply, sharp points of color staining his cheeks. He gestured for me to follow him into his office. He shut the door behind me and nodded at a visitor's chair against the wall. I glanced around the compact office where two black-and-chrome office desks faced each other. One held a scattered group of Little League, ballet recital, and soccer team pictures, used coffee cups, a crumpled McDonald's bag, a Beanie Baby snake, and stacks of files. The desk Detective Hudson sat behind contained only a green desk blotter, a black ceramic pencil cup filled with pens, a phone, and a picture of a redheaded girl about five years old sitting on the hood of his pickup truck. A sticker on his pencil cup showed a red circle with a slash through the word "whining." Between the two desks was a calligraphy sign that mocked the Serenity Prayer—"God grant me the serenity to accept the things I cannot change, the courage to change the things I can, and the weaponry to make the difference."

"Very inspiring," I said wryly, nodding at the poster.

"What did you find out?" he asked.

"Geeze, let me take a breath. What's the big hurry?"

"The big hurry is I'm getting my butt reamed out by my superiors because the sheriff is getting harassed from two prominent families—the Nortons and the Browns. One wants it solved, one wants us to quit poking around. I'll leave it to you to guess who's who."

"Well, sor-ry," I said, stretching out the word. "But that's still no reason to be such a jerk. In case you forgot, I'm not on the payroll, buddy. This is purely voluntary on my part, so save your nasty remarks and bad attitude for someone collecting a county paycheck."

He settled back in his chair, crossed his legs, and rested his hands across his flat stomach. Today he wore a pale yellow Arrow shirt and sedate, tobacco brown bullhide boots that looked like they cost a thousand bucks. "You're absolutely right, Benni, and please accept my sincere and heartfelt apology. I'm just feeling like the rope between the cow and the cowboy. Know what I mean?"

I nodded, suspicious at his suddenly genial mood.

"So, what do you have for me?" he asked, keeping his voice even and pleasant. But I sensed the tension and determination behind his good-ole-boy demeanor. He really, really wasn't going to like what I was going to tell him.

"I have the name and whereabouts of the nanny who worked for Judge and Rose Brown when she had the two sets of twins."

He sat forward in his chair, his face amazed. I have to admit one-upping him, to quote Dove, dearly gladdened my heart. "Shoot, that's great! But wait, that was back in the twenties. She'd have to be—"

"Ninety-seven and, according to my sources, still alive. Or at least someone is signing and cashing her Social Security checks."

He jumped up and grabbed his pale cowboy hat from the credenza behind him. "Let me have her address. I'm going to talk to her right now before she croaks on me."

I stood up and looked him squarely in the eyes. "No."

He stopped dead, his hat still in his hands. Anger flashed like a dust devil across his face, then was gone. He took a couple of slow, controlled breaths then asked, "Why not?"

I already had my answer thought out. "What's the difference between interviewing and interrogating?"

"What?"

"Tell me the textbook definitions."

"What are you talking about?"

"Tell me."

"Look, I'm not a barbarian."

"The definitions, please."

He gave a sharp, irritated sound, then said, "Interviewing is a non-accusatory, fact-finding mission where you let the suspect/witness do the talking. Interrogating is an active, confrontational method of questioning where you give the suspect a psychological reason to confess."

"Now how old did I say Eva Knoll is?"

"Ninety-seven, but what's that—"

"She's an elderly woman, Detective Hudson. And no matter what she's seen or done, I'm not going to let you browbeat her. I'm married to a cop. I've seen the techniques. I've *experienced* them. I know a so-called interview can turn into an interrogation in two seconds. I'm not going to allow that to happen. We'll go see her tomorrow. It's too late tonight and it's a bit of a drive. Please note the pronoun *we*. And one other thing. I'm going to do the talking."

He threw his hat down on the desktop. "There is no way you are interviewing this or any other possible witness. Give me that name and address now."

"No."

"I swear, if you don't, I'll . . . I'll . . ." he sputtered.

"You'll what? Call Gabe and tell on me? Inject me with truth serum? Lock me up for the night?" I held out my wrists. "Go ahead, book me."

He literally growled at me, "Don't think I won't call your husband. I'll tell him you've interfered in this from the very beginning, that I've asked you repeatedly to stay out of it, that you're jeopardizing my investigation, and that I'll have to go to my superiors if he can't control you. I'll embarrass you and him in front of all his colleagues."

I smiled serenely, knowing I had him. "And you know what I'll tell him and your boss? That you cajoled and harassed me into helping you on this case. That you didn't have the resources or feel confident enough to solve it without the help of a lowly civilian. Worse than that, a *female* civilian. And then I'll give the story to my cousin, the journalist. He's always looking for amusing things to make fun of in his column. He'll make mincemeat of your burgeoning career here on the Central Coast. You'll be the laughingstock of every police agency in the county. Nope, you got me into this, and now I've got the upper hand. I suggest you deal with it."

He gave a nasty smile. "With your reputation, who do you think they'll believe? Admit it, I have you there."

That's when I pulled the ace out of my sleeve. Or rather, the tape recorder out of my purse. "They'll believe me, Detective, because I've been recording key conversations with you for days, and the tapes are in my safety deposit box." I wiggled the tiny tape recorder.

He stared at the recorder, opened his mouth and started to say something, then closed it. His brown eyes were dark and angry, and I tried to quell the anxiety in my chest and the truth on my face. It was the biggest bluff I'd ever attempted, me of the billboard face.

Slowly a smile tugged at the corner of his mouth. Then he let out a small laugh. Shaking his head, he said, "Oh, man, you're good."

Surprised, I laughed, too, and said, "Yeah, I know."

"With an ego to match mine," he added.

"Meet me tomorrow. Nine o'clock at the folk art museum."

"I'll be there with my whips and thumbscrews."

"I told you, Detective, no browbeating on my watch."

He lifted his eyebrows slightly. "My dear Mrs. Harper, who said they're for the old lady?"

In the parking lot I called home again to see if Gabe was there. When the answering machine took the call, I hung up.

The driveway was empty. Inside the house, it was apparent Gabe hadn't been home yet—no briefcase or dirty glasses in the sink. Another dinner with Lydia? Annoyed,

I listened to my message to him on the answering machine, then the one after it.

"Sweetheart," he said. "I have a dinner with the city manager and then I'm going to drop by Lydia's hotel to talk about Sam. She and I have missed each other all day. I'll be home as soon as I can. *Te amo*."

"Yeah, me, too, Friday," I said, feeling sad rather than angry. I fed Scout, then heated up a can of soup and watched a couple of sitcoms on TV before falling asleep. The sound of the shower running awakened me, and I glanced at the bedside clock—ten-twenty.

"How was your dinner with the city manager?" I asked when Gabe climbed into bed.

"Fine," he said, turning to me and pulling me into his arms, nuzzling my neck.

I lay there for a moment, tempted by the masculine rasp of his beard, his gentle, seductive tongue, then pulled away. "I'm tired."

"All right," he said without argument. He kissed my temple, then settled into his side of the bed.

I lay there in the dark and listened to his breathing slow down until he fell asleep. The lacy curtains covering our bedroom window made snowflake patterns on the ceiling, and I watched them move and change, like all the lives surrounding me, like my own life.

SAM CAME BY the next morning and had breakfast with us, his dark eyes ringed blue with fatigue.

"How is Bliss?" I asked after Gabe left for work. I tossed some leftover bacon in Scout's dish. His happy tail beat against my leg.

"She's doing okay," Sam said, leaning his chair back on two legs. "She still won't talk about it, though. Says we just gotta move on." His young face looked troubled. "What do you think she means by that?"

"I have no idea, Sam," I said, taking his plate. "All I can suggest is give her time. Losing a baby and getting shot are both extremely traumatic."

"What should I do?"

"Just listen. Don't try to push her. Let her feel what she needs to feel. That's all I know to tell you."

"She told me last night she's thinking about taking a leave from the police department. She said she might go up north for a while with her mom and sister. Don't tell Dad. He doesn't know yet."

"How do you feel about that?"

"I don't want to go up north. I just got my life together down here."

I scraped a plate into the garbage can. "Only you can make that decision."

"Do you think it'll hurt our relationship?"

Determined to be honest, I said, "I have no idea, but it would be hard to build a relationship with someone if they aren't around."

"That's kinda what I thought. Maybe we don't love each other as much as we thought."

"Then again, maybe a separation will help you both see what you really want."

He nodded, his face miserable. "Like I said, don't tell Dad any of this. Or Mom. I haven't decided yet what I'm going to do."

"You have my word," I said, flattered he'd confide in me first. There was no doubt I'd miss him like crazy if he left.

He let the front of his chair drop on the kitchen floor with a thump. Scout went over and laid his head in Sam's lap, and Sam massaged his ears, causing Scout to sigh deeply. "All I gotta say, *madrastra*, is being an adult sucks. It sucks big-time."

"Yes, I know," I said and poured myself another cup of coffee. "This I do know."

DETECTIVE HUD ARRIVED at the folk art museum at five minutes to nine. He wore a pink shirt, another tweedy Western jacket and black-cherry-colored boots.

"Just how many pairs of boots do you own?" I asked, walking out to his truck.

"Twenty-two," he said. "But that's nothing. My mother owns forty."

"The infamous mother. I don't even believe she exists."

He opened the passenger door, a bland look on his face. "Oh, believe me, she exists. Where's your hound dog?"

"Left him home today. It's a long, hot drive."

He came around and climbed into the driver's seat. "Okay, enough small talk. Where are we going?"

"Mariposa Valley."

"Where's that?"

"Out on the Carrizo Plains. Eastern part of San Celina County. Just get on 101 North, and I'll tell you where to turn off."

He put the truck into gear and pulled out of the parking lot. "Put on some music, or I'll punish your insubordination by forcing you to listen to me sing."

With Dale Watson singing low-down, truck-driving, honky-tonk country, I directed him to turn off on Highway 58 outside of Atascadero and headed east on the winding, two-lane highway toward Mariposa Valley. In the distance, the Temblor mountain range rose stark and forbidding against the white-blue morning sky. We passed small herds of cattle grazing among the long grasses, bunched together around an occasional wind-carved oak. Then the land changed to pure prairie, and the sky turned a deep solid blue. Birds flew high above us, swooping in the currents, too far away to tell if they were peregrine falcons or one of the many types of hawks that live out here on the desolate plains—red-tailed, Cooper's, marsh, and rough-legged hawks.

"Hard to believe we're in the same county," the detective commented. "How far are we going?"

"It's about seventy miles to the fire station. That's where the post office and the library is, too. I'm hoping someone there will give us an address."

We passed a huge sun-faded billboard. He slowed down and read out loud, "WELCOME TO MARIPOSA VALLEY—2 1/2-ACRE PLOTS—GOLF COURSE, POOLS, SHOPPING CENTER, GOOD SCHOOLS—TOMORROW'S PLANNED COMMUNITY TODAY." He glanced over at me. "What *is* this place?"

"That sign is almost as old as me. Back in the early sixties Mariposa Valley was apparently being advertised as the up-and-coming place to buy property. There were twenty-five thousand acres to be sold, as the sign said, in two-and-a-half-acre plots, and a whole town was going to be built. They wanted to name it Paradise Valley, but I think that name was already taken. Anyway, except for some die-hard desert rats of the human variety, the only things that prosper out here now are a lot of mule deer, lizards, coyotes, sandhill cranes, and the occasional rattler. The only time it really gets crowded is when the bird-watchers flock out here to add to their life lists."

"What happened to the developer's great plan?"

I reached for my purse and dug around for a rubberband. This time of year out here, it would probably get close to ninety, and the sun coming in the window was already turning my thick hair into an uncomfortable blanket on my neck. "It was missing one important element—water." I zipped up my purse, irritated because I spend a fortune buying those fabric-covered hair scrunchies, yet never seemed to have one when I needed it. "You have a rubberband or a piece of string or something?"

"Check the glove compartment."

I opened it, and next to the neat black leather map holder was a bright pink Barbie scrunchy. Good enough. I pulled my hair into a high ponytail and turned to stare out the window. "It shouldn't be real hard to find her. I don't imagine there's more than a couple of hundred people who live out here these days."

"Then maybe we can get this cleared up today."

"I sure hope so," I said.

We passed only one other vehicle in over an hour, a San Celina Sourdough Bakery truck. Except for a couple of wind-blasted farmhouses, miles of black sage, manzanita, and chaparral, and a cluster of rusty combines laced with shiny-feathered crows, we could have been driving on Mars. Every once in a while we passed an abandoned car skeleton, bleached almost colorless by the harsh, prairie elements, squatting among the grasses—a twentieth-century reminder of nature's uncompromising power. The desolation out here had always slightly unnerved something deep inside me and though I'd eat a plateful of hay before admitting it, I was glad for Detective Hudson's presence and especially the gun underneath his tweed cowboy jacket.

"We're almost there," I said when we passed by the closed Butterfly Cafe and the graffiti-decorated, abandoned motel. I pointed to our right at a group of buildings about a mile away.

Outside the combination fire station/community building a single person stood watering a struggling section of lawn. We pulled into the parking lot next to the only other car, a tan Toyota pickup. I was right about the temperature. The hot and dusty air hit us with a slap when we stepped out of his air-conditioned truck. The person watering, a tall, proud-looking Latina dressed in engineer-striped overalls and a white tank top, watched us curiously. There was something vaguely familiar about her, but I couldn't put my finger on it.

"Let me do the talking," I said in a low voice.

"I will not," he replied.

"You'll blow it," I spat.

He grabbed my elbow, then swung around to the front of me so his back was to the woman watering, blocking her from my view. "Look, I've been extremely patient so far, but I'm not going to let an inexperienced civilian screw up this chance for me."

"*You* look. The people who live out here aren't like regular people. Many of them are hermits and other loners who are very skittish about anyone they don't know. I have connections with some of the ranching families out here and so have a better chance at getting them to talk."

He stood with his hands on his hips, a condescending sneer on his face. "You honestly think you can do better than me?"

I folded my arms across my chest. "Yes, I do. If they find out you're a cop, they'll clam up, and we'll never find out anything."

He stepped aside and swept his arm out dramatically. "Then by all means, go ahead. But I'm warning you, if you blow it, I'll—"

"Fire me?" I finished. "Detective, just follow me, keep your mouth shut, and your gun ready."

"You are really asking for it, Mrs. Harper."

I ignored him and started toward the woman in overalls, putting on a friendly smile. "Hey," I said.

"Hey," she repeated, her handsome face open but wary.

"My name's Benni Harper, and this is . . . my friend . . . uh, Hud."

Squinting into the bright sun, she nodded at the detective. The hose she was watering with sputtered, and she turned around, straightening the kink in it. "Harper," she said, when the water started flowing smooth again. "I used to know a Wade Harper when I was a bartender in San Celina. A place called Trigger's."

"Wade was my late husband's brother. Trigger's closed awhile back. Lost their liquor license."

"I heard. So, you're Jack Harper's wife? I remember him, too, 'cept he was a lot quieter than Wade. He left good tips. Nice eyes." She put her thumb over the hose's metal lip to make a thin spray.

"Yes," I said, remembering Jack's gentle brown eyes. "He did have nice eyes. He died a few years ago in a car accident."

"That's rough. I'm sorry."

"Thank you."

She peered at me closer. "You know, I feel like I've seen you somewhere. Did you hang out at Trigger's, too?"

"Not much. But I know what you mean. You look familiar to me, too. I grew up in San Celina. My dad and gramma own a ranch east of the city."

She walked over to turn off the spigot. "Cattle?" she said over her shoulder.

"Yep, some Angus, some Santa Gertrudis, some Hereford crosses. My dad likes to experiment with different breeds."

She turned back to face me, her brown, oval face thoughtful, then said, "I got it! We sat across from each other at a Cattlewomen's Association Christmas luncheon about five years ago. Over at that Mexican restaurant near the Goodwill store. A lady next to you was talking about antique buttons."

"That's right," I said. "She had one that was worth two hundred dollars, remember? We were flabbergasted."

"Yeah, I remember. That was when I was still with my first husband, Danny Wheaton." She made a sour face that was more telling than words.

"I know the Wheatons. They own a ranch north of the city. Nothing but Black Angus. Danny and I went to high school together." *And he was a spoiled, rednecked jerk if I remember correctly*, I added to myself.

"That's them. Meanest bunch of people you ever saw. Especially the mother. Danny was her pride and joy, and he took full advantage of that."

"How'd you end up out here?" I searched my brain for her name, it was something unusual . . . Danny and . . . Rolanda, Renata . . . Riccarla. That was it. "Riccarla," I said.

A big grin spread across her face as she wiped her wet hands on her overalls, leaving dark spots. "That's a pretty good memory you have. Met my current guy when I left Danny and was working at Trigger's. Bobby's great. He's the mailman out here. I run the library three days a week and spend the rest of the time making bay leaf wreaths. I sell them at the Farmer's Market."

"You make those! They're beautiful. I bought one for my gramma last year. She loves it."

"Thanks. It keeps me off the street corners."

Behind me I heard Detective Hudson impatiently clear his throat. Ignoring him, I said to her, "Being the mailman, I bet your husband knows everyone who lives out here."

"Yeah, he does. Lived here his whole life. His family's land goes back to one of the original Spanish land grants. We live out on the old place. Real log cabin. Takes us forty-five minutes just to get to the station here."

"Guess you really like your privacy," I said.

"After listening to those Wheatons yammer for six years, you betcha." She stuck her hands deep into her pockets. "So, what are you two doing out here? Going to see the petroglyphs on Painted Rock? I think it may be closed right now. They've been having some trouble with vandalism."

"No, actually we're looking for someone."

Her face instantly closed down. "Is that so?"

"Yeah, all we have is a post office box and we really need to talk to this person." I smiled my friendliest, most disarming smile. "I promise, we're not process servers."

She gave a small smile. "Who're you looking for?"

"Eva Knoll."

Her face definitely took on a cool demeanor. "Why?"

"Just want to ask her some questions."

She jerked her head over to the fire station, her friendliness gone. "Might be better if you talked to Lukie. She knows Eva best."

"Lukie?"

"She's the fire captain. Closest thing we have to the law out here. Talk to her." A few feet away a faded green Chevy pickup pulled into the gravel parking lot. Five children under ten scrambled out of the bed and ran toward the small door marked LIBRARY. She waved at them. "My public beckons. Nice shooting the breeze with you. Tell Wade hey from Riccarla if you ever see him again."

Behind me, Detective Hudson gave a mocking chuckle. "A half hour of playing 'six degrees of separation' and she tells you to talk to the fire captain. Very impressive interviewing. I was taking notes the whole time."

I turned around and, without a word, punched him hard on the arm.

"Hey, hitting a cop is against the law," he said, rubbing the spot.

"Yeah, yeah, yeah. Let's go see the fire captain."

"Are you going to let me do the talking this time?"

"No, I *still* know these people better than you."

"Fine, screw up our only chance to find this old woman."

"I'm not going to screw it up."

Inside the sparsely furnished fire station office, it took three minutes to get from the fire captain, a tanned, athletic-looking woman dressed in the neat, green uniform of the Forestry service, that yes, she did know Eva Knoll, and no, she wouldn't tell us where she lived.

Behind me, Detective Hudson started to say something. I turned around and held up my hand for him to keep quiet. He glared at me. I glared back.

"Why not?" I asked her. "Like I said, we don't want to hurt her or anything. We just want to ask her some questions. Riccarla can vouch for my identity and integrity." I decided to pull out what I hoped was my ace in the hole. "I'm married to San Celina's police chief."

"You're Gabe Ortiz's wife? He's a nice guy. Talked to him about old Chevys a while back at a Chamber of Commerce thing. He said he's restoring his son's Malibu. Sixty-five, I think it was."

"Yeah, Gabe loves old cars. We have a restored 1950 Chevy pickup. Original interior. His dad bought it in Wichita, Kansas, the same year Gabe was born."

"Cool," she said, nodding appreciatively.

"About Eva Knoll . . ."

"I'm sorry, but I just can't."

"But, honestly, we won't hurt her. We just want to ask her some questions."

A deep crevice formed between the woman's clear blue eyes. "I'm not questioning your identity or integrity and I'm sure you're a very nice person, but things are different out here. Our motto is 'Don't ask, don't tell.' Folks move out here because they don't want to be bothered by people, and we try to accommodate them. Sometimes it's for illegal reasons. I'm not saying we don't have our share of drug labs, but most times it's just that they want to be left alone. We're a tight group. We look out for each other because we have to. If we called the Sheriff's Department it would take an officer over an hour to get out here. That makes us pretty independent and self-sufficient. Eva's our oldest citizen, and we all feel real protective about her. I can give her a message, and if she wants to get back to you, then it's her choice."

"But it's very important I talk to her as soon as possible. It's a long drive out here. Does she have a phone? Can you call her?"

Lukie hesitated for a moment, then said, "Sure, I'll try."

She punched the number in and waited. "There's no answer. Guess she's out back in her greenhouse. She can't hear the phone out there. Like I said, I'll give her your number."

I bit my lip in frustration. "Isn't there any way I can convince you to tell me where she lives?"

"Like I said we feel real protective of Eva."

"Please, if I . . ."

Her eyes widened slightly as she peered over my shoulder. "Well, that would do it. Let me write down her address for you." She turned back to her gray metal desk and started hunting through a Rolodex.

I whipped around to look at Detective Hudson. He was holding up his badge and wearing a smug grin.

"Smart-ass," I muttered.

"Now, now," he said, patting me on the shoulder. "Let's not be a sore loser."

After the captain showed us on the huge wall map where Eva Knoll's house was, she said, "Please be careful. Eva's very fragile these days."

"I promise," I said, glancing over at Detective Hudson,

who was expressionless, "we will do our very best not to upset her."

"WE'D HAVE THIS interview done and eating lunch back in San Celina if I'd done that sooner," he said.

"Oh, pipe down," I said halfheartedly, staring out the window. At the side of the road a gray pronghorn antelope, its stomach open and raw, sat waiting for the elements to clean it to bones. No animal control officer out here to shovel up death and dispose of it neatly. "And I meant what I said to the fire captain. If Eva Knoll shows any signs of getting upset, I'm going to stop you."

He just shook his head and started humming the Dwight Yoakam song "A Thousand Miles from Nowhere . . ."

It took us forty-five minutes to find her place. For a little while we drove along the edge of Soda Lake. A silvery-white layer of water glimmered, miragelike, across the flat lake. The surrounding prairie mounds covered with bunch-grass were mirrored perfectly in the lake's glassy surface.

"Read somewhere that was an alkaline lake," the detective said.

I nodded. "Usually it's dry this time of year, but we had a rainy summer. In the winter, you should see the sandhill cranes. It's quite a sight."

Eva Knoll's house sat at the end of a half-mile dirt road. With only a lone cottonwood for shade, the tiny slat-board house and the occupant seemed defenseless against the frightening expanse of prairie. When we pulled up, a huge rottweiler mix bounded off the front porch, its large, powerful teeth bared. The dog jumped against the side of the detective's truck, its claws scraping down the passenger door with a sound like chalk on blackboard. I instinctively scooted across the seat away from the growling dog.

"He's scratchin' the paint!" Detective Hudson cried. "Dang it all, this is a custom job!" He leaned over me to pound flat-handed on the window. "Get back, you sorry piece of taco meat!"

"Maybe you should get out and stop him," I said, pressing myself against the seat and laughing.

The look on his face could have melted cheese. "You wouldn't be laughing if it were your truck he was clawin'."

"You're right," I said cheerfully, then instinctively jerked back against him when the dog hit the side of the truck again. I cracked my window and called to the woman standing in the porch's shadows. "Mrs. Knoll? Mrs. Eva Knoll?"

"Who wants to know?" her cracked voice called back.

"Benni Harper."

"Okay, then, come on out. Lukie called about you."

She moved out of the shadows, dressed in a flowered housedress and holding a double-barrel shotgun. So much for Mrs. Knoll's vulnerability. I eyed the growling dog, then called back. "Uh, could you call off your dog?"

"Heidi, come on, girl. These people won't hurt you." The dog turned and trotted back to Mrs. Knoll on the porch.

I laughed at Detective Hudson's stunned face. "She does kind of favor your girlfriend around the muzzle, don't you think?"

"Let's get this done," he said stiffly, opening his door and walking around the passenger side. The shredded paint caused a deep moan to erupt from his chest.

"Oh, cowboy up, city slicker," I said. "Better your door than your face."

Though the dog sat quietly next to the old woman, we were hesitant as we walked up to the shadowed porch. After a short introduction and a minute of letting Heidi sniff our hands, she rolled over and exposed her pale brown stomach, begging for a scratch.

"You're just an old fake, aren't you, girl?" I said, rubbing her muscled stomach. Detective Hudson stood a foot or so back, glancing over at his truck's ravaged door, still annoyed at the dog's disregard for his paint job.

"Oh, she can take a hunk out of you," Mrs. Knoll said. "Don't doubt it."

I straightened up and held out my hand. "I'm Benni Harper. You said Lukie called?"

Mrs. Knoll nodded, her short, white hair wispy about her dried-apricot face. Her handshake was firm and direct, like that of a young woman. "Said you needed to ask me some questions."

"Yes, if you don't mind."

She set her shotgun down on the corner of the porch. "Don't reckon I have much anyone wants to know."

"It's about Rose Brown," I said.

Her old face seemed to sink further into itself, and she stared out over my shoulder at something in the distance. She seemed lost for a moment in the past. She turned her ghost-lit eyes on me. "He the lawman Lukie was talking about?" she asked, nodding over at a silent Detective Hudson.

"Yes, he's with the Sheriff's Department."

"I don't have any use for the law. Won't talk to him. It's you or nothing."

I turned to look at Detective Hudson, raising my eyebrows in silent question.

He threw his hands up in frustration. "I give up."

"Come inside," she said to me. "You." She pointed at the detective. "Go sit in your truck. Sound travels around here, and this ain't none of your business what I got to say." The wooden screen door slammed shut behind her. Heidi remained on the porch, panting and watching me and Detective Hudson.

"I'm not sitting in my truck," he said. "I'm the one with

authority here. If that batty old woman thinks . . ."

I put a finger over my lips. "You want to blow this just because of your overinflated ego? She's agreed to talk to *me*, so just humor her and go sit in your truck."

Looking as if he'd like to take a bite out of someone's leg, he stomped back to his truck.

Inside the cramped house filled with the accumulation of a lifetime of possessions, Mrs. Knoll was already sitting in a ratty blue velour armchair with beige doilies on the arms. Heidi had followed me into the house and settled in what was obviously her accustomed spot in front of a fireplace filled with charred bits of wood.

"Over there." Mrs. Knoll pointed with a spindly finger to a Victorian sofa across from her. I moved a pile of ancient *Life* magazines and sat down.

"Sorry for the clutter," she said. "I don't get many visitors."

We sat there for a long, silent moment. Finally I said, "Mrs. Knoll, I have some questions about the years you worked with Rose Brown out at Seven Sisters ranch."

"That was a long time ago, young woman," she said, her thin arms resting quiet and still on the chair's lacy arms.

"Yes, it was. But there's been some . . . trouble out there recently, and Detective Hudson and I think it might have something to do with what happened back then."

"What kind of trouble?"

I quickly told her about Giles's death and the circumstances behind it. Her face never changed expression.

When I finished, she took some time to answer. The ticking of a large grandfather clock next to the door reminded me that an impatient Detective Hudson was fuming outside.

"Do you know . . . ?" I started.

She held up her hand. "That family will haunt me till I die. That's the plain truth of it."

"How?" I asked, hoping to get her started talking.

She gestured over at the table next to me. "See that picture?"

I picked up the round, copper frame and looked at the black-and-white photograph of a young boy sitting in the lap of an older woman who bore a striking resemblance to Mrs. Knoll. The boy appeared to be about two years old, and I recognized the facial features of a Down's syndrome child.

"That's my boy and my mother," she said. "He wasn't normal. Guess you can tell that. He had the best care, though. His whole life he did. Even when he got the cancer in his bowels. Had the best care. Private nurses. Big pretty headstone when the angels finally took him home. All because I kept quiet." She reached down and stroked Heidi's huge head, causing the dog to sigh deeply. "But now, I reckon there's no reason anymore. I'm old. I've been wanting to tell someone. You look like a nice young lady. Do you have any children?"

"No," I said. "No, I don't."

"Well, I'll tell you. You'll do anything for your kids. Leastwise, most folks would. Oh, you make your mistakes, all right. Maybe you're too easy or too hard. But most folks do their best. They *try*. Do you understand what I'm saying?"

"Yes, I think so."

"There's those, though, that just defy everything God ever intended. You want to believe they have a soul, but you can't imagine, can't imagine on this earth, why they do what they do. Do you understand what I'm saying?"

I nodded and didn't answer.

Then she told me a story that would darken a piece of my heart until the day I died.

14

"THOSE BROWNS NEEDED me, no doubt about it," Mrs. Knoll said. "Good nannies weren't any easier to find then than they are now, and the Browns really needed a good nanny, what with those three little girls under eleven and then the two sets of twins. Rose Brown had her hands full, and she wasn't raised to do nothing much but sit around and look pretty."

"When did you first come to work for them?" I asked.

"Right before the first set of twins was born. Oh, my, Mrs. Brown was big as a steamer trunk. By the time I came, those little girls of hers had been running wild for months. Took me a good long time, let me tell you, to get them civilized again. Especially that little Capitola. She was wild as a fox and liked it that way. Took me a week to comb all the knots out of her hair."

She shifted in her chair and wiped a bit of spittle that had pooled in the deep wrinkles around her mouth. I waited, trying to keep every part of my body still, though I was jittery with nerves.

"She was a handful, that little Cappy," the old woman reminisced. "The others, too, though not as much. That house was beautiful. It felt like a castle to me. I grew up around San Miguel in a little two-bedroom shotgun shack out in the middle of nowhere. Father worked for a farmer out that away. Mother was sick from the time I was real little. I started keeping house for Father when I was five years old. Could make a perfect angel food cake when I was seven, and that was on a woodstove."

"Incredible," I murmured. Then I asked, "How old were you when you went to work for the Browns?"

"It was in 1925," she said, almost inaudibly. "I was thirty-eight. Father said it was the best thing, what with Johnnie's condition and all. The Browns paid real good, and Johnnie's daddy took off right after he was born. Never saw him again. I sent money to my parents and visited when I could. The money helped a lot, Father said."

"Johnnie is your son?"

She nodded and pointed again at the picture on the dusty end table. "I visited him every chance I could get. He did okay out on the farm as long as Mother was alive. He didn't take much care, mostly just feed him and dress him, sit him on a blanket under a tree. I'd been with the Browns for about a year when Mother died. By that time, I'd already seen what I'd seen and I wanted to leave, but the judge offered to triple my pay, and with Father being all stoved up and not able to farm anymore, I was the only breadwinner. He and Johnnie moved to a little house near the San Miguel mission, and Father Xavier there gave him a job tending the mission gardens. It worked out real well because there was an old nun there who took care of Johnnie. I was real grateful for their kindness."

"What was it you saw at the Browns'?" I said, trying to focus her wandering attention.

Her age-spotted hand went up to her mouth as if wanting to physically hold back her words. "The first baby, Daisy, died of pneumonia," she said.

I nodded. That fit with the death certificate. "What about her sister?"

"Rose was so sad when Daisy died. Inconsolable. But the family and all her friends were right there helping her and taking care of things. Petted her and comforted her and told her she had to get up out of that bed, that her other little baby needed her, that her little girls needed her. Even her husband, the judge, started coming home at night. And her doctor, handsome fella, he came over every day, twice some days and talked and talked to her. They took to having tea in the parlor every day about four. She started wanting to live again, blossomed really. All that attention, she just craved it, and it fed her like an underwater spring feeds a lake. But then, like people do, they got back to their own lives. The judge started staying away again. He had his work and, though no one talked openly about that sort of thing then, his lady friends. Her doctor got busy with other patients and such. It was just me and her again, with the little baby and the girls and all the servants. The first time she came running down with the baby calling for me to fetch the doctor, the baby wasn't breathing, my heart just about broke for her. No one deserved that kind of sorrow. The doctor came, but by that time the baby was breathing again, and he sat with her down in the parlor and had his tea, and she laughed and carried on with him as if her baby hadn't been on death's door only an hour before. It didn't seem right to me, but I never was one to question about folks' ways much. They'd always been such a mystery. Still are for that matter."

She paused for a moment, breathing deep and hard. The effort of telling this story was wearing on her, but I didn't know how to make it go any faster. Like most things in life, it had its own pace, and I had to just let it unfold. She inhaled a phlegmy, rattling breath, and suddenly I was fearful that this might all be too much for her. *Should I stop?*

"Would you like some water?" I asked.

She motioned no with her hand and continued on. "It was after the third time the baby stopped breathing I got suspicious. It only happened when she was in the room, and since I tended that baby more than she ever did, it just didn't seem right to me. Every time the doctor came, and they talked and he fawned over her. I kept telling myself a mother wouldn't do that to her own child. Not just for a little attention. So I started kinda following her, watching her. Then I saw her do it."

"What?" I whispered.

"Hold the pillow over the baby's face. Her little legs just kicked and kicked. I screamed, 'Mrs. Brown!' and she looked up at me. Straight in my eyes she looked at me, set the pillow aside, and said, 'Yes, Eva?' Just like that, face as blank as a rock. 'Yes, Eva?' My blood ran cold as creek water."

"What did you do? Did you tell someone?"

Tears pooled in her pale eyes. "What could I do? Do you think anyone would believe me when I said Mrs. Rose Brown, wife of the richest man in the county, was a-tryin' to kill her own baby? So I made myself believe her when she said the baby had pulled the pillow over her face, and she was taking it off. I believed her because I wanted to. I had to. I kept telling myself that mothers don't smother their own babies. They just don't kill their own babies."

"Except she did," I said.

She nodded. "I was down at the stables with the girls, watching while they took their riding lessons. When I saw the doctor's car come barreling up the dirt road, and I knew in my heart this time it was bad."

"She killed Dahlia."

"Yes, and all the attention started all over again. Oh, such a funeral you can't imagine. Just like Daisy's. Hundreds of people. All the florist shops in town were empty. Judge Brown knew everyone, just everyone. A lot of people came, of course, trying to curry up to him. And during it all, I knew she'd killed that baby. At the funeral, she caught my eye and she knew I knew."

"No one suspected? None of the other servants? The judge?"

"Not that anyone said. To me, anyway."

"So, what about the other babies . . ."

"She got pregnant shortly after that. I stayed till past her delivering time. When she had another set of twins, I couldn't help but wonder what God was thinking, giving her those babies. They named them Bethany and Beulah. I struggled with what I should do, even went to the judge once, trying to tell him he needed to watch out for those babies, but I got too afraid, and my words got all jumbled.

" 'Eva,' he'd finally said in that gruff voice of his. 'I know working for Mrs. Brown's not the easiest thing in the world. I'll triple your pay if you'll stay. I know you need the money, what with your son and father. I'll see that Father Xavier at San Miguel gives him a little extra work, add to his pay. They'll be taken good care of, Eva. Trust me on this. I value your discretion.' "

She fingered the torn arm of her easy chair. "That's all he said. He valued my discretion. I had to look the word up to see what it meant. I knew then he was telling me to keep quiet. What could I do? If I lost my job with the Browns, there was no place to go. I was a good nanny, but by then it was hard times, and there was no work anywhere.

With my job and Father's tending the mission gardens, me and Father and Johnnie had it good. All I had to do was forget what I'd seen." She sighed deeply, causing Heidi to lift her head and whine. Mrs. Knoll patted the dog's head reassuringly.

"Things went okay for three months after the second twins were born. I'd even convinced myself that maybe I'd been seeing things. Then Beulah started having the breathing spells, and time after time Mrs. Brown would call for the doctor. I took to following after her, especially when she was around the babies. But she'd say, 'Now, Eva, let me care for my babies. Take the girls for a walk. They're looking a little peaked these days.'

"I'd take Cappy and Willow and little Etta for a stroll around the garden, and then, sure enough, the doctor would come driving up in his fancy car, spewing dust in his haste to get there. Finally Beulah died, and then Bethany. I was beside myself, not knowing what to do."

"Didn't anyone, Judge Brown, her doctor, *anyone*, suspect what was happening?" That seemed unbelievable to me, that all these babies kept dying and no one questioned it.

She shook her head slowly. "Lots of babies died back then. You go look at any graveyard and you can see that. If anyone else suspected she was killing her own babies, they never said anything. Like me, I reckon they just wouldn't, *couldn't* believe such a thing about anyone."

"Did you go to Judge Brown after the others?" I asked.

"I tried, but after Bethany, the last twin, passed on, he wasn't living at the house but one or two days a month. I think he knew something was going on. Maybe he just wanted to stay away from all that sadness. Maybe he didn't want to make any more babies for her to kill. I don't know. The one time I tried to say something, he stopped me and told me they wouldn't be needing me at the big house any-more. He gave me a year's pay and said he'd pay me a pension until I died. Got a check at the first of the month like clockwork. When my boy got sick, the bills were paid, and he paid for the funeral, too. Did the same when my father died. Then one day, after Father had been gone a while, the deed to this little house came in the mail. I moved out here around '42 and never saw any of the Browns again."

"And you never told anyone," I said.

Her glassy eyes seemed to clear slightly when they stared straight into mine. "Not until now. I figure there's no reason to hide it anymore. Those babies never got their justice, and I shoulder the burden for that. I should have told someone. I should have tried."

OUTSIDE, DETECTIVE HUDSON leaned against his truck, staring out at the bright, level horizon.

"Thought you'd never get through," he said, spitting a wad of gum out on the dirt. "So, what's the story?"

"She's ninety-seven. I'll be glad if I can even talk at that age." I looked back at the tiny desert house, bleached bone-white by the sun. A mental shiver rattled my brain. "Let's get on the road. I'll tell you on the way back."

We were halfway to San Celina by the time I finished my story.

"That's unbelievable," the detective said, his expression as incredulous as I still felt.

"I know. And somehow it's got to do with Giles's mur-der. I'm assuming he found out about this and was going to let it out. I bet you anything now that *Giles* was the anonymous caller to the newspaper the night of the party.

He was going to make sure this went public immediately if Cappy and the sisters didn't cooperate."

"And the great child-loving philanthropist, Rose Brown, would be exposed for what she really is—a baby killer."

I stared out the window. "The question is, what do we do now?"

He was quiet for a moment, then said, "I'm going to confront Capitola. Throw down the gauntlet and see what happens."

I twisted around to look at him. "I don't think that's a good idea. We don't know enough yet to confront her. We need to run this by someone who knows the legal stuff involved. You could blow it if you jump in too fast."

He thought for a moment. "Okay, I'll go talk to someone at the DA's office, then."

"That's still jumping the gun. I don't trust them to keep it quiet. I'm telling you, Detective, this is a very, very prominent family in San Celina. One whiff of this scandal, and the media will be all over you, me, the Browns, and Eva. If we found her without much trouble, so will they. I don't want . . . no, I *won't* let that happen. It might kill her."

Annoyed, he asked, "So what do you propose we do?"

"I know someone we can trust who'll be able to advise us without fear of leaks. Let me just run it by my friend before you set things in motion."

His face set hard and stubborn.

"Please," I said, ready to beg if necessary.

He hesitated, then said, "An hour. That's what I'll give this person. Then it's out of your hands, and I'm going to my superiors and the DA."

"Deal," I said.

⋆ 15 ⋆

As BEFITTING A good attorney, Amanda's expression didn't change while I told her Eva Knoll's story. For once Detective Hudson sat quietly and kept his thoughts to himself. When I finished, she waited a moment before speaking.

"I'll be flour-breaded and deep-fried," she finally said. "I know some research doctors back east who'd give their left nuts to hear this. There's always been speculation it happened before the seventies when it was given a name, but most doctors always considered it a modern-day disorder. I guess there is nothing new under the sun."

"A disorder?" I said. "What do you mean?"

"If what this Mrs. Knoll told you is true," she said, leaning back in her executive office chair, "then it appears that Rose Brown had a syndrome called Munchausen by Proxy."

"Don't give me any psychological crap," Detective Hudson burst out. "She killed those babies. That's homicide in my book."

Amanda's normally mobile and smiling mouth turned

grim. "I agree wholeheartedly, Detective, but it's not quite as simple as that, at least in the law."

He started to protest, and Amanda held up a hand. "Let me see if I can explain. I prosecuted a Munchausen by Proxy case when I was working for the DA's office in San Francisco. Young mother regularly fed her two-year-old daughter syrup of ipecac to make her throw up whatever she ate. The child inhaled her own vomit, causing pneumonia a couple of times. She was literally starving to death, but it took doctors eight months to figure out what was causing it. Since the pneumonia qualified as great bodily harm, we eventually prosecuted the mother under torture charges, simply because we couldn't figure out what else to call it and get a decent sentence." She picked up a small Beanie Baby panda from the top of a pile of Beanie animals and absentmindedly stroked its back with her polished fingernails.

"How about plain old child abuse? Assault? Attempted homicide?" Detective Hudson said bitterly.

Amanda nodded, still stroking the furry toy. "It's certainly a form of child abuse, but the problem is it doesn't fit neatly into what we call child abuse under the law or any of those other things. Once we had all these tidy organized categories: You had physical abuse, you had molest, you had neglect. Now all of a sudden we have this insidious type of child endangerment whose physical manifestations are hard to distinguish from the behaviors of good mothers who are simply caring for very sick children. You have to understand, the mothers of these children often appear to be extremely loving and deeply concerned. It's dangerous for doctors, nurses, or social workers to accuse someone of Munchausen by Proxy, because they might be accusing a mother who is innocent. There have been cases where a slow-growing brain tumor caused vomiting or other symptoms that only the mother observed, and it took the doctors some time to find the tumor. If those mothers had been accused of this disorder, it would have been tragic for them and their children. As a society we are hesitant to believe that a mother would harm her own child. It's only the worst of these Munchausen cases that even make it to court. Most are so borderline that the prosecutor doesn't have a chance convincing a jury that a mother deliberately tried to harm her sick child, that indeed she was the one making the child sick."

She set the toy panda down and picked up a turtle. She took a pair of scissors, cut the tiny tag off the ear and threw it away. "I give these to the deputy DA in charge of the child abuse unit. Helps the kids to have something to hold when they testify. They're the perfect size for little hands." She put down the turtle and picked up a pale pink pig. "I cut the tags off so crazy adult collectors won't steal them."

"So you're telling us that lots of mothers get away with killing their babies with this Munchausen thing?" Detective Hudson broke in.

She tossed the pig in the detagged pile and picked up a bright red lobster. "Look, child abuse cases, even ones with real evidence of physical injury, are hard for juries to watch and rule on. Like I just said, something deep inside all of us does not want to believe or face the fact that some mothers hurt their children. And when there's not always overt evidence of harm and the mother appears loving . . . well, what can I say? More often than not, they get away with it. That's if they're ever discovered, which in most of these cases they aren't." Her mouth turned down with sadness as she clipped the tag off the lobster's claw.

"But why would anyone do that to their own child?" I said.

"The question of the year," she said, leaning forward

and resting her elbows on the desk. "I'll give you the fifty-cent lecture. It has to do with power. Not having it and wanting it. Oh, there's lots of deeper issues, but it really comes down to that. Surprisingly, most of the mothers who do this have not come from overtly abusive homes. But they often come from homes where the father is emotionally unattached. Somewhere in the psyche of this young girl—and by the way, the majority of people who have this disorder are women—she develops what we call a 'character perversion.' In a nutshell, to get positive attention from her doctor, who is an authority figure substitute, she uses her baby and its imagined or manufactured illness. Their babies aren't even people to them, but more like objects used to gain them what they want, which is attention and praise. Some researchers have even gone so far as to compare the babies to fetish objects."

"But she killed her babies," Detective Hudson said. "If they were what she needed for attention, why would she kill them?"

"Very good, Detective," Amanda said, nodding. "You're right, most deaths in Munchausen by Proxy cases are accidental. Those mothers don't *intend* for their babies to die. But if they do, God help the next baby that comes along. They become the new fixed object."

I felt my stomach churn. Amanda was right; it was a hard thing to comprehend. The mother/child relationship was one we all idealized, even when we knew better.

"So, you're telling me," Detective Hudson said, "that she managed to kill four babies and no one had a clue? And why wouldn't she try harming the older girls?"

Amanda picked up a small moose with orange antlers, studying it critically. "He's pretty cute. I may have to buy one for myself." She looked back up at us. "First, it sounds like the first twin died naturally. Maybe the attention she received when the baby was sick set it off. As for why she didn't harm her older girls, who's to say she didn't and they survived whatever she did? We'll probably never know. The harm she did to them psychologically isn't as obvious. I'm telling you, Detective, I did extensive research on this subject, and there is very little information out there. As for people suspecting, there was one case file back in the fifties where seven children in the same family died from what they diagnosed as crib death before anyone started asking why."

Detective Hudson stood up and started pacing her small office in frustration.

"What do you think we should do?" I asked.

Amanda shook her head, bemused. "Accusing someone of this with so little proof, especially someone as prominent as Rose Brown, would only gain you a libel suit. Not to mention that it happened so long ago. I'm not clear as to why you found out this information."

I told her how we thought it was the reason Giles was murdered, that somehow he'd found out and was black-mailing the family.

"Then you've got a real sticky situation on your hands," she said. "It could be any of the family who killed him or none of them. And this could possibly have nothing to do with Giles's murder. It's intriguing, but I'd say it's infor-mation that, though troubling, is best filed under the good Lord's final judgment."

Detective Hudson let out a scoffing grunt. "I think I should confront Cappy Brown."

I looked to Amanda, questioning.

"That could be problematic," she said, watching him walk back and forth, finally saying, "Sit down, Detective, darlin'. You're makin' me dizzy."

He stopped, stared at her gorgeous, uncompromising

smile, then did as she said without a peep of protest.

"Here's the deal," she said. "Everything I told you is pure speculation. Ruining the reputation of someone like Rose Brown over something you have no substantial proof for would, as I said before, not only garner you a libel suit, but also might hinder you finding the real perpetrator."

He frowned, knowing she was right.

"So, what should we do?" I asked. "We should do *something*."

"My advice? Go light a candle or say a prayer for those sad, pathetic people and get on with your life, because it's way beyond your control."

I stood up, hitching my purse over my shoulder. "Thanks, Amanda. I appreciate you taking the time to talk to us."

"No problem," she said, coming around the desk and wrapping me in a Ralph Lauren–scented hug. "You do manage to get yourself into some interesting situations." She held out a hand to Detective Hudson. "Good luck, Detective. Hope you find your killer."

"Count on it," he said grimly.

She grinned at me. "God bless the eternal cockiness of the native Texan male."

"YOU CAN DROP me off at the folk art museum," I said, as we walked out to his truck.

"Fine," he said.

I glanced over at him. "You okay?"

The only reply I received was an almost imperceptible shrug. He was quiet the whole drive over to the museum.

"Got a john in there?" he asked when we pulled into the driveway.

"Sure, back in the workrooms."

I was listening to the message on the answering machine for the third time when he walked past my office. "Detective, come listen to this."

He stood next to me, listening to Cappy's gruff voice.

"We need to talk," she said. "Call me." The time of the call was three-forty-five p.m. The exact time we were sitting in Amanda's office. It was now almost five.

He picked up the phone and handed it to me. "Call her and see what she wants."

"I bet she knows we went out to see Eva Knoll," I said, staring at the phone he held out. "She probably had us followed or she has a contact out there."

"That's what I was afraid of. Call her."

After finding it in my Rolodex, I punched her number with a shaking finger.

"We need to talk," she said again. "Can you come out now?"

"Right now?" I asked, looking at the detective. He nodded yes.

"Yes," she said. "But alone. I will only talk to you alone. I mean it."

I hesitated, then said, "I'll be there in about a half hour."

"Fine." She hung up without saying good-bye.

"I'll drive," Detective Hudson said, starting for the door.

"She said she'd only talk to me," I called after him.

He stopped at the doorway and slowly turned around. "I will not let you go out there alone."

"But what if this is our only chance to get a confession out of her? Can't you put a wire on me or something? Park around the corner and come if I need help."

His face tightened. "This isn't television, Benni. If you got hurt, I'd never forgive myself. Not to mention your husband would kill me. Probably *after* he cut off my balls."

I grabbed up my purse and snapped. "Fine, come along.

It'll probably screw up any chance of her telling us anything, but far be it from me to endanger your masculine
appendages." Deep inside, I knew he was right. But I also
knew that Cappy most likely wouldn't admit to a thing with
him standing next to me.

When we drove the long, twisting entry road to the
ranch, we didn't see one solitary sign of life; the ranch was
eerily empty. Even the wine-tasting room had only one car
parked in front. Though Wednesday was not a busy day,
tourist-wise, I expected to see some activity, a vineyard
worker, a groom, or somebody walking around or working.
We passed the stables where the hot walkers stood still, the
chains swinging gently in the breeze, the training track and
corrals clean and empty. I rolled down my window, catching a strong whiff of horse, but not a single nicker came
over the breeze to shatter the immense silence.

We pulled up to the house and walked up the front steps.
Detective Hudson rang the doorbell once, and ten seconds
later Cappy answered the door. She was dressed in slightly
dirt-stained blue jeans and a pale blue, snap-button Western
shirt with the sleeves rolled up. Her brown, muscled forearms looked as dangerous as a man's.

"I said I'd only talk to Benni," she said, her gray eyes
flat as steel.

"Don't blame her," he said. "I wouldn't let her come
alone."

"Sit in the foyer, then," she said, pointing at a parson's
bench. "Come into my study," she said over her shoulder
as she strode across the glossy floor toward her office.

Detective Hudson hesitated.

"I'll be fine," I said in a low voice. "You'll be right out
here."

"I don't like this," he answered.

"We don't have a choice," I said.

"She's right," Cappy called from her office.

He glared in Cappy's direction and sat down on the parson's bench.

Inside her office, she was already sitting behind her desk, under her mother's Churn Dash quilt. "Please shut the office door," she said.

I did as she asked, then stood there, waiting. *Calm down,* I told my nervous stomach. *Nothing's going to happen. She's not a killer and even if she was, she's not going to pull a gun on you with Detective Hudson sitting right outside the door. Besides, he's just a yell away and he's armed and experienced at confrontations like this.*

"Please, sit down," she said, her voice amicable, as if all I was there for was to do a little horse trading or perhaps sell her a good load of timothy hay.

I sat down in one of the green leather chairs that Detective Hudson had used the night of Giles's murder.

"Would you like a drink? I've got some bourbon here in my desk."

I mutely shook my head.

"Okay, then," Cappy said. "Let's get down to business so we can get this wrapped up. I've got a trip to the Los Alamitos racetrack with Churn Dash tomorrow. He'll be running his first race as soon as he qualifies. We're expecting great things from him. Maybe he'll end up siring our next Futurity winner."

I nodded, not answering.

"You're a very clever girl, Benni Harper," she said, picking up a smooth wooden letter opener, running it back and forth through her strong fingers. "And persistent. I knew once you got your teeth in this I would have a hard time forcing you to let go. So . . ." She set the letter opener down and blinked her eyes slowly. "Blackmail's an evil thing, wouldn't you agree?" she asked, her mouth set in a grim, pale line.

I nodded.

"So anyone who would commit it would also be evil and deserve to be punished."

I shifted forward in my chair. Was she going to confess to Giles's murder? Reveal it was someone else? Was she covering for someone? That has always been a possibility. "Who are you talking about?"

She stared at me, her eyes as steady and reflective as a knife blade. She didn't answer my question, but instead said, "I have a story for you. Do you like stories, Benni Harper?"

Without thinking, I held my breath, mesmerized by her control. Her every deliberate movement, her unblinking eyes, reminded me of an ancient, battle-scarred rattler poised to strike.

She started talking, her voice cold and emotional. She told me a story that had I not already talked to Amanda, I would have never believed. A story about a terrified seven-year-old girl who watched her mother gently place a pillow over her little sister Dahlia's face, pressing down until her sister kicked and kicked her tiny legs in desperation to breathe. Then picking the baby up and running out in the hall and down the stairs calling for help, calling for someone to call the doctor, the beloved family doctor. How she saw her do it again and again, placing the pillow so lovingly, so gently over her sister's tiny face. Each time, stopping just in time to call for the doctor. The little girl told no one, but held the secret tight inside her chest, not believing her mother capable of that, not a mother, not her mother.

Then Dahlia died, and at the funeral she heard her mother whisper, *My babies are together again.*

Every night the little girl prayed that God would make things all right. That Daisy and Dahlia would not be dead, that the memories in her head of the pillow being held over Dahlia's face by her mother's delicate white hands would go away. A year later when another set of twins was born, the little girl was relieved because she believed that God had answered her prayers and that her mother had been given another chance. But she watched her mother, followed her constantly, until her mother said in her soft, gentle voice, *Don't be always hanging around me, go play like your sisters, get some fresh air, let me be with my babies.* Then the new twins, Bethany and Beulah, died, too, first one and then the other. Her mother both times came running out of the nursery crying for help, calling for the housekeeper to call the doctor. At the funerals, Cappy could not stop staring at her mother's delicate white hands.

"Then it was over," Cappy said, her voice emotionless and dry as a desert. "My mother never bore any other children, and she went on to become a great advocate for the welfare of children in this county. Without her, thousands of children would be much worse off, even dead, for lack of medical care. My father used his political influence to help her achieve her goals. I left home at seventeen to follow the rodeo and didn't come back until after Father died and Mother needed me to run the ranch."

I sat quietly—horrified. Horrified by the story of a sickness I still couldn't imagine, by the matter-of-factness with which Cappy told her story, and with the fact that a seven-year-old would have to carry a burden like that, a burden that twisted her own thinking and loyalties to the point of murder.

When I could finally speak, I asked, "Do your sisters know?"

"Yes, I told them years ago. But we agreed it should

stop there. Our children and their children have never known and never will. It needs to end when we die. And it would have . . ." She left the statement open.

"It would have, except Giles somehow found out about the murdered babies."

A muscle in her cheek flinched at my graphic words.

"Probably, because of her senility, from your mother," I continued, "and he was blackmailing the family to force you to merge your winery with his father's. You, or somebody in the Brown family killed him to keep him quiet."

Speaking slowly, obviously choosing her words with care, she replied, "Giles's death was a tragic event. I know his family will miss him. I wish it didn't have to happen."

"You know I have to tell Detective Hudson. I have to tell Gabe."

"What is there to tell? I'll deny anything you claimed I said about my mother and her babies. As for the rest . . ." She shrugged. "You and I were just lamenting over poor Giles's tragedy."

Our eyes met, and in that moment I knew she'd killed Giles and I knew she'd never get caught.

"Now you, too, have a burden to carry," she said, her voice not unkind, but firm and, it seemed to me, tired.

My heart pumped wildly out of control. It took me a moment to find the voice to ask the question I knew I had to ask. "Why would you protect her all these years when she murdered your sisters?"

An almost astonished expression crossed her old face, as if she couldn't believe I'd ask such a ridiculous question. "She's my mother, Benni."

"But she *murdered* your sisters," I repeated, my voice a whisper.

For the briefest second, her expression changed. All the years of fear and shame and grief and disappointment seemed to converge, and I thought for a moment she might lay her head in her strong, capable hands and start sobbing. Then her back stiffened, and cool resolve again blanketed her face.

"We've talked long enough," she said. "Please go."

I stood up, my knees trembling, wanting to say something, but not knowing what. Finally I said, "You won't get away with this forever."

"Good-bye, Benni," she said, then took a deep breath and turned her chair around, dismissing me.

Detective Hudson was pacing the hallway when I came out of Cappy's office.

"What did she say?" he demanded.

Stumbling over the words, trying to keep my composure, I told him.

He pushed past me and stormed into her office, his face white with anger. "You sick, sorry piece of human garbage," he said. "You'd protect a woman who murdered her own babies just for some attention. You'd protect a woman who's lived a lie most of her life, this woman who professes to be a great lover of children. You'd kill another human being in cold blood for a woman who'd do that! Why?"

She turned her chair slowly around, her face as expressionless and cold as a smooth river stone. Had I really seen all those emotions on her face minutes before, or had it just been wishful thinking on my part?

"I don't know what you're talking about," she said.

His breathing sounded loud in the quiet room. "You won't get away with it. I'll find a way to see that you or your mother doesn't get away with this."

"You don't have that kind of power, Detective," she said, unmoved by his anger. "And you never will."

"Maybe not," he said, his voice steel-edged, "but I have

time. And if it takes me the rest of my life, I'll expose you and your mother."

"Excuse me," she said, picking up the phone, dismissing us. "I have some important phone calls to make."

He started to say something else, but I laid a hand on his forearm. "Let's go, Detective Hudson."

He turned and looked at me, ready to snap a reply. We stared at each other a long moment, and I saw a small muscle flutter in his smooth cheek. Without a word, I took his arm and led him outside without looking back.

Swallowing the salt that coated the back of my throat, I willed myself to stay calm. *Get away*, a voice inside me kept saying. *Just get away*. Away from this house with its ghoulish secrets, away from a woman so tainted by the evil she saw as a child, it destroyed her, too. Having lost my mother so early and yet going on to live a fairly happy life, I once thought foolishly that perhaps a mother's influence was not as great as all the psychologists claim. That was until my experience last spring with my own mother's secrets. I realized then that our mothers set the stage so early for who we are, what we think of the world, of ourselves, of the bare facts of what we perceive as good and evil, that even their absence, emotionally or physically, changes the very fabric and landscape of our lives. We didn't have to be like them, but we never escaped them, no matter how swiftly we tried to run.

On the porch I gently squeezed his forearm and said, "Detective, you have to let this one go."

"No," he said, his voice still hard, though I thought I caught a tinge of agony.

"Amanda's right. There is no proof. And the Browns are too powerful. No one will ever believe us."

"So you're saying we should just walk away? That she'll never have to pay for killing Giles Norton? That her mother should never have to account for those dead babies?"

I flinched at his words. "She'll pay. And so will her mother. The babies and Giles will be given justice. Just not by us. Not in this lifetime."

His face contorted with disgust. "You believe that crap? You really believe they will stand before some almighty God when they die and answer for this?"

"Yes."

He slammed his fist against a wooden post. "Why? Give me one good reason why you believe that."

I thought for a moment, knowing that nothing I would say would satisfy him right now, but gave him the only answer I had. "Because the alternative—that this is all there is, that they will get away with it—is too awful to comprehend."

He shook his head, his face pale in the bright porch light. "That's some fantasy world you're living in, Benni Harper. Some pie-in-the-sky fantasy world for kids and dreamers." He ran a hand over his face. "But I swear, there are times I wish I could join you."

I touched his shoulder. "There's nothing more we can do here."

He turned back to contemplate the fancy, carved front door. "That is the only thing you've said in the last ten minutes I do believe."

As we were pulling out of the driveway, the front door opened, and Cappy stepped out on the front porch. At first her face was hidden in the shadows. She moved, and for a moment I could see her full face in the hazy evening light. Her hand reached up and touched her throat. Was that despair in her expression? Sadness? Regret? I still wanted to think so. I truly wanted to believe it was. In the truck's side mirror, I watched her standing alone, still as a granite sculpture, until we turned the corner and she disappeared.

On the way back, we were both quiet. When I opened my purse for some tissue, I spotted the small tape recorder I had bought to fool Detective Hudson. It hadn't even occurred to me to turn it on. Then again, maybe it was illegal, maybe it wouldn't have made a difference. Things happened in the way they were supposed to happen. She has had to and will have to live with what she'd seen and done her entire life and, if I truly believed what I told the detective, for all eternity. I closed my purse and stared out the window.

When we hit the city limits, the detective started to say something, stopped, cleared his throat and tried again. "What I said to Mrs. Brown, I meant. I'm not giving up on this case." His knuckles were white on the truck's steering wheel.

"I didn't think you would."

He cleared his throat again, keeping his eyes on the road. "So, if I needed, say, someone to help me. Research and stuff. I mean, since no one else knows about this but you and me . . ."

"Yes, Detective, I'll help you."

He smiled to himself. "Good."

"I've been thinking," I said. "If I were to get a bunch of people together like the folk art museum board, the Historical Society, the Cattlewomen's Association, maybe some children's rights groups, and all the wineries in San Celina County, and we organize a yearly benefit ball to help abused children, would you get the Sheriff's Department involved?"

He laughed out loud. "All the wineries so that if Seven Sisters didn't participate, they'd look pretty bad?"

I nodded. "We'll rub her nose in it every year. I'll use every society connection I've garnered in the last few years, call in every marker Dove and I have, and make it the biggest event of the year. Bigger than the Harvest Ball that Seven Sisters sponsors for the children's hospital wing. We'll make it less fancy so more average people can contribute and be a part of it. We could make it three times as big as the Harvest Ball."

"You do that, Benni, and I'll make sure every sheriff's deputy and police officer in the county buys a ticket."

We smiled at each other. It wasn't much justice, but for the time being, it was all we had.

It was dusk now, and ahead of us off the interstate we could see the flickering lights of San Celina. I hugged myself, my heart cold in my chest. Next to me, the detective's face, one I'd grown used to seeing jovial and laughing, was still and expressionless, except for an occasional swift blinking of his eyes.

When we turned off on Lopez, he said, "I'll take you to the museum."

"Would you mind driving by the police station first?" I asked, suddenly wanting to see Gabe, hoping he was working late. I wanted to feel his arms around me, wanted to hear him tell me that, yes, he agreed, there would be justice for Giles . . . and the babies. Maybe not man's justice, but eternal justice. My husband had his cynical moments, but on that one point we agreed.

"Sure," Detective Hudson said, swinging his truck over one lane.

Gabe was walking out to his parking space, his briefcase in one hand, his other hand loosening his tie. The detective pulled up behind Gabe's Corvette and said, "You gonna tell him what happened?"

"Yes."

"Are you sure? Maybe he'll feel obligated to do something, tell someone."

"It's up to him, but don't underestimate my husband's

wisdom. He'll know the right thing to do. And I know he'd never do anything that might hurt me."

His mouth turned down, impressed. "That so?"

I nodded.

"Well, ranch girl, go tell your husband I think he's a pretty lucky guy."

My mouth opened in surprise. "Is that a compliment? Someone record this and save it for posterity. Detective Ford Hudson actually said something nice to Albenia Harper."

He gave a weak smile and said, "I'll deny it under oath."

"You would." I sat there for a moment, my hand on the door handle. "Are you okay?" Something in me felt like I was abandoning a friend in deep distress. Though I'd eat penny nails for breakfast before admitting it to him, I had developed a bit of a soft spot for him and his cocky Texan ways. I might even miss him. A little.

His eyes flickered, then he smiled his wide, country-boy smile. "Now don't you worry about me. I'm gonna go downtown, buy myself a couple of long-necks, see what's playin' on ESPN. I believe I'll even spring for a chili dog." His face softened. "Then maybe I'll go see Maisie. Read her a bedtime story. One about a kingdom where the good knight always wins. You know how kids love fantasy."

"That sounds like a good idea. Be careful driving home."

"That almost sounds like you care."

"I'll deny it under oath," I said solemnly.

"Plagiarist."

"A three-syllable word. I'm impressed." I gave him a small salute. "Good-bye, Detective Hudson."

"Not good-bye, Benni Harper. More like see you around."

As he pulled out of the police station driveway, he hit

his horn. "The Yellow Rose of Texas" blared across the parking lot, and I laughed out loud.

Gabe was staring at Detective Hudson's truck when I walked up. It pleased me to see his expression was not entirely happy. Maybe even a little jealous. He shook his head and tossed his briefcase in the front seat of his car. "He's watched too many *Dukes of Hazzard* shows. What were you doing with him?"

The picture of the tiny overgrown graves of the Brown babies flashed through my mind. How petty my problems seemed now. I reached up and touched his strong jaw, scratchy with five-o'clock shadow. The rough familiar feel made me swallow hard, the tears I'd been holding tight inside myself coating my eyes like mineral oil.

"*Querida*," he said, cupping my shoulders with his warm hands, "what's wrong?"

"Have you got dinner plans tonight?" I asked.

His face looked chagrined. "No, and I know I've been neglecting you." He looked over my shoulder. "Why did you say you were with that guy again?"

"Yes, you have been," I said, not answering his question.

"Got a phone call today telling me so. I swear I was coming home to apologize and talk about it tonight."

I swallowed over the thick, salty lump in my throat. "Who called you?"

"I won't mention any names, but I really hate it when members of the press are right about something, though it happens so rarely."

"I know you and Lydia had a lot to discuss these last few days."

"Yeah, well as my little Arkansas Razorback told me, maybe I was too worried about proving to my ex-wife what a success I turned out to be instead of paying attention to what my wife was going through. I'm sorry, sweetheart. I feel like a fool for not seeing it myself."

I sighed and touched his cheek. "Forget it, Friday. You're a fool, but you're my fool. And I knew whose bed you were coming home to at night."

"Until the day I die," he said, taking my face in his hands. "Now, what's with you and Detective Hudson? Please tell me it was business, not pleasure. Is there something going on with the Norton homicide I need to know about?"

"First, how's Sam and Bliss?" I asked, not quite ready to begin the story I would tell him. There was one thing I was glad I'd learned from Cappy, that the family secret had not been passed down. Maybe Sam and Bliss still had a chance.

Gabe sighed deeply, his hands slipping down to my shoulders. "Bliss asked for a leave of absence today. She's going up north with her mother and sister. I have a feeling she's not going to come back. You know, there's things in that family that bother me, though I can't put my finger on them."

"What about Sam?"

"He says they're going to take a breather for a while. He doesn't want to leave San Celina. That's all he would say. At their age I wouldn't be surprised if it ended their relationship."

"I guess only time will tell."

"I suppose so." He squeezed my shoulders gently. "Now, tell me why you're so upset."

"I need to talk," I said, feeling as breathless and vulnerable as a child. A mental picture of a seven-year-old girl watching her mother place a pillow over her sisters' faces caused tears to finally flow.

"You can talk to me. You know you can always talk to me."

I looked up at this man whose face I'd kissed so many times. This man whose cries of passion were as familiar to me as my own. This man who knew me and loved me and had promised to stay with me until the day he died. This man I trusted like no one else.

"It's about Cappy. It's about Giles's murder."

"Yes, go on."

"The thing is," I said, my voice hesitant, knowing what I was asking might not be possible for him. "Right now I need to talk to my husband. Not a police officer. Not a government employee. My husband."

Still holding me by the shoulders, he looked at me a long minute. I wouldn't ask him again. If he couldn't, I would understand. I would still love him and I would understand.

He slowly reached into his back pocket and pulled out his leather wallet where he carried his badge. He opened the car door and threw it on the floor next to his briefcase, closed and locked the door. Then he held out his hand.

"Let's walk," he said.

Rick Smolen, editor, publisher and photographer, the guru and Godfather of all photojournalists.

Brian Leatart, food photographer.

Robert L. Grigg, car photographer.

Nancy Ellison, painter, fashion and personality photographer.

Victoria Cameron Pearson, fashion and personality photographer.

Susan Peters, wise woman, photographer and editor.

Karen Silverstein, photo editor at Condé Nast, L.A.

Karen Gillingham of Food Pages, food stylist.

Edwina Lloyd, my assistant and friend who reads all my pages first and never panics.

Medina Rosner and *Harris Rosner,* who provide pleasure and inspiration.

As I researched the background of *Dazzle* many generous people helped me by providing invaluable answers to my questions, others by giving me the chance to observe them at work. To all of them, I am wholeheartedly grateful.

Mrs. Alice O'Neill Avery, a truly great lady of California, whose memories of days long gone were fascinating, moving and inspiring.

Mr. Anthony R. Moiso, President and Chief Executive Officer of the Santa Margarita Company. Tony Moiso, Mrs. Avery's son, a seventh-generation Californian and a leading force in Orange County, is doing much to preserve the quality of a way of life that is fast disappearing.

Dr. William P. Frank, Associate Curator of Western Manuscripts at the Huntington Library, who helped me to solve pieces of the puzzle.

Dr. Judy Rosner, Professor at the Graduate School of Management, University of California, Irvine, who is a wonderful friend and a knowledgeable guide into the mysteries of Orange County.

Nancy Dackstrand, who knew so much about the search for Spanish land grants.

Gep Durenberger, antiquarian extraordinary of San Juan Capistrano, who opened many doors of Orange County to me.

Joanne Jaffe, Editor-in-Chief of *Angeles* magazine.

Tricia Burlingham, photographer's representative, a patient, enthusiastic source of information and explanation.

DAZZLE

A Bantam Book / published in association with Crown Publishers, Inc.

*PRINTING HISTORY
Crown edition published 1990
Bantam edition / February 1992*

*Grateful acknowledgment is made to PolyGram International Publishing,
Inc. for permission to reprint an excerpt from "Smoke Gets in Your Eyes."
Music by Jerome Kern and lyrics by Otto Harbach. Copyright © 1933 by
PolyGram International Publishing, Inc. (3500 West Olive Avenue, Suite
200, Burbank, CA 91505). Copyright Renewed. International Copyright
Secured. All Rights Reserved. Used by Permission.*

ISBN 0-553-29376-1

Published simultaneously in the United States and Canada

PRINTED IN THE UNITED STATES OF AMERICA

OPM 0 9 8 7 6 5 4 3 2 1

DAZZLE

JUDITH KRANTZ

BANTAM BOOKS

NEW YORK · TORONTO · LONDON · SYDNEY · AUCKLAND

He utterly forgot that he was being photographed while Jazz worked away in a hypnotic silence broken only by the languid melodies of the classical guitar. After minutes had passed, his memories suddenly faded and abruptly he noticed the intent, mesmerizing photographer, her skeins of hair rippling down on both sides of the camera, her tanned legs brazen and bare under the short skirt. Sam Butler moved restlessly on the velvet of the sofa, and Jazz got an entire roll of the most stunningly sensual and dangerously lustful pictures anyone was ever to take of him.

This sitting's over, she thought in alarm, as he began to unbuckle the belt of the raincoat.

"Time to change film," Jazz declared briskly, straightening up. But the tall Australian had moved quickly and caught her.

"Ever tried this sofa?" he asked, pulling her down beside him.

"You're being unprofessional," Jazz spoke haughtily, even as she tried to kick away his legs with her bare feet. He laughed, adroitly changed the position of his arms, slipped out of both sides of the raincoat and threw it down on the floor.

"I said to take off your clothes," Jazz cried in outrage, "not your underwear."

"You didn't ask if I wore any." Now both of his hands were busily taking off her clothes while the full weight of his muscular, naked body made her struggles futile. She should have taken that self-defense course, Jazz thought in panic, as she felt him quickly undo the one button of her smock and take one breast in his hand. . . .

DAZZLE

1

In California an earthquake isn't considered to have happened until people are able to get to a phone and discuss it. If friends aren't at home, any stranger who answers the phone will provide a satisfactory ear, so long as that person has also experienced the quake and can validate its existence. A dentist's answering service, a temporary file clerk, a children's nurse are all satisfactory repositories of post-earthquake exchanges. Only after such a conversation can a Californian be satisfied with the earthquake and put it into its right place in the scheme of things.

Today was such a day. There had been a distinct but insignificant temblor as Jazz Kilkullen drove to work and traffic had been tied up for an hour, but, alone in her car, with its long-unrepaired radio, she had only the irritated faces of strangers in other cars for verification. Finally Jazz pulled her classic 1956 turquoise and cream Thunderbird into her usual lot, vaulted out of the driver's seat and ran full tilt up the street from the lot to Dazzle, her photography studio.

Of all days to be late, she thought furiously, as she barnstormed past the occasional strolling couple who stepped back out of her way and stopped to stare at her. These tourists in Venice, California, already pleasantly alarmed by the minor but definite movement of the earth, were in a mood to be gratified by anything they encountered in this curious sideshow of a neighborhood. The sight of Jazz only confirmed Venice's reputation for eccentricity and authenticity.

On this slightly ominous but otherwise ordinary Friday morning in September of 1990, this girl in full stride, who ran as if the street belonged to her, wore the kind of improbable hat they'd seen in photographs of women at Royal Ascot, a big black straw cartwheel, its brim laden with giant, floppy red poppies. Her red wool skirt flared five inches above her knees, revealing long, glorious legs in black hose and high-heeled black shoes. She must be *someone* special, they decided as they looked after her. Who but someone special would sport such feature-concealing, outrageously big sunglasses, who but someone special would run with such a single-minded lack of awareness that anyone was in her path?

Jazz arrived at the street entrance to Dazzle, flung open the double glass doors and confronted Sandy, the receptionist.

"Did you feel the quake, Sandy? How long has he been here?" she demanded breathlessly. "Damn! I hate to keep people waiting!"

"It's O.K. One of his people just called from the limo. He'll be late, at least another hour, probably more."

"He'll be late? *He'll* be late? After I almost went starkers in that traffic jam? Didn't you feel that quake? He's got one hell of a nerve. I hope you told them that."

"Sure I felt the quake. It was just your ordinary shiver. I called my sister in the Valley and she didn't know there had been one. Jazz, if you had a car phone, I could have let you know that he wasn't here," Sandy complained. She lived basically by the grace and favor of the telephone, and the fact that Jazz refused to profane the interior of that old heap she drove so proudly with such an indispensable instrument was a constant irritation to her.

"You're right, as usual," Jazz replied, grinning like a cocky urchin who had just committed some undiscoverable mischief. She took a deep breath and recovered her habitual insouciance, holding herself with the invisible discipline and confidence of a bareback rider in the circus who makes the most difficult balancing act look easy.

She took the stairs two at a time to her second-floor studio where the walls of the outer office were covered with large framed photographs. Each frame contained two shots of the same subject, one taken during the first minutes of a session, when the subject was still suspicious, stiff and balky, determined to project a cherished persona, the other taken at the end of the session, when the subject had been transformed into a spontaneously reacting, openly human creature whose inner truth had been revealed by Jazz's camera.

François Mitterrand, Isabelle Adjani, Princess Anne, Jesse Jackson, Marlon Brando, Muammar Khaddafy, Woody Allen: the more difficult it was to establish a relationship, the more pleased Jazz was with the results. Pictures of subjects who had already established a deep complicity with the camera, from Madonna to the Pope, were never displayed on the walls of this studio in which she had become one of the most successful celebrity portrait and advertising photographers in the United States.

"Anybody home?" Jazz called as she entered the studio proper, kicking off her shoes, throwing her hat on the floor, and sinking down on a Victorian sofa, an incongruous prop in the enormous white-walled space whose huge windows looked out onto the Pacific Ocean, which was flat and soothingly blue.

Five years ago Jazz and two other photographers, Mel Botvinick, a top food photographer, and Pete di Constanza, who specialized in car photography, with their representative, Phoebe Milbank, had bought an empty building built in the style of the Piazza San Marco, on Windward Boulevard in Venice, right on the boardwalk, only steps from the beach. It had been a bank before it had been abandoned and allowed to run down for forty years. They were able to get a good buy on the noble hulk, which had been rechristened Dazzle and converted into a complex consisting of three large studios, an office for Phoebe and plenty of working room for their assistants and studio managers.

Toby Roe, Jazz's chief assistant, a slim young man wearing black from head to toe, emerged from behind the door that led from the studio into the offices, dressing rooms and filing space.

"Hey, are you O.K.? Was it the quake that made you late or is today's job that much of a bore?" Toby asked.

"We didn't blame you when you didn't show," Melissa Kraft added. Jazz's second assistant was dressed exactly like Toby, and like him carried three cameras. "When you think about it, what is he but just another lowlife macho creep with a good agent?"

"Scum," Jazz agreed. "Your basic theatrical slime. Let's never forget, this guy's an actor. *Just* an actor. You guys feel the quake?"

"Yep," Toby said. "Nothing to get alarmed about. I called my mom but I got her service so I left a message and phoned my brother and told him all about it—he'd slept right through it."

They smiled at each other, the earthquake disposed of and already forgotten. In spite of the wry objectivity that photographers traditionally prefer to maintain toward their subjects, as if they were puppetmasters to the world, all three of them knew the others were excited about the shoot scheduled for today.

In a series of startling performances, Sam Butler, an Australian, had suddenly eclipsed Tom Cruise as the most seductive and talented young actor to emerge from any country in years. Unlike most American stars, he had not yet consented to promote his movies with portrait sittings for magazine covers, so today's cover shoot for *Vanity Fair* was a coup.

"Sandy says he won't be here for an hour," Jazz told her assistants.

"She let us know when his people called," Toby answered. "That's why young Melissa here isn't foaming at the mouth. She's saving it."

"Toby's planning to ask him where he gets his hair cut," Melissa said, busy with a lens. Toby didn't bother to respond. He was looking at Jazz, relaxed momentarily on the sofa, as he repeated to himself the mantra with which he started each day of work:

"Thank God I'm never going to fall in love with Jazz. She's rich and famous and she's my boss. I'm never going to fall in love with Jazz." Armed with this mantra, which he sometimes had to repeat many times if a shoot was held up and his concentration on the job slackened, Toby had managed to stick out two years of hopeless lovesickness.

At least she'd never suspected, he thought as he glanced at her, trying, as he always did, to understand the riddle of her face. He'd been a photographer since his early teens and Toby still couldn't quite capture in his mind's eye, once and for all, what it was about Jazz that fascinated him so. The nature of his work had accustomed him to looking at women whose central fact in life was their beauty, many of them more beautiful than Jazz, and younger than she was at twenty-nine, but hers was the one face that he'd never been able to look away from with a sense of visual finality, of repletion, of aesthetic surfeit, as if he had seen as much as he needed to see.

Jazz, creature of flesh and blood that she was, had surfaces that could only be compared to a topaz, that rare gem flashing a rich gold with an undertone of warm brown, those precious crystals which the ancient Scots thought were a cure for lunacy. But had those ancients ever seen a woman with golden eyes, Toby wondered? Had they ever looked at a woman whose tawny plumage of golden brown hair looked amber in some lights and chestnut in another, hair that

hung all the way below her shoulders in the kind of
artless, childlike ripples that other women sometimes
possess, but only at their temples or foreheads? Had
they ever had to deal with a woman whose skin
seemed always faintly tanned, with a tint that gave her
cheeks the blush of an apricot-hued Brandy rose, a
golden pink blush very different from that of any other
rose in any garden? If so, he felt sorry for them, as
sorry as he felt for himself.

Above her golden eyes Jazz's brown brows
formed unusually strong and level lines, as precise as
those drawn by a ballerina. They shot straight up
when she was surprised, provoked or amused, and
often only the expression in her eyes would signal the
difference in her emotions. Below the firm, independent and potentially impudent line of her nose, her
mouth was a study in contrast, her upper lip delicate,
almost childish, her lower lip too full, too frank, too
swollen for classic beauty.

For with it all, Toby reminded himself, Jazz Kilkullen was a hussy, an electric hussy, a fabulous flirt,
a player of games, a mistress of disguise, a creature of
many moods, a teller of truths, a lady of accomplishments, and as hardworking a photographer as any he'd
ever heard of.

Thank God I'm never going to fall in love with
Jazz, Toby repeated to himself as he checked the cameras for the tenth time that morning. Jazz owned a
score of cameras she rarely used but today she'd told
them to load all six of her Canon T 90's with the multiple metering system that gave her three computer-
ized options for focusing. She was playing it as safe as
he'd ever known her to, for normally she scorned automatic focus.

While Melissa counted the host of easily movable
lights and tiny flashes, all self-powered by battery
packs, she observed Jazz's outfit, from the Cecil Beaton hat to the short, skittish skirt and thin red wool
blouse cut like an oversized smock, apparently held
together with one giant jet button. She'd expected that
her boss would think today's challenge called for the

combat boots, the Army-Navy store sailor pants and the five-hundred-dollar Harry Truman Hawaiian shirt, worn with dangling antique garnet earrings and delicate, precious old rings on each finger; one of the getups that she sometimes wore to confuse and control a new victim.

But apparently Jazz had decided on the ladies-lunch-at-the-Bistro-Garden approach, another manipulation tactic, relentlessly overdressed in a way in which no other photographer would feel comfortable.

Jazz never just put on her clothes in the morning, Melissa thought with exasperated admiration. She overdressed, underdressed, fancy-dressed, screw-you-dressed or didn't bother to dress at all in her brightly colored rugby shirts that she mixed with jeans when she wanted to look as if she could be safely ignored. Melissa was wise to her boss. She knew that if Jazz really intended to be ignored she'd wear all black as Melissa did herself. One day, when she too was a famous photographer, she'd throw out every black thing she'd ever owned, Melissa vowed silently as she went to answer the intercom from the desk downstairs.

"They're on their way up!" Sandy shrilled as the intercom rang again. "Now they're almost on time—honestly, don't you think they could have called?"

Melissa hung up without answering. "Battle stations," she said warningly to Jazz, who was still lying on the sofa. She raced into the office to summon Sis Levy, an efficient young redhead who was Jazz's office manager.

"I was almost asleep," Jazz protested, yawning, but she got up and into her hat and shoes two seconds before a group of people spilled out of the elevator.

"Come on in," she said, as Melissa and Toby faded into the background. She had never seen such a large entourage, not even when she'd photographed Stallone and Streisand together for *Rolling Stone*. And they were all female, like members of a cult that dooms young widows to wear deepest mourning, skirts falling either to mid-calf and worn with flat,

ankle-high boots, or cut just below the crotch and
worn with black tights and spike heels.

"I'm Tilly Finish, from the magazine," the oldest
of them said, coming forward to introduce herself.
"Sam will be right up. He saw some sort of car downstairs and he wanted to take a better look at it."

"That's my punishment for having a car photographer on the first floor," Jazz said pleasantly, as she
mentally damned Pete di Constanza for not hustling
the new Ferrari Testarossa inside his shop under
wraps the way he did when prototypes arrived. Sometimes the cars leaving and entering his studio became
such an attractive nuisance that she and Mel Botvinick
had to complain formally to Phoebe Milbank.

Tilly Finish started to introduce the other women
who gradually filled the entrance to the studio. Jazz
and Sis Levy shook hands all around. Three of them
came from the public relations agency that handled
Sam Butler; two more were stylists, each with an assistant, all holding garment bags with items from the
vast wardrobe Sam Butler might deign to wear; Tilly
herself had two assistants, both of them carrying cel-
lular phones; there was a hair lady and a lady makeup
artist. Jazz counted an even dozen, all young, all
pretty, all smiling tentatively, like a newspaper photograph of the wives of a renegade Mormon of the old
school.

Sis Levy took over the crowd, directing the stylists' assistants and the hair and makeup women to the
dressing rooms, so that they could dispose of their
burdens, but the others refused to move, standing
about, watching the elevator, like nervous Secret Service men who've lost the President.

Jazz looked at her watch. It was almost lunchtime
and they were far from starting. "Carry on," she told
Sis as she zipped out and clattered down the staircase.
On the street floor of Dazzle, Jazz rushed out of the
building and around to the side where Pete's studio
had its delivery entrance. The double garage doors,
big enough to accommodate the largest truck, gaped

open and inside she saw two men walking intently around the Ferrari as if it were the first car to have been invented. Henry Ford had a lot to answer for, she thought grimly, or was it the Wright Brothers?

Jazz walked up to Sam Butler, as bumptiously as a winning colt. "I'm Jazz Kilkullen," she announced, extending her hand. He took it without looking at her. "Right, I'll be with you later," he said, and turned his back, opened the door of the hundred-and-fifty-thousand-dollar car and slid behind the wheel. "Would you mind if I took this baby out for a spin? I've been wanting one but I don't know, it might be a bit too flash."

"It's perfect for you," Jazz said, firmly grappling him by his upper arm with her strong fingers, pinioning him by the tweed of his jacket. "If you don't drive the best, who should? Let's come back later, shall we? You have a fan-club meeting upstairs." Angrily he turned to look at her. She gave him a deadpan stare. He was so beautiful that it was simply silly, Jazz thought, a minor genetic joke. She refused to try to deal with this large blond creature visually until she was behind a camera.

"They can bloody well wait," Sam Butler said.

"But I can't."

"You have all day."

"Half of it's gone. This is a cover shot, remember?"

"I don't want to do the thing anyway."

"But I do." Jazz tilted her chin so that the brim of her hat no longer shadowed her face, looked him straight in the eye and smiled at him, half siren, half London bobby, wholly excessive. "Later you can have all the Ferraris you can eat," she said with a clear-cut twist of promise. "Let's let Pete do his job and we'll do ours, so you can come back to this car just as soon as possible. All right, Mr. Butler?"

"Call me Sam," the Australian said, leaving Pete without a glance. Jazz turned back to the car photographer. "If you do this once more, honey-child, I won't let you help audition the girls for the *Sports Illustrated* swimsuit issue," she warned him before she followed Sam Butler up to her studio.

Five minutes later, as the widows' club fluttered purposefully but distractingly around the actor, Jazz conferred with Sis Levy and appeared at Tilly Finish's elbow.

"This isn't going to work, is it, Tilly?"

"What do you mean?"

"Now, now, don't play innocent," Jazz said with a conspiratorial smile. "Obviously you've run into this before yourself, a woman of your sophistication. All these little girls are in heat. One can't blame them but they're useless. Total brain drain into the lower parts, wouldn't you agree? Look, if you could just take them all downstairs to lunch at 72 Market Street —I've reserved a table, and they'll put it on my bill— I'll send Sis and my assistants with you and by the time lunch is over I'll have the cover shot."

"Don't you need your assistants?"

"Everything's prepared. Six cameras loaded and ready. Anyway, I was an assistant for years. . . . I can still load film in the dark underwater upside down, and I always do all the lighting myself."

"But Sam isn't dressed yet," Tilly squeaked. "I haven't decided what he should wear. New York left it up to me."

"He'll look great, I promise. Anyway he doesn't need makeup or hair . . . you know they want a natural look. The important thing is to get the cover—I simply have to have the studio to myself for a few hours. Don't forget, we still have another outdoor color shot and three black-and-whites for the body of the story and he's only given us today and next Wednesday. We'll be lucky if he even shows up next week—he's not the most obedient boy, your Mr. Butler."

"My Mr. Butler," Tilly Finish said wistfully. "Wouldn't that be the day?" She clapped her hands. "Everybody, lunch break. Sam, I'll leave you here if you don't mind, to get started."

In minutes the studio was empty.

"Thanks," the actor said. "They were beginning to make me nervous. Why are they all in black? Did somebody die?"

"It's political," Jazz assured him, dismissing the whole question of young Hollywood chic. "If you're hungry I'll make you a sandwich before we start."

"I never eat lunch. It slows me down."

"Good. There should be a Versace raincoat in the dressing room. Would you try it on for me?"

"Yeah, right. I fancy that myself."

And well he might, Jazz thought. Sam Butler was the most astonishingly handsome actor she had seen since photographs of the young Gary Cooper. He must be the beginning of the swing of the pendulum away from the actors whose all-too-ordinary faces were described as "lived in": Richard Dreyfuss, Al Pacino, Robert de Niro, Billy Crystal and Donald Sutherland. He didn't suffer from the not-lived-in-enough syndrome that afflicted Tom Hanks, Tim Robbins, Charlie Sheen, Dean Stockwell and Michael Keaton, nor did he come under the heading of the neighborhood that was too marginally scruffy to be lived in at all, like Mickey Rourke, Patrick Swayze or Sean Penn.

Sam Butler was flawless, Jazz decided, and shrugged. A Grand Canyon of manhood, blond and blue-eyed in a way that defined those attributes for all time. Definitely not her type.

He returned with the raincoat tightly belted, the collar turned up.

"You're too bulky, Sam," Jazz said. "I don't want a stuffed-raincoat shot, I want a Butler shot. But I like the coat on you. Let me think . . . I know there's an idea in here somewhere . . . could you go back and take off that bulky jacket and put the coat back on? In fact, take off all your clothes while you're at it."

"Are you some kind of nutter?"

"Think of the raincoat as a bathrobe. You wouldn't be dressed in a bathrobe, would you?"

"Of course not."

"So what's the difference?"

"I don't know, but there's got to be one," the actor said, puzzled.

"Oh," Jazz coaxed, "just try it." She spoke capriciously, candidly inviting him to indulge her whim and join her in her wayward fancy. His resistance collapsed.

"What are you going to take off?" The actor was ready to bargain.

"My hat? My shoes? No? Not enough? What about my . . . pantyhose?"

"Done."

Jazz shook with laughter while he undressed. Sam Butler returned, belted, buckled, buttoned, looking fifty pounds lighter. His expression was set into a James Bondian toughness. By that time Jazz had rolled the Victorian sofa close to one of the windows. She was barelegged, and classical guitar music was playing on the tape deck.

"Better," she said, all business. "Lie down on this."

"Lie down on a sofa in a raincoat? I'd rather stand."

"I have to use this gorgeous light. See the way it's flooding in the window and pooling on the sofa? You can't get that quality any other place in the studio. The light'll be gone in half an hour or so and we'll be all finished."

"I had a dentist like you once. Quite like you, and quite unlike you," he remarked, sitting down on the sofa, bolt upright.

"Dentist? Where? Back home?"

"Yeah. Near Perth. He was my uncle so naturally I had to go to him, special family price. He was pretty good, actually. Painless. I'd never be in flicks without the job he did on my teeth." Butler's jaw had relaxed and he leaned back against the sofa, as if remembering, not too unhappily, the cut-rate work that had given him his twenty-million-dollars-for-three-pictures smile.

Jazz took a quick Polaroid and gave it to him. She believed in letting the subject know immediately that you were willing to let him see the work in progress, and veto it if he hated it. With image-exchanging you were halfway home.

"Not bad," he said, looking at it carefully. "It's . . . different, not one of those Christ-aren't-I-gorgeous shots that everyone else wants. Maybe it's the raincoat."

"Something about the neck is still too uptight." Jazz shook her head thoughtfully. "You look bunchy around the throat. Open about five buttons, spread the collar wide and put your head back on the sofa. Maybe put your feet up on the arm of the sofa there and stretch out all the way across to the other end—get comfortable and pretend it's a day at the beach, and you're lying in the sun at Surfer's Paradise . . ."

"You've been to Australia?" he asked, following her directions without question.

"Last year . . . I loved it . . ." Jazz said, moving around with her first Canon, shooting quickly, her movements minimal, unalarming and all but invisible. She loved what she saw. The open coat revealed his magnificent bare chest, the elaborately carved rosewood of the sofa was an inspired frame to the sleek Italian coat, his blond hair on the dark velvet created a devilishly tantalizing contrast.

"Don't you get homesick?" Her voice was low, without emphasis.

"Shit yes. I go home whenever I can."

"Tell me about your family."

"They're super. My mother still makes me take out the rubbish and my sisters still introduce me to nice girls and my dad still worries about whether I'm saving money, so I give him all my business manager's reports. Every weekend I play football for two whole days with the team I used to play center for. . . . Yeah, I've got to go home again soon."

His homesick voice trailed off, his expression vulnerable, wistful, yearning. Sam Butler looked as wildly romantic as Olivier's Heathcliff as he fell quiet, thinking of the great football matches of long ago. Jazz padded about noiselessly, picking up one camera after another whenever she came to the end of a roll of film. Sam Butler had stopped being laughably flawless and became entirely real as his eyes filled with memory of a place and people fifteen thousand miles away.

He utterly forgot that he was being photographed while Jazz worked away in a hypnotic silence broken only by the languid melodies of the classical guitar. After minutes had passed, his memories suddenly faded and abruptly he noticed the intent, mesmerizing photographer, her skeins of hair rippling down on both sides of the camera, her tanned legs brazen and bare under the short skirt, her full breasts swaying slightly under the red wool smock that was almost transparent in the light that flooded from the window. Sam Butler moved restlessly on the velvet of the sofa, refocused his eyes, returned to the present moment and Jazz got an entire roll of the most stunningly sensual and dangerously lustful pictures anyone was ever to take of him.

This sitting's over, she thought in alarm as he began to unbuckle the belt of the raincoat.

"Time to change film," Jazz declared briskly, straightening up. But the tall Australian had moved quickly and caught her.

"Ever tried this sofa?" he asked, pulling her down beside him. With one arm he pinioned her firmly down so that she couldn't move her upper body, and with the other he shrugged out of one shoulder of his raincoat.

"You're being unprofessional." Jazz still spoke haughtily even as she tried to kick away his legs with her bare feet. He laughed, adroitly changed the position of his arms, slipped out of both sides of the raincoat and threw it down on the floor.

"I said to take off your clothes," Jazz cried in outrage, "not your underwear."

"You didn't ask if I wore any." Now both of his hands were busily taking off her clothes while the full weight of his muscular, naked body made her struggles futile. She should have taken that self-defense course, Jazz thought in panic while she tried to find a way to thrash out at him and do some damage. She'd made sure that nobody would hear her if she screamed. Too clever by half, she thought confusedly, as she felt him quickly undo the one button of her smock and take one breast in his hand even though her arms and legs were still helplessly flattened to the sofa by the entire weight of his long body.

"Stop!" she shouted, looking for a part of him she could bite.

"No woman ever said that to me before."

"Egomaniac!"

"Truth," he said, shutting her mouth with a kiss.

Suddenly the sofa bucked beneath Jazz's struggling body, throwing them both to the floor. The entire studio swayed sickeningly around them, the floor lurched with a rending noise, doors banged loudly, the fearsome sound of heavy objects hurtling across the room was everywhere, and Jazz and Sam found themselves huddled together on the floor, clutching each other in speechless, shocked terror for endless seconds while the upheaval continued.

"What the fuck?" he whispered, when the building stopped moving. Jazz jumped quickly to her feet with the aplomb of a native Californian, checked first for broken glass and ran to the window, still wearing only her skirt.

"I'm getting the hell out of here," Sam Butler shouted.

"Stay where you are! It's not safer in the street. These old buildings can fall on you. We'd better look and see if a tidal wave is coming—in this neighborhood there's always that possibility."

"*Tidal wave?*" His voice rose.

"Damn right, it should be right out there," Jazz answered with conviction, pointing toward the ocean and leaning out of the window so he wouldn't see her lips twitch upward at the corners. Aftershocks, for certain, she thought, but not a tidal wave. Not this time, anyway. It hadn't been the Big One. From the dressing room she heard the unmistakable sounds of a man cursing as he hastily stuffed himself into his clothes.

"If you need more pictures, we'll do them on high ground," he yelled at her as he headed toward the door.

"And in a crowd," Jazz shouted after him. "Now I know why you have a reputation for being irresistible."

He turned, indignantly. "You haven't been very nice to me. Not at all. If I weren't too much of a gent, I'd tell you to go fuck yourself."

"*You*, Sam Butler, will never get another chance," Jazz laughed, arms covering her breasts. "And hey, throw me my hat, will you, on your way out?"

What *would* they do without me? Phoebe Milbank, partner in Dazzle, and business representative for Jazz Kilkullen, Mel Botvinick and Pete di Constanza, asked herself that familiar question as she spread a thick layer of cream cheese on an onion bagel. She envisioned herself wearing the trim, starched uniform of a proper old-time British nanny, pushing a large, gleaming, navy blue baby carriage, a Rolls-Royce of baby carriages. As she came to a street crossing, with her three infantile charges safely tucked under a monogrammed coverlet, cooing and burbling to each other, she would merely gesture with one hand and a policeman would salute her respectfully, bringing a line of impatient, speeding cars to a total halt until she had safely, and in her own good time, reached the opposite curb and remounted the sidewalk.

In her sharply critical mind, which was entirely free of any trace of an inferiority complex, there was no doubt that left to themselves her photographers would all starve. She was their all-knowing guide in a howling, unfriendly wilderness, that of the treacherous, complicated world of advertising and magazines in which photographs were offered for sale. All their creative powers would be as nothing if she were to desert them, for they were essentially helpless and hopelessly unable to manage their own affairs, like children in a burning building waiting for a fireman to come and save them. This situation was exactly as it should be and as she intended it to remain.

These pleasant thoughts occupied Phoebe during the first of the ten minutes that she scheduled for reflection, right before the monthly Saturday-morning meeting of the partners in Dazzle. This pre-meeting time with herself was sacred. It put her in the right frame of mind for any problems that might arise during the conference to come.

Phoebe got up and bounced around her office, rearranging the low-slung chairs that enabled her to look down upon everyone else from the tall chair that stood behind her desk. She was a tiny, shrewd, moppet-headed figure, with layer upon layer of bright yellow hair that had been fashionably distressed, at great cost, almost but not quite to the point of being ruined.

She was satisfied with her world. Her hair was ideal. Her pert, witty face that gave no clue to her crafty brain, was ideal. Her lean body was as close to ideal as any Twentieth Century Californian female could dream of. Every single one of her vertebrae was visible under her thin sweater, her hipbones poked sharp angles in her short knitted skirt, and no matter what she ate she never gained an ounce. At thirty-eight she knew that she could be mistaken, at first glance, for a cheerleader at UCLA.

Phoebe chose a fresh water bagel from the pile on the platter on her desk and larded it thickly with chive cream cheese. She was not, thank heaven, what she ate, she reflected. No, every photographer's rep was who she represented. Like a horse trainer, her own status was established by her stable.

Phoebe, for all her sense of superiority, was free of unwarranted conceit. She had an acutely accurate

notion of her worth, and of that of others. Her own
charges were the hottest trio in town, each at the red-
hot peak of the profession. Without her they wouldn't
have reached this point. Of course she wouldn't be
where she was without them. But that essentially was
beside the point. If not Jazz, Mel and Pete, three others would be in her stable.

Phoebe glanced at her watch. The meeting would
start in five minutes. Still time to take stock, as she
liked to do each month, to make sure that nothing was
gaining on her in a fast-growing business that changed
month by month.

Each one of her partners was a maverick, each a
demon when it came to getting the shot; and each—
and this was the most important thing about them—
each one of them was far, far on the other side of *safe*.

Safe, in photography today, was the only four-
letter word left, as far as Phoebe was concerned.
Every photographer with a decent portfolio could do
safe, but only a few photographers in the game would
consistently push beyond safe, into unexplored territory, and pull it off, without getting artsy-craftsy or
blurring the client's intention. And when they *did* go
beyond safe, didn't they always turn to her, their rep,
to bring them back home a little, to keep them from
being scared to death? Would they dare to be as controversial as they could be without knowing that she
approved?

It wasn't a question of technique, God knew. Two
hundred photographers had technique, and another
two hundred had taste; many millions—even civilians
—could take pretty pictures. But her guys? Each one
produced work that could be identified instantly by all
the best photo buyers and art directors in the business.
They were to the camera what any truly original
painter was to canvas.

It had to do with two things, Phoebe mused, with
two things she could identify: uniqueness of point of
view and knowledge of lighting. No good knowing
how to light anything from a spark plug to Michelle
Pfeiffer without having a point of view. No good hav-

ing a point of view without a total command of the
almost infinite possibilities of lighting.

And then there was that third thing she couldn't
exactly put a name to and neither could they. It was
that third thing—some people called it, tamely, originality—but she thought of it as *outrageousness*—that
made Jazz, Mel and Pete the best. There were too
many merely good, capable, proficient photographers
around today. Unless a photographer was willing, no,
not just willing, but absolutely desperate to *exceed* the
known limits of film, each and every time, he or she
could never command the highest fees. Mel, Pete and
Jazz had equals but no superiors, she thought, intent
on fairness. A handful of equals each, it went without
saying, belonging to a rep as good as she, of whom
there were but three in California.

Any would-be rep would have found it impossible
to find such photographers in Los Angeles fifteen
years ago, Phoebe thought soberly, glad but not surprised that she had been born in the ideal time and
place.

Almost all the top photographers used to live and
work in New York. But that had changed swiftly,
particularly in the fields of food, cars and celebrity
portraits, and now much of the major talent was concentrated in Los Angeles. She had been in on it from
the beginning.

Twelve years earlier, when she had just turned
twenty-six, Phoebe had worked as photo assistant to
Evan Jones, a portrait photographer who made a decent living taking flattering pictures of rich women to
give to their husbands for Christmas.

His real genius lay in retouching. He never
showed raw contact prints to his clients. First he made
his own selection, ruthlessly throwing out all but the
best photographs. Then he did some exceedingly discreet work with an airbrush, work so impossible to
detect that he presented the contacts as if they were
unretouched. Only after the flattered subject had chosen her favorite contact did he really go to town with

the airbrush and the tiny paintbrushes with which he added and subtracted; longer lashes, veinless hands, brighter pupils, thinner nostrils, lusher lips, smaller chins, perfect necks.

Though clever and kind, Evan had had a poor head for business. His accounts were badly kept and, worse, he had no idea of what constituted a fair price for his work. One day Phoebe, who had quickly realized that she didn't have the talent or the patience to become an outstanding photographer, simply took over Evan's office and began to run his business.

In a day she replaced herself with a far better assistant than she had ever been. She took his client list and called each of the women on it, reminding them that their old photographs were dated. She doubled his prices without asking him, knowing that his clients would only assume that he was asking more because he was worth more. Phoebe's sister, office manager for one of the top plastic surgeons in Hollywood, and a member in good standing of the office-manager mafia, provided an ever-fresh list of women who needed new photographs to replace those that revealed an older face.

Within six months Evan had a long waiting list for portraits, and Phoebe had tripled his prices, keeping twenty-five percent of what he made for her services, a standard amount.

Now she was ready to move Evan into the film industry. She made up presentation books of his most successful portraits and dropped copies off at the offices of every publicist, business manager, makeup artist and hair stylist in Hollywood. She quadrupled his prices.

Female performers of a certain age—an age that began younger and younger every year—began to see Evan's portraits. In less than a year he became the most popular photographer of that inexhaustible subject: women over twenty-one. His photos began to appear in magazine articles and on magazine covers, at the demand of his subjects. A great many women

had never looked so good, and quickly male performers joined their ranks. Phoebe bought herself a two-
door Mercedes 560 in bright yellow to match her hair.

Once Evan was firmly established, Phoebe lost
interest in him. There was only so far he could go,
only so much money she could make as his rep. He
didn't have the desire to change and only the new and
innovative interested her. She found him another rep
in 1980, opened her own small office, and set herself
to an analysis of the subjects of the ads in American
magazines.

There were more ads for food products than any
other category including cosmetics. Next came cars.
Automotive print ads were everywhere as soon as she
started to look for them. Phoebe made herself an expert on the relative merits of food and car photographers and picked out Mel Botvinick and Pete di
Constanza as the two of their species she was prepared to rep.

She bagged the two men quickly, setting her percentage of their fees at one-third. The more she did for
them, the more they needed her. The more she extended a hand, the tighter they grabbed on to it. Without her prudent management of their careers they
would never have dared ask for the money they now
commanded. Whenever there was a job going that
they really coveted, they grew anxious and overeager,
certain that someone else would nab it. At that crucial
point they were willing to cut their own established
fees.

Fat chance of that while she was around, Phoebe
said to herself, smiling. She kept their fees up at all
costs, turning down all low-ball offers even if it meant
an idle day for them. From the time she took them on
she steadily increased their earnings so that they all
commanded the maximum in the business. Pete made
well over a million dollars a year, Mel almost as much.

Jazz Kilkullen, because she shot so much editorial work for magazines, with her name on the photo,
was the only famous one of them. She earned about

four hundred thousand dollars a year, since editorial paid so much less than ads. Still, her potential was incalculable, particularly in cosmetic ads. If only there were two of Jazz: one who would just shut up and photograph models for major cosmetic advertisers, and another who could shoot magazine fashion and celebrities to her heart's content. But there was only one Jazz and that one insisted on doing editorial work because she liked the freedom.

In other ways too, Jazz was a different kind of cat than Mel, who did only the amount of editorial work Phoebe approved, and Pete, who did ads only. Jazz had a tendency toward that quality Phoebe resented the most: independence.

Yes, a damnable tendency, almost certainly due to her background, Phoebe recognized in familiar annoyance. Jazz's father, Mike Kilkullen, owned the last great cattle ranch between Los Angeles and San Diego, sixty-four thousand acres that remained virgin, intact, and undeveloped: a family-run empire as it had been since the days of the Spanish Land Grants. Jazz was an eighth-generation Californian, with old Spanish ranchero blood in her veins, as well as Irish and Swedish. She had always been a problem to control. Phoebe brooded, greedily eating some cream cheese straight, with a plastic spoon. Repping was like being a lion trainer. Just enough kindness, steady authority and fearlessness. *But above all, control.*

The three photographers straggled into Phoebe's office, irritated as usual at this invasion of their Saturday morning.

"How about that quake?" Mel Botvinick asked the group. "I'd just finished setting up to shoot a double spread on soufflés for *Bon Appétit* when it happened. We all had to stay till midnight to do it over. Talk about miserable timing!"

"That's nothing," Pete di Constanza replied. "I was standing on a ladder looking at the top view of the new Ferrari when the thing hit. If I didn't have such fast reactions, I'd be in the hospital today with a broken leg. But it could have been a lot worse—the car could have been hurt. Jazz, what happened to you?''

"Actually it came at a reasonably convenient time, all things considered," Jazz answered. "I wasn't doing anything special."

"Oh, you're all such babies," Phoebe said peevishly. "What's a little local earthquake? In Beverly Hills we barely noticed it."

"Shopping?" Pete asked.

"Getting my hair done, as usual. You know my Friday afternoons are sacred, Pete."

"Yeah, right. Like my Monday and Thursday hours with my shrink. I·can't believe him," Pete di Constanza complained. "The fucker makes a point of driving an old, ugly, beat-up Volvo, like there's something virtuous about it. So when I tell him I've just got the new Countach Anniversary account, guess what he says? 'I thought you only did cars.' The fucker doesn't know what a Countach is! Lamborghini brought it out in 1971, nineteen years ago, it's still the most powerful sports car on the road, and he doesn't fucking *realize*."

"How come you know what your shrink drives?" Mel Botvinick asked.

"I asked him."

"And he told you?" Mel said, puzzled. His shrink never answered questions.

"Yeah, he's not into that Freudian crap. You ask him an ordinary, acceptable question, you get an answer."

"Why are you so sure he thinks the Volvo is a sign of virtue?" Jazz inquired, laughing fondly. Pete di Constanza, from Fort Lee, New Jersey, dressed like a park ranger, looked like a lifeguard in a softporn beach-blanket movie, and lit hunks of metal like a god. He was one of the world's good people.

"I inferred it," Pete said with dignity.

"See, that's why my shrink won't answer questions," Mel said, with a superior sniff. "He doesn't want me to infer anything, he wants me to project."

"That's the guy who also told you not to write down your dreams," Pete objected. "How the hell does he expect you to remember them if you don't write them down?"

"He says I will if they're important."

"Boys, boys," Phoebe interrupted. "Could you save this fascinating discussion of your psyches for some other place?"

Pete subsided into silence. He wouldn't have to be at this time-wasting meeting if Phoebe hadn't persuaded him to invest in the studio. Sure, it was the best investment he'd made in his life, in fact it represented the only real money he'd ever kept, but being a landlord wasn't his style, not even of one-quarter of a building.

Since buying the old bank and converting it had been Phoebe's idea, she made them all show up to discuss the smooth running of Dazzle, on the theory that three photographers couldn't manage to get along without her monthly mediation. Airs and graces! As far as he was concerned, Phoebe had just one clearly defined function in life and that was to free him from petty details so that he could come up with killer shots.

Not just product shots. Any bum in Detroit could take product shots, and a lot of bums did, with cheapo colored smoke and firecrackers and mirror effects that made the car look as if it were part of a Vegas floor show. But if you wanted a shot of a car that caught the existential *essence* of the car? A shot that could convey the ultimate *emotional* experience of driving at 186 miles an hour and get that shot with the car standing still in a studio? A shot that was fucking romantic, a shot that was fucking poetic, a shot that made the car into a God damned icon? You simply had to come to Pete di Constanza.

By the time he spent a few weeks experimenting with some new lighting ideas he had, the new version of the great classic Countach would look as if it had just floated down from a spaceship and was lit from within, the kind of car your leading alien gear head

would be thrilled to drive. If they'd let him take the
prototype out on location there'd be no limit to what
he could do, but this particular prototype was too precious to be let out of doors.

"Minutes of the last meeting—" Phoebe began in
an official voice.

"Read and approved," Mel Botvinick interrupted
hastily.

"So moved," Pete and Jazz yelled simultaneously.

What was it with her, Mel wondered? Did Phoebe
think that she was running a Fortune Five Hundred
company? Come to think of it, with her one-third take
of everything the three of them billed, she made more
money than most top executives in big business could
dream of. She certainly didn't waste it on their re-
freshment, he noticed, looking with disapproval at the
meager platter of bagels, the half-empty plastic containers of cheese and the pitcher of iced tea which she
always insisted she'd brewed but which he knew was
Lipton's presweetened, right out of the can, into
which she'd brought herself to sacrifice a lemon cut
into four pieces and a few ice cubes. She couldn't give
a hoot about food. Mel shuddered as he looked at her
tiny waist and delicate wrists. She could certainly afford to fatten herself up until she'd appeal to a sensible
man, but no, she'd rather be painfully thin.

Still, why grumble? Phoebe was worth the money
she took from him. He shuddered at the thought of
having to go out and solicit an account, of being forced
to venture unprotected into the hard-sell world of
Wesson Oil and frozen pizzas and hustle his book by
himself. Phoebe didn't mind the horrible humiliation
of actually calling up prospective clients and proposing him for a job he'd never even heard of.

Phoebe had a sixth sense that told her exactly
when an account was looking for a fresh approach to
breakfast cereal and she never made him do more than
two fast food shoots a month. No artist could subject
himself to the kind of aggravation you'd have without
a rep and still keep himself in a condition to follow his

calling, for that was what it was. Food photography was a calling, nothing less, like ballet or brain surgery, just different in the details.

"Does anyone have any new business?" Phoebe inquired. Pete was slouched in his chair, making a ridiculous point of looking uncomfortable with his long legs in L.L. Bean hiking boots sprawled awkwardly in front of him. Mel was sitting, as he always did, as close to upright as he could in the slinglike chair, his delicate hands neatly folded on his plumply rounded belly, his light gray shirt uncreased, one black-trousered leg carefully crossed on the other. He dressed like a defrocked monk, she thought, and he looked like one too, with his smoothly barbered hair and his bland features in an egg-shaped face.

"No," they chorused.

"I do," Phoebe said briskly. "I've learned that the Purple Tostada Grande is thinking of selling their place." Moans filled the air.

Everyone who works in a photographer's studio is utterly dependent on take-out food for nourishment. Jazz, Mel and Pete each had a half-dozen different menus from local spots from which they ordered every day for the people who were working in their studios. The Purple Tostada Grande, an inexpensive Mexican place with a large patio directly across the street on the boardwalk, was everyone's favorite. Clients often walked in the door with their mouths already watering for stuffed quesadilla, that flour tortilla grilled and filled with green chilis, onions, sour cream, tomatoes and cheese; or the burrito combo with beans and beef, to say nothing of the famous shrimp in a basket served with fresh guacamole and fries on the side.

"How can they do this to us?" Jazz wailed.

"It's a disgrace," Pete sputtered. "I have clients coming from Japan and Germany who are already thinking about their Tostada lunches. I'll lose face with them."

"If we don't have Tostada, my clients may start eating the stand-in food," Mel worried. "As if I don't have enough trouble with clients who say they 'just want a taste' and pop the hero food into their mouths.''

"Look at it as an opportunity," Phoebe said. "Why don't we buy it ourselves? That way we can keep it in business and maybe make a little money."

"No way," Pete said promptly. "It's bad enough owning part of a building, but a restaurant, no way."

"Jazz?" Phoebe continued her poll.

"I'll pass. I'm not investment-minded at the moment."

"Mel?"

"You're kidding, aren't you? I shoot the stuff all day. I have the best-equipped kitchen in the world in my studio. I don't want to go into the food *business*." He looked offended.

"So you don't mind if I buy it myself?" Phoebe asked.

"Great!"

"Terrific!"

"Good show, Phoebe. Saved by our rep," Jazz applauded.

"Thanks, people. I'll make a note of your approval for the minutes." Phoebe looked cheerful. As she had expected, none of them had the native good sense to realize that every bit of Venice property was rapidly rising in value. Particularly a parcel right on the boardwalk. If she bought it today and didn't do a thing to it, the property could double in a year.

But better yet, the Tostada, with its big patio, was an ideal location for a totally new restaurant, a theme restaurant, something wildly different. Wildly expensive. Valet parking, of course, and a young top chef who was already firmly established somewhere in the American heartland, Chicago for instance, a chef who knew he'd never have arrived until he made it in L.A. Financing would be a snap. There were plenty of big shots who'd put up the money for the new place; everyone in this town wanted to be in on the ground floor of a new restaurant. Tony Bill wasn't the only person around who wanted to own pieces of Venice, California.

"Anyone have anything else to say?" Phoebe chirped.

"Uh," Mel said, and stopped.

"Mel? New business? Are you thinking of upgrading your air conditioning again?" Phoebe asked suspiciously. "We'll have to change the electric panel if you are, I warn you. And we have enough electricity coming in here already to operate a hospital."

"I'm, uh, getting married." He blushed violently.

There was a momentary silence of blank astonishment. Mel, with his total devotion to his work, had kept his private life so silent that they had finally assumed he didn't have one. How could Mel be getting married if none of them had heard about it on the studio grapevine?

"Who?" Phoebe said, startled. She should certainly have been told first, before he made such an important decision.

"Who?" Jazz asked in delight.

"Who?" Pete wanted to know. What kind of guy wouldn't have told him first, before the others?

"Sharon. You all know Sharon." Mel was beaming, now that the news was out.

"Sharon—I should have guessed. Who else is good enough for you?" Jazz said, struggling to get up out of the chair and kiss him. She doted on Mel. Her first job in the business had been with Botvinick.

"Sharon, what a great idea!" Phoebe exclaimed. *She* should have *told* him to marry Sharon, the best food stylist in the business. Now Sharon would know his shooting schedule and would always be available. Sometimes—not often but sometimes—Mel was smarter than she gave him credit for.

"Sharon! The last time you needed her for that *Bon Appétit* Christmas cover she was busy. I still remember the fit you threw. How come you decided to forgive her?" Pete wondered, amazed.

"That was kind of what did it," Mel explained. "When she didn't drop everything for that cover, I got too upset. I mean, let's face it, she's not the only food stylist in the business. I was overreacting. So I talked about it and talked about it with my shrink, because I couldn't figure it out. I don't usually overreact, you can't afford to with food, you have to have an unearthly patience. Anyway, I finally realized that I, uh, felt more than just professional regard for her.''

"What does your shrink think?" Pete wanted to know.

"I don't give a shit," Mel said calmly. "I haven't even told him yet. He probably won't say anything, anyway."

"Mine would definitely be thrilled," Pete affirmed. "He might even ask to see her picture."

"She's a wonderful girl," Jazz said. "Now I understand a discussion we had recently. I was saying that Mel Gibson and Mel Brooks had the same first name but somehow Mel sounded completely different when you thought of them, because you thought of the whole person, not just the 'Mel' part, and she said she thought Botvinick went better with Mel than either of the others. At the time I thought it was just a taste for the exotic."

"We should have a drink to celebrate," Phoebe remarked, getting into the spirit, "but I don't have any more iced tea."

"Remember when iced tea replaced Perrier as the power drink in Hollywood?" Mel's whole body quivered with happiness.

"Remember when Perrier replaced white wine?" Pete chimed in.

"Remember when white wine replaced the martini?" Jazz spoke dreamily. Her father still drank martinis.

There was a silence as they all remembered the martini, a drink lost in lore and fable. Maybe one day it would come back. In New York it had never disappeared, but those poor souls back there didn't care what they put into their bodies. Phoebe recalled them to order.

"If no one has any other business, happy or unhappy, I have a last item to bring up. I have more storage room than I need in my office. It's wasted space and there's a photographer who wants to come in and rent it. He's a photojournalist, does nothing but location work, but he needs an office and a secretary. I assume you have no objections to that. Incidentally, I'll be repping him.''

"Repping him?" Three voices shouted at her. Three bodies heaved themselves out of her sling chairs. Three photographers surrounded her desk and stared down at her in jealous fury.

"Hold it, children. Just hold it right there. No need to make such a thing out of it," Phoebe said in a gentle voice of hidden gratification. She raised her tiny hands in a gesture of command that should have quieted them but didn't. It was exactly as she thought. Sibling rivalry in great big so-called grown-ups. She had foreseen this reaction. What *would* they do without her when they reacted this way to the threat of having just a little bit of attention withdrawn from them?

"What do you mean, not a big thing? How many pieces do you think you can cut yourself into?" Mel said, madder than he'd ever been at Sharon.

"You're overextended with just the three of us! You'll have too much to do!" Pete shouted. "We'll get the short end of the stick.''

"It's not fair, Phoebe, and you know it," Jazz accused her.

"I haven't told you who the photographer is," Phoebe said calmly. "I'm talking about Tony Gabriel.'' She looked up at them with her most guileless and loving smile. They were all so deliciously predictable.

"Gabe—but—he's in Europe, isn't he? Or the Middle East?" Pete asked, suddenly speaking in an excited tone of voice.

"Tony Gabriel? How do you know Tony Gabriel?" Mel said, fury turning to awe.

"I know everybody," Phoebe said smugly. "Gabe's been working out of Paris for the last five years but now he's coming back. He wants to establish a home base in L.A. He'll be gone most of the time, of course, but you guys can understand why I didn't turn him down.''

"Wow, Gabe *here*. Great. That's sensational! I can't wait to talk to him," Pete said.

"I've always wanted to meet him," Mel said. "Tony Gabriel, wow, I've always admired the hell out of Tony Gabriel."

"Then that's settled and we can adjourn for this month." Phoebe stood up as Mel and Pete moved toward the door.

"Just a minute," Jazz said. "This meeting isn't over." Her voice was ringing with rage and she had become ten feet tall. "No way, Phoebe, no way you're going to pull this scam, no way you're going to railroad me into letting Gabriel into this building."

"What's the matter with you?" Phoebe blurted, genuinely astonished. Mel and Pete were silent in amazement at the metamorphosis that had turned Jazz into a pillar of wrath. What was biting her ass? Gabe was a genuine hero, one of the greats, to everyone in the business.

"Nothing's wrong with me. I'm the only one of you with any sense. Tony Gabriel is pure trouble. He's a taker, he's a user, he's a spoiler—he's a sociopath who doesn't happen to have murdered anybody."

"Jazz, you're completely nuts!" Phoebe sputtered.

"I don't give a flying fuck for your uninformed opinion, Phoebe. When we bought this building together we decided that if any one of us felt strongly against some other photographer coming in here and using anyone's space, that would be enough to stop it. So I'm stopping it. Cold stone dead. You cannot, repeat, *not,* rent or lend one inch of space to Gabriel. If he gets a foot in the door of Dazzle, he'll ruin it for all of us. I can't prevent you from repping him, that's your business, but if you do, I'll get another rep myself. It might even take me as long as one phone call. I mean that, Phoebe. Don't make the mistake of thinking I don't.''

"But Jazz, what the—"

"I don't have to explain myself to you or anyone else. You can make your choice." Jazz turned and slammed out of the office with a vicious bang of the door.

In the beginning, Jazz thought, as she rushed upstairs to her studio, shaking with fury, the Devil created the agent and the agent begat the rep.

Naturally he's late, Phoebe Milbank thought, with patience unusual for her, as she waited to meet Tony Gabriel for lunch at 72 Market Street. She frequented the restaurant as often as ten times a week. All her lunches and dinners were business-related and it was imperative to have one excellent place that would always create a table for her at the last minute without question, one place close to her office that would never present her with a check, but keep a well-itemized running account for her, including tips, and send it to the office each week for her IRS files. At Market Street she could call five minutes in advance, knowing that no matter how busy they were, they would find a way to squeeze in the twelve automotive executives from Japan she'd just decided to invite to dinner.

She ordered another iced tea and settled down to wait for Gabe. She could have arrived a half hour later and still been on time, but she wanted some minutes of solitary reflection in which to speculate on Jazz's bizarre performance earlier that day.

Obviously it was a personal matter and she'd get the truth out of Gabe when he came. But her own choice was clear. She didn't intend to lose Jazz. Gabe couldn't possibly make enough money out of photojournalism to replace her third of Jazz's earnings, particularly with her unlimited future.

A photojournalist was the prototypical rolling stone, ready at a phone call's notice to leave for any spot in the world where news was happening. Sometimes they got lucky and took a shot that would be reproduced in most of the newspapers and magazines of the world. It would become a classic. That could indeed mean a bonanza, for the photographer and the rep, but it was a crapshoot. Even for someone as famous as Gabe.

He must be forty now, Phoebe ruminated. Nineteen years ago, when he first went to Vietnam to cover the war, he'd been a kid. Twenty-one years old when he got there, as every student in every photo school knew, and yet, over the next two years, his credit had appeared on more of the great Vietnam photos than that of any other of the army of photojournalists who'd lived through it. After that, his reputation made, he'd roamed the globe: Iran, Poland, Israel, Nicaragua—it made her feel travel-weary just to think of it, but that was the way of his special breed. They were never happy except when they were on the move.

Gabe had an uncanny way of placing himself, camera ready, exactly in the right square foot of ground for the unexpected: the explosion of the *Challenger,* the aftermath of the Jonestown massacre, the fall of Saigon. There was no place he couldn't talk his way into, no plane he wouldn't parachute out of, no assignment too rigorous or problematic. And he had the essential gift of invisibility, that weird ability that the greatest photojournalists must have to stand inches away from a subject and shoot, undisturbed by the subject's awareness of a camera. Gabe had never covered anything as tame as the White House, but he was like that legendary Italian photographer who had managed, time after time, to become the undetected seventh man in the six-man official White House photo pool, the only one not pledged to share his shots with hundreds of other photographers.

"Phoebe mine, kiss me quick." Tony Gabriel had materialized on the banquette next to Phoebe, although she hadn't, she was certain, taken her eyes away from the restaurant door.

He kissed her lips twice, with careful attention, and then held her away from him at arm's length and surveyed her.

"Younger than springtime, you rotten bitch. Can I sleep in the coffin with you tonight?"

"Gabe. Honestly." Phoebe heard herself giggling like a teenager. She would have blushed if she'd had it in her.

Tony Gabriel hadn't changed since the last time she'd seen him, at least two years ago. Still the same rumpled, careless soldier of fortune, still too thin, with weatherbeaten skin, pockets bulging with God knows what—certainly his passport—dark hair that seemed to be mostly cowlicks, victorious brown eyes, a big nose and those two deep vertical creases in his cheeks on either side of his lips that had driven a hundred women bananas. Two hundred. But that didn't make him a sociopath.

"What's that stuff in your glass?" he asked her.

"Iced tea."

"You're a sick, poor, beautiful, pitiful child, I'm going to put you to bed and make you feel all better soon. Better all over, I promise. Trust me, as you people say to each other. Waiter, bring me scotch, neat, double, any brand. What's good to eat here, Phoebe? I'm starving."

"Most people order the meatloaf. It's what this place is known for."

"Ah, Hollywood. The mothers of most of the people who live in this place served them meatloaf because they were poor, they left home because of that eternal meatloaf, they made millions trying to get away from the memory of that meatloaf, and now they come back for it. I'll have a steak. Big, very rare. Now, what happened? Is it all set?"

"No, it is not. Just what did you ever do to Jazz Kilkullen? She doesn't have a high opinion of you, sweetie. In fact she won't let me rep you or even let you rent any space at the place."

"Jazz? Who made her the boss of you?"

"It's not that," Phoebe objected, piqued at his choice of words. "It's just the way we set things up when we bought the studio as partners."

"The renting I can understand. But the repping?"

"She convinced the others that I wouldn't have enough time to rep them properly if I took you on. What's the real story on you and Jazz?"

"Honestly, if I understood it, I'd tell you. Basically Jazz was another groupie. You know about me and my groupies. I don't do anything to encourage them, but how can I help it if they decide to turn me into something I'm not?"

"You've been known to fuck your groupies, Gabe," Phoebe observed gently.

"I didn't say I didn't. That's why God made groupies. But, Phoebe, what are friends for? Friends like us? Did you fight for me?"

"I totally went to bat for you. But it wasn't happening. I'm truly sorry, Gabe. You'd better try one of the big photo agencies. They'd jump at you."

"I don't want a big agency. I've had Gama, I've had Sygma, I've been a part of the best of all that and now I want something else. I want those choice fat, juicy assignments that make a ton of dough and I want you to pick the best of them for me. I want *Smithsonian* magazine, I want the *National Geographic,* I want *Diversions,* and all the other slick travel magazines that you steal from doctors' offices, magazines that send you to some luxurious resort and pay you in solid gold. Maybe I even want to be the Slim Aarons of the 1990s."

"Jesus, Gabe, you're a burnt-out case." Phoebe was stunned. She'd heard him for years ranting on the depravity of such lush assignments.

"Right on. You've got it. I always said you were smart. I've hit the wall. Nineteen years of risking my ass and now there are teams of television cameramen in there before I can even get close to the action. There's no room left for my kind of work, Phoebe. It's on the news before I can get the film back to my editors. Nobody wants actuality photographs anymore. I'm a dinosaur but I have the wits to know it. So go back to Jazz and set her straight and point me toward

the mating of pandas, the joys of snorkeling, inside
Wimbledon and 'A Day in the Life of a Duchess.' ''

"I can't do it, Gabe."

"She's that good, huh?"

"Yep."

"Well, what the hell, she should be. I taught her
everything she knows. Look, don't worry, eat your
meatloaf, I'll take care of it."

"How?"

"Jazz is a problem. A female problem. And I
never saw a female problem I couldn't fix. Just leave
it to me. This steak isn't bad. How's the meatloaf?"

"Just like Mother used to make."

3

Jazz shifted back to cruis-
ing speed, after she passed a truck on the Pacific Coast
Highway, driving south to the Kilkullen Ranch, and
reflected on the job well done for *Vanity Fair*.

On the second day of the shoot with Sam Butler
she had, in various small and subtle ways, allowed him
to feel dominant. She'd worn her Ralph Lauren gen-
teel, gentile, gentry gear, the ankle-length white flannel pleated skirt and high-necked, white Victorian
blouse with her grandmother's cameos, her hair in one
long braid down her back, and she'd spoken softly and
looked at him blushingly and bashfully, and all but
pawed the floor with her foot. Jazz thought she owed
it to him since, on reflection, just possibly, she might
have led him on. Some degree of mental seduction of
the subject, regardless of gender, was always involved
in any good celebrity shot, no photographer, male,
female or gay, could ever deny that, but it was presumed to stop there. God knows, no male photographer from Man Ray to Herb Ritts, on his best day,

could ever have come close to the shots that she had taken on the day of the earthquake.

Why did people say that the camera doesn't lie? It was ridiculously easy to make the camera lie, to project yourself into the image and create it as you thought it should be. Almost every celebrity portrait was a cleverly composed lie, hiding behind an appearance of super-reality. It was far more difficult to free the camera to tell the unvarnished truth, as she had with Butler. Yet there might be small, petty, picky, prudish, evil-minded folk who would claim that she should never have agreed to take off her pantyhose.

Sam Butler had shown up at Dazzle on time for the second day of photos the following Wednesday, as unruffled as if nothing had happened between them and apparently willing to take his chances on another quake. Jazz knew that she could never reach his vulnerability on this shoot, for he would never trust her again, but she hadn't needed to probe twice into his inner self. The essential elemental image that she always sought and always caught in a celebrity shot, that absolute *flare* of an individual personality behind the fame, had been captured in that first day's pictures of the homesick, horny actor. Drilling into the depths of a subject's psyche with a camera was something Jazz did as well as, and usually better than, any other great photographer in the world.

Mel Botvinick had been shooting a fast-food ad when Sam and his attendants had arrived on Wednesday, and in spite of the powerful vents in Mel's third floor studio, the smell of frying grease crept downstairs and distracted everybody.

Jazz had taken the actor outside, on the Ocean Avenue boardwalk, and let him wander, buying from the street vendors and talking to a flock of teenaged girls on roller skates. His face was still not so well known to the average movie fan that she couldn't trust crowd control to her assistants and the efficient, willing widows. The big Australian's beauty had become more animated as he talked to people and at the same time more awesome in contrast to the mortals who surrounded him.

They had finished just before twilight. Thursday had been spent by Jazz and Sis Levy, with a group of creative people from Chiat/Day/Mojo, the innovative advertising agency, scouting locations for a new campaign for Vacheron Constantin, the oldest Swiss watch manufacturers. Location scouting was something Jazz usually left to Sis, but the campaign was so offbeat for the conservative Swiss that the agency people had asked her to go along. On Friday Jazz had decided to book out of the studio and leave for the ranch a day early.

She should be there in less than an hour, she thought, in good time to help her father with the preparations for the great annual Fiesta that was being held Sunday as it had been every September since early in the 1800s.

Jazz's father, Mike Kilkullen, was the fourth in a direct line of Kilkullen men to own and run the ranch, a hundred square miles of property, roughly five times the size of Manhattan Island. This private empire lay south of the small town of San Juan Capistrano. It was an almost fan-shaped piece of land that stretched down toward the Pacific from the mile-high summit of Portola Peak, a summit that could be envisioned as the handle of the fan. From the heights of Portola, the boundaries of the ranch widened steadily on both sides, descending all the way down to the ocean, where the shoreline formed the uneven edge of the fan. Every wave for twenty miles crashed on the Kilkullens' broad sandy beaches; on their wide, horseshoe-shaped harbor; on Valencia Point, the natural breakwater that stretched far out to sea. Beyond Valencia Point waves exploded around large white rocks that stuck up from the ocean floor and defied the Pacific to grind their fantastic shapes down into pebbles. When Jazz was five and her father taught her how to sail her own small boat that was tied up on an inlet at the Kilkullen boathouse, he warned her not to venture out too far since the next landfall after Valencia Point was Hawaii.

One hundred and thirty-eight years earlier, in 1852, another Michael Kilkullen, Jazz's great-great-grandfather, had sailed to America from Ireland, an ambitious, industrious, unencumbered young man with a modest hoard of savings. Like so many others, he had heard that gold had been discovered in California, but unlike most, he was shrewd. Michael Kilkullen realized that he had more chance to make his fortune by selling hardware and lumber to the frenzied miners than by joining them in their hardships. In little more than a dozen years he had accumulated enough capital to venture south to follow his dream.

Land-hunger had always run in the young Irishman's blood, growing stronger by the year once he left the confines of his native island and realized the possibilities of the United States. In the tragic years of 1863 and 1864 the Great Drought had ruined almost all of the California cattle ranchers. Land was desperately cheap and Mike Kilkullen, like a few others, took advantage of it, paying fifteen thousand dollars in gold for the *mas ó menos* sixty-four-thousand-acre Rancho Montaña de la Luna, property of the family of Don Antonio Pablo Valencia. The flamboyant, hospitable, now-penniless Valencias had owned this land and lived on it in near-feudal conditions since 1788, when Teodosio María Valencia, an Andalusian veteran of the first Spanish expedition to set foot on the soil of what was to become California, had received it as a grant from the Crown of Spain.

There had been many other ranchos for sale at bargain prices in those days, but Mike Kilkullen fell in love with Don Antonio's only child, Juanita Isabella, who would have been heiress to the rancho had her father not been forced to sell. Doña Juanita Isabella Valencia Kilkullen had been Jazz's great-great-grandmother, and Jazz had been named after her, although only her father ever called her by that name.

Suddenly excited by her closeness to home, Jazz

turned off the highway below Three Arch Bay and
headed toward the ranch, swearing with impatience at
the fifty-five-mile-an-hour limit. Soon she was on narrow inland roads that earlier Kilkullens had built and
maintained, but the Orange County police were not
impressed by history, she reminded herself. Although
she couldn't bring herself to part with her T-Bird,
something utterly rakish about the car invariably attracted unwelcome attention from the forces of law
and order.

Jazz kept just under the limit along the miles of
strictly fenced-in land until she turned in at the massive open gates that were the main entrance to the
ranch. There, for five miles, she allowed herself one
satisfying burst of speed down the private driveway.
As she approached the hacienda she passed under an
avenue of two widely spaced rows of ancient and
noble Moreton Bay figs, natives of New Zealand.
There were ten trees in each row, trees so immense
that they seemed to come from prehistory, dark olive
green trees more than thirty feet in diameter that
arched overhead, branching so vigorously that they
touched each other and formed an enormous canopy
as they led to the courtyard outside of the front entrance.

Although it had been home to the Kilkullen family
for more than twelve decades, the hacienda, one of
the largest and best preserved of all the surviving landmark California adobes, was still called the Hacienda
Valencia and still preserved its basically Spanish
ranchero character. The one-story, thirty-five room,
whitewashed adobe had a long façade of simple and
deeply pleasing proportions. Stretching back from the
central structure were two wings separated by a large
patio and a central fountain. The dwelling was entirely
roofed in old, weathered red tiles; all the main rooms
opened onto broad, covered verandas beyond which
the patio, with its flower-filled beds, lay under an ever-
changing pattern of sun and shadow. The hacienda
had always been and still was far more of a manor
house, a *casa grande*, than a ranch house.

The hacienda was surrounded by ten acres of famous gardens, first planted by the Valencia wives, and later added to and embellished by the Kilkullen wives, the first two of whom had been of ranchero descent. This oasis was protected by thick plantations of trees that prevented any visible encroachment by the barns and stables that lay beyond their boundaries. The working ranch seemed to exist on a planet other than that green island on which winding, cypress-bordered walks led to a dozen different hidden gardens: a private world where many unexpected fountains played, surrounded by cascades of geraniums growing so rampantly that they almost hid their antique terra-cotta urns.

Jazz parked her car quickly in front of the hacienda and ran inside, delightedly aware of the familiar coolness of the air even in the heat of a California September. There was nothing unfriendly or damp about the slight chill caused by the two-foot thickness of the adobe brick walls for the air was impregnated with nostalgic aromas. In the air floated the immemorial scent of centuries of wood fires. Subtle, spicy fragrances, impossible to pinpoint, but which she had never smelled elsewhere, emanated from the huge Spanish chests, the massive carved sofas and high-backed chairs, the mahogany armoires, some still covered in the original leather, that had been sent to the Valencias on board ships sailing around Cape Horn. Persian rugs that had first covered floors of packed earth, in the earliest days of the hacienda, now lay over tiled and wooden floors. Each generation had added its own furnishings and art to the hacienda, but nothing had ever changed the essentially Spanish Colonial character of the interior, a rustic and solid character that was far more masculine than feminine.

Today, as happened each time she entered the hacienda after being away from it, Jazz was momentarily reminded of nights of her childhood when she lay tucked up snug and warm in a deep brown leather chair in the music room, watching the firelight reflected on the beamed ceiling, while both her parents listened to Beatles records. How many people felt a prickle of tears at the smell of woodsmoke and the memory of the melody of "Strawberry Fields Forever," Jazz wondered, and quickly put the thought out of her mind as she went directly to the kitchen to find her friend, the cook, Susie Dominguez.

"Susie, my one and only, how are you?" Jazz demanded, almost lifting her up in the air as she hugged her.

"Overworked for a change," the tiny woman replied with relish. Susie was of the breed of cook who was only happy when there was a dramatic bustle and flurry in the kitchen. If she had her way, Mike Kilkullen would give at least three dinner parties a week. The large kitchen, where once several Chinese cooks had prepared three hearty meals a day for a large family, would, if Susie had her way, still be filled with voices and people. Now her employer usually dined alone except on those weekends when Jazz came to visit, but today's planning for the Sunday Fiesta was up to her standards of hospitality.

"Where's my father?" Jazz asked.

"Up at the bowl, kicking ass. I don't have the time to worry about him—I've got my big chicken dinner to organize."

"But what about the caterer?" Jazz asked in surprise. "More than five hundred people are coming for a barbecue, Susie, not a chicken dinner."

"Oh, the caterer will be on the job tomorrow. His men are starting to set up already. But tonight it's my special saffron chicken with pine nuts and grapes, my Italian-style French bread, my multicolored coleslaw, my strawberry layer cake with a sauce of—"

"All that just for the two of us? Are you bucking to be voted the Martha Stewart of Orange County?"

"We're expecting company for dinner," Susie said mysteriously, and wrinkled her nose in a secretive way that succeeded in provoking Jazz as no man ever had.

"That's nice," Jazz said, as indifferently as possible. Susie would not be rushed when she was in the

mood to withhold information. "I guess you don't
happen to have anything for my lunch? Peanut butter
and jelly, or a slice of packaged cheese?"

"Look in the icebox. There might be something
for you to pick at on the bottom shelf, but don't dare
touch anything else."

"Gee, thanks, Susie," Jazz said, helping herself
to a large, carefully covered plate of sandwiches and
salad. "And I thought you didn't care."

Sometimes compliments worked with Susie,
sometimes insults, sometimes a judicious combination
of both.

"Nellie and Matilda are coming to set the table
tonight and serve," Susie offered as Jazz ate with
every sign of incurious contentment.

"Good. That'll make it easier on you, honey. At
your age you shouldn't be expected to do too
much. Slowing up is natural, Susie, after sixty.
You shouldn't feel badly about needing help with a
little chicken dinner," Jazz said solicitously. "I'll do
the flowers for you as soon as I've finished," Jazz
added, "and then you can tell me if you want me to
chop the cabbage. Or I could go into town and get
you some special-strength supplementary calcium.
Have you been taking enough calcium, Susie? You
certainly don't want to shrink any more. I'll bet you're
low on potassium too."

"Sixty!"

"Well aren't you over sixty? Or am I confused?"

"Damn it, Jazz, all right, I'll tell you. You've got
it coming. It's your sisters. And their husbands. And
their kids."

"SHIT!"

"Well, you started it. Sixty! I'm fifty-eight and
you know it."

"Who invited them?"

"Your father. You know how he is about the
girls."

"Oh, double trouble, triple shit. Shit in multiples.
Shit piled upon shit. Towers and turrets and pinnacles
of shit."

"Yep. I agree. We'll be knee deep. But it does give me a chance to do a little cooking around here. Thank God I'm not a member of this family."

"You might as well be," Jazz said gloomily. "You've been around long enough."

"No thanks."

"How wise you are."

Jazz's appetite almost disappeared at the mention of her half sisters, who were no doubt in mid-flight at this very moment from their homes in Manhattan. Of course she must have known they would be coming for the Fiesta. She just hadn't wanted to face the thought of the two daughters of her father's first marriage: Valerie, who was forty-two, and Fernanda, who was thirty-nine.

Throughout Jazz's childhood the two older girls had spent weeks at the ranch during each summer as well as a long week during both the Christmas and Easter vacations. They had gone to boarding school in the East, although their mother, Lydia Henry Stack, of an old Philadelphia family, had moved to Marbella, on the coast of Spain, after her divorce from Mike Kilkullen in 1960.

There was nothing that coven of two could do or say to her now, Jazz thought, that could hurt her as they had when she had been too young to defend herself, but their arrival meant a weekend of false and forced politeness covering dislike and mutual mistrust.

And all the sugar coating was put on for her father's sake, Jazz thought. He had never known how his older daughters treated Jazz. They had always made certain to be enchantingly sweet to her whenever he was around, and she, proud and stubborn, had chosen never to complain to him when they wounded her. Their weapons had been many, including jibes about her own mother, Sylvie Norberg, whom Mike Kilkullen had married immediately after his divorce. The Swedish actress, like a shooting star, had changed the face of film for ten years, until her death in 1969, when Jazz was eight.

"I forgive you, Susie," Jazz said, getting up abruptly and giving the cook a kiss on the top of her head. "You were only trying to hide the bad news. I thought you were up to your usual intrigues."

"A little of both," Susie said generously to the young woman she knew she loved as much as she would love a daughter, assuming she'd ever had one, instead of three sons.

"I'll go look for Dad."

Jazz went to her room to change into jeans, so that she could ride up to the wide, shallow, natural bowl in which the Fiesta would be held. The bowl lay high in the mesas beyond the hacienda, and her Thunderbird was too precious to be used on the dirt road that led to the Fiesta grounds.

In the stables Jazz looked for Limonada, her favorite horse, a strawberry roan her father kept for her although she hadn't lived at the ranch for twelve years. Limonada, he insisted, reminded him of Jazz, since her bright coat was a mixture of unnameable colors from dark honey to currant jam. Quickly Jazz saddled the fine-boned, alert mare, who curvetted and stamped and pranced in impatience. Riding like smoke, she reached the rim of the bowl in a few minutes. Jazz reined her horse in behind a sycamore above the bowl and, peeking out, surveyed the scene, looking for her father.

Dozens of caterer's workmen were busy, some hammering on wooden grandstands, some erecting tents made of blue and white canvas, others busy setting up dozens of round tables and hundreds of folding chairs under the tents, so that they would be ready for the blue-and-white tablecloths the next day.

Jazz recognized a few familiar ranch employees among them. She knew their names as a child would know their uncles. José had taught her how to rope a calf with a reata, Luis and Pedro and Juan had taught her rough-and-ready Spanish during those hours when they'd had time to go fishing and taken her along; twice she'd been allowed to go looking for a mountain lion with those great shots, Tiano and Ysidor. They

were all vaqueros, cowboys who worked on the ranch
year round, as had their fathers and grandfathers.

Yet nothing seemed ready, Jazz thought, as she
looked at the scene, not the dance floor or the horse-
shoe-throwing contest ground, not the barbecue pits
or the trapshooting area. Even the space for the grand
parade and roping contest hadn't been cleared. The
bowl looked as if anything could happen in it, a picnic,
a rodeo or a horse race, but Jazz knew that by Sunday
night the Fiesta would be as efficiently organized as
ever, and the guests, many of whom came from out of
state and even from foreign countries just for the occasion, would never dream of the amount of work that
went into this one remaining evidence of the scope of
old-time hospitality.

She searched awhile for her father, and once
she'd found him she remained where she was, watching him. Mike Kilkullen was a massive man, broader
and much taller than any of the other men around him.
He was so clearly in charge that only the fact that he
had been standing behind the grandstand until a moment before had kept her from spotting him instantaneously.

He was a chieftain, she thought, a chieftain born
and a chieftain bred. Could any photographer, even
Karsh of Ottawa, who had distilled all of Churchill's
fighting tenacity by snatching away the Prime Minister's cigar, have managed to search out her father's
essence indoors in a studio? Mike Kilkullen was utterly a man of the outdoors. He had been born to this
land just as he had been born to command. Right now
he was merely directing a group of men who were
putting up the long buffet tables, but from a distance
his rapid, positive gestures could have been those of a
general disposing his troops on the eve of battle.

His hair, so thick that he rarely covered his head
against the sun in a place where most other men never
went out without a hat, was entirely white and cut
very short, but his fierce eyebrows remained as black
as ever over eyes Jazz couldn't see from the distance,
eyes of a blue so incorruptible that they seemed fero-

cious to people who met him for the first time. Below
his aquiline nose, his mouth was set in a firmly uncompromising line unless he was smiling, and he was
slower to smile than most men were. To strangers he
would seem almost as intimidating as he was impressive. Only a few, more perceptive, would sense the
hidden sadness and sweetness in the man.

Mike Kilkullen, at sixty-five, cared nothing for
the pleasures of any city in the world. In recent years
he left the ranch infrequently, mostly to go to the bull
auctions in San Francisco's Cow Palace, or to attend
important Democratic state functions. Rarely did he
attend the many parties he was invited to by the growing number of accomplished hostesses of Orange
County.

Mike Kilkullen had been an only child, his parents had died early, his few friends were drawn from
the families of local landowners he'd known all his
life, but only his daughters called forth those deep
emotions that otherwise he invested entirely in his
ranch.

The Kilkullens of past generations had produced
numerous daughters but just one son in each of four
generations. These sons, whether firstborn or not, had
inherited the entire ranch, while the daughters had had
to be content with gifts of silver and jewelry on the
occasions of their marriages, and a portion of cash
when their parents died. British though it was, primo-
geniture, the aristocratic custom of the eldest male
inheriting all of the land, had somehow prevailed in a
now far-from-humble Irish family in Orange County.

Jazz waited awhile longer, until she saw her father mount his horse. Then she gently gave Limonada
a signal and, at a gallop, swooped down into the bowl,
stopping smartly level with his mount.

"What were you doing up there, Juanita Isabella,
counting the chairs?" Mike Kilkullen demanded as he
leaned over and wrapped his arms around her, almost
pulling her off her saddle.

"How did you know? I can swear you never
looked up."

"I'll teach you how someday. Old Indian lore."
He laughed at his youngest daughter, kissed both of
her fresh, sun-warmed cheeks, and all the sternness
left his face, all the sadness that underlay his com-
mander-in-chief demeanor disappeared. "What the
hell is that thing you've got on?" he asked. "It looks
like Halloween."

"You know perfectly well," Jazz said, preening
in the purple and gold satin official Lakers jacket that
her assistants had given her for Christmas. "You just
pretend to be ignorant."

"I like to tease you. What else is a worthless
daughter good for?"

"With Valerie and Fernanda coming, you'll have
your fill of daughters all weekend," Jazz answered.
"Why don't you hold it till they get here?"

"They'd never rise to the bait as easily as you do,
little girl. Anyway, they're perfect."

"True, too true," Jazz said.

"I hope you brought a dress. We have four bands
—two mariachis, one for country-western, and another for ballroom dancing."

"Why no rock and roll?"

"It's my party, Jazzbo, and I don't admit the existence of rock and roll."

"No reggae? No Top Forty?"

"I don't know what you're talking about. Anyway, ballroom dancing's back in style. I read about it
in the *Register,* so I figured I'd make you happy."

"Bullshit, you hired that band so you can dance
for a change. Lord save us, the former foxtrot king of
Orange County is back in town, and he's forgotten
nothing important. Ladies, lock up your daughters!"

Mike Kilkullen pinched her lightly. "You bringing a boyfriend?"

"Nope. Hoped I'd pick up some stray fella here.
A boyfriend'd cramp my style."

He eyed her covertly. Still no sign of getting married. What was wrong with the girl? Valerie and Fernanda had already produced six kids, but Jazz seemed
to waft from guy to guy without ever taking one seri-

ously enough to even think of settling down. It was probably the fault of her profession. He was damn proud of her, but twenty-nine was twenty-nine.

"Kid, do you ever give any thought to your—ah—biological clock?"

"Oh my God! You've been reading *Cosmo*!"

"No, listening to Susie. She's my window on the world."

"You're indecent! Whoever invented the biological clock should be chopped into sushi and fast-frozen."

"Just thought I should check up, make sure you knew about it. Doing my fatherly duty."

"Consider it done for the year. For the decade."

"Is that a hint?"

"*That's an order*. Race you back to the stable!"

Valerie Kilkullen Malvern stared expressionlessly and unseeingly out of the glareproof windows of the chauffeur-driven limousine that her husband, Billy Malvern Jr., had hired to transport their family from the San Diego airport to the ranch. She didn't join in the conversation her three teenagers were having with her husband, but wrapped herself in thought. Valerie knew that nothing she might observe on the trip could possibly interest her; it was an hour and a half to be endured without comment.

She sat erect, hands folded calmly in her lap, her profile betraying no emotion beyond a piercing self-assurance. She looked exactly like the pictures of her that frequently appeared on the society pages and in *Womens Wear*. Valerie Kilkullen Malvern, that well-known interior decorator, that powerful presence in New York society, had never been caught in an unflattering pose. She was always aware of her physical boundaries; she never lost a clearly directed consciousness of the impression she was making.

Years earlier she had decided on her look, knowing, as do all women of true style, that only one major visual impression can be made on people without confusing them and dissipating their interest. Valerie had

studied herself and understood that the shape of her
skull was so excellent that it allowed her to wear her
dark brown hair drawn back smoothly, totally flat,
tucked behind her ears and fastened by a neat bow at
her nape, a severe look that by its classic simplicity
would always be above mere fashion. Below her fine
forehead, her nose was entirely too pointed, too sharp
and too long for beauty; her chin several millimeters
too small.

Whenever she was anywhere near a camera—and
she was never caught off guard—she unsmilingly offered it that imperfect side view until it became her
trademark, and women with lovely noses and charming chins longed for an equally distinguished profile.

For daytime Valerie had adopted a deliberate uniform, wearing unadorned, dark turtleneck sweaters,
or collarless blouses, to emphasize the length of her
neck and the leanness of her torso, making her tiny
breasts into an asset. She tucked these tops into beautifully cut, totally plain skirts or pants, wrapped a wide
belt around her slim waist and never wore shoes that
weren't flat and brilliantly polished. She pushed her
tortoiseshell-rimmed glasses on top of her head when
she wasn't using them, and her collection of barbaric,
enormous earrings and wide cuff bracelets, studded in
huge semiprecious stones, made fine jewelry seem
fussy.

It was an enameled look that owed a lot to Diana
Vreeland, D. D. Ryan and Mrs. Winston Guest, Valerie would acknowledge to herself, but it worked. The
look sent its message to everyone and it awed many.
Above all it set her totally apart from her clients, those
women who, by definition, did not have enough style
sense to know how to arrange their own interiors.

Her look was inexpensive in the long run, something Valerie knew no one was shrewd enough to
guess. Not cheap, of course, for each separate piece
was the best of its kind, but since everything she
bought could be worn for years, no matter how fashion
changed, she had nothing that hadn't paid for itself
many dozens of times over. This left money for her

viciously expensive, handmade embroidered evening shoes; money for her collection of impeccable Hermès bags and gloves; money for the many brilliant evening gowns she wore for charity balls, occasions at which she was wise enough to know that her uniform wouldn't play.

Yes, she had money to dress in a way everyone associated with riches. She had managed that very well, Valerie reflected.

People thought that Mr. and Mrs. William Malvern Jr. were rich, and Valerie intended that they should never know otherwise. She too had believed, when she married, in 1969, that she would be rich, for charming, handsome, convivial Billy had inherited a fortune from his father, who had made a fortune in manufacturing during World War II.

William Malvern Sr. had been the first and only member of the Malvern family to emerge from the middle class, and he had taken pride in giving his son every advantage; he had shipped Billy off to as good a prep school as was willing to admit him; he had insisted on riding lessons and tennis lessons; he had sent him to the University of Virginia with a large allowance and overlooked Billy's indifferent marks when his son made the tennis team. After Billy's graduation his father had bought him a seat on the Stock Exchange. When William Malvern Sr. died in 1967, his son found that after the probate of his father's will he had inherited a tax-free income from five million dollars in municipal bonds.

William Malvern Sr. had achieved his goal of producing a son who was undeniably a gentleman and an amiable fellow. If he was aware that his son made up in good nature what he lacked in intelligence, he never revealed it to anyone but himself.

Billy Malvern had been a catch for clever, dominating Valerie Kilkullen in spite of his lack of background. She was never pretty unless she smiled, but easygoing, rudderless Billy, unlike other young men, had been captivated by her air of authority and her look of knowing exactly who she was. The Malverns

had married only three months after they met, and
Valerie, who had never dared hope for a handsome
husband, much less one with money, paid no attention
to his basic absence of intelligence until long after the
honeymoon was over.

Valerie had been as much in love as it was in her
nature to be, and during the years when Billy's income
had been riches, more than enough to buy everything
they wanted, his faults had not mattered. But now, in
the New York of 1990, there was little room for a man
without cunning or aggression.

Billy, for all his geniality, lacked the gut sense of
timing essential in the stock market, and he had actually managed to lose money for his own account
during years in which other men were becoming
wealthy.

He still kept a few clients, old pals who were as
conservative as he was, but his commissions were
negligible. Little by little he had sold some of his
bonds, and now the Malverns' unearned income was
no more than two hundred thousand dollars a year.
Inflation had made that a small sum indeed in Valerie's
Manhattan circle, which had been infiltrated, and
quickly taken over, during the last decade, by a class
of new people of impossible wealth, wealth on a
breathtaking scale that had not been known since the
heyday of the Robber Barons.

Incredibly, she and Billy had become *nouveaux
pauvres,* Valerie thought, with a familiar pang. Their
large Fifth Avenue apartment had been paid for in the
1960s, and their house in Southport, Connecticut, in
the early 1970s, but there was no possibility today
that they could afford to buy a vacation house in ski
country or the Hamptons. The Malverns were invited everywhere, of course, but it wasn't the same as
having their own place. Valerie had employed all her
ability in redoing their no-longer-highly-fashionable
Southport clapboard house so that it was occasionally photographed for magazines. In addition they
gave two large, well-publicized annual parties, one in
Southport and one in New York, without which they

would have no visibility as multiple home owners, the new coinage that signaled wealth.

Billy Malvern Jr. deeply cherished his position in the rapidly changing cosmos of New York, still seeing himself as the glamorous young man he had been in the 1960s. However, it was the money Valerie earned that now permitted them to stay in New York.

She had graduated from the New York School of Interior Design and apprenticed to an older decorator before she opened her own small business. Although Valerie would never have an innovative talent, she was able to create and supervise a workmanlike, professional job for women who craved the cachet of employing a "society decorator" from an old family.

Valerie charged her clients a straight thirty-three-and-a-third markup above wholesale on what they spent, plus a design fee. She did several jobs a year, as much as she could handle with one assistant and a secretary-bookkeeper. As long as nobody guessed that the Malverns needed the money, those jobs would continue to come her way.

Of course, Valerie mused, as the limousine proceeded north, she and Billy and their children could move to Philadelphia, her maternal ancestors' Philadelphia, where she could abandon the struggle to maintain a façade, where she never need set her feet in the abominable Decorating and Design Building again, where they could comfortably coast along on income and still take their place among the old families of the city. There, where New York values didn't prevail, where Valerie was related to half the town and friendly with the other half, they would be perceived correctly as having as much money as anyone really needed.

But Billy was the first generation of his family to attain a place in society. He had none of the attitudes of an old-money, bred-in-the-bone aristocrat, who would have scorned to maintain a position in the social-climbing Bedlam of New York in 1990. On the contrary, Billy Malvern was infatuated with his niche in society and he refused resolutely to move to Philadelphia, a city he considered stuffy, dowdy and unthinkably provincial.

There could be no question of divorce. Marriage to a presentable man, however ineffectual, however puffed-up, was far better, Valerie knew, than living on her own, earning her own keep as just another divorcée, while Billy was snatched up by some Fort Worth billionairess as any available man as attractive as he would inevitably be.

Whenever she thought of divorce, Valerie shivered in fastidious distaste, wondering how her younger sister, Fernanda, had endured, in her careening career, the disruptions of being once widowed, thrice divorced and now married to a fifth husband who obviously wasn't going to last any longer than the others. Yet Fernanda seemed to thrive on the hurly-burly of marital adventure, buoyed up by the money her first husband had left her, and a knowledge that she possessed an indefinable quality, beyond charm, beyond beauty, beyond cleverness, that guaranteed that she would never be without men vying for her attention. . .

It was a lucky thing that magazines and newspapers invariably referred to the two of them as the "Spanish Land Grant heiresses," Valerie thought with a quickly repressed, acrid twist of her mouth. Most people assumed that she and Fernanda had already inherited large, romantic funds. All that was very well, except that in both their cases "heiress" merely meant expectations. Neither she nor her sister nor their children had had anything from their father, except for the normal birthday and Christmas presents.

Mike Kilkullen's money was all tied up in unsold land. If you kept an eye on Orange County land values, and she did, oh, she did indeed, then the Kilkullen Ranch was worth billions to investors who would stand in a long line to buy and develop virgin acres on that Platinum Coast.

But their father would never sell as long as he was alive. He had made up his mind to it from the day on which he was first old enough to think, and Valerie knew that stubborn, unreasonable, unreachable man would never change. His land was himself, and he'd far sooner cut off an arm than part with as little as five thousand acres.

Valerie glanced briefly at Billy, charming as ever, she acknowledged, and still lovable, but in the final analysis a rather disappointing husband who worked in a business in which he was not bright enough to compete, but not quite stupid enough to be found out. Billy Malvern, whose genes had managed to produce three daughters! Not even the grandson who might have somehow caught her father's fancy.

The last stretch of highway to the ranch turnoff seemed endless. This weekend, thank heaven, would be particularly short, involving them only until the Monday morning after the Fiesta, since both she and Billy could plead their work as a reason for their return, and the children had to be back in school. She'd hoped to be able to avoid the annual Fiesta this year since there was a particularly good dinner party in New York on Saturday, until her mother had phoned from Marbella and told her that it was out of the question.

"You and Fernanda haven't visited the ranch for almost eight months," she had said sharply to her eldest daughter. "I don't understand how either of you girls can be so foolishly neglectful, Valerie. Don't fall into the trap of thinking that just shipping your children out to California from time to time is enough."

"Father's very fond of my girls," Valerie had objected.

"Nonsense. You and Fernanda are his flesh and blood, not the girls. Why do you think Jazz is down there almost every weekend? She's no fool, she understands that man, and if we don't take care she'll turn herself into the son he never had. How would you two like to be supplanted in his will by Jazz, Valerie?"

"Father would never do that," she'd answered, attempting to don the confidence of the oldest child, while she wondered, with a familiar rage, how her domineering mother, stuck away in Spain, always managed to know exactly what was going on in her life.

"I'm far better aware than you ever will be of what your father is capable of doing," Lydia Stack Kilkullen had responded. "He'll do whatever suits him and just when you least expect it. How often do I have to tell you that he's a monster of selfishness and a slave to any impulse that may strike him? I don't doubt that as he gets older he gets more selfish and more impressionable. He's sixty-five, Valerie, he can't live forever."

"He hasn't aged a day in ten years. He'll live to be a hundred, Mother."

"All the more reason to remind him of how devoted you both are. Consider, Valerie, what if he should marry again? There will always be plenty of women quite willing to become the third Mrs. Michael Kilkullen. How can you forget for a single minute what he did to me?"

"No one's managed to catch him in twenty-one years," Valerie had reminded her mother, but an irritated hiss had told her, without words, how lacking in foresight she was.

Her mother was probably right too, Valerie admitted as they passed the Carlsbad city limits. How many sixty-five-year-old men in New York, widowed or divorced, took young brides? It was standard procedure, so expected, so natural that it caused next to no notice. If a man of sixty-five had married a woman of his own age it would have been the talk of Manhattan, a nine-and-a-half-day wonder. Why had she not thought of the possibility herself? And Fernanda, that self-educated expert on divorce, why had she too ignored it?

Valerie bit the inside of her lip, thinking that she'd allowed herself to slip where her father was concerned.

It hadn't always been that way. After her parents' divorce, her mother had insisted that she and Fernanda spend weeks out of every year at the ranch. It

had been banishment for the teenagers to be sent out
to Southern California when they had been invited to
stay with their relatives from Philadelphia during
school vacations. In the summers, when they longed
to be with their peers on the East Coast, sailing
and going to parties in Long Island or Maine, where
so many of them spent the summers, they'd been
forced to sweat it out for weeks at a time in that old-
fashioned, gloomy adobe her autocratic father was
so ridiculously proud of. They'd had to put up with
Jazz, that humiliating new baby, and, worst of all,
Sylvie, her father's second wife.

Valerie couldn't remember a time when she'd believed that her parents were happy together. Her
mother's sense of alienation in California had been
passed on in hundreds of subtle ways to her daughters. Valerie had been twelve at the time of the divorce, thirteen when Jazz was born, and she had seen
it all through her mother's demonically bitter eyes.
Nevertheless, Liddy Kilkullen had insisted that her
daughters "preserve their place in the family." The
Kilkullen family! As if she'd ever cared about them.

She, Valerie Malvern, whose mother had been a
Stack of Philadelphia, whose maternal grandmothers
had been a Greene of Philadelphia and a James of
Philadelphia, who could count among her ancestors
five Philadelphia gentlemen—a Dickinson, a Morris,
an Ingersoll, a Pemberton and a Drinker—five Tory
loyalists who had had the class and convictions to
refuse to bow to pressure to sign the Declaration of
Independence, why should she think of herself as a
Kilkullen? What was there to admire in that half of
her background? How could a single poor Irish immi-
grant of 1852, a shopkeeper before he bought land,
compare to the founding fathers of the most proper
city of the United States, men with such close ties to
the great families of England that they refused to re-
volt against her?

And what were succeeding generations of Kilkullens but cattlemen who had known their share of bad
times? She knew little about the Valencias, the far-

away source of the Spanish land grant. The family seemed to have melted away after one of their daughters had married the first American Kilkullen. They were lost in the rough stream of California history, complicated history that had always seemed too foreign to stir her interest. And as for their taste in furniture!

"Mother! We're almost there," exclaimed Holly, her oldest daughter, who at seventeen showed no signs yet of becoming either a beauty or a brain. Valerie, jolted out of her brooding, passed her hands quickly over her hair in an involuntary grooming gesture, checked her dark red lipstick and made herself ready to face a father she had been taught to blame for her mother's unhappiness. Nevertheless, in her unemotional way she had always longed to love him. She had never been able to admit this to herself, for Valerie had also been taught to believe that he had never loved her.

Fernanda Kilkullen Donaldson Flynn St. Martin Smith Nicolini, so often married that she was known to the readers of society pages from Bar Harbor to La Jolla simply as Fern Kilkullen, was accompanied by her two sons, Jeremiah Donaldson and Matthew Donaldson, offspring of her first marriage, a marriage that had left her, at twenty-five years, a widow with a sizable fortune. The boys were nineteen and seventeen, more than grown up enough to handle any transportation while she sat in the backseat of the Chrysler Imperial and mentally prepared for the weekend.

Her father, of course, would want to know why Heidi Flynn, Fernanda's fifteen-year-old daughter, had not come to the Fiesta with her. He expected Heidi, as usual, and he probably even expected Nick Nicolini, much as he disapproved of his daughter's latest husband, who was only twenty-nine and hadn't had a serious job in his life. Mike Kilkullen would be satisfied by nothing less than the attendance of his entire family at the Fiesta, but Fernanda and Nick had reached the point of divorce after the battlefield of their two-year-long marriage and she didn't want her father to know about this latest mess until it was necessary. As for Heidi, she had simply grown too pretty in the past six months for her to be included.

Only a dermatologist could have come close to guessing Fernanda's age, and only in a bright light. She knew, without vanity, that she looked as if she were in her late twenties. But if she were seen next to Heidi? The difference between being far and away the prettiest thirty-nine-year-old woman in the world and being a normally pretty fifteen-year-old girl is encompassed in just one word: youth. And youth, authentic, heartbreaking, flushed youth, was the only thing she could no longer attain.

Fernanda had never been a great beauty—she was a perfect miniature in the sheer intensity of her prettiness, widely skirting the more serious realm of beauty—but as far as men were concerned, and her concerns had always begun and ended with men— being pretty was far more to the point than being beautiful. Beautiful could frighten them, pretty made them approach.

Fernanda had been at her teenaged prime in the mid-1960s and she had kept a sixties look stubbornly and instinctively, without any of the thoughtful premeditation with which Valerie approached her appearance.

She was five feet five and her silver-blond hair hung long and straight, almost to her waist. She needed to have her brown roots lightened every two weeks, but staying blond was worth any amount of trouble, in Fernanda's opinion. Shorter strands of hair were encouraged to fall over one eye or even into her mouth, to be casually puffed away in charming impatience. Her eyes, as bright and vividly turquoise blue as the tile in a swimming pool, were always heavily fringed in frank layers of black mascara; her small, fine nose and tiny, delicate nostrils had the charm of a child's. Her mouth was dainty yet deeply curved and it pouted in an enchantingly infantile way above her well-formed chin. Her skin was so perfectly pink and white that it gave her the quality of a very expensive doll who had been dressed as a hippie by accident rather than design.

Fernanda always wore tight, low-slung jeans or the shortest of leather miniskirts with close-fitting vests that were cut to deliberately reveal the exquisitely feminine curve of her belly and the dimple of her belly button. She had dozens of pairs of pointy-toed Western boots in every kind of leather, a closet full of lavishly decorated cowgirl jackets, and pounds of silver and turquoise jewelry. Her furs came from the Fendi sisters, dyed in mad colors, worked with beads and insets of fabric.

Rounded, appetizing, tiny-waisted, a lush little tidbit of a female with delectable breasts and bottom, Fernanda could still display every inch of her slender and rigorously trained body. Her midriff, her inner thighs and her upper arms, those places where skin texture first changes as the tightness of youth is lost, were still in splendid shape. She had worked for that body, taking everything nature had given her and maintaining it with daily exercise classes and a strict diet, as vigilant as an obsessive curator of rare manuscripts.

She knew, for Fernanda was shrewd, that she dressed right on the borderline of bad taste. She produced herself in the wild-thing spirit of the girls in the ads for Guess?, except that she didn't reveal glimpses of her lingerie since she never wore any. When she checked herself out in her full-length mirror she made sure that she looked like a biker's wet dream, yet Fernanda Kilkullen could never be mistaken for a slut. Headwaiters, doormen and salespeople knew instantly that they were confronted with the kind of woman for whom they reserved their best service. Only a supremely assured thirty-nine-year-old who looked, in all the essentials, like a kid, could get away with that stunt.

It would, of course, have been simplicity itself to slide gracefully into a way of dressing that was fashionable, suitable and yet youthful, but youthful wasn't *young*. Young was Fernanda's operative word. Young meant men, constantly available men, lighthearted men too young to have ever considered that one day they might find themselves on the verge of middle age. Everything she put on her back, every hair on her head, every fresh coat of mascara, was intended to signal to these men that she was fuckable.

Fernanda was ruled by the pursuit of sex. A few centimeters of flesh between her legs explained her actions, her motives, her directions, her past and her future.

Her earliest memory was of her first orgasm, self-induced when she was supposed to be taking an afternoon nap. She could tell, from remembering the cot and the very color and texture of the blanket, that she had been less than three years old at the time, yet as soon as the wondrous surprise faded she had realized, with the kind of absolute knowledge that is inborn, that no one must find out what she had just discovered.

As a child she had shared a room with Valerie, and her biggest problem had been to find excuses to lock herself securely in the bathroom so that she could give herself up to the slow process of bringing herself to the peak of pleasure, for an orgasm was never quick with her, but required long, gentle, well-lubricated, carefully heightened, deliberately quickening strokes of her fingertips, and if she was distracted by footsteps in the hallway outside she had to begin all over again. Worst of all, she often had to give up entirely because Valerie, impatient, would demand to use the bathroom.

After the divorce and her mother's move to Marbella, they had both been sent to a strict, New England all-girls boarding school, with roommates and no locks on the doors. There Fernanda discovered the safe retreat of the reading room of the school library. She staked out a deep, comfortable chair in a half-hidden corner. She would grab a book, throw a raincoat or a polo coat over her lap, let the book fall open on the arm of the chair, close her eyes as if she'd gone to sleep and, undisturbed, spend hours surreptitiously bringing herself to an orgasm. She would pretend her fingers belonged to a man, a faceless, nameless man, a man who was her absolute and adoring slave, a man who wanted nothing for himself, who existed only to bring her bliss. No one watching her could have guessed what she was doing because she had so mastered the art of concealment that when she finally reached the ultimate moment only her lips tightened as she held her breath.

Fernanda's clandestine activity in the reading room was the focus of her days. She did her studying in the dorm, after dinner, with enormous concentration, so that her late afternoons were always free. She had little spare time to make friends with her classmates. During those heady years of change in the sixties that even reached their secluded campus, at meals she half-listened to girls debate issues that seemed utterly unimportant to her.

Only sexual gratification interested her deeply, but she never betrayed herself. Her need to hide, born in infancy, had been reinforced year after year by her mother's demeanor. Fernanda had been deeply marked by the emotional atmosphere in which her mother moved: cool and reserved except when she spoke so bitterly about their father. Valerie, in many ways an imitation of her mother, only made things worse. Vacations and summers at the ranch had certainly not led her to confide in her father, and year by year an unreasoning fear of him grew, for, more than anyone else in the family, Fernanda had the feeling that he could somehow sense her one preoccupation.

A week after graduation from boarding school, Fernanda met Jack Donaldson, who had been out of Harvard Law School for five years. Almost thirty, the brilliant lawyer had been incredulous when he realized that this ravishing morsel of an eighteen-year-old had never had a serious boyfriend. Such girls, in his experience, weren't supposed to exist in the era of Woodstock. He proposed marriage immediately, before anyone else found out about her.

On their honeymoon Jack Donaldson began to wonder if his fantasy of awakening an ignorant virgin had been foolish. He used every technique that had ever worked with other women, he was as gentle and tender with Fernanda as possible, but soon, intoxicated by her body, he wouldn't be able to stop himself from entering her and, aroused by a half hour of foreplay, coming quickly. Once he'd reached his own climax he'd try to satisfy Fernanda with his fingers and his mouth, but she always pulled away. It doesn't matter, darling, she'd say, it's just not that important, I don't care, honestly.

When Fernanda became pregnant with their first child, Jack Donaldson put the problem on hold. Perhaps the hormones of motherhood would provide the answer to her lack of arousal. Was she always going to be frigid, Donaldson asked himself wearily after their first son was born.

Their second son was born in 1973, when Fernanda was twenty-two and by that time he had almost stopped caring. She was utterly faithful as far as he knew, she was always pliantly available when he wanted her, but she couldn't respond beyond a certain point and there was nothing more he could do about it.

Other men lived with the same situation, with wives less adorable than Fernanda. He never knew that after he'd made love to his wife and had fallen soundly asleep, she left their bed and made her way to her bathroom—dressing room, where she gave herself the slow, gradual, practiced, stealthy orgasm that she couldn't have with him.

If only, Fernanda would think, oh, if only she didn't *know* each time Jack started making love that no matter what he did to her, his aim was to come inside her. If only she weren't conscious of that need beating away under every caress, inspiring his every touch, if only she weren't so aware of his attempts to hide his impatience, if only she weren't perfectly aware that he was wondering when he could decently allow himself to enter her. *If only he didn't rush so.*

He honestly thought he gave her plenty of time, more than enough, but he never, ever did and she really couldn't expect him to, not the way men were. No matter how hard Jack tried, she could never *count on him,* as she could count on the faceless, nameless, selfless slave in her fantasy.

When he died in a car accident in 1976, leaving Fernanda millions, Jack Donaldson hadn't worried about her sexual inadequacy in years. He had other girls who responded lustily to his advances, and toward Fernanda he felt only faint resentment, and the love of a man for a sweet child.

Briefly Fernanda had mourned him, or rather she had mourned their seven-year marriage, not one day of which had fulfilled her. Then, free, rich and twenty-five, she set forth on a quest to find the right man for her needs. A young man, a man who could last and last forever. Somewhere there had to be a man who would make her have the orgasm she'd never had except by herself.

Why had she actually *married* any man, Fernanda asked herself now, on the way to the ranch, as Jeremiah turned the car radio to one of California's New Age music stations and synthesized harpsichord music filled the car.

Four young husbands and dozens of young lovers in the last fourteen years—it wasn't the life her mother had brought her up to have, God knows, but each time she went to bed with a new man some constantly renewed spring of optimism, or perhaps mere desperation, made her hope that this time it was going to be right, going to work, going to be magic.

Jim Flynn, Hubert St. Martin, Hayden Smith and Nick Nicolini had all been younger than she when she met them. Each of them had been so entranced by her exquisitely sexy prettiness that they had been capable of miracles. At first each one had made love to her three or four times a night. Always, that last time, they were slow to arousal, almost lazy, almost not caring, without the fatal urgency that chilled her, and sometimes she experienced a small, brief spasm that was—

almost—an orgasm. Perhaps it was actually a real orgasm, she wondered, the kind other women had with men, but there was no way to know. Certainly it didn't come close to what she could do to herself.

Soon, oh much too soon, each of her husbands, like each of her lovers—like every damn man in the world—wanted to make love less frequently. If she was dealing with a lover, Fernanda simply dropped him. But with a husband she found herself faced by the need to pretend to have an orgasm or else deal with an utterly predictable discussion that reminded her of the unbearable tedium of her first marriage. Sooner or later, when she couldn't endure faking orgasms anymore, divorce became inevitable.

Thirty-nine, Fernanda thought, and still chasing an experience she *had* to have. Thirty-nine and still feeling that heavy, tormenting, almost crampy fullness, like a bowl of warm water carried between her legs, whenever she thought about a man who could last long enough in bed.

Thirty-nine was a sickening age, the worst age she could imagine. One day, not so long from now, she'd wake up to find she was forty-three, forty-five, even forty-seven. One day she wouldn't be able to pass for a pretty girl no matter how well she took care of herself. And only a *very, very rich* woman could hope to attract young men after a certain age.

She hadn't reached that age, not yet, oh no, not nearly yet, that fearful juncture of time and gravity was still far away. But a number of Jack Donaldson's millions had been spent in the circuit from one playground of the world to another. She was still well off, no question about it, still able to buy everything she needed, but not nearly as rich as she'd *have* to be as she grew older. Everything was a question of degree, wasn't it? It was unbearably difficult to be facing her fortieth birthday except as a very, very rich woman.

As they turned off the highway and the car began to climb the road that led to the ranch, a familiar thought crossed Fernanda's mind. One day, when her father died and they could sell the ranch, she and her sisters would become so rich that she could scarcely imagine it. Hundreds of millions, for each of them. But when? How long would she have to wait? Would the money be there before she needed it, while she still had her looks? Or would it only come when it was too late?

4

As darkness fell on Sunday night, the Fiesta was approaching its height. The big band had struck up a medley of Glenn Miller arrangements, and at the first notes of "Midnight Cocktail" a mob had taken to the dance floor. Each of the families that received an invitation to the Fiesta was allowed to bring all their children over sixteen, and the teenagers were wildly rediscovering Swing, their parents were energetically trying to remember it from old movies and everyone over fifty was showing them how to do it as it was meant to be done. The Fiesta guests always dressed up for the occasion: the men in elaborate cowboy gear even if they never rode; the women in outfits that ranged from four-thousand-dollar fringed chamois dresses to Scarlett O'Hara–inspired hoop skirts.

Mike Kilkullen decided to draw back into the shadows under the grandstand and just observe his party for a while. He could see clearly across the width of the great natural hollow in the mesa, for it was illuminated by the flames of the glowing barbecue pits, by thousands of candles in windproof glass hurricane lamps and by twinkling white lights that had been strung everywhere. Every precaution had been taken against fire, but he had stationed vaqueros along the perimeter of the bowl lest an airborne spark escape and start a blaze.

How he wished his grandfather could be with him tonight, he thought with a sudden and unexpected ache. Hugh Kilkullen was the first Kilkullen child born on the ranch, in 1867, and he had lived to be eighty-five. He had been in his still green and vigorous sixties when he started taking his six-year-old grandson out on a pony, beginning to train him in the many duties of a rancher as they rode the seemingly endless pastures that rose gradually upward from the bluffs above the Pacific, the rounded, grass-covered mesas separated by the steep-sided, wooded arroyos where oaks, sycamores, laurel and melaleucas grew.

Hugh Kilkullen had grown up in the era when the ranch was run much as it had been from its first days; he had seen the coming of the Santa Fe railroad and the passing of the great teams of forty-two horses that drew a single giant threshing machine during the grain harvest. He remembered the decades when there was no running water inside the hacienda; when kerosene lamps were lit at sundown; when a year of low rainfall meant that the women of the family had to sacrifice their precious flower beds while water, stored in great tanks aboveground, was used only for the cattle. He had seen stately stags and the honey-stealing bears who once inhabited the lower slopes of Portola Peak.

Portola Peak rose abruptly near the inland border of the Kilkullen Ranch. It was an unexpected mountain to find so near the coast, a mountain that was geologically considered the westernmost extension of the Santa Ana range. The mountain, which had given the ranch its original name, Rancho Montaña de la Luna, pointed one steep finger toward the sky, and from certain angles observers could see the moon rise directly behind the summit of Portola. Every soul who lived within sight of the summit, up and down the coast, had been marked by the glory of sunrise as it touched that point, beyond which range after range of the higher, snow-capped mountains in the Cleveland National Forest were often clearly visible.

Sometimes, as they rode back to the hacienda, Mike Kilkullen's grandfather had told him stories of the era before and after the turn of the century when he and his wife and children had filled the many rooms of the Hacienda Valencia with his own four married sisters, their husbands and their children, as well as with two of his beautiful, unmarried sisters-in-law who lived with them while they waited to be claimed by suitors. Hugh Kilkullen had married Amilia Moncada y Rivera, who was descended from another old California Spanish family, rancheros like the Valencias and related, in one way or another, to a number of the few families who had once owned all of California: the Avilas, the Ortegas, the Vallejos, the Corderos and the Amadors.

The Hacienda Valencia itself had stood firmly at the center of their family traditions, a home place which had been, during the time of the Valencias, a small village. It had possessed its own school, a family chapel, a smithy, a tannery, a slaughterhouse and a dairy. Almost a hundred employees had worked for the family alone: shoemakers, cheesemakers, seamstresses, carpenters, bakers and even a resident jeweler.

Sailing ships frequently rode at anchor off the Valencia harbor, bringing ice from Alaskan glaciers to cool their summer drinks, a grand piano from Germany for Mike's great-great-great-grandmother, Irish crystal and English porcelain for the dinner table. That lavish and intensely hospitable epoch had vanished when Spanish ranchero life had ended, as dead as plantation life in the South after the Civil War, but much of its open-handed spirit lived on into the late Victorian and Edwardian days. Hugh Kilkullen, a dedicated amateur photographer, had captured it in thousands of photographs which were now preserved in their own fireproof storeroom.

Those rooms of the hacienda spilling over with children and their nurses, relatives and friends who visited for months at a time, those days of merriment, of passionately contested horseraces, of day-long picnics, of great balls, of brilliantly celebrated marriages, of music-filled evenings and weekly fiestas—how had all that fun and life so quickly dwindled down to himself, one solitary man who gave this big party once a year so that he could have an excuse to gather all his daughters and grandchildren around him? Shouldn't something more of the past have been preserved for his children's generation than photographs and his memories of his grandfather's stories, Mike Kilkullen asked himself.

But something did remain, he answered silently and defiantly, something that was infinitely more important than the individual history of any one family. The land itself remained, the land itself was unchanged, the land that his grandfather had always told him must never be sold, because the land would always take care of the Kilkullens. Yes, the land had been preserved for the future.

From his vantage point in the shadows he picked out Valerie at a table surrounded by a group of his neighbors and oldest friends. Most of them had become millionaires many hundreds of times over in the last thirty years, turning their land into shopping malls or industrial parks, or developing it into vast housing tracts. There was no end to the hunger of people to live in Orange County. Whenever new homes were to be sold, huge crowds would gather at special lotteries to allow them a fair chance to buy. They undoubtedly considered him a backward fool for not joining them in that certain route to membership in the Forbes Four Hundred, but the Kilkullen ranch still belonged, every last acre of it, to the family. It would remain a working ranch as long as he had anything to say about it.

Watching Fernanda, clad in deerskin jeans and a denim halter embroidered with turquoise beads, dancing with an eager boy half her age, Mike Kilkullen wondered, with a familiar pang, what the future would hold if he had had a son, someone to carry on the hardworking tradition of the cattleman.

What if he and Lydia had never been divorced? Or what, for that matter, if they'd never met back in 1947? He'd been a big, cocky, lusty kid of twenty-two, who joined the Army at seventeen and emerged, three years later, with a chestful of medals and the idea that he was an adult. Seven-league boots would have looked too small to him then, he remembered grimly.

Before his mother died during the war, she had often told his father that young Mike must get an education when the war was over. Although he'd wanted to get back to the ranch as fast as possible, his father had insisted on carrying out his mother's wishes. He'd spent two years at Stanford, and it was during the late summer vacation, just before the start of his junior year, that he'd been invited up to the party in Pasadena where he'd first laid eyes on Lydia Henry Stack.

She was just eighteen, blooming with the perfection of a flower that had been cultivated for a flower show, her eyes brimming with calm self-confidence, as she waited for the beginning of what was certain to be a triumphant debutante year in Philadelphia. Her best friend from Foxcroft, the Virginia boarding-school, had persuaded her to come out West to visit for a few weeks. It had taken him only a half hour to talk her into leaving the party with him.

He could still remember how entrancing Lydia had been in her full-skirted, pale blue taffeta dress with its matching jacket; so maddeningly proper with her little white gloves and her satin pumps; so enticingly graceful in a slender, reined-in, precise way; her shining dark brown hair falling in absolutely disciplined waves to her shoulders, her smiling lips a perfect shade of pink that made all the other girls look overly made-up.

Yes, she had knocked the daylights out of him with her finishing-school sophistication, a unique brand of polished poise, an unmistakable stamp of class, for want of a better word, than he'd ever seen in any of the nice Southern Californian girls he'd dated up till then.

And he must have represented something equally fascinating, new and irresistible to her, or else why would she have allowed him to take her away from a party? Why would she have spent every day of her visit with him, permitting him to kiss her for hours on end in the front seat of his convertible, until their lips were abraded and swollen and they were both feverish and sick with desire?

He'd never been allowed to touch her naked breasts. No contact below the collarbone had been her rule. Oh, he could still remember the violence of that frustration, more powerful than the best fuck he'd ever had, a frustration that neither of them knew what to do about because in 1947 anything more than kissing was unheard of for a Philadelphia aristocrat. Or for a nice Californian girl, for that matter.

So they had eloped, Mike Kilkullen and Lydia Henry Stack. Two criminally stupid, infatuated, sex-obsessed kids who should never have laid eyes on each other, let alone gotten married, had eloped because they couldn't jump into the sack and screw themselves blind for a few weeks. Half his generation had probably done the same thing, but that didn't mean, looking back, that it wasn't a catastrophic way to make a decision, particularly when an easy divorce was out of the question with his Catholic background and her strict Episcopalian upbringing.

Looking back, he knew that he hadn't realized to what extent their marriage had been a mistake until far later—years later—than she had. It had seemed to him to be working in the beginning, when they rented a little apartment in Palo Alto after college started. True, once it was legal to go to bed, the lovemaking was never as wonderful as both of them had ignorantly imagined it would be. Liddy, who had so loved to be kissed, didn't enjoy sex. The real thing frightened and distressed her, and no matter how gentle he was, she never got over an essential distaste for what she considered a messy, intrusive act. But he was convinced

that her attitude would change in time, especially
when she became pregnant so soon.

During those early months he often found her
weeping, hidden away in the bathroom so that he
wouldn't hear. She'd insisted that she was only upset
because she hadn't wanted to have a baby so quickly,
or because her parents were still furious with her for
eloping, but later he'd understood that she was in a
hopeless, unending, voiceless rage with herself for ruining her life, getting stuck in an impulsive, *unnecessary* marriage when she should have been back East
where she belonged, in the city she loved, among people of her own kind, with everything ahead of her.

They had been far, far too young to get married
without a great passion. Or even *with* a great passion,
Mike thought bitterly. Their attraction was based on
incomplete arousal and equally incomplete fantasies
about each other. She'd been the princess treasure
he'd won from the Eastern heart of American civili-
zation and culture; he'd been the embodiment of the
phonied-up glamour of the Wild West, heir to a great
ranch, a wartime hero, already a man in her inexperienced eyes. Their great romance had been nothing
more than a better-dressed, richer version of the Cowboy and the Lady.

It had been one woeful big bitch of a mistake, but
Valerie was born eleven months after their elopement.
Then, before the last year of college started, his father
had had a fatal stroke. Overnight, prepared only by
what he had learned before he'd gone into the Army,
he, the last male Kilkullen, had become the big boss
of the ranch. Emilio Hermosa, an old man, had been
the Cow Boss at the time, and he'd attached himself
to Emilio to absorb every detail of the operation of the
ranch. During those early days they'd driven a pickup
truck, for the area he needed to learn about was too
great to cover on horseback. Liddy had found herself
in charge of the running of the big hacienda, supervis-
ing the servants and the gardeners as well as caring
for Valerie. Both of them had been too busy to face
their misery with each other. Fernanda had been born

two years later, and the girls had managed to hold them together for a few years longer.

"Dad, what are you doing standing back here?" Jazz said, appearing at his side.

"Remembering," he said, startled into honesty.

"What?"

"Anaheim red wine. All that champagne and vodka and white wine that everybody's drinking tonight—do you know that once the only stuff anybody ever drank here was a plain red wine from the vineyards in Anaheim?"

"Disneyland rouge?"

"Disney wasn't born. And ladies didn't drink except maybe once a year or so."

"You're having an attack of ancient racial memories."

"Probably. It was something your great-grandfather told me."

"How about a dance?" Jazz asked.

"Nothing I'd like more," he said, and led her out of the shadows onto the dance floor.

I fancy myself madly tonight, Jazz thought euphorically, as she moved through the crowd after dancing with her father, stopping to greet everybody, for not one guest was unknown to her.

She had decided to wear a precious and seemingly simple dress that she'd bought at a fiercely contended auction of great old clothes, bidding with a reckless determination to win. It was from Madame Grès and dated from the early 1960s, a long dress made of white silk chiffon, classically Grecian in style, with one shoulder draped and the other bare. This understated triumph of the most elite house in all of haute couture was so finely worked that dozens of yards of pleated chiffon fell into a slim column that moved around her gently as she walked or danced. Even standing still, Jazz seemed to be touched by a lyric breeze. Yet to the uninitiated it was just another evening gown, appropriate for any big party.

The night air had dampness in it, as it always did

so close to the ocean, and over her shoulders Jazz had thrown a magnificently embroidered black Spanish silk shawl that her great-grandmother, Amilia Moncada y Rivera, had worn a hundred years ago as she presided over special occasions at the Hacienda Valencia. It was a coveted family heirloom; none of the three sisters owned it, but her father had let her borrow it for tonight.

She had piled all of her hair high on her head, experimenting until she found a look that somehow suggested Spain, with the help of a few invisible tortoiseshell combs. All I need is a rose in my teeth and three feverish bullfighters throwing themselves at my feet, Jazz mocked herself, but she was thrilled by the romance of the effect she had achieved, for it seemed to be in perfect harmony with the benign spirit of the evening, a spirit that hung over the golden, firelit bowl of the Fiesta and sang of another century, a spirit rarely captured in Orange County, where only a few social traditions dated back before 1950.

Jazz moved almost to the edge of the bowl, where there were few people, and looked at it in meditation. If only it were possible to capture this instant in a picture, Jazz wished briefly, but she knew it was impossible because if she were in the photograph she couldn't take it, and so much of the joy she was experiencing was tied to being in her own skin and looking outward, knowing that she was in her own beloved home place, wearing a dress whose value only she appreciated, as well as the priceless family shawl. And carrying it off with a flair that no other woman there could match—why pretend to false modesty on such a night? Or on any night for that matter?

Unable to resist framing the scene in her photographer's eye, Jazz made an improvised viewfinder of the circle of her thumb and forefinger and peered through it, framing the scene. Impulsively, moving toward the last row of lights, to widen the focus, she took three quick steps backwards.

A sudden impact jarred her so abruptly that she almost tripped. She had backed into someone who

was—no, make that someone who *must have been*—
eating an enormous plate of chili, she realized in horror, as she stood stunned into immobility, feeling a
mass of the semi-fluid concoction spreading in a hot,
oily, quickly widening splotch of tomatoes and beans
and hamburger down from the edge of the shawl to the
bottom half of her skirt. Slowly, ever so slowly, as if
that could minimize the damage, she turned her head
over her shoulder and looked down her back.

"No, oh my God, no, tell me I didn't do this!" It
was a man's voice.

She raised her eyes from the appalling mess to
look at her assailant. The oaf, the clumsy, unforgivable klutz was an absolute stranger, flushed with
dismay, a big redheaded lunkhead in a navy blue
pinstriped suit and black city shoes, more out of place
among the men of the party than a clown. Would it be
unladylike to kick him in the balls?

"But—you—did," she said, so stunned that she
could barely get the words out.

"I'll get club soda, I'll get salt, just don't move,
stay there, I'll be right back," he implored her.

"Club soda? Salt? They never work, not even on
a little spot on a tablecloth. *You've ruined everything.
For good!*"

"No, wait a minute! Don't get so upset! I'll buy
you another dress, I'll find another shawl, I promise
you I'll replace them as good as new. Better!"

"Oh, will you really? You think it's that easy?
Listen, dickhead, one of the ten best-dressed women
in the world would have to *die* before another dress
like this becomes available, assuming she didn't will it
to her daughter, and as for the shawl—it belonged to
my great-grandmother—it's one of a kind, irreplaceable, an heirloom. That is, it used to be, before you
took a shot at it."

"Shit!"

"That's the first halfway intelligent word you've
said so far. Shit is exactly the word for it. What kind
of a cretin eats chili standing up? You're like a highway accident just waiting to happen. Don't you see all

those tables and chairs over there? Haven't you ever been to a party before?'' As she spoke, Jazz got angrier and angrier. The chili was now puddling on the ground, and she could feel its wetness under her hem.

"Look, I'm as sorry as I can be, I couldn't possibly feel worse, but I was just standing there, out of the way, minding my own business, watching the crowd, when you came out of nowhere and backed into my elbow with a hell of a jolt. I had a good grip on the plate, but you just popped it out of my hand. I take all the blame, every bit of it, but to be fair, it wasn't a hundred percent my fault.''

"Aha! Let's play 'blame the victim'! The next thing you'll say is that I was trying to attract your attention and couldn't think of any other way to do it.''

"No, the next thing I'll say is that if you tried to exercise some tiny sense of perspective, we might agree that this isn't exactly the Exxon oil spill,'' he said, finally furious himself.

"Great. Let's intellectualize this out of existence. It isn't Three Mile Island either. Or Chernobyl. Your turn. What else isn't it?''

"The fucking end of the world,'' the stranger said quietly. "Let me try to get some of that stuff off the shawl before it sets. I'm going to lift it off you as carefully as I can.''

He walked forward, his arms outstretched stiffly, and lifted the shawl from her shoulders. Its wet pointed tail hung down and dripped repulsively as he turned and stalked slowly toward two trestles and laid it across them. Jazz darted to the nearest table, grabbed two knives and a handful of napkins and joined him. They both bent over the big black silk triangle.

"Try to flip the visible bits off,'' he instructed her, "but don't scrape the silk. It looks awfully fragile.''

"What are you, a dry cleaner?'' Jazz muttered, but she followed his directions.

"Jazz, Casey, what are you doing?'' Suddenly Mike Kilkullen's voice sounded behind them. They both straightened up and arranged themselves side by side in front of the shawl.

"Don't tell me you two have something to hide already?" he said, grinning at their guilty faces.

"An accident, Mike. I'm afraid I spilled chili all over this young lady's antique shawl," the stranger said.

"Damn." Mike grimaced in dismay. "Every time I serve chili, something like this happens. Never again." He bent down to inspect the shawl. "Oh Lord! But what the hell, I guess something can be done. I don't think you should touch it—leave it to an expert."

"See," the stranger said, turning to Jazz, "I knew there had to be a way."

"And that makes you feel just fine? I know, I know, you said you were sorry! Why don't you suggest that I dye my dress brick red while you're at it. That'll make everything perfect." Her voice was still dangerous, but her father's presence had made her modulate her tone.

"Juanita Isabella, is that any way to talk to your long-lost cousin?"

"Cousin? No way," Jazz said flatly.

"Cousin? She can't be," the stranger said at the same time.

"Didn't you introduce yourselves? Jazz, this is Casey Nelson. His great-grandmother was a Kilkullen. Casey, this is my youngest daughter, Jazz. She's your third cousin, as I understand it."

"Who was this great-grandmother?" Jazz demanded, arms akimbo. "I've never heard of her."

"I hadn't heard either, until Casey tracked me down and wrote me a few weeks ago."

"Wrote you?" Jazz asked her father. "Wrote you out of the blue? What for?"

"I didn't expect you tonight, Casey," Mike Kilkullen said, ignoring Jazz's question. "Not till next week. But I'm delighted you could make it for the Fiesta."

"I finished my business in Chicago early, so I

took the first plane out. I didn't bother to change, just dumped my bags at the house and rushed up.''

"Why don't you go get yourself another plate of chili? I'll take care of the shawl.''

"You're sure? O.K., I hate to admit it, but I'm still hungry.'' He walked off, leaving Jazz and her father alone.

"Dad,'' she asked casually, "you said that Casey Nelson tracked you down and wrote you. What did he want, anyway?''

"A job,'' her father answered.

"So the boyo is out of work and needs a job, does he? How did he think you could help, I wonder?''

"He wants to work here, on the ranch.''

"Oh sure,'' Jazz giggled. "I can just imagine him polishing tack in a brand-new, all-but-threadbare, super-macho Ralph Lauren cowboy outfit.''

"Don't make the mistake of thinking he's a dude, honey. He isn't.''

"How much do you actually know about him?''

"After he wrote, I made it my business to find out. My grandfather had a younger sister, Lillian, who married a boy named Jack Nelson. He came over from Ireland back in the 1880s. Grandpa told me that this Nelson didn't like California so he and Lillian went to New York and he got into the tugboat business. Had a lot of kids. Grandpa stayed in touch for a while, but after his sister died, maybe sixty years ago, he stopped writing. He mentioned her to me a couple of times way back, but I'd completely forgotten that we had relatives in the East. Casey's great-grandmother must have been my great-aunt Lillian.''

"And that makes him a cousin?''

"As close as I can figure it out. Definitely a relative.''

"Are they still in the tugboat business?''

"Casey's father has done very well in tugboats.''

Jazz gaped at him. Her father used the expression "doing very well'' for neighbors like the Segerstroms, of whom he'd said, "They've done very well in retailing,'' only after the South Coast Plaza, the biggest and most luxurious shopping mall in the United States, had done close to a billion dollars a year in its location on what used to be their fields of lima beans. The first John D. Rockefeller would be, as far as Mike Kilkullen was concerned, a man who had done very well in the oil business.

"Then why is he looking for a job on a ranch? Why isn't he carrying on in tugboats?"

"It seems he's always wanted to be a cattleman. Since he was a kid. Who knows, maybe it was that bit of Kilkullen blood? He's been getting experience working ranches on and off for years; wrangler up in Wyoming, buckaroo in Nevada, jackeroo in Australia, assistant Cow Boss of the Stanton ranch in Texas—graduated Texas A&M. He's planning to buy a big spread in Nevada, but he wants a solid year of on-the-job training first—that's why he wrote me."

"Nevada? Good land there's worth a fortune. Stocking it's another fortune."

"Casey's done well—in fact, I'd have to say that Casey's done very well—in business. He went to Harvard Business School after college. Has a knack for investing, it seems, but his heart is in ranching."

Jazz digested this information. If her father said it was true, it was.

"What are you going to do with him?" she asked, wonderingly.

"Cow Boss," her father said shortly.

"Come on, Dad," Jazz laughed. "What are you really going to do with him?"

"Jazz, I told you. Cow Boss."

"You can't possibly mean that!"

"Why not?"

"Because that's *your* job! You've been Cow Boss here for forty years! That's insane. Absurd, impossible! You don't even know this guy. Cow Boss! *You must be out of your mind!"*

"Don't talk to me like that, Juanita Isabella, and don't try to tell me how to run my ranch." His voice was quiet but deeply angry.

She looked at her father in a mixture of bewilder-

ment and outraged shock, her whole being absolutely
rejecting the idea of anyone but her father as Cow
Boss of the ranch. She struggled to find words, but the
look on her father's face warned her not to continue
to protest. After a few seconds of silence he continued
to speak, his anger quickly gone.

"Hell, Jazz, I can use him. I haven't been covering the ground the way I used to. Not for quite a while
now. We lost the grass on a couple of mesas last
month to wild English thistle because I hadn't been
around to those pastures recently—damn it, Jazz, just
last Tuesday I finally discovered two windmill pumps
that must have broken down God knows when. And
those damned vandals—they're coming in on motor-
cycles, destroying the fences, shooting the cattle and
blowing up the water troughs. It's their idea of fun,
and it's getting worse day by day."

"But still—why call him Cow Boss?" Jazz ventured, gaining courage from this list of normal rancher's complaints.

"No other title will give Casey the authority with
the vaqueros. He'll need it to keep them hustling,
being a stranger to the place. It's my ranch, so where's
the problem?"

"No problem, Dad," Jazz said hastily. "I'm just
surprised, that's all. It . . . happened so quickly."
Her father had said nothing about Casey Nelson all
weekend, and he'd clearly been expecting him soon.
So he couldn't bring himself to tell her, she realized,
and he wouldn't have done so until the oaf actually
arrived. Mike Kilkullen had decided to replace himself
—even if only for a year—in the only job he'd ever
wanted in his life.

Being the big boss, or the owner, or however else
he cared to phrase it, might be good enough for most
other cattlemen, but it had never been sufficient for
Mike Kilkullen. Nothing but the nominally lesser title
of Cow Boss would ever be the right title for him, a
man who had gloried in the responsibilities only the
Cow Boss commands; who rode out at sunup and gave
orders till sundown; who could do every single job on

the ranch himself, from fixing fences to bidding on prize steers at the Cow Palace in San Francisco; who could ride into a herd and pick out a sick cow with one glance and doctor her in less than a minute; who was the leader, the unquestioned and absolute and proud leader on the land, living all day on horseback among the cattle and the vaqueros, a leader without peer.

A Cow Boss was always a general in the midst of a constant struggle that had not changed much since the first man on a horse fenced in the first cows. A big boss could be any city man in a Stetson and a cigar who liked the idea of owning cattle. Her father would never give up his title of Cow Boss because of a mass invasion of English thistle or a dozen broken pumps. He must be feeling—what? Jazz's heart raced in near-panic as she searched his face. Weary? Tired? He certainly didn't look it, but yes, that must be it, he must be just plain tuckered out for the moment to even think of letting Casey Nelson become Cow Boss. But did that make sense? Would Mike Kilkullen give up being the Cow Boss of the Kilkullen ranch because of simple fatigue?

"Honey, haven't you got something else to put on?" her father asked. "You can't go around like that."

"I'll find something," she said absently.

"Now."

"Yes, sir." Could a man of sixty-five be having a midlife crisis?

Back at the deserted hacienda, few of the lights were on. Susie, who had a nature that was frugal in a few small ways, could never leave the place at night without saving electricity. Jazz drove the Jeep she had commandeered as close to the back gate to the patio as she could so that she wouldn't risk getting any of the still-wet chili inside any room but her own. She navigated the garden paths carefully, holding the dress up with both hands, found her way to the covered veranda that led to all the family bedrooms and, pushing open her door with her elbow, went into her own room. She'd left a light on by the bed, but trust Susie to have turned it off, she noted, annoyed, as she stepped inside. In the dark she took four steps toward the bathroom. A violent pain slammed into her shin just below her left knee. She teetered for an instant on her high heels, still trying to hold up her dress, before she fell forward onto a mass of hard, angular objects, hurting an elbow and an ankle.

"I DON'T FUCKING BELIEVE THIS!" she informed the silence in a shriek. Slowly she picked herself up from the ambush, letting her dress drop, and with her hands stretched protectively in front of her, sweeping the darkness for any further obstacles, she groped her way toward her bed table and switched on the light.

A pile of Vuitton suitcases, the ungiving, hard-sided kind with lethal metal corners, lay in a careless heap on the floor of her room.

" 'I just dumped my bags at the house,' " she said out loud. "I just dumped my bags . . . *just . . . dumped . . .* ! Does this look like a guest room, dickhead? Answer me! Does it?" She looked around the room fiercely. As usual, when she was home, she neatened up after herself as she'd been taught to do as a child. Tonight she'd been especially careful since there was always the possibility that some of the guests might come back after the party for a last drink and a tour of the landmark adobe. After she'd dressed for the evening, she'd put all her accessories away in the top bureau drawer, and the bathroom was equally, impersonally neat.

"Yes, Jazz, it does indeed look like a guest room, a very nice guest room, particularly to the dim, sub-human mind of cretinous cousin Casey," she muttered as she rubbed the shin where, fortunately, the layers of pleated fabric had prevented a bruise from forming, although it hurt like hell.

Jazz managed to release herself from the ruined Grès gown and rolled it up tenderly in a towel. She pulled the combs out of her hair, found her brush and lashed and bashed at her Spanish confection ruthlessly

as she stood in front of the closet door and considered
what to put on. Jeans and a shirt would do on any
other night, but not for the Fiesta. She changed her
beige pantyhose for a pair in gold, and quickly she
grabbed a hanger from which hung, on tiny straps, a
short, shapeless little piece of gold cloth. She slipped
it over her head and, in an instant, Jazz was reborn,
all tits, all ass, all gams. Glorious old-time Hollywood
gams, Betty Grable gams, Ginger Rogers gams, Cyd
Charisse gams, the kind of great gams that are the stuff
of dreams.

The piece of cloth turned into Calvin Klein's newest slip mini-dress, as short as a dress can be, the most
fiendishly difficult-to-wear item in American design, a
garment brought out every season, always in a different fabric, but otherwise identically styled, a dress
seemingly designed to mock every woman whose
body is less than perfect. A dress that challenged all
women, especially those who should never wear it.

Jazz had been born to wear that dress, and after
she had photographed it on a model for an Absolut ad,
she had called the designer in New York and got him
to send her one months before it went on sale all over
the United States. She reached into a pot that she'd
bought at the Soap Factory on Melrose, and threw a
handful of gold dust over her hair, which now rippled
down her back like autumn sunshine in the woods.
"Go the distance," she muttered to herself, not without a touch of pleasure. She changed her white sandals
for a pair in gold, and hung long, dangling, flashy, fake
yellow diamond earrings from her ears.

Jazz left her room in a state of maximum disorder,
stalked back to the Jeep, and within minutes she was
back at the party. She surveyed the crowd for a moment before plunging back into it. Her eye was
abruptly caught by the back of a woman's head, a
woman with red hair cut so short that it almost looked
like a boy's, a woman she hadn't noticed earlier.
Surely there was something that tickled her memory
in the particular poise of that head, in the long line of
that neck, in the lovely shape of those shoulders?

Yet, just as surely, Jazz knew that whoever that woman was, she had no connection with any previous Fiesta. She was from another world than that of the ranch. As she walked forward, curious, she noticed that her father was talking with unusual animation to the woman whose face she hadn't yet seen.

Mike Kilkullen looked up and saw his daughter approaching. Jazz waved, he waved back, beckoning to her, his expression suddenly changing to a look Jazz didn't understand, a look that mixed the amused welcome she expected with something else that seemed to be a kind of—was it anticipation, was it confusion, could it be embarrassment? The woman turned around.

"Red!" Jazz yelled and rushed toward her, flinging her arms around her and hugging her tightly. "Red, my darling Red, I would have recognized you right away if you hadn't cut your hair, what on earth are you doing at this hoedown?"

"Mike invited me," Red answered, returning Jazz's hug.

The two women fell silent for an instant, gazing searchingly at each other, looking for signs of change, as women do who haven't seen each other for six years. Jazz had been twenty-three when they last worked together during the leaping early stages of her professional progress. Red Appleton had been one of the greatest models of the early 1970s and a top fashion editor by the 1980s. At the peak of her magazine career she had been about to retire to married life.

"Red, where *have* you been?" Jazz demanded. "You just vanished, totally disappeared into the jet-set zoo."

"Cap Ferrat, St. Moritz, and a dozen other low-life, high-rent places." Red spoke in a Texas drawl that had been imitated by half the girls in the business. She had been everybody's pet, an all-time favorite model, a brilliant editor, and always the center of fun on every shoot, good-natured, unflappable, and without ego.

"Where are you off to now?"

"I'm not going anywhere. I'm never going to pack another suitcase. I've bought a divine place on Lido Island."

"You? Living in Newport Beach? You, a neighbor! I can't believe it. How come? Where's that husband of yours?"

"He's a chapter out of an old paperback I left on a plane." Red grinned that huge Texas grin that nobody could imitate.

"Divorced?"

"Definitely."

"Well, welcome back!" Jazz was delighted. She and Red had shared the one thing that two women who are able to feign just about anything, as all women can, cannot ever feign: genuine liking. She'd vaguely resented Red's obscenely rich husband because he had taken Red out of the magazine business in which she'd been a star, and whirled her away into a life of migratory pleasure-seeking. But then Red, so independent in most ways, had always had one weakness: she'd been a sucker for older, bossy, dominating men.

"Dad, you're full of surprises tonight. Where did you run across my darling Red? Or is she another long-lost cousin too?"

"We met at a party," Mike answered.

"When?" Jazz asked, startled. Her father almost never went to parties.

"A couple of weeks ago."

"Well, you could at least have told me," she said, obscurely annoyed. "I didn't have the slightest idea that Red was living here."

"I didn't know she was 'your darling Red.' Am I supposed to make weekly reports to you on my social life? Now listen, Jazzbo, you run along and have fun. Red's my date, she couldn't get here earlier, and now we're going to dance till we drop." Mike Kilkullen grasped Red firmly and walked toward the dance floor with her. Red fluttered her hand at Jazz over her shoulder as she allowed herself to be led away, bending gracefully into Mike Kilkullen's side.

Jazz stood openmouthed. His "social life"? Her

father didn't have a social life, not that she knew of. He didn't go to parties. He didn't invite one of the most beautiful women in the world to his annual family-and-old-friends Fiesta. *He'd never brought a date to the Fiesta.* A couple of weeks ago? How many times had they met in the interval? What was going on? Could anything be going on? Could anything *not* be going on? Why shouldn't something be going on? Her father was still a magnificent man. Red was what? At least into her forties, in any case. And divorced. Thus available. And she'd always been a total sucker for men who told her what to do. Her father told everybody what to do. Red only went for men much older than she was. He was that for sure. SOMETHING WAS GOING ON.

Well. Well. Well. Jazz's head and heart did a zigzag, flip-flop, upside-down twisting turn as she considered what she had just learned. She struggled to be fair. To be broad-minded. Was there a single reason she could think of why her father shouldn't have invited Red to be his date tonight? Wasn't this his party, his ranch? Didn't he have every right to a social life? Wasn't he entitled to the pleasure of—flirting—with a beautiful woman? Surely Red had let him know that they were old friends. But that didn't make it a crime that he hadn't told her about knowing Red for two weeks, during which time she, his darling daughter, must have spoken to him by phone on a half-dozen occasions. He had a right to some privacy, didn't he?

Yes, yes and yes, to all of the above, but what about that look he'd given her as she approached them? She had thought at the time that it was embarrassment or confusion and perhaps it had been a little bit of both, but mostly it had been—pride.

And why not pride? What man wouldn't be proud to escort Red Appleton. She mustn't jump to crazy conclusions on no basis, and it wasn't any of her damn business anyway, and even if something was going on, so what, why shouldn't it, Jazz told herself severely. She thrust her heart back in its place, grabbed her questioning brain and slammed it shut, arranged a smile on her face and, resolutely turning her back on the dance floor, studied the tables, deciding which group to join.

Not far from where Jazz stood, Casey Nelson was seated, calmly eating dessert with Valerie on one hand and Fernanda on the other. Both of them were bending toward him in obvious fascination. Of course, Jazz thought, if Charles Manson were out on parole and could still get it up, Fernanda would be making goo-goo eyes at him, but Valerie always reserved her interest in new people until she had an inkling of how they could be useful to her.

Jazz slipped through the crowd, refusing all invitations to dance, and eased herself into a chair at what seemed to have become the family table. She was a mistress of the art of joining a group without disturbing it, making herself almost invisible until she wanted to be noticed. She set herself to an imperceptible study of this new joker in the pack.

After what her father had told her, she'd have to consider him as more than an aberrant irritation who would disappear in the morning. He wouldn't last long, of course. This was, had to be, some sort of experiment on her father's part, a momentary whim about this investment-minded tugboat heir out of the Bad Apple. Perhaps he even had a subconscious notion he could make this unlikely lad—who had to be thirty-two or thirty-three if she was any judge, and she was—into a substitute for the son he'd never had. Jazz brightened, and the panic she'd felt a few minutes before oozed away. Of course! That was it! Casey Nelson was a Kilkullen male. Only by a relatively minor tributary of the bloodstream, but still there was that essential connection. Hot damn, she had it!

He didn't look like a Kilkullen except for his hair, she thought, flicking her eyes at him for an instant in a way that couldn't attract anyone's attention. His crisp, dark red hair that curled here and there was family hair; Mike Kilkullen had had hair like that before it turned white. But no Kilkullen had ever looked like a grown-up lion cub, with a forehead that fur-

rowed in intensity as he spoke. This Nelson person
had a thick sprinkling of freckles on the kind of white
skin that would probably burn easily; heavy, unruly,
red-gold eyebrows over bold hazel eyes and a nose
that was rather too broad at the base. To her trained
eye his features were both obstinate and generous. He
probably wouldn't photograph interestingly, his face
was too blunt, too no-bullshit, without enough angles,
yet, if you just looked at him, there was a certain
individuality that the camera could seek out. Not the
distinction of the almost decadent, old-school British
look that was still sought in male models, but a conservative, old-fashioned kind of—for want of a better
word—decency. Didn't he know that just plain decency was out? Just like his bloody Ninja luggage?

"Oh, Jazz," Valerie said, turning to her and putting a proprietary hand on Casey Nelson's arm.
"Have you met our newfound cousin, Casey Nelson?"

"We're old cronies," Jazz said. "In fact, Casey
seems to be sleeping in my room."

He looked up and noticed her for the first time
since she'd sat down. "I'm sorry . . . again . . . I
thought it was a guest room."

"Understandable mistake. That makes two tonight, Casey . . . so far." Jazz threw him a gratui-
tously wanton smile, a shameless, thoroughly naughty
smile she reserved for special occasions, just to keep
in practice. It was a pity to waste one speck of gold
dust on her sisters.

"I've just been telling Casey that I know his father, Gregory," Valerie said, refusing to sound puzzled at Jazz's acquaintance with Nelson. "He's
president of the committee for the Madison Avenue
Settlement House. You remember, Jazz, it's that
dreaded charity thing I have to do every year."

As to many decorators, the coveted culmination
of Valerie's year was the invitation to create a model
room for the Madison Avenue group. The settlement
was an Old New York, society-backed charity devoted to after-school education for gifted but poor

children. Each year the committee took over the finest
empty house on the real-estate market and asked a
selected group of eager decorators, who would tear
each other apart for the honor, to design one room
apiece.

"I had no idea Gregory Nelson had a son who
was interested in ranching," Valerie continued. "I've
just had the most amusing inspiration. This year I've
been assigned a child's room, and now that I've met
Casey I'm going to do a young boy's room. Can't you
just see him tucked up in bed with his little head
crammed full of Western fantasies? I happen to know
where I can lay my hands on two of the most extraordinary, museum-quality, antique rocking horses—
then Navajo rugs, of course, and piles of Navajo
blankets in the corner. I can do the upholstery and
bedspread in leather, even the walls if I can find just
the right color. Cacti everywhere, in big square terra-
cotta pots. Barn-door red for the moldings, don't you
think, Casey, and coils of rope piled on top of each
other for lamp bases? A saddle mounted into a night
table—why not?"

"Will there be a bookcase for comic books and
Western magazines, Valerie?" Casey asked. "That's
all a kid really needs."

"I shouldn't think so. No, absolutely not. A
bookcase, certainly, but not for comics. He can keep
them in the bathroom. They'd spoil the look."

"Mustn't have that," Casey said. He drank half
a glass of red wine and refilled his glass, the expression on his face carefully unreadable.

"You *do* see. I knew you would." Valerie looked
about, smiling, aware of the becoming color of her
leaf-green pants and shirt, so satisfactorily crushed in
that superior manner that only pure linen has. Gregory
Nelson actually her distant cousin? What a piece of
luck. Imagine Great-Grandfather having let the connection drop and Father having managed to forget it.
Trust Californian cattlemen for that kind of insular
social myopia. The Nelsons must own every tugboat
in the New York Harbor, to say nothing of Hoboken,

Boston and Lord knew where else. Tugboats weren't oil tankers, of course, but oil tankers weren't what they used to be.

"Cousin Casey," Fernanda purred, "now that we've discovered each other, I have to tell you that nothing, absolutely nothing you read about me in Andy Warhol's diaries is true. How he could have dreamed up that business about me and Joe Dallesandro and Mick I can't imagine, but—"

"I didn't read it," Casey Nelson said tersely.

"I was thinking of suing the estate when the book came out, but I took my lead from Halston, when he was still alive. He said it wasn't worth it—it simply spreads the original lie. Do you think that if Andy were still alive he'd be dropped by all his friends, the way Truman was? Poor Truman—he always said that I was exactly the way he'd imagined Holly Golightly. The movie part was originally written for Marilyn Monroe anyway, not Audrey Hepburn. Don't you just adore Tru?"

" 'Adore' isn't a word I'd pick for Capote." He sipped more wine.

"Well then, just who is your favorite author?" Fernanda asked, leaning forward so that the luscious half-moon of her almost-uncovered breast nudged the back of his hand.

"Louis L'Amour."

"Who?"

"L'Amour. Louis L'Amour."

"Hmmm—but that sounds utterly fascinating. Where do you find his work?"

"Everywhere."

"Oh," Fernanda said in disappointment, "I thought it might be something special."

"It is," he told her, and gulped the rest of his glass and refilled it again.

I'd better rescue the poor slob, Jazz decided. Nobody deserved both Valerie and Fernanda trying to impress him at one time, no matter what he'd done.

"Casey," she said imperiously, standing up and tossing her hair so that for an instant she scattered a

gossamer cloud of gold dust on her shoulders.
"Dance?"

"Christ, yes!" he said fervently, and rose immediately, still holding the wineglass. Jazz approached
him with little importunate dancing steps, her sliver of
gold no more than a blatant invitation to easily imaginable delights, and for a time-stopped moment everyone at the table gasped at her. Casey Nelson took one,
big, fast, eager step forward, tripped over Fernanda's
foot and sent the glass of red wine flying. It covered
Jazz's dress from top to bottom.

"That's three," Jazz announced with an unsur-
prised hoot of laughter. "With six you get egg roll."

5

Fernanda dug her nails into her palms in annoyance at finding herself so unceremoniously deprived of her new cousin. He was difficult to talk to, but a man as clearly masculine as Casey Nelson was worth working on. It was only a question of finding out what plucked his banjo, catching his full attention, and then watching him fall. Obviously he felt that he had to watch his step with his new and distant relatives, or he wouldn't have been able to conceal some reaction when she had allowed her breast to touch his hand.

Casey had potential, enormous potential, Fernanda reflected, as she watched him dancing with Jazz. He moved well, with an aggressive grace. But he was dancing with that bitch of a Jazz who looked determined to keep him all for herself, Jazz who had ten precious years of youth more than she had, Jazz who had committed the unforgivable sin of becoming world-famous, so famous that men would always find her fascinating no matter how old she grew. As much as she had disliked Jazz as a child, she really loathed her now, Fernanda thought broodingly, her infantile mouth compressed into a thin pink line, her rosy pink skin going white with a wave of envy.

Restlessly, trying to shake off her darkening mood, Fernanda looked around the dance floor. Orange County gentry were not her usual style. Every man seemed to be a contemporary of her father's, or a kid who belonged to some local family. She sighed and resigned herself to a dutiful-daughter evening, although how she could be dutiful when her father was dancing away, absorbed by some redhead who looked vaguely familiar, she couldn't imagine.

"Excuse me, ma'am," a man's voice said. "Would you mind if I sat down?"

Fernanda looked up at a very young man in chinos and an open-necked khaki shirt that he wore with a military air. He was unsmiling, almost severe, his jaw firm and his broad shoulders thrown back as if he were standing at attention.

"Wait a minute—it *is* Sam Emmett—isn't it?"

"Sure is, ma'am. I didn't think you'd remember me."

"I can't believe how you've grown! Come on, do sit down, Sam. How old are you now, anyway? I'm all confused. I haven't seen your mother in so long."

"I'm almost seventeen, ma'am. Nobody else can believe it either. I've been growing about a foot a year, I guess, and I haven't seen you in three years. I was just a kid then."

"Indeed you were," Fernanda murmured. Sam Emmett, the son of an old friend, had been sent away to a military academy in the East when he was thirteen and a half, a pudgy brat with a shock of surfer-bleached hair, and freckles scattered all over his bold little face. He'd been such a discipline problem that his parents had sent him away as a last resort.

"Well, am I still talking to terrible Sam, the holy terror of Laguna Beach?" Fernanda asked, amused.

"No, ma'am, I've shaped up. Next year I'll be captain of cadets," he replied in his new man's voice.

"Your mother must be very proud." He was one

of those teenagers who age as you look at them, Fernanda realized.

"Yes, ma'am. She says she is."

"What's all this ma'am stuff, Sam? I've known you for years."

"That's the way I address a lady, ma'am," Sam Emmett said stiffly, sitting very straight.

"Is it indeed?" Fernanda chuckled. "That's very reassuring. I feel safe knowing that there are still young men who know a lady when they see one. But please stop. Call me Fern or I'll feel too ancient."

"You could never be ancient, ma'am," he said shyly.

Fernanda looked him up and down. Sam must be six feet tall. His rapid growth had left his frame appealingly gangly, his blond hair hadn't yet darkened, although it was so short that it was almost a crewcut. He was a few months younger than her son, Matthew, yet in every other way in the last three years he had moved from the last border of childhood to the beginning of manhood, while Matthew was still firmly a teenager. Sam's deep voice, the strong structure of his face, the determined set of his lips, the intense definition of his features, all set him apart from other kids of his age. True, he was shy. But that was to be expected.

"Are your parents here, Sam?"

"No, they're out of town, so I drove over alone. I've had my license for almost a year," he said, pride showing through his military varnish.

"Sam, listen, I have to go back to the hacienda to get a jacket—it's so damp here. Could you drive me back in one of the Jeeps—"I don't like that road at night."

"Sure thing, ma'am."

Fernanda led the way to the Jeep that Jazz had used earlier, and soon they were back at the deserted hacienda.

"I'll wait out here for you, ma'am," Sam Emmett said.

"Oh, please come on in, Sam," Fernanda replied.

"I don't like going into an empty house by myself. It's silly, but I always worry that there might be somebody hiding there."

He jumped down from the Jeep and followed her to the door to her room, where one lamp was lit, standing outside as she entered. Fernanda opened the closet and fumbled around, searching for her jacket.

"Damn, I can't find it—Sam, come here and look for my red jacket, will you? There's not enough light in this room and, believe it or not, I'm color blind."

As soon as Sam busied himself in the closet, Fernanda quickly and quietly locked the door of her room. She snatched a towel from her bathroom and threw it on the bed. Then she went to the closet and touched the boy on the elbow.

"Never mind my jacket, Sam. I don't really want it."

"Huh?"

"I just wanted to get away from that crowd and be alone with you, didn't you realize that, Sam?"

"You're kidding!" He stood still, half in, half out of the closet, too amazed to move.

"Yes, alone like this," Fernanda said, and reached up and put her arms around his neck. Her pink tongue peeked out and tasted her pouting upper lip as she looked up at him with anticipation in her wayward turquoise eyes. A mischievous half-smile lit her face as she savored the novel idea that had brought her to her room.

"I never thought . . . you wouldn't want . . ." The cadet backed away, still stiffly military, with an expression of alarm in his stern young eyes.

"Sam, stop. You might as well relax. Now sit right down here on this bed. I want to talk to you." Fernanda employed the commanding tone of voice she used with her children, and he responded to her authority, lowering himself awkwardly onto the quilt that covered her bed. She sank down six inches away from him.

"Now Sam," Fernanda continued, in a lowered

voice that no longer held any maternal note, a voice designed to forge a joking bond between them, a smiling, conspirator's voice, "do you believe that I don't know that before you came over to the table tonight you'd spotted me sitting there by myself? Didn't it cross your mind at that moment that you'd like to— oh—I don't know—kiss me, maybe? Touch me? Even . . . do certain things you've probably never done to any woman. Certainly not to a lady. Didn't you have those thoughts earlier, Sam? Tell me the truth, on your honor as a cadet."

"Damn! You're teasing me, aren't you? You only remember me as a brat. You don't realize I'm grown up now. You think it's funny to play this game with me, right, and then you're going to tell my mother that I had dirty thoughts about you, aren't you?"

"Neither one of us is going to say one single word to your mother. *Ever.* And I don't play games with tall, grown-up guys like you. Did you have thoughts like that, Sam? You still haven't answered me."

"Well . . . maybe something about dancing with you, that's all," he mumbled.

"That's better, Sam. Much, much better."

"I don't get it," he muttered, but he did not rise from the edge of the bed. He sat up straight, his feet squarely on the floor, one hand flat on each thigh, looking straight ahead, at attention.

Fernanda made no attempt to touch him again, although he looked adorable and sulky and frightened, the lamplight reflected on his young skin, his young lips, the nape of his young neck. She lowered her eyes while she spoke so that she could watch the effect of her words on him. Her voice had become very soft and she was careful not to move, to preserve the distance between them.

"Hasn't it ever occurred to you, Sam, that a woman like me might find something very . . . interesting . . . about a young man of your age? When you're still as young as you are, Sam, you have . . . powers that older men don't have. But you don't have the opportunities, do you, especially in military school? It doesn't seem fair to me. All that power going to waste.''

She paused for a minute and caressingly repeated, ''All that power.'' She watched the boy tremble and grip his thighs with his hands as hard as he could. Such big hands, she thought, the hands of a full-grown man.

''Tell me something,'' Fernanda asked, drawing out every word cajolingly, whispering as if she were begging him to tell her secrets. ''Have you ever had a woman, Sam? On your honor? Have you ever had a naked woman in your bed, a woman who would let you do anything to her? Hmmm? I think I know something private about you, Sam. I think that in that military academy of yours, night after night, you get into bed and then you can't fall asleep for the longest time because you get hard, Sam, your cock gets so terribly hard, so terribly big, because you need a woman so much, and the more you think about it the bigger and harder you get, so very hard that you think you're going to die if you don't have a woman . . . isn't that true, Sam?''

''Stop,'' he groaned, ''please stop.'' His legs were still firmly planted on the floor, but Fernanda could see that under the taut crotch of his chinos a heavy ridge of flesh was lengthening up flat against his stomach more than halfway to his belt. Sam sat completely immobile except for his hands punishing his thighs, afraid to make a move in her direction, too embarrassed to look at Fernanda but terribly aware of the uncontrollable excitement that her whispered words were causing. He still looked straight ahead into the dimness of the bedroom but he knew that his penis was jerking against the fabric of his trousers in a way that nobody could miss. Fern Kilkullen had dominated his sexual fantasies for years, but he was so shy that it had taken the greatest effort to speak to her tonight. Now he was terrified that he'd come in his pants if she kept on speaking to him like that.

''Do you know what I think, Sam?'' Fernanda said in her teasing, little-girl, secret-telling voice. ''I think that in bed at school, you imagine a woman, a woman who's only wearing a tiny pair of panties, so transparent that you can almost see through them, almost but not quite, but you can see that there's a darkness between her legs. And then you let yourself imagine that this woman is pushing her panties down, very slowly but very deliberately, so that you can get a really good look at the wonderful hair, blond hair, like mine, so soft and secret between her legs, and then you get harder and harder and you can't stop yourself from putting your hand on your own cock and rubbing yourself, just a little at first, and then more and more, and then you let yourself imagine that the woman pushes her panties all the way down and kicks them off so that they don't hold her legs together. She's completely naked now but she doesn't say anything, she doesn't make a sound, she just lies there with her legs spread a little bit apart and she's moving her ass around on the bed, she can't help it, Sam, because she's so hot knowing that you're looking at her and seeing that you're getting more and more ready for her, oh, so hard, Sam, so ready and then you finally can't help it either, you imagine yourself reaching over and putting your fingers on her pussy and the woman still doesn't say anything but she can't stop squirming, trying to lift herself up toward you, and then she puts her own hands on her pussy, right over your fingers, and ever so slowly she opens her legs so that you can see what the hair is hiding and you know that now, now you can stick it inside her— oh, my goodness . . . Sam, I'm going to have to take that big cock of yours out of your pants or you'll be in trouble, won't you?'' Fernanda whispered.

She leaned over quickly, deftly unzipped his fly, took out his straining, painfully tumescent penis. "Oh, it's so big, so beautiful and big," she said and held it in her palms, not moving her fingers. As she spoke the boy, goaded beyond any restraint, reared backwards and fell onto the bed, biting his lips together to stifle his cries. He flooded immediately into her cupped hands in quick, huge spurts and with each spurt he bit his lips harder so that no sound escaped him. Finally his penis lay heavily in Fernanda's palms. She let it fall forward onto the quilt while she leaned over to the towel on the bed, and wiped her hands dry. The boy pushed himself back onto the bed, clutching his trousers, his eyes still firmly closed, panting in relief. Fernanda bent over him and realized from his expression that he still didn't dare look at her, that he was embarrassed by the quickness of his spasms.

"Oh, Sam, you did just what I wanted, exactly what I wanted you to do," Fernanda assured him. "You're going to come again and again, until you think you can't come anymore. *I'm going to milk you dry.*"

"I don't get it," he said breathlessly, almost sobbing. He opened his eyes and looked at her. "Why did you do that to me? You made me come so fast, those things you said, you knew I would, I couldn't help it. You treated me like a toy!"

"Listen, Sam," Fernanda said, in a low but relentlessly carnal tone, "I'll let you do and see all sorts of things you've dreamed of and some you haven't—and if that's not good enough, you can leave. We're just beginning, that was just a sample. You don't want to leave now, do you? Wouldn't you rather stay here with me, Sam?" While she was talking to him she was unfastening her halter and unzipping her deerskin pants so that they slid to the floor. She stood totally naked in front of him and he rose up on his elbows, gaping in astonishment, too stunned to say a word.

"Now, Sam, just watch, don't you dare move," she warned him as she let her hands wander down her body, lifting and cupping her marvelous breasts and squeezing them enticingly together, and then smoothing herself caressingly over her slightly rounded belly and her delicately full hips until she brushed her hands enticingly over her pubic hair, her thighs parted a few inches. "Ah . . . yes . . . I knew I couldn't trust you," Fernanda said, even as she displayed the softness and shape of her body, fingering herself shamelessly. "You're getting hard again, Sam."

She had no intention of letting the boy touch her until he was so spent that he'd be ready to take her directions. She licked her fingers and teased her nipples until they stood up hard and firm and pale brown on her rosy, lush breasts. The cadet began to breathe with difficulty. "Take your clothes off but don't get off the bed," Fernanda told him. She watched him as he struggled quickly out of his clothes, her hands never leaving her tense nipples, breathing deeply as he revealed his lanky but powerful naked body. "Now lie back on the pillows and say, 'I'm your slave,' say it out loud."

"No!" he protested.

"If you don't say it I'll leave. Say it and play with your cock while you say it. Rub yourself the way you do when you're all alone, show me how you do it."

"Oh God!"

"Say it!"

"I'm your slave, I'll do anything, just let me put it in you."

"Oh no, no, not yet. You still have to do what I want, Sam. Don't worry about it, just look at me, watch what I'm doing, and keep playing with your cock. I want to watch you do it. Don't stop, don't stop and don't try to touch me no matter what I do."

Fernanda stood close to him as he lay on the bed, so that at eye level he could see her sucking the middle finger of one hand and putting it between her legs. She rubbed it back and forth, returned her finger to her mouth, sucked on it and then put it back on the fattening, succulent bit of flesh.

"What are you, Sam?"

"I'm your slave," he moaned through dry lips, feeling his penis fill and rise under his rapidly moving fingers.

"What am I doing, Sam?"

"Touching . . . yourself. Oh God, let me stick it in you, please, just once," he implored.

"I'm all wet inside, Sam—but you can't put it in me, you can't touch, you can look but you can't touch. Keep playing with yourself."

"No," he said unsteadily. "I won't. I'm not a baby."

"Then I'll have to do it for you," Fernanda said ruthlessly, leaning down so that her hair brushed his testicles. She took the jerking, rearing, meaty penis in her hands and with sure, swift, merciless strokes massaged it up and down, with a knowing, dominating rhythm, until he fell back on the bed, giving himself up to her without resistance, moaning for her not to stop, not to stop, not ever to stop. He came in seconds, not flooding into her hands with the ease of the first time, but spurting separate convulsive contractions that were so powerful that he could do nothing to keep himself from uttering cries of abandon.

"Good, Sam, that was very good," Fernanda praised him as she wiped her hands on the towel. "My slave, that's exactly what you are. And you've finally learned to obey me."

She lay down next to him on the bed, and looked at the boy. The cadet was utterly limp, almost as if he were unconscious, every muscle, every joint, every tendon of his young body relaxed, his head and his body turned away from her, as he lay on his side.

Yes, he was the nameless, faceless, devoted slave she had fantasized about for so many years—or as close as she was ever going to get. He was exhausted, all desire gone. In a minute she would allow him to touch her, make him follow every direction she gave him. When he finally got hard again, he'd know that he had to wait until she was ready. He belonged to her, he'd learned his lesson, she'd trained him. Why had she never tried a boy before, a slave boy, Fernanda wondered dreamily, and for a few minutes she drifted off to sleep.

She woke to find herself pinioned under Sam's body. His penis, enlarged with the almost impossible growth of a man aroused for the third time, was pulsating at the entrance to her vagina and her legs were spread apart by his knees. With a grunt he pushed the swollen tip roughly into her, grinding it forward until he filled her completely.

"So I'm your slave, am I? I'm fucking you good, you cock-tease. Can a slave do that?" he asked ferociously. "I'll show you what kind of slave I am."

"Stop! Stop or I'll scream."

"I don't give a shit. You'll take my cock and you'll like it."

"Sam, I'll tell your mother!"

"Oh sure. How did I get to your room? Shut up. You want it, I know you do."

"I don't!"

"Yes, you do!" He fell silent, gritting his teeth as he pulled his penis back violently so that he could shove it forward with all his strength, grinding it into her body with the crazed, untutored power that only a very young man has. His breathing was uneven, he didn't touch her with his lips or his hands, all his frenzied concentration was on his penis, and although Fernanda fought in an effort to stop him, it was as if he had jammed a rod into her. Faster and faster he labored, thrashing about on the bed, as unconcerned about the woman he was in as if he were in a whorehouse. Finally he rode her into his racking, torturous, short orgasm. He lay heavily on her, still swollen, until finally, as she pummeled him, he pulled out, falling away from her without a word.

Fernanda jumped up, trembling with fury and shock, ran to her closet and hastily put on a robe.

"Get out of here, you filthy little bastard!"

"Christ, give me a break. You got what you wanted, didn't you? Whatever it was. I'll bet you don't get it like that every day, either."

"Just get out!"

"Sure." He stumbled about, putting on his clothes, so weak that he could hardly stand. "Wow, when I think of the things I imagined—nothing came close. Say, Fern, O.K. if I take the Jeep? I've got to get back to my car."

"Take it," Fernanda mumbled. "Hurry."

"I'm going. Listen, don't worry, I won't tell. Nobody'd ever believe this anyway. How lucky can you get?"

=====

"It was one of the best Fiestas I can remember," Jazz assured her father, after the last of the guests in the hacienda had finally taken themselves off to bed toward three in the morning.

"You still look as if you could stay up all night," he said, "but not in that dress."

"No, Cousin Casey finished off this one too. I would have changed again, but I didn't have anything except jeans to wear, and if I had had another dress, who knows what he might have done to it? I couldn't risk it."

"He didn't do it on purpose," Mike Kilkullen protested, sitting relaxed in one of the two armchairs in his bedroom, where he and Jazz had retreated while Casey moved his luggage from Jazz's room to the guest room that would be his for the year.

"Freud says there are no accidents," Jazz said, her eyebrows high in amusement.

"Total bullshit," he answered lazily.

"You tell him, Dad."

"So you and Casey made friends, after all?"

"The guy can dance, if that's what you mean."

"Well, you two danced all night."

"So did you," Jazz answered tartly. "With Red."

"So I did. I hadn't thought you'd noticed."

"Nothing escapes my eye. Listen, Dad, I'm going to bed. I have to go back to L.A. tomorrow morning, damn it."

Jazz got up from her chair and bent to kiss her father on the top of his head. As she turned to leave his room, she saw the picture she had taken of her mother that always stood on his night table. For one instant it was like looking at a picture of herself, and then quickly it dissolved into the familiar enlarged snapshot that was one of the first photographs she had ever taken. Jazz had inherited the precise set of her mother's eyes and the shape of her eyebrows, nothing more, but in a quick glance that was always the first thing she noticed. Strangers sometimes noticed it

too, but the differences between her coloring and
Sylvie Norberg's, the differences in the shapes of their
mouths and the ways their hair grew, often made them
miss the resemblance.

Did her father ever sit and gaze into the eyes of
that photograph, she wondered, or was it just habit
that made him keep it there, the only photograph in
the room?

Sylvie Norberg arrived in California in January of
1959. The Swedish drama student, who was not yet
twenty, had been discovered by Hollywood after she
appeared in an Ingmar Bergman film. She was the only
child of a pair of Stockholm intellectuals, her father
an art critic and her mother a set designer of repute.
They lived an intense bohemian life that was centered
on their daughter. The Norbergs had consistently nur-
tured Sylvie's early evident talent and encouraged her
strong, inborn sense of selfhood.

Her parents had given Sylvie the kind of personal
power that only comes to someone who has never
known what it is to need or to seek approbation. Approval had always surrounded her, unnoticed and totally accepted and expected, taken for granted like the
law of gravity.

Sylvie Norberg had a flawless confidence about
the choices she made for herself, a confidence that
would be rare in a mature woman. Throughout her
childhood and girlhood, her free-thinking parents em-
phasized that her obligation was to exist in the way
she felt was right for her. Sylvie Norberg was so quietly certain of her decisions, and so winning in her
imposition of them, that no one ever questioned her
entitlement.

She became an international star in her first
American film, the kind of star who becomes, quite
simply, *inevitable,* as soon as she is properly presented on the screen, just as Audrey Hepburn was in
Roman Holiday. Sylvie accepted stardom with a luminous and supremely modest grace, no more awed

or surprised by this turn of events than would be a young princess who has known since birth that she is destined to wear a crown.

The very texture of her attitudes, her foreign upbringing, her foreign standards, her enchanting gravity, were so different from that of other young Hollywood stars that the press treated everything she said with serious respect. She conquered journalists without making the slightest attempt to do so. She spoke English slightly too well, in a slight Scandinavian accent that gave her words a weight of charm and meaningfulness that no other accent in spoken English can produce.

Sylvie Norberg was not a flaxen Swedish blond. She had soft dark blond hair with a slight natural wave, cut simply just below her chin. A light as changeable and mysterious as a combination of moonstones and moonbeams poured from her clear gray eyes, a light that could be kindled by a word, extinguished by a word, a mesmerizing light that made everyone who saw her wonder what she was thinking. Except for her supremely interesting regard, Sylvie's beauty was untheatrical, touchingly simple and uncomplicated, the look of a woodland dryad, with a freshness that was exactly right for the dawn of the 1960s. She looked like a sensitive tomboy with a mind of her own, a quality that was the essence of the way women wanted to look in a reaction against the sophisticated, mature stars of the past.

Indifferent to public opinion and free of any sense of the limitations that life imposed on ordinary people, Sylvie's personal motto was simple. What she wanted, she would have.

Throughout her youth she had a history of taking the right turnings on the paths of life. But Sweden, she knew, was not as complicated as Hollywood. In the film industry she would have to stand up for herself or come to belong to a system whose ideals didn't match hers.

After her second film was completed, the summer of 1959, Sylvie Norberg took a holiday at exactly the moment when an ambitious American actress would have thrown herself into her career without a thought for anything else. But Sylvie had just completed two major pictures, back to back, with all the obligations of interviews and photo sessions attendant on the emergence of a new star, and she decided that she wanted time off to absorb her new experiences.

It wasn't possible to spend the summer in Sweden because she had a movie commitment for September which would require several costume and wig fittings in Hollywood during the months of July and August. Still she was conscious of a deep need to hear Swedish again, to speak Swedish again. She missed the cadence of her native tongue far more than she had expected she would. Sylvie accepted a standing invitation to stay with a cousin of her father's, Sven Hansen, who ran a small Swedish coffeehouse in San Juan Capistrano.

In San Juan she would be near enough to Los Angeles to take the train up for the day, but the tiny old town, built around the ruins of its great Mission, was so quaint, so old-fashioned and so far off the beaten track, that summer there would be as refreshing as a trip to a foreign country. Her first picture hadn't reached the one movie house in San Juan yet, Sven assured her, and her second wouldn't be released until the fall. "Some folk may recognize you, particularly after that *Life* magazine cover," Sven said, "but they won't bother you if you don't want them to. And you can count on me not to boast about my famous cousin."

In the spring of 1959, Mike and Liddy Kilkullen finally admitted to each other that they had reached the end of their marriage. The upbringing of their daughters had provided the thin glue that had kept them together for so long. They had never been able to paper over the fact that they had each, quite simply, married the wrong person.

Her thirtieth birthday had galvanized Liddy, forc-

ing her to focus on her discontent, and had made her
decide to get out while she still could. Valerie was
eleven and Fernanda was eight, and she nourished
flint-hard, lofty ambitions for them. She intended them
to have all the things she had given up, things they
would never have if they continued to grow up on the
ranch. She had endured its isolation from a major city
for ten endless years, but if she didn't take them East
now and put them into good schools, they would never
have the polish necessary to take their proper places
in the world.

Liddy gathered up her daughters and returned to
her parents' house in Chestnut Hill, near Philadelphia,
to spend the summer before filing for divorce. She
wanted to consult her family's lawyers before she took
the final step.

Mike Kilkullen did not try to stop her. It was far
too late for that, he thought with a mixture of acqui-
escence and a deep sense of failure. If it were not for
the children, he and Liddy would have been nothing
more than memories to each other for the last decade.
They would work out an arrangement so that the girls
would spend as much time with him as possible, but
he had long known that she would one day go back to
a life she should never have left.

It had been more than two years since she had let
him touch her. He didn't blame Liddy any more than
he blamed himself for not agreeing to her repeated
suggestions that he sell the ranch and try to make a
life for them in Philadelphia. Even the fact that she
could come up with such an insane notion showed how
pitifully mistaken they had been to get married in the
first place.

The weather that spring had been as good as his
inner climate had been dismal. After heavy winter
rains, the mesas of the ranch had turned as green as
Ireland, the cattle had eaten their fill, and after the
roundup in March, the crop of healthy, well-grown
young calves had fetched record prices. Mike Kilkullen bought two prize bulls at the auction in the Cow
Palace in San Francisco and put the rest of his profits

for the year in the San Clemente Bank, where he did all his banking.

You couldn't get rich as a cattleman, Mike reflected, not in California, but if you didn't live too high, if you took care of your land and your stock and you kept enough flat crop land rented to provide you with an annual income that you could count on—well, you'd never starve, that was for damn sure.

In Texas the sixty-four-thousand-acre ranch would be considered a small spread, yet at thirty-four Mike Kilkullen found himself one of the major landowners in all of Southern California. The ranch covered almost one-sixth of Orange County, and even though he voted Democratic, he was considered an outstanding citizen—if you forgot the fact that his personal life was as dry as a sinkhole and as bleak as the land above the treeline on Old Saddleback.

Self-pity makes me want to puke, Mike said to himself, and drove into San Juan to see if Sven Hansen's coffeehouse was still open. He could use a piece of cake and a cup of coffee. He wasn't in the mood to mingle with the merry, thoroughly sloshed crowd that hung out at the Swallows bar tonight, but the hacienda was so empty after dinner, without his children, that he had to get out or risk feeling sorry for himself. The trouble with cattle, he thought, was that the critters were inclined to sleep at night. If they didn't, he'd never have to stop working and start thinking.

The coffeehouse was empty when Mike looked in, but behind the counter he saw a girl in a summer dress washing a cup and saucer. Sven must have hired a waitress, he thought, and went in and sat down.

"Miss? Is it too late to order?"

"What is your pleasure, sir?" Sylvie asked. She'd come down from her room for a cup of coffee and was about to close for the night, since Sven was out. But she'd played a waitress once, and suddenly it amused her to play one tonight. The thought filled her eyes with a wanton light.

"Coffee, please, and some of Sven's seedcake if you have any left."

Holy Mary, Mother of God, what was his pleasure? Show him another waitress in all the world who looked at him with such delicate mockery, who asked that question in that wonderful accent, using those insanely inflammatory words, and he'd show her what his pleasure was. His pleasure was to kiss her until she was dizzy, to start with . . .

"May I offer you cream, or do you prefer it as it comes?" Sylvie asked.

"Black's fine. Have you worked here long?"

"Only a week. Sven is my father's cousin."

"Are you here for long?"

"I am visiting for the summer only," Sylvie said regretfully.

"Do you have a name?" asked Mike Kilkullen.

"Sylvie . . ."

He was splendid, Sylvie thought. After six busy but lonely months in Hollywood she had begun to wonder where she would find the only kind of man who attracted her, the fully adult yet uncomplicated, utterly masculine men she'd found in Sweden. She had no time for the actors or the producers, directors and writers of Hollywood. They all were too fragmented, too artificial, too preoccupied with the silly, necessary business of movies.

This stranger reminded her of the giants of mythology that she had studied at school, so tall, so broad, so commanding. He looked like a leader of men, he looked like a lover of women, he looked like a man who never put a foot inside a house if he could help it. She studied his strongly hewn features in his square face, his ferociously blue eyes, his fine, aquiline, aristocratic nose and thatch of thick red hair, wondering what background had created this man. She would have him, she decided. She wanted him. Now.

"I'm Mike Kilkullen," he said, getting up and shaking hands. "Would you care to sit down and have a cup of coffee?"

"Is it permitted for a waitress to join a customer?"

"In San Juan Capistrano, everything is permitted," Mike said, with his slow smile. "Welcome to Liberty Hall."

"Do you live in this neighborhood, Mike Kilkullen?" she asked gravely, sitting down. Of course he had to be Irish. Why had she not known at once? A creature of the north, like herself. A man with hot blood and no doubt a bad temper, given to deep loyalties, intense stubbornness, sometimes abandoned to melancholy, living always with a touch of madness.

"I own a ranch about five miles south of town."

"What do you grow?"

"Grow? I'm a cattleman," he said with a surge of pride in being able to so present himself to this lovely woman, for she was too composed, too sure of herself, to be considered a girl. "Would you like to visit my ranch? Someday soon? I can arrange it with Sven. Do you ride?"

He was as anxious as a boy asking a girl to the senior prom. Did this woman have any idea how beautiful she was? It puzzled him enormously to find her working in such a simple place, at such an unexpected job, but he thought it would be rude to ask her personal questions.

"I love to ride. Can you provide me with a mount?"

"No problem."

"Tomorrow is my day off," Sylvie said.

"But that's Saturday. Won't Sven need you?"

"Perhaps he will, but I won't be here. I will be riding with you, won't I? In Liberty Hall?" When Sylvie smiled, the little pockets of flesh under her eyes, those expressive puffs of amusement, suddenly changed the quality of her gravity to sheer joy.

"You've picked up the customs of the country already."

"I've been told I'm a quick study."

"I'll come by for you whenever you say. I can pack a lunch and we can ride out to the ocean and have a picnic by the bluffs."

"Oh yes! That is exactly what I want to do to-morrow—and I always do what I want."

"My father used to come down here, wade in and practically scoop the lobsters up in his bare hands," Mike told Sylvie as they galloped up to a cove set into yellow bluffs down which tumbled a blaze of magenta and purple bougainvillea. They dismounted and Mike threw a blanket, a package of sandwiches, and a thermos down in front of a pile of driftwood where they could eat sheltered from the breeze that blew steadily along the shore.

To their left the Pacific broke in a never-ending chevron of foaming waves and high-tossed white spray against the boulders of Valencia Point.

Between the cove and the water lay a wide, firm beach on which the darkish sand, at low tide, was webbed with a network of seaweed and fringes of foam, bubbly threads of kelp, and the furze of tide plants. Above them floated an endless sunny tent of sky agleam with the particular gauzy, intoxicating lightness that only forms where sky and ocean meet.

Mike unsaddled the horses so that they could wander at will. Sylvie ran out onto the beach, where drops of water sparkled on the sea's leavings, and stood just clear of the low-tide mark, shading her eyes with her hands as she slowly turned in a full circle. The ocean, the beach, the miles and miles of green hills, the tip of the mountain that was visible in the far distance above the edge of the low bluffs—she spun around and around and looked far out to the horizon and opened her arms in delight at the limitless freedom of this place that stretched from sea to mountaintop.

"It's heaven!" she cried, and began to run wildly up the empty beach toward no particular destination, a reaction common to many humans when they find themselves standing on the edge of a continent. Mike Kilkullen laughed at the sight of the two horses, who broke into a gallop as she ran, all three creatures at one with the sea, the sun, the air and the eternal rhythm of the breakers. He ran out to join Sylvie, and the two of them raced up and down the beach, changing directions unexpectedly, swerving and skidding and bumping into each other as senselessly as unleashed puppies, until they had to stop because they were breathless and gasping.

They fell onto the sand, immediately discovered that it was soaking wet, helped each other up, laughing helplessly, and tottered up the slope to the cove, where they collapsed on the blanket, still laughing.

"Don't you want to kiss me?" Sylvie asked when she could talk.

"That's the dumbest question I ever heard," Mike answered, and pinioned her in his arms. She was finely made and slender, he was big and solid, but they were both strong and equally given over to a madness that had possessed them both since they had laid eyes on each other the night before, a need that had kept them both up all night, filled with feverish imaginings.

Impetuous, clumsy, awkward in their frantic eagerness, they kissed and embraced with a hastiness that bruised their lips and made them bump their noses and chins together until they found the right way to fit their faces together.

Sylvie started to unbutton Mike's shirt while he was kissing her. She had to see the whiteness of his skin where the line of tan stopped below his open shirt, she had to put her hands flat on the muscles of his great chest and feel their strength, she had to rub the texture of the hair on his chest against her open palms. She had taken lovers since she was just sixteen, but not one of them had ever made her feel so ravenously, mindlessly urgent, as if this act had to take place before the rest of her life could begin.

"Wait!" Mike said as she began tugging impatiently at his belt. "Are you sure you know what you're doing?"

"The *dumbest* question—why don't you help?" He looked into Sylvie's eyes and there he saw the answer to his question, there he saw that with this

woman he had entered a strange and foreign world in
which no more questions were necessary. He had only
to follow her lead.

"I'm helping," Mike said, and stripped naked in
seconds. He laid Sylvie down flat on the blanket and
undid her white linen shirt and unzipped her white
slacks deftly, although his fingers were trembling.

"Hurry," she commanded, wriggling out of her
clothes without the slightest hesitation.

"Hurry?" He wanted to explore the marvels of
her body slowly and carefully.

"I want you now," she said, in a low, vibrating
voice that brooked no argument, and in a supple, sudden movement she sat up on the blanket and launched
herself over him, toppling him down so that she was
perched on top of him, her legs parted, pressing his
thighs together. She took his erect penis in her hand
and paused a moment, glorying in its bulk and readiness, and then, without a word, she moved forward
and upward, and slowly, unhesitatingly, impaled herself on it, a slim, firm, white column of flesh, braced
on the heels of her hands, her breasts pointing upward, her head thrown back and her lips parted in a
grimace of mingled pain and victory, as if she were
a runner who had broken the tape at the finish line of
a race.

Then she lay forward on his chest and stretched
her legs straight out over his, her full weight on him,
so that their two bodies were together, flesh to flesh,
for their entire length. He was so much larger than she
was that her weight felt like nothing, and he lay back,
willing himself to control, waiting to see what she
would have him do next. She rested for a minute,
feeling him swelling steadily and ever more tightly inside of her, listening to his heartbeat, measuring the
sound of his breathing, feeling the beat of his pulses.

He was like a huge untamed animal she had
hunted on a savage shore and brought to ground, she
thought, with the sun hot on her back and the taste of
salt on her lips. Now there was no hurry, now she all
but owned him. What she wanted she would have.

Now she could give herself up to the play of luxurious and deliberate movement, squeezing her pelvic muscles together so faintly that the change she made might not have been perceptible to a man less aroused than Mike Kilkullen.

That tiny tingle of a signal was all he needed. He put his arms around her slight, perfect body and, without withdrawing from her, he lifted her easily and placed her under him so that he was gazing down at her. They looked at each other and he saw that she understood that no woman was going to ride him into submission, no woman was going to rush him into a climax for which he wasn't prepared.

Slowly he eased himself completely out of her body and guided the underside of his penis deliberately and carefully back and forth across the fiery axis of moist flesh between her legs. Then he entered her again, pushing into her steadily, pausing between each inch of progress, coming to rest solidly inside her while she clenched and unclenched her muscles against him. No word passed between them as he pulled out again and rubbed himself slowly against the tender, burning, most secret place of her body, feeling her lifting her hips higher and higher, listening to the rhythm of her breathing quicken and catch and hold as she squeezed her eyes tightly shut. Only when he felt the first unmistakable tightening and lunging of her buttocks, only when he heard her begin to cry out, did he allow himself to quickly reenter her warmth and give himself up to the rhythm that would bring them both to the fullness of their passion.

They lay on their sides, clasped in each other's arms, his penis still inside her.

"This can't have happened," Mike said in a voice that seemed to be that of a stranger.

"It usually doesn't," she answered, laughing softly.

"Don't laugh, I'll slip out if you do."

"Sooner or later you will anyway," she assured him, still laughing.

"Are you such an expert?" Mike asked, suddenly

alert, and there was an undertone to his question that made her pull away immediately and sit up, a creature from a magic wood who had ventured out of the protection of the forest into the full sun of day, her arms clasped around her knees, hiding her breasts.

"There is no better sport I know in which to be an expert." There was no challenge in her voice, only a serene certainty of the truth of her statement, but her eyes were no longer laughing.

"What I mean . . . what I'm trying to say . . . you—" Mike sat up too, suddenly feeling that lying down he was at a disadvantage.

"What you're trying and failing to say, my darling, is that you're surprised—no, shocked—to find that a woman you have known only since last night gives herself to you so freely. And that she considers making love a sport that one should do well. Isn't that so? You don't even have to answer, I can see it on your face. You expected to have to pay court to me for weeks before I might—just might—let you have me like this, and even then I would not be the one to choose the moment. And it would have been at night, wouldn't it? According to your expectations, I should have had to 'get to know you' first."

"You're putting words in my mouth," he protested, but he knew that everything she said was true.

"No, not at all. I'm reading your mind. You're an American male, and I have learned to understand them, how they think, what they believe, how they feel women should behave. I didn't expect you to be the single exception in this country."

Sylvie's dignity was total and touching, her gentle sense of authority implicit in every sentence she spoke, although she was still flushed in the aftermath of love and so tousled that she looked even younger than her twenty years.

"Damn, I don't understand you!" Mike exclaimed in the frustration of incomprehension. "You told me you were some kind of relative of Sven's, here on a short visit, you're working for him at the coffeehouse—now you're an expert on American male behavior and thought. But you're too beautiful to be a sociologist or an anthropologist or a professor of some kind. You're altogether too beautiful and too sure of yourself and too damn knowing about sex to be any ordinary woman. What's going on here?''

Kneeling, he grabbed Sylvie by her shoulders and pulled her close, tipping her chin up with his thumb and fixing her gaze. ''Just what *is* going on here,'' he repeated. ''Are you a mermaid or some kind of changeling or elf in human disguise?''

''Only an actress,'' she told him, lowering her lids and smiling innocently.

'' 'Only an actress'? Only an actress where?''

''Stockholm . . . and . . . Hollywood.''

''A movie actress? I've never seen you. What have you done in English?''

''Only two movies. The first was *Perfect Strangers*. The second one, *The Inconstant Wife*, hasn't been released yet.''

''I haven't seen a movie in six months, but I read the papers from time to time. *Perfect Strangers* was a huge hit. What part did you play?''

''The lead.''

''The girl they called the new Ingrid Bergman, the girl they . . .''

''Yes, yes, yes! I was going to tell you anyway, so you can stop this interrogation. I'm a movie star, not just an actress. Does that bother you?''

''I have the feeling that it should, but I don't exactly know why,'' Mike said slowly, trying to absorb this oddly unwelcome information. He felt surprised, confused and disoriented, as if something had shifted and dimmed, as if a cloud had passed over the sun. ''Does it bother *you*?''

''It's my work,'' Sylvie answered lightly, casually, ''but it isn't easy for other people to see me clearly when they think 'movie star'—that's why I pretended to be a waitress last night—although I wouldn't have bothered for anyone but you.''

"Is Sven really your father's cousin?"

"Oh yes, that much was true. And the coffee was real coffee."

"What else should I know about you that I don't?" he demanded, roused to impatience by her teasing.

"You know more already than any other man in America. And I know nothing about you, Mike Kilkullen, except that you make love marvelously. And that you can blush under your tan. Remarkable."

"I'm married, Sylvie, but my wife and I are separated. She's going to file for divorce in the fall. Sven doesn't know that. Nobody does. I have two daughters, eight and eleven. I'm thirty-four. Except for the army, I've lived here all my life. I'm a simple man, Sylvie. I don't know anything about your kind of life."

"Why should you? You are planted like a great tree here in this marvelous, *marvelous* place. You are in your element, bossing everyone around—oh, I saw how quickly you were obeyed when you ordered the horses saddled. This is your place, Mike, your home place. It must be so good to have land that no one can take away, a beach on the edge of the ocean, a mountain and all the miles and miles that lie between the two. You felt so solid, so real when I was lying on you, like the earth itself."

She sounded wistful, he thought, and almost forlorn. "Do you miss Sweden?" he asked. "Are you homesick, my beautiful crazy little movie star sweetheart?"

"I was homesick until today. I won't be if you hold me in your arms. I won't if you make love to me again. It's the only cure I know."

"Shall we make love as a cure or as a sport?"

"Both," Sylvie murmured into his lips. What she wanted she would have.

During the next two months, Mike Kilkullen hurried through his duties on the ranch, delegating authority freely for the first time since his father's death, so that he and Sylvie could spend as much time together as possible. He spoke immediately to his friend Sven Hansen, to tell him about his separation and the planned divorce, news that Sven accepted with little surprise and kept to himself.

However, Mike knew that he couldn't be seen again picking Sylvie up in front of the coffeehouse without involving the whole small town in a flurry of speculation and gossip. The hacienda was staffed by a new cook, Susie Dominguez, and two maids who were delighted to be told to go home early every evening, leaving the house empty and dinner on the stove. Sylvie bought a little car and at dusk, when the light was at its most beautiful, she drove out to the ranch to be with him. Their meetings were wild with an intemperate hunger that swiftly grew from passion to love.

At night, before they slept, they often walked around the vast private paradise of the peaceful, enclosed, unexpected gardens, a secret pattern of greenwalled rooms, stopping here and there to touch a white rose that signaled to them in the moonlight, to pick a few leaves of lavender and rub them between their fingertips, to dabble their hands in the fountain that stood in the center of the main patio, to sniff the many perfumes that the night released, finding all the hidden garden seats on which they could silently contemplate the immensity of their happiness, the nights so quiet that every whinny from the stables was clearly audible. With an unspoken, mutual mixture of superstition and willful blindness, they refused to discuss the future until it was almost time for Sylvie to go back to Los Angeles and start work on her new picture. Their nights had no edges or boundaries. Although their time together was circumscribed to the kingdom of the ranch, these hours of perfect happiness spilled over into their days, during which their love for each other was a constant, obstinate, aching presence in their bloodstreams, blurring the threadbare, ordinary, outside world.

On a Friday late in August, Sylvie finally broke the silence. "One more week . . . after the Labor Day weekend I must start work," she said tonelessly, and pulled at the petals of a faded ivy geranium, adding to the shower of pink that lay at her feet like confetti.

"Don't you think I know? I know to the hour. To the minute."

"What are we to do? It's unimaginable. I don't know how to start to think about it."

"Darling, it's very simple. I had a letter from my wife's lawyer last week. She's going to fly back to California and file for divorce. In a year from that day the divorce will be final. Next year, at this time, if you still love me, we'll get married."

"Nothing can be that simple," Sylvie said longingly.

"But it is," Mike answered with conviction, pushing aside the thought of the details of the letter he'd received.

He would pay Liddy twenty-five thousand dollars a year in alimony for life or until she remarried; he would assume all the children's expenses, including clothes, medical costs, private schools and eight years of higher education after high school. He would pay three hundred and fifty dollars a month per child in child support when the girls were out of school, unless they were with him. Liddy would take one-half of all his ranching profits since they had married. The only reason she wasn't entitled to half the ranch and half the house was that they belonged to him by inheritance.

His lawyer had protested angrily that he was being robbed blind, that the alimony and child-support payments were far higher than any court would award, higher than those imposed on any man except a rare millionaire, but Mike had accepted all the conditions.

He had his land, he had his herds, he had the Hacienda Valencia, he would always be able to take care of Sylvie, and he was willing to give Liddy whatever she asked in exchange for his freedom.

"It is that simple," he repeated, since Sylvie was looking at him with disbelief clear in her gaze.

"Mike Kilkullen, you oversimplify."

"I said, if you still love me . . . I'm not taking anything for granted. What more is there?"

"I will still love you."

Sylvie Norberg had never been as beautiful as when she said those words, nor had the mysterious, mesmerizing light that came from her eyes ever been so disturbing as when she slowly continued. Her self-confidence, always so reliable, was profoundly shaken as she realized the gravity of this decision.

"There are so many other things we haven't talked about," she said haltingly, as one detail followed the other. "My new film—I didn't want to spoil our time together with the details—but my new film is to be shot on location in England and Italy. That means I'll be away for three months. When I come back, I'll have a few weeks to be with you and then—after Christmas—there is another film I have accepted in Hollywood. We shoot every day during the week. Oh, my darling, I'll only be able to be with you on the weekends. Three months, Mike, three months apart—only a few weeks together before I start to work again, and then—only weekends. Are you willing to live like that?"

"I am, if you are," he said carefully, trying not to sound as grim as he felt. He hadn't made a serious effort to comprehend what a movie star's work meant in terms of sheer time. He had refused to face something he hoped would disappear by itself. But he could never let her go. That was not an option.

"But, Mike, do you think that you'll still mean that in the future—say five years from now? I warn you, my darling, it's not easy for an actress to be a good wife. Acting is not merely what I do, it's the one thing I absolutely *need* to do and *I must feel free to do it*. Free, Mike, really and truly free, without any guilt, without being torn apart by compromise, without ever looking over my shoulder at a part I turned down because I knew that it would upset you if I took it. *What I want, I must have*. The only way I know how to live, the only way I intend to live, is fully and deeply, taking everything I can from existence. It's as simple as that for me—I'm selfish, you see, dreadfully selfish, the kind of selfishness that it's fair to call ruthless. I'm determined to live exactly as I choose, no matter what anyone wants of me, no matter what anyone says. This summer, these months with you—they've been —outside—the rest of my life. I may never *be* like this again. We may never have months like these again. If you change your mind about me, I will never blame you.''

"I'm willing to take my chances," he replied confidently. He could tear out his heart with his bare hands more easily than he could change his mind now. And how could any twenty-year-old girl—even this beloved, fierce, eloquent nymph—possibly imagine how she would feel in five years? She thought she was a philosopher, she thought she could see into the future, she thought she knew exactly how she wanted to lead the rest of her life, but already she had been changed by love more than she guessed. How could she imagine that she was selfish and ruthless? Those ridiculous words alone proved that she was overdramatizing the situation. Of course she'd always be free to act, but didn't she realize that love inevitably took away perfect freedom? That no one had *ever* had both? She'd find that out sooner or later, God knows, for marriage changed women even more than it changed men.

"I think," Sylvie said, so thoughtfully that she sounded sad and somber, "that perhaps a woman like me should never marry. Perhaps it is not fair to any man."

Now he was sure that she was a little cockeyed, Mike Kilkullen told himself as he shut her up firmly with a storm of kisses. A woman like her was meant to be married if ever a woman was. If his darling Swede were allowed to run around without a wedding ring on her finger, no man was safe. If she wanted to go away from time to time and do the work she loved almost as much as she loved him, so be it. In any case, what choice did he have?

6

In the summer of 1960, Lydia Henry Stack Kilkullen flew out to California to pick up her final divorce papers. She rented a car at the airport and checked into a room she'd reserved at the Beverly Wilshire Hotel. This was, she realized, the first time she'd ever spent a night on her own in Los Angeles, a city that was an hour and a half's drive from San Juan Capistrano, but a galaxy apart in attitude.

During her early years of life at the ranch, Liddy had been aggressively antisocial. Since she knew in advance that Orange County would never provide the kind of society she belonged in, she had turned her back on it. Orange County had never noticed. However, in the sixth year of her marriage, she had formed a friendship with a childless couple from San Clemente, Nora and Deems White, the son and daughter-in-law of Henry White, who had long been the Kilkullens' banker.

Nora was an immensely rich girl, an orphan who had inherited a vast fortune from her San Diego family, but to Liddy she had always been without interest, in spite of her money and the good schools to which she had been sent. Nora was lumpy and irredeemably plain, with no charm or conversation. She adored her husband and harbored great ambitions for him, which she shared with her father-in-law.

Deems White, a lawyer, was an exceptionally attractive man, indeed so attractive that it was apparent to anyone who met the couple that he could only have married Nora for her money. Yet such was Deems White's charm that people not only didn't hold the cold-blooded marriage against him, but thought that Nora had been damned lucky to get him.

Deems White was of middle height, with straight sandy hair above a finely molded, sensitive yet somehow impish face. He resembled a young English university don in a 1920s photograph, with his long, mildly crooked nose, his reluctant, sideways grin, his ever-present pipe and his way of casually wearing his well-chosen clothes.

Deems couldn't make himself take the legal profession seriously, although he was as clever as any well-connected lawyer needed to be. However, it was one way to pacify his father about his future, since Henry White, the dominating parent of an only child, never ceased to insist that Deems had the capacity to do something important with his life. Indeed, Henry White had engineered his son's marriage with the thought that Nora's money would help Deems's future, and he had found it useful to go along with his father's plan.

If Deems White had had his own private income, he would have drifted to Europe and fallen in with a raffish, rich, bohemian group who lived off their unearned wealth, who painted a little, who wrote a little, who skied a little, drank a lot and didn't care with whom they slept. Nora's income was the closest he'd come to inherited wealth, since his father gave him nothing more than the legal business he steered toward his son. The young Whites' large house and frequent trips to Europe were the nearest equivalent to the life Deems felt he had been born for.

Fortunately for Deems, Nora was a worshipful woman, painfully aware of her plainness, who was easy to please, and easier still to ignore. She was convinced that it was entirely her fault that her husband made love to her only on the rarest of occasions. Sex, she decided, wasn't important to her, but it was essential to be able to live in Deems's beloved shadow and she was grateful to spend her large income keeping him happy.

In 1953, Henry White gave a dinner party to celebrate his fifteenth year as president of the San Clemente Bank. Mike Kilkullen insisted that Liddy make an effort and go with him to honor the man who had been his father's banker, and whose grandfather had been his grandfather's banker.

Liddy agreed, although an evening with San Clemente's small and provincial business community made her turn up her nose. She was twenty-four at the time, the mother of one five-year-old child with a bad cold and another who was two and teething, but as soon as she applied makeup and dressed, Liddy became utterly un-Californian, a sophisticated woman who was far more brittle and hard-edged than she had been when Mike Kilkullen first laid eyes on her. Her mouth was firmly painted in scarlet now, her skin powdered uncompromisingly white, and she had learned to use eye makeup in a discreet but striking way. She was aware that she reminded people of a young version of the Duchess of Windsor, and did nothing to diminish the resemblance.

Liddy came from a background in which women rarely departed far from the hairstyle they wore in their debutante year. However, the waves that had once fallen to her shoulders had been cut so that her neat cap of hair was chin-length and parted in the middle. Her profile was cosmopolitan in its severity, and her inborn, un-Philadelphian sense of style was kept up to date by the fashion magazines she devoured in grieving frustration every month. For the Whites' dinner party she decided to wear a Donald Brooks black linen dress, a completely self-confident, East Coast dress that she had ordered from Bullock's in Los Angeles, without any real expectation that she might need it.

Liddy found herself seated next to Deems White at the dinner. The two of them, evenly matched in age, equally disappointed in their lives, equally unable or unwilling to do anything about their unsatisfactory situations, immediately fell into a deep and intimate conversation which they both knew had to be resumed as soon as possible.

From that first night they divined things about each other that they hadn't yet spoken of; they sensed clearly that they would become important in each other's lives; and, without a word, they shared a mutual knowledge that it was essential to hide this sudden, intense affinity from the eyes of the world. It was too strong to be analyzed, too strong to be given a name. It was more than a friendship, more than a flirtation, it had nothing to do with sex. It was a meeting of two people who needed each other emotionally for reasons they couldn't explain, didn't need to explain, didn't want to explain. But the need was painfully real.

There was no business reason which could explain a future meeting between Liddy Kilkullen and Deems White. Only a social occasion that included Mike and Nora was possible, and that evening Liddy invited the Whites to come and have dinner with them the following Saturday. The invitation was reciprocated, and soon the Whites and the Kilkullens became a recognized foursome.

Mike Kilkullen, who found neither of the Whites particularly interesting, went along with the arrangement out of hope that through them Liddy would be drawn into accepting the social life of Southern California. Nora was flattered to be treated as a friend by glamorous Liddy Kilkullen, whom everyone considered an East Coast snob, although they couldn't help but admire her.

"I don't understand what you have against Deems White," Liddy reproached her husband.

"I don't think he treats his wife well. And what's more, I don't think he likes women."

"That's absurd! Women are crazy about him."

"That's not what I mean, Liddy. I think he's not physically attracted to women."

"What kind of basis is that on which to judge someone?"

"Never mind, Liddy. You're right. It's not important."

Oh, but it was important, Liddy thought. If Mike was right, it meant that no other woman could become more important to Deems than she was already. No other woman would come into his life and lure him by the promise of sex, that unfastidious, muddled coupling she occasionally had to perform with her husband no matter how little pleasure it gave her.

Since the Whites, thanks to Deems, were a popular couple who knew everybody, the Kilkullens inevitably found themselves invited to parties. Liddy even began to give dinner parties herself, because only in a group could she and Deems find the occasions to carry on their increasingly necessary and increasingly intense private dialogue. It was not what they said that was meaningful, but the fact that they said it only to each other.

They did not touch in the same frankly sensuous way that two young people might, not even when they danced together. A strong inhibition, an inability to speak with utter frankness, kept them from arranging for a contact that they both craved, a different kind of physicality than any sexually attracted couple could have accomplished by a rendezvous in a motel.

Liddy and Deems both wanted the freedom to hold each other silently, tightly, for a long, long time, and comfort each other for everything that had gone wrong, everything that they had been robbed of, every compromise they had made. They wanted to hold each other as if each were the other's mother and each were the other's child.

If there had been an attraction of the flesh between them, they could have gratified it easily, but their needs were too complex, too strange. When a young man and woman need to be alone together without sexual intercourse, and when it is impossible for them to explain to each other precisely why sex is not an aim, they are doomed to a frustration of this need that makes it all the keener.

Except for the conventional hug and peck on the cheek as the two couples parted after an evening together or at someone's home, she and Deems had never touched each other, Liddy reflected as she sat in her room at the Beverly Wilshire, on the day before her divorce became final.

Liddy had kept in touch with the Whites by phone during the last year in Philadelphia. They were the only people in Southern California to hear from her, and she always managed to call at a time when Deems would be home. Now she tried to think of a way to get Deems to come to Los Angeles by himself to see her this evening. She should have managed to arrange it before her quick trip out, she realized, but now it was too late, too much at the last minute. She resigned herself to a lonely evening. Tomorrow she'd make the obligatory trip to the courthouse in Santa Ana, the county seat, pick up her final divorce papers, and return to Philadelphia the following day.

As Liddy was packing for her return flight, a reporter from the *Los Angeles Times* reached her by phone in her hotel room.

"Mrs. Kilkullen, what do you think of your former husband's marriage to Sylvie Norberg yesterday afternoon?" he asked.

"What?"

"You know about it, don't you?"

"Why, yes . . . yes, of course." In the astounding black ambush of his words, she had only one thought: she must not seem surprised.

"Could I trouble you for couple of quotes, Mrs. Kilkullen? How did your ex and Miss Norberg get together? How long have you known about this romance? What kind of stepmother do you think she'll make, considering that she's fifteen years younger than he is?"

"I have nothing to say."

"Come on, Mrs. Kilkullen! Your husband married the hottest star in the movies a few hours after the two of you got divorced, and you haven't got a word to say? I can understand your desire for privacy, but Sylvie Norberg's public property."

"In that case, why don't you call her?"

Liddy hung up the phone and told the operator not to put through any more calls. She fell into a chair, so penetrated by shock that there was no room for emotion. Only slowly did her mind begin to work as she tried to put things together. Mike couldn't have known Sylvie Norberg before she and the children had left the ranch last summer, or she would have known about it. At some point during the last year they must have met, and managed to keep it quiet. *A movie star. Fifteen years younger.* A shattering hatred, a corrosive bitterness that would not die until she did, became part of Liddy Kilkullen at that moment, falling over her shoulders like an invisible mantle of heavy, dark fabric.

She got up and locked the hotel room door, without knowing why, and returned to her chair, huddled into a ball, trying to gather her wits, trying to find out where, precisely, she stood.

While Liddy was waiting out the time for her divorce, she and her daughters had lived with her parents in Quaker-founded Philadelphia, a city run by men so conservative that they made old-line Bostonians look frivolous. If she had made her debut, as had been planned before her marriage, at The Assembly Ball in the Bellevue-Stratford, she would have been bowing to society at a ball that was founded in 1768, a ball to which no divorced and remarried people were ever invited. Philadelphians loathed nothing more than public scandal; Philadelphians took no pity on people betrayed by romantic love, an emotion that played havoc with the preservation of family and class.

Liddy had taken great pains in the way she had presented her coming divorce to her circle of friends and family. Over tea at the Acorn Club on Locust Street, the female equivalent of the aristocratic Philadelphia Club, she had confided, one by one, in each woman she knew, from her great-aunts to her Foxcroft classmates.

"I was so young and inexperienced when I met Mike that I made the worst mistake of all—I married a man with whom I had nothing in common," she had admitted, knowing that each of them would shudder at this unthinkable gap in a city in which common interests were the coinage of most marriages. "I thought that he'd try to change, he promised me he would, but now I've faced the fact that he simply hasn't got it in him. I would have endured it for myself, but it isn't fair to my daughters to bring them up without any cultural opportunities, without the right kind of education."

She had painted a picture of a husband who, for all his decent personal qualities, had no life beyond his cattle, no imaginative life, no artistic interests, no interests in the ruling Philadelphia hobbies of art, literature, antiques, gardening, and that great gourmet cooking which was almost always the domain of the husbands.

Each of her women friends and relatives had been warmly understanding and sympathetic, doubly so as they silently congratulated themselves at having avoided such a fate. Liddy had been willing to be pitied rather than cast out of the world to which she belonged, and could belong again in spite of her divorce, with any luck, for there were a multitude of bachelors in Philadelphia.

How those women would be gossiping about her now! Gossiping in the deadly nice Philadelphia way that almost couldn't be called gossip: a few hushed words exchanged just before a meeting of the Board of the Philadelphia Museum of Art; a discreet conversation carried on in an antiques shop on South 17th Street as two women considered a piece of Chinese export porcelain; another heart-to-heart talk at Bailey, Banks & Biddle as engraved invitations were ordered; a murmured discussion during the intermission of the Friday afternoon concert at the Academy of Music, or over a lunch table set for two in a house in Chestnut Hill. Every woman who mattered in Philadelphia would read today's newspapers and remember her words of explanation with scorn.

If Mike Kilkullen was the hopeless clod, the country bumpkin Liddy said he was, then exactly how had he managed to win the heart of the fascinatingly elusive Swedish star, the child of Stockholm intellectuals as they all had read, the great actress, the great beauty? *How and when?* Everyone had to believe that she had been lying. They had to assume that Mike had fallen so hard for Sylvie Norberg that he'd been willing to break up their marriage to marry her, to marry her only a few hours after it was legal.

Liddy moved to the dressing table and studied herself in the mirror. She was only thirty-one and far more striking than she had ever been. She was still marked with all the desirable, impossible-to-imitate stigmata of someone born to the old-money inner circle of the East Coast upper classes. There was nothing wrong with her at all, Liddy thought, except that she was damaged goods. She'd been dumped, as publicly and as humiliatingly as any woman could be dumped.

Every man in Philadelphia who didn't know it this morning would learn before dinner tonight that Lydia Henry Stack, the woman who, only twelve years ago, was about to reign over her debutante year, the girl who could have married any bachelor in the city, had been thrown aside for Sylvie Norberg. Yes, Sylvie Norberg, the movie star, the women would say excitedly to their men, is there *another* Sylvie Norberg? Liddy certainly had me fooled, they would add. Poor Liddy, why did she bother with that pathetic charade about her husband when she must have known that it was all going to come out anyway?

If she had only known. Nothing on earth would have convinced her to divorce Mike if she had imagined for a minute that he would remarry someone like Sylvie Norberg. She would have left him and taken the children, but kept him chained to her, chained forever with no recourse at all, rather than let him put her in this position. No wonder he'd agreed to the conditions of the divorce without a struggle. Her own lawyer had advised Liddy that in his opinion she was asking too much, but she'd insisted that he make the attempt to obtain the maximum in alimony and child support. *If only she had known.*

Liddy got up and began to walk around and around the room. The time to leave for the airport was approaching, but she knew absolutely that she must never go back to Philadelphia. That was the one place on earth in which she would never show her face. She called the airline, canceled her flight and told the phone operator that she'd take calls now.

Where could she go? Philadelphia was self-absorbed, God knew, but not so stick-in-the-mud that its citizens didn't gossip with their friends in other cities. Any place on the Eastern Seaboard was out of the question for a few years. Europe, of course, but where in Europe? Money was not a problem. Her half of the ranch's profits had come to a substantial sum, and last winter she'd received an inheritance that gave her an income of an additional ten thousand dollars a year. With thirty-five thousand dollars a year she could live very well in Europe.

When the phone rang again, she was ready.

"Mrs. Kilkullen, this is Hank Jamison of the *Herald Examiner*. Would you mind if I asked you for a few comments on your former husband's marriage to Sylvie Norberg?"

"Not at all, Mr. Jamison."

"What's your reaction to the news?"

"I hope that they'll be very happy. In fact I'm sure they will be."

"Did you know this was going to happen yesterday?"

"Naturally I did. My former husband and I remain very good friends."

"What do you think about Sylvie Norberg?"

"I haven't met her, but I admire her work enormously. She's talented and lovely."

"So you're not upset about the age difference?"

"I'm a modern woman, Mr. Jamison. Why should it matter to me if it doesn't matter to her?"

"What do your children think?"

"That's hard to say now. They'll have to get to know her first. You know how children are."

"In other words, you have no hard feelings?"

"Mr. Jamison, I was the one who asked for this divorce. I left my husband long before he met Miss Norberg. My reasons were purely personal and private. I want him to have a happy life, and I'm sure he wants the same thing for me."

"Thank you, Mrs. Kilkullen. It's a pleasure to talk to a real lady."

"Thank you, Mr. Jamison."

No matter how well she handled reporters, no one she knew in Philadelphia would believe what they read in the papers, but this story would be seen on every continent, and one day, when it had been repeated often enough, it would become the truth.

Soon after Sylvie and Mike Kilkullen were married, Sylvie was amazed to discover that she was going to have a baby. "But I've never wanted a child before, I've never even thought about it," she told him, as bewildered by this unexpected development as if she had suddenly developed a taste for playing high stakes poker or breeding Great Danes.

"I'm willing to bet that you unconsciously wanted to have a baby," Mike told her, gleefully watching the beginning of his private predictions of change coming true.

In January of 1961, their daughter was born and named Juanita Isabella after Mike Kilkullen's great-great-grandmother, at Sylvie's insistence. She craved that continuity with the family and the land to belong to her daughter in a way it could never truly belong to her. Sylvie turned her back on Hollywood after her child's birth, for she had a longing to experience motherhood.

Ten months later she had assimilated the experience and duties of motherhood. It was delightful, but no longer a novelty . . . no longer . . . quite . . . *enough.* The itch to return to her work began to trouble Sylvie as she played with the lively, pretty blond baby she and Mike had decided to call Jazz. Impatiently, Sylvie brushed the familiar craving aside for weeks, until it became so strong that she realized she must fulfill it if she wished to be true to herself.

Every woman *must* have a baby, Sylvie told the press of the world as she finished her new film in London. It was a brilliant experience. Absorbing, unique. No woman could realize her full potential until she had given birth.

Did she plan to have only one child? Ah, but who could answer such a vastly difficult question, she replied, with her low and wonderful laugh. She reserved her right to have a dozen children, oh, certainly, a dozen, if she wanted them. Everything was possible —marriage, motherhood and necessary work—because she was married to a unique man, a man who understood a woman's need to fulfill herself as a creative artist. Yes, her husband was more than strong enough to make a new pattern of life, a new way of being married, which permitted her to leave home from time to time to make a film while he stayed on the land he loved. When she made a film in Hollywood she lived in a little apartment near the studio and spent weekends at the ranch. As for her baby, Jazz was beloved and happy in that stable environment everyone knew was necessary for a child's development.

Everywhere women envied her.

When Sylvie returned to the ranch between pictures, she changed every room she entered. Her mere presence gilded the atmosphere of the hacienda more brilliantly than sunlight, and the life of everyone who lived there danced to a thrilling rhythm. Sometimes she stayed there for a month or two at a time, occasionally a little longer. During these periods of relaxation, Mike and Jazz were the center of the enchanted universe she had arranged for herself.

Her imprint was everywhere, like the fragrant smoke of a scented candle: books and magazines lay open on the floors; the music of the new records she brought home filled the house; her marvelous dressing gowns were flung about like tapestries over the arms of her favorite chairs; the armfuls of flowers she cut from the garden stood artfully thrown together in containers on every table; she baked large Swedish cookies and simmered rich Swedish stews and turned dinner into a festival. She sat in the old family rocking chair on the patio, took Jazz in her lap, and told her ancient folk tales and fairy stories for hours. Even Susie Dominguez, who disapproved of Sylvie's absences, fell under her spell. Often, after Jazz had learned to ride a pony, Sylvie rode with her on the bluffs above the beach, cantering alongside the fearless child, controlling her own mount with hands so light that no horse, no man, no child could gainsay her.

Sylvie happily entertained the neighbors at dinner parties; she loved to hang out at the Swallows bar, where Liddy had refused to set foot; she was a superb hostess at the annual Fiesta, and she never missed Jazz's birthday party, even if she had to fly across oceans and continents for those two occasions. She visited her parents at least once a year, and on three occasions, when she knew she was going to be at the ranch for a six-week period, she sent them tickets to fly over from Sweden so that they could spend a few weeks getting to know their son-in-law and their granddaughter. When Jazz started school, Sylvie joined the PTA. She got to know every member of the families of the vaqueros on the ranch. She refurbished many rooms of the Hacienda Valencia, without dimming any of their evocative Spanish Colonial character, and she worked side by side with the gardeners to restore the gardens to their full splendor, as much the mistress of the ranch as the wife of any Kilkullen had been before her.

Yet, inevitably, one day her agent would dare to interrupt Sylvie Norberg's country idyll, sending her a script that she would push carelessly away. Another script would come in the mail a week later, and again she wouldn't open it. After a pile of scripts had lain on her desk for a while, under Jazz's anxiously watchful golden eyes, the day would come when Sylvie Norberg would reach for one, feeling the prompting of that glorious, edgy desire she knew so well, a life-giving desire she could not help but welcome. She'd read the script and throw it aside with an exclamation of disdain. Soon she'd read another, and then another, until the day came when she found a script that contained a role she wanted, a role that would take her away from home for months. Soon she would begin to pack the bags she had never unpacked for good. What she wanted, she would have.

Every marriage is a bargain, almost always unspoken. When Sylvie Norberg, who did not believe in such tacit pacts, had told Mike Kilkullen exactly what to expect before they married, she had not misled him by one word. His tragedy was that he had not believed her. His fate was to live with the bargain he had made.

"Wave good-bye to Mommy," her father's voice said in Jazz's first clear memory. He held her high and moved her hand back and forth. She could remember nothing more, not where or when it happened or what her mother looked like at the time. Only her father's arms and his words.

Many other similar memories were superimposed on this first one, many sharper memories of her mother's longed-for returns and painful departures. Jazz could never recall a time in her childhood during which she hadn't lived with the understanding that whenever her mother was home, there would come a day on which she would go away. Her father told her, when she was old enough to ask questions, that for almost a year after Jazz's birth, in 1961, her mother had remained at the ranch, and turned down all scripts in order to be with her new baby. "But you were tiny then, of course you can't remember," Mike Kilkullen would add, and lose himself for an instant in the past.

Jazz Kilkullen learned abandonment before she could walk. Her mother left her before her first memories began, disappearing forever, as far as her infant brain could comprehend.

All the years of her early childhood were a series of contradictions. Sometimes her mother reappeared, brimming with love, her attention focused on her daughter, filling Jazz's days with games, waking her in the morning with playful kisses, putting her to sleep at night with a Swedish lullaby. Sometimes her mother disappeared, taking with her the love and warm arms and lips and the songs, leaving behind an inexplicable world that had grown gray, empty and sad beyond tears. Jazz accepted this as normal, for she knew no other life.

When she grew older and she could begin to understand the explanations her parents repeated to her about the reasons her mother had to go away, she denied the depth of the emotions she felt. Since children fear abandonment more than anything else, since being left forever is the worst thing they can imagine happening to them, it becomes the most important thing to deny.

Yes, of course she didn't like it when Mommy had to make a movie, but that was Mommy's work. She had her father and Susie and Rosie, her nurse, to take care of her, she had her own pony to ride, and every single one of the vaqueros played with her when they had time. Mommy would come home as soon as the movie was finished. There was nothing, really, for a sensible little girl to feel bad about.

Mike Kilkullen helped her to deny her grief, for he was far too grown-up to be able to hide his emotions as well as the child could. Jazz tried to make up to him for her mother's absence. With a stout heart and a talkative tongue she kept him company, eating an early dinner with him in the brightly lit kitchen,

with Susie and Rosie both busy bustling around, so
that they wouldn't be alone together in the dining
room, just the two of them, at the table at which Sylvie
had sat, laughingly and lovingly, only a week ago.

After dinner, her father would sometimes invite
Jazz to look through the Kilkullen family pictures, his
grandfather's great collection of photographs that was
kept in the long-unused archive room at the far end of
one wing of the hacienda. She was the first of his own
family to be interested in them. There, behind fireproof doors to which he had the only key, stood a long
wooden table, well lit by green-shaded lights, in front
of deep shelves of dusty portfolios. He would ask her
to pick a year, any year, as long as it wasn't before
1875, when her great-grandfather, young Hugh Kilkullen, had been given his first camera, and the little girl
would cry out "1888" or "1931" as if it were a magic
trick.

And indeed it seemed like magic to her to be
transported suddenly back to the ranch she already
knew so well, and see the familiar buildings as they
had been then, mysteriously almost the same as today,
yet so different in certain small details. It was a miraculous alternative world: certain saplings were now big
trees; what had been tiny vines now covered walls;
men she knew as ancient were mere boys; the fathers
of these same men—sometimes, she was sure, wearing the same hats that their sons now wore—rode
horses she had never seen; an old well, now covered
with morning glories, had once served as a source of
water; a newly planted rose garden was now enlarged
by hundreds of bushes; long-dead women, plump and
pretty in their white, floor-length summer dresses
trimmed with lace, sat under their parasols and drank
tea on the patio; children on ponies that looked so
much like her own pony sat mounted in front of the
same stable, yet they wore more clothes than any
child she knew had ever worn, and had odd ways of
parting their hair.

Jazz was fascinated by the photographs of weddings, baptisms, fiestas and funerals, photographs of

harvestings and fishing and hunting parties. Her great-grandfather had worked only with natural light for most of his life, but he had been singularly gifted in his feeling for composition, and there was a density and clarity in these old photographs that had great power to stir her imagination. She wanted to know everyone's name and how they were or were not related to her. What kind of food was in the cookpot around which the vaqueros were standing with plates in their hands? A White Steamer?—who had owned that car with such a strange name? Had her great-grandfather learned Chinese from the Chinese cooks, or could they speak English? Why was the roundup the most important event of the year? Did the calves really have to be branded? Didn't it hurt?

Best of all, Jazz loved the Kilkullen ranch sagas, the year-long battles against hoof-and-mouth disease and the Texas fever tick; the weekly baths and flea-removing that the children of the ranch endured; the annual black bass fishing contests in the reservoirs tucked into the hundred square miles of pasture.

There were even legends that might or might not be true, such as that of the Franciscan shrine that dated so far back that nobody knew its age. The shrine was supposed to exist somewhere on the heights of Portola Peak, and her great-grandfather had been certain that he had found it when he was a young man. Her grandfather had never gotten around to climbing up to look for it, so her father couldn't promise her the story was true.

Alone in the cozy archive room, after Susie and the two maids had all gone home and left the hacienda, after Rosie had been persuaded to go to bed, Jazz sat perched on a footstool by her father's feet, and entered a brightly peopled universe of history which became far more real than the present. Mike Kilkullen allowed his daughter to stay up much later than Rosie approved of, and the man who would never speak of his loneliness and the child who couldn't allow herself to acknowledge it, forged a bond that grew ever deeper. When he reluctantly realized that he had to put her to bed, he sang one last song to her after he'd tucked her in: "Clementine" or "Oh, Susannah," or her favorite, "On Top of Old Smokey," the songs he'd grown up on. When Jazz remembered the tune of a Swedish lullaby as she lay there, she never hummed it to herself until after he had left the room.

At some point in the early years of his marriage, Mike Kilkullen began to hear about items in movie gossip columns that hinted that Sylvie Norberg was having an affair with the male star of her latest film. Although he didn't read gossip columns himself, no husband of a famous woman is spared knowledge of what is being said or written about her. Before their marriage, Sylvie had prepared him for such innuendo. "If they don't say I sleep with men," she'd told him, "they'll say I sleep with women. You must be able to ignore gossip if you want me."

There had actually been surprisingly little gossip about his wife, considering her youth, her beauty and the fact that she lived alone so much, he thought, hoping that Susie and Rosie weren't hearing or reading the same lies. Of course they would believe them no more than he, but it disturbed him to think of such ugliness touching anyone who shared his daily life.

The stories continued, like a slowly bleeding wound that could not be staunched, during the next several years, but he refused to so much as comment on them to Sylvie when she was at the ranch between pictures. Her quality of radiant existence in the present had not changed. Mike had never observed her in a moment of remoteness or dissatisfaction or absent-mindedness, as if she were thinking about someone else, or even something else. Her smiles were never self-contemplating. When she was at the ranch she was totally *there*. She mended him with her love, and even to speak of gossip, he told himself, was to dignify it.

In 1967, Mike Kilkullen realized that Jazz, who was in the middle of her first year of grammar school, soon would be reaching the age when some word of gossip must eventually touch her, through the mothers of the children she went to school with in San Juan Capistrano, through one teacher overheard talking to another, through God knew what malignant source.

He did for his daughter what he was too secure to do for himself, and spoke to his wife. Wasn't there something she could do to stop these columnists, he asked. Didn't the public-relations people assigned to her pictures have any way of stemming the lies that were bound to reach Jazz someday?

"There is nothing you can do about the press except to rise above it," Sylvie said with a weary, exasperated sigh. "I warned you, darling, remember? The only way ever to stop such stories would be for me to retire, to give up acting, to stay home forever. Those wretched newspaper columnists and movie magazine hacks would have nothing to print if they stuck to the truth. We love each other, we each need to do our work, and we can't expect not to have to pay a price for living as we do."

She hated to lie, Sylvie thought, no matter how easy it was. She would scorn to tell an unnecessary lie, but to protect her two universes she had to admit that deception was essential.

She could never expect any husband, and Mike in particular, to understand that she owned two universes, two separate and utterly different universes that had nothing to do with each other, two universes that must continue to have no impact on each other in order to remain perfect.

It had been almost two years after Jazz's birth that she had first been—to use that absurd American word—"unfaithful" to Mike. She had been on location in Paris when she had an affair with her costar, an affair that stopped on the day the film was finished. It had been so very necessary.

Not that she needed to experience passion to act it, she reflected, remembering that summer. She wanted that actor, it was as simple as that, wanted him badly, from the very first day of shooting. And he wanted her so much that he couldn't even remember his lines when they had a scene together.

She could have denied herself and remained aloof, but that would have been to impose a needless limitation on her existence, it would have constricted and lessened the freedom in which she deliberately gave herself permission to conduct her life. It had been a purely physical relationship, almost wordless, but he had been a superbly gifted lover, and she had found that she was more than ready for this kind of sex, sex without marriage or parenthood or responsibility, sex without emotion or permanence or the slightest guilt.

Yes, Sylvie thought, she had learned an important lesson that summer in Paris. She had discovered that she was capable of redefining her life, enriching it. She *needed* to have lovers, she decided, knowing that she always made the right choices for herself.

Other affairs had followed the first one. Sylvie felt as young and ripe and hot-blooded as she had before her marriage, when she had been free and footloose in Stockholm. Once she had known the pleasures of sex with a man she'd never have to see again after the wrap party, she had almost always taken a lover with each new film, or, if not an actor, a director.

She played by the unspoken but well-understood rules of filmmaking romances; no participant ever wanted these affairs to intrude on his or her home life. Their families, those families who didn't breathe the air of the studio, the lot, the set, the location, those families who waited for them at home, were never to be involved. The only way gossip got out was through those sharp-eyed, sharp-eared informants on every film—a wardrobe assistant, a script girl, a makeup artist—who acted as paid pipelines to the columnists. No one knew who they were, and there was nothing anyone could do about them but ignore them.

But oh, how exciting it was to know, even as she reveled in being a wife and mother, that her second universe existed, that her life knew no boundaries, that within weeks of making a phone call to her agent she could be off to make another film, to meet another stranger, to share a secret intensity with him that could never hurt anyone.

It was well worth a few lies.

Valerie and Fernanda, Jazz's half sisters, had been a constant in her life throughout her earliest years. They came to stay for almost a month every summer and for at least a week at Christmas and Easter. Liddy Kilkullen, in her self-imposed European exile, had not neglected to keep herself alert to all the details of the boom that was taking place everywhere in Orange County.

Sitting well protected from the Spanish sun, a Los Angeles newspaper in her hands, she brooded over the bitter fact that in 1960, the year of her divorce, the master planning for the University of California at Irvine, not too many miles to the north of the Kilkullen Ranch, had just been set in motion. The plan included urbanization of 35,000 virgin acres that ran inland from the coast to the future university. Her former neighbors, the Irvines, Lydia knew, would soon be richer than ever, and God knew they'd been rich for a long time, almost as long as some new Philadelphians.

It was obvious to her that it was only a question of time before some enterprising developer would strike a deal with her ex-husband for part of his land, particularly the most desirable acreage on the twenty miles of beach which were not useful for ranching, but only for growing lima beans. If she knew Mike, he would never sell outright, but would retain an interest, almost certainly a controlling interest, in whatever portion of the ranch such a change would involve. Perhaps he would even develop the land himself.

Previous generations of Kilkullens had rented large parcels of their lowland to small farmers to ensure a good, steady annual income during the highs and lows of the cattle-ranching business. Many acres of the Kilkullen Ranch were covered with fields of flowers and groves of citrus and walnut trees. Mike

Kilkullen had built homes on land he owned for the farmers who rented those acres, and in time he certainly would build homes for strangers. There would be an immense fortune in that, now that the new freeway from Los Angeles was open.

Not only had she been fool enough not to marry for money and position, Liddy told herself, with an agony of self-blame that was more difficult to endure than any outside reproach, but she had decided to get a divorce at the very moment when the ranch was about to be worth a fortune. If she had hung on, she would have *made* Mike Kilkullen sell some of his land, she told herself, sick to the depth of her being at her lost opportunities.

She had not been clever, she had not been lucky, she who deserved by birth and beauty to be both. But now, while it wasn't yet too late, she must be foresighted. Liddy vowed to herself that her daughters would not be alienated from him when Mike Kilkullen struck it rich.

When Jazz was tiny, her sisters ignored her, absorbed in their own teenage activities, out riding for most of the day. She was always hopefully aware of them when they visited, trying to tag along after them as soon as she could walk. They ignored her until her fourth year, when Rosie decreed that Jazz was old enough to be left in their charge from time to time. Then they began to torment her, for their mother's unrelenting influence had taught them to believe that Jazz had no right to be alive. She was the child of the evil and powerful woman who had taken their father away from them, the woman who was responsible for the fact that their father had to be courted and catered to as if he were a king, for if they neglected him, he would no longer care about them at all, engrossed as he was with his new wife, his new child.

Fernanda and Valerie, spiteful and jealous, pretended to give Jazz a new hairdo and braided her hair into so many tiny braids that the rubber bands at the ends pulled out hundreds of strands; they stole her favorite dolls and returned them subtly changed in various horrible ways; they removed the bulb of the night-light that she was used to having in her room, and replaced it in the morning so that Rosie wouldn't notice; they played hide-and-seek and disappeared for an hour at a time.

In front of their father, the two girls left Jazz in peace, and although they could always manipulate Rosie, they never dared to practice their tricks if Sylvie was at the ranch. Jazz wanted to win the acceptance of the big girls so much that she pretended that their cruel games were games indeed. She never told on them to her parents or her nurse, because telling on people was always sneaky. Somehow, somewhere, she had absorbed that version of the rules of fairness. She thought that if she held her tongue, Fernanda and Valerie, who were goddesses to her, would realize what a good girl she really was and let her into the longed-for, private world of their eternal, smirking secrets.

As they grew a little older and realized that Jazz would not let them provoke her, they tried other tactics. Whenever they were alone with her, they pretended that she was invisible. They passed each other the butter or the salad across her, so that she had to draw back or be hit, while they discussed her in the third person.

"Did you know that the little Orphink Annie got a terrible report card?" Fernanda would ask.

"It's because she spends all her time training her dog, that filthy Sandy," Valerie would reply. "That Orphink girl will never amount to much. That's what I heard Susie saying just yesterday."

"It's not true!" Jazz would cry, her words snatched out of her mouth, vanishing.

"They say the Orphink has a mother who's away somewhere doing something important, but I don't believe it, do you?"

"If she really had a mother like that, then she wouldn't be an Orphink, would she?" was the ritual answer.

"She is away, she's in England! I have a letter from her!" Jazz screamed.

"Did you hear a dog bark?" Fernanda asked Valerie. "It must be that ugly old Sandy again."

"If the Orphink really has a mother, she's certainly not a good mother."

"She must be a very, very bad mother if she goes away all the time. Except that I don't believe she's real."

When one of them passed her in the garden, the big girls would hiss "Orphink," without looking at Jazz. "Orphink," they would silently mouth at her across the dining room table when their father wasn't watching. In front of him, they would call her "Annie" and tell him that it was their pet name for her.

Jazz blinded herself to them, mute in misery. Didn't they like her, not even a little bit, she wondered endlessly? What was wrong with her for them to be so mean? Yet she never told anyone. She was filled with a kind of shame, the shame of the persecuted. She didn't want to make things worse. If she didn't repeat the words, they wouldn't exist. If she didn't show that she minded, it wouldn't be real.

Jazz knew nothing of the history of the divorce. Brought up to speak out freely by both her parents, Jazz's first experiences in duplicity and cruelty were learned at the hands of Fernanda and Valerie, hands that were guided by Liddy.

By the time Jazz was eight, her older half sisters had stopped trying to bait her. She was too dull-witted to bother with, they decided, and their own lives were too full. For the next few years, now young married women, they rarely visited the ranch in spite of their mother's demands that they do so.

In Jazz's eighth year, Sylvie Norberg decided that she felt like taking time off from moviemaking. She had never been more in demand, her agent was driven almost mad by the opportunities she missed, but she forbade him to so much as send her a script, no matter who had written it. Sylvie wanted a respite and if her agent didn't understand that, so much the worse for him.

Jazz's life entered a period of paradise. Rosie left, briefly mourned, to take care of another little girl, for Jazz was too grown-up for a nurse, and besides, now she had her mother at home.

During the summer of that year, when Jazz was out of school, she and Sylvie spent more time together than they ever had before. Jazz was her mother's companion during the days, while her father rode the range, and together they made plans for each day. Often they took their horses and went to the beach for a picnic, using the private road that had been constructed to pass under the San Diego Freeway, which now ran the length of the ranch almost two miles inland from their shoreline. They went sailing together, Jazz handling the boat more expertly than her mother, and frequently they drove into San Juan Capistrano in the afternoon for ice cream.

Afterwards, as likely as not, they were drawn to visit the Mission compound surrounding that enormous stone church that had been laboriously built over a nine-year period and, according to family legend, contained stones that had been taken from Valencia Point. The ambitions of its builders had been mighty, too mighty, as Sylvie pointed out in the only moralistic phrase she ever uttered, for only six years after the church was finished, its bell tower was destroyed by an earthquake, toppling down while mass was being celebrated and killing forty people.

Both mother and daughter loved the astonishingly European atmosphere of the Mission grounds, the monumental, vaulted ruins that would have looked equally at home in Italy as in Spain; the narrow, friendly, charmingly humble chapel in which mass was still celebrated; the flocks of absurdly tame, white pigeons who never hurried as they marched in tiny, officious steps over the old paving, the warbling of the thousands of swallows who nested in the buildings of the Mission, still returning on March 19 of every year and inspiring many different and contradictory theories to explain their migratory schedule.

Jazz and Sylvie often brought their ice cream cones and sat on the wooden bench that they found on the far left side of the Mission. From this favorite bench the view contained only a giant, ancient California pepper tree, a wishing well, a wall covered with bright red bougainvillea, the ruined arches of an arcade, and a rose garden that had certainly seen better days, but as they sat there they were conscious of a particular deep, resonant peacefulness that seemed to exist in no other place.

"Someday we'll go to Europe together," Sylvie promised, winding a strand of Jazz's hair around her finger. She made a ringlet and let it slip off her finger, the curl immediately slipping back into a wavelet. Where did those golden eyes come from, Sylvie wondered, as she looked at her daughter? She knew that they were her own eyes in shape and placement, but the chiming topaz of Jazz's pupils was not to be found in anyone in Sylvie's family, or in Mike's, as far as he knew. She'll be tall, Sylvie thought, taller than I am, and lovely. Yes, she had been right not to have other children. One child was enough when that child was Jazz. How well she had managed her life!

Month after month passed when Jazz was certain of exactly what would happen tomorrow, when she would be allowed to curl up in an armchair after dinner and watch her parents dance together in the music room under the huge, low beams of the ceiling. The heavy twelve-by-twelves had been fastened together before there were nails on the ranch. Rawhide straps still held them together, thongs of such sturdy leather that time had no effect on them, and only changes in the weather caused them to make a creaking noise, as if the Hacienda Valencia were a ship at sea. *Oh, how she wished it were.* A small, safe little ship, sailing on and on, with just the three of them aboard, through the moonlight and the sunlight, day after day, night after night, with nothing ever changing, not even the music of the Beatles. Forever and ever. Strawberry fields *forever*.

That blissful summer when she was eight, Jazz began to take photographs. Her father bought her a Kodak and a few rolls of film, since a child should start with a minimum of equipment, particularly when her enthusiasm might not last.

Jazz's first subject was Sylvie, sitting on the broad veranda of the hacienda, in dappled morning sunlight, reading a book and wearing a blue and white flowered dressing gown.

The first time she looked into the camera and saw her mother's profile and shoulders framed by the lens, her eyes lowered toward the book, Jazz was overwhelmed by a great and unforgettable burst of joy. She pressed the button and knew that now she *owned* that instant in time, she *owned* that image of her mother, it belonged to her, to no one else in the world, and it could never be taken away.

Sylvie looked up and smiled, as photographers always asked her to do, and Jazz took another picture. Sylvie kept smiling, holding still and looking at the camera, cooperating with the little girl, but Jazz, who didn't want to waste her precious film on a duplication of her second picture, said, "Mommy, just pretend that I'm not here."

Sylvie grinned at this precocious command. Jazz sounded just as sure of herself as she must have sounded herself when she was a child, she thought, and returned tranquilly to her book, concentrating on it entirely, while Jazz circled round and round, coming closer and then standing back, all the while peering into the viewfinder to see what she could see, without taking a picture.

The novelty of reducing the broad range of what her eyes normally could take in, down to the limited scope of the lens, fascinated her. She could, if she wanted to, photograph only her mother's hands, or her feet, or her sleeve. She could stand at a distance and reduce her mother to a tiny part of a big picture and yet contain her from head to toes, or she could come in very close, until all the lens held was her mother's head, oddly distorted.

She knew nothing about focus or exposure. She didn't even know that there was anything to know, nor did she wonder. Even pressing the button and taking the picture was far less important than her utter absorption in her newfound ability to *capture life,* to hold it tightly inside a square or a rectangle; then to move a little in another direction and make it change according to her will; to place the borders of the picture where she wanted them to be, to pin things down in just the way she chose.

Jazz had never felt totally powerful before. For the rest of her days, so long as she had a camera, she would never feel totally powerless again.

"Jazz, are you ever going to finish that roll?" Sylvie asked gently. "It's almost time for lunch. I have to get dressed." She turned her head in inquiry to Jazz, who had crept up behind her, and in that instant Jazz snapped her third photograph, as Sylvie started to rise.

"One more, please, Mommy," Jazz implored her. "You were moving. Just one more." Sylvie laughed out loud at that familiar command.

" 'One more,' " she echoed. "My poor baby, born into the ranks of paparazzi—it must be prenatal influence."

"Oh, Mommy, hold still! I want to get it just right," Jazz begged, and Sylvie stayed in her chair. "No," Jazz said, shaking her head vigorously, "not exactly like that, put your eyebrows back up, please Mommy, the way they were a second ago when you asked me when I was going to finish."

"Not just a paparazzo, but a perfectionist too! That sounds like trouble," Sylvie commented as she complied, mildly wishing that her husband had asked her first before he had decided that Jazz was old enough to own a camera. She had never played with a camera when she was a child, and in all her years of being photographed, she had never been at all curious about what went on behind the lens. She was the eternal subject, never the recorder of the subject, and unlike many camera-wise stars, she was concerned only with emotions, not with lighting or angles. My child, she thought, could learn more if she belonged to Sophia Loren.

After lunch, when Sylvie went shopping with Susie, driving to a local farmer's roadside market for corn that had just been picked and perfectly ripe peaches for pie, Jazz was so absorbed by her new camera that she didn't go with them for this shopping treat that normally she would never miss.

Instead, she wandered through the hacienda gardens, trying to see if a flower or a tree would provide her with the same sensation of owning a moment of life that she'd had in the morning. She slipped outside the green oasis of the gardens, and since the barns and stables were empty, with all the vaqueros out on the range, she pointed her camera at her pony, at the dogs that roamed the stables, at a row of old iron rakes that hung on a wall, at some of the buildings that her great-grandfather had photographed when they were new. She used her film stingily, afraid that it would run out before her father got home and she could take pictures of him.

By the end of the afternoon, Jazz had decided that she only wanted to take pictures of people. The command and possession of a special moment in time, the new excitement that she had felt when she first photographed her mother, didn't exist for her in inanimate objects, and she couldn't tell the animals what to do.

And photograph people Jazz did, all the rest of the summer, dragooning Susie, the vaqueros, the farmers who rented land on the ranch, their children, the mailman, the milkman, and every salesman who appeared. No one escaped. The friendly, well-known inhabitants of San Juan and their children, her school-

mates, were persuaded to pose, whenever she rode
her pony into town, her camera hanging around her
neck.

By trial and error she taught herself as she began
to work with a little more speed and accuracy and a
little more understanding of light. Composition and a
sense of exactly the right moment to press the button
came naturally to her. Her very first picture of her
mother reading was such a success that it was deemed
good enough to be enlarged and placed in a position of
honor on her father's bedside table.

Sylvie searched stationery stores in San Juan
Capistrano and Laguna Beach and San Clemente until
she found a portfolio that looked almost like those of
Mike's grandfather, and Jazz began to keep her pictures and negatives there, filed in big envelopes that
she labeled and dated carefully. Her father had another key made to the archive room and gave it to her
solemnly. Jazz hung it around her neck on a piece of
string until Sylvie persuaded her to put it in a special
box in her chest of drawers.

"I wonder if this is just a phase," Mike wondered
aloud to Sylvie.

"I started acting before I was eight," Sylvie answered. "You can't tell anything from just one person's experience, but I knew what I wanted to do with
my life that very first time. I didn't have a moment's
doubt."

"When I was seven I won the roping contest at
the Fiesta," Mike added thoughtfully. "Beat all the
vaqueros and my own father."

"Come on, cowboy," she giggled, "you couldn't
have."

"Honestly. It's not a question of how big or
strong you are, but how well you throw. It's the angle
at which the reata wraps itself around the hooves that
stops the calf."

"What a family of prodigies. I'm glad she hasn't
been roping calves all summer," Sylvie laughed, and
kissed his lips.

"Oh, darling, must you . . ." Mike caught himself, ashamed that the words had escaped. He had promised himself so long ago that he would never ask her not to leave the ranch, not to make another movie, but Sylvie had been home for so long now that for just a second he'd forgotten the stern prohibition which made their life together possible. Sylvie caught his tone and understood the words he hadn't said.

"I told you yesterday that I was ready," she said gently, tenderly, but implacably. "I phoned my agent this morning."

"Did he have anything interesting?"

"Lots of things. He's sending the scripts by messenger tomorrow."

"Isn't the mail fast enough for him?"

"For me, yes. Evidently not for him."

Another necessary lie, Sylvie thought. She had requested the messenger. Her need to be back doing her work had been growing and building for weeks, a pressure as solid, as internal and as restless as a child wanting to be born. Only the evident happiness of her husband and daughter had prevented her from making the phone call she'd made today.

It was if a spell had been cast over her, putting her will to sleep. The longer she didn't work, the more difficult it became to disturb the status quo. In another week, two weeks at the most, she'd start to grow bored and boring, irritating and irritable. Their pleasure in her being home would be destroyed. But why on earth was she actually *justifying* herself to herself like this? It was proof, if she needed proof, that staying away from work for too long was wrong for her.

Jazz was happily awaiting the beginning of third grade at the grammar school at the Mission in San Juan. Mike was always busy, no matter what the season. Her own time to bask in the sun, growing mentally fat and lazy like a declawed kitchen cat fed too many scraps, was over. And no matter what script she picked, no matter where it took her, she knew that she could safely promise Mike and Jazz to be back by Christmas. Not that she would ever promise, not out loud, for to promise would be to limit her freedom, to be false to her beliefs. It was compromise enough to have told another lie.

Sylvie Norberg shut herself in the bedroom and attacked the pile of scripts. Usually so difficult to please, she was tempted by each of them at first reading. The sane simplicity of life at the ranch had become a prison the moment the scripts had been delivered. The soothing rhythms of a quiet, predictable, healthy life for which she had yearned last winter were intolerable at the approach of this new autumn. She ached to bend to the discipline of her craft. Her art. Her only art.

At second reading, only two of the scripts still appealed to her, and the third time she read them she was sure which role she wanted. And what she wanted, she would have.

She phoned her agent and told him her decision. As she had been certain, the part had not been cast. The director, an old friend, had been waiting for her, putting off the studio from month to month, so sure was he that only Sylvie Norberg could do justice to his film. Preproduction had been so thoroughly planned, even in the absence of the hoped-for word from the star, that he could begin filming in Greece by the end of September. That meant she had to leave at the end of this weekend to go to Los Angeles for meetings and costume fittings and makeup tests and rehearsals and—oh, all the thrilling, buzzing, entrancing multitude of things she had missed without knowing that she was missing them.

For once in her life, Sylvie Norberg's confidence in her power to make the infallibly correct choice was mistaken. For twenty-nine years she had existed according to her own rules, living by her own freely made decisions, expecting and receiving the self-fulfillment that was her right. Chance, always random, chance that cares nothing for rules or freedom, had always been on her side. She never gave a thought to the laws of chance. It was benign, and she believed she lived under a lucky star. Yet the only law that rules chance is its eternal presence in the affairs of humankind.

On the night of the wrap party, at the beginning of the third week of December of 1969, Sylvie and her costar drove back to the small hotel in which the cast was staying while they were on location on a Greek island. They had left the wrap party early, anxious to get back to the hotel unobserved for one last night together before they said good-bye and returned to their separate homes, he in Rome, she on the ranch. The night was dark, the road was bad, the curves were unmarked and the Italian actor drove dangerously fast. He overshot a steep turn and the car went off the road, landing far, far down the cliff. Neither of them survived the crash.

Sylvie Norberg Kilkullen was not home for the Christmas of 1969. For once in her life, what she wanted she would not have.

7

Neither Mike nor Jazz
could have endured the years after Sylvie's death
without the comfort and nearness of each other. Beyond their most immediate and hideous grief came
a profound and lasting loss that no one else could
possibly share. They were utterly necessary to each
other, two people who knew that the other still listened for the same rapid step to approach, for the
same light silver laughter to sound in the next room;
two people who saw the same slender figure bending
intently over a heap of freshly cut flowers, hesitating
for a thoughtful instant before she began to fill a vase;
two people who knew which records they could never
dare to listen to again, which books had to be packed
away, which familiar groupings of furniture should be
rearranged so that Sylvie's empty chair would no
longer be a constant reminder of an absence they must
attempt to learn to accept.

For the next six years Jazz went to the public
school in San Juan Capistrano, riding her pony back
and forth every day from the ranch to the history-filled

town, so calm that it didn't even have a policeman until she was ten. As she grew older, the wives of Mike Kilkullen's neighbors began advising him that Jazz should be sent to boarding school when she was ready for high school, suggesting that he enter her at the excellent Santa Catalina school, far up the coast. Although he couldn't imagine life at the ranch without his daughter, Mike knew that his well-meaning friends were right. When Jazz first heard of this impending separation, she refused violently, but by the time she was fourteen, after years of a running battle, she had finally been persuaded to go to the all-female Bishop School in La Jolla, which was near enough so that she could board during the week and still come home every weekend.

In the spring of 1978, as Jazz approached her graduation from the Bishop School, she made plans to enter Graphics Central in the autumn. This school of the applied arts, located in Los Angeles, near UCLA, had a reputation for teaching photography that was as impressive as that of Brooks in Santa Barbara or the Art Center in Pasadena.

Many years had passed since Sylvie's death, and the "mourning process," as people had decided to call it, Mike Kilkullen thought grimly, should have been over long ago.

God knows, about four years after the car crash he had started to look around, honestly started to try to find a woman he could care about. There had never been a shortage of possible candidates once it became known that he was again available. No single man could escape a rain of invitations from well-meaning hostesses, particularly not a man who lived so close to growing centers of hospitality like Newport Beach and Laguna Beach. Mike Kilkullen had ventured out to parties up and down the coast from San Diego to Los Angeles whether he felt in the mood or not, considering it his duty not to become a hermit.

He'd had a series of affairs, discreet, well conducted, non-compromising affairs, but none of them had grown into an emotional connection. Sooner

rather than later, each attempt to create anything more
than good times, goodwill and physical satisfaction
faltered, withered and was abandoned.

By the time Jazz graduated from the Bishop
School, Mike Kilkullen realized that his heart died
with Sylvie. His love was concentrated on Jazz, although he had never stopped wishing that his older
daughters would spend more time at the ranch, so that
he could somehow reestablish the relationship he'd
had with them before the divorce. Foolish though he
knew that hope was, given Liddy's dominance over
the girls, he had never abandoned it, as each autumn
he lured them and their children out to the Fiesta.

The Kilkullen Ranch, and its preservation as open
range, had become more essential, more fundamentally necessary to Mike with each passing year, as he
witnessed the carving down and paving over of Orange County. It seemed, from the freeway, to have
turned into one inhuman, gigantic, heartless assem-
blage of tract houses, malls and office towers, a man-
made money machine that defiled the ocean and the
mountains on its borders. The bastards had turned
paradise into a parking lot, all right, he thought in fury,
as he turned down one offer after another for his property. *Somewhere,* for Christ's sake, *somewhere* they
had to be stopped.

Jazz was thoroughly dashed by the disappointments
of her first year at Graphics Central, yet she knew that
in order to pursue a career as a professional photographer she needed more technical training. She must
be able to solve any problem that could be presented
during any photographic assignment.

She entered school with a hunch that she would
easily master the purely technical aspects of photography, since she had already taught herself so much,
progressing from simple cameras to more difficult
ones, reading everything she could find, taking and
developing many thousands of pictures. Everyone
who had seen her work had thought that she was
gifted, but none of them had been professionals.

Jazz realized she was still an amateur, a hobbyist who had had no one to guide her. She needed teachers and the kind of focus that she would find at Graphics Central: the Zen Workshop, in which you took pictures without ever looking through the viewfinder; the Choreography courses, which taught focus on a moving target so that it became a totally automatic skill; the controversial Confrontation Class, in which each member took portraits of each other member in a style of his own choosing, attempting to delineate character.

However, Graphics Central did not offer these esoteric courses to first-year students. Jazz's first year was spent learning the basics as if she were a would-be automobile mechanic who'd never been under the chassis of a car. She learned to load and unload every kind of camera in the dark, with a stopwatch held by the instructor; she took a course in the most basic details of darkroom technique, although she'd had her own darkroom at home for years; but the main thrust of the first year was the rudiments of lighting.

Indoor lighting, Jazz thought broodingly, never natural lighting, but one hundred million varieties and combinations of every kind of artificial illumination ever invented, from a bare lightbulb to the most advanced strobe. And the severe simplicity of the subjects that had to be lit! A tube of toothpaste was the most exciting assignment they were given, for at least they were allowed to squeeze some of the toothpaste out and coax it into the shape of their choosing, but the toothpaste tube came only at the very end of the year, as the grand climax to the course.

This beginning lighting course would lead directly, in her second year, to tabletop photography, which would probably become the financial mainstay of many of the students, Jazz realized, even as she groaned at the prospect.

Tabletop included anything that could be photographed on a stationary surface, from a perfume bottle to a toaster, from a diamond necklace to a pot roast. But until then, Jazz and the other first-year lighting students, ninety percent of them male, illuminated and photographed nuts and bolts, literally nuts and bolts, and dollar bills and thumbtacks and grains of salt. They were given nothing that could spoil or rot or grow mold, no flower or apple, for each object was intended to last for years, as generations of students lit them in dozens of different, textbook-designated positions, none of which left room for improvisation.

The lighting assignments were so exhaustive and difficult that the course was considered the photographic equivalent of being a first-year hospital intern. None of the students got more than a few hours' sleep at night for weeks at a time as they struggled to find the solutions to lighting nails and buttons and pieces of thread. "Bread, not thread," was the class's wistful rallying cry, but with a few exceptions, like impatient Jazz, who knew she'd never want to do tabletop photography, the students were grateful for the strict training that would leave them equipped to light anything on the face of the earth, or indeed in space, if they could get up there with a flashbulb or a light box, or even a match.

Jazz, at eighteen, found herself far more mature than her teenaged classmates, almost all of them boys, and she took no interest in any particular one of the mass of males who sweated and tinkered with lenses and fuses and talked about Nikons and Leicas with worship. If only one of them had cared about the Lakers, she thought, as she listened to her fellow students . . . but no, they were hopeless nerds who would have looked at her in astonishment if she'd asked them what they thought about the chances of that new rookie from Michigan State, Earvin "Magic" Johnson. He struck Jazz as too tall for a point guard, more likely to become a power forward, but her father, who had followed basketball all his life and had taken Jazz to hundreds of games, assured her that if Jerry West, manager of the Lakers, had chosen Magic as the first pick of the college draft, he must have a damn good reason.

Tony Gabriel never really could find out why he accepted the invitation to lecture at Graphics Central in the late spring of 1979. It wasn't his bag to spend time pontificating and answering questions, but he had a couple of days in L.A. before he was due to leave for Nicaragua, and the new dean of the school, Davis Collins, was an old buddy who'd burned out after his fourth divorce and decided to take a job that would keep him home nights in case he ever got married again.

"If you'd never started that marriage stuff, Dave, you wouldn't have racked up four divorces," Gabe advised him kindly. "You should give it up."

"We don't all have your guts, Gabe. Some of us fall in love."

"Four times?" He was incredulous.

"Don't ask me to explain. Come on down and let the kids hero-worship you, Gabe. They've been working so hard all year that they've just about forgotten why they came here. They need some inspiration."

The lecture hall was jammed, kids practically hanging from the ceiling, as he did an improvised slide show and explained when and where and how each world-famous image had been shot. For an hour afterwards he fielded questions, waiting for one from a girl who sat silently in the front row, looking as if she'd drifted in from some woodland wild, never taking her eyes off his face. She was dying to ask something, he could tell, and he found himself glancing at her, waiting for her hand to be raised, but she sat without moving, her long, wiggly hair falling in careless squiggles around her face, her eyes glowing in repressed curiosity under her level brows.

Finally Gabe announced that the lecture was over, and that there would be absolutely no more questions. He accepted the storm of applause, and turned to gather up his stuff while the hall emptied behind him. When he was ready to leave, the girl was still sitting quietly, looking at him, alone, a question still in her eyes. He could guess what she wanted, he realized with pleasure. Groupie time.

"Excuse me, Mr. Gabriel, may I ask you something?"

"I'm on my way, cutie, but why not?"

"Would I be right in saying that the craft of photojournalism is ninety percent lying and cheating and talking people into letting you into the right place; nine and nine-tenths percent the pure chance of *being* in the right place at the right time; and one-tenth of one percent actually taking the picture?"

"You could say that." A novel approach, but no question she was hitting on him.

"That's what I figured. I knew I didn't want to be a photojournalist, but I wasn't entirely sure why. Thank you for being honest." Jazz rose to go and was halfway down the aisle when he stopped her.

"So how come you stayed till the end?"

"I didn't want to ask you that in front of everybody. It might have sounded rude."

"*You* were afraid of embarrassing *me*?" He found himself suddenly indignant.

"Well, of course." She walked more quickly toward the exit to the hall. He followed her and grabbed her arm.

"So how come, if it only takes one-tenth of one percent of what I've got going, that I'm the one who comes up with the killer shot and not the next guy?"

"I would assume that you've been extraordinarily lucky."

"You think there's no craft to what I do?"

"Craft? Absolutely yes. It's *all* craft. That's the problem. I like a little something else mixed into my work."

"Jesus. An arty one. You take pictures of weirdly shaped trees at sunset, and reflections of mountains in ponds, and prairie grasses waving in the wind and shit like that."

"Not exactly. Look, I have to go."

"So go."

"You're holding on to my sweater."

"So let's have a drink. You can show me your work."

Yeah, that was how it had started. He'd never known if she'd hit on him or he'd hit on her, but probably it was what he got for doing a favor for old Dave. No good deed goes unpunished, as his grandmother, may she rest in peace, used to say.

Human charm, in its superficial manifestations, can be conjured up by a well-worded recollection of the timbre of a voice, the particular quality of a laugh, the contrast of an unexpectedly beguiling glance in an otherwise ordinary pair of eyes, the recollection of the play of humor or the music of whimsy. Yet charm is essentially inexplicable and resists description.

Tony Gabriel had been blessed by immense charm, that unfairly distributed blessing. He had charmed from his cradle. His con-man performances rested far more on his charm than on his shrewdness, persistence, courage and skill, all of which he had legitimately. Part of his charm was that he never exercised it deliberately, as do those semi-charming people who can rise to charm when the occasion demands it.

Tony Gabriel couldn't turn it on because he couldn't turn it off.

Many photojournalists referred to him as "the Hungarian," because in the history of the western world, Hungarians have been and remain the most notoriously charming people who have ever lived. Tony Gabriel knew of his nickname, knew the meaning behind it, and since he was the kind of charmer who had never had to work deliberately at being charming, it puzzled him slightly. What element of his personality were they picking on, anyway? At the same time, he saw no reason to be offended. Hungary was close enough to his family's mixed-up, much-traveled, middle-European background so that his family tree, if it could be constructed, which it couldn't, probably contained a Hungarian here and there. He was pragmatic about charm and believed that the only important thing to remember about it was that it worked.

=======

"I feel an interesting preference for being exactly where I am," Tony Gabriel said to Jazz.

"Is that so unusual?"

"It's . . . new. Sort of . . . agreeable. I don't normally sit and just . . . sit."

"Maybe it's the lighting," Jazz suggested. "Imagine thinking of putting candles on the tables. That's exceptionally authentic. And semicircular red leather booths and paper napkins. You almost never see anything like that in a bar."

"Yeah, and laminated plastic tables and Tou-louse-Lautrec posters on the walls. We could be anywhere. Mexico City—Kansas City—even Jersey City."

"I noticed that too," Jazz said, "as soon as we came in. Down-home credibility. That probably means there isn't too much water in the booze, unless it's all done to lull suspicion."

"Since when is white wine booze?"

"I meant your scotch."

"Booze is from before your time."

"My father says 'booze.' "

"Mine too."

"How old are you?" Jazz asked.

"Twenty-nine," he answered.

She inspected him carefully. Unkempt but very clean, rough and ready yet somehow sophisticated, an outdoor look because of his tanned skin and skinny frame, more lines on his face than a twenty-nine-year-old should have. "You look older. Definitely older. About thirty-two."

"Yeah? So how old are you?"

"Eighteen. Should I call you Tony?"

"Gabe."

"Do you get to Jersey City often?"

"Often enough. So why do people call you Jazz?"

"Because Juanita Isabella is unwieldy, as names go."

"So you're basically Spanish?"

"Some. Mostly Irish and Swedish, all Californian."

"A *native?*"

"The first you've met?"

"I think so. Wait a minute, I used to know a guy, he was born in Vegas. Nope. And there was this girl, she was from Corona Del Mar. Nope. You're my first native. Did you know that the first time you meet anyone of an absolutely new ethnic background you get to make a wish?"

"You're perfectly aware that Del Mar is in California. No wish."

"So I've never been where the turf meets the surf. Not my gig."

"That's the good news."

"You're a fresh kid. Why aren't you slithering all over me? Why aren't you asking me about how I walked into Tibet or rode a camel through the Gobi or how many times I've climbed out of a helicopter and just let go? Where's the respect a mere first-year student should show a big-shot, famous photojournalist?"

"You should have asked one of the boys out for a drink."

"Actually, I'm not in the mood for mindless adoration. I get too much of it. Your subtle disdain is refreshing. But you could try to flirt. We belong to different genders. Maybe even totally different species. It's only polite to indicate that you recognize the difference."

"I never flirt," Jazz said righteously.

"I know. Why should you have to? You're too beautiful to flirt. Too intelligent to flirt. Too snooty to flirt."

"I am not snooty," Jazz said, sipping her wine with a larky glint in her eye.

"I just said that, I didn't mean it. Beautiful and intelligent, but not snooty."

"Well put. Also I'm exceptionally modest."

"I think I like you."

"I know you do." Her voice was amused.

"So do you like me? *Forget it!* I never asked anyone that in my life."

"Don't be frightened, I won't hold it against you." Jazz giggled at the expression of horror on his face. "I sort of like you. You're more or less basically likable. What's not to like?"

"Well, you don't know me yet. There could be a lot."

"I'm sure there is. But how bad could it be?"

"There's only one way to find out. Dinner?"

"Of course," she said without hesitation. She had assumed that drinks would lead to dinner.

"So you don't have another date?"

"No. So why do you start a lot of your sentences with 'so'?"

"Do I?"

"Never mind. I'm afraid it's catching. So where are we having dinner?" Jazz asked hungrily. She knew she was dressed presentably for any restaurant in California in 1979, in her white trousers and heavy, hand-knit, cable-stitched white sweater.

"I was thinking about your place."

"Seriously. Oh, you *are* serious. I share a place with two roommates. We have peanut butter, bananas and skim milk. My roommates don't mind sharing. Sound good to you?"

"Not even for breakfast," Gabe said, shuddering. "That leaves Thai, Chinese, Indian, Moroccan, Japanese, Italian, but not French, I hate French. All truly civilized people hate French, especially the French, whose dream meal is a steak and fries, washed down by two bottles of red wine, accompanied by a pack or two of cigarettes. Of course there's always pizza. Or we could make a gesture toward simplifying life, stay right here and have a hamburger."

"We could. Let's. Their hamburgers are probably as authentic as the scotch." Jazz was decisive.

"There's something . . . different . . . about you. I don't get it and I'm not used to not getting things. It makes me nervous. I can't exactly figure you out—there's something . . . something particular, not peculiar, but I don't know, something . . . about you that I can't quite put my finger on."

"Take your time. I'm not going anywhere." Jazz shrugged in an especially provoking way because it told the shrugged-upon person that she was indifferent to being analyzed and that she would never modify her behavior to suit anyone, but she sweetened the shrug with a smile that was as much at odds with her shrug as it was almost impossibly seductive. It was a smile that stopped the clock.

"I've got it! That number about being Spanish and Irish and Swedish—it's a scam—you're *Hungarian*! Oh my God, am I in deep shit."

"I don't know," Jazz laughed, "are you?"

"That wasn't a question," he responded. "It was a statement of fact."

Jazz knew that she had never been in love. She'd had a crush on one of her teachers in sixth grade and felt a flutter for three weeks for the boy who acted opposite her in the eighth-grade play, but the Bishop School had contained no possible love object, nor had she had time, in the rigorous first year at Graphics Central, even to think about men.

Nevertheless, her memory of her emotions from grammar school was enough to inform her, as she tried and failed to eat the hamburger for which she thought she had been so hungry, that the way she seemed to be bending her attitude toward Tony Gabriel had something to do with her heart.

When he picked up a strand of her hair, looked at it with intense concentration, and asked, "What do you call this color—cornbread with maple syrup?" she felt as if he'd fallen to his knees and told her she was far more lovely than a Botticelli Venus.

She found herself studying the two deep vertical lines on either side of his mouth, which remained whether he smiled or not, as if they would provide a clue to her inability to look away from his perfectly ordinary nose, very big but not remarkable in any other way, and his bright, clever brown eyes, no different from anyone else's bright, clever brown eyes, and his rather humorous mouth, which was just a man's mouth with a nice ordinary upper lip and a nice ordinary lower lip and nice ordinary teeth. There was nothing about the ensemble of his features, either separately or taken as a whole, that she could honestly pick out as special, and the topography of the human face was the area on which she had concentrated her interest for years. Gabe was . . . attractive, very attractive . . . and somehow interesting looking, but so were a million men. He certainly couldn't be called handsome or striking, she told herself, desperately trying to hold on to reality. It must be all those silly cowlicks.

She couldn't stop staring at him.

"Something wrong with the hamburger?" he asked.

"No, it's fine. I'm just . . . not hungry."

"Neither am I," he said, looking in some surprise at the almost untouched hamburger on his plate. "Maybe we should have gone for something more exotic."

"I don't think that . . . would have helped." Jazz found that she had to force herself to speak. Her lips seemed frozen and her mind wasn't working normally. In fact, it was barely working at all.

"I'm not hungry," Gabe said in wonder, "and I haven't eaten since breakfast." He sounded bewildered, a man who has made a discovery he knows is momentous although he doesn't yet know why.

Jazz made a noncommittal noise that indicated a response. Something about the way he'd offered this piece of information made it seem as if invisible, golden trumpets had blown a glorious fanfare. He wasn't hungry and she wasn't hungry. She felt a rising, choking, dangerous tightening in her chest, as if she were about to burst into tears or laughter and be unable to stop.

"Don't take this personally, but do you believe in love at first sight?" Gabe asked, with an expression of shocked and terrified disbelief as he listened to his voice saying words he had never said before and never expected to say.

"If you'd asked me that five minutes ago . . ." Jazz hesitated and lowered her eyelids, unable to meet his gaze.

"Yes?"

"I would have said that I doubt it . . . but I suppose anything can happen . . ."

"Don't stop . . .". Gabe implored her. "Just say whatever comes into your head."

"Now . . . I'm beginning to . . ."

"To what?" he asked, taking her hands in his and holding the shaking fingers tightly.

"Beginning to wonder . . ." Jazz's high color grew higher.

"Wonder what?"

"If maybe it's . . . possible," she whispered, overcome by a sudden new bashfulness, her chin lowered so that she was looking only at the table.

"For some people or all people?"

"No idea." Jazz shook her head.

"For you and me?"

"How would I know? Why do you expect me to know everything?" Jazz said, lifting her head in protest against this blissful, pointless interrogation.

"Because I'm crazy nuts in love with you, I have been since the minute I saw you and it doesn't seem possible, it's never happened to me before, so *you* have to tell me it's true."

"Oh," Jazz said, feeling the heart she had judged cool and unready slip easily free of the cords that bound it and dance wildly to the music of the trumpets that blew and blew again their announcement of joy.

"Are you just going to sit there and say 'oh'?"

Jazz nodded, incapable of speech.

"That's good enough for me. You didn't say no, did you? You feel the same thing? It's not just me? It can't possibly be *just* me, can it?"

Jazz could not even make a gesture. She just sat there, immobile, knowing that it was enough for her to accept his words and wait. His hands were trembling as badly as hers, but his were warm and hers were cold.

"So that's settled. Love at first sight, that's what it's called, that's what's happened to us."

Jazz tried to smile. She failed. She felt so frightened that she didn't know what to do. She could never get up and leave the safety of this red leather booth. She'd have to spend the rest of her life here. How had she managed to talk to him before? What part of her brain had permitted all those words? Just so long as he didn't let go of her hands, she'd be all right.

"Did you know in the lecture hall?" he demanded tenderly.

"I don't remember. It was too long ago. Yes. Maybe. I don't know."

"But you kept walking away, Jazz. What if I'd let you go?"

"You couldn't have."

"I couldn't have," Gabe agreed. "No way. Do you realize that I haven't kissed you yet?"

"It doesn't seem to matter," Jazz muttered timidly.

"You're right. We should give it a chance to matter."

"There's no rush," Jazz said, almost unable to breathe.

"Don't you care?"

"I care too much."

"Me too. We'd better get it over with. The longer we wait, the tougher it's going to be," Gabe said with the determination and knowledge of a man who made his living taking risks no sane man would take. "Will you come back to my hotel?"

"Of course. But you have to hold my hand the whole time. Don't let go."

As soon as they reached the hotel room, Gabe dropped Jazz's hand, which he had clutched except when he had put his key in the ignition, and put his arms tightly around her, standing up with his back to the door.

"You're safe now, we're home free," Gabe told Jazz, who was shivering in spite of her heavy sweater.

"Just keep holding me." Her voice was low and tyrannical. She buried her head in his chest.

"Are you that afraid?" He spoke to the top of her head.

"Yes," she answered, as resolutely as if she were denying any fear.

"Me too."

"But you're much older than I am. You have to be brave," Jazz argued, stubbornly bashful, clinging to bashfulness as if it were familiar, although she had never been bashful in her life before.

Gabe held Jazz a few inches away from him, tilted her head upward and touched her lips softly with one finger and grinned.

"I'd damn well better be brave enough to kiss you."

Gabe inclined his head and placed his mouth slowly on her mouth, and his delicate, almost humorous kiss allowed some of the muscles in her shoulders to release a little of their tension. "I'm even brave enough to kiss you a lot," he whispered, and he kissed her again and again, feeling her cold lips turn warm and her shivering grow less, as he learned the feel of the shape of her mouth. It felt even fuller than it looked, he thought, even fuller than he had imagined, succulent, tender, firm, fresh, a mouth like none other he had ever known.

Jazz responded with an awkward willingness, beginning, little by little, to match him kiss for kiss, as if kissing were a marvelous game at which the players never lost or won, a game that could be played indefinitely.

"We just can't stand here necking," Gabe finally said, between kisses.

"Sure we can," Jazz murmured. "There's nobody to stop us."

"It's not comfortable. Want to . . . sit down?"

"I want to do whatever you want to do."

He'd never had a girl in his room before, Gabe thought—and God knew there had been more than his fair share of girls in his rooms—who wanted to keep on kissing standing up all night, but he'd never been in love before, so maybe that accounted for it. All the old rules were changed. This was a whole new ball game.

"So how about the couch?" he suggested, feeling ridiculous but willing to feel ridiculous.

"What about it?" Jazz landed a kiss on his nose.

"We could look at it or we could talk about it or we could reupholster it—or we could sit down."

"Oh, let's sit," she said, laughing for the first time since the door had closed behind them. "Isn't that what's it's there for?"

Gabe took Jazz firmly by the hand and led her over to the couch and watched as she sat down neatly, almost primly.

"Like this?" Jazz asked. She was playing dumb, Gabe decided. His darling dumb some-new-sort-of-blond.

"For a job interview, yes. This isn't a job interview." Gabe rearranged her until she was in a semi-reclining position. "O.K., now hold still. There's this particular place right behind the top of your ear where the hair starts to ripple—I've been thinking about that place all night. I want to kiss you there. You're not ticklish?"

"Only on the soles of my feet."

Gabe sank to his knees on the floor, since it was a foam-rubber couch, both low and narrow, and leaned over Jazz. He slid one arm under her head to support it, and held the hair off her neck with the other hand, rummaging around behind her ear with his lips, kissing her with tiny, tasting, peregrinating kisses along the length of her hairline to the nape of her neck.

They hadn't turned on any of the lights in the room, and he could only see her dimly, her head half-turned away from him so that he could have complete access to her hairline, but the tactile contrast of the softness of the skin of her neck with the springy birth of her hair with its promise of a thousand discoveries to come, was almost as exciting as her lips. Jazz, utterly silent, half-opened her mouth in delight and closed her eyes so that she could concentrate on his warm, moving mouth as if she were listening to music too important to permit visual distraction.

Gabe's lips ventured slowly upward, behind her ear, and crossed her temple to her eyelid. He slid the tip of his tongue across the curved line where her eyelashes grew from the skin of her lids, skin so delicate that he dared only to brush it with the lightest of touches. He flicked his tongue over the tips of her lashes and she cried out suddenly, the first sound she'd made since they'd moved to the couch.

"You like that," he muttered.

Jazz broke out of her trance and grasped him around the neck, drawing his head down. "Lie down next to me," she begged.

"There's no room."

"There's room on the bed," Jazz said.

"That's a wonderful idea. I wish I'd thought of it." Gabe marveled at his delicious dumbbell.

"You're the one who said the couch," Jazz replied, almost reproachfully, getting up, crossing the room, kicking off her shoes and lying down on the bed.

"It's all my fault. I won't make it again. Straight to the bed from the door. What was I thinking of?"

He stood over her, studying her. "White pants and white sweater on a white bedspread? This won't work. How can I find you—it's like looking for a white rabbit in a snow bank."

"Look for a pink nose," Jazz answered, sitting up and pulling her sweater over her head.

He gasped at the sight of her breasts. The sweater was such a thick knit that there had been no way to even imagine breasts like these, so utterly young, yet heavy and opulent; ripe breasts that were so firm they rode high on her chest, lifting upward with their big rosy nipples hardened and pointed.

Gabe slid down and pulled Jazz over on top of

him so that her breasts were above his face. She
leaned on her elbows as she gazed down at him, a look
of intent curiosity on her face. He moaned and with
his large hands he took her breasts and pushed them
together so that he could take both her nipples into his
mouth at the same time. With all the pulling, sucking
force of his lips and tongue and cheeks, he feasted on
those hot buds as if he could make them open and
flower inside his mouth.

For many minutes his whole being was concentrated on the nipples he held so firmly enclosed. He
suckled at her unmercifully, teasing her with tiny nips
of his teeth, causing her a pleasure so wonderful that
she bit her own lips as she tried to force even more of
her breasts into his mouth. She pressed down on him
with her hips without realizing what she was doing,
rubbing and pushing so urgently, with such insistence,
that finally he knew that it was time to tear himself
away from her breasts. Gabe took her by her shoulders, turned her over on her back and, with the boldness of an outlaw, stripped off what was left of her
clothes, intent, possessed.

Jazz lay spellbound, suddenly stilled, with only
her hair to cover her shoulders, watching him, a question again glowing in her eyes. He stood beside the
bed while he tore off his own clothes. Jazz stared at
Gabe, her eyes widening at the sight of his tanned
body in the dimness of the room. He was as thin as
she'd thought, but she hadn't imagined that his arms
and legs and shoulders would be so unexpectedly
sinewy, or his chest so broad. Nor had she tried
to picture to herself the powerful, heavy, masterful
penis, thicker and longer than she could have believed, that stood out and up from the dark hair between his legs. She drew in her breath, stunned,
incredulous, unable to look away, shocked into immobility.

Gabe knelt on the bed, his knees holding her
thighs apart, kissing her open, panting mouth many
times, making sounds she couldn't understand. She

threw her arms around his neck as she tried awkwardly, but with all her strength, to pull him down on top of her, desperate to be crushed under him, to feel his skin everywhere on her body.

Finally Gabe sat back on his heels, consumed with a need so savage that he spent no time on her voluptuous, abandoned nakedness but reached one masterful hand straight toward the curly, abundant tangle of her pubic hair and pushed forward with a questing finger. She was ready, oh yes, very ready, more than ready for him. He held the weighty heft of his penis and steadily, relentlessly pushed it deep and deeper into her body, so harshly inflamed that he didn't listen to the indrawn breaths that now broke her silence. "Ah, ah, ah!" Jazz cried out, on a wild and rising note, but he didn't hear, for he had become finally deaf in his intention to have her. He might have attempted the inhuman task of holding back so that she could catch up with him, but he knew that he would take her many times this night, oh, she would get it, she would get it, but now he could wait no longer. He gave himself entirely to the burning, imperative flood that forced itself upward, swelling, growing, tightening, hardening, until he burst inside of her in long, excruciatingly good spasms of fire that brought a great animal scream of ravening triumph to his lips.

Gabe still penetrated Jazz when he finally fell on his side, holding her tightly against him. He gradually became aware of sound and sight. Jazz, her breath heaving, was weeping in loud gulps. "Oh God, I'm sorry," he said, deeply contrite, "but I couldn't stop. Christ, that hasn't happened since I was a kid."

She gasped, sobbing, inconsolable.

"Jazz, Jazz, darling Jazz, don't cry! It's not a tragedy. I'm going to love you again, just for you, and then again and again, all just for you. Don't cry!"

Gabe hugged her and caressed her hair and kissed her all over her wet face, but still tears spurted out of her eyes. Finally she yielded to his pleas and little by little she wept less and less until she sniffed and complained in a tiny voice. "I didn't expect it to hurt so much."

"Oh shit! I hurt you! Shit! *How could I?* Will you ever forgive me?"

"Of course I will . . . don't feel bad . . . it's supposed to hurt, isn't it . . . the first time?"

"The *what?*"

"The first time."

A vast astonishment whirled into his brain like the twister of a tornado, and everything fell together in one click. Her fright, her cold lips, her prim posture on the sofa, her clumsy attempts to pull him down on top of her, her combination of shyness and boldness.

"Why didn't you tell me!" he demanded, torn between rapture and guilt.

"Don't know," Jazz muttered, trying to bury her head in his shoulder. He held her off.

"Why? Why?"

"I was . . . afraid . . . that you wouldn't want to . . . that you'd make too big a deal out of it . . . oh, you know."

"You're damn right I would! I'm so much in love with you—I sure as hell wouldn't have hurt you. Oh, my darling baby, I would have been so gentle. And now it's too late. Too fucking late," he mourned.

"Don't feel bad," she comforted him. "It's stopped hurting."

"Oh yeah, sure, just like that, I'll bet it has, poor love, poor sweet dumbbell."

"I wish you'd stop blaming yourself and do something useful," Jazz said with a return to cheer that told Gabe that he might have missed one train but another one was steaming into the station.

"So I'm going to have to kiss it and kiss it and make it well. That what you had in mind?"

"Something like that. Yes . . . definitely. That."

Together, forgetting any other reality, Jazz and Gabe lived through the next week without asking questions

of the future or directing a thought to the past. Only
the uncomplicated completeness of the lavish present
existed, perfect days and perfect nights, which would
mark all days and all nights to come in their memories;
days and nights in which detail flowed into detail to
make a seamless, splendid whole; days and nights that
are granted to a few fortunate people once in a lifetime, but rarely twice. They shared one consciousness; they woke at the same minute and slept at the
same minute and grew hungry together and thirsty together and needed to touch each other, even if it was
only to hold hands, at all times.

After a week the world refused to stand still for
them any longer. Gabe had to leave for Nicaragua and
the new assignment for which he was already several
days late. There was no question of his giving it up;
there was no doubt that Jazz would go with him; there
was no reason for her to remain in school. Even if
there had been a compelling reason, she would have
ignored it. The only person who had to be told about
their plans was Mike Kilkullen.

"We'll drive down and see him," Jazz said.
"Today."

"Can't we phone?" Gabe asked hopefully.

"Coward."

"Shouldn't I be?"

"I can't go away without telling him everything
and saying good-bye to him, you know that," Jazz
replied. "He won't bite. I hope."

"I don't think he'll be thrilled." Gabe looked at
Jazz. She was so vivid in the directness of her happiness that she flew where other people walked, blazed
where other people breathed. What father in his right
mind would want to see that?

"He'll be happy for me. I hope."

"So let's go."

"Maybe tomorrow?" Jazz suggested, suddenly
feeling a twinge of anxiety about her father's reaction.

"Today," Gabe responded. One of them had to
be the grown-up. "But first we'll both take a shower.

You smell like me and I smell like you. Then fresh clothes all around. Don't dare touch me again until we're on the way home. No reason to flaunt it."

Beirut, Belfast, the Gaza Strip—they hadn't turned out to be so dangerous after all, Gabe reminded himself as they drove through the wide avenue of giant figs leading to the Hacienda Valencia. This should be a breeze. After all, what conservative Orange County rancher wouldn't be tickled pink to send his adored eighteen-year-old daughter off to the trouble spots of the planet with an imperfect stranger?

God in heaven, had they no common ordinary decency, Mike Kilkullen raged to himself. To show up here, obviously just out of bed, with that unmistakable fucked-out look and that smell clinging to them like a cloud of gunpowder, practically unable to keep their hands to themselves, and announce that they were going off together? Did they think he didn't remember and recognize that look, that smell, that he'd never experienced it himself?

Jazz didn't even look like herself anymore. He didn't want to think about the new way she looked or the way she couldn't take her eyes off that big-nosed bag of bones she called Gabe—what kind of name was that, anyway? Why did men have to have daughters when this was what always happened sooner or later and in this case much, much too soon? And when there was nothing, absolutely nothing, that you could do to stop it in 1979? If he could, he'd brick her up in a tower and lower the portcullis, or send her to a convent for a few years or take her on a long, slow trip around the world or, better yet, get out his hunting rifle and blow this daughter-stealing shitass bastard Gabe straight to hell for which no jury in the world would convict him. Christ, why did the sixties ever have to happen? That was what was wrong with the world. The fucking sixties. Now every eighteen-year-old believed that she was in charge of herself and her destiny and even when it was your own daughter you had to go along with it because you had no choice.

"Do you have everything you need, Juanita Isabella?" Mike Kilkullen asked, sounding thoughtfully polite but not concerned. "Plenty of money and a return ticket and stuff like that?"

"Don't worry about any of that, Dad. I don't need much. Gabe's taking care of everything. And I have traveler's checks, just in case."

"You're not going without your camera?" Mike asked.

"Of course not. Gabe's going to teach me everything there is to know about photojournalism."

"Well that's just fine, kid. Fine and dandy. Do you have a telephone credit card? No? Well, just call collect whenever you happen to feel like it, don't worry about the time difference. I'd like to hear from you when you get a chance."

"I'll make sure she calls, Mr. Kilkullen."

"You do that, Gabe. You do that."

Or I'll come over there, no matter where you are, and I'll find you and put a pistol to your head and pull the trigger, or take a knife and gut you up the stomach like a fish. What the hell Jazz sees in you I can't begin to imagine. That fat-assed Billy Carter is a damn sight better looking, and for sure the Ayatollah Khomeini has more charm. Nobody will ever miss you or even notice that you're gone, you thief, you villain, you filthy son of a bitch.

"Oh, Daddy, we've got to be going back to L.A.," Jazz cried, looking at her watch. "There's so much traffic on the road and I still have to organize a couple of things and pack and catch a plane first thing the day after tomorrow."

"Did you remember to tell the school you were dropping out?" he asked evenly.

"I called the registrar. They said they'd send back your deposit for next year. I'd learned everything they had to teach me, Daddy, the rest was just trimming. You know, most real photographers say that you should never stay in photo school too long or you lose your originality."

"It's lucky you found that out before it was too late."

"I'd really like to look at Jazz's work," Gabe said. "She's told me about the archives. Don't we have enough time, Jazz?"

"I suppose," she answered reluctantly. What if he didn't like it? What if it wasn't as good as she thought it was?

"I've lost my key," Mike Kilkullen lied. "Do you have yours, kid?"

"No, I left it back in L.A.," she said, relieved.

"Tell you what, Gabe, I'll show you something you ought to see." Mike got up and left the living room abruptly, returning in seconds holding the framed enlargement of the snapshot of Sylvie that never left his bedside. He gave it to Gabe.

"That's one of the first pictures my daughter, Juanita Isabella Kilkullen, ever took. With the first roll of film I gave her. With the first camera I gave her. That's her mother, of course. My daughter was eight at the time, only ten years ago. It was the last summer of my wife's life. She went off to Europe. Only she went off alone. But, of course, you know that story."

"Daddy!"

"What's wrong? I thought Gabe should see at least one picture you took. Before you go away too."

"That's not fair!" Jazz shouted. "How can you say such an awful thing to me?"

"Because it's true. Going away is going away," Mike Kilkullen said, standing as immovable as a boulder.

"I get your point, Mr. Kilkullen." Gabe was standing. "I won't presume to say I understand how you feel, but I know I'd feel the same way too if I had a daughter. I'll take good care of Jazz. I promise you that on my life. And she'll call home every week."

"Yeah, you do that, Gabe, you do that. I understand that the phone service from Nicaragua is top-notch, especially during a civil war."

8

Gabe and Jazz were there when the Sandinistas hoisted their red and black flag over the National Palace of Managua in July of 1979. A month later they were among the first journalists to reach Ireland the day after Earl Mountbatten of Burma was killed by Irish Nationalists; within two weeks they flew into Afghanistan as Premier Amin took over after President Taraki had been killed in a coup.

Later, Jazz was to look at her rookie summer of '79 as her personal boot camp and almost her Waterloo. She learned that photojournalism wasn't a superior form of photographic con game, but a job that demanded more guts and stamina than she believed she could possess; a job for the perpetually jet-lagged, the eternally footsore, the utterly focused and, particularly, a job for people to whom fear, sensible, rational, normal, life-saving fear, was nonexistent.

At first she thought her feeling of being overwhelmed was caused by the sheer size of the celebrating Nicaraguan crowds who had overthrown

Somoza's forty-six-year-old dynasty. In the bitter aftermath of the Mountbatten killing, she attributed her storm of emotion to the cruelty of the death of a wartime hero on board his fishing boat in an explosion that also took the life of his grandson. By the time they reached Afghanistan, Jazz had decided that her anxieties were based on the fact that she wasn't entirely sure who was who, what was what, or why. A month later, in October, back in the United States, as Gabe covered racial violence in Boston high schools, a subject on which she could get a clear grip, Jazz was finally forced to admit to herself that she was in far over her head.

She had never imagined that she would come quickly to expect danger everywhere, no less in Boston than in Managua. She felt as if she had sprouted antennae on the alert for danger, not just in the back of her head but on the soles of her feet, on the points of her elbows, and at the back of her shoulders.

Anywhere, in any of the emotion-swept, often violent mobs that Gabe moved through so purposefully, there could be someone with a gun or a bomb who would choose a man and a girl with cameras as a target. Or else someone might throw a bomb for an entirely different reason, and they would find themselves in its deadly path. Mobs of people were dangerous in and of themselves; Gabe's style of photojournalism meant getting as deeply into the crowds as possible.

So far, Jazz had managed to hide the nature of her feelings from Gabe.

She told herself that either she must learn to live with fear or go home; get her shit together or get out.

Jazz decided to stay, because she was more afraid of being without Gabe than she was of some as-yet-unthrown bomb. The way to stay was to keep so busy that she didn't have time to think; staying meant shooting almost as much film almost as fast as Gabe, even if she didn't know or care what side the people she was shooting were on, or why they were intent on demonstrating. Shooting meant concentration on getting a powerful image, no matter the circumstances.

Her work improved, in her opinion anyway, and the antennae on the soles of her feet, which warned her that the next step might be fatal, bothered her less. Perhaps it might be coincidence, she thought, or it might be due to the fact that she was wearing filthy socks inside of even more filthy boots, with no hope of doing her laundry for days. Dirty hair, unwashed clothes, blisters on her feet—Gabe didn't care what she looked or smelled like so long as she kept up with him but never got in his way, and that was all that mattered. She carried his spare camera bodies and lenses in their foam-rubber-padded case, she loaded film for him, and she kept a watch out for portable food and drink when he would have forgotten about both. He wasn't used to having an assistant, and she had to fight to do anything for him, but eventually he gave in and let her take over in these areas.

Jazz still managed to do a great deal of shooting on her own, pictures that would never be developed or used, since she was not on assignment, but pictures that Jazz knew were steadily inching closer to the emotional center of the action. The antennae on the backs of her shoulders grew less watchful as her eyes became quicker to pick out the single most mean-ingful grouping of people in any hurly-burly, from Tehran while Shiite students set fire to an American flag on top of the United States Embassy, to Lake Placid after the American ice hockey team won the gold medal.

In the last days of March 1980, while Gabe was getting entirely too cozy with Mount St. Helens, Jazz, finding herself on the West Coast for the first time in almost a year, decided that the increasingly restless volcano was far less important than going home to visit her father.

Mike Kilkullen was stunned by the changes in her, both visible and nonvisible. The daughter he'd been forced to allow to go off to wars, riots and terror-ism had been the same girl he'd watched grow up, day by day for eighteen years, reserved, almost enigmatic, quietly humorous, changed only by her first experi-

ence of love. At nineteen, Jazz had been many years
less mature than her mother had been at nineteen.

Until she met Tony Gabriel, she had lived absorbed in the two strongest forces in her life: her tie
to her father and her photography. In many other
ways she had been a late bloomer, not interested in
entering into the mating dance of adolescence; incurious about the lure of big cities or travel; content with
the small excitements of life on a relatively isolated
ranch near a small town; a girl, he felt, who still
needed to be surrounded by the safety and protection
of daily routine. Hadn't she fought to stay on the ranch
with him instead of being sent away to boarding
school? Hadn't she driven back home every weekend
during her year at Graphics Central, turning down invitations that any other girl of her age would have
accepted?

Mike Kilkullen had been worried about Jazz for a
long time. He didn't understand the dynamics of
everything that could happen to an eight-year-old
child when her mother dies, but he knew that there
had to be a basic connection between the brutal explosion of that worst of all possible losses and Jazz's
passive lack of interest in the world outside of the
ranch. Jazz had never, it seemed to him, truly taken
possession of a secure sense of her own self that he
believed only a mother can give a child. From her
birth until Sylvie's death, Jazz had managed to grow
up in spite of Sylvie's frequent absences, for three
reasons: her firm base in his own love, Rosie's devoted care, and Sylvie's absolute emotional availabil-
ity when she was at the ranch. It was far from a perfect
way to be brought up, he reflected, but many children
had far less.

But for years after Sylvie's death, Jazz seemed to
have been frozen, as if she couldn't quite take the next
steps with only his support. Her adolescence had not
contained a minute of rebellion, which certainly
seemed odd, according to what he read and heard.
Even her consuming passion for photography, he suspected, might somehow be tied to her loss of Sylvie,

for only in memories and in photographs could she recapture her mother. And memories fade faster than snapshots.

Now, ten months after Jazz had so suddenly left home at eighteen, it seemed to him that a woman had returned to the ranch, in place of the girl who had left. This woman walked with a far more confident stride than Jazz ever had; she spoke up far more frequently and with more conviction; she was suddenly aware of the absurdity of life and the impossibility of doing very much about it, yet she hadn't become a cynic. She was far more animated than Jazz had ever been, a hundred times less inclined to accept his opinion on everything, but she didn't make a point of insisting that she was right. Right or wrong, she seemed to think, no matter what he thought or what she thought, it would all work out one way or another—or rather it would all probably *not* work out—and they had to accept the fact that they couldn't do much about it.

"Are you still a Democrat, at least?" he asked sharply.

"For sure. But where would I register to vote?" Jazz grimaced at the fact that now that she was old enough to vote she never stayed long enough in one place to have an address.

"At the American embassy of whatever country you go to most often," Mike Kilkullen answered her indignantly. It was tough enough being a Democrat in Orange County without losing a single potential voter.

"That would be Paris," Jazz said thoughtfully. "Photojournalism has always been centered in Paris, ever since the great days of *Paris-Match,* and it still is, oddly enough. You'd think it would be New York, but Paris is the red-hot center."

"Well, damn it, Jazz, then register at the embassy in Paris. You can get them to give you an absentee ballot if necessary. Or do you feel that you're just a mere spectator at the great scene of world events, with the planet as one big photo opportunity?"

"You mean do I still care who wins? Not just the election but in general? Of course I do, Dad, but if I

stopped long enough to think about it, I'd just keep
Gabe from doing what he has to do."

"Are we talking heavy-duty camp follower
here?"

"Very heavy-duty. But a happy camp follower."
Jazz grinned at him in a way he had never seen before,
and which the father in him instantly wiped out of his
mind.

"Why the hell did you cut your hair?" he said
irritably, instead of asking her why she smiled like a
satisfied female animal. Of all the physical changes in
Jazz, what upset him the most was that her magnificent head of hair, which had always made him think
of the beautifully streaked pelt of a golden sable, had
been cropped to a shaggy urchin look that was as short
as a boy's at the back and the sides and fell over her
forehead every which way in front.

"Cooties," Jazz answered.

"I don't believe you!"

"Relax! I didn't actually ever *have* them, but
after a week without a good hot shower, I sort of
began to wonder about the possibility. My hair got in
my way. Anyway, I like it like this—don't you?"

"I liked it better before," he said, as gently as he
could. I liked it better before you met Gabe, I liked it
better when you didn't strut like a champion after a
good game; I liked it better when you didn't move as
boldly as if you were wearing a full set of chain-mail
body armor, when you didn't look as determined as if
you'd been born on a kibbutz, when you didn't have
that invulnerable set to your mouth and chin, when
your face hadn't changed to a woman's face, but still
had a little of the baby in it; I liked it better when the
sun rose and set on me; I liked it better when you
didn't feel really happy anywhere but at the ranch; I
liked it better when you were still my baby. I liked it
better before you met that reckless shit Gabe and grew
the fuck up.

"Hey, Daddy, if I can vote, I can drink in a bar
in California. Come on, let's ride into town. I want to
buy you a drink at the Swallows."

"Oh yeah?"

"Yeah."

"O.K., let's go."

If Jazz had to grow up, at last, why couldn't she do it at home, where he could keep an eye on her?

By the middle of April, Jazz and Gabe were back in Paris with a week to spare before they were due to go to Rome to join Pope John Paul II's tour of Africa.

"We've got to go register to vote at the embassy, before we leave," Jazz informed Gabe as they ate ham sandwiches at a café and counted the number of different ways Frenchmen, as style-obsessed as their women, had invented to hang mufflers around their necks.

"What's this 'got to' stuff? I never vote, cutie. Who has time?"

"That's disgusting. My father will be very upset if you don't register." Jazz fluttered her eyelashes disapprovingly at him through her tangled bangs.

"So I'll go, I'll go," Gabe said hastily. "Just tell me what party he prefers."

"Do you think the embassy will mind that we're living in a hotel? Does that count as an address?"

"Beats me. Let's rent an apartment."

"Gabe! You've never lived anywhere except hotels."

"I never had a girl like you before." He brushed away her bangs and studied her excited, vivid face, her bloom of a mouth, the sumptuously full lower lip flirting with the devastatingly delicate upper lip, her cornflake-colored crop of hair, her jeweled eyes. He'd never be absolutely sure he knew what she was thinking, he realized with delight and ever-renewed curiosity. "A babe who looks like you deserves a permanent address. A babe like you should have a place to hang her hat. You should *have* a hat, now that I think of it. We're always passing through Paris—we could leave all our clothes here, if we had any clothes. Have you still got your *Tribune*? Let's look in the classified. So what have we here? A place in the eighth *arrondisse-*

ment, no way, too close to Dior; a place in the six-teenth—that's the ultimate in boring; the thirteenth, nope, sort of not my favorite neighborhood; here's something on the Ile St-Louis. Quai de Bourbon. Out of the way, awfully far downriver, but a good view. I'll call the real-estate lady.''

"Do they have real-estate ladies in Paris?"

"I keep forgetting how young you are," Gabe said, searching in his pocket for a telephone token. "How inexperienced, how innocent."

"How virginal?" Jazz asked.

"Complaining? Been feeling too virginal lately?"

"On the contrary."

"Good. Stay that way."

Gabe disappeared into the café to make the call, and returned with an appointment to view the apartment that afternoon. After one quick look they rented the little second-floor walkup for its view of the tree-bordered Seine. The furnishings that came with the apartment weren't as bad as they might have been.

"If I take all the little bits and pieces off the tables and hide them in a closet, buy some plants, take down the curtains in the living room, put up new curtains in the bedroom, get a decent frying pan, maybe give the walls a coat of fresh white paint—oh, Gabe, it's going to be fabulous!"

Jazz whirled around from one room to another, afire with joy, a nesting instinct she'd never had before suddenly awakened.

"If we buy plants, who's going to water them when we're away?"

"I'll make a deal with the concierge."

"Then why are we still standing here?" he asked. "There's a plant market on the Ile de la Cité. After-wards, we can buy all that other stuff and have it delivered to the concierge."

"Couldn't we start on the walls right away?" Jazz begged. "With rollers we'd be finished almost before we start."

"Good thinking. Where's the nearest paint store?"

"How would I know?"

"When in doubt, find a café, order coffee and ask. That's the sum total of my knowledge of how to get things done in Paris."

"Where's the nearest café?" Jazz asked, willfully, blissfully, enchantingly stupid.

"Just where it always is. Around the corner. Any corner. Come on, toots, you're a housewife now. No time to waste mooning out the window. The view will still be here when you get back."

Before they left for Rome and Africa, Jazz and Gabe had made the apartment their own and discovered a bonus that the real-estate lady hadn't mentioned. At night the lights of the *bateaux mouches,* the sightseeing boats that passed by on the Seine, gently floodlit the windows of their apartment at regular intervals as they floated by, since all the banks of the Seine in the heart of Paris were a historic monument, as treasured as the Grand Canal in Venice. The approaching floodlights would just touch the trees on the riverbank while the boats were still at a distance, and gradually, as they came closer and the lights grew brighter, the tops of the trees outside of their windows were illuminated as magically as if they were on the set of an old-fashioned ballet. The lights poured into their bedroom, as if the moon had drifted down from the sky and was peering in at them, and then, just as softly as the light had come, it started to disappear, to be soon followed by the lights of another boat, on many of which dance music played.

They made love every night to the fairy lights of the *bateaux mouches,* knowing that they were the soul of the eternal spectacle of Paris. Occasionally, during these hours, Jazz gave a passing thought to the tourists sitting stolidly on the boats, dutifully observing the elaborate stone façade of their ancient building, listening to the guide recite facts and dates, but never knowing the beating, thrilling pulse of the life on the other side of the wall, the life of the bed on which she and Gabe, enraptured and in love forever, lay intertwined, too happy to sleep.

For the next six months, as they shuttled from Gdansk
to Paraguay, from Algiers to El Salvador, Gabe found
himself looking for the' assignments that would mean
a stopover in Paris. In February of 1981 he turned
down a job covering the trial of Mrs. Jean Harris in
New York to do a photo story on the new Archbishop
of Paris, Jean-Marie Lustiger, a convert from Juda-
ism; in April they went to Rome, a short flight from
home, to follow the capture of the Red Brigade leader
Mario Moretti, rather than cross the ocean to cover
the first space shuttle flight at Cape Canaveral; in
May, when six soldiers were arrested in San Salvador
for the murder of American church workers, he decided to turn down the assignment and wait in Paris
for the election, a day later, of François Mitterrand,
France's first Socialist president.

The summer of 1981 found Gabe uncharacteristi-
cally lazy, content to let the world go to hell in its
normal, predictable way, unchronicled by him, as he
and Jazz spent their vacation in a farmhouse that
friends lent them in the hills behind St. Tropez. In the
autumn, Gabe promised himself as he relaxed in the
lavender-blessed air of Provence, he'd get back in
stride, but for the first time in his life he found himself
reluctant to contemplate the complete disruption of
their Parisian life that each new assignment meant.

Suddenly the thought of throwing his stuff into a
shoulder bag and taking indefinite leave of the little,
white-walled, plant-filled apartment on the old island
in the center of Paris was utterly untempting. He
found himself looking forward three days in advance
to the weekly roast chicken at the roaring, busy Brasserie Alsacienne on the tip of Ile St-Louis, he who had
never bothered what he ate or when he ate it. He
established a favorite among the cafés that opened
early on the Rue St-Louis-en-Ile, and he went there
each morning for breakfast while he read the *Tribune*.
Afterwards, he bought two croissants for Jazz, whom
he had left asleep in bed, and brought them back to

the apartment for her, waking her with a cup of tea and minutes of kisses.

Now that they had their own place and spent so much time in Paris, Jazz turned one small inside room of the apartment into a darkroom. She started getting jobs taking portraits of children of the large diplomatic colony in Paris, through a friend who was a secretary to the popular and delightful Canadian-born Jean Bakker, the wife of the Dutch ambassador to France. Jazz's prices were reasonable, and her pictures were marvels because they showed the children in moments of action, instead of the traditional forced repose.

Children in movement, unaware of the camera, are hard to capture on film, but it is the best way to show them as their parents know them best. Jazz's experience following Gabe in crowds stood her in good stead, for she could shoot faster and more accurately than any living specialist in pure portrait photography. Even more important, by watching Gabe closely, she had learned how to work without the subject being aware of her, for all great photojournalists have that unique trick of disappearing even as they shoot, so that they can catch people at their most human and natural, in those all-important unguarded moments in which they think they are unobserved.

Jazz took her young subjects to the parks swarming with children playing games, or to the zoo or to open-air markets where birds and rabbits were sold, and let them loose to enjoy themselves. She shot them in repose only if they stopped moving without her asking them to, and those unposed portraits were often the most interesting of all.

She shot in black and white only and developed her own film, carefully cropping and enlarging the best pictures, no matter how many there were. Then she turned them all over to the parents at one price for the lot, instead of demanding that they pick their one or two favorites, as so many photographers did. If they wanted duplicates, she charged only for the cost of the film and her time in the darkroom. Her business quickly grew by word of mouth, and it fit in well with Gabe's schedule, since it didn't demand that she stay in one place for a specific period of time.

Now the waiters at the many restaurants of the Ile St-Louis knew them by name, as did the jovial bandit who owned the one hardware store on the island, and the women who ran the gourmet delicatessen where Gabe and Jazz went to buy provisions for the weekends. The island was a village, and most of its inhabitants rarely crossed its many bridges into the city of Paris, but they knew each other as villagers do all over the world. The newsstand owner knew which magazines to save for them, and they found a dry cleaner, a laundry, and a drugstore. Gabe began to make occasional plans for dinners with friends on the vague assumption that he and Jazz would still be in Paris; when he opened his closet he wasn't surprised to find clean clothes; from time to time he remembered to get his hair cut, and once in a while he bought fresh flowers at the stalls on the streets. Sometimes he even remembered to stick them in water when he got home. On Sunday afternoons, he and Jazz often would go to an American movie in its original, unsubtitled version on the Boulevard St-Germain, and afterwards wander the streets in the direction of the Rue des Canettes, where there was a choice of six pizza places, each one better than the last, and one old-time French bistro, their favorite, Chez Alexandre.

As photo editors began to realize that they could often manage to contact Tony Gabriel in Paris, more and more assignments came in to do local stories such as the inauguration of the TGV, the first high-speed train service in France.

The Poles of Solidarity were waging a dangerous campaign against the Soviets, the Russian troops were massing near the Polish border, while Mitterrand made the first TGV trip from Paris to Lyons, with Gabe and Jazz among the photojournalists on board.

In October of 1981, when the Egyptian leader Anwar el-Sadat was assassinated in Cairo while watching an air show, ten other people were killed and forty wounded. Gabe's first thought on hearing the news was relief that he hadn't been there, because Jazz might have been among those killed or wounded. His second thought was regret for the photos he'd missed.

In November, as the Parisian days grew shorter and the apartment became more agreeable than ever, in contrast to the cold, damp weather outside, Gabe realized that it was almost two and a half years that he and Jazz had been together. In January of 1982 she'd turn twenty-one, and her father had long ago written her about making plans to celebrate her birthday at the ranch with a big party.

"When do we have to fly back to L.A.?" Gabe asked Jazz, thinking about the unwelcome trip. His tone was a resigned grumble.

"I have to go," Jazz said mildly, "but you don't have to come, not if there's a good story somewhere else."

"You'd celebrate your twenty-first birthday without me?"

"I'd rather not—but a story's a story. I don't want to cramp your style," Jazz said understandingly.

"What if I don't mind if you cramp my style? What if I don't want you to have a birthday party without me?" He felt violently jealous at the idea.

"Then be there . . ." Jazz, who wasn't really listening to the conversation he was trying to have, didn't look up from sorting through a set of contacts of her latest job.

"So let's get married."

"What?" He'd finally captured her attention.

"Let's get married," Gabe repeated.

"But . . . we were talking about my birthday. Married?" Jazz paused and let the slippery contact sheets drop to the floor. She had trained herself not even to think about marriage to Gabe. She'd wanted to marry him, it seemed to her, ever since the first night they'd spent together, but that first knowledge had been linked to an immediate understanding that it would never happen. No sane woman would think of

clipping Tony Gabriel's famous wings. He wasn't remotely a candidate for the wedded state. Photojournalists as a group lived in a state of delayed
adolescence. When they were with you they were totally there, and when they were gone they were totally
gone. She had accepted that idea long ago, absorbed
it and remained with him in spite of it. Now her fingers
were beginning to tremble, but she answered carefully.

"Gabe, you don't really want to get married, even
if you think you do. You're not the type."

"Forget my type. Don't tell me how I feel. Don't
you want to get married?"

"I don't . . . I'm not . . . I'm O.K. with the way
things are."

The cautious, gradual and decidedly minor-league
domestication of Tony Gabriel had been a series of
small changes, not one of which Jazz had initiated.
She had consciously forced herself to live in the present for so long that the racing of her pulse and the
intimations of splendid possibilities that suddenly beat
in the air of the room scared her. She had a strong
instinct not to commit herself to wanting anything
from him but a continuation of what they had.

"Well, I'm not," Gabe insisted.

"Hmmm." Jazz shook her head, so perplexed
and astonished that she couldn't find words to fit the
situation. This amazing leap, Gabe's readiness to talk
about marriage, seemed too much. Yet his expression
was as fixed and serious as she'd ever seen it.

"What the fuck is that noise supposed to mean?"
Gabe demanded.

"I'm thinking, that's all. What do you want me to
say?" she asked plaintively. "That this is so sudden?
Actually, that's exactly what it is."

"So? *Think!*"

"I wouldn't marry anyone else," Jazz said
slowly, picking over a minefield of possible responses
to find one that seemed safe, that wouldn't leave her
out on a limb, admitting to an inadmissible longing.

She wanted it too much. She couldn't let him know how much.

"Swell." Gabe scowled ferociously.

"But—what kind of husband would you be?" she blurted out.

"My God! We've been living together for over two years. If you don't know now . . ." He was outraged.

"Living together isn't the same as being married. Married gets . . . sticky. Married means making all sorts of promises and compromises and one person getting the short end of the whole deal . . . married ain't all that . . . grand . . ." Jazz's voice trailed off as she thought of her parents.

"Look, forget about your mother. It wouldn't be the same at all. You'd be with me wherever I went. I would never, ever go off and leave you behind, waiting till I was finished working."

"It's a risky business, highly risky," Jazz murmured, almost to herself, and lowered her eyelids to hide the flaming speculation she knew was in them, to hide her wonderment at his making her so specific a promise. Photojournalists were like sharks that remained in constant motion even while they slept. Life for them was so spontaneous that this week's cover of *Time* would be only a dim memory in a few days. She concentrated hard on trying to make her fingers stop trembling, linking them together so that he wouldn't see and know.

Gabe, trying to look into her mind, was doubly frustrated. He studied the perfect shape of her dark golden head bent thoughtfully downward, and never had he felt such a stubborn, absolute need to conquer her, to make sure of her. Jazz seemed so far away, so inaccessible, so caught up in memories he could never share that she had become a stranger again. He stood up suddenly, lean, rumpled, dark, tough, more intent on having his way than he'd ever been in his life, and crushed Jazz in his arms, forcing her to look up at him.

"You can't possibly not marry me, and you know it!"

"I . . . probably do," Jazz admitted, feeling an unanticipated miracle of certainty begin to invade her prudent, eager, disciplined, ardent heart. "I just never thought . . ."

"No more thinking. It's bad for you," Gabe muttered, leaning down to her lips. "Let's just do it, not talk about it."

"Just do it?" she gasped between kisses, trying, in this moment of victory, to hold him off so that she could test the glorious reality with a flurry of last-minute objections. "You can't just do a wedding—you have to *plan* it—I have to call my father. I have to get a dress we have to find someone to marry us someplace to get married invite people to the wedding —oh, it's so complicated," she complained in delicious deviousness. She wanted him to persuade her one more time. He owed her that.

"We'll make it simple. We'll get married, and have a big party right afterwards—we'll take over Chez Alexandre—and announce it to everyone when we get there." His voice rang with triumph.

"A surprise wedding?"

"Right. Just us and whoever marries us. Just you and me. Jazz, Jazz, we don't need anyone else."

"But my father—"

"And your father."

"Yes," Jazz said. "Yes, yes!"

In spite of Gabe's simplifications, it was several weeks before the surprise wedding could take place. The French have never made it possible for anyone to get married on impulse in their officious, permit-obsessed country, and for Americans in Paris, it is more complicated rather than less. Jazz was a half-Lutheran, non-practicing Catholic. Gabe was nothing in particular, so no priest would marry them. Finally they found a minister affiliated with the American Church in Paris who agreed to perform the ceremony in his study after he got permission from his parish. He also agreed to provide his wife as a witness, along with Mike Kilkullen, who was planning to fly to Paris several days before the wedding. The date was set for the second week in December, before any of their friends left for Christmas vacations.

The day before the surprise wedding, while Jazz was busy making sure that all was in order at Chez Alexandre, Gabe went for a drink at the Press Club to calm what he diagnosed as an unusually severe case of bridegroom's nerves. Either that or a very bad clam, he thought to himself, trapped in a toilet stall from which he'd already attempted to emerge twice, only to be forced to return in haste.

"I thought I saw Gabe at the bar," he heard a familiar voice say.

"I did too, Herb, but when I turned around, he'd gone," said another voice. Both of them were long-time photojournalist pals of his, but Gabe was in no condition to greet them. "Probably rushed home to Jazz. I know I would."

"You going to their Christmas party tomorrow, Herb?"

"Wouldn't miss it."

"I wouldn't either. Imagine Gabe and Jazz giving a Christmas party—that's a first for him. I'd never have believed it, not in a million years."

"Domestic bliss, Herb, old man."

"What the hell's happened to him anyway, Jim? In your professional opinion."

"Early burnout, very, very early burnout, I might add, or else it's the slavery of true love, take your choice. The end result's the same."

"Jim, I understand all about love, I've been in love myself, more often than not, but love doesn't mean that you lose your edge, lose the thing that makes you different from everyone else. Gabe had two Pulitzers, and now? It's been almost a year since I even stopped to admire somebody's great shot and noticed his photo credit on it."

"Yeah, when you remember the stuff he sent back, Cambodia in '75 and the boat people shots in '77—"

"The Patty Hearst scoop—"

"Hell, Herb, what about his coverage of the surrender to the Commies of Saigon in '75? The airlift of the last marines off the roof of the embassy?"

"How about the Black September massacre at the '72 Olympics—remember that, Jim? Gabe almost got himself killed there—"

"And those pictures from Biafra? They accounted for one of the Pulitzers, and Kent State the other."

"That's all history now, Herb. Ten will get you twenty that one day soon Gabe'll be covering some Baroness de Rothschild's fancy-dress ball. He's dug in here in Paris now, settled down with the girl of his dreams, and once that happens . . ."

"Well, what the hell, love can hit the best of them, or maybe it *is* burnout—Gabe's been around awhile—every one of us is going to have to quit sooner or later," Jim said.

"Not everybody quits. What about Capa? He landed on the beach in Normandy on D-Day, and he was still working when he stepped on that Thai mine, poor bastard."

"Capa was generations—eons—before Gabe," Jim said. "They don't make them like that anymore."

"Anyhow, there's no question that Gabe's left a body of work, you can't deny that . . ."

Herb's voice was abruptly cut off as the door opened and closed behind them. Envious cocksuckers, Gabe thought, envious, envious, *envious,* you couldn't even have a personal life without incurring their poisonous envy. All they were really saying was that they hoped he'd lost it, the sanctimonious bastards, the cocksucking, motherfucking pricks. They were hoping, not predicting or commenting, but *hoping* with all their envy-ridden hearts that there was one less photojournalist in the world who could show them up for the amateur snapshot album hacks they were, one less photojournalist who they knew would always be better than they were on the worst day he'd ever had.

As soon as he could, Gabe left the Press Club and walked blindly across Paris, not waiting for stoplights, plunging through traffic, paying no attention to the alarm of the automobile horns, not seeing the gray city that was decked out for Christmas, not noticing the rosy children or the lazy pigeons or the flocks of pretty girls, not buying flowers or stopping for coffee or lingering on a bridge, a man whose bridegroom's nerves had been forgotten in the awful birth of a far greater fear.

On the morning of her wedding day, Jazz woke up late. The night before, her father had insisted on taking them to dinner at Taillevent, so that instead of their usual quick brasserie dinner they had stayed up unusually late eating and drinking. Oh, but it had been so good, Jazz thought as she stretched and yawned, reluctant to get out of the warm bed, yet anxious for the jubilant day to begin.

Finally she put on a heavy robe, socks and slippers, for Paris was as cold as Finland in December, and twice as damp. She rushed to the kitchen to make herself a cup of tea. Gabe had forgotten to leave her croissants, she saw with a twinge of disappointment, but he'd been so absentminded yesterday evening that he was capable of forgetting to have any breakfast himself. Warmed by the tea, she brushed her teeth, washed her face and sat down at her small dressing table in the bedroom to inspect her face in the dim light of the thick gray haze that lay outside, hanging over the Seine. Propped up in front of her mirror was a blank envelope. Puzzled, Jazz opened it and two folded sheets of paper fell out, covered in Gabe's handwriting. There was no salutation on the first page, and no date.

*I've been up all night trying to wake
you up and talk but I can't. I've realized
that we can't get married.*

*I'm so much in love with you that I've
stopped doing good work. I've stopped
taking risks because I'm afraid that
something might happen to you. I've
avoided travel so we could stay here
together. I've looked for the easy
assignments instead of the tough ones. I
haven't done anything I'm proud of in the
last year. I've been incredibly happy every
minute since I met you.*

*I'm 31 and I'm a photojournalist.
That's all I can be and all I ever want to be.
If we get married I'll never be any good
again.*

*I'm getting out while I still know what
the fuck has happened. I'm getting out while
we're still happy. I'm getting out before I
start to blame you for something that's a
hundred percent my fault. You deserve
better than me.*

*If we got married you'd understand
what I'd done to myself. Because I love you
too much.*

                                        Gabe

Automatically, Jazz turned the sheets of paper
over to see if there was anything more on the back of
them. She peered inside the empty envelope and re-
read the letter. She got up and looked in the closet in
the hallway. Gabe's clothes were there, except for his
heavy coat, his sturdiest boots and a pair of corduroy
trousers. She looked in the dresser and found that his
warmest sweater was gone. She didn't bother to look
for his cameras. She wandered around the bedroom,
backtracking and stumbling as if the small room were
a forest and she were a lost child. Finally she got back
into the bed and pulled the quilt up over her face. Her
mind wasn't working. All she could think was that it

wasn't possible. It just was not possible. It could not be possible. He'd left her, left her on their wedding day, because he loved her too much. Did it make sense? Was there any twisted way in which it made sense? He was getting out while they were still happy. He'd been incredibly happy since he met her. Therefore he'd left her. He loved her so much that he had run away from her. Did that make sense?

I should cry, Jazz thought. People cry. Her eyes were dry, but she felt as if they were bleeding. Her heart was thumping with sickening heaviness and her hands and feet were freezing.

The doorbell rang and she was out of bed in a second, racing to answer it. Gabe hadn't left after all, she knew he couldn't, it wasn't possible, it never had been. She flung open the door. Mike Kilkullen stood there, his arms full of packages from Fauchon, blocks of foie gras for the wedding party.

"Daddy!" Jazz screamed. She pulled him inside, ran to the bedroom and came back with the letter, holding it out to him. "Read it!"

Quickly, Mike scanned the two pages. He pulled Jazz close and held her as tightly as he could as she began to shake as if she were coming apart. She was not weeping, but terrible noises came out of her throat, sounds of an inhuman keening, a lost howling. There would be plenty of time later, Mike thought, to tell her that Gabe had been right about one thing in his life. Jazz deserved better than him.

9

In the years to come, her departure from Paris never became any clearer to Jazz than a blur of dank, dark fog, in which the only reality was the figure of her father, to whom she clung, physically unable to let him out of her sight. She felt like a small, crushed animal who'd been run over and thrown to the side of the road to bleed to death all night long.

Mike Kilkullen threw a change of clothes and all the files from her darkroom into a bag, slung her camera bag over his shoulder, and watched over her all night in his hotel, until they took off for California the next day. Years later he told her that he had remembered to telephone Chez Alexandre that afternoon to tell the proprietor to carry on with the party and to explain that the hosts had unexpectedly left on assignment in the Middle East.

In the ever-shifting world of photojournalism, a world in which the divorce rate for photographers for the *National Geographic* had almost reached one hundred percent, if attention was paid when the couple formed by Jazz and Gabe never resurfaced in Paris, it didn't reach beyond a small circle of incurious men with no long-term memory, men who forgot their best friends and lovers with each new job, men to whom a lasting relationship was as unthinkable as having only one single photo assignment for the rest of their lives.

Jazz remained at the ranch for weeks. She rode every day, packing a lunch so that she didn't have to return before sunset. As she guided her horse through grassy pastures, moving among the large, calm herds of grazing cows and nursing calves, or picked her way along the edge of the harbor, looking for seashells, or cantered along the beach, the sun and the rain and the rising and falling of tides slowly began the process of mending that could not have taken place in any city on earth.

By the end of January she knew that she couldn't stay on at the ranch forever. She had taken from it what she needed, but now she had to continue her life, to begin to be independent for the first time. Nowhere on a working ranch was there a place for her to do anything useful, and it was important to her to get back to work. She wanted to earn money, something she had never done except when she was doing the portraits of children in Paris.

Jazz put together a book of her work, using the best work she could find from her first year at Graphics Central, and from all the Paris files, the best of the film she had shot when she was with Gabe and the finest of her portraits of children. She borrowed her father's car and went to consult the placement office at Graphics Central.

Cathy Prim, at the placement office, had been an acquaintance of Jazz's when she was at Graphics Central. "You're kidding, right?" Cathy asked her after she'd looked through the book.

"No? Why?"

"Look, Jazz, your work is astonishing, but this book is simply a mess. You've got the tabletop stuff you shot here, you've got photojournalism from hell and gone, incredible shots that should have been published but never were, and you've got *uncanny* children's protraits. What you don't have is one clearly defined area in which you can display exactly what kind of photographer you are. This is an age of specialization—all I deal in are entry-level jobs, and nobody's looking for an overqualified, Renaissance-girl assistant—the Pope in Africa, for heaven's sake!—who shoots everything in sight. This stuff, fabulous as it is, cancels itself out.''

"What do you think I should do, Cathy?"

"If you seriously want the kind of job I can steer you to, and I'm not sure you do, you've got to prune this book back to tabletop . . . that's where ninety percent of the work is, and even your first-year stuff was excellent. Too bad you quit school.''

"What about the portraits?"

"You'd have to have a rep, and anyway there's no real demand for children's portraits—their parents take them with cameras any idiot can use. Have you ever tried to get a rep to even look at your work? You could get old and gray while you waited, and then there's no guarantee that the rep would be effective.''

"Tabletop,'' Jazz said slowly. "Cathy, to be honest, I'm . . . I'm not wild about tabletop.''

"But you're great at it. What can I tell you? Unless you want to try to sign on at a photo agency and look for work in photojournalism. Now there's a field that's always wide open, and you're meant for it.''

"Photojournalism is absolutely out for me. *Over*. I included it only to show that I can shoot fast.''

"You're sure about that? It's a major waste of talent, Jazz.''

"Positive.''

"How did you get to all those places, anyway?'' Cathy asked curiously. "I've never seen anything like those shots in anybody's book before.''

"Dumb luck,'' Jazz said hastily. "Look, I'll take your advice about tabletop. Have you got any openings?''

"Only one single opening at the moment, and it

just came in. A food photographer needs a Girl Friday. I could fill it with twenty different candidates, except they're all Guy Fridays. It's a real break, Jazz. If I were you, I'd try to grab it while it's still available.''

''Does it involve doing dishes?''

''Could be. Also silver polishing, and probably sweeping up. When the word 'Friday' is in the job description, it means everything but life-threatening situations.''

''Does it involve cooking?'' Jazz asked cautiously. She could handle sweeping up.

''You're insane! All the cooking is done by the professional food stylists, who are home economists, gourmet chefs and highly trained in the art of food presentation. They won't let you *near* the food.''

''That's the good news. What's the salary?''

''The minimum. Girl Fridays always get the minimum.''

''Where do I go to apply?''

''Mel Botvinick's studio. He's on Olympic and La Brea.''

''What do you know about him, Cathy?''

''He's great. He graduated from here about nine years ago—one of our stars. Tops in the field. Two of his Girl Fridays have gone on to open their own studios.''

''Doing food?''

''What else? Food photography is serious big business. Listen, Jazz, don't futz around. It's a job, and you can't imagine the competition for any kind of job in photography. You can use my phone to call, and then I'll call them and put in a good word for you.''

''Cathy, you're an angel.''

''What I'd really like to know is how you got those incredible pictures from all over the world.''

''I happened to be in the neighborhood.''

As Jazz walked through Mel Botvinick's studio to the studio manager's office where she was going to be interviewed, she had the impression of a tranquil convent combined with a laboratory in which competent, silent people were engrossed in contemplative creation of some mystery known only to themselves. It was a large, high-ceilinged, windowless space lit mainly by a few strong worklights over a big wooden table where three women were seated on kitchen stools, intent on some detailed work she couldn't observe. There was no smell of cooking, she couldn't spot the large, elaborate kitchen she had expected, nor could she see any photographic equipment except one huge camera mounted on a tripod. The atmosphere of the studio gave Jazz an instant sense of security and serenity. In the middle of busy Los Angeles, it seemed an island of peace and calm. Suddenly, getting this improbable job became very important to her.

Jilly Hexter, the young studio manager, had an office in a loft above the studio proper. She leafed slowly through Jazz's hastily reassembled book of her first year's lighting assignments, which, to Jazz's critical eye, looked boringly technical.

"What have you been doing since you left Graphics Central?" Jilly asked, closing the book with an approving nod.

"I had a chance to go to Europe for a few years."

"Lucky you. What were you doing there?"

"It's a little embarrassing to admit, but I ate my way from one city to another, from one country to another. Once I started, I couldn't stop. It seemed more important than anything else. I'm passionate about food."

"We all are here. Mel says that food photography is as much a calling as an art."

"I agree entirely," Jazz said fervently.

"Do you cook?"

"I can open cans, including sardines, I can make myself a sandwich if I'm starving, but I feel that serious cooking is too important for amateurs to meddle in. What I really love to do, when I get a chance, is clean up a kitchen."

"Isn't it *satisfying* when it's all sparkling again?" Jilly said devoutly.

"It answers a deep need for me," Jazz answered. "And the best part is that you know that it won't stay that way long."

"When can you start?" Jilly asked.

"Right now."

"Good. Come on downstairs and I'll introduce you."

Jazz followed Jilly and met the head food stylist, Sharon, and her two assistants, Molly and Barbara, the women who were working at the wooden table. Each of them had a pile of mint leaves in front of them, which they were examining for the most microscopic of flaws, discarding hundreds of leaves before they found one that was absolutely perfect in shape, size, texture and color. At their feet were piled dozens of cases of various fruits which were to undergo the same selection process.

"We're doing a fruit bowl for a cover shot," Sharon told Jazz. "I need stand-in leaves for Mel to use while he composes the picture, and hero leaves for the actual photograph." She looked at the three piles. "I think that's enough, gals. Let's put them in the fridge and get started on the strawberries." There was a muted whisper of a sigh from her assistants, a noise somewhere between pleasure and pain.

"Strawberries are utter hell," Sharon informed Jazz, with a calmly proud smile, like someone showing off a splendid baby and complaining that it has learned to walk sooner than its peers. "It's almost impossible to find a perfect strawberry, and when you do, the little ruff of leaves at the top is never just right, or else the stem is damaged in some way. If we were doing just one small fruit cup, I'd have to buy a case of each kind of fruit, so that I'd be sure to get one good stand-in cup, one hero cup and three backup heros. With a bowl, it's ten times as much work. But at least we're not doing raw mushrooms. There is *no* such thing as the perfect mushroom. Of course, the worst of all is a decent slice of packaged bread. Once I had to go through five hundred loaves to find a good-looking one."

"Holy moley," Jazz murmured. "And then you have to do all that cooking too."

"Cooking? Nothing to it. It's the way the stuff *looks* that drives you mad." Sharon smiled beatifically.

"Shall I get rid of all this mint you've discarded?" Jazz waved at the heaps of green that lay on the studio floor among the fruit baskets.

"Good idea. But first pass up the strawberries, will you?"

As Jazz carefully placed dozens of baskets of strawberries in front of the three food stylists, she asked, "Where's Mr. Botvinick?"

"Over there." Sharon pointed to an almost invisible figure in gray who had been sitting in front of the tripod, motionless on the floor in a yoga position. Jazz realized that she had seen him there out of the corner of her eye when she first entered the studio almost an hour earlier.

"What's he doing?" Jazz whispered.

"He's conceiving."

"In the dark like that?"

"He has to figure out a way to shoot a fruit bowl in a way that's never been done before."

"Never ever?"

"Exactly. As if it were the first fruit bowl in creation. He may be there all day."

"The poor man," Jazz said sympathetically.

"That's why he's a genius," Sharon explained reverently, as a red hailstorm of defective strawberries rolled from her adept fingers onto the floor. "The rest is purely technical, and ninety-five percent of it is lighting. You need one kind of light for mint, another for strawberries, another for grapes, another for kiwi, another for the bowl they're in, another for the tabletop, another for the accessories, and so on. But it's the conception that makes it or breaks it."

"A fruit bowl from hell," Jazz said, almost to herself.

"We did that one last year," Sharon said kindly. "For Halloween."

Within a few months, Jazz had made herself indispensable at Mel Botvinick's. During the first weeks, no one let her do anything but pick things up and put them down, but when they were sure she wasn't clumsy or reckless, they gradually gave her more and more to do.

She was allowed to unroll the bolts of fabric that were thrown over the tabletop to simulate different tablecloths—although the fiercely elegant prop stylist, Tinka, a beautiful Japanese woman, actually arranged the folds of the material. Jazz was permitted to take Sharon's heavy metal work kit from her hand when she arrived at the studio, to unlock the various hinged drawers so that the complicated battery of dozens of knives and scissors, pipettes, atomizers, bamboo shoots and tacky wax were revealed. Eventually, as Sharon came to trust her, Jazz might be instructed to hand over one or another piece of equipment, like a surgical nurse in an operating room.

After Jazz had demonstrated her ability to clean the eight-burner Wolf range, the microwave and the double sink to Sharon's satisfaction, these jobs became her undisputed province. She was sent almost daily to the supermarket to buy the paper towels, sponges, Windex and plastic bags that the studio consumed in huge quantities; she was given the opportunity to put ice cubes into Baggies that were destined to be hidden under salads to keep them looking fresh under the lights. When Tinka arrived with her arms filled with twenty different bunches of fresh flowers, in case one or two were needed in a shot, Jazz's job was to put them into deep containers of water. Sometimes Tinka let Jazz carry back the packages from the trade shows, retail stores or antique shops where she bought or borrowed the plates, silver and serving pieces that were used to create the mood of the picture. Soon Tinka added Jazz to her two free-lance assistants, who built the sets which were sometimes needed in the background of a shot; everything from a tropical beach to a Tuscan farmhouse kitchen.

Jazz became the unquestioned source of the vital Q-tips that Sharon dipped into a mix of chemicals and concealed in the food so that they simulated rising steam; she learned how to crouch under the table and pop up between shots to pump up the foam in glasses of beer with a turkey baster; she was entrusted with the secret of the mixture of Angostura Bitters, Kitchen Bouquet and detergent with which all roasted fowl were painted and then browned with a little torch to make them look cooked.

"If I really roasted them for more than a half hour," Sharon explained, "they'd shrink and look dried out."

"But what about the women who wonder why their chickens don't look like yours?" Jazz asked.

"Food pictures are fantasies, like the photographs in fashion magazines, or rooms in interior design magazines. Nobody looks like that, do they? Nobody really lives like that, do they? But they do give you an idea of the potential, of the way to go."

"I guess," Jazz said, realizing that food pictures had the same relationship to reality that a publicity photo has to a movie star's face when she wakes up in the morning. At least it wasn't photojournalism.

As Jazz slowly came to know round, Buddha-like Mel Botvinick, she discovered him to be a gentle, shy, lovable man with a never-satisfied passion for his work. He allowed nobody to approach the tabletop on which he composed and lit each food photograph, working with the stand-in food until he had taken enough eight-by-ten Polaroids with the big Toyo on the tripod to be satisfied with his conception and start to shoot color film.

Soon, Mel let her take the Polaroids, and when she proved equal to that task, he reluctantly entrusted her with a Hasselblad and permitted her to take small detail shots of a single egg yolk in a cup, of a whisk, of a sack of rice, of a slice of cut onion.

"Mel, why won't you let me light these detail shots?" Jazz asked.

"I'm sure you know how, but I can't."

"Mel, they're going to be less than half an inch square on the page," Jazz objected.

"The client is paying for my lighting," Mel said, in a kindly but uncompromising voice.

When he was working on lighting, Mel was as set apart as he was when he was conceiving and composing the shot. Jazz studied his techniques as intently as possible. She realized that what she was learning from him more than made up for the second year of tabletop lighting she had missed when she dropped out of Graphics Central.

She hovered, unseen, as she watched him bring to life the sparkle of the crystal of a wine goblet, the patina of the skin of a purple grape, the heavy brilliance of a well-polished silver fork, the contrast between the surfaces of a boiled shrimp and the mayonnaise in which it was dipped, not in a series of shots but in one single shot which contained a dozen other elements as well.

Often, when Jazz was left to close the studio at the end of a long day, she'd relight the detail shots she'd taken during the day, experimenting with ways to do it better than Mel, but she never found a method that made a slice of onion more vividly onion-esque than he had. He had a magic she didn't yet understand that made food more real than it looked to the naked eye. Every bit of food jumped out of his pictures, as if it were alive and would eat you if you didn't eat it first. She could light small food shots almost—but not *absolutely*—as well as Mel Botvinick, but she couldn't improve on him, Jazz admitted to herself.

Dissatisfied, she started practicing on the various tabletops laden with stand-in food that remained in place overnight, gathering dust, until the hero food was ready to be photographed. Endlessly she rearranged platters, plates, table decorations and flowers, struggling to find greater excitement and harmony and graphic power than Mel had. Sometimes, looking at her efforts upside down in the Toyo, she decided that she had managed to achieve a more interesting composition than Mel's. When this happened she quickly shot the picture with her own color film and labored for hours to restore the setup to exactly the way it had been when she started.

Later, when she compared her shots with Mel's, Jazz was forced to admit that hers were almost as good—but never *absolutely* as good—as his. In spite of the sober deliberation with which Mel plotted each photograph, he made a clear leap into new, uncharted territory each time he finally shot the picture. His mind worked with dazzling innovation within the possibilities of food photography, in a way hers did not and never would. All she could do was learn from him.

She had rented a one-room furnished apartment near the unfashionably located studio. When Jazz got home at eight or nine at night, weary and footsore from the miles she walked every day, both inside the studio and running errands, she was content to make herself a light meal, take a hot bath and go to bed. Everyone at the studio ate a huge lunch and a high tea, ordered in from a variety of places. None of them would dream of tasting the food they were working with, since they knew too well what had been done to beautify it. It would have been, Jazz thought, like a plastic surgeon wanting to make love to a woman whose breasts he had enlarged, whose saddlebags he had diminished, whose kneecaps he had lifted.

She felt tranquilized by the work she had been doing for the first six months of 1982. No matter how good a food photographer and everyone who worked with him were, they all had to have enormous reserves of patience. Two long days, often three, of painstaking, detailed preparation were normal before a single major photograph could be taken.

Yet the relaxed, humorous patience that permeated the studio was the reverse of laziness. There was absolutely no slackness; the studio hummed with an undercurrent of disciplined determination to finish each tiny job at hand and get on to the next tiny job. At all times they worked under deadlines fixed by the advertisers or magazine art directors who counted on getting the finished pictures on a certain date.

This was the first time that Jazz had ever worked with a team, a dedicated, cohesive team, in which ego could play no part. Mel Botvinick, shy and modest as he was, was a leader who knew how to inspire total loyalty in his troops.

When an important detail proved faulty and had to be done over, as was bound to happen in each and every separate food shot, Mel stayed so calm that he never allowed an atmosphere of crisis to develop. There was no blaming of individuals when things went wrong, no competition for getting things right; nothing short of an invasion of roaches would have provoked anger. Botvinick's studio was a supremely *safe* place to be, a cosmos into which no discussion of the riots and terrors of the outside world ever made their way. When Sharon announced that she had decided never to eat anything that had eyelashes, this was as close to a political statement as anything Jazz had heard since she started as a Girl Friday.

Jazz wasn't sure if this was the atmosphere in which she always wanted to work, but she knew that there was a quality about it that was supremely right for her now. It made her flourish, it helped her grow the skin of a fresh experience over the tumult of the past two years. In shopping for unusual bread baskets with Tinka, in learning how Mel would go about lighting a dish of bouillabaisse or how Sharon would use her skills to beautify an artichoke, Jazz could, for minutes at a time, forget her horribly wounded heart.

"I can't find Mel's birthday card," Jilly said to Jazz, looking unusually distracted, as she rummaged in bulging file cabinets, on a day in June of 1982.

"How can you find a card in there? Those are the negatives of stuff he took last year. Do you want me to go to a card shop for you?"

"No, that's not it, Jazz. Every year on his birthday, Mel sends a food shot to all his clients and all the art directors who might become clients, and all the photo buyers for magazines—to everybody in the magazine and advertising businesses. They don't even know it's his birthday. You know how shy he is, but he likes to do it. And Phoebe says it's great for getting new business.''

"Just one shot?"

"Yes. He has it enlarged and printed on the world's most expensive, heavy, glossy paper and signs it on the bottom. A lot of people frame them. It's become a tradition.''

"Shall I help you look?"

"Thanks, but it won't help. I've shown him fifty great shots and he's turned them all down. He says they don't say anything new. Now I'm starting on last year's work. He's been doing this birthday-card thing since he opened the studio.''

"With due respect, Jilly, why don't you try something different?''

"Jazz!"

"Think about it. Something that could personalize even a . . . a bowl of Jell-O?"

"Jell-O! Mel *hates* Jell-O. How many new ways do you think he's had to find to shoot Jell-O?''

"O.K., not Jell-O. What I mean is, what about doing pictures of all the people who work here, showing how each one contributes to a single food shot, with a line saying that this is the team that works for Mel Botvinick? It could be laid out as a sort of . . . booklet . . . right, a booklet with the food shot itself on the last page. Nobody really appreciates the effort that goes into food photography.''

"Wouldn't it cost a fortune to do?" Jilly objected.

"Not if you got the pictures for nothing and didn't print it on such expensive paper.''

"Who's going to shoot the pictures for nothing?"

"Me."

"You?"

"Sure. I've had experience in doing photo stories. It's fun for me, and you can buy the film.''

"Gee, I don't know . . ."

"You, for instance, Jilly, I'd shoot you talking on the phone to Phoebe or running up and down the stairs, or conferring with Sharon on the next job, or explaining to Tinka what Mel's conception is, or organizing the lunch orders, or handling the billing, or chatting up one of the clients, or digging up negatives like today, or any one of the hundreds of things you do every day, managing the studio."

"Hundreds?"

"You're like a perpetual-motion machine. This place would stop functioning if you took a day off."

"I never thought about it that way," Jilly said, entranced by Jazz's vision of her, the kind of vision based on truth that a photojournalist conjures up to convince an unwilling subject to allow a photograph to be taken.

"That's because you take it for granted. I'm a fresh eye. For example, in this light, I can really see the fine bones in your face and the fascinating set of your ears—you have perfect ears, did you know that?"

"Well . . . I have been told that they're pretty . . ." Jilly blushed with pleasure.

"Not pretty. Perfect. Almost no one in the world has perfect ears. I'd never shoot you on the phone unless you held it in the off-camera hand."

"Wouldn't all this mean a lot of posing, Jazz? I feel self-conscious already."

"Jilly, I promise you won't even know I'm working. I'll only take informal, working shots. When do you have to mail out the birthday card?"

"In a month."

"No problem. Let me see that ear again, Jilly. *Oh yes!* An ear for the ages. If you say to go ahead, you'll have contacts in ten days and then you can decide if it's a good idea. If they don't look good, you can always go back to your usual approach."

"Let me ask Mel. It all depends on what he decides."

"Tell him it says something interesting about the power of people working together."

During the next week, when Jazz found herself with a rare second to think, she would wonder why she had deprived herself of using a camera of her own for so long. As she took her first tentative shots of Sharon icing a cake, she felt as if a part of her body that had been numb had started to function again, more alive than ever. The thrill of capturing a human image, that thrill she had first known when she was eight, was not only undiminished by the passage of time, it was enhanced by all the other work she had done in the last few years.

Jazz hadn't realized how much she had learned until the week she shot Botvinick's birthday card. The personal invisibility, the speed, the accuracy, so perfected that they had become second nature, and the ability to see and seize the perfect moment, all of which were essential to a photojournalist, belonged to her.

The awareness of the importance of motion, the meaning of facial expressions, the understanding of the playfulness of activity, the sensitivity to mood and fleeting thoughts, all of which were essential to a photographer of children, belonged to her.

The vision of the most eye-catching and original graphic composition of a variety of elements, which was essential to a food photographer, belonged to her.

Her understanding of lighting had grown a thousandfold, so that Jazz was able to use whatever light was available without resorting to flash, which would have been a disruption of the mood of the studio, where everyone was deep in preparation for a double spread of a post-football-game buffet supper.

She did her own work in effortless triple time, her loaded Nikon F-2 around her neck, and shot whenever she could steal a moment, flitting back and forth, here and there, an inquisitive winged creature, wearing her uniform of jeans and work shirt, tireless, exhilarated, finding angles she hadn't known existed, seeing her co-workers in ways she'd never seen them before, and always, during that week, aware of the love she had for all of them, a love that had been growing during the six months she had worked in the nurturing, beneficent atmosphere of the studio.

Each one of the three food stylists was beautiful in her own special and different way, Jazz realized as she looked into the viewfinder. Tinka, the prop stylist, and her two equally elegant assistants were whirling, high-stepping creatures who seemed to have danced in from the pages of fashion magazines; Jilly was everything Jazz had told her she was, and more, for she was the energetic element of the real world of business in the quiet creative buzz of the studio.

Although Mel Botvinick had agreed to Jazz's idea for his birthday card on the stipulation that she not do a portrait of him, he hadn't specifically excluded his hands, Jazz thought, as she shot away, nor had he mentioned his unmistakable shadow, that of the only man in this world of women.

By the end of the week she had a great bagful of rolls of black-and-white film, for it had been agreed that the only color picture in the birthday booklet would be the food shot. Jazz drove home to the ranch, as she had been doing every weekend since she moved to Los Angeles, and stayed there developing film in her darkroom night and day, from Friday night, when she arrived, until early Monday morning, so excited that she felt no need for sleep. Susie brought her trays of food, and Mike Kilkullen looked in on her from time to time to make sure she was all right, but Jazz just waved them away, the expression on her face reassuring them more than any words.

She left the ranch before dawn on Monday morning and drove straight to the studio. Mel and Jilly were discussing a billing problem in the loft office when she climbed the stairs and put the sheaf of contacts down on the desk.

"Done," Jazz said, as calmly as she could.

"Well, I suppose we'd better take a look," Mel Botvinick said heavily and reluctantly, putting out his hand for his magnifying glass. Jilly hesitated, looked nervously around the room, but found no way out, and slowly forced herself to pick up another magnifying glass. As the two of them began to inspect the contact sheets, they maintained a guardedly noncommittal silence, for the two of them had agreed that if the pictures weren't acceptable, they couldn't use them, no matter how much it was certain to upset Jazz. They both regretted the sudden impulse that had made Mel first agree to Jazz's proposal. When their first enthusiasm wore off, they realized that being a splendidly willing Girl Friday did not make a photographer.

Jilly and Mel peered long and closely at each small contact, cagey and vigilant, determined not to express any premature judgment, tensely mindful not to relax their circumspect attitudes. They exchanged no words or glances, they never looked up at Jazz with an approving smile, but the gathering speed with which they began to slide their magnifying glasses from one image to another, the growing swiftness of the rhythm with which they passed the contact sheets back and forth to each other, gave away their rising excitement.

Jazz watched their hands, not their faces, and started to breathe again. She leaned back against one of the walls of the office, her arms folded, her feet crossed at the ankles, an expression as calculatingly blank as theirs on her face, so that when they finally both looked up at her in wonder, they didn't see the great wave of triumph that was holding her up.

"You . . . you . . ." Mel Botvinick breathed, and then stopped, shaking his head in a mixture of awe and utter astonishment.

"*You never said.*" Jilly's words tumbled out of her mouth, accusingly.

"*Where* did you come from?" Botvinick demanded, as if he'd never seen her before.

"You never—I didn't know—why didn't you *tell* me?" Jilly asked, as wonderingly as if Jazz had lifted her up, twirled her overhead and revealed that she was Misha Baryshnikov in drag.

"I did, I told you I'd had experience with photo stories." Jazz tried to maintain her cool, but she couldn't prevent a tear from rolling down each of her cheeks as she looked at the absolute delight on their faces.

"Experience!" Botvinick exploded. "If I hadn't seen you with my very own eyes, shooting these all by yourself, I'd swear that they were taken by one of the best photographers in the world."

"Why, thank you, Mel. That *was* a compliment, wasn't it?" Jazz grinned, wiping away her tears.

"Huh? Oh. You know what I mean." Mel Botvinick's round face turned bright red as he heard his own words.

"Jazz, there aren't any pictures of you here," Jilly realized.

"I'll do a shot of Jazz," Botvinick announced. "I've been dying to try to light her hair for months now. It looks like French toast, a little burned around the edges, with melted butter streaking over it. And her eyes . . . they'll be tricky. Christmas-tree ornaments? Yellow diamonds under water? Pieces of eight? Leave that to me. In color, of course. No other way to do her."

"Mel, how are we going to pick the best picture of each person?" Jilly asked. "There are just so many I wouldn't know where to start."

"Process of elimination," Botvinick said briskly. "Let's say each page is ten by twelve; let's say we can get nine clearly visible pictures on a page and still leave room for the person's name and what she does at the bottom; let's say three pages for the food stylists, three pages for Tinka and her assistants, one page for you, Jilly, and the last page for the food shot, with Jazz's picture on the back and her photo credit for the booklet and mine for the food shot, that's eight pages in all, plus a cover shot of . . . well, maybe . . . sort of a tease, nobody'd have to know what it was, of course . . ." His voice trailed off. "Sort of an inside joke," he said at last.

"This one?" Jazz asked, pointing to her favorite picture of the tabletop where the hero food for the football game feast was laid out. Mel's hands were making a final adjustment in the placement of a fork, and his shadow loomed over the entire scene.

"As a matter of fact . . . yes. I mean, it is my birthday, so why not go for it?"

"Are you sure you wouldn't rather use this one?" Jazz pointed to another picture of Mel, seen from the back, sitting on the floor in the process of conception.

"Oh no," he said hastily. "Somebody might recognize me."

"Mel," Jilly protested in her office manager's voice. "That makes a nine-page booklet. Even with the least expensive paper we can decently get away with, it's going to cost a bundle to do this."

"What are you talking about? We'll use the paper we always use, of course. It would be criminal not to. Criminal! With these pictures! And it's a legitimate business expense."

Jilly made a muffled noise of agreement. She was taking another look at the shots of her making phone calls. Jazz had been perfectly right. Her ears were perfect.

Three weeks later, hundreds of art directors and photo buyers all over the United States and Europe were looking with stunned fascination at the phenomenon of Mel Botvinick's birthday booklet. Each and every one of them knew immediately that it was destined to become a collector's item. Only every two or three years did their jaded eyes see the work of a photographer with a fully formed style that was entirely original, a style that owed nothing to any other photographer, a photographer capable of work that had never been done before. Jazz's work, as new and fresh as the day after tomorrow, revealed a strong personal point of view that turned a static portrait shot of someone into a virtual conversation. This unknown photographer, with her total mastery of technique, a photographer who had jumped into center stage as a fully formed star, was as young as she was beautiful, to judge by the small, exquisite color portrait of her that Mel Botvinick had taken. They called every photo rep they dealt with and asked only one question.

"Who the hell is Jazz Kilkullen?"

Only one rep, Phoebe Milbank, knew the answer to that question, and she had signed Jazz to a contract before the booklets were mailed.

Phoebe Milbank represented only Mel Botvinick and the car photographer Pete di Constanza. After signing Mel and Pete, Phoebe had deliberately refused all other clients, although dozens of hopefuls came knocking at her door every month, carrying portfolios of their best work.

It was infinitely more important, Phoebe decided firmly, to spend every available second of her time doing an outstanding job with her two major photographers, who together billed over a million dollars a year. Phoebe didn't believe in the quick buck, although she worshiped the steady one. There was plenty of time to choose, with close evaluation and hardheaded conviction, a third and probably final client after she had steadily boosted Mel and Pete's prices and multiplied the number of people vying for their work.

Jilly phoned Phoebe to update the final list of people who would receive the birthday booklet. Crafty and ever on the alert when her clients were concerned, Phoebe had heard a note in Jilly's voice that made her curious enough to drop by Botvinick's studio to take a look at the booklet before it was mailed. Electrified by what she saw, not taking the time to ask a single question about Jazz, the skinny blond whirlwind had pounced, for she knew that as soon as the booklet was in circulation Jazz would be the target of every rep in the business. By the end of the day, with the help of Mel's unqualified blessing and his strong recommendation of Phoebe, Jazz had agreed to sign with her.

Phoebe, giddily astonished at her own uncharacteristic impulsiveness, talked her new client into going out to lunch with her the next day to celebrate. Jazz was still working as a Girl Friday until Jilly could replace her, and she insisted that they eat at the little Chinese joint around the corner from the studio, so that she could get back to work quickly.

"You're pretty cool for a girl who's going to be awfully rich and famous," Phoebe probed, looking Jazz over with the avid curiosity of a mail-order bride who has just married a perfect stranger.

"Phoebe, we're going to work together very closely," Jazz said tightly. "It's important that you understand some things about me that aren't general knowledge. Fame will never be my motivation. My mother was Sylvie Norberg."

"Oh my God, Jazz, I'm sorry!"

"Thank you, Phoebe."

"But no one at the studio said . . ."

"I never told them. It's an old story and a sad one. There was no need to talk about it."

"I should have guessed. You have her eyes, her look . . . you're so much like . . ."

"I know." Jazz closed Phoebe's rising excitement down by her tone. "I'm very close to my father," Jazz went on quickly. "I spend most weekends down at our ranch near San Juan Capistrano—the land is important to me, more important than you can realize. I don't want to lead a life in which I find I don't have time for my father or the ranch. So if there's a job that pays a ton of money but takes me away from California for a very long time, turn it down."

"Just like that?"

"*Faster* than that, Phoebe."

"What about my possible buyer's remorse here? My new client doesn't want to be rich or famous! This could cut into my piece of your action."

"Change your mind, I'll understand. And nothing's been signed yet."

"No way. I said 'could,' not 'would.' We'll work around it. Leave that to me. Is there anything else I should know?"

"Now that you know that being rich and famous aren't my priorities, what else is there?"

"Men?"

"Nothing important. I'm married to my work."

"Of course." Phoebe tossed her banana-yellow

hair and every one of her pointy bones expressed disbelief.

"You'll see." Jazz laughed at this improbable creature who had swept in, scooped her up and declared that she could orchestrate a great career for someone about whom she knew nothing. If Phoebe hadn't been Botvinick's rep for two years, Jazz would never have agreed to get involved with a rep who was so grandiose in her thinking.

"Listen, Jazz, when will Jilly get a replacement for you?"

"She's interviewing this afternoon. No reason she shouldn't find someone right away. It's a marvelous job."

"Good, because I have your first assignment."

"What?"

"Last night I had dinner with a photo editor from *Esquire*. I showed him the booklet—you have a way of digging out and illuminating a woman's inner sensuality, even if she isn't a recognized sexpot. Most women can't tell when or how another woman is sexy —it's a gift. I'd never noticed how deeply sensual Sharon and Jilly are—Sharon icing a cake was positively *carnal,* and Jilly on the phone—she gets an X-rated expression on her face. So you're set to photograph two, let's call them . . . middle-aged . . . women for a cover story for *Esquire*—going right straight for their hidden sensuality, the guarded, deep, but *intensely* private and *privately* intense sensuality that people miss in them, but that is brought out by their work. That's the only angle *Esquire* wants. Sexy middle-aged broads."

"Who might they be?" Jazz asked. She knew that Phoebe, for all her elaborate stage directions, had to mean Linda Evans and Joan Collins. So this was what a rep did.

"Margaret Thatcher and Nancy Reagan." Phoebe watched Jazz out of the corner of her eye to catch any surprise.

"Why'd they leave out Mother Teresa?" Jazz asked with unblinking curiosity.

Phoebe gave her an appreciative, tinkling giggle, a mixture of fluff and flint. Jazz was a quick learner. "You'll do Mother Teresa for the Christmas cover of *Vogue.* She represents the spirit of this year's ultimate chic, or so they told me over the phone this morning. And since your fashion stuff with Tinka was as sensational as your portraits, they want you for fashion as much as for celebrity portraits."

"How could they have possibly seen the booklet yet?"

"Condé Nast has an L.A. office." Phoebe crunched an egg roll with self-satisfaction.

"What else did you do this morning?"

"All in good time," Phoebe answered. The sixteen-page portfolio for *GQ,* showing twenty-five years of Warren Beatty's women, hadn't firmed up yet. She never told a client about a job that wasn't a sure thing, because they'd blame her if it fell through.

Phoebe had been up all night, feverishly plotting the moves for Jazz's immediate future. She intended to have Jazz concentrate exclusively on editorial work for the next year. That was the way to make her famous fast. Lucrative advertising contracts would follow the editorial work, but they could wait until next year, when Jazz would be firmly established as the most interesting new celebrity photographer in the business. Tonight, when Phoebe saw Jann Wenner for drinks, she'd clinch the *Rolling Stone* cover shot.

"I suppose you're a Republican?" she asked Jazz. "Being from Orange County."

"Why do you ask?" Jazz quirked an eyebrow at Phoebe. What did her politics have to do with anything?

"It's something you could knock off on a weekend without missing your visit with your father."

"How so?"

"San Juan Capistrano is just a short drive from San Clemente, isn't it? *Rolling Stone* wants a portrait of Nixon for the tenth anniversary of Watergate."

10

After the Fiesta of September 1990, Jazz's life at Dazzle grew busier than ever. For a month she was booked so steadily, with each shoot starting so early and lasting so late, that she had been able to go down to the ranch only twice: unsatisfactorily short visits that lasted from Saturday lunch to late afternoon on Sunday, when she had to start back to L.A.

Casey Nelson hadn't been visible on either of the two Saturday nights. Mike Kilkullen reported that he got up long before sunrise to conduct his business affairs, using the fax machine he'd installed in his room. The two men had been having dinner together at the hacienda almost every weekday night, but when Casey knew that Jazz was expected, he tactfully took himself off so that father and daughter could spend what little time they had without the constant presence of a stranger.

Jazz was feeling city-bound, pushed to the limit and ragged around the edges. The time she usually reserved to spend at the ranch, riding and walking and sailing, renewing her contact with the land, was essential to balance the taut, breathtaking pace of her work, the pitiless pressure of the clock, the need to stretch and stretch again for each new assignment so that her work never became repetitive or predictable.

Jazz complained to Sis Levy about her workload, but her studio manager answered that the fault lay with Phoebe. The next time Jazz found that she had a minute to spare, toward twilight on a Thursday in late October, she confronted her rep with the overscheduling.

"Land sakes, Miss Jazz, you're a caution," Phoebe replied, blinking in amazement. "Here I work my dialing finger to the bone to make sure that you get your choice of all the prize jobs, and what's my reward? Of course you're busy. If you weren't, I wouldn't be doing the job you pay me for. Mel and Pete are perfectly happy, and they work as hard as you do. Incidentally, do you know how many years you've been going home to Daddy on the weekends?"

"I haven't counted," Jazz flared.

"Well, I have. It's been eight years. Some people might . . . just might . . . say it was—oh—a bit unusual. You're a big girl now, Jazz."

"What are you trying to say, Phoebe?"

"Frankly, Jazz, I've been concerned about you for some time now. I understood perfectly when we met, but you're twenty-nine, and you've never been seriously involved with a man. Could it be because of your tie to . . . the ranch?"

"I don't believe this," Jazz said incredulously. "You're trying to meddle in my private life—you?"

"Why not me, Jazz? I know you as well as any woman does, maybe better. We've been working together for a long time, and I have your best interests at heart."

"Why do I suddenly not believe that?"

"Maybe you don't want to hear what I said."

"Phoebe, stay the fuck out of my head," Jazz said in a deadly voice, "and clear every single booking with me before you accept it. That's an order, not a request."

As she slammed out of the office Jazz missed seeing the tiny, vindictive twitch of Phoebe's lips.

My, my, Phoebe thought, oh my. Ever since Jazz threatened to leave if she repped Gabe, that girl had been getting more and more independent. But someday, someday for sure, that girl would want something badly, and then, if her rep didn't get it for her, she'd realize where the real power lay.

Things like that had a way of happening, Phoebe decided, in high spirits. They always did when she started to concentrate on them.

Jazz ran up to her studio in a cold fury, sent Sis, Melissa and Toby Roe home early, locked up the studio herself and found herself in her car driving north toward Trancas, way beyond Malibu, before she collected herself enough to decide to go home.

Suddenly she felt that she needed something like a nice cup of tea, or at least something that would produce the vaunted effect of a nice cup of tea. A martini, if she only knew how to make one. She hoped that she had teabags in the kitchen, for usually she ate breakfast at the studio. Maybe she would get into that old quilted bathrobe she'd been trying to throw out for five years and make a few friendly phone calls. She was too angry at Phoebe to drive around aimlessly. She shouldn't be behind a wheel when all she could think of was taking that skinny wretch by her skinny tentacle of a neck and doing something unspeakable and final to her.

She turned the Thunderbird and headed back to her apartment in Santa Monica. There was little traffic as she left the 405. Anxious to find herself in familiar surroundings, she shifted into third. Her car responded instantly. Nothing wrong with this old beauty, Jazz reflected, no Anniversary Countach for her. What was the point of a car that could do 186 miles per hour when the speed limit was 55? If she asked Pete a question like that, he'd just look at her pityingly. Obviously, if you had to ask, you didn't need to know. Weren't worthy of knowing.

The sound of a siren and the sight of a flashing light in her rearview mirror brought her hastily back to the present. She braked the instant she heard the siren, but a glance at the speedometer told her that all was lost. She was only down to forty, and seconds had passed. She pulled over to the curb, rolled down the window and prayed. "Hey, *great* car!" the policeman said with enthusiasm.

"Thank you, Officer," Jazz replied, with a stirring of hope.

"See your license, please?" he asked in a friendly way.

Jazz handed it over obediently, hope killed. Friendly or not, there was absolutely no point in sweet-talking or trying to vamp him. She knew. Oh, how well she knew. He disappeared, went back to his car and radioed in her number to the computer at headquarters. He returned, busy writing out a ticket.

"How fast was I going, Officer?" Jazz asked politely, out of resigned curiosity rather than any hope of redemption.

"Fifty."

"But that's five miles *under* the limit," she objected, as boldly as she dared. "Under, Officer, not over."

"You're in a residential zone, lady. All residential zones are posted at twenty-five miles an hour. You were twenty-five miles an hour over the limit."

"Twenty-five miles an hour?" She was incredulous. "Nobody goes twenty-five miles an hour! If they did, you'd pull them in for obstructing traffic!"

"They're all just as guilty as you are."

"Oh God. Why are you so mean?" It was a whimper, not a question.

"You've had two moving violations in the last year. If you go to Traffic School, you can get this ticket off your record. Otherwise your insurance rates go up. One more and we take away your license."

"Traffic School. Please, no, *not Traffic School,* anything but that."

"Your choice. Say, you wouldn't want to sell that T-Bird, would you? No? Didn't think so. Well, have a nice night." He handed her the ticket, returned to his car and, Jazz thought, undoubtedly vanished into the hiding place where he must wait like a bloodthirsty leech for just such another innocent one as she, so that he could fill his quota of tickets before he went home for the day.

Jazz's small apartment was in a large, luxurious, expensive old apartment building, The Penthouse, in Santa Monica. She had picked it for several reasons. It wasn't a real home, and unlike a home, she could leave the apartment without worrying about anything happening to it while she was away. Someone else worried about the roof and the landscaping and the pipes. Jazz could stay away for a weekend or two weeks and it would always be there. The building had optional maid service, valet parking, and high security —a reception desk for all visitors, an elevator man in each elevator twenty-four hours a day—and a view of the ocean.

Except for the view of the ocean, the apartment meant little to her. It was like a particularly comfortable hotel suite. Jazz's real home was the ranch, and when she couldn't be at the ranch, her home was her studio. Most of her evenings were taken up with dates and parties and restaurants, when she wasn't too tired to go out. Basically, her apartment served as a bedroom and dressing room into which she dashed to change for the evening, then dashed out again and returned only to sleep.

Tonight, however, Jazz found herself wondering if she should spend some time redecorating the place, warm it up a little. It would repay a little loving kindness, she thought, feeling as sorry for the neglected apartment as she did for herself. Traffic School lay in her immediate future. She dared not attract the attention of the insurance company.

Jazz made a cup of hot tea and poured vodka into it until it was cool enough to drink quickly. Perhaps she was reinventing the martini. Traffic School. The perfect end to a perfect day. She'd never had to go before, but she'd heard horror stories from everyone. On any shoot, the mere mention of Traffic School turned the most frostily remote movie star into an instant buddy of the humble pizza-delivery man. It was like root-canal work. Everyone in California seemed to pass through its hell sooner or later.

Jazz decided to call her father and tell him. He'd had to go to Traffic School twice. He'd comfort her. He'd tell her what she should have said to that cop. Once he'd given her the ticket, was there anything worse he could have done if she'd told him what she thought of him? Could you be cited for verbal assault of the LAPD? Probably.

She dialed the hacienda number and let it ring. There was no answer after a dozen rings. Where could her father possibly be? No father, no Susie, not even Casey Nelson to talk to. Jazz was willing to accept his condolences on the subject of her ambush and entrapment. If he was there, surely he'd answer the phone, unless he was laid up in bed with saddle sores. Nobody to home at home, Jazz thought mournfully.

She called Newport Beach information and got Red Appleton's number. No answer except a recording on a machine. She hung up hastily, without leaving a message. Red not at home, and her father not at home. They had to be out somewhere together, having dinner, sharing jokes and confidences. They must be having a marvelous time, Jazz thought. She didn't begrudge it to them, but still, where were they when she needed sympathy? It wasn't as if she came around demanding sympathy on a regular basis.

She put the phone on the bedspread and looked at it as if she'd never seen it before. Tears blurred her eyes, and she brushed them away impatiently. This was absurd. Traffic School was only eight hours. No picnic, agreed, but then not even a picnic was a picnic. How many people really liked picnics? Why, then, did

the prospect make her feel so utterly . . . abandoned?
As if she'd lost her best friend?

She couldn't call Mel, he'd be all wrapped up in
Sharon. She couldn't call Pete, he'd roar with laughter
at the idea of her getting caught driving at five miles
under the speed limit. She couldn't call any of
her friends because—she didn't know why, but she
couldn't possibly call at this time and intrude on anybody. Whoever wasn't out on a date would be making
dinner at home with some man or other. It was amazing, just when you felt like calling people on the phone
you couldn't reach anybody, yet when they called you
it was always at an inconvenient time.

Maybe she would write somebody a letter, Jazz
thought gloomily, giving the ocean an indifferent
glance. It was fascinating by day, but dark and unfriendly by night. Perhaps it would be better to have
an apartment that looked out on city lights instead of
the uncaring blackness beyond her windows. She
could put the letter in a bottle and throw it in the ocean
like the little girl in a story she'd once heard from
someone, who sent a message in a bottle that said,
"Whoever gets this, I love you."

Jazz padded into the kitchen in her bare feet, the
old bathrobe tied securely around her waist, planning
to make another cup of tea and maybe look for a
cracker. She was too gloomy to feel hungry. The
house phone rang, and she jumped at the sudden
noise. It rang again, aggressively, and she answered
it.

"Miss Kilkullen," said the voice of the receptionist, "there's a visitor here for you."

"Thank God," said Jazz. "Who is it?"

"A Mr. Gabriel. Shall I tell him to come up?"

Jazz gaped at the house phone as if she'd found
herself fondling a snake.

"Miss Kilkullen? Shall I send Mr. Gabriel up?"
the receptionist repeated patiently.

"Hold on a minute." Jazz was transfixed by confusion, not knowing, for one frightening moment of
time, what year it was or why she was barefoot in this

kitchen. She was thrown back to the rending pain of
the wedding that hadn't taken place, to the months of
recovery in Mel Botvinick's studio, to the astonishing
shot of Richard Nixon lying relaxed in the sun on the
sand of the San Clemente beach and reminiscing about
Diane Sawyer with a lazy smile no one had ever seen
on his face before, the shot that had made her famous
all over the world when it was published in magazines
in every foreign country, everything jumbled together
as if they were happening now, simultaneously.

She looked at the calendar on the wall: 1990.
Jazz's sense of time returned, steadied, settled in. She
knew who she was. She couldn't behave as if she were
afraid of Gabe, that mixed-up guy with the emotional
age of an eleven-year-old, whom she had loved in her
own foolish immaturity. If she ducked him, he'd think
she couldn't face him.

"Tell him to come up in seven minutes, Joe," she
instructed the receptionist and hung up.

Five minutes were enough for Jazz to compose the
perfect outfit in which to greet, after nine years of
silence, the first man she'd ever loved, the only man
she'd ever trusted with her whole self, the man who'd
left her waiting at the church. Every girl was entitled,
she told herself as she dressed, to one gigantic mistake
in her life.

She concentrated on her clothes, beating down an
attack of nerves that could only be an aberrant, irra-
tional form of stage fright left over from another life,
another girl, an innocent, gullible person she barely
remembered. Gabe could never happen to anyone but
just such a dumb kid.

Jazz pulled on the purple and gold Lakers T-shirt
she always wore to the games—the glory and power
of the splendid team, led by Magic Johnson, the most
valuable and charismatic player in NBA basketball,
would isolate her from Gabe as a necklace of garlic
protected a sleeping person from a vampire.

Being dumped by Gabe had been the most important favor anyone had ever done her. If, God forbid,

they'd gone through with that mad marriage plan of his, she would have continued to live in his shadow, without a career of her own. Impossible as she now knew that would have been, Jazz was annoyed to realize that she still didn't feel as totally invulnerable as she was. As she had been for years.

She pulled on a well-worn pair of black leather biker jeans, with studs on them that would keep a member of the Hell's Angels at a respectful distance. Black high-top sneakers, an extra layer of mascara, a quick brush-through to make sure that her hair was as disorderly as possible, a smudge of lip gloss, and she was almost ready to open the door.

She surveyed herself critically in the mirror. Don't mess with me, motherfucker, said her image. But, silly as it was, Jazz decided that if this were a picture and she was taking it, she'd know that something else was needed—some kind of prop. Jazz ran to her fridge and got an apple, took a bite, carefully removed it from her mouth and put it in the garbage, went to the front door and opened it a fraction. She turned on the television set in the living room and fell into her usual, cross-legged perch on the rug, propped up on half a dozen pillows, apple in hand.

The doorbell rang. "It's open," she called, nipped a tiny bite of apple and chewed vigorously, never taking her eyes off the set, trying to ignore the agitated pounding of her heart. It was no more than a reflex reaction, the proverbial chicken with its head cut off.

"So," Gabe said, stopping in the hall at the entrance to the living room.

"Oh, hi, Gabe. Come on in. I have to see the end of this show—it'll be over in a minute," Jazz said as she chewed, gazing intently at the screen and waving vaguely at the couch behind her. He sat down and waited silently for three minutes as the episode of a television series came to an end. Jazz picked up the remote control and snapped off the set. She glanced up at Gabe. He hadn't changed, she thought, except that his eyes were world-weary and his mouth sardonic in a way it never had been before. Such an ordinary man. "Sorry, but 'thirtysomething' is the one show I watch religiously," Jazz said. "Do you like it?"

"Huh?"

"Never mind. Apple?"

"No. Thanks." He fell silent as Jazz nibbled away unconcernedly. "So," he said at last.

"You sound like Mary Tyler Moore. Remember, on her show, how she always said 'So,' with that big, bright, nervous smile, whenever she couldn't think of anything else to say? Blair Brown does it too."

"Is this the television trivia quiz night?"

"I forgot you haven't had a chance to see American television in a long time."

"So you've become a Lakers fan?"

"If you're tired of the Lakers, you're tired of life," Jazz said with mocking eyes. "You'd probably think it's not enough of a contact sport. After all, nobody gets killed. There aren't any riots. No bombs are thrown. There's no blood on the floor. Still, as someone once wrote, when Cooper guards you, it's like the worst wet kiss you ever had. You should be at the Forum when the Lakers have to get physical. I wouldn't want to be out there then, not even if I were as big as Michael Jordan or Charles Barkley."

"Barkley?"

"Of Philadelphia," she said patiently. "You sound like someone from outer space. How've you been keepin'?"

"Fine. And you?"

"Never better. Busy, up to my eyebrows in work, but then aren't we all?"

"Jazz!"

"What?" she mumbled, through a bit of apple.

"Just stop. I came here to talk to you, not play games."

Jazz let his words hang in the air as she chewed and swallowed. She turned around on the rug and put some pillows behind her, hugging her knees with her arms and looking up at Gabe on the couch. Her cloud of wavelets, streaked with every color from chutney to tortoiseshell, fell back from her open, flower-fresh face. She spoke lazily.

"Well, sure, Gabe, say whatever you have to say. I'm not stopping you." Jazz kept her expression benignly neutral, even though she was thinking that if what he had to say was too difficult to confront her with, he could always write her another lovely letter.

"I had dinner with Phoebe a while ago. She told me you don't want me in the studio and you don't want her to rep me. I told her you were just another groupie, because I didn't want her to know anything about us."

"I'm amazed that you didn't tell her the truth. Phoebe usually insists on knowing all."

"Since she obviously didn't know we even knew each other, I assumed you hadn't told anybody here."

"You can't expect that experience to be—how can I put it?—the favorite item in my memory book. Those years seem to have happened to somebody else. No one but my father knows what kind of human being—no, strike the word 'human'—what kind of being you are."

"It's about time you got hostile." Gabe leaned forward. "Now we can get this out in the open."

"Wrong. I'm not hostile. That was merely the most friendly way I could think of to describe you. A being. You exist. There's plenty of room for both of us in L.A., but there's no room *on my turf*."

Jazz took another bite of the apple. There was another silence as she chewed methodically. "Want to watch 'Nightline,' with Ted Koppel?" she offered finally, in a friendly tone. "Wherever you've been, it's probably the best way to catch up. That and 'Washington Week in Review.' That way you won't have to spend as much time reading the morning papers."

"I do not want to watch 'Nightline.' I do not want to catch up. I do not want to know what's going on in the world. I've seen too much of it."

"I'll bet you've never bothered to vote again, after that one time in Paris," Jazz remarked with a lightly scornful edge to her voice.

"Fuck! I didn't come here for Civics 101."

"I don't remember inviting you. On television night I try to stay home."

Gabe got up and sat down on the floor near her. She edged away immediately.

"Jazz, I can find other office space, that's no problem at all, but I need Phoebe to be my rep. I've known her for years, I trust her judgment, and I don't see how that can intrude on your territory."

"Any connection between us is out of the question," Jazz said coldly. "Your old pal, buddy, sidekick, Phoebe the know-it-all, is nothing if not a connection. She's like some gonzo computer hacker who can sneak in everywhere and stir up trouble. It would be impossible to maintain a distance between us once Phoebe was involved in your work."

"Jesus, Jazz, you're still hooked on me!"

Jazz jumped up from the floor when she heard the faint but unmistakable note of not-quite-hidden triumph in his voice. She stood over him, flooded with the rage she'd been suppressing since he'd walked in the door.

"Hooked on you? *I hate you, Gabe.* I hate you for what you did to me when I was a twenty-year-old kid, too young to know that no one should ever believe one word that came out of your mouth. *It was so desperately cruel.* What kind of contemptible bastard is capable of getting a girl to say she'll marry him, against her better judgment, and then disappearing at the very last minute, leaving nothing behind except a shit-eating letter of shit-eating, trumped-up, so-called explanation? You couldn't even find the little bit of guts you needed to tell me face-to-face."

Jazz turned away from him and stalked over to the window, shaking with the adrenaline of her pent-up fury. Gabe got up and followed her, and when she heard his footsteps behind her she turned a frightening face on him.

"You left Paris in the one way that had to hurt me the most. I'd turned over my life to you. It was your idea to get married, not mine, God knows. I never tried to tie you down, you did it to yourself and then—*then* you tried to put the blame on me. Somehow what you did became my fault! It was so cheap, Gabe, cheap beyond cheapness, so utterly unfair. *You disgust me.*"

"I've disgusted myself ever since. Good God, Jazz, don't you think there isn't one thing you've said that I haven't said to myself a thousand times, night after night—and ten times worse? Every word of that letter was the cold, hard truth, but that doesn't excuse it. Nothing can excuse my gutlessness. *But you're still hooked on me, Jazz,* no matter what you think of my character."

"*That's sick!*" she cried. "Really sick! I know what kind of vile coward you are, I know how cruel you can be, but I didn't think you were egomaniacal enough to think I couldn't get over you."

"You wouldn't be so determined to avoid any contact with me if I were just a bad memory. You wouldn't still be so defensive, Jazz, if you'd really forgotten me."

"I honestly think you believe that revolting crap," Jazz taunted him. "I hear you talking yourself into it. You've actually convinced yourself." Her voice was corrosive, jeering.

"You're not over me, Jazz." Gabe's lean, dark face was insistent and certain of his words.

"It's been years and years since I wasted a minute thinking of you," she said contemptuously.

"Prove it," Gabe challenged her.

"I don't have to prove anything to you!"

"Then prove it to yourself. If you don't, you'll never really trust yourself again."

"I trust myself plenty," Jazz said coolly, in control of herself again. "Get out of here, Gabe, I want you out of my house. You make it stink."

Gabe grabbed Jazz roughly, pulled her into his arms and kissed her with all the immoderate passion that he'd felt since he came into the room and saw her again, so much more beautiful than he remembered. Jazz punched him in the face with her fist, as hard as she could.

"I knew it!" he cried. "You'd never bother to hit me if you didn't give a damn!" Gabe held her arms pinioned to her sides and kissed Jazz again, over and over. He stopped for a minute, released his grip and gave her a clean chance to beat him up in any way she chose.

"Obstinate bitch," he said, when she didn't move, or change her stony expression. He held her unyielding body close again and bent to her cold lips once more, his whole being concentrated on making her acknowledge his mouth. Finally he felt her lips responding, just the merest flicker of a response, a tiny quiver, a faint pressure, a warming, a hint of a yearning, which grew and grew until it became a kiss that met his kiss.

They stood in front of the window by the ocean, clasped in each other's arms, kissing silently, tentatively, each unwilling to make a sound or say a word that might break the unexpected magic of this isolated moment in which the past and the present met and all the joy of their years together was distilled and all the pain of the ending forgotten. But when Jazz felt Gabe pressing against her so tightly that she couldn't ignore how aroused he was, she pushed him away and stood apart, tall and proud and defiant.

"Oh no. Definitely no, not that," Jazz said in a strong, clear voice. "You've proved your point, Gabe. I'm not physically indifferent to you. There's still something there, I'm only human. But it's just an unimportant something, a bit of the past that somehow . . . *survived* what you did to me."

She shook her head sadly and reflectively. "Whatever it is, it's not strong enough so that I'll let you make love to me, Gabe. Oh, I admit that I want to, Gabe, don't think that I've forgotten the way it used to be when the lights of the *bateaux mouches* lit our window and we lay in bed, invisible, listening to the dance music on the river, with you so deep inside me that I knew absolutely and forever that nothing in the world had ever been that marvelous for anyone else but us."

Jazz put her hands on his shoulders and spoke gently, the light of her eyes so incandescent with memory that he couldn't meet her gaze.

"They say that there's nothing to beat an Auld Lang Syne fuck, Gabe, and you were the best, the very best lover I've ever had. Not just because you were the first—I've had a chance to compare." Jazz cocked her head and gave a complex, unconsciously infuriating smile, full of memories that Gabe suddenly knew had nothing to do with him. "The problem is I can't trust you. And I won't make love to a man I don't trust."

"Can't you believe that in nine years I could have changed?" he said in anguish. "That I *must* have changed? That you can trust me?"

Jazz laughed abruptly at his words. " 'Trust'? Trust *you*? Trust is out of the question. Even you must know that. But I don't care anymore if Phoebe reps you. In fact, you can rent the space too. You've just proved something to me that you didn't intend to prove. You don't have power over me anymore, poor Gabe."

She patted him on the cheek and he started to speak. Jazz raised a finger in a way that stopped him cold. "*Don't say it!* Don't make me hate you again by saying that if I were truly sure that you didn't have power over me, I'd let you make love to me. No, Gabe, no, you can't use that frat-house argument all night. It would be unworthy, even of a Hungarian. You've got what you came over here to get. And a little extra. Be satisfied."

Gabe looked at Jazz speechlessly. Christ, he'd really done himself in this time. Fucked himself up good and proper. He'd thought he was over her, mostly anyway. He must have been completely insane. It hadn't been an acceptable risk to so much as shake hands with this incomparable girl. He'd taken it, and now he was stuck with the consequences. Stuck for good, stuck forever, if he knew anything about it. She'd always been the only one.

"So I guess we've missed Ted Koppel," Gabe managed to say.

"Chances are." Jazz gave him an amiable and impersonal smile. "Want to watch Jay Leno?"

"No, I've got to go. Thanks, Jazz, see you around," he said, and fled.

She was going to be late for class, Jazz thought in a panic. On top of everything else that was revolting about the prospect of Traffic School, there was no place to park near the building in which the school was located. *Late for class.* She could feel anxiety sweat bursting out all over her neck and forehead. Late. For. Class. The mere sound of the words brought with them all the feeling of a particular kind of nightmare.

Jazz had reluctantly investigated the options available in Traffic School after she had received her speeding ticket. Obviously she wasn't the only automotive offender in town, since there were dozens of different schools, a California cottage industry, as thick on the ground as meetings of Alcoholics Anonymous in Beverly Hills. Some schools advertised that they were especially for singles, others promised pizza for lunch; schools lured customers with magic tricks and Disney movies, and many billed themselves as comedy schools. The only school located not too far from her apartment was called "Fabulous Comedians Entertain U."

Gritting her teeth at wasting a Saturday, Jazz had called and signed up at Fabulous Comedians to expiate her ticket. When she arrived, thinking that she was in good time, she found that the parking lot behind the building was closed on Saturday and the streets around the school were all filled with cars parked next to meters. "Teacher's pets," she snarled out loud, feeling the sweat begin to trickle down her sides as she sought a space in growing alarm.

Eventually, three blocks from the school, she wedged her car into the last space available and ran back as fast as she could to the unprepossessing two-story building on Pico Boulevard. There was no one in the halls or on the staircase, and when she crashed into the room in which the class was held, a round of mocking catcalls and applause greeted her.

"You're two minutes late," the instructor said, locking the door behind her. "Another second and it would have been too late."

"Thanks," Jazz gasped, and looked around for a seat. Only one chair was empty, on the aisle in the front row, obviously right under the nose of the instructor, and the last place anyone would want to sit, if schoolday memories were any guide. She slunk down the aisle and sat down next to a messily dressed man with an enormous black handlebar mustache. He had a grubby crew hat pulled down over his hair, and he wore dark glasses.

The tiny chair was even harder and smaller than she had expected. Jazz looked straight in front of her, pulling her streaky ripples of hair over her eyes in an attempt to create a private space. She should have postponed coming to Traffic School as long as possible, she realized, now that she was actually there. Not that it would have been any better later in the allotted period of two months, but she had been feeling unusually down since the night, a week ago, when Gabe had shown up at her apartment. She had no wellspring of energy during the day, although she managed to function more or less normally in the studio. She'd caught Toby and Melissa exchanging concerned glances, although neither of them had actually mentioned anything. She'd turned down dates in order to go to bed early, and then she'd slept badly, with unpleasant dreams, although she couldn't remember what it was about them that made her feel bad.

In the morning Jazz felt more weary, more bruised, than when she went to bed. She felt obscurely damaged in some way, as if she'd gone through a far more brutal experience than the actual meeting with

Gabe had been. She felt older than twenty-nine, unpleasantly streetwise, and totally cynical. Every time she read a newspaper or watched the television news, she wondered why she'd even bothered to drag herself out of bed. It all seemed so . . . hopeless, so endlessly hopeless. If this were depression—although she couldn't think why she should be depressed—how could she get rid of it?

Whatever was causing her to feel this way, it couldn't be Gabe, Jazz was certain. She finally put that ghost to rest. She'd seen him again, she'd kissed him again, and she'd found out that she was over him. She'd had a chance to confront him with some of the accusations she'd been storing up for eight years, and he'd had to admit that she was right. He'd been reduced to nothing more than what he was, a part of her past, a part that had been far more good than it had been bad, in spite of its traumatic ending.

To be logical, Jazz ruminated, to put things in the correct balance, it was only fair to admit that Gabe had taught her an enormous amount just by his example. Her ability to shoot straight from the gut under any circumstances, and her methods of manipulating any subject, could only have been learned from a photojournalist. She should be grateful to him.

She *was* grateful. Their years together had been a time of invaluable experience. Of course, there had been a price to pay for that education. No realistic woman could have expected anything else. She couldn't go back and relive her life, that was for sure, and meanwhile there was Traffic School to survive, in an airless room that was jammed with people. Jazz surveyed the perimeter of what she could see through the protective wings of hair she had pulled together so that they almost met at her nose.

Her scruffy neighbor was a tall man with long arms that invaded her space, but because of the way in which the chairs were crammed together, he couldn't move in any direction to give her more room. Thank God, on one side there was the narrow aisle, although she couldn't move her chair because it was bolted to the floor. Jazz pressed her lips together in useless disgust, but she was careful not to look at the man on her right. There must be absolutely no eye contact between them, as if they were in the New York subway. It was the only way to maintain any psychic distance between herself and someone to whom she was destined to be all but chained for the next eight hours. The slob was three times too big for his chair. He came into direct body contact with her, all the way from his shoulder to his knee. She'd worn her jeans and work shirt from her Girl Friday days, but now she wished she had worn something with spikes on it, to fend off his hideously unwelcome closeness.

The man who had locked the door mounted the podium and began to speak.

"I am LAPD Officer Muffet, your instructor for today. You are here for eight full hours. Any attempt to cheat me of your attention before your four hundred and eighty minutes are up will be regarded with grave prejudice. Do not even *try* to ask me if you can leave early; that will be construed as a bribe." The instructor, a middle-aged man, looked as pale and tough as a prison guard, Jazz thought. Where were the fabulous comedians? Why was this room filled with hulking, ugly men and only one other woman?

"This class is subject to monitoring by the Department of Motor Vehicles," Muffet continued. "If you come back late from lunch, you will find the door locked and you will have to repeat the class. There will be one fifteen-minute break in the morning and one in the afternoon so that you can feed the meters. These breaks will *not*—repeat, will not—be deducted from your four hundred and eighty minutes of Traffic School. The door will be locked as soon as the break is over."

Holy shit! She had plenty of singles in her wallet, but no change. Could you get a parking ticket while you were in Traffic School? Unquestionably.

"The officer who was supposed to teach this class has a cold. I'm replacing him at the last minute, and I don't do jokes."

A chorus of outraged protests broke out from the imprisoned souls in the room. Muffet listened impassively. When it died down he said, "Anyone who wants to leave is welcome to do so. I don't advise it unless you have another Saturday you want to clear for Traffic School, or unless you want to waste the part of the morning you've already devoted to getting up and getting here and getting your seats. The rules for the comic Traffic School are exactly the same as mine."

Jazz heard a few people getting up noisily and leaving, but she stayed put. She'd given up a weekend at the ranch for this hell, she'd found a parking space, and she was damned if she'd go through that drill again.

Muffet waited impassively until the last defector had left, and began to speak.

"A trial by jury does not apply to your infractions. When you get a ticket, you're guilty until you're proven innocent. Unless your time is worth less than twenty dollars an hour, don't fight the ticket. That's my first lesson."

Muffet looked around the room with a grisly smile. What had happened to the Bill of Rights, Jazz wondered?

"O.K.," Muffet said. "Now who knows what Selective Enforcement is? Nobody? I thought so. Nobody ever does, except repeaters, and they won't admit it. Selective Enforcement is the right of an officer to pull you over when *everybody else* is doing the same thing you're doing. Every single car is doing sixty on the freeway, and you get a ticket for doing sixty. You don't think you're guilty, but you are. Why? Selective Enforcement is practiced by the LAPD because there is only one chance in *twelve hundred* that you'll be picked out to get a ticket. In other words, if you get one ticket, *we know* that you have committed that particular violation twelve hundred times *without* getting caught. So, no matter what the circumstances, you're guilty. That's my second lesson."

Muffet hitched up his pants, his authority established as thoroughly as if they had all been deposited on Devil's Island for the rest of their lives.

"How many people in here are single? Raise your hands," Muffet continued. The rustle of hands was clearly audible. "How many are married?" Again she heard hands raised. "How many don't know?"

Jazz's hands were clenched. She hadn't raised one for any category. Her private life was none of his concern. What did it have to do with getting an outrageously unfair ticket?

"Now I'll ask each of you your name, what you do for a living and how you got your traffic citation," Muffet continued.

I'm not here, Jazz thought, this is not happening to me. Behind her, people were giving answers to his questions. All their violations, without exception, were far greater than hers. The advantage of being in the first row was that when her turn came she was able to reply in a low voice. The man next to her said, in a mumble even lower than hers, that his name was Leslie Duff, that he was a construction worker and he'd been cited for running a stop sign.

"Why didn't you stop at the sign?" Muffet asked.

"I did," Duff protested gruffly. "But there was nobody coming in any direction, not a single car anywhere, so I looked around carefully, came to a rolling stop, and crossed the street. I thought that was good enough."

"A stop sign means three full seconds at a full stop," Muffet said disapprovingly. "We call those three seconds 'the eight-hour decision.' If you'd stopped, you wouldn't be here."

Duff subsided into a sullen silence. What a goon he was, Jazz thought. No way she would give Muffet any backtalk. The LAPD had its national tough-and-rough reputation to protect, and this class was clearly taking place somewhere beyond the territorial waters of the United States.

"You," Muffet demanded, pointing at Jazz. "Do you know the only two things that can be thrown from your car legally?"

"No, sir."

"Water and feathers of *live* poultry."

"Yes, sir."

Muffet paused, and Jazz could see him tempted to actually make a joke, just to see if it was possible. "I don't want to ever catch you on an overpass with a pillow," Muffet told her. In disgust, Jazz heard herself giving a nervous giggle.

Muffet began to berate the class with a series of warnings about pedestrian rights, and Jazz's eyes began to close. She was appalled by the prospect of at least seven and a half more hours of enforced confinement in this crowded, claustrophobic room. The small windows were closed and there was no air circulating; the chair was growing harder by the minute, and it felt as if Duff were taking up more and more of the little space she occupied, although he hadn't actually moved as far as she could tell. If she could only put herself onto a higher astral level, remove herself completely, have an out-of-body experience. This would never be happening to Shirley MacLaine.

Suddenly Duff laid a piece of paper on her lap. Startled, she looked down and read the words, "Hi, gorgeous."

She almost shrieked out loud. This weirdo was trying to pick her up. For the whole gruesome, penitential day she was going to be subjected to his harassment with no hope of escape. Jazz took a pad and pencil out of her purse and wrote, "I'll tell Muffet if you don't stop," and passed it to him when Muffet wasn't looking.

He scribbled busily and slid her another scrap of paper. "I thought you'd want to know that I forgive you."

Duff was also crazy, Jazz realized. A sex fiend

and a nut case, and a very large-sized one. He might lash out quickly and do her some damage before Muffet could protect her. "Thanks," she wrote. Perhaps that would pacify him.

"How about lunch?" the next note said.

Jazz was about to get up and remove herself to a safe distance and then tell Muffet what was happening, when she suddenly realized that this horrendous creature might have his uses.

"No thanks. My husband's taking me to lunch. Do you have change for a dollar?" she wrote.

"Plenty," was the answer.

"That's very kind," Jazz wrote, and sat undisturbed until the break. Everyone rose quickly as soon as Muffet announced it. Jazz held out some dollar bills but Duff simply poured quarters into her hand, turned his back, and started down the stairs. Jazz sped to her car, put in three quarters, and started running back toward the school. The street was empty, she was still two blocks away from the school, when Duff, even bigger than he seemed sitting down, materialized in front of her.

"Can't stop," she said, and kept on running. He caught up with her quickly and grabbed her arm.

"Come on, be nice," he said. "You weren't always so stand-offish."

Perhaps sweet reasonableness would get her safely back to Fabulous Comedians, Jazz thought frantically. Muffet would take care of him. Muffet unquestionably had a gun and would love to use it. "We're going to be late if we don't get back to class right away," she puffed.

"The last time we met, you were more friendly," Duff insisted, still holding her arm.

"I'll scream for help," Jazz said wildly.

"No woman ever said that to me before."

Something about his voice was weirdly familiar. He had an accent that wasn't quite American, and even those exact words rang a distant but clearly remembered bell, Jazz realized. She looked at Duff for the first time. He didn't have on his sunglasses. With-

out the mustache . . . without the dirty crew hat . . .
he would be not that bad . . . no, he would be . . .
memorable . . . he would be . . .

"Sam Butler," Jazz snapped accusingly. "What
the hell are you doing clowning around with that ridiculous hair on your face?"

"You mean you really didn't recognize me? I
thought that with your eye you must have spotted me
—aren't you the lady who sees around corners? I figured you were just giving me the cold shoulder." The
Australian actor smiled his twenty-million-dollars-for-
three-pictures smile, and Jazz realized that if she'd
been paying any attention to her surroundings, she'd
have recognized him immediately, mustache or not.

"You scared me to death," she said severely.
"Who's Leslie Duff?"

"Me. I changed it for the movies."

"I thought you were a mad rapist." Jazz was furious at having been so frightened.

"That happened before too. Do you assume that
every man is hot for your body, or is it just something
special about me?"

"It's definitely you." Jazz bit her lip to keep from
smiling at the way she'd frightened him with the men-
ace of a tidal wave after that earthquake weeks ago.
"Something about your attitude."

"Do you really have a husband taking you to
lunch?"

"No," Jazz admitted. "I wanted to make you
stop writing notes."

"Then is lunch on?"

"I have to eat anyway . . . so all right. What did
you mean, you forgive me?"

"I forgive you for being so unfairly sexy when
you photographed me. You *were* sexy, you have to
admit it. You really had me going. It was the first time
a photographer ever got me to strip for a shoot."

"Oh. That. Yes. Well, maybe I did take advantage of you. I guess actors are considered fair game.
But what would have happened if there hadn't been

an earthquake? You were on top of me, for God's
sake! Naked!"

"I would have let you go," Sam Butler assured
her. "I made an honest mistake. And I apologize. I
was absolutely wrong."

Studying him and trying to size him up, Jazz knew
that for some reason she believed him. A man like
Sam Butler didn't have to go around forcing himself
on women.

So many actors were chameleons, depending on
the part for their appearance, but Sam Butler could
only look like Sam Butler. He couldn't disguise the
absolute masculinity of his features, the strong, square
jaw, the straight nose, the thick, almost flaxen blond
hair, the resolute blue-beyond-blue eyes, the wide, determined mouth, all arranged in a way that would have
left a crowd of Victorian maidens in a mass swoon
. . . what could he do about it? Sam Butler's features
said things about him that didn't necessarily have to
be true, but which no actor's craft was powerful
enough to deny or change. He would inevitably be
cast as a romantic hero. Like the young Olivier, to
prove that he was a good actor, he would always have
to hide behind makeup.

It had been too easy for her to categorize this
actor as another guy who didn't understand a "no"
when he heard it, to overlook the loving and homesick
heart he had revealed when he talked about his family
back home in Australia. The attitudes of Planet Hollywood were getting to her, Jazz thought, and that
wasn't good news.

Butler looked at his watch. "Run for it. We're
going to be late for class."

They arrived, winded, Sam pulling Jazz by her
hand to speed her up the last flight of stairs, just as
Muffet was about to lock the door. Sheepishly they
regained their seats.

"I've seen this before," Muffet said severely. "I
don't allow socializing in my class. No profane language, no chewing tobacco, no spitting, no Doritos,

no disgusting noises.'' He pointed at Jazz and Sam. ''And particularly no sucking face. If you wanted to meet someone, you should have gone to one of the singles Traffic Schools.''

''We're cousins,'' Sam assured him.

''First cousins,'' Jazz said hastily.

''Our mothers were sisters,'' Sam embroidered.

''Twins, actually,'' Jazz added.

She couldn't seem to shut up. Siamese twins? She felt hysteria mount. A crazy laugh was about to overtake her, the kind you couldn't bring to a halt, the kind that hadn't happened since high school, the insane laugh that came over you at the most solemn and inappropriate places and that fed upon itself. High mass, graduations, weddings, funerals—oh God!

She felt Sam Butler's fingers pinch her upper arm, and she was able to control the fatal laughter until a sideways peek at him revealed that he was also shaking with suppressed mirth, which he was trying to conceal by hiding his lower face. He was having trouble tucking his long, unwieldy mustache away inside his collar. This absurd sight put Jazz over the top. She hunched up her shoulders, looked blindly at the floor and gave herself up to a full-fledged fit, weeping with unstoppable laughter.

''What's going on here?'' Muffet demanded.

''It's . . . a . . . comedy . . . school . . . sir,'' Sam Butler managed to choke out. ''My cousin's . . . very . . . susceptible . . . to jokes.''

''Well, O.K.,'' Muffet said grudgingly. ''But don't let it happen again.''

Jazz finally gained control of herself through the realization that if she didn't stop, she'd pee in her pants. It was an instantly sobering thought, and she concentrated on it until the lunch break, her eyes almost shut as she shrank her attention down to this one strong possibility, willing herself not to be aroused by the fits of giggles that shook Sam from time to time, and which were communicated to her by the quivering of his body.

Finally the lunch break came. Jazz and Sam dared to look at each other.

"Why were we laughing?" Jazz asked soberly.

"I don't know," Sam said.

"It wasn't that funny." Jazz looked puzzled.

"Not nearly funny enough. What's so funny about twins?" Sam agreed solemnly. The word "twins" set them both off again, until they staggered out of the classroom, gasping, headed hastily for the restrooms on the ground floor.

"Got to put in some quarters before lunch," Jazz reminded Sam when they rejoined each other on the street.

"I'll come with you," he said companionably.

"Where's your car?"

"There." Sam pointed to a black stretch limousine that was following them as they walked. "The studio didn't want me driving to Traffic School. They were afraid I'd get another ticket on the way here."

"I wish someone took that kind of care of me," Jazz said enviously. "I almost couldn't find a parking place. Was it their idea to send you out in disguise?"

"No, mine. It's the only way I can have any privacy now. Since my last flick . . ." His voice trailed off, embarrassed.

"You mean you're drawing crazed crowds in *Hollywood*? Nobody gets a second look in this town. We locals pride ourselves on that."

"Well . . ." he mumbled, looking away from her.

"My God. I'll bet you do. Women going apeshit every time they see you. I can see it now. If there had been more women at Traffic School—it makes perfect sense . . . they haven't seen anything like you in generations."

"I hate it," he said simply. "Come on, let's have lunch. We deserve it after four hours of Muffet." He handed Jazz into the limo.

"Where can we go? We have to be back in about a half hour, and there's nothing around here but a Pollo Loco and a McDonald's."

"All taken care of." Sam Butler opened a big wicker picnic basket that was lying on the floor of the limo, and revealed a large array of plastic containers and flat parcels wrapped in aluminum foil.

"I told them to order a little of everything from Nate n' Al's deli—good tucker there—and we've got lashings of Australian white wine to start with." He pulled off his false mustache, took off his crew hat and dark glasses, and shook his head in relief.

"Wine, please," Jazz said, stretching her cramped muscles and lying back on the cushions of the limo. "Wine, strong wine, and lots of it. Were you expecting a guest, or did you order all this for yourself?"

"Just for me. I hated the thought of Traffic School so much that I thought it might be a good idea to drink my way through it, but that wouldn't go down well with Muffet, would it?"

"Don't say his name," Jazz begged. "With only a half hour, let's not spoil it. I smell pastrami . . . oh, Sam Butler, for a simple country boy from Perth, you learn quickly."

There were two bottles of wine, pastrami, corned beef, bagels, rye bread, mustard, pickles, French dressing, smoked salmon, cream cheese, sliced turkey, rare roast beef, and even a container of chopped chicken liver, which they both agreed should be saved for dessert because the cheesecake that the studio had ordered was fattening and they'd each had three sandwiches and almost all the wine.

Never in their lives had they needed food and drink so much. They ate in greedy, hasty silence except for moans of delight with each new sandwich combination, and when they were absolutely full they rolled down the limo windows to get some fresh air before the second half of Traffic School.

"I'm not going," Sam Butler suddenly announced.

"Not going where? Where are we, anyway?" Jazz said, oddly disoriented.

"Back. I'm not going back to that room. I can't stand it. We don't have bloody Traffic School in Australia. I'm not even an American citizen. What can they do to me? I'll go home to Perth. They can't extradite me, and no jury in Australia would convict me."

"But this morning won't count if you don't go back. You'll have to do it all over," Jazz objected sleepily.

"That's O.K., but I'm not going back now. This morning was a small price to pay."

"Pay for what?"

"You. I'd do two weeks of Traffic School to meet you again. Three. Four. A fucking year of bloody Traffic School just for you, cobber."

"You could have phoned, if it meant that much." Jazz giggled at his histrionics.

"I was afraid you'd hang up on me. Would you have?"

"Probably. What's a cobber?"

"A friend . . . a buddy."

"How sweet, how very sweet," she said sentimentally. "Sooooo sweet—but I think I've got to go —don't I?—go back to school or whatever? Could you tell the driver?"

"Driver, back to the school, please," Sam said.

"We've been parked in front of it for more than fifteen minutes," the driver answered.

"NOT POSSIBLE!" Jazz screeched. She looked at her watch. She ran up the stairs with Sam following. The door was locked. They pounded on it, and the only response was Muffet's sadistic shout. "I warned you two, don't say I didn't warn you."

"Oh SHIT!" Jazz almost burst into tears.

"It's all my fault."

"Damn right it is!"

"I'll make it up to you."

"How?" she demanded. "Just tell me one way you can make up four wasted hours of Traffic School!"

"I can't make it up to you," Sam muttered,

abashed. "Not ever, not if I tried for the rest of my life."

Jazz looked at his face, set in lines of genuine and total dismay. His eyes were screwed up with self-reproach, every bone in his body expressed his honest distress.

"Cheer up," she said, "I forgive you. It's not the worst thing a man ever did to me."

"If it isn't, I'd like to meet the bloody bastard who did."

"Are we a little drunk, Sam?"

"Not possible on Australian white. That never gets to me. I'm no two-pot screamer. But it's not a bad idea. Want to go drown our sorrows?"

"In the afternoon?"

"Right. Much too early. Let's go to that old-fashioned circus. You know, in that tent on the beach . . . I've been wanting to go ever since they got here—fire eaters, sword swallowers, jugglers—how about it?"

"I'm too sleepy. I need a nap."

"Poor cobber, you're not used to Australian wine," he said. "I'll take you home."

"What about my car? I can't drive it like this, I'm a teeny-weeny bit smashed, I do believe."

"I'll have it taken care of, just give me your keys."

Limply, Jazz let Sam help her back in the limo. She fell asleep immediately from the combined effects of four hours of Traffic School, a huge lunch, a bottle of wine and all the emotions of the morning.

When she woke up, on top of a strange bed, under a strange quilt, Jazz could tell from the darkness outside that it must be night. She lay very still, certain that if she tried she would be able to remember where she was and how she had come here. There was a small lamp on in the room, and she could make out a window with trees beyond it. What little she could see of the room looked as if it were located in the Yukon, about a hundred years ago. She smelled a wood fire burning and the sounds of a man's footsteps quietly crossing another room. She closed her eyes again and tried to free-associate. Yukon, wood fire, quilt, trees, nothing. She ran her hands over her body. Jeans, work shirt, Girl Friday, Mel Botvinick, Pete di Constanza, Dazzle, automobiles, Traffic School. Bingo.

Jazz threw off the quilt and realized that she felt as refreshed as if she'd just had the best night's rest of her life. She padded across the dim, wood-paneled room and discovered a bathroom. She splashed her face for a long time with ice-cold water, used a new toothbrush that she found there, and inspected herself in the mirror.

She couldn't help smiling. She looked, to her critical and habitually appraising eye, at least eighteen. It was probably the deep sleep, the fact that she hadn't put on any makeup this morning, or the anarchic disorder of her hair, but she recognized a girl she hadn't seen since she'd worked on her first-year lighting assignments at Graphics Central. Her eyes were untroubled, her cheeks flamed pink, she looked like the girl she'd been before she met Gabe. Better yet, she felt like her.

Her sneakers had disappeared, Jazz discovered, back in the bedroom, but she was still wearing her socks. She cracked open the door of the bedroom and stood there without making a sound, peeping through the slit she'd made and surveying the empty living room where a fire was burning low, providing the only illumination.

Sam Butler came through a door at the far end of the room, carrying an armload of logs. She watched him renew the fire as quietly as possible and sit down patiently in front of it, obviously waiting for her to wake. From the way he sat, from the severe look on his face, Jazz knew that he'd stay there all night if need be. He'd been guarding her while she slept the afternoon away in this mountain retreat or wherever it was.

"Good evening, Sam," she said sedately.

Sam Butler started violently. He'd been somewhere else, Jazz realized, and her sudden words had jerked him out of a dream.

"Jazz!" His expression changed from severity to happiness as he looked at her. "I was getting worried. You passed out, I couldn't wake you up."

"I don't usually drink a bottle of wine before lunch. Also, I don't normally get kidnapped."

"I didn't know where you lived, or I'd have taken you home."

"Why didn't you look at my driver's license?"

"I didn't want to look in your handbag without your permission," he said gravely. "It didn't seem polite."

"That was very . . . delicate of you. Is this your place?"

"Right. I found it a few months ago."

"Where are we?"

"Way far up in the Hollywood Hills. This place was built about eighty years ago. I have deer in my backyard."

"What time is it?"

Sam Butler looked at his watch. "It's almost seven-thirty and it's Saturday night—I'm sure you have to be somewhere . . . you're probably late already. I'll take you home right away."

Jazz sat down in front of the fire. "I don't have a date, but I'll bet you do. Why don't you just call me a cab?"

"I was planning to stay home alone tonight, it's been a busy week." He folded his arms resolutely, a man with nothing to do but look into a fire and think idle thoughts.

"Then I'll get out of your hair," Jazz offered.

"No, I didn't mean it like that. I—I could make you a drink."

"That you could," Jazz said thoughtfully.

"Or I could broil you a steak."

"You could do that too," she agreed.

"I can't put on telly. My set's broken."

"That's fine," she said equably. "No telly to-night."

"But I could put on some music."

"Music's fine. I've always liked music."

"That's about all I can do to entertain you."

"Can't you think of anything else?"

"Not at this late date. We're not dressed to go out."

"Nothing at all? Not one single other thing?"

"Nope . . . I don't have any imagination," he said with a flicker of mischief in his eyes.

"You certainly don't," Jazz said, shaking her head in commiseration. She crawled forward, turned around and lay back across his lap, looking up at him, her head resting on his folded arms, her lips tilted toward his chin.

"How about a kiss, cobber?" She put up her arms and pulled his head down. "That's what people used to do for entertainment before there was television."

"Oh, Jazz," Sam said, resisting the pull of her arms, "I want to so much."

"Then why don't you?"

"I want to start all over again with you. And I don't want to go barmy and swarm all over you like I did the first time, and I don't want to act like a bloody nitwit who thinks he's a hotshot movie star."

"Is that what's stopping you from kissing me?"

"Yeah."

"You think too much," Jazz said, and pushed herself up far enough so that she could plant a hasty kiss on his mouth. "Now I'm the official aggressor. You can make the next move and it won't count against you."

Sam held her at arm's length and studied her face intently in the firelight.

"That doesn't count," he decided, finally. "That was just a little quick peck. Where I come from, that's the way you kiss your brother."

Jazz launched herself at him, wrapping herself around him, giving him a long, warm kiss that could never be considered sisterly.

"No, sorry, but that just won't do," he panted. "That's the way you kiss your cousin."

"Don't say you didn't ask for it," Jazz warned him in a tyrannical whisper. So he was a game player. And good at it too. Well, so was she, if the game was worth the candle. She pushed Sam down on the rug and bent over him. He lay quietly, watchfully, questioningly looking up at her as if he were taking her measure. Jazz realized, in this spell of consideration that held her motionless, that never before had she been so aware of the shape of her mouth. Kisses were something she was used to being given, not something she had ever had to take.

As she watched Sam seeming to wait so patiently for the touch of her mouth, she visualized what he was seeing, she saw her own sudden birth of sensuousness, the ardent fullness, the promise of warmth, and she felt her lips parting in response to the genuinely reined-in desire she saw in his eyes. Jazz brought her mouth down on him like a gift, gently, tenderly, with a steadily increasing pressure until she couldn't wait any longer to learn his mouth with the firm tip of her tongue. She thrust it slightly between his lips and stopped, waiting for the answering thrust she expected. When it didn't come she searched for it in an exquisitely invasive rush, until she had captured his tongue firmly between her teeth, and had abandoned herself to a long discovery of its wonderfully sensitive surface.

Sam was kissing her back now, kissing her back powerfully, but still he was not advancing beyond the boundaries she established, Jazz understood in a flame of delicious, incredulous impatience. She could just go on kissing him like this—or she could stop, which was the silliest idea she'd had in a long time—or she could do whatever she wanted to do to this big, beautiful, tricky creature who claimed that he wanted so badly to start out all over again with her. But she had to show him what she wanted to do, or he would restrain himself. He'd make good his threat, or was it a promise? A matter of national pride, no doubt.

Jazz leisurely unbuttoned Sam's shirt all the way to the waist and started to kiss her way with agonizing deliberation down the warm, good-smelling, good-tasting flesh of his throat and his chest. From time to time she stopped, as if she had decided to go no farther, testing him, and then, as if she were almost reluctant, she continued, until she reached his nipples. With a teasing lack of haste she fastened her mouth on one of the points and took the other gently between the first three fingers of her left hand, rolling her fingers around the tiny, sensitive bit of tissue that was almost lost in the blond hair on his chest. Instantly they both became stiff, and as she sucked on his right nipple, he gave a great groan, which only made her fasten herself on him more closely, playing with him, flicking hard with her tongue, withdrawing it, then attacking again, meanwhile never letting up the growing pressure of her rolling fingers, which she had moistened in her mouth.

Jazz felt Sam's whole long body pull together, every muscle tensed as he held himself resolutely still under her aggression. He didn't permit himself another sound, but he couldn't control the mad pace of his heart or the wild sound of his breathing. She felt her whole body trembling with this new experience of making a man *take* more pleasure, controllingly, unrelentingly, than he should be able to endure without moving. She felt herself swelling and growing wetter, as she realized again that he was there for her to plunder as she willed; she grew even more purposeful as her curiosity leapt ahead of her actions and she wondered, in a bewilderment of anticipation, if he was ready for her, if it was difficult for him to contain himself, if it was hurting him to lie there so rigidly, if this was a game he had invented or if someone had taught it to him.

Jazz raised her head inquiringly, but his eyes were squeezed closed. "Is this . . . too much?" she murmured.

"God no . . . no . . ." he replied in joyful, shuddering supplication.

At least he wasn't wearing a belt, Jazz thought, as she unzipped his jeans. She went still, holding her breath. He wasn't wearing anything but his jeans, and the open fly revealed a penis so thick, so long, rearing so strongly upward from its tangle of blond hair, that she was unable to go any farther.

"I . . . can't . . . you have to," Jazz said in awe, even as her shaking fingers began to undo the buttons of her work shirt and liberate her breasts.

"No . . . you have to . . . I have to know you want me." Sam's voice was strangled but adamant.

"Oh, I want you, all right," Jazz muttered as she stood up, never taking her eyes off him, and stepped out of her jeans and her panties. He'd won this game already, by whatever rules there could be, but since he still insisted on playing, she'd give him a match to remember, she thought, in luscious vengefulness, and she lowered herself until her knees were on the rug. She opened her thighs wide apart just in back of his head so that her mound was placed above his mouth, but she held it high enough so that his tongue couldn't possibly reach it as long as he lay where he was. Jazz bent forward over his body so that her hair would fall and touch his penis. Then she moved her head gently from side to side so that his straining, jerking organ was lashed softly by a million little whips. Her hips swayed in supple unison with her head and, once again, she had the feeling of knowing exactly what he was seeing above him in the firelight.

Now she heard him groan again and again, but she didn't falter in her teasing rhythms, nor did she approach any closer to his body. She knew that the revealing moisture of her parted lower lips must be clearly visible to him in the leaping flames, but she continued her shameless, slow motions. She knew that he could see her whole body above him, the full, hanging globes of her breasts, the swollen circles of her nipples, the taut swell of her belly, the whiteness and softness of the insides of her thighs.

No man could stand this forever, she thought, as she moved more purposefully, lowering her head so that her lips were almost on top of his penis, so that he could feel the warmth of her breath and die for the

touch of her tongue, a touch that didn't come. She
was right, as Sam reached one long arm up and pushed
her carefully down to the rug, turning her over and
holding her down while he pulled off his jeans. He
opened her with one hand and entered her with one
steady push, for she was so ready for him that there
was no resistance. Then he stopped and held steady,
although the need on his face matched that on hers.
Still he didn't move, although he was inside her as far
as he could go. For the last time he asked, passion
now unmistakably bright in his eyes, "You're sure?"

"You win, you bastard! You win! Yes, I'm sure!"

Liberated at last, steadily, strongly in command,
thrusting deliberately and knowingly, Sam Butler gave
Jazz the long, piercing climax that she was so instantly
ready for, waiting until she was in the middle of her
splendid, frenzied release before he allowed himself
to grind into her body without holding back and join
her own spasms to the first mighty, relentless strokes
of his masterful orgasm.

11

Valerie Kilkullen Malvern and her sister, Fernanda Kilkullen, temporarily Fernanda Nicolini, lived in a chronic condition of mutual disapproval, yet, in the manner of so many sisters, found each other indispensable. No other friends in their individual worlds could be trusted so implicitly. No other friends could be so counted on for sound and shrewd advice as could these two women who shared a common history. No other friends could understand and feel true sympathy for certain of their basic points of view. Mutual disapproval was an insignificant price to pay for their deep complicity.

They knew many of the same people and traveled in many of the same circles, although Valerie's life had been one of a single conservative marriage and Fernanda's one of constant upheaval and travel. More often than not, they made the time to end their afternoons with a quick telephone call before dressing for dinner, so that they kept informed of each other's activities.

Several months after they had returned from the

Fiesta at the ranch, they spoke together as the New York twilight, exciting with the promising glow of a crisp winter, deepened outside their well-lit apartments.

"Did Mother reach you on the phone today?" Fernanda asked.

"Yes, but I was out," Valerie replied.

"Lucky you. Unfortunately, I wasn't. Poor timing on my part, so you owe me one."

"What did she have to say, besides making sure that everything's in order for her visit?" Valerie asked.

"How do I always manage to block out the date of her arrival?" Fernanda giggled.

"How is it that I always get stuck with having her stay with me?"

"Now, Val, you know I can't have a guest the way things are with Nick right now. Especially not Mother."

"But you must admit that it's utterly unfair. You always have the same excuse, Fern. One day even you will run out of husbands, and I'll make you take her for keeps."

"But those men gave me so much trouble," Fernanda said plaintively.

"Fern, that just doesn't impress me. I think you do it on purpose, to provoke."

"Oh, Val darling, I'll send tons of caviar and flowers and champagne and I'll take her for lunch and dinner as much as possible but I just can't face having Mother living in my guest room, the way Nick is carrying on."

"Damn the department stores," Valerie hissed.

"And their damn sales," Fernanda concurred. "It's too much, four times a year."

The sisters paused, a pause that admitted that there was nothing that would stop their mother from descending on them for one of the three or four visits to New York that she made each year.

Lydia Stack Kilkullen had made her permanent home in the Spanish resort of Marbella for three decades.

After her divorce and Mike Kilkullen's immediate re-marriage to Sylvie Norberg, she had devoted long hours of calculating thought to the problem of where to establish her future home. She didn't take her daughters into consideration, since she planned to send them to boarding school in the United States, no matter where she decided to live.

London, although there would be no language problem, was totally out of the question. It was Philadelphia society's favorite port of call. Historic friendships and close family relationships existed between London and Philadelphia, London was the foreign city in which a Philadelphian would feel the most at home, and Liddy had determined, in the hours following the discovery of her utter humiliation, to get as far away from her native city and its gossiping citizens as possible.

She eliminated Rome for another reason. It was the period of *La Dolce Vita;* in that noblest of cities, international moviemaking was at its height, and Rome was known as "Hollywood by the Tiber." Liddy had no intention of finding herself in the same city in which her husband's new wife would reign as a queen whenever she chose to arrive there. *Two* Mrs. Kilkullens? Impossible.

Paris presented other problems. Liddy still could speak some Foxcroft French, and she imagined that she could conquer the language if she applied herself. She had an ear for languages, and she'd heard enough about Paris from her mother and her aunts to understand that without French she could never live there happily. It was the only key to the city. But Parisians, of the kind she would hope to move among, Parisians of the upper class, simply did not get divorced. Religion and tradition combined to make even the most unhappy marriages last forever, and she, an unknown American divorcée, would find herself very much the odd woman out. She assumed that even in Paris, given enough time, she'd find a few friends, but why set herself up in a position in which she would start out as an underdog?

At last she decided to move to Marbella rather than to any large, cosmopolitan center. In 1961 it was barely a year since the Austrian prince, Alfonso Hohenlohe, had begun to make the little fishing village into an international resort, and three hundred million dollars was earmarked to be quickly invested in Marbella and its surroundings.

Marbella, the ancient home of a few fisherfolk, was a port on the Costa del Sol of Andalusia that had never before existed in the eyes of the world. Liddy cleverly understood that she would be among the first residents, a distinction which would give her an instant, established position among the visitors, as well as put her on a basis of equality with the European aristocracy, largely Austrian, who were busily developing the resort.

Just as important was the fact that in any resort, by its very nature, there would be no line drawn between the divorced and the married. Languages would be no problem, since most of the people whom Hohenlohe would attract spoke English as their second or third language. And the stream of temporary visitors would be so full of lively, ongoing gossip that no one would bother to remember or repeat anything as essentially dull as the story of a cast-off wife who'd lived in the outback of Orange County and had been raised in Philadelphia's equivalent of cold roast Boston. Nobody would have heard of the Kilkullens, or even of the Stacks, strange as that might seem. It was the perfect chance for a fresh start.

Liddy found a rambling white villa, in rather poor condition, but with a view of the sea. She bought it in the nick of time, before the prices started to go up and continued to rise for decades. The villa was within a short stroll of the hub of all activity, the lively hive of the Marbella Club, which she joined instantly, for she saw that it was going to become a magnet for the fun-loving world.

One of the worst deprivations of her married life had been that of lively company, Liddy had realized during the year she had just spent in Philadelphia.

Even the muted, feminine hum of the Acorn Club had been like Mardi Gras compared to the stillness, the remoteness of the ranch. Except for Deems and Nora White and the people she had come to know through them, she would, by choice, have had no social life at all. And of all the Whites' group, only Deems had been important to her. She missed him terribly, she missed him every day, but she could hardly have remained linked to Mike Kilkullen just to continue her burning, ardent friendship with a married man she could only see in public.

Now, in Marbella, Liddy found that lively company was what the place was about, the grail of both the aristocratic Europeans who followed the lead of Prince Alfonso and came to Marbella in increasing numbers, and the bands of international sybarites, beautiful and famous moneyed drifters, who asked nothing more than sun, sex, drink, dancing and a bit of dinner, so long as it wasn't served a minute before ten-thirty at night, when the languid, possibility-filled night of Marbella officially began.

All over the western world there are a few women like Liddy Kilkullen who can astutely analyze the problem of what to do with their otherwise unsatisfactory lives, and decide, with all the facts laid out hardheadedly before them, that the answer is to become a certain kind of hostess.

Single, widowed or divorced, such women judiciously and prudently accept the fact that they must not lead their lives in expectation that a man will come to their rescue. They determine, as Liddy did, to rank among the famous hostesses—not an easy métier, nor one for a woman who is lazy, inefficient, or without connections and iron nerve.

Within their different means, these clever women entertain with rigorous regularity; some give modest cocktail parties, some give grand dinners, some can afford to invite people to country weekends; knowing that if the fashionable world can be lured to gather at their homes, eventually there must be reciprocity.

If hostesses set themselves up to wait patiently, and never falter in the *dependability* of their entertaining, soon they will be asked here and there, and eventually everywhere. Liddy never had any intention of settling down in Marbella and staying planted there. Her villa was designed to become the vehicle by which she would eventually regain all the potential worldliness she had forfeited when she married Mike Kilkullen.

Liddy allotted herself the most insignificant bedroom and bath in her new home. She spent most of Mike's settlement money on restoring the villa, putting in a swimming pool and doing up the three large guest suites she carved out of the various rooms of her large establishment, turning them into accommodations so well conceived that in them the most world-weary guests would feel pampered.

Each suite had a big, pretty bedroom, well lit for reading, with deep chairs, wonderful beds, and a dressing table with a comfortable bench and a big triple mirror. French doors opened to a private balcony that looked out at the ocean. Each bedside table held a large carafe of cool bottled water, an airtight tin of freshly baked cookies, a new box of *Boules Quies*—the French wax ear plugs that had saved many a marriage—an unopened box of tissues and another of imported chocolates. The sitting rooms were as spacious and comfortable as the bedrooms, for Liddy knew that no couple wanted to spend all the free time of a holiday holed up together in the same room; that sometimes one or another would want to nap or read without disturbing the other.

The new bathrooms she had designed were conceived with every thought for convenience and luxury. The towels were the thickest in Europe, the plumbing was up to the minute, the bidets and the toilets each had their private cubicles.

These suites were designed for visits of at least two weeks; the closets held dozens of padded hangers, the embroidered Spanish bed linen was more luxurious than anything that could be found in the Uni-

ted States, the pottery vases of fresh flowers were
changed every other day, and the magazines, from
many countries, were replaced every week. Liddy's
Spanish chef was trained to cook in an international
style, and when she had guests, she always gave parties in their honor, asking the most impressive of the
local residents and their guests: the Bismarck clan,
Prince and Princess Alfred Auersperg, the Baron Guy
de Rothschild and his wife, and Baron and Baroness
Hubert von Pantz.

Liddy started entertaining slowly. She had to be
careful with her invitations so that she didn't bring the
infection of Philadelphia gossip to Marbella. Her first
guests were Deems and Nora White. From the moment they arrived, she and Deems fell back into their
mutual obsession with each other, and Nora, fascinated by Marbella, never noticed it in spite of the fact
that Liddy was now without a mate. She asked long-
unseen friends from Foxcroft and older, established
European friends of her family's. Everyone accepted
her invitations, for Marbella had quickly become the
most desirable destination of the International Set.
Soon Liddy began to make friends among the many
aristocrats, both British and European, who came to
stay at the Marbella Club, and added them to her
house parties.

In a matter of only several remarkably discrimi-
nating and well-managed years, Liddy Kilkullen's
house parties during the Marbella high season became
an institution, discussed on the society pages of newspapers, and written about in magazines. Her unfortunate divorce was overlooked in Philadelphia, as her
old friends wrote to her in her alluring exile, hoping
for invitations.

Liddy always filled all three guest suites since, in
her opinion, less than six guests didn't provide enough
gaiety or variety. She rose hours before they did to go
over the menus with her chef, to give orders to her
industrious little maids, to buy the best produce at the
local markets, to arrange the flowers, and to telephone

to check on the day's arrangements, making sure that the invitations to tennis, lunch and cocktails, on one of the yachts anchored in the harbor of Porto Banus, were all organized satisfactorily. Of course, there was always the Marbella Club, the blessed club where everyone ended up sooner or later, but the bills there had an unpleasant way of adding up, and although no one ever realized it, Liddy had to be careful how she spent her money.

Since visitors to Marbella had nothing to do but amuse themselves, entertaining was the primary occupation of every woman who had a house there. With the energy and attention to detail that Liddy expended, she could have run an excellent, small Swiss hotel. Once the house had been done over and furnished, none of her guests would have guessed that she could entertain in her lavish, openhanded style merely on the alimony she received from Mike and the additional ten thousand dollars' income she had inherited.

In return, Liddy was invited to stay at great houses all over Europe, England and the Eastern Seaboard. She was as marvelously professional a guest as she was a hostess. Although she remained beautiful, she never threatened any woman's marriage; sexual intrigue only interested her in the form of gossip; she quickly picked up as much Spanish, French and Italian as she needed to make conversation with any bore in any civilized country; she could be counted on to play tennis and bridge expertly and to charmingly animate any dinner table.

But Lydia Henry Stack Kilkullen, in spite of the success with which she established herself in the whirlwind of international society, never forgot the period of her life when only her wits, luck, timing and hard work had enabled her to rise from the ashes of her divorce.

She was *owed,* she would brood, when she had a moment to herself, *she was owed.* No matter how successful she was now, no matter how many invitations she received or issued, no one could ever repay her for those years of her marriage, the forever lost, wasted, joyless years of what should have been her glorious young womanhood. She should never have been forced to cater to guests, she should have been —always—the one who was catered to, the one about whose comfort others worried. Even now she had to keep careful books, to worry about the rising cost of living in Spain, where it had once been so cheap; even now she had to think about pleasing, always pleasing, in her own house or in the houses of others, for she was a single woman, and a single woman must always please.

There was no financial revenge, she realized bitterly, nothing she could do to claim what should have been hers, as the rapidly developed land all around the Kilkullen ranch turned to pure gold in the hands of builders. But through her clever tongue, her network of friends and her knowledge of the inside workings of her world, Liddy did manage to take a steady revenge for the disappointments of her life.

If a woman she didn't like was foolishly indiscreet and Liddy Kilkullen heard about it, the news found its way back to her husband, although no one ever knew how he had learned the truth. If a new hostess attempted to establish herself in Marbella, and she was someone without sources of power, she found herself frozen out, and never suspected what Liddy had said about her. If a married man preferred men and thought it was a secret, he was unmasked by Liddy Kilkullen if it suited her purposes, but no one could ever point to the source of information. She knew who took drugs, who drank too much, who cheated at cards, who had married for money and regretted it, whose sexual tastes were unsavory or criminal, who owed too much money and to whom it was owed.

She was like a clear, ever-flowing well in a village from which all the inhabitants dipped their pitchers, never knowing that the water they drank might make them ill. As she grew older, Liddy grew more vengeful, more sophisticated, more amusing, more poisonous.

Only one human being besides her daughters was entirely safe from Liddy's evil: Deems White. He and Nora were invited to Marbella at least twice during the season, and soon Nora became addicted to what she considered her unique position as part of the Marbella set, and made no objection to the frequency of their visits, which cost no more than the price of the airline tickets.

Nora White and Henry White, Deems's father, had good reason to feel that their ambitions for Deems were prospering. Henry White was a leader of the Orange County Republican Party, and Nora could be counted on for heavy and steady contributions to anyone her father-in-law favored.

Deems raised no objections to their newly formed political ambitions for him. It was more congenial, and more amusing, for such a charming man to win votes than it was to litigate. During the 1960s he had held a number of local offices, each one more important than the preceding one. Nora drew the line at his running for statewide office, for she couldn't imagine herself living in Sacramento, but Congress was altogether a different matter, she realized when her father-in-law raised the possibility.

If Deems was elected to Congress, the Whites would live in Washington part of the year and in San Clemente for the remainder, and in both places, with Nora's well-invested, ever-increasing income, they could cut a splendid figure. Her exposure to the pleasures of Marbella had induced Nora to pay more attention to her looks and her clothes, and she had transformed herself into a perfectly acceptable-looking woman who was, if nothing else, instantaneously perceived to be rich. Since she was good-humored and polite, people spoke well of her, as people always enjoy speaking of their rich friends, feeling the richer themselves.

Deems White, in his early forties, was easily

elected to Congress. He was a natural candidate; he spoke extremely well in public, and his grasp of issues was clear and sensible; he was a part of a Republican family who had lived in Republican Southern California for generations; and he charmed the voters as he charmed everyone else. The only surprise was that he hadn't run for the office sooner. Nora was a happy woman, thrilled by the success of her ambitions for her husband and certain that this was only the beginning of an honorable career.

Liddy watched over Deems's rise in government from Marbella, now far closer to him than ever before. On the first visit the Whites had made to Marbella, right after she had finished her villa, she and Deems had finally found the blissful solitude they had never been able to establish in California. Nora never grew accustomed to the late Spanish nights that ended after three in the morning. Every afternoon, after the late lunch out by the pool or at the club, she slept deeply until it was time to dress for cocktails. Deems and Liddy, unlike Nora, drank nothing at lunch, and unlike Nora, they needed little sleep.

During each of those afternoons, when all of Marbella was still, Deems would come to Liddy's room, where she waited for him, the shutters drawn against the sun, her piqué bedspread removed by her maid in preparation for Liddy's siesta, her embroidered silk sheets freshly changed each morning. A creamy ocher light shimmered in the corners of the room, where drops of sunlight pooled on the terra-cotta floor, but otherwise the room was almost as dark as night. It was never too warm in the cloistered room, nor was it ever too cool; lilies and jasmine perfumed the air.

Liddy wore her dark hair shingled as short as a boy's now, but she always changed into one of the superbly made, modestly cut, satin-and-lace nightgowns that she ordered in Madrid. When she let Deems in, after his single tap, she locked the door securely behind her.

Wordlessly, without any explanation, they slipped into Liddy's open bed together, Deems wearing nothing but the accepted houseguest uniform of swimming trunks. Usually they were utterly content just to lie intertwined, close, close, in the miraculous twinship of their dreams, Liddy's face buried in Deems's neck, his face touching the smoothness of her short hair, so intimately connected by the contact of skin on skin, breath on breath, sigh on sigh, that they wanted nothing more.

When he was at home in San Clemente, Deems White was in the habit of leaving his office several times a week, giving one of a hundred reasonable and uncheckable excuses, and driving rapidly to San Diego. There, in the depths of the dark, squalid bars near the port, he would rapidly select and pick up a young, unknown sailor from the naval base. For enough money the sailor would follow him to a cheap hotel, where Deems would penetrate the young man in furtive, frantic, potent secrecy and exquisite pleasure. He would stay with the sailor as late as he dared, using him often and purposefully. On these frequent trips to the nearby port, Deems found the absolutely necessary relief for the inadmissible longing that he had hidden all of his life.

Now, when he had not bent over a young and willing man in a few days, now when he was a houseguest at Liddy's, now when he was lying in her bed, utterly safe from the world, now when he became aware of the muscular firmness of Liddy's buttocks and the strength of her legs, sometimes he would feel his penis rise and fill as they held each other so chastely. Deems would wait until he was certain that he had an erection that would not go away. When he felt himself in the sure grip of a ferocious impatience, he pulled off his trunks.

When she realized that he was naked, Liddy would turn her head away, never looking down. Silently, with only a touch, Deems would indicate to Liddy that he wanted her to turn around in the bed, so that her back was toward him, and pull up the hem of her nightgown so that she was exposed up to her waist. She moved as elegantly and deliberately as an athlete as she raised one of her long, smooth legs so that she was spread open far enough to receive his penis. Her eyes closed, her breathing scarcely quickened, she refrained from a single movement that would indicate that she had any other expectation of him but this silent, slow, sweet intrusion. Sometimes he simply remained inside her for a long, long, close time without thrusting at all, clasping her from behind with his arms. She would relax backwards into him with a sigh of pleasure, but she never rocked her buttocks in an insinuating way that would have suggested that she wanted him to do anything more. Sometimes they fell asleep in that position and woke later, with a feeling of mysterious joy.

Yet on other occasions when Liddy held herself still in that undemanding position, Deems would reach down and pull up her nightgown so that he could caress her between her legs, touching her body with so little aggression, almost absentmindedly, for such a long time and with such great delicacy, that she would be unable to hold back the noiseless, subtle, but profound climax that Mike Kilkullen had never been able to win from her.

More often, as the days of his visit went on, and Deems lay there with his eyes closed, pressed up against her firm rear, as far inside her wet softness as he could go, it would happen that he imagined that she was a young sailor, a very young and tender sailor in whom he had engulfed himself more easily than most, and then he would come to plunging, sudden life inside her with an urgent vigor that would have astonished his wife. When he finally poured himself into Liddy, a smile of utter contentment would cross her lips, but she never claimed any matching satisfaction.

No matter what took place during their siesta hours in Marbella, Liddy and Deems never spoke of it to each other afterwards, just as they never parted their lips when they kissed. Whatever it was that they had together was perfect for each of them. Its precise nature would have been disturbed by words, its marvelous mystery dissipated. They had always understood each other. Now, every afternoon of every Marbella vacation, year after year, they could touch each other in ways that satisfied them both utterly. It was enough to know that it would continue forever, as long as there was a room in which they could lock themselves away while Nora slept.

Clothes had always been a problem for Liddy Kilkullen. The rich European and American women who became her closest friends dressed with enormous expense and rarely had to repeat a dress. No matter if they spent their days in bathing suits and tennis clothes, their evenings demanded elegance and lots of variety.

Eventually, Liddy Kilkullen realized that the big sales at New York department stores provided her with the only way to dress almost as well as her friends. Since European haute couture was completely beyond her means, she contented herself with the best of American ready-to-wear. Once her daughters were married, when she stayed with them in New York there was the additional economy of the hotel bill. And, of course, it was nice to see the girls in person instead of just keeping in touch by phone, no matter how annoying they usually managed to be.

Fernanda's marriages were a disgrace, but it wasn't her fault that she was so attractive that men wouldn't leave her in peace. Valerie was stiff and dogmatic, but she'd never let anyone guess that she didn't have the marriage she'd expected, and that, as Liddy well knew, was a quality much to be admired.

In any case, it was her clear duty to stay with them in New York, to keep her eyes open, listen well, test the waters around them and then tell them the things that children unfortunately never wanted to hear. If a mother couldn't rub her daughters' noses in a few home truths, who could? Who would bother? Everything she said to them was for their own good, and at heart she was sure they knew it and took her advice and warnings seriously.

A saleswoman at Saks and another at Bergdorf's

were instructed in Mrs. Kilkullen's needs and her schedule of visits. Pleased and flattered by her confidence, for she told them exactly where she went, whom she saw, how she needed to dress and, especially, exactly how much she had to spend, they set aside clothes for her as soon as inventory-taking began and last season's garments were marked down. Often, when a dress came in that was clearly a buyer's over-enthusiastic mistake, a dress they knew would be hard to sell because it was hard to wear, too highly styled for the average woman, they would keep an eye on it for Liddy. If it was snapped up by some clever woman before it was marked down, they felt a genuine pang. Soon they started to put those garments away in their private "hold" bins, before anyone else had a chance to buy it. Liddy never failed to write to her two sales-women from Europe, on letter paper that bore the names of great houses, and give them the latest gossip and tell them how successful her clothes had been.

They knew her size, which had remained a perfect eight for the last thirty years, and they knew she wouldn't buy any dress that demanded great jewels to make it work. They knew that Mrs. Kilkullen no longer liked to expose her underarms or her elbows; they knew that her slim waist, her magnificent shoulders and small bosom had remained highly presentable, that her legs were as good as ever, and that she didn't have to wear a bra in an evening dress, so that she could afford to reveal a smooth and well-muscled bare back. Liddy had always watched her diet, and she swam two hundred laps daily in her pool. Mrs. Kilkullen was a pleasure to work with, each of them thought in satisfaction, and neither of them guessed at the existence of the other. They looked forward to the big sales as a chance to be of service to her again.

"After all, she is our mother," Fern sighed finally, holding the telephone idly.

"There ought to be a statute of limitations on having given birth—it's not that major an achievement.

Even you managed to do it three times without too much confusion.''

"Red Appleton, Val, that tramp Father's been seeing—have you heard anything new about her lately?'' Fernanda continued, ignoring Val's words.

"I talked to a friend in Newport Beach this morning who said she'd bumped into them last night at some great little Chinese place called Five Feet. She said they were very, very cozy,'' Valerie replied crossly.

"I don't like the sound of that. Not at all. We've been hearing about them every week since the Fiesta.''

"She's half his age,'' Valerie estimated, "and gorgeous.''

"And there's no question that Father's crazy about her,'' Fernanda ordained in a disapproving voice. "I wonder what he's like in bed?''

"Now *that* is truly disgusting,'' Valerie said. Fernie was so predictable.

"I couldn't agree more, Val darling. Still, wouldn't you like to know? No, you probably wouldn't. Not an ounce of normal curiosity in your long, chic bones, is there? Anyway, talk to you tomorrow.''

Valerie began to change for another ordinary dinner with Billy, ordinary Billy, handsome Billy, none-too-bright Billy Malvern, who had always been good in bed, as Fern had managed to worm out of her years ago. At least she didn't have to cope with that dreadful Nicolini person. She hoped Fern would get rid of him quickly. She was quite enough of an embarrassment all by herself, without her latest husband.

The next day, Valerie, who had reinforced her preferred mode of impenetrability by shielding her eyes with her wide-rimmed, lightly tinted tortoiseshell glasses, sauntered around the site of the future Madison Avenue Settlement show house. From time to time she gave a glance at the list of the rooms that had been assigned and the decorators to whom they had been given, all based on a lottery system because of the impossibility of any committee making such decisions without a full-scale war.

One year Valerie had received a tiny maid's room, tucked away at the top of the house, one year a ballroom, and yet another year, the most difficult of all, a kitchen. She was pleased with her assignment of a child's room since it was neither too small, like the maid's room, nor too technical, like the kitchen, nor too big, like the ballroom, which had been a nightmare to fill. People were so unreasonably sentimental about children that her second-floor bedroom would be seen by everybody.

Since her rude but potentially useful cousin, Casey Nelson, had been cool to her idea of a little boy's Western room, Valerie had decided to go in a totally different direction. She would design a room for twin girls of ten. Ten was the ideal age at which all children should be quick-frozen. It avoided all the messy problems of puberty, so that the fantasy wouldn't be interrupted by parents wondering what might be happening in the room while they were away on weekends in the country. It also bypassed dealing with the clichés of a small child's room.

Valerie moved through the chaos of the house, wearing her useful glasses. She had perfect eyesight, but with her glasses on she could seem to be inspecting something with nearsighted attention while she was actually listening to what people around her were saying. Not eavesdropping, of course, but just keeping informed. It was amazing how invisible she could become by wearing glasses, and a blouse and skirt of flat beige, unrelieved by a handsome belt or interesting jewelry.

Experience with doing a room for a show house had taught Valerie the value of casing the competition during the first hour, while everyone's guard was down. All the other decorators were standing in their stripped and often unpromising rooms, most of them complaining about the location, the size, the number of windows, the height of the ceiling or some other undesirable feature they had just realized they were stuck with. Valerie had only given a quick look at her second-floor room, although her assistant, Crumpet Ives, was busy taking measurements there. While there was time, she wanted to cull hints about what her neighbors and competitors would be up to. There was much to be gained in testing the waters of today's newest "ins" and "outs," for in the world of interiors these could change overnight.

Valerie Malvern knew that she wasn't an originator. If she occasionally wished that she were, it was in the abstract, the way a man might idly wish he were Kevin Costner, without bitterness or a spark of useless hope.

Her comfort was that there had only been a few genuinely original talents since the days when a young American woman, Elsie de Wolfe, created a new profession: that of a person who takes over an entire house and decorates it for money. Until that day the insides of houses fell within the province of cabinetmakers, architects and tasteful amateurs, Madame de Pompadour first and greatest among them.

Valerie was quite aware that her work was competent, so long as a client didn't want the contemporary and innovative. Rare was the woman who had the stomach for contemporary, and even rarer was one who demanded innovation.

"I tell you, John, chintz is out. O-U-T. Oh, it's still all right in England, if it's been in the house for decades and has a faded, dusty patina. Your great-grandmother's chintz is still acceptable, but in New York it's become a joke. Remember what Rebecca West said, 'The chintz was singing its old vulgar song'? It's not even nouveau riche now, no matter how much it costs, just O-U-T."

Valerie edged closer to the two men, who were standing by a bay window against which a new building had just been put up, posing the problem of how to block out the lack of view.

"I don't care what you think, Nicky, this room

isn't doable without pattern everywhere. And that means chintz. It's less of a yawn than toile de Jouy, for Pete's sake, and people have used it for three hundred years. Doesn't that tell you something? It's timeless, not in or out.''

"Bore, bore, *bore*. That's what it tells me, John. Saturation. I say we do this as a garden room. Outdoor furniture and trellises on the walls. We can bank these windows with marvelous trees—really big ones. It doesn't matter that they'll die without light; they won't croak until the show is over. I see it as part of the whole new feeling about ecology. Didn't you read that quote of Mark Hampton's? It's so delicious. 'Even people who feel incapable of being natural should strive for natural interiors.' ''

"What the hell do you suppose that means? Give me a break, Nicky. Cecil Beaton did the ultimate garden room a hundred years ago. What's O-U-T are trees and green plants of all kinds. *That's* what's reached the point of no return. Also big bouquets of massed roses, all that Victorian starched white linen on tables and beds and pillows, and, need I say, the whole ghastly country-western look.''

Valerie moved on. Whenever decorators started griping about country-western they grew unreasonably nasty, since so many of them had installed vacation house interiors that were inspired by New Mexico just before the fad ended.

She collected a number of overheard tips in the next hour, each one negating another. What seemed to be in, Valerie decided firmly, pushing her glasses back on her head and putting on the earrings she'd left in her purse, was utter confusion about what was in and what was out.

New Yorkers put a monstrously unreasonable burden on having the perfect interior because the minute they set foot on the street they were confronted with the dehumanization and degradation of their city. Even the few steps from apartment house to limo exposed them to things they couldn't allow themselves to see. The square feet of private space they owned or rented gave them the only refuge they had from the crumbling outside world, and their frantic, obsessive efforts to turn their homes into islands of comfort and peace had seeped down to the decorators who catered to them.

Once decorators had been calm tyrants, semi-benevolent dictators for whose smile a client was grateful. Now the clients were so rich and so demanding, so aware of what other rich people had, thanks to *HG* and *Architectural Digest* and *World of Interiors,* that members of the decorating community were scrambling to keep ahead of each other, in much the way that the residents of the Hamptons did.

There was nothing to be learned from her colleagues, Valerie thought, as she confronted her own allotted space for the first time since she had taken a rapid glance at it earlier. It must have been a dining room at one point in its history, since it had two double doors on each side of the wall at the far side, doors which the fire laws dictated must be kept open, but otherwise it was a good size and shape for what she had in mind.

"We'll simply have to work around those doors, Crumpet," Valerie said to her young assistant, whose boarding-school nickname, Muffin, had become so common that she'd changed it officially, with a party at Le Club. "But otherwise the room seems adequate."

"You won't say that, Mrs. M., when you hear what's going on in the next room," Crumpet said, a look of alarm crossing her unexceptional features.

"What have you heard?" asked Valerie. That was the utter hell of show houses. Adjoining rooms could kill each other if there wasn't some element of visual harmony between them, since you could see from one to another so easily.

"It's been assigned to Lady Georgina Rosemont, and she intends to turn it into a man's playroom paradise . . . a man whose hobby is electric trains. She's planning tracks that will go up for seven levels across the back of her room, which means that our own open double doors will be crisscrossed by the tracks up to eight feet."

"She can't do that," Valerie snapped. "The fire marshal won't let her."

"He's already been to see it. She promised to leave six feet open behind the tracks and he gave her permission. The trains will be running all .day long, state-of-the-art electric trains with a whole miniature landscape built around them. They'll be a terrible distraction, don't you think, Mrs. M.?"

"That's one way to put it, Crumpet." Valerie looked for a windowsill on which to sit. She was weak in the knees.

Lady Georgina Rosemont was the new and uncontested winner in the top New York wives' race, taking the prize the first year she had lived in the city. No, not just taking the prize, but being *accorded* it, Valerie thought, faintness turning to nausea. Only twenty-nine, she was more beautiful than Blaine Trump, she was richer than Carolyne Roehm Kravis, and she entertained more frequently than Gayfryd Steinberg, yet she had been entirely spared the habitual nasty sniping in the press that was growing more outspoken week by week, as envious journalists snarled, spat and bared their teeth at the ladies with new money.

Lady Georgina's recent and worshipful husband, Jimmy Rosemont, who bought companies for breakfast and sold them for dinner, had given her a decorating business as a toy for Christmas. She operated it with the massive help of talented assistants lured away from the best firms in town by doubling their salaries.

She was also, most unfairly, an earl's daughter, with a family tree that went back to William the Conqueror, which really, truly was the final, utter, bitter end, because who, among all the women jockeying for position at the top of the ladder, could tell you their grandmothers' maiden names?

Valerie's mind raced, trying to think of a way to somehow block out the noise of electric trains, but she knew that unless she turned the twins' room into a

nursery for quintuplets and managed to keep five live
and identical babies penned up in a crib in the middle
of the room, she was doomed to failure. In any case,
you couldn't have animals in a show house, so that
rule probably applied to babies too, assuming they
could be procured.

"Mrs. M.," Crumpet's worried voice said, "are
you all right?"

"No, Crumpet. Would you be?"

"We're in an unenviable position, aren't we, Mrs.
M.?"

"Please, Crumpet, I'm thinking," Valerie said
absently, while she watched Mrs. Rosemont in animated conference with three assistants in the next
room. It was a *fait accompli* that her man's playroom
was going to be the hit of the show, both from the
point of view of the public and the publicity. The
media were fascinated by Lady Georgina. It was a
new idea for a show house, and with unlimited funds
and assistance there was no way she could go wrong.
But, to look on the bright side, if Mrs. Rosemont could
somehow be persuaded to give up the electric trains,
the contrast of a grown man's fantasy and the twin
girls' ballet fantasy might, just possibly, complement
each other, since they both had a childlike element,
and yet were so different.

Valerie got up and walked rapidly into the next
room.

"Lady Georgina, I'm Valerie Malvern." Valerie
extended her hand, smiling.

"Well, Mrs. Malvern, how very nice. I understand we're to be neighbors."

"Yes, we are. And, like all neighbors, we're facing a tiny problem. I do hope we can solve it."

"I hope so too." Valerie studied Georgina Rosemont, her heart falling. This was a really secure
woman. All the top New York wives were tall, and
added the highest of heels to make them look even
taller, even though they towered over their husbands
in their bare feet. All the top New York wives were as
thin as women could get without perishing of hunger.

All the top New York wives wore expensive, magnificently tailored designer suits in the daytime, and had a hairdresser who came to the house every morning to ensure that they were always perfectly coiffed in case a photographer happened by.

Georgina Rosemont was petite and wore sensible, low-heeled, highly polished walking shoes. She was gently and delicately rounded, from her rosy, smiling face to her shapely calves, and looked happily well nourished. She wore a well-cut tweed skirt, neither too long nor too short, a gray cashmere sweater, and no jewelry but pearls at her ears. Her auburn hair was parted on the side and fell simply to her shoulders in a way that betrayed nothing but a good brushing. If you ignored her astonishing beauty, so great that she used almost no makeup, she looked just like a sensible citizeness of . . . Philadelphia. Damn the Brits! When they did it right, they were superlative.

"Lady Georgina—"

"Oh, please, just Georgina. And I'll call you Valerie, shall I? So much simpler."

"Georgina, the electric trains—"

"You've heard already? I must admit, I am totally enthralled by it. The idea came to me in the middle of the night, my very own brainstorm. When I thought of the trains, I knew immediately that it was perfection. Jimmy, my husband, used to have a passion for electric trains when he was a poor boy and his parents couldn't afford them, but somehow I hadn't thought that a grown man would adore to have the trains he wasn't given as a child."

"It's a marvelous idea, I do agree," Valerie said hastily, "but I'm afraid that you'll, well, to put it bluntly, wipe out my room with the sight and sound of your trains."

"Oh, Valerie, surely not! As I understand it, we're all supposed to do whatever fits into our spaces and just let the public be entertained by it. I'm sure that whatever you have in mind will stand up beautifully to the background of my sweet trains."

"I'm planning a room for ten-year-old twin girls,

with a ballet theme," Valerie said, smiling with as much conviction as the earl's daughter.

"You see, I knew it! Your twins would love to be ballerinas, and my man would love to have been an engineer. It goes awfully well. Our two rooms will bring out the buried child in men and women. Why, Valerie, it's not a problem at all."

"But the noise—"

"Think of it as background music. In fact, why don't you have something from *Swan Lake* playing in your room so that no one will notice the sounds of the trains? Oh, but you're so clever, why should I be giving you suggestions? I know you'll find the perfect solution. I have to be on my way, but I'll be back tomorrow at about this time. Will I see you then? Yes? Splendid. Till tomorrow, then."

Valerie Malvern watched the retreating form of Lady Georgina Rosemont. There'll always be an England, she thought sourly. But for every one of her ancestors who had refused to sign the Declaration of Independence, there had been at least two who'd fought in the Revolution. That battle wasn't over yet. It had not even been joined.

Fernie had her uses, Valerie had conceded long ago, and helping with the show-house problem might be one of them. Fern's daughter, Heidi, had gone through an acute attack of balletomania that had lasted almost four years before she grew out of it. Surely she would have some suggestions for the show house, or even an idea of something entirely different to do that would trump Georgina's ace. Sometimes, oddly enough, scatterbrained Fern came up with an original idea that she, Valerie, might have overlooked. She telephoned her sister and asked her to meet her at the house the next day.

"You have to do something with *this?*" Fernanda said in dismay as she looked around the room, seeing the walls on which paper hung in tatters, and the ugly, chipped radiators under the windows.

"Don't concentrate on the wrong thing, darling.

It's always a mess until we get started. I'd visualized it perfectly—very Old Vienna, two dear little gilt four-posters draped in great poofs of the kind of tulle they use for tutus, masses and masses of tulle at the windows, sheet music scattered on a stenciled and lacquered floor around a marvelous old harpsichord—pianos are madly fashionable again, even if you don't play, so a harpsichord would be even better—and wreaths of dried flowers in shadow-box frames on the walls—romantic and girlish and fairy tale-ish. But that Englishwoman, who should have stayed where she came from and wowed the competition in her own backyard, is going to ruin *everything* with her electric trains. A delicate room like mine will fade out entirely."

"What if you had huge racks made and put them in front of those double doors and hung all the girls' clothes on them as if they didn't have closets?" Fernanda suggested. "You could create a sound barrier if you hung school clothes, dress-up clothes and all their ballet stuff, toe shoes, leg warmers, costumes, just massed in."

"I thought of that. It's a good idea, but not good enough."

"Why not do the room you thought of for Casey Nelson, and add a mechanical bucking bronco like the one in that movie with Debra Winger and John Travolta—remember, it was about a bar in Texas?"

"It's a possibility," Valerie said. "But I'd need two mechanical broncos, one in front of each door, and that would be painfully obvious. Broncos don't make sense without people on them. No, it's loud and distracting, but it doesn't work either."

"Isn't that Lady Georgina?" Fernanda asked, nodding in the direction of a woman who had just walked into the next room.

"Yes. I think that's her husband with her."

"The famous Mr. Rosemont?" Fernanda asked thoughtfully.

"Why famous? Just because of his corporate raiding or greenmailing or whatever they call it now? Surely that's nothing at all these days, if you keep out of jail. He just does it better than the others.''

"Val, you amaze me. That man is famous for his love affairs. Even you should know that. Apparently he's the heir to the Aly Khan's ability to keep it up for hours and hours . . . something to do with mind control. Eastern religion—mysticism—''

"Darling, do you think you could keep your mind on *my* problems for a minute?'' Really, Valerie thought, in the midst of this catastrophe, could Fernanda find nothing better to do than to meditate on the eternal subject of her pelvic region?

"Fernie, where are you going?'' she cried in alarm, as her sister started resolutely in the direction of the other room, her dark green lizard cowboy boots clicking on the bare floor, her blond hair tossed about defiantly, her body flamboyantly encased in a burgundy suede jacket and tight trousers, lavishly trimmed in silver. Fernanda didn't stop to answer.

"Hi,'' she said, walking up to the Rosemonts. "I'm Valerie Malvern's little sister, Fernanda. Val, poor dear, is too shy and reserved for her own good, which is what comes of being from Philadelphia, so she didn't want to say anything about your trains, but I just know that you'd simply never, ever do something that wasn't sporting, would you? Even inadvertently.''

Fernanda turned from one to the other, her face alight with vivid, urchin conviction. She was a compelling mixture of girlishness, coquettishness, worldly wisdom and rascalry. "I do love your idea, Lady Georgina, it's so much fun, but let's face it, a whopping monster set of trains next to *any* room, not just my poor sister's, wouldn't be considered quite—well, quite playing the game. It's going to sound as if a street carnival is going on in here, all that hooting and tooting and whistling and stopping and starting and general clanging around. It would be the *greatest* thing at a private party, Lady Georgina, but I'm afraid you might find that there will be a lot of carping from the other decorators—the trains will have an impact on every room on this floor.''

"Oh dear," Georgina Rosemont said, blushing. "I hadn't really thought of that—but perhaps you're right. I don't know . . .''

"I think—it's Fernanda Kilkullen, isn't it?—is right, as a matter of fact," Jimmy Rosemont said. "I thought you might be getting a little too ambitious, pet, but I didn't want to spoil your fun.''

"Well, I'll just do without the trains, then," Georgina decided, looking plaintively at Fernanda. "Oh well, so much for brainstorms in the middle of the night.''

"Oh, you are a perfect darling!" Fernanda exclaimed. "I knew you'd understand, once I'd explained it to you.''

"Your father's Mike Kilkullen, isn't he?" Jimmy Rosemont asked.

"Yes, he is. How'd you know?''

"We sailed our yacht up the coast of California last summer, and when we passed your father's property I asked what it was—you could see Portola Peak all the way out to sea for over a hundred miles. It was a most beautiful sight. I was amazed to learn it was part of one huge ranch that was still privately owned. Did you grow up there?''

"Yes indeed.''

"That must have been marvelous," Georgina Rosemont said.

"Oh, it was . . ." Fernanda replied automatically, as she took a rapid inventory of Jimmy Rosemont. His reputation as a cocksman was obviously not going to be explained by his exterior, she thought. He must be at least forty-five, perhaps older, fairly short and a little too plump in spite of his well-tailored suit. Still, he was a most attractive man if you liked the devilish look. He had devilishly pointed eyebrows over devilishly lively black eyes and a devilishly lubricious mouth in a foxy, clever, alert face. If you were any kind of a hound, you'd chase him on sight. If you were any kind of a woman, you'd lie down and spread your legs.

Valerie joined the group.

"Val, Lady Georgina isn't going to have the trains after all," Fernanda said. "And this is Mr. Rosemont. He's seen the ranch from the ocean, and knows who Father is."

"Should I apologize for my sister?" Valerie asked, hiding her relief. "I can't imagine what she's been saying to you."

"Nothing that didn't need saying," Georgina Rosemont replied. "I do hope I didn't worry you with my mad train idea."

"Well . . . yes, a bit. But I'd never have said more than I did yesterday. I hope you're not too disappointed."

"Of course not. Tell my husband what you're planning—it's a lovely idea, Jimmy."

"Listen, why don't we all go have lunch together?" Jimmy Rosemont proposed. "I'm starving, and I can only listen to decorating talk for so long before I get antsy. You two ladies can go at it to your heart's content, and I'll talk to Fernanda about life at the ranch."

He shooed Valerie and his wife in front of him and stopped Fernanda from following them. "I understand your father has about sixty thousand acres," he said, as Valerie and Lady Georgina walked toward the door.

"Uhmm, more or less."

"That's interesting."

"Fascinating," Fernanda agreed. Jimmy Rosemont had taken her by the arm in such a way that he had brushed her ass with the heel of his hand for the briefest of instants. There was no possibility that the contact could have been inadvertent, but also no way in which it could have seemed deliberate except to someone who wanted it to be. Fernanda leaned her body into his side just a trifle more than was necessary, and looked him straight in his rakish eyes. A smile of impure temptation formed on her pouting lips at what she saw there.

"I thought you were starving," Fernanda purred, and released his arm slowly. "Shall we join the ladies?" she suggested.

"May I call you for lunch someday? I'd love to hear more about growing up on the ranch."

"What a good idea," Fernanda agreed, and hurried after her sister, her boots clicking a tattoo of savage anticipation on the uncarpeted floors.

12

Jazz leaned back in her favorite chair at the ranch, a worn leather armchair that had somehow escaped being re-covered in seventy-five years, and surveyed the three people gathered around the great fireplace in the living room, where one of the first fires of the California winter blazed.

There was her father, looking fifteen years younger than he had at the Fiesta only a few months earlier. Maybe it was because his new tweed sport jacket of subtle shades of dark gray, in an inadvertent trick of contrast, caused his thick white hair, cut in an even shorter crewcut than usual, to look almost blond. Maybe it was because the winter rains had started heavily, with much more rain predicted, so that Mike could begin to relax about the eternal water problem; maybe it was the notoriously flattering firelight; maybe it was just that he was glad to see his darling daughter safely back from the Land of the Rising Sun; maybe —and there was always that possibility—maybe he was feeling the benefits of passing over certain daily responsibilities that he had hoped for when he made

Casey Nelson Cow Boss. Whatever it was, Jazz decided, it was real, not just something in the flickering orange light, and she found herself puzzled, for her father looked not just younger but, in some subtle way, *different*.

Jazz hadn't seen Mike Kilkullen in weeks. She had returned four days ago from a trip to Japan, where she had shot three separate portrait and life-style stories for *Connoisseur, Vogue* and *Sports Illustrated*. All three commissions had come in simultaneously, right after Traffic School, for interest in the new Japan was growing steadily as it established its economic presence in the United States.

Vogue had assigned her to photograph the ten most beautiful women in Japan in their own homes; *Connoisseur* had wanted portraits of the outstanding figures in Japanese literature and art, and *Sports Illustrated* had needed action pictures and informal portraits of the Japanese baseball, golf and swimming champions.

Jazz had taken along both of her assistants, and left Sis Levy to coordinate everything from Dazzle. It had been an exhausting, fascinating trip, and she'd spent every night since her return at home in Santa Monica, trying to arrive at the other side of a massive case of jet lag.

Sam Butler had telephoned her almost every day while she was gone, and he'd met her at the airport and whisked her home. For one glorious hour of fervid reunion, Jazz thought that Sam had invented the quick cure for jet lag, but the next day she'd been totally wiped out, and since then she had functioned in a semi-fog, doing nothing more than shoot two fashion spreads for Barney's new Beverly Hills store, before she went back to her apartment, falling asleep before dinner, waking up at three in the morning and staying up, unable to fall asleep again until it was time to go back to Dazzle. She'd booked herself out yesterday, a Friday, and arrived at the ranch in the late afternoon, falling asleep immediately after dinner with her father last night. When she woke up at noon today, she felt rested for the first time since her return.

Earlier this evening, Red Appleton and Casey Nelson had joined Jazz and Mike Kilkullen for dinner at the·El Adobe in San Juan Capistrano, a landmark that had been built of adobe bricks in 1778, by far the best restaurant in town and Mike's favorite. Jazz had been so hungry, after a reviving afternoon galloping around the ranch, that she had barely paid attention to the conversation of her three companions while she devoured the great Mexican food in the restaurant that was uniquely agreeable on a wet night.

Richard O'Neill III owned the El Adobe as a hobby. His historic ranch, the Mission Viejo, was almost as large as the Kilkullen Ranch. Once the O'Neill family and their cousins, the Baumgartners, had owned the Santa Margarita y las Flores, a vast possession of some 230,000 acres, but the Marine Corps had taken over more than half of it at the beginning of World War II, turned it into Camp Pendleton, and never given it back as it had first promised to do. Richard O'Neill, like Mike Kilkullen, belonged to an old family, woven into the fabric of the land, a family that had also married Land Grant aristocrats. They had developed some of their land for residential and commercial use, but they had retained the largest part of it as natural ranchland on which they continued, like Mike Kilkullen, to raise cattle.

Now, in the firelight, Jazz observed that Red Appleton looked subtly different from the way she had looked at the Fiesta. Although she knew that her father and Red had been seeing a lot of each other, somehow Red, like Casey, hadn't been around on Jazz's weekends at the ranch during the early fall. Meanwhile, Red had let her hair grow so that, instead of a severe boy's cut, it now curled whimsically in casual bright wisps around her face. For another thing, Jazz noted, she'd gained weight. For Red to gain weight had to mean something important.

During Red's years as a great model, she'd always been as underweight as the métier demanded, a good fifteen to twenty pounds too little for her height, judged by any reasonable calculation. Even after she became a fashion editor, during the period when Jazz had first known her, Red had fanatically maintained her model's figure, so brainwashed by the discipline of years that she was convinced that if she dared to relax for a single decent lunch or, heaven preserve her, an honest dinner, she'd wake up the next day with a body fit to float overhead among the balloons of the Macy's Parade on Thanksgiving Day. At the Fiesta, Jazz had noticed that Red was even more willowy than ever—approaching scrawny—as if her fast-track married life had not permitted any time to eat.

But tonight, at the El Adobe, she'd kept pace with the rest of them instead of pushing food around on her plate, and although she was wearing black slacks with an easy cut, and a dolman-sleeved black silk blouse, garments which conceal the shape as much as anything can, Jazz's eye could spot the fact that Red, like a girl of fourteen, had sprouted new, unmistakable and very becoming breasts. She even had a nicely rounded bottom where once she had only had bones.

Was Red letting herself go at last, Jazz wondered, after the discipline of over twenty years? It must be the relief of getting rid of her husband. Or perhaps it was the influence of the good life on Lido Island, that pure platinum spit of land off Newport Beach, where almost every one of the four- or five-million-dollar houses on the bay side had its own yacht landing; Lido Island, where the outboard-motor-powered "cocktail boats" rocked gently next to the yachts, and were used far more often as their owners visited each other each evening, their little boats gaily strung with multicolored lanterns and stocked with what were perhaps the last cocktail shakers in California.

Yes, Red had changed, mysteriously changed, in ways that weren't limited to her hair or her weight. An expression of . . . contentment . . . or was it peacefulness . . . had replaced the permanent look of underlying tension Jazz had always seen on the face of her old pal, her old buddy, her dear old Red, who had given her such a lot of work when she was just starting out after Phoebe started to rep her.

Yes, Red looked different and her father looked different. Why not admit it, Jazz asked herself suddenly. Why not admit that they looked different because of each other? Why was she looking for explanations beyond the obvious? On the night when she'd been ambushed with a speeding ticket, on that dismal night when Gabe had had the nerve to show up at her apartment and talk her into letting him move into the studio, on that altogether curious night when the LAPD had lobotomized her, she'd been unable to reach either of them on the phone, but she certainly hadn't begrudged either of them a little friendly meal together.

But it was one thing to know, as she did now, that they saw each other—you certainly couldn't say that they "dated," because they were far, *far* too old to date—on some sort of regular basis, and it was quite another actually to see them together. *Quite another* thing to see them touching each other's shoulders or arms or hands or knees, as if to emphasize a point in conversation—but with far more frequency than could be considered within the range of normal behavior, unless you happened to be a member of the Yiddish Art Theatre; quite another thing to see them catch each other's eye and smile privately or, worse yet, not even smile, just exchange a wordless glance for a little too long; quite another thing to catch a tone in her father's voice when he talked to Red that she, his very own daughter, couldn't remember hearing before in her whole life; quite another thing to watch Red sneak a look at Mike Kilkullen when he wasn't looking at her, and *quite another thing* to watch her father mooning at Red when he thought he was unobserved.

Just what the fuck is going on here, Jazz asked herself, getting up from her chair and wandering around the room. Can't they behave like grown-ups, for God's sake, if not in front of me, then at least in front of Casey? Have they no shame? What on earth can make people lose all sense of human decency and carry on like teeny-boppers at their advanced ages? Haven't they any idea of how ridiculous they look? No wonder Red hadn't been around when she'd visited the ranch these last few months—if they didn't have the self-restraint to keep their hands off each other, they probably were so ashamed that they didn't want her to see them together. God almighty, you'd think that they had invented sex, or whatever it was they still did at their ages. She expected more dignity from her father, more class from Red, more maturity, at a very minimum from them both. He was sixty-five, for Christ's sake, and she had to be forty-one. Didn't anybody *ever* become an adult?

Casey put another log on the fire without being asked, looking relaxed and altogether too much at home, Jazz thought wrathfully. He certainly had changed since the night of the Fiesta. Now that he was wearing the most thoroughly broken-in boots she'd ever seen, a flannel shirt that had faded until she couldn't make out its original plaid, and clean but ancient jeans. Yet his clothes suited him. He looked like a Cow Boss. Everything about him was of a piece now, and he moved with unconscious ease and the same easy grace with which he had danced with her on the night of the Fiesta. Casey might be a city boy and a clever investor, Jazz admitted to herself, but horses and cattle were clearly his game too.

These three people, lounging in front of the fire, were the most boring, bovine bunch she'd ever spent time with, Jazz decided, her peregrinations around the living room bringing her to a stop in front of the fire. The backlighting brought out a nimbus of crisp, bright hairs around her head, and her golden eyes shot topaz sparks. She treated them all to a determined smile.

"Wouldn't it be wonderful," Jazz said, "if there were sixteen different types of men and women, instead of the hideous boredom we're condemned to with just two? As an example, let's say that you, Casey, happened to be born a Type Nine. You'd go to a cocktail party and you'd get into conversation with a girl and pretty soon you'd exchange numbers. She'd say that unfortunately she was a Type Five or a Fourteen—clearly out of the question for you—but that her friend over there was a Type Eight or a Seven or a Ten or an Eleven, or even—jackpot!—just like you, a Nine. Now you'd have the whole range of types from Seven to Eleven to pick from—five different types of girls with wonderfully different and amusing . . . attachments . . . diversions . . . surprises . . . variations . . . but each one just enough *alike* so that with a little goodwill and minor adjustments, everybody could manage to get it on. Maybe, if you were particularly broadminded and athletic, a Nine, like Casey, could establish imaginative and rewarding consensual sexual relationships with a range of types all the way from a Six up to a Twelve. At least he could give it a shot. I can't imagine why the Almighty stuck mankind with so little choice. He did a hell of a lot better with Chinese menus."

"Hmmm," Red murmured.

"Brilliant," Casey observed. "Tallulah Bankhead used to say that she'd had men and she'd had women and there had to be something better—I think you've just figured it out."

"Jazz," Mike Kilkullen said, "the way I look at it, two is just perfect. The Almighty couldn't have done better if He'd tried. In fact, I believe He did try, and two was His best shot. Come on, Red, I'll take you home. You look sleepy."

"Good night, Red, 'night Dad, I'll see you in the morning," Jazz said.

"Don't count on it, honey. But I'll try to be back before—well, I may not make it for lunch—but definitely before you have to leave for L.A."

"Right. Well, I'll see you when I see you."

Red and Mike both kissed Jazz quickly, waved at Casey, and left in unceremonious haste. There was an instant of total silence in the living room of the Hacienda Valencia.

"A Nine, huh? Is that what you'd think I'd be?" Casey asked.

"Oh, shut the fuck up!"

"Would you be a Nine too?"

"Stop trying to change the conversation!"

"What conversation?"

"You know what I mean."

"Oddly enough, I do."

"You couldn't possibly. You haven't got a clue, Casey Nelson."

He walked over to the music room and sat down at the concert grand that had been Jazz's great-great-grandmother's pride and joy, and lazily played a few elegant chords that quickly resolved themselves into "Smoke Gets in Your Eyes." Casey sang quietly, in a rusty but true baritone.

> "They asked me how I knew
> My true love was true,
> I of course replied,
> Something here inside,
> Cannot be denied . . ."

"Did you hear me?" Jazz said furiously, rushing to the music room, "I said to shut the fuck up, not to do a piss-poor Bobby Short impersonation."

"Just sending a message," Casey said, continuing to play. "Since Western Union stopped delivering and I can't fax you because you don't have a fax except at Dazzle."

"Casey," Jazz said in bewilderment, sitting down on the piano bench next to him. "You've been here for months while my father's been carrying on with Red. Tell me what's happening."

"I just did." He stopped playing and turned to look at her.

"True love? Red and my father? You can't *mean* that!"

"That's the way it looks to me."

"How would you know? What makes you an expert? It's just a fling. Look at how they behaved— they're so . . . so blatant! Why don't they take out an ad, for Pete's sake. 'Hello world! Guess who just rediscovered their long-lost hormones?" It makes me want to throw up."

"Listen, Jazz," Casey said gently, "let's imagine that you're truly in love. Are you in love, by the way?"

"Certainly not," Jazz said indignantly. She definitely wasn't what she'd call in love with Sam Butler. She wouldn't let herself be in love with the love object of tens of millions of women, no way—absolutely not. Only civilians fell in love with actors.

"Well, let's try to imagine that you're crazily in love with . . . oh, just about anybody . . . for the sake of argument, let's say that you've fallen for me, since I'm the nearest able-bodied male in the neighborhood. Now you're convinced, by your foolish heart, that I'm the best-looking man in the world, brilliantly intelligent, incredibly sensitive, sexy beyond sexy, a Fred Astaire on the dance floor and . . ."

"Well, you do dance very well, I'd have to agree with that," Jazz said grudgingly.

"Try to extrapolate, Jazz. I put it to you that you also believe everything else I just mentioned. All for love, and the world well lost—that bit. Naturally you couldn't help showing how you feel."

"Just where is this improbable scenario going?" Jazz was suspicious of every word Casey said. It was probably no more than an elaborate pass.

"Would the way you felt about me be a reason for you to love your father any less?"

"Of course not," Jazz said calmly. "In your heavy-handed way—your *habitually* heavy-handed way, I might add—you're suggesting that I'm afraid that my father might love me less because he's got the hots for Red. You're missing the point—it's the juvenile way he's acting that shocks me. My father, the Mike Kilkullen I've always known, would never, *ever* have been so obvious about the fact that he was staying at her house tonight. He just about drew a picture, for God's sake!"

"Were you ever madly in love?"

"Maybe . . . maybe when I was a kid, years and

years ago. Everyone's been in love once, for heaven's sake," Jazz sputtered. "What does that have to do with it?"

"Did you *behave* as if you were in love in front of your father? Did he ever notice it?"

"I suppose he must have been aware of it." Jazz suddenly remembered her father, in a white fury, showing Gabe the photograph she had taken of her mother when she was eight, when she and Gabe had come down to inform him that they were taking off for Nicaragua together.

"But didn't you still love your father just as much as you ever had? One love didn't cancel out the other, did it?"

"Not . . . exactly . . ." Jazz said thoughtfully, ruefully. "Not really, not ever, nothing could."

"I rest my case."

Jazz burst into tears, wailing inconsolably, her fists beating on the top of the piano. Transfixed and astonished, Casey put his arms around her and she huddled into his chest, contorted by deep waves of sobs that had in them a mysteriously mournful violence he couldn't understand. He stroked her hair as if she were a little girl, holding tightly to this grown-up woman who had so quickly become a miserable bundle of childlike grief. Casey made the kind of little understanding noises that he hadn't known he was capable of, and patted her patiently and comfortingly. Eventually her tempest of misery began to die down to individual sobs and sniffs. He didn't dare ask any questions. He seemed to have done enough harm already.

"I was a total *shit* . . . total, total," Jazz gulped. "It was almost as if Dad didn't exist . . . he was lucky if I telephoned to tell him I was still alive . . . for more than two whole years! I can't believe the way I treated him . . . oh, Casey, whatever he does, he'll never do that to me, will he?"

"Jazz, baby, come on, make some sense. Your father isn't an innocent eighteen-year-old girl in love for the first time in . . ."

"How did you know how old I was? How did you know it was the first time? How did you know I was innocent?"

"Ah . . . I . . . it's . . . *fuck!*"

Jazz rose accusingly from the piano bench and stood furiously, arms akimbo, looking at Casey.

"Haven't the two of you great, big, strong, silent goatherds got anything better to do than sit around discussing the old details of something that happened to me years and years ago? Which you don't have any right to know about at all because it's none of your damn business and he should have known it! Damn it all to hell, now I'm really pissed off!"

"Oh, *damn.*" Casey closed his eyes and beat himself over the head with his closed fist. "Damn it! You don't understand at all. It just—well, it just happened to come up one night . . . you know how people get to talking very frankly about themselves and their families when they start to get to be really good friends . . . and sometimes they say something they shouldn't have said, in passing, by accident, Jazz, only once, honestly—we never talked about you and Gabe again. I swear it."

"Gabe. You even know that," she raged.

"Is Gabe some kind of sacred name? Cool down, Jazz, please. I beg you. Now listen to me. One night when your dad was talking about your mother, he told me how you'd consoled him, kept him company, just about kept him from going mad after her death, even though you were only a little girl yourself—and then he happened to say something about this guy Gabe who came into your life. He said that you grew up all at once in an awful rush, and for a couple of years he was worried sick about you, terrified that you'd always be rushing around from one riot or war to another, but there wasn't anything he could do about it, he couldn't stop you any more than he could stop your mother from going away and doing what she had to do."

"Dad talked about my mother?" Jazz asked in

great wonder. "He never even used to mention my mother . . . we never . . . we just never could . . ."

"Well . . . he has."

"I don't understand it. How could he talk about her to you, to someone he hardly knows, when he's not even been able to say her name for years and years to me?" Jazz's voice was lost.

"He doesn't say a whole lot, and not often, either, but sometimes he will mention something, something she did or said that was special. My own guess is that it's because of Red. It doesn't have anything to do with me. Now that your father's able to love someone else, he can bear to talk about your mother."

"Twenty-one years," Jazz said falteringly. "He spent twenty-one years with only a daughter to love."

"Yeah, but a real interesting one."

"But I'm a selfish bitch!"

"No."

"It was *vile* of me to be jealous of my father and Red. I've been thinking such rotten, unfair things about them. I've been behaving like the worst kind of dog in the manger."

"No."

"Why not?"

"Because."

"Grow up, Casey, 'because' is not a satisfactory answer."

Casey Nelson stepped forward and put his arms around Jazz again. He picked her up and carried her over to the sofa and sat down with her in his lap, still holding her so tightly that she couldn't wriggle or even squeak. Then he started to kiss her tear-stained face and lips and he didn't stop until he felt that he had thoroughly made her understand what "because" meant to him.

"Wow," Jazz whispered.

"There's only one thing wrong with you," he said, and kissed her for another five minutes.

"What is it?" Jazz asked when she could breathe.

"You talk too much."

Jazz studied his face. She had decided on the night of the Fiesta that this lion cub of a man looked obstinate and generous, and she hadn't changed her mind. But at close range there was far more to be observed on his blunt features. He had a reckless mouth capable of the most ardent, full-hearted, brimming kisses, kisses of a power that she would never have guessed at. His freckled white skin was so much more . . . intriguing . . . than skin without freckles. It made you want to . . . touch it? Maybe. See how far down the freckles went? Possibly. But it was the furrows of intensity on his forehead that made the tips of her fingers itch. Those furrows were as irresistible in a man as dimples or a cleft chin—particularly since a dimple or a cleft chin had clearly specific limits, and furrows suggest a thousand possibilities for caresses. Of course, he looked like nothing much compared to Sam, but what man did? Just a little touch wouldn't hurt. Would it?

"Jazz?"

"Hmmm?"

"I'm coming up to L.A. next Wednesday to see my accountants. Could we have dinner together?"

"You mean like a date?" Jazz said, in the ingenuous manner that was as close as she came to a mating call.

"Exactly like a date."

"Wouldn't that be sort of weird?" she asked in an irreproachably naive complaint. "You live right here, you're the Cow Boss, you're a member of the family—I'm going to be coming back next weekend anyway, and I think the Lakers are playing the Supersonics Wednesday. Isn't it a little artificial to go out on a date?"

"I don't want to wait until next weekend to see you again," Casey said, as deliberately obtuse as she.

He rubbed her level eyebrows the wrong way with one finger, and she shivered in delight. Jazz tightened her arms around Casey's neck and kissed him with all the imperative witchcraft at her command.

Casey Nelson stood up abruptly, holding her steady by the elbows so that she wouldn't fall.

"Are you going somewhere?" Jazz asked in a little, larky voice of exemplary virtue and ingenuous wonder.

"To take a cold shower."

"Why?"

"Because I'm not going to try to seduce you under your father's roof while he's away."

"What on earth makes you think that you could possibly seduce me?" Her voice was offhandedly wanton, dangerously gentle. She wasn't all that easy to seduce, Jazz thought, not under any roof. Not at all. Just let him try and he'd find out how impossible it was.

"Good night, Jazz. Sleep well."

"Well, Mel, what do you think? Is Gabe humping Phoebe or not?" Pete di Constanza asked, as the two men met outside the entrance to Dazzle.

"You'd have to be pretty desperate . . ."

"Or pretty horny . . ." Pete agreed.

"Or generous," Mel suggested kindly.

"Or ambitious—yeah, ambitious," Pete said suspiciously.

"Maybe he likes very bony ladies." Mel shook his head disapprovingly.

"Nah, it's not the bony part that turns me off about Phoebe, I could live with bony, and Phoebe's not bad looking when you think about it. It's her attitude," Pete di Constanza insisted. "I mean how can you *begin* to imagine doing it with Phoebe, she'd be telling you where to put it and how you were doing it wrong, and how you could do it better, and how long you had before she was going to lose interest, and how much she was going to take off your fee unless you got it right . . . you know."

"I can't possibly consider it, Pete, not in such lurid detail—God, man, you're *perverted*—but face the facts. He's getting more than twice—maybe three times—as much of Phoebe's attention as we are, or Jazz for that matter, and we're the moneymakers around here. Gabe still hasn't done any major shoots —he's been away too long to have really caught on yet.''

"She suddenly doesn't have the time to make phone calls for me—she's always on the phone about Gabe.''

"She hasn't bid out some important shoots for me, she's too busy getting Gabe off the ground. I almost lost the Campbell's Soup account last week,'' Mel agreed.

"And they have lunch together three times a week,'' Pete said. "Not take-out either, but Market Street. I'll bet she pays.''

"He's gotta be humping her,'' Mel decided. Lunch was conclusive.

"What a price to pay,'' Pete observed with gloom.

"We're the ones who're paying the price, Pete. For Gabe it may come under the heading of animal gratification.''

"Food photographers!'' Pete snorted. "You all think you're the philosopher kings of the world of commercial photography.''

"You asked me what I thought. No need to insult me.''

"Sorry about that. Just me being macho again. Occupational problem, comes from always working with heavy metal.'' Pete gave Mel a fraternal hug and the two men parted ways, content in their old friendship.

"Gabe,'' Phoebe said, pausing as she unhooked her bra, "have you ever covered a housewarming?''

"Come on, Phoebe, I asked you to rep me, not pimp for me. Come on, get naked. A broad of your wide experience should know that this isn't a time to talk business.''

"I will in just a minute, I promise, on my honor,

sweetie pie, but first, about this housewarming, it's going to be a very special occasion and they're only going to allow one photographer."

"So who's having a housewarming?" Gabe asked without interest.

"I can't tell you yet, lover, but it will be major news."

"News? A housewarming? I don't even do weddings. Cutting the cake, flower girls, throwing the bouquet. Spare me, kiddo. It's not my style. And don't call me 'lover.' "

"How do you know so much about weddings?" Phoebe asked suspiciously.

"I went to Monaco once to play blackjack, got trapped into Princess Caroline's first attempt. What a bummer. Never again. Get me a good funeral, I'll say yes, but if you don't stop trying to talk me into a party, I'm gonna lose interest in this other little matter we came here for."

"One last word, Gabe. *Money.*"

"Money?"

"The most you could get for covering any party in the world. Your shots would be everywhere from *People* to the front page of *The New York Times*, with tremendous international syndication guaranteed."

"So I'll do it. Now lie down."

Phoebe complied rapidly. Gabe had just made half her day, now he'd finish the job. Make haste while the sun shines. Gather ye rosebuds while ye may. Waste not, want not. Gabe was every bit as good in bed as rumor had always had it. No. Better. Much, much better.

Lydia Kilkullen and her two daughters settled into a banquette at La Côte Basque and glanced quickly and without the slightest interest at the menu. No matter what differences of opinion the three women might find on each occasion they met, they were in perfect accord on one thing: lunch was a meal of maximum lack of interest. The need to fuel the body during the day was the only excuse for the existence of lunch—

that and gossip. Anyone so misguided as to eat lunch for pleasure clearly didn't understand the first thing about upkeep.

For form's sake, Fernanda, who was paying for this lunch, consulted her mother and sister. Quickly they made their decisions.

"We're all having the same thing," Fernanda told the headwaiter. "First, cold asparagus without any dressing, and then the filet of Dover sole, off the bone, dry, no salt, with extra lemon on the side."

"White wine, madame?" the headwaiter asked.

"A large bottle of Evian, please."

"Yes, madame." He had lost any illusions a long time ago. At least these ladies understood that it was proper form to order bottled water. Some clients, tourists perhaps, just drank the stuff from the tap.

"It's a treat to be with both of my daughters again," Liddy said. "You both look marvelous."

"You're the best looking of the three of us," Fernanda said sincerely. She only hoped that when she reached her mother's age she'd be as chic as Liddy, since nothing else but staying in style would mean anything in that hideous, faraway, unimaginable future.

"Thank you, Fernanda, but after the frightful morning I've spent, I'm amazed that I haven't torn my hair out."

"Bad luck at Bergdorf's?" Valerie asked sympathetically.

"There were some good enough things, but I can't believe how expensive they are. What on earth has happened to prices? Even on sale, at close to half-price, there's almost nothing I can afford—there wasn't a single simple daytime dress for under seven hundred dollars, no long dress I would care to be seen in for less than twelve hundred."

"I'm sure tomorrow Miss Kelly at Saks will have a better assortment for you," Valerie said hastily. "Everyone says that Bergdorf's has become the priciest store in town."

"Let's hope so," Liddy said, trying not to sound

as discouraged as she felt. After one of her maiden
great-aunts had died, her fixed income of thirty-five
thousand dollars a year had grown to almost sixty
thousand. Her parents lived on, as healthy as ever,
controlling what little remained of the Stack estate.
Her family had always had far more history than
money, and even when they died, she couldn't expect
much. However, prices had continued to rise steeply
in Europe as the value of the dollar steadily lessened,
so that now Liddy could no longer live in Marbella in
anything approaching the style she had established
when she first went there thirty years ago.

   She hadn't so much as changed a slipcover or
bought new towels in ten years; she hadn't been able
to give the pool or the guest bathrooms the major
overhaul they needed; she had reduced her staff so
that now she ran her villa with only the help of one
maid, one gardener, and a cook. Liddy spent more
and more time every day filling in for the servants she
no longer had. She had reduced the number of house
parties she gave each year, although, of course, they
were the last economy she could make, for without
them, where would she be? Indeed, *who* would she
be? Incredulously, Lydia Henry Stack Kilkullen
began to feel as if she were the proprietor of a small
business who saw herself being steadily but surely
forced into bankruptcy.

   Worst of all, Marbella was no longer the drawing
card it had been for so long. She traced it to the evil
day when Prince Alfonso had sold much of his ownership in the Marbella Club to a fabulously rich Saudi
Arabian, Al-Midani, who, to the universal dismay of
the residents, had allowed so much development to
take place that the town was now disfigured by tall
apartment buildings and shopping centers. Almost all
of Liddy's friends had abandoned their homes on the
coast and moved inland to the hills behind the Cadiz
road, building mansions worthy of Beverly Hills in
new residential developments.

   The town of Marbella itself was still full of people,
but they weren't the right people anymore, Liddy

thought acidly. The new visitors were unspeakably awful. They made the invasion of rock stars and back-gammon professionals of the seventies look as brilliant as the truly golden, glorious sixties. Her friends continued to come to her house parties, but the day would soon come when an invitation to her villa would no longer bear any cachet.

In fact, that day had come already, if she were to allow herself to face the truth. It was only habit that made her friends return each year. What did they say to each other at night, in their guest suites? Had they noticed all the signs of deterioration that she knew were there, or did her still-meticulous hospitality outweigh the fact that the Marbella Club was no longer glamorous, the fact that although the Archduchess von Hapsburg, the Bismarcks and the Rothschilds were still coming to Marbella, their main topic of conversation was how much it had changed for the worse?

"I'm counting on Miss Kelly," Liddy said, as lightly as possible. "I won't begin to really worry unless Saks lets me down too. Now, Fernanda, what's new in your life? Exactly what is going on with you and that husband of yours?"

"Nothing much," Fernanda said with false calm. It certainly hadn't taken old Mum long to get down to the most unpleasant subject she could have raised.

"From what I hear, I have every reason to be concerned about you."

"No, really not, Mother. Val, do tell Mother all about the show house and the great electric train victory."

"Valerie told me the whole story last night at dinner," Liddy said. "I think you did well to speak up, Fernanda. Lady Georgina sounds like a most agreeable person. And her husband seems a sensible man, in spite of all the things one hears about him."

"He knew it was absolutely wrong even before she did," Valerie remarked. "We'll go over to the show house after lunch, shall we? The Rosemonts have turned out to be charming, both of them."

"Actually," Fernanda said, delighted that the

conversation had turned away from her troubles with her husband to the Rosemonts, "I bumped into Jimmy Rosemont the other day on Madison Avenue and we had a quick drink together."

"Did you indeed?" Valerie said with quick curiosity. "A quick drink?" How come this was the very first she'd heard about this meeting, she wondered. Fernanda had never been known for afternoon drinking, nor, she imagined, would a man as busy making billions as Jimmy Rosemont be strolling idly around the streets of Manhattan looking for people to pop into bars with. But even Fernanda couldn't have . . . yes, Fernanda not only could have, she *had,* Valerie realized, looking at the fugitive expression that was crossing her sister's face. My God, was there nothing she stopped at? Didn't she realize what a ghastly idea it was to mess with Georgina's husband? If it got out—and how could it not?—the whole city would be talking about it. Her damned sister was in heat every day of the year. And just when she and Georgina were getting on so well, too.

"When was that, Fernie?" Valerie probed casually.

"Oh, last week, I don't remember exactly. But he did say something I meant to discuss with both of you when Mother got here. He wants me to introduce him to Father."

"Why?" Valerie asked sharply, her fury at Fernanda's sexual activities forgotten for the moment.

"What else did he say?" Liddy asked intently.

"He said he had a business proposition that he'd like to put before Father, and that he thought it was always better to meet a man through a member of his family or a mutual friend."

"What did you tell him?" Valerie demanded.

"I said . . . I said that Father wasn't the easiest man to meet when it was a question of business, but I'd do what I could. Actually, I was stalling to see what you thought."

She could hardly tell them that she'd already

promised to introduce Jimmy Rosemont to her father, Fernanda thought. Their lunch, in the small, luxurious apartment she knew he kept for just such secret meetings, had been a disappointment sexually, but curiously enough she felt most kindly toward him. No man had ever showered her with such intelligent and detailed praise for the specific beauties of her body. More important of all, no man had made her feel so young in a long time. There was a great deal to be said for older men.

It wasn't Jimmy's fault that he'd been so excited from the moment they started to make love that he couldn't hide it. It wasn't his fault that she'd noticed the state he was in—who could miss it?—it wasn't his fault that she'd been overcome by that familiar disappearance of her desire when she realized that even if his endurance was as prodigious as it was reputed to be, he was basically just like all other men. All Jimmy Rosemont really wanted to do was put it in her and get his own satisfaction, and no amount of his elaborate foreplay could disguise that brute aim.

She'd been convinced that if she didn't fake an orgasm, he'd keep her in bed all afternoon, trying one thing after another to pry it out of her. He certainly got the prize for persistence. And she deserved one too, Fernanda thought, for the sheer artistry of the orgasm she'd produced. He, the legendary cocksman, hadn't been able to tell it from the real thing any more than any other man ever had, and she'd managed it with elegant dispatch, as soon as she realized that he'd never give up on her although she had been turned cold by his robust, athletic eagerness.

They'd parted in mutual good humor. He'd been delighted by her performance and she'd been pleased with his astute and discerning compliments. She'd told him that she couldn't meet him again because she liked Georgina so much that her conscience would bother her. A nice touch, that, Fernanda thought. It got her off the hook of having to go through another such experience, and it kept his self-esteem intact, always important with any man. If he wanted to meet her father, why not? That introduction, she knew for certain, wasn't why he'd asked her for lunch.

"Did he say anything about buying land?" Valerie asked.

"No, Valerie, a cow," Liddy said witheringly. "Of course he wants to buy land. Everyone has wanted the same thing for twenty-five years, and the answer has always been the same. Your father won't sell."

"I wonder," Fernanda said slowly, as if she were thinking out loud, "if Father marries Red Appleton, won't things change? Maybe he'll be ready to sell—won't he want to have more time to enjoy life? After all, Red's loaded, everybody knows that. It wouldn't be fair for him to ask her to give up her way of life and live on the ranch—and at the same time, how would it look if he lived on her money?"

Liddy choked on her Evian. "Marry!" she hissed when she'd regained her breath. "You talk about it as if it were a minor thing! What have the two of you not been telling me? How far has this business gone?"

"Fernie's talking off the top of her head, Mother," Valerie said hastily. "They've just been seen a lot together."

"Over a period of months and months, Val, and suspiciously often," Fernanda objected. She didn't like to hear her speculations dismissed so quickly.

"Neither of you has the slightest common sense," Liddy said angrily. "If there's any chance that your father might remarry, don't you realize what it would mean to the two of you? This Red person is only forty-one. What's to prevent her from having a baby or two, for pity's sake? And how do you know that the ranch wouldn't be left to any male child she might have? That's been the Kilkullen tradition since they came here out of the bogs and began to act like the British aristocracy."

"You don't really think that Father would cut us out of his will?" Valerie said incredulously.

"Why not?" Liddy said, trying to rein in her impatience with these criminally ignorant, naive children. "If he had a son, he'd be perfectly capable of leaving you and your children some worthless souvenirs and keeping the ranch in one piece, in trust for his son. He thinks both of you have quite enough money —which you do—and he's already paid for your expensive educations, thanks to me."

Valerie and Fernanda sat in stunned silence. With all their chat about the Red Appleton developments, neither of them had thought the matter all the way through to its logical possible conclusion. They were too accustomed to thinking of themselves as the inevitable Land Grant heiresses to imagine a Land Grant heir ever being born and taking their place. This was the modern world. Such things simply didn't happen. But they knew Mike Kilkullen and they knew he didn't live in the modern world.

"Naturally, you two haven't planned any counteraction," Liddy said scathingly.

"What can we do, Mother? We can hardly go to California and break up his little romance," Valerie managed to say.

"Both of you should be busy planning to spend Christmas at the ranch, you and every *single* one of your children. Fernanda, your Jeremiah is nineteen and Matthew is seventeen. Your Heidi and Valerie's three girls are all adorable. With six grandchildren, two of them young men, swarming all over him, your father won't have much time to see this Red creature, and he most certainly will realize that he has heirs already."

"My kids are planning to go skiing," Fernanda wailed.

"My girls have sub-deb parties all during the Christmas holidays, Mother," Valerie said.

"Absurd! None of that matters. They *must* be at the ranch. And in good spirits about it. No whining," Liddy snapped.

"Mother, it was one thing when you sent us to the ranch every time you possibly could—we understood why—but our children weren't born there, they don't know much about you and Father, we haven't brought them up the way you brought us up—how could we explain it to them?'' Valerie asked.

"I don't know and I don't care, but you've got to do it! If your father marries again, you'll have to share his estate with his wife even if he doesn't have any children. And then there's always Jazz, Jazz who practically lives there! A man can make a will any way he chooses. What if he leaves you practically nothing? What if Jazz and his new wife get the ranch and you get the cash in his account at the bank, the way I did? *I'm talking about billions of dollars*. Don't you two nitwits have the sense to understand that?''

Valerie and Fernanda exchanged a quick glance of terror. Ever since they could remember, their mother had drilled into them the fact that she had sacrificed her marriage to enable them to get the education and the advantages that good Eastern boarding schools and friendships with nice girls from nice families would mean. They knew that they owed her their escape from growing up as a pair of Orange County country mice. It had always been understood that when they did become heiresses, they would provide Liddy with a handsome percentage of their inheritance in return for all she had done. Both Valerie and Fernanda had never questioned this future arrangement, nor did they now, but they realized that their mother's panic was not just for them but for her own future as well.

Panic was not an emotion they had ever heard before in Liddy Kilkullen's voice, but as they heard it now, it infected them instantly. The three women sat silently, staring at the tablecloth as the waiter removed their half-eaten fish. Fernanda and Valerie were both frantically trying to decide how they could change their children's Christmas plans and force them to accept the trip to the ranch.

Liddy's mind was speeding far ahead. Deems White was now in his second term as Governor of California. He and Nora still came to Marbella when he was able to get away, even if it was only for a week at a time. The intense quality of their marvelous affinity had never diminished. The infrequency of their meetings only made them more important, more filled with meaning. Liddy never changed the severe, shingled haircut that Deems loved. Her body, fanatically exercised, remained as firm and muscular as ever, for she never wanted to change from the woman Deems had met one night in San Clemente and adored instantly.

Now, in the publicity that his office attracted, Deems White dared not find an outlet for his homosexuality. Liddy's room, with its shadowed, mellow afternoon light, its heavy scent of flowers, was the only place in the world where, in fantasy, he could become again the carefree young man he had been when he first entered her bed. When he came to her room every afternoon, he never left until both of them were satisfied. Although Liddy never guessed it, she had become his sailor.

Nora White, Liddy thought, had taken advantage of her position as First Lady of California, to give herself airs and graces that Liddy had been careful never to discourage, for Nora was a loyal friend. The Whites maintained a home in San Clemente, where they spent almost as much time as they did in Sacramento, and Nora, who had bloomed in sophistication as a politician's wife, knew all the gossip of California society. She would have every access to people who knew all about Red Appleton. Perhaps she had some information about Red, information that could be used against her. Liddy resolved to telephone Nora as soon as she returned from lunch. How could she have failed to do it sooner?

The waiter briefly considered asking if any of the three ladies were ready to order coffee—obviously they would never order dessert—and thought better of it. Perhaps in a minute or so, but not now, not while they were sitting there without speaking, as if they were angry with each other. They were very different, he thought idly, the beautiful young one with the long blond hair, the other one with her hair pulled back, the big nose and not enough chin, and the older one with a kind of unsmiling hardness in her face that you didn't often see when ladies lunched, yet there was also something alike about them. Something in their expressions, perhaps?

13

"**D**on't fly too low," Jimmy Rosemont instructed the pilot of the small helicopter he had rented at John Wayne Airport. "This thing makes too much damn noise as it is." In his hand he held a fold-out Thomas Guide map of Los Angeles, Orange and San Diego counties that he'd carefully marked the night before, in his suite at the Ritz-Carlton Hotel facing the ocean in Laguna Niguel. It was a fairly small map that covered a great deal of territory, so that only the crude outlines of the country below were indicated, but it served his purposes. He had already flown over the partly developed areas where the Irvines had once ranched, land now owned by Donald Bren.

Now there was a man he admired, Jimmy Rosemont mused, there was his kind of guy, worth zip thirty-two years ago, many billions now. The color photo of Bren in the *Forbes* annual issue of the richest people in America, in the small section devoted to multibillionaires, showed him wearing a rancher's cotton shirt, faded jeans and a conqueror's thin smile,

standing in the sunlight amid orange trees, looking
every inch the former champion skier and marine he
had been before he borrowed $100,000 to build his first
home way back in 1958. By 1977, when he had become
an extremely successful builder, Bren and four partners bought the Irvine ranch for a laughable $337 mil-
lion. When the partners hadn't been able to get along,
Bren had bought them out for $518 million in 1983.

Only seven years ago, Jimmy Rosemont thought,
his rascal's eyes dreamy, Bren had been able to buy
one-sixth of Orange County for that incredibly low
sum. How could his partners so have lacked vision?
Hadn't any of the other four hardheaded rich men with
whom Bren had co-financed the purchase been able to
see that they were making the sucker deal of a lifetime
when they sold the land back to him? So what if they
didn't get along? For the kind of money they each lost
by selling out to Bren, they could afford a little ego
conflict, for Christ's sake. But Bren had been the only
Westerner in the bunch, probably the only one who
realized the potential of the land he was acquiring. Al
Taubman of Bloomfield Hills, Michigan, one of Bren's
former partners, made $150 million on selling his share
of the Irvine ranch back to Bren, a lousy $150 million
for losing control of land that must be worth ten times
that now, and would be worth twenty times that in a
few years.

Jimmy Rosemont snorted in disdain and then forgot his fellow billionaire, Al Taubman, as he leaned
forward to look at the Kilkullen Ranch, which lay just
ahead, below the tiny helicopter that had wraparound
windows and a floor that was largely transparent, so
that anyone flying in it had an exceptionally wide
view.

"Head out over the water first," he told the pilot,
and the helicopter swooped out to sea, turned and
followed the coastline of the ranch. Jimmy Rosemont
held his breath as the vision of the virgin coastline
unfolded under his eyes. He knew he was looking at
twenty miles of empty beach on a typically California
winter day, brilliant with sun and blue sky, but if he

had been introduced into Ali Baba's cave, and all the barrels of the riches of the Orient had been spread open before him, he would not have been nearly as excited.

The inhabitants of the South of France would long ago have seen their tourists depart and now would be settling in for a rainy, increasingly uncertain winter; Provence would be empty except for farmers for the next months of mistral and cold; Florida would be in the grip of possible hurricanes and certain humidity, but here, during the winter, would rule the best weather of the entire western world. And there, just below, was the perfect natural harbor he had heard about, the wide, horseshoe-shaped curve which the Pacific waves had scooped out over the millennia. It must be at least a mile and a half across.

Like the rest of the beach, the harbor was deserted except for a tiny structure that he knew must be the Kilkullen boathouse, located in an inlet at the most protected part of the harbor. On both sides of the harbor, the wide strand of the gray-brown sandy beach spread in a long, undulating line, the waves beating against the shore. Here and there, well out to sea, were outcroppings of great rocks against which the ocean, now at high tide, flung up wild horses of white spray. And there was Valencia Point, just as it had been described to him, reaching out into the waves like a finger pointing westward.

"Make another pass and then go in and fly right over the beach," he ordered. "But stay high." In the next ten minutes he saw that the beachfront property of the Kilkullen land was broad and unblemished, backed by high bluffs behind which some two miles of flat, treeless land was planted in a crop he couldn't identify.

Rosemont instructed the pilot to fly inland, over the rich green lowland acres that were planted in many different crops, dotted at wide intervals by the farmhouses of the men who worked the land. Then they flew yet farther inland, over the heart of the ranch, the miles and miles of rolling, rising pastures and deep, shaded arroyos, where only herds of cattle and the occasional man on horseback could be spotted, where the trees were fewer and most of the thousands of acres were given over to pasture. Narrow dirt roads, windmills, fences and five reservoirs were the only marks to be seen on the majesty of the uplands.

"Do you want me to circle all the way around Portola Peak?" the pilot asked.

"Don't bother, I can see it easily from here," Rosemont replied. The peak itself was the least interesting part of the fan-shaped ranch from his point of view. Above the treeline it was rocky and steep, the most difficult part of the land to develop. On the other hand, Rosemont realized as the helicopter rose and gave him a better view, if the peak was carved out properly, the views from the lower and even the middle parts of the mountain would be so magnificent that they would more than repay the huge expense of the infrastructure. The peak could be as valuable as the beachfront. In some ways more valuable.

"Go back to the airport," he told the pilot. *Infrastructure,* Rosemont thought, who the hell had invented that awful word? It was so unnecessarily intimidating. The infrastructure of any piece of land was much simpler to understand than the complexity of any human hand.

Roads, water supply, sewers, telephone lines, gas lines, electricity, and there you had it. Every homeowner presided over a piece of infrastructure, although he never thought of it that way. If you had vision and weren't afraid of the word *infrastructure,* if you were a Jimmy Rosemont or a Donald Bren, you were as much at home with infrastructure as you were with yourself—maybe more so—because without it you couldn't put up anything more complicated than a tree house.

Jimmy Rosemont stepped down from the helicopter and walked across the circle of the heliport into the waiting limousine that would take him to his meeting with Mike Kilkullen. He was early, he thought as he looked at his watch. Time for a cup of coffee before he met with the man over whose property he had just flown. It was more valuable than he had ever expected, he thought with certainty, far more valuable than even his partners had suspected. And these partners, a consortium of the richest bankers of the Hong Kong Chinese community, were the smartest men, in his opinion, with whom he'd ever done business.

Mike Kilkullen walked out of the front door of the hacienda when the limousine drove up. He always received guests, no matter how unwanted, at the entrance to the Hacienda Valencia, but his daughters Fernanda and Valerie had made such a point of their friendship for the Rosemonts, when they telephoned him last week, that he wanted to be particularly gracious for their sake. Normally he would never have agreed to a business meeting in the middle of a working day on the ranch.

The two men shook hands, taking each other's measure. Neither liked what he saw. Kilkullen looked too much the lord of the manor for a man who had never done anything with his life but raise steak on the hoof, Rosemont thought, too imposing, too damn tall, in his gray flannels, his open-necked blue oxford shirt and his gray tweed jacket, for someone who never traveled, whose farmer's life was limited to a daily round that didn't include the only excitement worth having, the power to make things happen in the great world. And he hadn't expected the absolute grandeur of the approach to the hacienda, the giant avenue of trees, the perception that the hacienda was surrounded by acres of old, well-tended gardens, the size of the hacienda itself.

Mike didn't like men who couldn't drive their own cars, no matter how rich. He didn't like men who wore dark gray, pinstriped, three-piece suits during the day. He didn't like men with darting eyes and smiles that they must practice before the mirror every morning to make sure that none of the charm had worn off overnight. He didn't mind fat men or thin men, but he didn't like plumpish men who thought they could

conceal a slight paunch under the excellence of their
tailoring. He particularly didn't like men who came to
him on "business" through members of his family and
made appointments at an hour that guaranteed that
he'd have to invite them to lunch or seem inhospitable.

"I'm delighted to meet you, Mr. Kilkullen. It's
most kind of you to make the time for me."

"Not at all, Mr. Rosemont. Come on in. I think
it's about time for a drink before lunch."

Mike led Jimmy Rosemont quickly through the
long living room of the hacienda and out to the broad
veranda supported by beams that were covered with
winter-blooming jasmine. They settled down in comfortable old chairs in front of a table on which an array
of bottles, glasses and an ice bucket had been set.

"What can I give you?" Mike asked.

Rosemont never drank at lunch, but he decided
that even though there were bottles of Perrier on the
table, he didn't want to ask for it with a man who must
be a two-fisted drinker. "Scotch, please, no ice."

Mike poured from a bottle of Glenfiddich, gave
himself a Perrier on the rocks, with a half a lime, and
the two men raised their glasses in a silent toast.

Rosemont's eyes darted around the patio. He
hadn't dared to fly over the hacienda itself for fear of
being spotted, but he was fascinated by the view from
the veranda: the wide fountain surrounded by pots
overflowing with purple vinca, pink geraniums and
huge blue and white pansies, the paths of formal cypress that led in many directions, indicating the existence of a number of separate gardens, each one
hidden from the others.

"What a marvelous place you have here, Mr. Kilkullen."

"It's my pride and joy, Mr. Rosemont."

"There's nothing like a garden, is there? My
wife's English, and she lives for her days digging in
the dirt at our country house. Georgina told me that
you have a famous rose garden."

"Thank you. It's trouble, but worth it. Now what

was it that you wanted to talk to me about, Mr. Rose-mont?'' Mike asked, trying to cut through the horti-cultural bullshit as quickly as possible.

"Your future, Mr. Kilkullen."

"Selling life insurance, Mr. Rosemont?".

"Not exactly. Mr. Kilkullen, you've been a very astute man all of your life, you don't need any insur-ance."

"How so?"

"All around you, up and down the coast, people whose families settled here in the late 1800s, and even in the 1900s, have been selling their land and getting rich, while you've been sitting tight on your land, liv-ing in comfort and not parting with an acre."

" 'Living in comfort.' Is that the way you see cattle ranching?"

"As I understand it, in the cattle business, if you own your land free and clear, and if you haven't bor-rowed against your stock, you're doing fine. Let's say you run four thousand head of cattle—that's about right, isn't it, Mr. Kilkullen?—and ninety percent of them calve every year. That's thirty-six hundred calves. In a good year, by the time they're ready to go to market, they'll weigh four hundred and fifty pounds a head and you'll sell them for five hundred dollars a head. It costs you four hundred and fifty dollars to raise each one, so you make a net profit of fifty dollars per calf, or two hundred thousand dollars a year."

"That's in a good year," Mike said softly, furious that this stranger was in possession of accurate facts that he couldn't possibly have found out without the assistance of an expert. Rosemont was putting his hand in his pocket and counting his money.

"Even in a bad year you still have your steady income from your tenant farmers, your flower grow-ers, your strawberry growers, your citrus growers. And you've been smart enough to stay out of the horse-breeding business, which eats up profits like nothing else."

"Now that you've explained my own business to me, why don't you explain *your* business to me?"

"I'm a man who helps other men to maximize their assets. Obviously I do it for profit, but I make people rich, Mr. Kilkullen. Incredibly rich, totally independent of anything that can happen to them in life except death. Taxes aren't a problem, if you're rich enough. As we sit here, you could become, with a single decision, one of the richest men in the entire world because you've been smart enough to hang on to your land, instead of selling too soon."

"Some people don't call me smart, just stubborn," Mike said lazily.

"No doubt. But I'm sure you're a man of reason as well. Look around at your neighbors, your old friends, the families you've grown up with. Take the Segerstroms, for instance. They were lima bean farmers until the end of World War II. Now the family's worth well over half a billion dollars in real estate and shopping malls. Have you ever visited South Coast Plaza, Mr. Kilkullen?"

"As a matter of fact, I have. Henry invited me to the opening of the Noguchi sculpture garden there—I particularly liked the rock formation Noguchi called *The Spirit of the Lima Bean*—a long-awaited tribute to an underrated vegetable, wouldn't you say, Mr. Rosemont?"

"Magnificent, splendid. But I'm just as impressed by what the Segerstroms have been able to do for Orange County. They're the spirit behind the opening of the Performing Arts Center, they gave the land and six million in cash—the Center has been internationally acclaimed, and it will mean *immortality* for the Segerstrom name. They couldn't have done that if they'd been content to stick to growing lima beans."

"You won't get an argument from me on that."

"Take the Irvines as another example. When they gave the land for UC Irvine, before they sold, they created a great university where nothing had stood before. Today, as you must know, Mr. Kilkullen, UC Irvine attracts some of the greatest scholars in the world, to say nothing of one hell of a football team.

Even though they no longer own the land, the Irvines too have achieved immortality.''

"Are you trying to make me rich, Mr. Rosemont, or immortal?'' Mike asked, opening another bottle of Perrier.

"Rich, Mr. Kilkullen. Very rich. Immortality is something many rich men seek when they have all they can spend and as much as they want to give their heirs. Immortality is an option.'' Jimmy Rosemont shrugged eloquently.

"I'm here to point out," he continued, "that you have in your immediate grasp every possibility that any man could ever dream of. There would be nothing on earth you couldn't do with your life. You could become a great collector, you could sail your own yacht around the world, you could establish your own charities, you could do what Bren does and become the largest contributor to the Republican Party in California, you could buy a football franchise—the whole wide world is there for you, Mr. Kilkullen . . .''

"And all I have to do is sell you my ranch.''

"Precisely.''

"Why would I want to do that now, when I've refused to do it over and over again for the last thirty years?'' Mike asked mildly.

"Because you can't live forever, Mr. Kilkullen. I'm old enough myself not to feel uncomfortable saying that to you. In twenty-five years you'll be ninety, and if you're still here—and I heartily hope you will be—you can't deny that you'll have lived your life. Will it be the same routine life you've known, day in and day out, for as long as you can remember, or will it be a life full of rich memories of the amazing potential that is open to you right now, while you're in the best of health and have many of your best years to look forward to?''

"You make a sound case, Mr. Rosemont. You're a most persuasive man, and you're not afraid to mention the unmentionable. No one who has ever tried to buy me out has mentioned death before. Taxes, yes, but not death. Tell me, purely out of curiosity, where would I live if I did decide to sell the ranch? As you point out, I'm sixty-five, and naturally I'm deeply attached to this family home. There's no other place in the world where I'd rather live—and die, for that matter."

"That wouldn't be a problem. You'd decide on the limits of your private property, and it would be excluded from the sale. You could live right here, and never notice any change around you. With these gardens and trees protecting you, there's complete privacy."

"Just a little noise, I suppose? Construction work and so on?"

"Well, naturally, there would have to be that. But if you kept out, oh, let's say a hundred acres for yourself, enough for a huge spread, you wouldn't notice anything much, if at all."

"And my cattle business?"

"You'd no longer be a cattle rancher in Southern California. But you could buy another ranch, Mr. Kilkullen, there are ranches for sale all over, ranches that could use men of your experience to run them properly."

"Montana, Texas, places like that?"

"Exactly!"

"Inland ranches. No seacoast, no mountains."

"True, but the country is magnificent."

"Like in the Marlboro ads?"

"Even better, greener, and it goes on forever, not like here."

"Why don't *you* buy one of those ranches, Rosemont?"

"An amusing idea, Mr. Kilkullen, but we're both busy men. I'm interested in your ranch because it has possibilities that I can't find inland. Obviously I want to develop your land for residential use."

"Rows of identical houses, Rosemont, without even a backyard for the kids to play in? Maximum land use?" Mike's voice was still lazy.

"Nothing like that," Jimmy Rosemont said hastily. "I'm interested only in fine properties. It's ten percent more expensive to build an expensive home than to build a moderately expensive home, but the profit is vastly different."

"I'm aware of that. You have the same infrastructure expenses either way, but the trimmings are where you make your dough. The marble baths, the granite countertops in the kitchens, the two-story entrance halls, the family media room, the ma-and-pa baths, and all that relatively cheap icing on the cake."

"I didn't know you followed real estate, Mr. Kilkullen."

"I don't. My Cow Boss put me in the picture."

"Well, then, you realize that it would be unprofitable for me to use the land for low- or even moderate-income use. The Kilkullen Ranch would always be the ultimate residential property in Orange County . . . if you sold it to me."

"I'm not going to sell, Rosemont. Not to you, not to anyone, not one acre or ten thousand. This ranch is the only place between L.A. and San Diego that has remained as nature made it. Everything else is new and *it is shit*." Mike Kilkullen rose to his feet.

"The only option I want for the rest of my life, Rosemont, however long I live, is to keep riding my range, to keep breeding my cows, to run my roundup every year, to be able to gallop along my beach at sunset, to repair my fences, to worry about rain, to sail my boat from my own boathouse, to doctor my cows, and, at the end of the day, to sit in front of my own fire in my family's place and know that all around me lies the land that my great-grandfather bought from my great-great-grandfather, and that I've preserved for my children."

"I'm sorry to hear that," Jimmy Rosemont said, rising in turn. "I don't think I'll take up any more of your time, Mr. Kilkullen. I'll skip lunch, if you don't mind—that way I'll get back to New York and still be in time for dinner."

"Certainly not, Rosemont. I understand. Let me walk you to your car. And don't forget to give my love to Fernanda and Valerie when you see them."

"Without fail."

"Oh, yes, one more thing—that was your helicopter I noticed inspecting my ranch this morning, wasn't it?"

"Ah, that . . . yes, as a matter of fact, it was."

"I imagined so. Well, have a safe trip back, Rosemont. I hope you enjoyed the view."

Casey Nelson had insisted on taking her to Spago for dinner, Jazz thought, as she began to get dressed, in spite of the fact that she knew he wouldn't get a good table there. Only regular customers, almost always customers who were in show business, could expect a decent table in the famous, trend-setting restaurant that gained and gained in popularity as each hot new place in L.A. opened and closed to make way for another.

Wolfgang Puck's first restaurant, Spago was the "21" of California, the one absolute establishment place, the place you had to go to in order to retain your membership in the hierarchy of L.A. glamour. It was not meant for the new Cow Boss of the Kilkullen Ranch, even if his father did own a mess of tugboats in New York.

She had been tempted to call Bernard, the maitre d'hôtel, or pretty, dark-haired Jannis who worked with him, and tell them that she was Casey's guest. That would have ensured a well-placed table, but Jazz had decided that since Casey had been so pigheaded about the restaurant, she wouldn't make things easier for him. Let him be aware, when they were led all the way back to the far right end of the front room, instead of to the left near the bar, or even worse, back to one of the rooms she'd never set foot in except for a private party, of his presumption. Any man who dumped her out of his lap deserved severe humiliation.

She felt pretty, Jazz decided, oh *so* pretty, with Sam Butler panting after her and Casey Nelson so smitten that he was insisting on showing off with dinner at Spago. A girl should always have two beaux to her string. Or three.

What do you wear to indicate such a furiously pretty mood, given that getting seriously dressed up for Spago wasn't done except on Oscar night? Casey could hardly appear in public in that Cow Boss garb that had been acceptable at the El Adobe, so he'd probably wear the same dark suit in which he'd ruined her Grès gown and her Spanish shawl.

A problem indeed. An overdressed escort for the most conspicuous restaurant in town, where casual elegance was the norm. First, Jazz decided, you start with black pantyhose, black wool trousers and flat black velvet shoes. That takes away immediately from the relative formality conferred by any skirt. Then you look through your closet and muse, ponder, ruminate, speculate, meditate, and go into a trance until you find the right top. Nobody sees anything but your top once you're seated at the table anyway.

Jazz's fingers flipped through dozens of hangers on which hung an amazing number of wrong blouses and wrong jackets. She searched through the piles of sweaters which lay folded on her shelves, wrong sweater after wrong sweater, sweaters which had once been perfect for Spago but which weren't tonight.

Nothing! She had nothing to wear! Oh, God, wasn't that always the way? She'd been so busy for a year that she'd hardly had time to shop. There was only one thing to do, Jazz realized, as she stripped off her trousers and shoes. She had to dive immediately into total Chanel. When you had nothing to wear, that meant that only Chanel was possible, old, new, old and new mixed, it didn't matter. Chanel was for all seasons, all trials and tribulations. It wasn't imaginative, it didn't show any vision of personal style, it didn't match her emotional state, but everyone from the editor-in-chief of *Vogue* to the rich Japanese wives on the Ginza still wore undiluted Chanel.

Casey's female relatives, if he had any, probably wore Chanel from dawn till dusk, Jazz thought grimly, pulling on a red and black suit from the new ready-to-wear collection. She rummaged in her accessory drawers for five or six Chanel pearl necklaces in different lengths, a pair of earrings and a black satin camellia that had cost her $250. She threw it all on and looked in the mirror. She squirmed out of the suit as quickly as possible. It looked totally pulled together, not casual, not easy, not Spago. You could wear it to a power lunch. *Phoebe* would wear it.

She had ten minutes till Casey arrived. She could decide how to dress five models in ten minutes, Jazz reassured herself, trying to calm down. The important thing was not to lose your head. When Chanel didn't work, the Hanes T-shirt ploy was the way to start. She pulled a boy's white T-shirt over her head, added purple suede trousers, and threw a Chanel jacket over the whole thing, the off-white jacket trimmed with pearls instead of braid, which Lagerfeld had shown last year on thirty different models simultaneously, wearing everything from bathing suits to evening gowns, the famous jacket that you couldn't go wrong in. Nothing really dumb about the outfit, Jazz decided, except that there would be at least two other women at Spago in the same jacket, and she looked like a version of Murphy Brown on one of her more frazzled days.

Naked except for her pantyhose, in a frenzy of inspiration, Jazz grabbed a miniskirt made entirely of forest-green sequins, tucked in a sheer organza shirt in the same color, plucked an ancient dark green velvet blazer from the pile of clothes she'd been planning to give away for two years, found some very high-heeled black pumps and a pair of huge, chunky glass earrings from Yves Saint Laurent that had cost her a thousand bucks three years ago and had been well worth it. Perfect! It had everything, the throwaway cool of the old jacket, the tease of the shirt, the audacity of the skirt, and the deliberate mismatch of the much-too-glitzy earrings.

She pranced to the door when she heard it ring.

Casey Nelson stood outside, in cord slacks, an Armani jacket and a thin brown wool turtleneck.

"Hi," she murmured. "You're right on time." How, she wondered, did he know exactly what to wear for Spago?

"You look like . . . a tree . . . a gorgeous Christmas tree," he said admiringly, twirling her around.

"I felt sort of seasonal," Jazz said lightly. How could she have forgotten that Christmas was less than a month away? She made it a point never to dress to fit the season. Now she looked as if she were in costume for a Christmas play in kindergarten. Tacky, tacky, tacky, but too late to change.

"Ready to go?" he asked.

"Let's," Jazz agreed hastily. If he walked into the apartment he'd see into her bedroom, beyond which lay her huge closet. She'd forgotten to close the closet door, and it looked as if a rummage sale had been going on in there.

Casey drove to Spago in the kind of silence frequently described as "companionable," although silence like that made Jazz nervous. They weren't old buddies, they weren't intimate friends, they weren't lovers. What was it with him and his comfortable silence? They were third cousins who had exchanged a few words and a few kisses, kissin' cousins, about as tenuous a relationship as you could imagine, and it was clearly his duty to entertain her.

They left the car at the lot above Spago, with its many security guards, and started down the steep sidewalk to the entrance. At the top of the sidewalk, the usual crowd of paparazzi were waiting to shoot the stars.

"Hey, Jazz, where's Sam?" one of them called.

"Is Sam coming in tonight?" another asked.

"Jazz, you two-timing Sam?" inquired a third.

"Ignore them," Jazz instructed Casey. "They invent stuff like that to annoy me. Professional jealousy."

Inside, the usual crowd waited at the bar. Bernard

spotted Jazz and came over immediately to give her a
kiss on the cheek. "You look great, Jazz—set for
Christmas already, huh?" he said. He turned to Casey
and put a friendly arm around him.

"I have your table waiting, Casey," Bernard assured him, and led them into the front room, turning
to the left. At the end of the front room was the open
kitchen. To the immediate right of the kitchen counter
was the best table in the house, always reserved for
parties of six or eight, and next to that was the second-
best table, which could accommodate four or even five
people. Tonight they had set a smaller table for two
there, right in the curve of the window, turning it into
the "lovers' table" that always got more scrutiny than
any other table in the house. Bernard led them directly
there, and, as usual, everyone else in the place
checked them out until they reached the table. At
Spago it is never rude to stare, and table-hopping is a
way of life.

"I gather you hang out here?" Jazz asked Casey,
once they were seated.

"Whenever I get a chance to eat dinner in L.A. I
wanted to invest with Wolf when he started this place,
but he didn't need my money. I have a piece of the
new brewery, and he knows I want in on anything else
he does. The man's a genius."

Well, that explained it, Jazz thought. Casey was
an investor. Everybody knows that investors get good
tables, that's usually why they invest. Casey had
bought in—not against the rules, but not a legit way
to get a table position either, in her book.

René, the aproned, handsome waiter, appeared,
carrying a platter. "Wolf saw you come in, Mr. Nelson, so he sent over your Jewish pizza. Oh, good evening, Miss Kilkullen, back so soon?"

Jazz nodded. *Casey's* Jewish pizza? What about
her Jewish pizza? She was the one who always ordered the pizza covered with the finest quality of
smoked salmon spread over a thin layer of what cream
cheese might taste like if it were elevated to something
ten times better than cream cheese.

"Jazz, how about aquavit from the freezer with this?" Casey asked.

"Definitely."

"Let's not bother to look at the menu until we've finished the pizza, O.K.? Who knows what we'll be in the mood for?"

"Who knows indeed? Dad said you'd tell me all about the latest guy who tried to buy the ranch."

Jazz listened intently as Casey told her the story. "When the bastard finally took off," Casey concluded, "Mike had a double shot of bourbon to get the taste of the Perrier out of his mouth and spent the afternoon in the Jeep, checking the fences to make sure that Rosemont hadn't been tunneling under them, digging for oil."

"That's not so!"

"Honestly. He said Rosemont made him paranoid, something weird about his eyes, plus the way that helicopter kept flying back and forth over the land. He said that he knew exactly how Faust must have felt when he met the Devil, the only difference being that Mike didn't want to sell."

"It's not easy to hang on to a way of life that's over and gone everywhere except at our place and at Dick O'Neill's," Jazz said slowly. "But Dad will never change, and he'll live to be a hundred, like his grandfather. I suppose to some people it could seem almost . . . well, almost selfish, one man living on land that thousands of people could live on, but Dad knows that once that ranch is gone, it's gone for keeps, and there'll be nothing left but some old photographs to show people how life used to be in California. He feels so fiercely that it's up to him to preserve something of the past, he knows that he's the last one who refuses to let it vanish, who's holding back so-called 'progress,' and I understand him."

"I do too," Casey said fervently.

"Oh, there's Shirlee," Jazz said, waving at her good friend, Henry Fonda's beautiful young widow. She made a come-on-over gesture, and Shirlee left her companions to say hello.

"Jazz," she said in her deliciously squeaky voice, that sounded as if she had a permanent case of low-level, sexy laryngitis. "At the lovers' table two nights in a row? What goes on here? Does Sam know?"

"This is Casey Nelson, Shirlee. He's my cousin."

"Hello, cousin." Shirlee's eyes were full of mischief. "What degree of consanguinity are we talking about here?"

"Third cousin, Mrs. Fonda," Casey said. "I don't think that counts, do you?"

"Certainly not . . . only first cousins count. I've got to get back to my table. 'Bye, you two, don't worry about incest."

"I like her," Casey laughed.

"Everybody does," Jazz said, annoyed. Shirlee was usually supremely discreet, but Casey, too busy looking at Shirlee's famous legs, hadn't noticed her reference to Sam.

"Jazz, when are you coming back down for the weekend?"

"Probably next weekend, and of course for Christmas. I'm going to be very busy for the next few months . . . I probably won't be able to come home as much as I'd like."

"How so?"

"A new client, a major job. Diet Pepsi is going to go all out on a print campaign that'll get the attention that Annie Leibovitz's stuff gets for American Express, and they've hired me."

"Naturally."

"Naturally." Jazz grinned. She and Annie had been pals, equals and rivals for so long that it felt like having a twin.

"What's the thrust?" Casey asked.

"Simplicity itself. Double spread shots of celebrities with cans of Diet Pepsi."

"That doesn't sound new to me."

"But it will be. There's a twist. First of all, you'll have to really search for the can. It's going to be practically invisible, truly hard to find, like the piece of the jigsaw puzzle that's right under your eyes while you're going crazy looking for it because you know it absolutely has to be there. There's going to be no copy at all to explain the shot, just that pesky, damn near camouflaged can—maybe even only half of the can—that people will expect to find but can't unless they honestly try—it'll turn into a kind of game. That means that the shot will get an immense amount of time and attention . . . it'll stop the reader cold. And I'm going to shoot all the celebrities in rumpled, mellow, sweaty, intimate action—Michael Jackson in a recording studio on the twenty-fifth take; Don Johnson and Melanie Griffith in bed, with a trickle of cola running down between her breasts into the nightgown, as if he'd just upset it; Madonna in her dressing room, half-in and half-out of her makeup and clothes, such as they are; Arsenio Hall wearing only a shirt, trying to make up his mind between a dozen new suits at his tailor's—you get the idea.''

"How do you get people like that to pose in these situations when you're not using their names?''

"Pepsi gives them $250,000 for their favorite charity.''

"I'd do it for less.''

"Yeah, it's generous. But it's the least part of the expense of the campaign.''

As Jazz spoke, she saw a tall, smiling redhead approaching behind Casey, putting her finger to her lips for silence as she looked at Jazz meaningfully. The woman looked familiar, but Jazz couldn't immediately place her. The stranger put her hands over Casey's eyes and said, in a voice that was obviously disguised, "Guess who?''

Casey sat still and then raised his hands to his eyes and carefully touched the hands that covered them, exploring the palms, the fingers, even the shape of the redhead's wedding ring.

"Fauve Avigdor, what are you doing here?'' Casey said, jumping up and folding her in his arms.

"How the hell did you know who it was?'' the woman asked.

"Your hands," Casey answered. "Only one pair in the world like them."

Fauve Avigdor, Jazz thought—but she lives in Provence. And how could I have missed knowing who she was? I'm losing my grip.

"Fauve, this is *my* cousin, Jazz Kilkullen. Jazz, this is *your* cousin, Fauve Avigdor."

"My *what*?" Jazz exclaimed. Fauve smiled without surprise.

"Where's Eric?" Casey demanded.

"At the bar, waiting for our table."

"René, please bring a chair for the lady," Casey asked the waiter.

"Casey, have you taken leave of your senses?" Jazz insisted as Fauve sat down.

"You Californians don't know your own family history. If you were my father's daughter, you'd be aware that sixty years ago one of his great-grandfather's sons, Perry Kilkullen, had an illegitimate daughter, and that baby was Fauve's mother. Poor Perry died before he could marry Fauve's grandmother, Maggie Lunel. So we're all definitely cousins, in a vague sort of way, but brave, brawny, lusty Kilkullen blood runs in all our veins."

"In Casey's anyway," Fauve said to Jazz, laughing. "We must meet again and discuss him behind his back, in brawny, lusty detail. Now I have to go back and find Eric."

"What brings you both here?" Casey asked.

"Eric's designing a new housing complex in San Diego. Casey, where can I reach you?"

Casey scribbled a number on a piece of paper and handed it to Fauve, who made her way composedly back to the bar.

"My God, Mistral's daughter is a cousin of mine, and I didn't even know it," Jazz marveled. "I should have recognized her, but she looks older than I remember. Of course, there haven't been any photos of her in magazines for years—since Mistral died. That must have been about fifteen years ago . . . I was only in high school."

"Just about. I'm one of the collectors of Fauve's paintings. Someday I'd like to show them to you— they're remarkable."

"You collect paintings, you invest in restaurants, you have a fax in your bedroom at the ranch so that you can communicate with your broker in New York before dawn, you have the good kind of Vuitton luggage—just what kind of Cow Boss are you, Casey Nelson?"

"A damn good one, according to your father."

"How can it be more than just another game to you, Casey? Ranching isn't an easy life, and you've obviously got more money than you need."

"Should I let money stop me from doing what I want to do?"

"That's no answer."

"Jazz, I'm a cattleman. I've been one for years. What do I have to do to prove it to you? Can't you just believe I have the same reasons to love it that your father has?"

"No, because he was born on the land, our family land, and that makes an immense difference," Jazz persisted.

"I fell in love with ranching when I was a kid destined to run a tugboat fleet. What if Mike had been born on the ranch, hated it, and run away to sea? Would that invalidate his life's work?"

"Why don't I trust you when you sound as if you're making sense?"

"Why don't you trust me at all?" Casey sounded unexpectedly somber.

"Where did you get that idea?"

"It just came to me. You don't really trust men in general, do you?"

"No. No, I don't," Jazz said slowly.

"Gabe. He's the reason."

"Casey, *do not start*."

"Sorry. Forget I said anything. Let's order."

They plunged into an inspection of their menus. After they'd ordered, Barbara Lazaroff, who was Wolfgang Puck's wife and a professional restaurant designer and architect, came over to greet them. As always, she was an exotic work of art, her brilliant eyes and long black hair set off by fantastic antique jewels. She dressed in a collage, a pastiche of elaborately decorated pieces of clothing like none other in the world, combinations that could only exist in Barbara's lively fantasy.

"Jazz," Barbara asked, "that jacket? Is it a political statement? All that green . . . the environment? Anyway, it's really great on you. That reminds me—we have to start baking our Christmas cakes or they won't be ready in time. Oh listen, yesterday when you promised to get Sam's autograph for that waitress, I hope it wasn't an imposition. She knows she isn't ever supposed to ask for autographs in here, no matter what the provocation, but she just couldn't restrain herself. I almost asked for one myself, but I decided Wolf wouldn't approve."

"Right, Barbara."

"Since you're coming in with Sam tomorrow, there's plenty of time. I promise not to let that waitress near this table again. She might have an attack, jump the guy."

"Right, Barbara."

"Thanks, kid. 'Bye, Casey, see you next week. Same time, same place. Remember, you get a Christmas cake too."

"Sam?" Casey asked. "It seems to me that I keep hearing that name tonight. Who is he?"

"An actor. Sam Butler."

"Sam Butler, *an* actor? Or Sam Butler, *the* actor?"

"The," Jazz replied.

"You had dinner at this table with him last night. You're having dinner with him at this table tomorrow?"

"So it would seem."

"I wish I hadn't asked. Actually, I had decided not to, but it kept coming up so often that I figured no one could be as stupid as I was trying to be."

"He's just a friend," Jazz said hastily.

"Oh, I know that. A girl who doesn't trust men in general certainly isn't going to trust—of all the kinds of guys in the world—an *actor*."

"God, you're a shit." Jazz was obscurely pleased at his words.

"The day we met, you told me I was a dickhead. Is that better than a shit, or worse?"

"It depends on my tone of voice—don't bother to split hairs, you're both," Jazz said with a generous smile.

"You're too kind," Casey replied, and for the rest of dinner they engaged in a volley of talk too tiny to be called small.

On the way out of Spago, Jazz found herself embraced by a lovely blond girl who looked ten months pregnant. They talked for a few minutes in the crush around the bar, and then parted.

"Not possibly another cousin," she informed Casey. "That's why I didn't introduce you."

"But what a raving beauty. Is she an old friend?"

"Yes, Daisy Shannon. She's having her second set of twins."

"Good Lord, Princess Daisy. It's lucky Pat likes kids."

"Oh, you know Shannon?"

"We do some business together from time to time."

"Small world."

"Isn't it?"

Jazz and Casey drove back to her apartment in a charged silence, an uncomfortable silence, an uncompanionable silence. She couldn't think of any way to break it, and after a while she decided that there was no reason to do so. She felt righteously aggrieved that after all the immense trouble she'd gone to to dress up like a Christmas tree, to salute the festive season, Casey Nelson had decided that he had a reason to be jealous of Sam Butler. After all, it wasn't as if she were spoken for, as if she belonged to Sam.

Casey escorted her to her door. Jazz put her key in the lock, opened the door, and was about to give him the basic absolute minimum thank-you-for-a-lovely-evening, when he put a restraining hand on her shoulder, gathered her in his arms and brought his reckless mouth down squarely on hers. He'd kissed her for minutes before Jazz, out of breath, was able to break away and put a little air between them.

"May I come in?" Casey asked urgently.

"I don't think that's a good idea."

"Couldn't I just come in for a minute? It would be nice to talk without everybody in Spago joining the party. We've hardly been alone all night. I promise never to take you there again."

Jazz looked up at him, sorely tempted. Those furrows on his brow, those freckles, those lips . . . but she'd been out with Sam last night and she was having dinner with him tomorrow and . . . and . . . no, it was positively not a good idea.

"Casey, I wish I could let you try to seduce me, now that we're not under my father's roof, but I'm not that kind of girl," she said softly, regretfully caressing his lips with the tip of her finger.

"What! I haven't heard anyone say that in years."

"Takes you back, doesn't it?" Jazz agreed sweetly. "Good night, Casey. Sleep well. And thank you for a lovely evening."

Jazz shut the door behind her, shaking with silent laughter. She wasn't that kind of girl, not now, not ever. Never would she get involved with two men at once, back to back as it were. But could she ever be a hundred percent sure, in her heart of hearts, absolutely and positively, what terrible, awful, unthinkable thing she might just possibly have been tempted to do if she hadn't remembered what a mess her closet was in?

14

Mr. and Mrs. William Malvern Jr. were sitting at the table in the kitchen of their Fifth Avenue apartment, drinking their second round of martinis. The chicken-and-rice casserole, which their housekeeper had left for their dinner on her day off, was slowly heating up in the oven, for neither of them had managed to master the operation of their microwave.

Even in the kitchen, with an apron around her waist and a pair of comfortable shoes on her feet, Valerie maintained her brilliantly simple and severe look, although she didn't bother to wear her unnecessary glasses at home.

"Valerie, I never thought I'd say this, but—alone at last," Billy Malvern drawled out the last three words with a particularly unfortunate Anglo-Saxon attempt at a French accent.

Valerie didn't deign to look at him down her too-pointed nose. "If you're trying to let me know how thrilled you are that my mother is out tonight, don't trouble. I'm as relieved by her absence, Billy, as you are, perhaps more. It's always easier for you to deal with her. After all, she's not your mother."

"I don't believe in taking cheap shots, Val, but you're tempting me."

"Look, I'm aware that she's stayed on longer than she usually does. But what can I do, throw her out in the street? If only Fernie would get rid of Nick, she could go there. In any case, Mother is definitely leaving next week."

"No fool, that sister of yours. By the time Liddy makes her next visit, Fern will be embroiled with another impossible young husband, so we'll have to take her again. I see it coming."

"Oh, shut up and drink, Billy. Stop whining." Valerie lifted her inadequate chin and glared at her husband. "Can't you talk about something agreeable? I'm rather pleased about going to the Rosemonts' party tomorrow—it should be the party of the year."

"I'd be more pleased if Rosemont would throw a little business my way. It seems to me the least he could do, the way you and Fern have become such great pals of Georgina's."

"Jimmy Rosemont does his own investing," Valerie said dryly. Jimmy Rosemont hadn't become one of the richest men in the world by taking advice from brokers like Billy, she thought. And just what, she wondered, was going on with Fern and Georgina? They had lunch together twice a week, seeming as close and giddily foolish as two schoolgirls sharing secrets. Obviously, Georgina didn't have a clue about Fern and her husband. What a fool she must be, not to guess. Or perhaps Georgina was just so sure of herself that it had never even occurred to her. In any case, since the show house, both of the Rosemonts had been more than kind to both of them, even including Liddy in several of their smaller dinner invitations, in spite of the fact that the introduction to their father had, as Valerie had expected, led to nothing.

"I wonder what the Rosemonts' party is going to cost?" Billy said, fretfully peering into his glass. "A hundred and fifty people at a sit-down dinner at home with dancing afterwards—what do you think, Val?"

"I can't imagine. A few years ago I could have made an educated guess, but now the best caterers, florists and party decorators have become so unbelievably greedy that it could cost almost anything. Of course, Georgina's style isn't pretentious, it doesn't have to be. Doing it at home is always preferable, if you have the space and can afford it."

"And they can."

"And they can."

The Malverns sat silently. In the early years of their marriage, twenty-one years ago, when Billy's income had been half a million dollars a year, and they had been indisputably rich, they had found the subject of other people's money delectable, a never-failing occasion for self-congratulation, larded with condescending pity for their less-fortunate friends who had to make do on salaries, who had to pay taxes, unlike Billy, whose money was all in tax-free municipal bonds.

They had spent hours estimating the net worth of their friends, speculating on who among them was in line for an inheritance, who had a trust fund that couldn't be broken, who was living over his income and who was lucky enough to live under his income and still spend freely.

As Valerie was guiltily aware, this kind of discussion was the old-money equivalent of talking the vilest kind of trash, far worse in every way than almost any social sin, but she had indulged in it nonetheless, since Billy, whose money was only one generation old, couldn't guess how obscene it was. Billy thought these orgies of gleeful discussion both instructional and fascinating.

For Valerie, the speculations were as pornographic as they were irresistible. Her Philadelphia values were deeply offended, but she was only part Philadelphia. She had been influenced deeply enough by Liddy Kilkullen's money hunger, and her sense of having been cheated out of what was owed her, to enjoy the reassurance that Billy's wealth gave her.

Now the Malverns could only circle wearily around the subject. Billy's lack of success in business, in addition to his sharply diminished income caused by the sale of some of his bonds, created a gnawing imbalance in their marriage as Valerie earned more and more of what they lived on.

It had been a decade since the Malverns had felt the sensual glow of being more secure than the people they knew, for the way Manhattan's new society spent their riches made the Beverly Hillbillies look like Cabots and Lodges.

Old money, unable even to attempt to compete, had retreated. Either its possessors resolutely stuck together and disappeared gracefully from social sight, or, like Valerie, they joined the parade and put up a reasonable show of welcoming the newcomers, with the pragmatic excuse that New York's cultural and charitable institutions needed the absolute monarchs of new money, who had not the slightest trouble in buying themselves entry everywhere.

Valerie got up to poke irritably at the casserole, which was taking its own good time. She didn't dare turn the oven up higher than 350 degrees because she was afraid the rice would dry out, but the inside of the dish was still barely warm. She poured them both fresh martinis and sat down at the kitchen table again, wishing they could leave the casserole and sit in the drawing room like civilized people, but she was certain that if she did, dinner would burn. They'd both been too tired tonight to bother to go out, and she'd be damned if she'd descend to sending out for food.

"How's it going with your new client?" Billy inquired, hoping to change his wife's mood.

"I may not take on Sally Evans," Valerie answered.

"But you told me she was ready to spend almost anything . . . what's wrong with her?"

"She's a third wife . . . as if a second weren't bad enough. Sally's all of twenty-six and Mr. Evans is sixty-two . . . she used to work for him, although in what capacity she won't say. She's well put together in a vulgar kind of way, I'll say that for her, but she has the delusion that because her husband owns a big chain of Midwestern grocery stores, she's going to be welcomed into what she calls 'the charmed circle' by having a marvelous apartment and wearing the right clothes. It's hopeless, of course. She's so ignorant that she doesn't have a clue that a net worth of a hundred million will sound like the life savings of the manager of a family drugstore to the women she wants to get to know.''

Nor did she realize, Valerie thought, that the media had declared open season on the style of the new-money circles to which Sally Evans aspired. At about the time of the Malcolm Forbes birthday party, as nearly as she could figure, the ostentation of the newest billionaires had started to be ferociously attacked by the same journalists for whom they had been a favorite subject only months earlier.

Media voices of a new decade, finally able to express their repressed covetousness, had dubbed the 1980s the "Decade of Greed and Glitz." The wives of the new-money men had pulled up their recently erected drawbridges against a continued invasion of any more of their own kind, hoping to become "establishment" if they minded their manners, lowered their profiles ever so slightly, turned to "good works" in the Lady Bountiful tradition, and hung in without complaint as they were pummeled in the press.

It might take a period of delicate readjustment, in which the spending of money was varnished by a coat of social conscience, but people of privilege knew that the media couldn't exist without them. Readers everywhere felt momentary pangs of loss at the righteous bashing of the rich and famous, but soon they recognized that their favorite newsmakers had not been swept away in the tide of recently assumed journalistic virtue. Given the immutability of human nature, short of a revolution, there would be plenty of delicious excess to look forward to in the 1990s.

"How did this prize land on your doorstep, anyway?"

"I'm not sure," Valerie answered shortly. She couldn't tell Billy that her potential new client had tried to hire other, better known decorators, and had been told that they were too busy, any more than she could tell Billy that her room at the show house, for all the pretense she had put up for her family, had not been a success.

It had been entirely ignored by the press, although the only reason for her having put so much time and effort into the project was to gain publicity and clients. The crowds at the show house had passed it by quickly, in their search for the spectacular, the lavish, the thrill of the never-before-seen, all of which Georgina's room had provided. Valerie realized that she'd made a mistake in judgment. Her twins' bedroom had been too whimsical, too pastel, too well bred; all that girlish tulle and dried flowers had made women think they could throw together such a room themselves.

"Are you going to give her the heave-ho?" Billy probed.

"I haven't decided," she said, quickly drinking half a martini. If only, Valerie thought, Billy didn't think he had to demonstrate supportiveness of her work by asking maddening questions that she had no intention of answering.

In other days—as recently as five years ago—she would have given Sally Evans the back of her hand, but times had changed drastically with the explosion of New York riches. Only the decorators with major names were passionately sought after now, like that young man Peter Moscino, who boasted so odiously in *Women's Wear Daily* that he didn't work for the people who *had* only fifty million dollars, but for the people who wrote checks for fifty million dollars.

The fact that he was probably telling the simple truth didn't make his statement any less disgusting, Valerie thought, nor did it change the fact that her reputation as a society decorator had simply stopped being enough to lure clients anymore. People might be afraid of the press, but they still wanted decorators who created excessively lavish interiors, and excessive in any direction was something she couldn't be, any more than she could be original.

At the moment, if facts were faced, she didn't have another single potential client in line except Sally Evans, who had opened their interview by saying, "I want instant background and I want drop-dead chic and I want it to look like *me*, not as if I'd had a decorator at all. My husband has said that we can shop Europe together as much as we want—I need three chateau fireplaces and rooms and rooms of *boiserie*."

Could she possibly endure doing a job with the client glued to her side, particularly one like chattering Sally Evans, who had that most dreaded quality in a client, indecision?

Outright, full-blown bad taste was easier to deal with than indecision. At least, with bad taste, you knew your client's point of view, but Sally Evans had arrived with a notebook filled with pages torn out of magazines, each one an interior she'd admired, each one an interior she wanted, each one in an entirely different style. Did she, Valerie wondered, have the patience to try to train a twenty-six-year-old third wife, to educate her—assuming that it could be done —or was no amount of money worth it?

On the other hand, did she have a choice? Billy's income and earnings were simply not enough to cover the way they lived, and everything, from a head of lettuce to her daughters' shoes, was getting steadily more expensive. How had she imagined for a minute that she could afford to turn Sally Evans down? Indeed, why not admit it, she was lucky to get her, and that was the hardest fact to swallow.

"What's that odd smell?" Billy inquired languidly, finishing his third martini and pouring another.

"Rice burning," Valerie snapped. If he wanted his God damned dinner, why the hell didn't he get up and check the God damned casserole himself? Nothing, no power on earth, would make her look in the oven one more time.

Valerie poured another drink, walked out on her irritating kitchen, her irritating husband, her unquestionably dry casserole, and retired to her dressing room to take refuge from life on her chaise longue.

She tore off her apron and her shoes and flopped down on the chaise, covering her feet with a soft mohair throw, and just lay there for a minute, contemplating nothing at all, sipping gin.

After a while a familiar picture formed in Valerie's mind, the picture that never failed to calm her. It was a vision of a two-story fieldstone country house in the suburb of Chestnut Hill, on the Philadelphia Main Line. The house belonged to Martha and Wheelwright Stack, the parents of her distant cousin and schoolgirl best friend, Mimsie Stack.

Mimsie and Valerie had been in the same class at Foxcroft, and the Stacks had treated Valerie as a second daughter, since her own mother was so far away, in Spain. They had arranged for her debut at The Assembly the year that Mimsie made her own bow to society, and Valerie loved them both dearly. Each year, during school and summer vacations, she had spent every minute that she didn't have to be at the Kilkullen Ranch or Marbella with the Stacks in Chestnut Hill. Even now, she and Billy returned there four times a year to spend weekends with the elder Stacks, in spite of Billy's protests that they bored him. Valerie had kept up all her contacts with the girls of her debutante year, and from time to time she went to Philadelphia for some particularly important lunch party.

Her mother had cheated her of Philadelphia, Valerie brooded. If Liddy hadn't decided to live in Marbella, out of pride and anger, she could have brought up her daughters in the city that Valerie loved. If her mother had been able to endure a brief period of post-divorce embarrassment, her daughters wouldn't have had to grow up eternally shuttled about, without a real home. She would have been a Philadelphian who had just happened to spend her first twelve years in California. She would have grown up there, in a secure and familiar atmosphere of confidence that should have been her right, and married someone who belonged by birth to old Philadelphia, just as she herself did. But she'd met Billy Malvern while she was at the New York School of Interior Design, and now Philadelphia was a place she returned to only from time to time, a semi-lost paradise that she had never truly possessed.

But, oh, how she loved the Stacks' house! It was of a medium size, some fourteen rooms, but utterly *substantial*. It had small, cozy windows made of small, cozy panes of glass, framed by cozy white shutters. The fieldstone itself was dappled in shades of gray and beige, and the roof of the Stack house was weathered brown slate. An undiluted plainness of weathered, first-class surfaces was the characteristic of the exterior that Valerie valued the most. Mature trees grew on the surrounding four acres of lawn, there was a proper English garden, the driveway was bordered by weeping cherry trees, and the front courtyard was paved in brick.

There was not one inch of the Stack house that failed to breathe dignity and serenity, not one room that was not, in a mysterious way, exactly the right size for its function. To Valerie it was the most perfect shelter she'd ever known.

Once inside the house in Chestnut Hill, she had always known that she was safe, in a way she had never felt in any other dwelling, no matter how massive. The house itself had been built in the early 1800s on the model of an unpretentious English country manor; it was comfortably and solidly furnished with well-cared-for but nondescript American antiques; it contained no rare collections or particularly good art or fine examples of anything at all.

The elder Stacks were a comfortably thrifty couple, in the Philadelphia manner, which some misguided people mocked as stingy. Martha Stack saved string and tissue paper, and directed her cook to rinse off and reuse aluminum foil and plastic wrap. She'd never throw away the tie of a Baggie until it broke. She tore her Kleenex in half, horizontally, because otherwise most of it went to waste; she recycled her Christmas wrappings, and she wouldn't part with a bar of soap until it fell apart.

Martha Stack was a knowledgeable gardener who wouldn't have dreamed of planting her annuals close together, for the gratification of a quick mass of bloom. She preferred to delay that pleasure until the well-spaced-out seedlings naturally reached their destined size. Once, in a moment of particular intimacy, she'd confided to Valerie that she'd always wanted to plant annuals from seed, rather than spend the money to buy plants at the nursery, but the spring weather in Pennsylvania didn't last long enough for her to risk such a delight of sensible economy.

Economy, Valerie thought dreamily, such a pleasant word, so soothing and sensible. She practiced it herself with her smile, her goodwill, her invitations and her endearments, but in her slice of New York, economy was suspicious and hinted at some carefully hidden impoverishment, instead of intelligent husbanding of bounty.

When Martha and Wheelwright Stack gave a dinner party, she put fresh candles in the candlesticks on the dining room table, and saved the candle ends that were removed, no matter how short, for family dining. Only the prospect of damaging the top of a candlestick could force her to remove a candle that retained a quarter-inch of usable wax.

Martha Stack's guests were always family and old friends; the Stacks had not invited recently met people to dinner in the course of their marriage, for they had not had occasion to encounter any.

They owned a summer place in the lovely seacoast town of Camden, Maine; they employed a full-time live-in cook-housekeeper; they were generous to their two children and seven grandchildren; they were mainstays of Philadelphia cultural life, an enormously popular couple who considered themselves indecently rich while living within an income that was no more than Billy's alone.

Was it the fact that there were no surprises in the Stacks' life that made it seem so desirable, Valerie asked herself. Was it the lack of challenge, the calm, the routine, the pleasantness, the expectations that were never too large to be met, the knowledge that they wanted nothing they didn't have? Was it a smallness—or was it a . . . *rightness?*

She sighed as she finished her martini. Whatever it was that the Stacks had, it appealed to some deep need in her. But whatever it was that the Stacks had, it couldn't be found in New York at any price.

Valerie got up to go back and rejoin Billy. After all, she didn't want him to have to eat that casserole alone. As she passed her dressing table, she stopped for a minute to contemplate a bud vase. It held the last yellow chrysanthemum of an arrangement that someone had sent her well over two weeks ago. Valerie always took apart flower arrangements the minute they arrived, separated the flowers, recut their stems, and put them in bud vases so that they could be distributed all over the apartment. This mum had another good three or four days left in it, she thought, and, considerably heartened, she returned to feed her helpless husband.

Pete di Constanza hadn't smiled once, Jazz noticed, during today's monthly meeting in Phoebe's office, nor had he taken the name of the Lord in vain, nor had he complained about the stale doughnuts and lukewarm coffee Phoebe served. This was so unlike her old pal that when she finished shooting the following Monday, she decided to try to find out what was up with him. The double garage doors of his studio weren't locked, and when Jazz peered inside, she saw that although the overhead worklights were off, Pete was still there, all alone, sprawled full-length on the floor, leaning on one elbow and looking fixedly in front of him. This was his normal, visionary position, in which he remained for hours at a time as he pondered the lighting of a car, no less intent than Mel had ever been, but the vast studio was completely empty of automobiles, none of Pete's four muscular assistants was in evidence, and even his studio manager had gone home for the day.

"Business slow?" Jazz asked, as she walked over to him, safe in the knowledge that Pete was booked a year in advance, sometimes two years, by clients who would accept no other car photographer.

"Yeah, sure." Pete looked up with a doleful attempt at a smile. He was wearing his favorite Patagonia parka, designed for serious mountain climbing, although the December day had brought with it a typical pre-Christmas heat wave and hot Santa Ana winds. Pete thumped the floor next to him in invitation to Jazz to sit down next to him.

"Listen, Jazz, how do you feel about vets?"

"Vets—as in soldiers?"

"No, honey, vets as in dogs and cats."

"I don't get the question." Jazz sat down and looked at his downcast face. He was huddled in his parka as if it were a security blanket, the collar turned up around his chin. "Do I like them better than dentists or less than doctors?"

"Do you think they're incredibly sexy?"

"Aha, that BMW campaign is bugging you again," Jazz said. For the last two years, BMW had been doing car photos in outdoor settings, at polo clubs and yacht basins, the pictures swarming with elegantly dressed people photographed in a muted pointillist way, with the actual car deliberately downplayed, shown merely as a prop that glorified the lifestyle of the crowd that surrounded it. Pete, like all of the three or four other great car photographers, loathed this approach because it diluted the purity of the automobiles, those splendid machines that inspired aesthetic emotion.

"What are they doing now, showing a BMW filled with a sobbing family rushing its sick cat off to a vet?" Jazz asked sympathetically, for she knew how seriously Pete took his work.

"It's not that. It's Marcia. She's just ditched me for a vet. And eighteen months ago, exactly the same thing happened with Samantha. Jazz, I just don't get it! I was nuts about each of those bimbettes, damn it, I was just about getting ready to do some major thinking about proposing to each of them, and suddenly I hear, 'Pete, I'll always love you but I'm going to marry this wonderful man and I never dreamed this would happen to me and I know you want me to be happy and I'm sorry, Pete, but would you be a darling and help me move my suitcases into the car?'—and they're out of there like I never was happening. And both times—*vets*. Is this sinister, or what?"

"Ah, Pete, I'm really sorry. I liked Marcia so much." What could she do besides sympathize, Jazz wondered. If she were a man, she'd offer to go out and get drunk with Pete . . . wasn't that what men traditionally did at a time like this?

"So did I, kid, so did I. What I'm looking for is a dose of woman's intuition. I don't want this to happen again. Got any to spare?"

"Vets," Jazz said thoughtfully. "Did Marcia and Samantha have pets?"

"I suppose . . . yeah, but I never paid much attention. You know I'm a motorcycle man myself. Marcia has one of those shitty little dogs, you know, the kind you can sneak into your purse and try to take on a plane . . . used to drive me wild when she pulled that . . . and Samantha kept a horse at the Equestrian Center in Burbank . . . she used to go exercise him three times a week and take dressage lessons, dressage lessons . . . big deal, how to make a horse walk backwards on its hind legs." Pete snorted in disdain.

"I'll bet you never saw *National Velvet?*"

"Nah, I had a misspent childhood. I don't think *National Velvet* even played Fort Lee, New Jersey. And we sure as hell didn't have horses."

"Were Samantha and Marcia's pets ever sick?"

"*Ever* sick! They were sick all the damn time! What a turnoff—maybe I'm not so unlucky after all," Pete said miserably.

"Pete, consider this. A woman with a sick pet is like a woman with a sick baby. She's at her most vulnerable, and you can't give her any emotional support at all. Meanwhile, the vet is becoming a hero; he's caring, warm, capable, providing security, advice and reassurance. He's healing her baby. But where are you when you're not in the studio, big guy? You're sitting next to a fancy set of wheels on top of a mountain, waiting for those first three crucial minutes at sunrise which give you the light you need for your shot. Or you're lying in a road while a stunt driver drives in tight circles around you, so you can get the shot of the rear wheels of a car kicking gravel in your face. So who did Samantha and Marcia turn to in their hour of need? The vets."

"But they knew where I was," Pete protested. "And what could I have done anyway?"

"Pete, listen," Jazz continued. "Who can make a house call at any hour of the day, when a woman's all alone with her sick dog? The vet. Who exudes the sexually charged aura of a doctor, so that he benefits from the kind of emotional-erotic transference that's inspired by a shrink? Yet a woman *can* have sex with him because he's not *her* doctor? The vet. My God, Pete, they've got to catch more girls than any other specialty in medicine!"

"I guess I never had a chance." Pete looked at Jazz with the first signs of cheer on his face.

"What you need is a girl who doesn't have any animals."

"A girl who promises *never* to have any animals," Pete agreed. "Like you."

"Something like me," Jazz agreed, reflecting that the amount of travel she did for her work effectively prevented her from keeping so much as a guppy.

"Why didn't we have a great, mad, flaming romance when we first met?" Pete demanded. "I kept offering you my heart and my body, but you were never interested. Was it another guy?"

"No," Jazz said dismissively. "You and I were meant to be friends, not lovers."

"Bullshit. We would have been great together. We still would be. That invitation is permanent, honey. It must have been Gabe."

"What are you, nuts?" Jazz sputtered.

"Ah, come on, kid, it's the way he looks at you —angry, bitter, wistful, *hungry*, all that good stuff— and the way you went up in smoke when Phoebe wanted to bring him in, remember? Mel and I knew almost right away."

"The two of you old gossips think you know everything!" Jazz said furiously. "You're like a pair of ancient biddies sitting on a stoop somewhere, peeking through the neighbors' curtains. Every man I know is a gossip! Don't you have anything better to do?"

"It's a necessity for us to exchange information," Pete said calmly. "We have to know what the women in our lives are up to so they can't surprise us. We have great respect for your power to disrupt our lives."

"Well, you didn't know shit about vets."

"Unworthy of you, Jazz, but I'll forgive you this once. How are you and Sam making out? Industry sources report a major passion."

Jazz sighed with exasperation, but she couldn't stay angry with Pete. He'd been a buddy for too long.

"Sam's a good guy," she answered. "I like him a lot."

"But?"

"No 'but.' Simple statement of fact."

"I heard a 'but' in your voice," Pete insisted.

"Pete, there's something you have to understand about Sam. He lives in a world other men will never live in, not you, not Mel, not anybody we know."

"Huh? He just bought that Ferrari I advised him on—what are you talking about?"

"The world of beauty, Pete," Jazz said patiently. "Sam is so beautiful that nobody can relate to him in a normal way. He says that it's easier for a woman to almost get to understand him, but it's just too tough to

ever explain to a man. He'd never get any sympathy
from a guy, so how can he even complain?"

"Give me a break," Pete said. "I relate to him
fine. Of course, I'm gorgeous too."

"Did you talk about anything except cars?"

"What else is there?"

"You might have tried to get to know Sam, but
you didn't, did you?"

"I will, next time I see him."

"No you won't, he's too beautiful for any man to
want to get to know him. It's the unconscious, or conscious, envy factor." Jazz sighed. "Sam says that all
exchanges of small talk he has with other men are
always stiff, or at best superficial, because they can't
look at him—I mean literally look at his face or into
his eyes—the way they can with other guys . . .
they're afraid they'll seem to be staring. And they
can't talk about girls with him because they assume
that he'll always have the edge on them with any
woman. And they think he's too beautiful to have any
brains, so they don't discuss serious things . . . only
sports, cars, and the weather. The only man who talks
to him semi-seriously is his agent, and then only about
money. It's a terrible thing to be that beautiful."

"No shit," Pete said kindly.

"It gets worse. Sam says that he didn't ask to be
born beautiful, that it's a kind of curse, but that there's
nothing he can do about it except to accept the fact
that no one outside of his family will ever, *ever* fully
understand the real him. It's like being some kind of
freak, set apart from the rest of the human race. People sneak peeks at him as if he were an animal in a
zoo. He intimidates most people, you know—too
much beauty scares people—they flutter around him
all flustered, as if he weren't flesh and blood, but what
can he do or say to reassure them without admitting
that he knows *why* they're acting that way? So it's a
double bind. God, I feel so sorry for him."

"You two talk about this problem a lot?" Pete
inquired.

"Naturally . . . it's always on his mind, and with

all the massive publicity he's been getting lately, it's going to be worse and worse, with no end in sight."

"But *you* understand him, don't you? Isn't that enough?"

"Sam says that even I can't really, truly understand what it's like. He thinks I'm so lucky just to be very, very pretty—because that's on an understandable human scale—but that if I were really beautiful, like Michelle Pfeiffer, I'd *almost* be able to feel the reality of what he goes through, even though it's much more culturally acceptable to be a beautiful woman than a beautiful man."

"He *told* you that you weren't as beautiful as Michelle Pfeiffer!"

"Pete, I appreciate the compliment, but face it, I'm not."

"Look, honey, if I get to come back in another life, I want to be Michelle Pfeiffer, but to me you're more beautiful than she is because I love you, and we don't even fuck, so to a guy who—enjoys your favors —you should be much, much more beautiful."

"Sam's just being realistic. He's an honest guy, and I don't mind his being analytical, explaining it to me."

"Yeah, over and over and over, it seems to me."

"Not that often," Jazz said with exasperation. "It's not the only thing we talk about."

"What else do you talk about?" Pete asked casually. He could hardly wait to tell Mel all this stuff.

"His work. The different scripts he turns down. What would be the next right career move for him— that's critical when you're so beautiful, because you don't want to be cast *just* as a beauty—Sam has to do some serious decision-making. He's thinking that maybe he should do a character part, even play a second banana in a serious political statement film with a major European director—like a Costa-Gavras—to try to break the mold. He'll never get an Oscar if he isn't accepted as an actor first, a beauty second."

"Good thinking."

"Yeah, but will anyone ever give him credit?

Look how people still talk about Paul Newman's blue eyes before anything else, and they aren't half as blue as Sam's. Critics call Sam things like 'painfully beautiful,' whatever that's supposed to mean.''

"You going to bring him to Mel's wedding?'' Pete asked hopefully. This he had to see with his own eyes.

"It wouldn't be fair—he'd upstage the bride.''

"I guess you're right,'' Pete said. He looked at Jazz sitting next to him, her bare legs drawn up so that her chin rested on her knees, her arms clasped around her calves. She had on white shorts, a navy camp shirt and bright red Keds. Her hair had been pushed back and tied in a knot of string, and her profile was grave and concerned. Now this girl, he thought, was painfully beautiful, if he'd ever seen that sight, because it gave him such a permanent and acute pain that he'd never had a decent shot at her. If only he'd met her when she wasn't getting over another man, their lives would have been entirely different. Maybe he wasn't right for Jazz, probably he wasn't good enough for her, but, oh, how he wished she'd had a fair chance to find out before they became "just friends.''

Next chance he got, Pete thought, he was going to throw Gabe down a flight of stairs. Or run him over. Whichever was most likely to kill him. And hurt the most.

Jazz sat on a bench watching the shoppers stream into the South Coast Plaza at the entrance opposite I. Magnin's, where a hillside of weeping ficus trees were planted, their festive leaves still as green as springtime in the early, still-slanting light of a cool December day.

Two days ago, Mike Kilkullen had driven up to Los Angeles to take Jazz out to dinner. Such an action Jazz had found uncharacteristic of her father, particularly since he expected her to come down to the ranch for the weekend. He had picked Le Chardonnay, on Melrose Avenue, one of the best and most charming French restaurants in the city, ordered a particularly good bottle of wine, and, under her amused, suspicious and loving eyes, proceeded to discuss nothing of importance for the next half hour. There was no way to rush him into whatever he wanted to talk about, Jazz decided, without seeming to be meddling in his private life.

When Mike Kilkullen gathered up his courage and announced to his daughter that he and Red Appleton were going to get married, Jazz felt a rush of unequivocal delight. She'd suspected that this development was in the wind for many weeks, but she hadn't been sure how she'd feel when she heard the actual words. Now she was swept by joy for the two of them and something more: relief from a heavy responsibility she had accepted but never fully admitted to herself, a responsibility for shielding her father from his essential loneliness.

In the years following her mother's death, Jazz had missed her desperately, but as she grew older, her emotions had grown less and less violent, until she had finally accepted and absorbed her loss. But Mike Kilkullen had never seemed to be able to let go of Sylvie, even after twenty years. There had always been an underlying melancholy, an ache of unresolved pain that Jazz was keenly aware of, a sadness no daughter could or should ever be dear enough to dispel.

But now, at last, there was Red and his almost boyish love for her, dear Red, so newly relaxed and radiant, Red with her growling, sweet-ass Texas drawl and her gift for salty wisecracks, Red who so visibly adored him; Red, sophisticated but essentially downhome, who would fill his life with unexpected, spontaneous fun and leave no room for him to grow into the hermit rancher that he might well have become without a wife. With Red, Mike Kilkullen would never again be all alone, except for a daughter who visited on weekends. He would rely infinitely less on Jazz for his happiness, and that, she thought, was a good and necessary thing, and yet it would never alter her own special relationship with him.

Jazz had immediately telephoned Red from the restaurant to tell her how happy the news had made her. As they talked, they realized that they hadn't spent a minute alone together, without men around, and they decided to meet to do some Christmas shopping together this Friday.

Red must be late, Jazz told herself, and looked at her watch. No, she was just impatient to set her eyes on the new bride-to-be. This morning, with beds of freshly planted snapdragons all in bloom, with its scented air and cheerful crowds, felt like an unexpected school holiday, and Jazz was doubly glad that she'd been able to close the studio yesterday, on Thursday night. Next Monday she had to leave for New York and conferences with the Pepsi people.

Phoebe had insisted that Jazz go to New York now, instead of waiting until early January, when the Pepsi advertising agency's creative team would come to California where most of the campaign would be shot. Phoebe had decreed, in her most knowing and impressive manner, that it was vital for Jazz to meet certain of the Pepsi executives on their home ground.

"You've got to get to know all the key players in advance, press the actual flesh, so that if you run into any trouble, you have personal relationships to fall back on in the client's camp," Phoebe had instructed Jazz, so emphatically that Jazz didn't argue.

Her rep was a control freak, Jazz thought, but since it was just for this ability to see wheels within wheels that she paid her, and since Phoebe had negotiated the highest fee for commercial work that Jazz had ever been paid, she had reluctantly agreed.

As highly visible and expensive as the campaign would be, Jazz anticipated no problems on the creative side. She had done some trial shots, using her studio assistants as stand-ins for the celebrities, employing the new, seemingly off-the-cuff, casual, Peeping Tom technique that the agency and the client had loved for its innovative freshness. However, Phoebe had been adamant that she spend three days in New York, so depart she would.

"Jazz!" an excited voice called, and pulled her out of her thoughts. She jumped up and ran to meet Red, who had just turned her car over to the parking attendant. The two women embraced each other with that flustered mixture of complicated and not easily expressed emotions that affect a man's grown daughter and the woman who is going to marry him, but whatever they saw in each other's faces instantly assured them that their new relationship was going to be a heightened continuation of their old, easy friendship.

"Jazz, I can't tell you what I was going through until you phoned the other night! I was sitting at home without a single fingernail left to gnaw on, imagining how you were going to take the news. Sweetie pie, I had some real scary Tennessee Williams scenarios going through my head."

"I wish you'd been there to see Dad working himself up to it." Jazz laughed at the memory of her sheepish father, who had suddenly turned grimly formal, almost Victorian. "He all but asked me for your hand in marriage. I wonder why he thought I'd be surprised or anything but thrilled?"

"Some daughters have been known not to be so generous with their daddies. Mike wanted to tell you without me there. Just the two of you."

"But it's been just the two of us for much, *much* too long. Oh Red darling Red, it feels so *right* to have you in the family! The Kilkullens need you. But look, we can't just stand here, people are beginning to fall over us. We'd better walk as we talk."

The two women strolled along the wide, tree-lined entrance to the vast shopping complex, an enclosed space that was far too grand to be called a mall, anchored by six large department stores, among which ran three levels of row upon row of world-famous boutiques; an Orange County version of all the streets of Beverly Hills' Golden Triangle.

They stopped in front of Alfred Dunhill of London, struck immediately by the window display of handsome leather jackets. Red started to enter the store.

"Red, don't move!" Jazz said in a voice of authority. "Remember, on the phone we promised each other that we'd get the bulk of our Christmas shopping done today, and if we go into a store before we know what we're doing, chaos will follow. Now, I assume you have a list of the people you're buying presents for, with the approximate amounts of what you want to spend alongside each name."

"Why, Lord have mercy, I wouldn't leave home without it. I assume you have a list like that too, sweetie pie." Red looked haughty.

"Naturally."

"Then show it to me," Red demanded.

"I believe I forgot to bring it . . . in the excitement of the moment . . . a perfectly natural omission. In fact, I forgot to make it."

"Me too."

"I knew it! And I was worried that you might be totally organized, like Phoebe."

"Who's Phoebe?"

"Oh Red! Somebody new I can complain to about Phoebe! Heaven! Bliss! But I'll save it for the next time . . . you won't believe the sheer horror of Phoebe without an hour of details, and I don't want to distract us from making headway with Christmas. There are only ten days left."

"I don't really need a list," Red confessed. "I ordered the presents for my folks and my brothers and their kids in Texas by catalog long ago, so I'm just shopping for Mike, and a little something for Casey."

"Would you believe that I have to get presents for five men?" Jazz asked. "Mel and Pete, my partners; Sam, my . . . I suppose you'd have to call him my boyfriend—more or less; Casey, my I don't know what, but he's a cousin anyway and I have to get him some tiny little token; and Dad."

"What about this Phoebe? Does she get a present?"

"A canary. To match her hair. Or maybe I should just stuff it in her mouth, as a small warning. Hell! I forgot Valerie and Fernanda and all their kids! At the

ranch for Christmas week—Dad told me but I blocked
it out as usual. That means—oh, no!—that makes ten
more presents on top of the five men!''

"Why did you have to remind me?" Red moaned.
"If I was terrified of your reaction, how do you think
I feel about your sisters? They couldn't be coming at
a worse time. I haven't seen them since the Fiesta . . .
they're going to sincerely hate me, I just know it, but
Mike says I'm being silly. He hasn't even told them
yet, just you and Casey."

"What's Dad planning? Not, I hope, a surprise
announcement on Christmas Eve? Please, Red, darling, please promise me it isn't something like that."

"I have the awful feeling that it is. He's been
resolutely mysterious and humming to himself. Carols, Christmas carols . . . they make my blood run
cold. You know how stubborn your father is, sweetie.
I've never loved another man, not really, not like I
love Mike, but even you've got to admit that he has
one minor fault—he likes to have his own way. I can't
get a word out of him about what he's going to do, and
I've tried every which way. He never realized it, but
at the Fiesta those two vixens were sitting there glaring at me like Cinderella's wicked stepsisters, when
all Mike and I were doing was dancing together.
What's it going to be like when they find out?"

"Red, remember the first time we worked together, the time you were the editor and I was the
photographer and we took three models to the Virgin
Islands to do resort wear? A hurricane struck, the
electricity went out, there wasn't any running water,
the makeup artist and hair stylist broke up their long
love affair and the models all got food poisoning?"

"How could I forget?"

"It probably won't be quite that bad." Jazz
grinned fiendishly.

"Gee, Jazz, thanks."

"I'd be wrong not to warn you . . . and we survived the hurricane. And we got the pictures. Personally, I can't wait to see my sisters' faces, but you'd be
better off averting your eyes. Look, they'll never dare

be nasty to you in front of Dad. And I promise, on my honor, I'll never leave you alone with them. I'll buy you a whole set of Lakers sweats and a purple satin jacket. You can wear them the whole time and I'll wear mine. We'll form a Gang of Two.''

"Thanks . . . but I hate it that Mike's caught in the middle. You know how much store he sets by his family.''

"That he does, little as they deserve it, but they'll hardly ever be around . . . a maximum of twice a year for brief appearances, duty visits. If you'd just do the right thing and have a baby, they might boycott the ranch for a while.''

"What?''

"You heard me.''

"You want me to have a baby?'' Red asked, astonished.

"I'd *adore* it. You've never had any children— don't you want one?'' Jazz asked. After all, Red was forty-one and presumably she should be fixated on immediate reproduction, if the television show "thirtysomething,'' her chief sociological guide, was right about what women of that age really wanted.

"I'm . . . honestly not sure. I want to be with Mike, always, all the time. Wherever he is, whatever he's doing, I'll be keeping busy and waiting, more or less patiently, until he shows up. That's the only thing I'm positive of right now. Why would he want a baby around now, distracting me from him? And why would I want to divide my time?'' Red looked puzzled. Should she want a baby? Wouldn't she have had one by now if she did?

"Hold those thoughts . . . my TV-network primetime sources say you've got three or four more years to decide. Now I think it's safe to go into Dunhill's. Since you've got practically nothing to buy yourself, you can advise me.''

The two women entered the shop and circled around with the narrow-eyed, radar-like, concentrated gaze of expert shoppers, a look that keeps equally experienced salespeople from approaching them too quickly. Women like these two, the Dunhill salesman knew, didn't want to be interrupted until they saw something they liked, and then, at that very instant, they would expect to be waited on. One alone was bad enough; two together were certain hell, since that meant both of them had to be convinced. They were the kind, he guessed from their sternly critical expressions, who believed that a good opinion was too precious a thing to waste. What's more, from the way they were both dressed, in those easy, flapping, slouchy, on-the-verge-of-sloppy trousers, vests and jackets that screamed genuine Armani, they'd only want the very best.

"Jazz . . . what do you think?" Red held up a cashmere cardigan in a subdued Argyle pattern.

"He'd never wear it. Too busy."

"I didn't think so either. What about this?" She held up a solid blue cable-stitched cashmere pullover.

"Yes indeed," Jazz approved.

"May I help you?" the salesman asked, seeing his opening.

"Do you have this in a forty-two?"

"Certainly, madam."

"Good. I'll take it. Jazz, what about these Glen plaid cashmere mufflers?" Red asked.

"Dad's not the muffler type."

"But they're so beautiful! I love them."

"I know. Men's clothes are so much nicer than women's. I'd get one for Pete, but it's too elegant. He dresses as if he's leaving on an Outward Bound expedition, even when he goes dancing. Especially when he goes dancing. Look, if you give me this one and I give you that one, we'll have finished our shopping for each other—does that sound too unsentimental to you?"

"You're on!" Red was enchanted to find another female who understood that the only gift to give a woman you really cared about was something you were dying to buy for yourself. She handed the two splendid lengths of cashmere to the salesman, who was beginning to reconsider his opinion of these ladies.

"Jazz, just look at the honey color of the wood on this box." Red turned to the salesman. "What is it?"

"It's a game set, madam. You have all your chips, your cards, your dice, everything you need to play any kind of game, and the box itself is olivewood burl."

"Wouldn't it be great for cold winter evenings?" Red asked. Jazz nodded enthusiastically, picturing Red and Mike playing cards in front of a fire. "We'll have poker parties too. The hacienda needs to have parties in it again." She gave the large box to the salesman to put with the other things she'd found.

"May I show you some leather jackets, madam?"

Jazz and Red both looked at him in amazement. Neither one of them would have presumed to buy Mike Kilkullen a leather jacket. He *had* a leather jacket, a well-seasoned leather jacket that he'd worn forever, and if he ever decided that he needed a new one, which seemed highly unlikely, he'd certainly buy it for himself. Who knew what a man who lived on horseback would want in a leather jacket? It was an absolutely personal purchase.

"You've bought my present, I've bought your present, and you bought Dad two presents. That leaves me right back where I started," Jazz said plaintively.

"Why don't you get Casey another one of those mufflers?" Red suggested. "He dresses so well."

"No way—didn't you see the price tag?"

"Sure—two hundred and ninety-five dollars," Red said.

"I can't possibly spend that much on him . . . he'd misunderstand, and I have a law about not creating misunderstandings with Casey." Jazz shook her head with determination.

"It's a delicate problem," Red mused, "spending money on a man unless you're engaged or married.

Too much and you look as if you're overboard, too little and you look as if you don't really care. In fact, you look downright cheap. I'm so glad Mike agreed that I could spoil him as much as I wanted . . . if we hadn't gotten engaged until after Christmas, I'd only dare to give him a book. Oh, maybe two books, the big, expensive, coffee-table kind."

They walked briskly along the wide interior streets of South Coast Plaza. Mountains of beige marble in three different colors had been leveled to cover the walls; more marble, in shades that contrasted from light to medium gray, were inlaid underfoot. Forests of slow-growing fishtail palms, fifty-foot giants, grew from the lower level of the plaza to the skylights of the upper level, so that walking from shop to shop made them feel as if they had been airlifted to Hawaii. Round topiary trees constructed from gilded branches and covered with tiny, clear Christmas lights were everywhere, and a ring of glittering ficus trees circled the Jewel Court, where the wide network of marble walks met under a canopy of stained glass.

At Vuitton, Red found a majestically simple eighteen-karat gold fountain pen designed by Gae Aulenti, the Italian woman architect who had designed the Musée d'Orsay in Paris. Jazz pronounced it just right for her father, but the only item she saw that she wanted to buy was a soft cowhide bag, called a Keepall, without any initials on it, that would break Casey of his hard-edged, initialed Vuitton luggage habit. However, it was far too expensive. But she could buy it for her father, she realized. He didn't have any decent luggage.

"Where are you two going for a honeymoon?" she asked Red.

"Oh, Jazz, I don't know. I've been absolutely everywhere five times over, and I don't care, really and truly, if I never see any of it again." Red turned her lovely face shyly toward Jazz. "I want to start taking riding lessons—I grew up in the heart of Houston, but I've never been on a horse—I want to learn how to sail a boat so I can help crew when Mike takes the boat out, and I'm dying to get to work on the gardens—they're the only thing at the ranch that I almost understand. In theory, all Texas gals can tell a weed from a flower. So I don't think I could *stand* to have to go on a honeymoon. Once in any lifetime is enough. Is that awful of me? I haven't actually told Mike yet. There's so much we haven't talked about, because how could we until we actually knew we were going to get married? What do you think he'll say?"

"He'll be overjoyed," Jazz said, putting the bag down on the counter where she'd found it. Her father wouldn't have to take the hated vacations he had never taken, she thought. If she had needed any additional proof that Red was the perfect woman for him —and she hadn't—this was it. "Why did you wait so long to decide?" she asked curiously.

"I suspect Mike thought he was too old for me. There's a twenty-six-year difference."

"Twenty-four, I do believe."

"Oh, all right. Twenty-four. That's the trouble with old friends . . . they know to the minute how old you are. But, sweetie pie, the only wisdom I have to pass on to you is that age is relative as well as irrelevant, particularly in Mike's case."

"I don't even know when you're getting married," Jazz said, surprised. "Have you gotten around to talking about that, at least?"

"We thought after Christmas, when your sisters and their kids will be gone, so that it wouldn't be a big deal, just us and you and Casey and a judge, of course."

"Casey?"

"Mike wants him to be his best man, and naturally I want you to be my maid of honor, and that's all. Afterwards, we'll go to the Swallows for drinks and the El Adobe for dinner. No fuss."

Jazz frowned. How could it be a real wedding without a production, without problems, without confusion?

"It's exactly what I want," Red said, understanding her thoughts. "Believe me, I've gone the other route and it's hell. Whatever is low and unworthy in people is brought to the surface by a wedding. They play out all their long-hidden family resentments in fighting about things like the color of the tablecloth or what kind of cake to have. As for what to wear—it's out-and-out warfare, like *The Godfather,* only with women."

"I'm going to shoot Mel's wedding . . . I'll keep your words in mind. Sort of a Freudian subtext . . . the inner hostile meaning of the marriage ceremony."

"Oh, Jazz, don't."

"I was kidding. I'll know what to avoid, that's all. Shooting Mel's wedding will be sheer pleasure for me, because it's all about people I love. Come on, Red, I still haven't accomplished anything."

Jazz and Red took an escalator down one level to Tiffany's, which glittered so much that they didn't even enter. Across from the jewelry store, a storefront painted dark green, in the style of a small, old-fashioned English inn, beckoned. It was a men's shop called Rosenthal Truitt. Jazz scrutinized the window carefully.

"This is it!" she exclaimed, as soon as she spotted a pair of suspenders made of braided leather.

Inside she bought the suspenders for Pete, and a belt in the same leather in case he wanted to switch, and three sturdy plaid flannel shirts. She pounced on brass-and-beechwood shoe trees for Sam, buying him four pairs. "Just the right amount to spend, suitably impersonal, yet totally useful," Jazz announced. "It's a triumph of exactly the right thing. And did you ever hear of a man buying himself shoe trees, or a woman, for that matter?"

"Why don't you get them for Casey too?" Red asked. "They don't know each other."

"No, somehow . . . they're not Casey. *This* is Casey," Jazz said, holding up a supple suede vest in a neutral shade of taupe, with oxhorn buttons. The back of the most pleasing garment was silk, printed with a tapestry-like design of a pheasant against dark green and red autumn foliage.

Red sighed in admiration of its elegance, understated from the front, flamboyant from the back. "He'd look wonderful in it. But look, it's three hundred and ninety-five dollars—that's too much to spend, according to your own law."

"Ah, I know, Red, darling, but now the poor lout has to have something special for your wedding, and after all, he'll never guess in a million years what it cost, I'm taking the price tag off myself right now, and you'll never, never tell, you have to promise, and how can I pass it up, I'm so tired of shopping that I'm doing myself a favor, and my feet hurt. Look, I'll give him this too." Jazz held up a small book called *A Gentleman's Wardrobe, or, Good Clothes Open All Doors.* "See, this makes it into a joke. He can't take any gift too seriously if I give it to him with this book."

"I see," said Red. "Dimly."

"That just leaves Dad and Mel," Jazz gloated. "I'm almost done with the hardest part. Come on, let's go into Georg Jensen."

Even worldly Red was astonished at the expense of the great Danish handmade silver.

"Let's get out of here," she said to Jazz.

"Don't you like the silver?"

"The prices!" Red exclaimed.

"I'm getting Mel that tea-and-coffee service."

"Are you completely mad?"

"It's a wedding present for him and Sharon, not just for Christmas. Mel gave me my first break, and I'll never forget it. Just don't look at the price tag."

"I didn't plan to."

"But you do think it's nice, don't you? Mel and Sharon should like it, shouldn't they?"

"It's without question the most beautiful silver I've ever seen, except for that other set on the tray, which probably costs twice as much." Red sounded limp.

"Red, darling, you look tired. Sit down over there and rest your feet while I give the salesman my Visa card. You can be my character witness, if I need one.'' Rapidly, Jazz bought one service for Mel and the more magnificent one for her father and Red. They were getting married too, weren't they? And she could damn well afford it.

"That finishes my list," Jazz said to Red as they left Jensen's. "I'll get Dad something in New York."

"What about your nieces, your nephews, your sisters and their husbands?"

"I'll buy the teenagers' stuff in Beverly Hills too, more fun for them to exchange, which they always do, plus it will get them out of the house for a day, and I've just thought of a truly . . . compassionate present to give Fernanda and Valerie."

"What?"

"Individual subscriptions to *Lear's*."

"The magazine that says on the cover, 'For the Woman Who Wasn't Born Yesterday'?"

"The very one."

"If I weren't too happy to be as much of a bitch as you, sweetie pie, I'd go fifty-fifty on them."

15

After two busy days in New York, Jazz decided that she had made enough blood brothers and sisters among the Pepsi brass to cut her visit short by a day and return to Los Angeles on an early morning flight, picking up three hours on the flight west. She took a taxi from the airport directly to the studio, so that she arrived well before lunch on the Friday preceding the Christmas weekend.

Although Friday was nominally a day of business as usual, Jazz knew that at Dazzle, as in offices all over the country, the mood would have already swung to the holiday mode and no one would be making an attempt at work. The usual Christmas party had been voted down at the last partners' meeting, but she wanted to tell her assistants to go home whenever they chose, and to give everyone a hug before she took off for the ranch, where she could stay for a four-day weekend. Christmas didn't actually come until Tuesday of next week, and she'd drive back in leisure Wednesday morning. People would be digging themselves out from Christmas and beginning to think about getting ready for the long New Year's weekend. Perhaps, Jazz ruminated, the two-week holiday season of 1990–91 would turn out to be the final reason for the decline of the West, the excuse for never working a five-day week again.

As she opened the glass doors of Dazzle, she almost collided with Gabe, who was loaded down with two camera cases and a third case that held his collapsible lights.

"Why all the equipment? No rest for the weary?" Jazz asked pleasantly.

"Just a gig," he said, pausing for a moment.

"With Christmas on a Tuesday and the whole country shutting down even as we speak, how come?" Jazz asked, more out of a desire to seem normally friendly at this time of the year than from real curiosity.

"Gigs don't respect holidays, not this kind anyway. It's a party, a Christmas housewarming."

"You? *Shooting a party?*" Now she was truly disbelieving. Why should Gabe bother to lie to her about a job? The only kind of party he'd ever deign to shoot would be a Summit Meeting.

"Yeah. Listen, gotta go. I don't want to be late."

"O.K. Gabe. Anyway, merry Christmas and have a good time." Jazz's expression had changed from skepticism to a flash of astonishment that she quickly attempted to conceal with an overly bright smile. She had just realized, from his sheepish manner, that he truly had been seduced into shooting a party. It probably involved some major movie star and a gigantic fee, but still, for Gabe to rush off, at Christmas, for something so undemanding, so pathetically ordinary, showed her the extent to which he had lowered his standards since his return. Although he'd been getting an increasing number of good, if not great assignments since Phoebe had become his rep, apparently he couldn't afford to turn this job down.

Gabe caught the expression she'd tried to hide, saw that her smile was false and that she was pitying him. To spare his pride Gabe tried to enhance his assignment in a flurry of the very details he'd been pledged not to reveal.

"Seriously, Jazz, it's a story every photo agency in the world would kill to cover. Magic Johnson is throwing a Christmas housewarming tonight in his new house. He didn't want mobs of media attention so he's kept the party a secret for months. He's invited all the guys who play in the charity game he puts on every summer for that Negro College Fund—the top stars in basketball and their wives, plus all the Lakers, of course, including their kids. He's flying them out to L.A., but nobody knows who else is coming, so it'll be a surprise party . . . a gathering of the greatest. Naturally he's got to have shots of the action so I was tapped for the job."

"Hey, feel free to fantasize about a lot of things, Gabe, but not about something like that." Jazz spoke with bravado mixed with the beginnings of incredulous suspicion.

"So don't believe me. Anyway, I'd better hit the road. I can't even bring an assistant, but naturally he wants shots minute-by-minute—the guys' expressions when they walk into his place and see who else is there, the gorgeous wives getting to know each other, the pick-up game in the backyard court, the slam dunk contest, Magic and Michael Jordan playing one on one . . . you know, all that regulation, traditional stuff that everybody does, plus a few unique touches like Jack Nicholson and Arsenio Hall playing twin Santa Clauses, Jerry West and Jerry Buss costumed as Santa's helpers and the Laker Girls in reindeer outfits—your average monster Christmas housewarming. Somehow I'll survive it."

"Just another Christmas housewarming?" Jazz asked Gabe, her voice unsteady. "That's really all this means to you?"

"Come on, Jazz, you don't expect me to pretend I'm emotionally involved, do you? It's a question of the photo credits and the money—major money, major credits. For what I'm making . . . let's just say that there isn't a photographer alive who wouldn't take this gig. Merry Christmas, Jazz. See you next week.'' Gabe turned and walked quickly toward the parking lot.

Jazz stood just inside the doors, looking blankly at the unmanned receptionist's desk. She felt Gabe's words take possession of her, leaving her filled with a clear vision of the wonderful surprise party; the new house overflowing with epic heroes, dozens of magnificent champions united in a special championship that they could find only among their peers, glorying in a rare few hours of mid-season relaxation with their beautiful wives and swarms of excited children. The thought of the great photographs she'd never get to take traveled down through her heart and landed in her belly, where she finally experienced it fully, as if she had received a violent punch from a huge fist. She walked slowly to an upholstered bench and sat down heavily, clumsy with a complex feeling of utter betrayal and outrageous disappointment. She felt like a three-year-old who had just been smacked across the face. The feeling grew and grew until she had to press on her stomach as hard as she could with both hands in an attempt to counteract an emptiness that existed with more reality than any pain.

Jazz sat and tried to make logical excuses, in a desperate effort to be adult, to be sensible, not to take this as a personal rejection by Magic who she had photographed more than half a dozen times during his glorious career. She didn't own Magic, Jazz told herself, just as she didn't own the Lakers just because she'd devoted a week to shooting them for an entire special issue of *Sports Illustrated* in 1988, the year in which they'd won the back-to-back championships; she didn't have a right to *expect* to be treated as special just because she knew every team member personally, just because all the dramas and changes in the last two years of Laker basketball had been played out in her mind and heart. Just because she was as lunatic a fan as there was in L.A., just because she felt that each Laker was part of her own family, didn't give her a guaranteed first crack at shooting Magic's party.

Gabe would do a brilliantly professional job and
the fact that he didn't give a damn wouldn't show in
the pictures. She had no exclusive or official position
with the team. She didn't need the money or the
credit. Gabe, a great, award-winning photojournalist,
was an understandable choice for Magic to have
made, assuming he had made that decision. And Gabe
certainly had every right to take the job when it was
offered to him. Yes . . . every right.

When it was offered to him. When, exactly when,
had that been? How could she not have heard some
rumor of it in a studio complex in which news of what
each photographer was doing might well have been
broadcast on loudspeakers every morning, for the
amount of privacy that existed?

Where was everybody? Although Sandy, the receptionist, was not anywhere around, it was still far
too early for the studios to be closed. Jazz sniffed the
air and realized, from the smell of cooking and the
sound of voices, that there were certainly people,
many people, in Mel's studio on the third floor of Dazzle. She'd been too deep in thought to notice. Now
she took the stairs running, seeing as she passed that
her own studio was deserted.

A crowd filled Mel's studio, where a huge tree
had been set up and decorated while Jazz was away.
She pushed through the celebrating horde. Every assistant was there, as well as a large number of clients
from all the ad agencies in town and a surprising assortment of her favorite models. It sounded as if the
party was just getting started; there was a mob by the
bar and Sharon and a group of free-lance food stylists
were already busy serving up genuine hot dogs
and cheeseburgers under a banner that proclaimed
"REAL UGLY FOOD."

"Jazz, great! You got back for the Christmas party we swore to each other we weren't going to give! Hey, this is terrific!" Pete grabbed
her and gave her a kiss on each cheek. "Mel was
the first to crack. How come you're here? Nobody
expected you."

"Pete, do you know anything about Magic's big housewarming?"

"Magic's giving a party? Where'd you hear that?"

"Some crazy rumor. Where's Phoebe?"

"Over there in a corner talking business with a poor bastard she's trapped from an agency. She hates Christmas, says it's a waste of time and money but trust her never to pass up a free meal. Come on, pretty female, let's do the dirty hula."

"Later, Pete," Jazz managed to smile at him. She looked in the direction he had indicated and spotted Phoebe, almost hidden by a man in a gray suit. Phoebe's hand was poised persuasively on the man's arm and she wore the dangerous look that all clients inspired in her, halfway between a needy orphan and a greedy strumpet. Jazz made her way rapidly through the Christmas merry-makers, waving at everyone who greeted her, but not stopping until she reached the corner of the studio.

"Excuse me," Jazz said to the man in the gray suit. "Would you mind terribly if I had a quick private word with our little Phoebe?"

"No problem," he said and took off in the direction of the bar.

"Jazz . . . you're supposed to be in New York." Phoebe's animated face shaped itself into a concerned look. "Didn't it go all right?"

"For an utterly unnecessary trip," Jazz said, standing in front of Phoebe, backing her into a corner and spreading her arms toward each wall so that she had her rep trapped. "It went beautifully. I bumped into Gabe on the way in here. He told me about the surprise housewarming."

"Oh. Yes. That party. Cute idea."

"Thrilling."

"Jazz, there's someone over there I simply have to nab while I can. Let's have a good chat later." Phoebe bent rapidly, trying to duck under Jazz's arm, but Jazz intercepted her move and forced her back against the wall.

"Phoebe, how did Gabe get that job?"

"Some fellow from the Laker management phoned on Magic's behalf and asked if we had a photographer to cover the party. Since you were out of town, I talked Gabe into it."

"Someone called you? Was that yesterday or the day before?"

"Yesterday. Unexpectedly. After all, it's a surprise party."

"And just asked if you had a photographer available?"

"Right. It was one of those crazy last-minute sort of things. If only we'd had a little notice . . . well, I know you'd have liked the job but you just weren't around and I had to give them a quick yes or no."

"You could have phoned me in New York yesterday. I could have taken the red eye, been back in plenty of time, or I could have flown directly to Detroit." Jazz said with calm precision.

"I didn't think of that . . . and the phone call came awfully late in the day, New York time. I'm really sorry Jazz, I guess that should have occurred to me, but I knew how busy you were with the Pepsi people and there was Gabe with nothing special to do—"

"Every word you've said is a lie."

"Jazz, I see you're upset, but that's no reason to insult me!"

"Shut the fuck up, Phoebe. Are you trying to tell me that Magic would attempt to give a surprise party on the spur of the moment, considering how complicated, how damn near impossible it is to get players here from other teams all over the country?"

"You know me, Jazz, I try to rise above the unimportant details—I just look for the essential point of the job." Phoebe tossed her blond split ends vigorously. "Even if he had been planning this in advance, he only needed a photographer yesterday. Somebody must have let him down at the last minute, is all I can imagine."

"No possible way, Phoebe. It could never happen. If Magic had a photographer set, he'd have had one in reserve, maybe two. Few things in life have to be as carefully planned as a surprise party, any surprise party, and certainly one like this."

"Oh, Jazz, you're blowing this entirely out of proportion."

"Magic asked for me first, didn't he Phoebe?"

"Honestly, Jazz, just because you're a big fan . . ."

"He did, didn't he? I can check it out with one phone call."

"Oh, so what if he did, Jazz! O.K.? Are you satisfied now? Honest to God, you make me sick! Here I just got you the biggest commercial account you've ever had, you're going to be making more money than anyone else has ever made on commercial print ads, and you begrudge Gabe one little job, just because you want to be at the party yourself. Talk about selfish!"

"How long ago did you throw the job to Gabe?"

"I didn't 'throw him' the job—I made a career decision based on what was best for you, which, I might remind you, is the reason I've been so successful as your rep ever since you started in this business."

"You made a 'career decision'? No, Phoebe, you talked me into going to New York on an unnecessary errand. You got me out of the way so I couldn't hear anything about the surprise housewarming until it was too late. You *gave* Gabe an assignment that Magic wanted me for, a job I'd give anything to be doing."

"As usual, you're overdramatizing, Jazz. You're making more of this than it deserves because you're seeing ghosts, the unlaid ghosts of you and Gabe." Phoebe flung her head back and looked Jazz straight in the eye, daring her to make more of a fuss.

"What did you say?"

"You and Gabe. Do you really think I didn't know? That's what this childish fuss is all about, isn't it? Not one job, not one party, but Gabe and you and the way it was between you, way back when. Poor Jazz—I had no idea that you still cared so much."

The two women stared at each other in silence for a second, Phoebe with a small, knowing look of amusement that tried to taunt Jazz into thinking that the only way to retire from this struggle with her pride intact was to abandon it. Instead Jazz took Phoebe by her prominent shoulder bones and held the skimpy flesh steady with her fingers. Her voice was calm and low and unmistakably truthful.

"It has nothing to do with Gabe. It has to do with trust. We're through, Phoebe. You don't represent me anymore. I'll send movers to clear out the studio next week. Merry Christmas."

Jazz released Phoebe gently and walked out of the door of Mel's studio knowing that she would never enter Dazzle again.

"More stew, Casey?" Susie Dominguez asked.

"No thanks," he said, looking at Jazz sitting with him at the kitchen table. Red and Mike were spending a last night at Red's house, which had been put on the market. Jazz had arrived an hour ago, in time to join him for dinner, but she'd been so choked with outrage that she hadn't tasted the excellent lamb stew, so furious about being cheated out of her chance to photograph Magic Johnson's Christmas housewarming that she literally hadn't been able to stop talking about it for a minute.

"If you want my opinion," Susie continued, finally able to break into Jazz's monologue, "why blame the whole mess entirely on Phoebe? You're being much too easy on that bum."

"Gabe?"

"You know perfectly well I've never said his name since"—Susie glanced at Casey—"since that misunderstanding you had with him. But to my way of thinking, it's impossible that he didn't know exactly what it meant to you."

"I told you, Susie, he's not interested in basketball."

"How long has he been back in Los Angeles?"

"I haven't kept track," Jazz said mulishly.

"Months?" Susie persisted.

"I guess."

"And in all these months, working out of the same place as you, surrounded by the people who know you best, he hasn't even heard how hooked you are on the team? You've never mentioned the Lakers in his hearing? Listen, Jazz, you've been a hero-worshiper since Magic was a rookie more than ten years ago. I don't even follow basketball, but I feel as if the whole team grew up in my house, I even got a contact depression from you when Kareem retired, I know exactly how to pronounce Vlade Divak's name, I hear about it every time A. C. Green gets a haircut, not to mention the wonders of gravity defying Orlando Woolrich, bicep-and-tricep king of the NBA, and I try not to pay attention, because, as I keep telling you, football's my game, but I'd have to be deaf for it not to sink in. Casey? Has Jazz ever mentioned the Lakers to you?"

"Constantly. Do you want to know how many triple-doubles Magic and Worthy have this season?"

"No thanks, I'm aware of them. Now let's say that someone asks you to be the official photographer at Magic's party—wouldn't you absolutely have to at least wonder if that wasn't a job that should go to Jazz?"

"Susie, stop badgering Casey. He doesn't have to have an opinion on this. We're not taking a vote here."

"I'd know," Casey said. "I wouldn't wonder, I'd know."

"But Gabe wasn't told about the job until the last minute," Jazz objected. "Phoebe set the whole thing up."

"How could she have counted on that bum being around and available?" Susie asked. "If he really didn't know about it, he might have gone out of town for Christmas. Then Phoebe would have had to turn the Lakers down, and they'd have used another photographer. She'd have lost her rep's fee, which would be cutting her own throat. So, according to your own reasoning, when Magic asked for you and she gave it to that bum, it must have been a sure thing, set up a long time in advance."

"Good God, Susie, you sound like Agatha Christie," Jazz objected vehemently. "You should have been a rep yourself."

"Insults so soon, and the weekend hardly started."

"I'm sorry, Susie—I should stop talking about it. At least Bill Laimbeer won't be invited either. I'll put it behind me. Sorry to be so boring. I'll see the pictures in the newspapers."

"You just don't want to blame him," Susie insisted rebelliously. "You still buy his line."

"Damn it, Susie, stop nagging at me!" Jazz jumped up from the kitchen table, turned on her heel and took off in the direction of the living room.

"Now I've gone and done it," Susie said to Casey after a minute's remorseful silence. "I made her feel even worse. But that bum—between us, that bum's strictly a no-good son of a bitch!"

"Mike told me about Gabe," Casey said.

"Then you understand my feelings. How she can even talk to him after what he did, I'll never understand."

"Susie, aren't you being . . . overprotective? Their romance, or whatever you want to call it, took place more than ten years ago. Weren't they allowed to fall in love and fall out of love just like other people do?"

"Sure. When Jazz went away with him, that's what I told Mr. Kilkullen. I said all the kids are doing stuff like that, you've got to accept it. But when they were planning to get married and Mr. Kilkullen flew over to Paris and then came back almost before he'd left, with poor Jazz—looking like she'd never recover —*deserted by that bum the night before the wedding* —no! That's where I drew the line. Nobody can do that to my girl! That's not falling out of love, Casey, that's unforgivable."

"Mike never actually said they were planning to get married." Casey spoke slowly.

"That's not the sort of thing I get wrong, Casey. I don't know how long it took Jazz to get over that louse."

"Maybe she never did."

"Who knows? What a family! How about some cherry pie, as Agent Cooper would say."

Casey joined Jazz, who was deep in thought in front of the fire. He could see from her brooding expression that she hadn't been able to take her own advice and put the matter behind her. Her face was pale with fatigue, she obviously hadn't thought about touching her makeup since she'd left Mel's studio, and her eyes were tight with unshed tears. He imagined that she'd looked like this when she'd been a little girl and someone had hurt her feelings but she'd refused to cry. He felt that he knew things about her that no one had ever told him, least of all Jazz. Had she always been so proud, so defended, so difficult to reach, so burdened with memories? He had to make her smile.

"Would you like to hear me sing again?" Casey offered. "I know the lyrics and music to everything Rodgers and Hart ever wrote—also Harold Arlen, the Gershwins—anything Ella Fitzgerald can sing divinely, I can sing badly."

"You're being very sweet." Jazz looked up and really noticed him for the first time that evening. "The multitalented Casey Nelson, snappy dresser, Cow Boss and occasional troubadour."

"I can tell you're not in the mood for music. Would you like to play two-handed solitaire? Saddle up a couple of horses and go for a moonlight ride? Play spin-the-bottle?"

"Nope."

"We could go to the Swallows and trade the world's oldest dirty jokes. *Muy atmosférico.* We could watch television—I'd let you flip the channels. Or we could take a hot bubble bath. My tub is plenty big enough for two."

"Nope."

"We could trim the tree."

"It's all trimmed. Who did it?"

"Red, Mike, Susie . . . I strung the lights."

"Oh, you sucker," Jazz said mockingly. Casey felt triumph. Mockery was close to smiling.

"They saw me coming," Casey admitted. "Next year I'm going to get new lights."

"Next year you won't be here."

"Right."

"You'd really forgotten, hadn't you?"

"Yeah, I was thinking of something else."

"How come you didn't go home for Christmas?" Jazz asked.

"It seemed like too long a flight for just a weekend," Casey replied.

"Too long for a four-day weekend? Wouldn't Dad give you any extra time on either end?"

"I didn't ask—figured I'd better stay here. A Cow Boss should be constantly available, like a gynecologist. Come on, Jazz, let's go and poke around in the archives. There are some photographs of yours I'd like to look at again."

"You've finally made the right offer," Jazz said, with determination to change her mood. She unwound herself from the depths of the chair in which she'd been huddled as Casey tried to get her to cheer up. "I'll go and brush my hair and splash some water on my face and I'll join you there—Dad said you had a key."

A few minutes later they sat on the bench beside the long wooden table, opening a portfolio of Jazz's photographs from 1976, the year Jazz was fifteen.

"Those five little kids are Fernanda's boys and Valerie's girls," Jazz explained. "Heidi, Fernanda's youngest, wasn't born yet. They were here for a few weeks during that summer and I never stopped taking pictures of them. There's nothing like shooting kids before they're old enough to be self-conscious. You'll meet them all on Sunday, when all the family descends on us, but you'll never be able to recognize them from these shots.''

"I saw them at the Fiesta, all but Heidi—but I was a little confused that night.''

"You were a perfect asshole that night!'' Jazz smiled at last, and Casey shoved the portfolio gently out of his way. He was going to seduce this foul-mouthed, sad, magnificent, obstinate, antic girl under any roof in the world including the Sistine Chapel, he thought as he began to slide toward her on the bench.

"Anyway,'' Jazz continued, "Sam will be meeting them for the first time. I pray that the girls don't act too impressed, but that's probably too much to hope for. Fernanda, of course, can be trusted to make an utter fool of herself.''

"Sam?'' Casey's progress along the bench halted.

"I felt sorry for him, all alone at Christmas, homesick for Australia, so I invited him for Christmas Eve and Christmas Day.''

"That was thoughtful of you.''

"It seemed like the decent thing to do,'' Jazz answered with what seemed to Casey to be a smug, shifty, self-satisfied look. He closed the portfolio and went over to the shelves on which all the others were ranged by the hundreds. He fumbled as he returned it to its place, stunned by the emotion he felt. At random he started poking around among the portfolios, his back to Jazz, afraid that if he turned to face her, she'd be able to read the jealousy he knew must be visible on his face, a jealousy he had no right to feel. No right at all.

"Come on, let's see something from—I know— 1910, before World War I,'' Jazz commanded, as she had once conjured up past worlds from her father after dinner, and lived for hours in Hugh Kilkullen's photographs.

"Let's see . . . 1910 . . . that should be on the top shelf,'' Casey said, relieved by the distraction. He searched at length for the 1910 portfolio, and as he finally pulled it out, he noticed another portfolio that had slipped down behind the shelf and had become wedged in behind the many albums that covered the wartime period at the ranch. It was not green, like the others, but brown and almost invisible against the wood. He would never have noticed it if he hadn't been deliberately taking longer than he needed so that no trace of his jealousy would remain for Jazz to read. "Look, Jazz, here's a lost sheep." He put it on the table in front of her. "Have you ever seen this before? It doesn't seem to belong with the others."

"No! Never! How strange, it's not even the same size as the others. Wait a minute, Casey—look at what's written on it—'Amilia Moncada y Rivera'— my great-grandmother! That was her maiden name. She must have owned it before she married Hugh Kilkullen. And look, it has a date on it—1883. He was born in 1864, so she must have been a very young woman then. Help me get this open, for Pete's sake," Jazz said excitedly, struggling with a ribbon that threatened to crumble as she tried to untie the complicated knot.

The ribbon yielded finally, and Jazz opened the portfolio with impatient fingers. It had four accordion-pleated compartments, and she saw immediately that although two of them contained photographs, the others held various kinds of papers, most of them brightly colored. "Some things never change," Jazz sighed with pleasure, recognizing what they were as soon as she saw them. "Amilia kept her valentines. Look how beautiful they were. Have you ever seen valentines like these?" She lifted each elaborate, lacy, embossed card with the tips of her fingers, scanned their old-fashioned designs and opened them up to see the different names that had been signed to them. "Amilia has always had a reputation as the flirt of the family. Oh, and Casey, look, a bundle of letters. Maybe they're love letters. I hope they're all from Hugh Kilkullen, but I wouldn't bet on it. This ribbon is just too pretty and too tightly wound to tackle now. I'd make a mess of it. What's this?" She held up two sheets of yellowed paper. "It's in Spanish, but look at that complicated handwriting. It would take me a day to try to figure it out. I can speak ranch Spanish with the vaqueros, and I took traditional Spanish in school, but I don't think I could translate this. It's to Amilia from, oh, Casey, it's signed Juanita Isabella—my great-great-grandmother! She was Valencia's daughter, the girl Michael Kilkullen married when he bought this ranch. Now, why do you suppose Amilia kept a letter from her mother-in law?"

"Maybe it contained a list of suggestions for keeping Kilkullen men happy, from a Spanish woman's point of view."

Jazz lifted her eyebrows pityingly at him. "For some reason, that seems to be a typically unimaginative male remark." She put the valentines and the letters scrupulously back inside the portfolio and pulled out the photographs that were in the other compartments, and laid them out on the table. There was a silence as she and Casey studied the pictures that were over a century old.

"It's a good thing she labeled them," Jazz finally remarked.

"What a large family," Casey said.

"And what terrible pictures! My God, these people look as if they'd been electrocuted first and stuffed afterwards. And the lighting is so bad you can barely make out their faces. They're almost all members of her own family. Look, here's one of Hugh Kilkullen. I've never seen him look so young in any of his self-portraits. Amilia must have taken it before they were married. He looks dashing, from the little you can see of him."

"He looks like your father would if he had dark hair and a mustache," Casey said.

"Doesn't he, though? Hugh Kilkullen's own pictures make you realize how far ahead of his time he was. Well, even if these aren't good pictures, it's fascinating to have them. Look, here's one of Amilia's parents, my great-great-grandparents on the Spanish side. I think the Irish genes dominated." Jazz sighed. "It would have been great to discover a great-grand-mother with talent."

"That way you could say it came down from the female line."

"Right. Well, let's put everything back. I'll show them to Dad when I get a chance."

Jazz closed the portfolio, not daring to try to tie the ribbon. Casey put it back on the shelf with the larger, green portfolios from 1910.

"I don't think I've ever been so tired, Casey," Jazz said. "I just realized that I'm still on New York time—my day started a dozen years ago. I'd better try to get some sleep."

"Next time I go on a treasure hunt, I'll take a girl who can stay awake later than eight o'clock," Casey grumbled as he turned off the light of the archive room and locked the door.

How many points do you get for being a good sport, he asked himself. Jazz designed a weary good night in the air and started off to her room. Two hundred? No, dickhead, *minus* two hundred.

Although she had felt a wave of utterly draining fatigue in the archive room, Jazz realized that it was still only nine in the evening as she finished her bath and got ready for bed. She didn't know whether to push herself to stay up until a reasonable hour and get back on California time, or to give in and go to sleep early. Absently she opened the Christmas present Pete had thrust into her tote bag as they talked in Mel's studio during the party. Black satin pajamas and a matching robe, man-tailored and bound with an edging of white satin. Pleasure lit her face. In the language of lingerie, this ensemble made an open but nonaggressive decla-ration of desire. Good old Pete. He never stopped trying. She put them on, and they felt so delicious, slithering over her body, that she decided that nothing was more important than going to bed.

Jazz woke up with a bump three hours later, an abrupt surfacing into total consciousness that informed her that there would be no easy return to sleep, not even in this bed, in which she usually slept better than anywhere else in the world. It was midnight on her alarm clock, so it was three in the morning in New York, and everyone knew that the worst possible time to wake up was three in the morning, an hour that had a way of distorting thoughts, of bringing up ideas that would never be given house room during the day. And yet, as she lay in bed, her eyes wide open, she was aware that she felt mysteriously and deeply happy, as if she'd had a marvelous dream that she couldn't remember, which had colored her awakening.

Jazz reached down and picked up some of the patchwork pillows she had pushed onto the floor just before she dove into sleep, stuffed them behind her, and sat up in bed to check out her thoughts. Happiness like this, after her hellish morning, had to be accounted for. She probed gently at the whole mess of Gabe and Phoebe and their heist of the party shoot.

Of course, Susie was right; she just hadn't been able to face the whole truth at dinner. Gabe must have known what he was doing. Almost the first words she'd said to him when he'd shown up at her apartment had concerned the Lakers. She'd even been wearing her Lakers T-shirt. Of course, Gabe would always behave in a Gabe-ish way, Phoebe in a Phoebe-ish way. The only method for dealing with people like those two was either to accept them with a shrug or stop having anything to do with them. Like bedbugs.

She had chosen the latter course. It had been a clean decision, instantly arrived at, and in a final way, Jazz realized that they were truly out of her life. The bruised, battered emotions she'd brought back to the ranch had vanished. She still yearned to see Magic's housewarming surprise party, but that wish had been relegated to the never-never-land of unfulfilled wishes, the equivalent of owning good season tickets to the Forum. Wishes? Had she dreamed about wishes? The word had rung a tiny, maddening bell of dream memory as it came into her mind, Jazz thought, but she couldn't capture anything more, although her feeling of unaccounted-for happiness remained as strong as ever.

Jazz's thoughts turned to Sam Butler. Perhaps she felt happy because he'd be coming down to the ranch for the first time on Monday. He'd been in a tormented state the last time she'd seen him. He'd agreed to do a comedy for Guber-Peters in which he'd play a male model who confounds expectations by becoming a real-estate tycoon, but he'd been overcome by contract-signer's remorse.

"It was the worst career move I could have made," he insisted miserably to Jazz. "I still don't know how those brass assholes convinced me that it would be good for me to play against the typical thinking about male models, but I was bloody well had. Then I talked to this interviewer, and he told me that actors invariably expose their real selves, not in an interview, where they can hide, but in their choice of roles, which is, according to him, a *fatal* revelation of who they really are. So I had to ask myself if Redford would ever have agreed to play a male model, and I had to admit that he wouldn't. In fact, no bugger of a producer would have had the bloody nerve to ask him."

Jazz smiled at the thought of Sam and his career agonies. Oh, they were real, all right, as real as the agonies of any ordinary-looking man, and she tried to be as sympathetic as she would be to Mel or Pete, but he had a way of—was it just overdramatizing them? A way of making them seem not quite real. It wasn't anything he could help, she thought pityingly, poor Sam, a very large, very normal Australian trapped in the face and body of a great beauty. Ancient Greece would have been the right time and place for him to have been born, she decided, although it would never do to tell him that. His sense of humor wouldn't make the stretch.

No, thinking about Sam only made her queasy. The almost-unprecedented gathering of the whole family over Christmas had never promised to be a feast of good feelings, and the addition of Sam, an unknown element, might prove a welcome distraction or it might prove a disaster. She wished that she hadn't impulsively invited him when he'd told her so plaintively that he couldn't go home for the holidays, home where he was treated just like everyone else. How would her father take to Sam? But why should she worry about that? He only had eyes for Red. Why not worry about something real, like whether or not Sam and Casey would be civil to each other?

Casey! Jazz sat bolt upright in her bed as a fragment of her dream came back to her. She'd been sitting on the piano bench with Casey, and he'd been singing "There's a Small Hotel" and he'd just finished the second line, about the wishing well, and then— she couldn't remember beyond Casey singing, "I wish that we were there, together." Her chin had been leaning on his shoulder.

Jazz closed her eyes tightly and concentrated hard, but no additional image came into her mind. However, the feeling of happiness intensified and focused, as if she were looking into an emotional viewfinder. *Casey*.

She had barely paid attention to him tonight. All through dinner he'd just been a suitably outraged audience, after dinner he'd been a kindly, warming, patient presence who would have followed any of her whims to distract her from her anger, and yet . . . and yet . . . what if he hadn't been here tonight? Would she be wide awake at midnight, alive with an absolute understanding that if truth be told, Sam Butler was just a little bit—well, a little bit self-absorbed, that Gabe was nothing more than a hopeless Hungarian, that even Phoebe was basically a bad joke? Casey had a way of putting things into perspective, not by what he said, but by what he was.

Integrity. That was it. Casey had integrity, Jazz decided. On impulse, she got out of bed and put on her new robe. She wouldn't be able to get back to sleep for hours now, she told herself, as she hesitated in front of the door to her room. Should she go into the kitchen and make some warm milk? It was the classic remedy for insomnia, but it seemed like too much work. Should she turn on the light and read until she felt sleepy? No again.

It was so cold in her room. All of Southern California was having one of its classic fits of miserable winter weather, for which the natives were never prepared. She should go into the living room and see if the embers of the fire were still burning, add some logs and build up the fire, Jazz thought, as she realized that she was humming the tune of "A Small Hotel." Hadn't Mel and Pete once had a long discussion about how all they had to do was listen to what songs came unbidden to their lips, to know what was really on their unconscious minds? Mel had called it "tune therapy," and for once Pete had agreed with him. If what they said was true, then it followed that what she needed to put her back to sleep was to hear Casey singing at the piano.

It sounded right. Yes, here was the ring of truth to the idea. A few verses of his barroom ballads, and she'd be yawning. The only problem was that Casey's room was in the guest wing at the end of the long, covered veranda that ran along the hacienda, and she'd have to go outside, walk there and get him, possibly wake him up, explain the situation, invite him into the music room and let him sing.

Still, he had offered to do anything to cheer her up after dinner. Now that she had cheered up, in fact, cheered up remarkably, what was to prevent her from telling him that she was more upset than ever, and wanted to take up his offer to do Ella? Nothing, Jazz admitted, except a regard for his uninterrupted sleep and a minor question of telling the truth. If she looked at it another way, Casey would probably be so pleased to know she felt better that he'd be glad she had roused him to tell him, and the news would put him in the mood for singing. Yes, that was, in fact, the only considerate thing to do. For all she knew, he was still awake himself, worrying about her as if she were a sick cow.

This was truly thoughtful of her, Jazz thought, as she walked barefoot along the veranda where the winter-blooming jasmine perfumed the air with sweet nostalgia. There was an unhealthy, penetrating dampness in the night air, and a gusty wind, and here she was, risking catching a cold just to put Casey's mind at rest. An angel of mercy, very properly clad in black satin. Of course, if she'd been wearing a lacy nightgown she would have changed to something less revealing, but in a robe like this she could go out dancing.

There was no light under Casey's door. Obviously he hadn't been concerned enough about her to keep him from sleeping, Jazz thought, as she shivered. She rapped on the door several times, but she didn't hear him stir. She called his name but there was no answer. The wind blew nastily through the layers of satin, and her feet were freezing on the cold stone floor. Pneumonia weather. Jazz twisted the knob impatiently. The heavy old door opened with a creak of wood and she stepped quickly into the room and closed the door behind her. She waited a minute to get accustomed to the darkness, remembering her first painful encounter with Casey's luggage.

There were lanterns that were always kept lit in the patio, and they cast enough light so that soon she could see fairly well. She went over to Casey's deeply sleeping form and hovered over him, trying to decide on the best way to wake him up. She could pull on his big toe, which was the kindest way, because the toe was so far from the heart that it didn't cause alarm, but Casey's toes were covered by a blanket. She could stroke the back of his hand, but the hand nearest her was under the blanket too, and the other was flung so far on the other side of the bed that she'd have to lean far over him to reach it, and risk falling on top of him.

Jazz sat down on the floor while she considered what to do. Her face was level with the mattress, and she studied Casey as he slept. The covers were pulled all the way up to his chin so that only his face was visible. He looked like a little boy, she thought, a freckled boy of summer. His furrowed forehead was smooth, as it so rarely was during the day, and his habitually intense expression was absent. He seemed almost to be smiling in his sleep. Perhaps he was dreaming the same dream she'd had?

Jazz's eyes, so obsessed by the design of the human face, wandered slowly, judgmentally, from Casey's chin to his hairline, from his nose to his eyelids, from his ears to his mouth, all of them colorless in the dim light. His red hair, with its occasional curls and cowlicks, could have been any dark color, yet each individual feature was agreeable to her, deeply agreeable, even the nose that was too broad at its base. Each of them was solid, each arranged in an excellent relationship to the others. His features were unquestionably blunt, but their bluntness was not that of insensitivity but that of strength.

Still, with his eyes closed he wasn't at his best, Jazz decided. She missed the flashing brightness of his pupils, which were the interesting brown of a ripe hazelnut, and she missed the stubborn lion cub look that he had when he was speaking. Yes, he was better awake than asleep, no question about it, but had any man ever slept so deeply?

With an exasperated little noise, Jazz leaned forward and kissed Casey on his faintly smiling mouth. He showed no signs of waking up. She kissed him again, at length, the kind of a kiss no real, red-blooded man, in her opinion, should be able to sleep through, and all he did was try to move away from her lips. This was really getting annoying.

She could whistle piercingly right into his ear, Jazz thought. That would get his attention. But with Casey's propensity for clumsiness, he'd probably punch her out before he realized who she was. Jazz considered for a minute and then held Casey's nostrils together with her thumb and forefinger, so that he couldn't breathe through his nose, and fastened her lips tightly to his lips, so that he couldn't breathe through his mouth. Still asleep, he tried to twist away, but she had his nose so firmly in her fingers that he couldn't move.

As he started to smother, Casey's eyelids flew open and Jazz pulled away quickly.

"It's just me," she said.

"Huh? Huh?" He was utterly confused.

"It's me, Jazz."

"What are you doing here?"

"I . . . I wanted to tell you something." Why had she come, Jazz wondered in a fluster. She'd had a very good and important reason for her presence in his room, but in the long interval between leaving her own room and waking Casey up, she'd lost her earlier train of thought.

"You wanted to *tell* me something?"

"Yes . . . something about a dream. I'm absolutely freezing. Can I get into bed with you?"

"What!"

"Just to get warm. Come on, let me in. I'll catch something if you don't."

"I will not."

"Why not?"

"I don't wear pajamas."

"Well, I'm fully dressed and I won't look. Don't be such a prude." Jazz dove under his blanket.

"Ah. Better! It's nice and warm in here."

"Jesus, Jazz!"

"What's the matter?"

"What have you got on? It feels like ice."

"Pete gave it to me for Christmas. It's gorgeous . . . a black satin robe with matching pajamas."

"Pete gives you black satin underwear? I thought Pete was your business partner."

"He is, and this isn't really underwear, it's lingerie. Anyway, Pete's such a darling—he has this longtime fantasy about me . . . a kind of harmless, permanent yen that doesn't mean anything . . . could you move over a little? I'm on the edge of the bed here."

Casey slid into the far middle of the bed, and Jazz promptly rolled over so that she was lying as close to him as possible. He was very warm, very naked and very standoffish.

"Jazz, what the hell are you up to?" Casey asked sternly.

"Why are you so suspicious? I had something to tell you about a dream, but I can't exactly put my finger on it now . . . you know how dreams are."

"If I showed up in your room in the middle of the night and flung myself into your bed, what would you think?"

"That would be entirely different."

"In what way?" Casey demanded.

"Well, you'd probably have . . . something else . . . in mind," Jazz quavered. Now that he put it so crudely, without any understanding of the now-misty inner logic that had somehow brought her here, it probably would seem a little odd to him. She wished he'd shut up and be more . . . hospitable. Jazz put up her arms and locked them around Casey's neck. "You could kiss me, at least," she murmured.

"Great. Just great." Casey captured her arms and held them firmly so that they didn't touch him. " 'At least.' What do you think I am, some sort of life-sized toy? You spent the whole evening ranting obsessively about a man you'd once been planning to marry, you've invited your latest lover, major movie star Sam Butler, here for a family Christmas, and now you want to do a little bit of cuddling with me to show off how cute you look in the pajamas darling old Pete, with his unquenchable yen, gave you."

"Oh! You shit!" Jazz jerked away and sat up in the bed. "That's the most unfair, unfounded accusation I've ever heard in my life."

"Yeah? You say that I'd only want one thing from you, but all you want from me is a kiss. What are you doing in my bed, unless you want me to make love to you? Truly make love, seriously make love, for-keeps make love. But you don't, do you?"

"What do you expect me to say?" God *damn* him, Jazz thought, that had been exactly what she wanted, the lousy bastard, but she'd burn in hell before she told him so. And she'd never, ever, in a million billion years, tell him her dream. Didn't the stupid schmuck know anything about women?

"You're the damnedest tease I've ever come across. One more scalp for your collection, that's what I'd be. Well, you can forget that. I won't play. Just leave me alone and go back to tormenting lovely Sam and sweet Pete and unforgettable Gabe."

"Go to hell!" Jazz cried, popping out of bed and scurrying across to the door. "You fascist pig!"

"Would you say that the words 'painfully polite' are appropriate?" Red asked Mike in a quick, low whisper, as they preceded Jazz and Casey into the restaurant in Laguna Beach on Saturday night.

"I think 'the triumph of dignity' is more like it," he answered.

"It's not as if they're not speaking," Red said, rolling her eyes.

"Not speaking," Mike muttered, "would be an improvement. Who needs the younger generation?"

He was benignly amused by the way Casey and Jazz were behaving. He'd never seen his unpredictable daughter so blandly agreeable, so monotonously pleasant, so downright boring. As for Casey, he was as stiff as a career diplomat making his first visit to the protocol-crazed emperor of a foreign country.

As he pulled out her chair for Red to sit down, she leaned toward him and summed up her opinion. "Either they did and it was a bummer, or he wanted to and she wouldn't."

"Nothing else would explain it," Mike Kilkullen agreed. "I wish they'd stayed home and taken another shot. They shouldn't expect to get it right the first time . . . they're too young."

He had made reservations at L'Ambroise, one of the few expensive, elaborate and formal French restaurants in this casual beach community. Normally they would have dinner at the hacienda, but Mike wanted to give Susie extra time to get a jump on tomorrow's cooking, when the rest of the family, ten

strong, would arrive. She had hired two of her local
kitchen helpers and two waitresses to come in daily
for the next week, but Susie, being Susie, was busy
doing the major preparations herself.

The Saturday night before Christmas was no night
to leave home, Mike Kilkullen reflected. They had had
trouble finding a place to park in a crowded mall lot
where many of the stores would still be open all evening, but at least this restaurant, with its resident pianist who knew all the great old standards, could be
counted on to serve excellent food in an atmosphere
that relentlessly excluded small, boisterous children.

"Let's celebrate, darling," Red said to him.
"Caviar and vodka, don't you think, and lots of it?"

"Good idea." He pressed her hand tightly, divin-
ing her intention. If Red thought that food and alcohol
might lighten the air between Casey and Jazz, what
better, more rapid way to go than caviar and vodka?
The combination must possess an invaluable quality
that smoothed the edges of even the most hostile of
adversaries, or the Russians wouldn't always use it to
break the ice on official occasions.

"What are we celebrating, Daddy?" Jazz asked,
after Mike had ordered.

"Life in general, kid. Health and love and friends
—all those good things."

His daughter must be really pissed at Casey, he
thought, for she had gone to considerable trouble to
be at her most wickedly wonderful. She wore a very
short dress that, in any other era, would barely even
have been considered a teddy, much less a slip, an
alluring wisp of spidery brown lace over nude chiffon,
with only the thinnest of straps to hold it up over her
breasts. She had, damned if he knew how, arranged
her hair in the Veronica Lake style of the 1940s, so
that its waves flopped over one side of her face, and
when she sat down she managed to place herself so
that she gave Casey not only her bare back and her
cold shoulder, but also her blind eye.

A waiter brought them all footed crystal schnapps
glasses and filled them from a carafe that had arrived

at the table encased in a block of ice. Mike Kilkullen listened carefully to the pianist playing a great song from 1936 before he raised his glass in a toast to Red.

"The night is young and you're so beautiful," he said, and swallowed the vodka in one gulp.

"Sing it to me?" she suggested.

"Not me . . . I can't carry a tune."

Red raised her glass and drawled, "May I have the next romance with you—from that same year." She downed her glass and held it up for more.

"Hey, let me in on this," Jazz demanded, raising her glass to the two of them. "A lovely way to spend an evening—no, wait, I want another chance—my heart belongs to Daddy—and Red too." Attentively the waiter refilled her empty glass.

"My turn," Casey said. "All or nothing at all."

Red gave Mike a self-congratulatory pinch under the table. She was never wrong about sex, and if she'd needed confirmation, she had it now.

It was Mike's turn again, and they all turned to him. "The loveliness of you," he announced, looking into Red's beautiful face, enormously pleased with himself. Songwriters, those of long ago, were definitely on his side.

"When my dream boat comes home," Red toasted him.

"I've got my love to keep me warm," Jazz tossed off, blowing Mike a kiss.

"Fools rush in," Casey offered. His choice was greeted by a chorus of boos from Red and Mike, and silence from Jazz. "Can I have another try? O.K.— for Red—there's something nice about everyone, but there's everything nice about you."

"Now, where did that come from?" Red asked with a disbelieving laugh.

"Nineteen twenty-seven," Casey answered, showing off his esoteric knowledge.

Mike Kilkullen held his glass up again. "Happy days are here again—for all of us."

As he swallowed, he saw himself, year after year, for forty-five years, saddling his horse at sunrise and riding out with his vaqueros to the upper pastures and the waiting cattle; he saw Sylvie, holding Jazz in her lap in the old rocking chair, singing her baby a Swedish lullaby. It hadn't always been a happy life, or an easy one, but he wouldn't trade it for the life of any other man on earth.

The waiter made the round of the table again. This time, Jazz was the first to raise her glass. "I want to marry a male quartet," she announced with a wide, defiant grin.

"The lady is a tramp," Casey countered.

"Just hold it a minute, you two," Red objected. "We're getting off the track here. A little respect, please. All right." She turned to Mike, having restored order among the young. She lifted her glass. "More than you know."

"With a song in my heart." He grinned at her, clinking crystal on crystal before he poured the vodka down his throat.

"I had the craziest dream," Jazz toasted the table with an enigmatic gesture.

"Not allowed, it doesn't make sense," Red, a self-appointed referee, spoke up.

"Does it have to make sense?"

"If you're going to play, absolutely yes."

"O.K. A lemon in the garden of love. No? Come on, it's from 1906, honest. Ah, Red, you're rough. Life is just a bowl of cherries—that suit you?"

"Much better," Red approved.

"Not for all the tea in China," Casey volunteered emphatically, tossing off his glass.

"Casey, you're as out of line as Jazz. You get another chance," Red said through her laughter.

"She wouldn't do—what I asked her to."

"You made that one up," Mike said accusingly.

"Written in 1923, same year as that immortal song, 'I won't say I will but I won't say I won't'— from *Little Miss Bluebeard*, music by Gershwin. Must have been another prime year for confused females. Ask me anything, Mike, this is my field of real expertise. Cows are as nothing compared to this."

"You have a gift for the unexpected." Red made a toast to Casey, although there was no song to match her words.

"Let's call the whole thing off." Jazz drained her glass and slammed it down on the table with unnecessary force. "I need caviar," she added. Her attention was still focused on Red and her father. She hadn't favored Casey with so much as a toss of her head.

"We all need caviar," Mike said. They had drained the carafe of vodka so quickly that the waiters were only now serving the caviar from the big blue tin nestled in a silver bowl of crushed ice, being careful not to bruise a single one of the large, fragile gray eggs.

Red had been wrong about the mellowing effect drink would have on Jazz and Casey, she reflected. It seemed to have had the opposite effect. In a minute they'd be passing the ammunition and forgetting to praise the Lord. Well, the adults had done as much to help the children as they decently could.

Actually, he thoroughly enjoyed watching another generation play out a variation of one of the classic dramas, Mike Kilkullen admitted to himself, as he took in the table in a long, happy, reflective look. Why should they have their way smoothed over too easily? His wayward daughter was at her most glorious when she was in one of her cheeky snits; it was good for Casey to be so obviously smitten and so clearly rejected. They'd work it out or they wouldn't, and either resolution would be the right one as far as he was concerned, for the only essential was that Red would be by his side, his own Red, his unique darling, who would always remain a loving, adult woman, no matter how the kids kicked and screamed and reinvented the wheel.

Mike Kilkullen chuckled inwardly at his own philosophical distance. It felt like being in the middle of a warm, golden circle of light, as if he were pausing, at high noon, on the uplands of the ranch, and looking around for miles and miles in every direction over his empire, from the blue, beloved distant shores all the

way up to the top of Portola Peak, aware that even
beyond his view, it all belonged to the Kilkullens. He
had often done just that, but in earlier years those
splendid moments had rarely stayed with him for long.
Now, for many months, this feeling had become his
inner climate. It had taken him a lot of years to
achieve this state, he thought, but now that he'd arrived, it was one hell of a great and joyous place to be.

The rest of the meal passed in lively pleasure as
Casey and Jazz, in a state of temporary truce, applied
themselves to the spirit of the festive occasion.

"Where to now?" Red asked Mike as they made
ready to leave the restaurant.

"Home, darling. This town is too full of people,"
Mike answered.

When they reached the parking lot, Mike decided
that he and Casey should go and get his prized car, a
vintage 1966 Mercedes SE white convertible that Sylvie had given him. Jazz and Red waited on the sidewalk at the entrance. There was so much confusion,
with shoppers carrying large bundles of packages and
trying to fit unwieldy loot into their trunks, that progress toward the valuable car he had carefully parked
at the very far edge of the lot would be difficult.

Red and Jazz waited, arm in arm, their warm
coats wrapped snugly around them, in companionable
silence.

Minutes passed and a number of cars left the lot.
It shouldn't take this long, Jazz thought impatiently.
Suddenly she heard her father's voice, shouting
from a distance, raised in unmistakable anger. There
was a yell from Casey, interrupted by gunshots. Both
women, with the same instinct, raced through a mob
of shoppers.

They reached the edge of the lot where the car
was parked. Red and Jazz plunged into the crowd,
clawing, shoving, elbowing their way through the
crowd that had gathered, each of them growing more
frantic by the instant. At the edge of the crowd, men
held back the press of curious people, as if to prevent
them from reaching the small cleared space around

Mike Kilkullen's car, preventing them from seeing the
bodies on the pavement. Jazz and Red shrieked at
them with words they were never to remember, and
the men let them through immediately.

Casey was lying spread on top of Mike's body,
his arms flung up as if to shield Mike's head, his own
face flat in the dirt, blood spreading out from his side.

Mike Kilkullen lay on his back, his short white
hair wet in a pool of his own blood, his eyes open.

Jazz looked into their calamitous emptiness, and
long before Red, she smelled the truth. She put her
fingers onto his neck, just inside his collar, where she
had always pressed against his strong pulse when she
was a child carried in his arms. There was still
warmth, but no flicker of a pulse. She heard Red im-
ploring the crowd to call the paramedics, and she
heard people yelling for the police, but she knew already, as if she had received a semaphore signal from
the far ragged edge of her existence, that her father
was dead.

She turned to Casey. He was still alive, still
breathing, but unconscious. There was no way to
move him off of her father's body until the men came
with stretchers, no way she knew to find out how he
was wounded. All she could do was hold his limp hand
and wait for the help she knew must eventually arrive.
Even on the Saturday night before Christmas.

16

"**M**r. White is reading the will in San Clemente this afternoon," Jazz informed Red, as the two of them sat on a bench in a deserted children's playground overlooking the water at Lido Island. "Valerie and Fernanda don't intend to stay here a minute longer than they have to. When Father Joseph told them that he wouldn't hold the funeral on Christmas Day itself, they couldn't decently object, but anybody could see on their faces that they felt righteously inconvenienced. They wanted Mr. White to read the will this morning, but he said he wouldn't be ready until the afternoon, and he's a law unto himself, probably because he's about a hundred and two years old. He seems to have been ancient ever since I first met him and I was just a kid. The whole lot of them are planning to go back to New York tomorrow morning, first thing, which is the only good news I've heard."

Jazz listened to herself rattling on in a desolate skein of wonderment that she could sound so prosaic when she wanted to lose herself in endless, keening

lament. She found herself thrust into the position of
comfort-giver, although she had lost the most important person in her life, the father in whose love she
had been secure from the day she was born. But Red
was now so much less able to manage the most basic
motions of life than she was. This helplessness was
the only thing that kept Jazz from slipping into a bot-
tomless pit of mourning the incomprehensible cruelty
of his death. Her responsibility to Red had enabled
her to survive through the past three bitterly demanding days without giving up, throwing herself on her
bed and howling in a hideous grief that would have no
end.

She and Red watched the sailboats and yachts
riding at anchor, registering nothing but a gray shadow
of that sunshiny, shimmering holiday scene on the
morning of December 27. The previous day, Mike Kilkullen had been buried in the family plot in the graveyard of the Catholic church at San Juan Capistrano.

Every one of his children and grandchildren had
been there; all the vaqueros and their wives and children had attended, almost the entire population of the
town had thronged to the churchyard; leaders of the
Democratic party had flown in from different parts of
the country; ranchers from all over the West, who'd
made friends with Mike Kilkullen during more than
forty years of convivial auction weeks at the Cow Palace, had made the trip to San Juan; everyone who
worked with Jazz at Dazzle had driven down for the
funeral, except for Phoebe, who had had a sudden
attack of flu. After the funeral it seemed as if most of
them had come to the Hacienda Valencia to pay their
respects to the family, an endless stream of visitors
repeating the same words of utter disbelief and sorrow.

Only two people Mike Kilkullen loved had not
been at his funeral. One was Casey Nelson, who was
still confined to the hospital, beginning to mend from
the massive loss of blood and the bullet through his
lung that he had taken as he tried to shield Mike. The
armed thieves had been surprised as they tried to steal

the twenty-four-year-old Mercedes for the sake of its parts, which were highly valuable to professional restorers.

The second absent mourner was Red Appleton, who was too locked in the shock of her incredulous heartbreak to endure the sight of the man she loved being buried. She wanted to remember him laughing and happy, the way she had seen him only minutes before his death, she explained in the emptied, ragged voice that remained to her, and Jazz, thinking of the coldness that Valerie and Fernanda would certainly display toward Red, had agreed it was best that way.

Since the night of the killing, Jazz had been sleeping at Red's house on Lido Island. No less than Red, she could not face being alone with her stupefying grief, and Red needed her for survival through these first days. She had packed an overnight bag and shuttled the short distance up and down the coast highway between San Juan Capistrano and Newport Beach.

"Old Mr. White," Jazz repeated, when Red didn't respond to her flood of information on the reading of the will, "is that retired banker, the Governor's father. Dad did all his banking in Mr. White's bank in San Clemente, and for some reason or other, it seems that he gave him the only copy of his will. I guess it's because he never trusted lawyers."

"Oh, Jazz, you don't have to take care of me," Red said. "I know you don't feel like talking."

"Ah, come on, Red, darling, you're taking care of me. I couldn't stand being in the hacienda with six teenagers who hardly knew Dad, all trying to be well behaved while they're wondering why this had to ruin their Christmas. Poor Susie, she can't break down until they leave—that's all that's keeping her going."

"Susie was going to teach me . . . how to cook," Red said, as thinly as if she were trying to remember something that had happened a hundred years ago, to somebody else.

"That's more than she ever did for me. That means she really approved of you."

"We were planning . . . parties . . . I never gave Mike his Christmas presents . . ."

"Red, Red! Give them to me, I'll take them back. It's not good for you to have them around."

"All right," Red agreed emptily. "The packages are in the hall closet. Jazz, we opened the silver service. I knew what that box from Jensen's had to be when it arrived last week, and I couldn't wait till Christmas to show it to Mike. He was so . . . so proud of you . . ." Red burst into a racking spasm of sobs that doubled her over while she beat her fists weakly on her knees, trying to control herself.

Jazz wrapped her arms around her as tightly as she could. There was nothing she could say to help Red when one of these attacks of grief ambushed her, but she hoped that being held must be some tiny comfort.

"I'll take it all back to the store, don't worry, darling, I'll take everything away," she repeated over and over, meaninglessly, as if crooning to a baby, until Red finally was able to straighten up and dry her eyes.

"God, I'm so selfish. Look at you being brave," Red reproached herself when she was able to speak.

"I'm lucky, I have things to keep me busy, and you have nothing to do but think. In fact, I have to get started for San Clemente now. It wouldn't do to keep Mr. White waiting."

"I didn't know that they actually read wills anymore," Red said, trying to show some interest in Jazz's affairs.

"Neither did I. I thought you just got a letter from the executor, or something like that. But Mr. White is of the old school. I'll be back as soon as it's over and I've checked on Casey at the hospital. Tonight you're going to eat a decent dinner—I won't let you get up from the table till you do. Come on, walk me back to the house."

The two women walked slowly back. Jazz wondered, from a far distance, how she was managing to put one foot in front of the other in her state of emptied, abandoned stupefaction, of wanting to be dead.

═══════

Mr. Henry White, in spite of his years, still kept an office in San Clemente, on the same street as the bank he ran for so long. There he read five newspapers every morning, looked after his investments for several hours every afternoon, and maintained his network of political contacts by telephone. The combination, in his case, had ensured a lively, contented and healthy old age that had been crowned by his son's reelection as Governor of California.

After Mr. White had led Jazz, Valerie and Fernanda to the chairs arranged in front of his desk, he sat behind it as he addressed them. Since he had talked to each of them individually after their father's funeral, he wasted no time in formal condolences.

"Young ladies, I never expected this occasion to arise, I never expected to outlive your father, but since it has, I would like to say, before I read this will, that I disapprove of it. I do not believe in holographic wills. 'Homemade wills,' I call them, and legal or not, I've never trusted them."

Valerie bit her lips in irritation at his pedantic, fussy manner, and swung her foot nervously. Fernanda's hands were twisting in her lap, and she blew her hair away from her face with a quick puff. Jazz sat in frozen stillness.

"I told your father many times," Mr. White continued, "that his will should have been drawn up by a lawyer, and kept in a lawyer's office, but he refused to listen to me. I had been entrusted with his own father's holographic will, and he felt that what was good enough back then was good enough today. I did not agree, but that's as may be."

Fernanda looked at Valerie and raised her eyes heavenward in a manner that indicated clearly that she was practicing the utmost in self-control. Mr. White ignored her and kept on speaking at his own pace.

"This will, in spite of my objections, is, I assure you, perfectly legal in this handwritten form, and I have had some considerable experience with wills. Ha! It was written three years ago, on January 15,

1987, and I was present the entire time. Although the law doesn't require it, I insisted that it be witnessed by my secretary and the present manager of the bank. As far as I am aware, no other will exists."

He pushed his glasses down from his nose and looked from one to another of them, noticing the expressions of undisguised impatience on Valerie's and Fernanda's faces, and paused a moment before going on, speaking in the slow and distinct voice of someone who intends to make himself plain under any and all circumstances.

"Now, young ladies, there are several bequests of cash, primarily to Susie Dominguez, who has cooked for you for many years, and to each of the vaqueros who have worked for your father much of their lives. These are very generous, but not surprisingly so, considering their length of service to the Kilkullen family. However, none of these bequests are significant in the context of the estate, and I will read them to you later.

"What you young ladies are anxious to learn, I should imagine, is the disposition of the residue of the estate, which consists of a savings account in the San Clemente Bank and the sixty-four thousand acres of land known as the Kilkullen Ranch."

Henry White scrutinized all three of them from under his wrinkled lids. Only Jazz returned his look in a friendly way. She knew that her father had regarded Henry White as a most trustworthy friend, she had met him a number of times when her father happened to take her with him on his visits to the bank, and in spite of Henry White's dry manner, she was fully aware of his real sadness at Mike Kilkullen's death. Finally he began to read from the document he held in his hand.

" 'In the absence of a male heir, I, Michael Hugh Kilkullen, leave the money in my savings account in the San Clemente Bank, to be put into a trust to pay for the upkeep of our family home, the Hacienda Valencia. My daughter Juanita Isabella Kilkullen is to decide how this money should be spent.

" 'I leave the Hacienda Valencia, designated a California Historical Landmark, all of its contents, the entire area of the driveway from the road to the hacienda, all the gardens that surround the hacienda, the stables, the outbuildings, and the archives of photographs taken by my grandfather, Hugh Kilkullen, solely and unconditionally to my daughter Juanita Isabella Kilkullen. The Hacienda Valencia has always been her home, and I know that neither of my other daughters regards it as such.' "

"That's indecent!" Valerie interrupted explosively. "How could he decide that I wouldn't want to have a place in California? Or Fernanda? That couldn't be more unfair!"

"Valerie, could I ask you to reserve your comments till later?" Mr. White said severely.

"It's an absolute disgrace, and I won't put up—"

"Val, shut up. I want to hear the rest of the will," Fernanda said, tapping her sister sharply on her knee.

"To continue," Mr. White said, looking reprovingly at the paper he held.

" 'In the absence of a male heir, I leave all of the remaining land, known as the Kilkullen Ranch, in three equal parts to my three daughters, Juanita Isabella Kilkullen, Fernanda Kilkullen and Valerie Kilkullen. I hope, trust and believe that my daughters will possess the ability to do the proper thing with this inheritance.' "

The old man stopped reading and put the document down on his desk. The three women waited for him to resume. He looked calmly from one to the other and finally broke his silence.

"That's all."

"All?" Valerie asked suspiciously. "As simple as that?"

"As simple as that. Aside from the bequests I mentioned earlier," Mr. White assured her, "you have just heard the contents of the entire will of your father, Michael Kilkullen. He told me, when he wrote this will, that he had been as fair to his children as he knew how to be, and the rest was up to you. Ha! I hope that you will be equal to the task. Now I will read you the individual bequests to his employees."

Valerie stood up abruptly, a victorious expression dawning on her face, replacing the rage that she had shown when she heard that Jazz alone owned the hacienda. Now that she understood that she had, at last, inherited a third of the ranch, her words rushed out imperiously. "Could you send all that to me and my sister in a letter, Mr. White? We're both pressed for time, and we don't need to know the details of these small bequests right now, do we?" Fernanda also stood up and both of them, without ceremony, started toward the door of the office.

"One minute, young ladies," Henry White said sharply. "The two of you come back and sit down. I'm by no means finished."

Valerie spun around. "Is there some law that says that we have to sit through the reading of all the other bequests?"

"No, this has nothing to do with those bequests. There is one more piece of information that I should give you at this time, so that you'll be able to understand the position in which you now find yourselves. In the case of a will like your father's, which was made without naming executors—which, again, was against my advice—there will have to be a special administrator appointed as soon as possible until a permanent administrator is named."

"Why?" Fernanda demanded.

"The Kilkullen Ranch is a going business. There must be a caretaker to ensure that expenses are met. For example, many dozens of people work on the ranch, and there is a considerable payroll to be met; various bills have to be taken care of on a weekly or monthly basis; there is the question of the citrus and truck farmers who pay rent to the estate, and then, of course, there is the problem of how best to dispose of the cows, most of whom are in calf, as well as the herd of bulls. Don't forget, young ladies, I was your father's banker for many years, and there's nothing wrong with my memory."

"Who . . . who appoints this special administrator?" Jazz felt bewildered. Four thousand head of cattle, thousands of calves to be born, hundreds of bulls —there must be a million details she had never thought about that were involved in running the ranch.

"The Orange County Superior Court. Normally I would expect them to appoint someone from the trust department of a bank that has experience in the ranching business, Wells Fargo, for instance."

"So some stranger from a bank . . . ?" Jazz asked.

"Exactly. Unless, of course, one of you should petition the court to become the administrator herself, and the others agree."

Jazz glanced at Fernanda and Valerie and saw that they were as negative about such a suggestion as she was. All three of them shook their heads.

"I think you've made a wise decision. It's a complicated job. Of course, this special administrator is not empowered to sell any of the assets of the estate. However, all three of you must agree on the appointment. It should only be a matter of a few days."

Henry White sat back in his chair. "You're all free to leave now."

"Jazz, I hope you don't mind our taking up room in your grand old Historical Landmark for one more night," Valerie said, piercingly spiteful at the injustice of being cut out of the hacienda. "We'll pack up ourselves and the children and be out of your hair first thing tomorrow morning, won't we, Fernanda?"

"For God's sake, Valerie, you're all more than welcome to stay as long as you like! You know that perfectly well!" Jazz cried.

"I wouldn't dream of it. We'll be a great deal more comfortable at the Ritz in Laguna Niguel anyway, until this administrator business is settled."

As Valerie and Fernanda clattered down the stairs, they exchanged rapid, short phrases uttered in low, excited voices that Jazz was glad she couldn't overhear. She sat still, humiliated for them, knowing that old Mr. White was far too shrewd not to have noticed the instant glee, the greedy, grabby, almost out-of-control avariciousness that she had seen so clearly on their faces, replacing the conventionally sad faces that they had worn for several days.

"Well, Jazz, my dear, you don't seem to be in as much of a hurry as your sisters. I'm glad for that. There were a few other things I wanted to say before they left, meditations of the voice of experience you might call it, but I didn't feel it was advisable or even possible—ha!—to detain them any longer."

"I'd be interested in listening to the voice of experience," Jazz said gravely. Fernanda and Valerie had not even thanked Henry White for his services.

"I hope you and your sisters are aware what a responsibility this inheritance will be," Henry White said. "I'm sorry they felt that they had to leave so quickly. I knew them as children, of course, but only slightly. I knew their mother well. She and my son, the Governor, and my daughter-in-law are still close friends. They might, it seems to me, have taken a minute to acknowledge that."

"I'm sure they didn't mean to be so abrupt," Jazz said. "Valerie was upset about the hacienda."

"That's as may be. One-third of the Kilkullen Ranch is a princely inheritance. My own impression was that they were each in a hurry to broadcast the news," he said with a sharp look at Jazz.

"Or pack," she said disgustedly. Trust Valerie to act as if she were being put out in the snow with a babe in her arms.

"It was only due to my constant, nagging insistence that this will was made at all. Your father was a man who denied his own mortality. Like many men, even many of the very same lawyers he mistrusted, Mike Kilkullen had no intention of ever dying. He rejected the thought of how best to dispose of his ranch, because he couldn't bring himself to consider that a day would come when he was no longer in control. This will is a hasty will, made by a man who wanted to get it over with as quickly as possible. It is a will that makes the implicit assumption that you and your sisters will get together and agree on how to proceed with the division of the estate.''

"We have no practice in agreeing," Jazz said. "You may have noticed that."

"I was aware that might be the case." He studied her astutely. "I was his banker through the period of your father's first marriage, of his divorce and of his remarriage to your mother. I know that your sisters have been brought up on the East Coast, that they have made their lives on the East Coast, that they will have no interest in the ranch except to sell it as quickly as possible."

"But—" Jazz started to speak out, but suddenly found that she couldn't collect her mind. Her violent grief robbed her of any clarity of thought. She struggled to find words.

"Yes?" Mr. White asked, sitting patiently back in his chair.

"It's just that—you make it sound almost as if— as if the ranch *had already been sold*—so quickly, just like that." Jazz snapped her fingers with a sound of finality. "It's everything my father lived to prevent— and now—going, going, gone! Sold. It seems so heartless, so . . . cut-and-dried, as if he'd lived for nothing, as if now . . . now that he's not . . . here, nobody has anything to say about it."

She hadn't begun to realize fully that her father was dead, Jazz thought, and she hadn't had time to mourn him, yet this wise old man had already taken it for granted that her father's ranch, a hundred square miles, land that had belonged to the Kilkullens, and the Valencias before them, for seven generations, was in the hands of unknowns. How Mike Kilkullen would have raged at such an idea. No wonder he fought the process of making a will, no wonder he couldn't endure thinking about a time when he would no longer be able to protect his property.

"Instead of a stranger, couldn't the Cow Boss, Casey Nelson, be appointed as special administrator?" Jazz asked. "Wouldn't that be the logical choice?"

"I don't know, Jazz. It would depend on the court. It would depend on your sisters' agreement. And it would depend on his willingness to take on the job. In any case, we are talking about a temporary appointment. The real aim of the court is to find an administrator, technically called an 'Administrator with Will Annexed,' who can negotiate the sale and division of the estate. The court will make every attempt to do this as quickly as possible, within six weeks to two months."

"Oh, why didn't my father leave the whole ranch to the state as a park? Isn't that what he should have done, damn it?" Jazz cried with her whole heart.

Henry White cocked his head in surprise. He considered Jazz's words for a minute.

"Certainly that would have solved a lot of problems. Ha! But it would have disinherited his children. Few men do that, unless they have a very good reason."

"But I wish he had!"

Henry White permitted himself a smile. "Jazz, my dear, if I may give you a piece of advice—?"

"Yes?"

"Get a lawyer, Jazz. A good one."

"Casey, I just can't get my mind around it," Jazz said in bewilderment. "I'm trying, but I can't. I understood the words Mr. White used, but I can't make myself accept them. I feel as if I've been pulled off my feet by a giant, turned upside down, whirled around the giant's head, and shaken up and down like a rag doll until I've lost all sense of direction. I'm . . . reeling."

Jazz slumped in a chair by Casey's bed in the hospital, a forlorn figure, her gilded surfaces all dulled and tarnished. The golden topaz glint of her eyes had turned the color of smoke, her skin was paler than he'd ever seen it, her hair fell with unusual lifelessness and docility around her face, its color more tortoise-shell than golden brown. She wore gray flannel trousers and an ancient gray turtleneck sweater he'd never seen before.

"These have been the worst days of your life," he said gently. "You can't expect to absorb everything all at once."

"Casey, today I felt . . . as if I'd lost Dad all over again. When I realized that the sale of the ranch was just a question of time—oh, Casey, I'd never faced that before. I can't stand to think about the future any more than Dad did. When my mother died, I had to believe he was immortal, because if he weren't I would have truly been an orphan, truly been alone." Jazz spoke in a toneless reverie of lament.

"When I grew up, I was still convinced that my father was immortal. And nothing Dad ever did made him seem less . . . eternal. He didn't believe it any more than I did." She shook her head and seemed to shake herself away from her anguished dream with an effort of will.

"Can you imagine my father leaving his will with a man as old as Mr. White?" Jazz asked. "It must have been his way of making a will without admitting it to himself." She spoke as much to herself as to Casey.

"Mike probably realized, somewhere down deep, that Mr. White would have made arrangements to have the will transferred to safekeeping. Your Mr. White sounds like a very practical man to me."

"Oh, that he is. He told me to get a lawyer. Why do I need a lawyer?"

"You're an heiress, and every heiress needs a lawyer."

"For what?" Jazz seemed willfully childish to Casey. Admitting that she needed a lawyer was admitting that Mike was dead, he realized. But she had to be sensible.

"I'm very serious, Jazz. I'll bet that as soon as Valerie and Fernanda got back to the hacienda, the first phone calls they made were to lawyers."

"What kind?"

"Jazz, look, I know you don't want to think about

it, but you've just inherited one-third of sixty-four thousand acres of the most valuable undeveloped land between Los Angeles and San Diego. And your two sisters together control the other two-thirds. Haven't you ever heard of something called 'protecting your interests'? There are lawyers who specialize in inheritance and real-estate law. One way or another, you're going to need lawyers. For the entire rest of your life."

"Casey!"

"Christ! I'm sorry—I guess I shouldn't have been so blunt. But you can't be *allowed* to be naive. Jazz, remember, I'm a hard-headed businessman when I'm not playing cowboy."

"Hard-hearted too?"

"If I have to be, but only then."

"I still can't understand how you persuaded the hospital to let you put a fax in this room," Jazz said, changing the subject. She didn't want to hear another word about lawyers.

"As soon as I could talk, I convinced them I'd never get well without it. I found a temporary secretary who comes in at six every morning and faxes for me. By lunchtime the stock market in New York is closed, and I shut up shop for the day. My doctor wasn't thrilled, but he says he'll probably let me out of here in two or three days. I walked around this floor six times this morning . . . felt pretty good."

"Casey, there's no right way to say this, but . . ."

"Then don't." He put up his hand like a traffic cop to stop her, but Jazz paid no attention.

"You almost died trying to save Dad. The doctor told me that you could easily have been shot through the heart, not the lung. Saying thank you isn't enough. The right words don't exist, but I can't *not* thank you, no matter how ridiculously inadequate it is."

"It was a reflex. I didn't think, I just acted. I don't get credit for that, Jazz, and I don't want thanks. My only feeling is the greatest, the deepest—the most . . . *unutterable* regret that I failed."

"You . . . loved him." Her voice, as low as a whisper, answered the unspoken question in her words.

"I hadn't realized how much. I think we became closer, even in these last few months, than I've ever been able to be with any other man. Sometimes we talked most of the night . . . it was like being back in college with my best friend, if my best friend had had sixty-five years of experience to draw on. I'll always, always miss him, Jazz, miss him terribly."

Jazz put her hand on Casey's shoulder and they sat in grieving silence for a few minutes. Finally she roused herself from the murderous sadness of her memories. If she started to cry now, she would never, never stop.

"Casey, Mr. White told me that the court would appoint someone to run the ranch on a caretaker basis until they find a permanent administrator who will handle the sale. Would you be willing to stop being Cow Boss and take on that job? I know it's an indoor job, and tedious, but it would mean so much."

"Of course. I'll do anything I can to help. How do I get appointed?"

"Apparently I can ask the court to appoint you."

"Well, go ahead and ask. And, Jazz, *get a lawyer.*"

"I will. Just don't tell me again."

There was a tap at Casey's door. As it swung open, Jazz looked up, expecting to see a nurse who would, in the time-honored fashion of nurses, tell her not to tire the patient. Instead, a handsome, middle-aged man in a well-cut New York suit looked at Jazz with instant recognition as he advanced toward Casey's bed.

"Jazz, this is my father, Gregory Nelson," Casey said, in introduction. Jazz jumped to her feet and put out her hand.

Gregory Nelson took Jazz's hand and held it tightly between both of his. "I'm terribly, terribly sorry, Jazz," he said, and then pulled her into a warm hug. So this was what a lion cub would look like when he grew up, Jazz thought confusedly, taken off guard by his informality. Gregory Nelson, whose wife had been dead for three years, was a little shorter than Casey, and his features were different, but he had the same look of honest concern, and to Jazz, whose emotions had been sharpened by her grief, he radiated fundamental goodness so strongly that he made her feel as if she had been taken into the circle of protection of a powerful ally. She had to blink back tears at the unexpected comfort the greeting of this stranger had given her.

"When did you get here?" she asked, taking refuge in banality in order to regain her equilibrium.

"As soon as we got the news," Casey's father said. "I've been making sure that Casey obeys orders. He's almost as good as new, assuming that he was ever any good in the first place."

"That's my dad," Casey said proudly. "The old man never misses a chance to remind me that I used to be a little shit."

"Why should I treat you better than you treat me?" his father asked.

"You give me a fresh perspective," Jazz said. "I wish I'd met you sooner."

She took her leave, wanting to stay longer and talk with Gregory Nelson, but knowing that she had to settle matters with Valerie and Fernanda.

Jazz drove from the hospital to the ranch, turning into the avenue of venerable fig trees and parking in front of the Hacienda Valencia. Before she went inside, she stood for a moment, uncertainly, and looked around reflexively, squinting here and there at the scene through her thumb and forefinger as if she were planning how best to photograph the exterior of the hacienda. She tried telling herself that this belonged to her now, but the thought had no resonance, no faint echo of significance. The view was drained of three-dimensional reality, as if she were looking at façades of make-believe buildings and surveying cardboard trees and flowers. As she searched the familiar yet suddenly meaningless surroundings, she vowed to guard them always as they were today, as they had been during her father's lifetime, and his ancestors' before him.

When Jazz finally stepped inside the house and heard the unexpected crackle of a fire burning in the living room, her heart contracted violently and she almost cried out loud. Although the scent of Mike Kilkullen's pipe tobacco lingered in the air, the sound of a fire he could not have lit told her, finally, that he would not rise from his chair by the fire to kiss her when he heard the sound of her step. She walked resolutely toward the living room, trying to push from her mind, until her mission was completed, the adored image of that tall, white-haired chieftain with his slow, dear, loving smile.

Fernanda was lying comfortably in Mike Kilkullen's favorite chair, her high-heeled purple lizard boots up on his ottoman, a glass in her hand. Valerie was sitting in the brown leather chair that Jazz considered her own, her long, lean legs crossed under her, yoga-fashion, her flat shoes on the floor beside the chair, another glass balanced on the wide arm of the chair.

"I hope you don't object, Jazz," Valerie said coldly. "I didn't think you'd begrudge us a few sticks of wood for the fire, and a drop of your scotch."

"Be my guest," Jazz said equably, choosing another chair and pouring herself a drink. She was determined not to let Valerie provoke her.

"You know, Jazz, no matter how much money Father left for the upkeep of this manse, it isn't going to go very far. You'll be lucky if you can redecorate in any sort of style, even Southwestern. If I were you, I'd check the roof for leaks before I touched anything. Just a hint."

"I'm not planning to redecorate, Valerie."

"You have to. This place hasn't been touched in years, not since your mother died. Just look at this chair—the leather's all cracked."

"I like it that way."

"Well, far be it from me . . ." Valerie shrugged.

"What are you going to do with this big old place?" Fernanda asked. "Live in it?"

"I haven't decided anything. I didn't know it was going to be left to me until you did."

"Father expected you to keep this white elephant going, that's clear," Valerie said. "As he said, it's your home."

"Yes, Valerie, so it is. Listen, I came here so we could discuss this caretaker appointment."

"I thought the court would take care of that," Fernanda said.

"It will," Jazz replied. "But I have a better idea. Luckily for us, Casey Nelson is willing to take over the administration of the ranch. I've just seen him, and he'll be out of the hospital in a few days. He knows far more about running the ranch than anyone the bank could possibly find. Can we agree on his being given the job?"

"You must really think we're a pair of fools, Jazz," Valerie said scornfully. "Casey Nelson, indeed!"

"He's not just a Cow Boss, Valerie," Jazz said patiently. "The guy is much more than a plain rancher, he's a serious, successful businessman. He's involved in major investing in many different businesses. He'd only be doing it as a favor."

"A favor? To whom?"

"To all of us, Valerie. Casey would maintain the ranch in peak operating condition until the permanent administrator took over."

"I see three women in this room, Jazz," Valerie drawled, "and only one of them has been fucking Casey Nelson."

"What!"

"In my book, that gives you an unfair advantage. Doesn't it, Fernie? Haven't you had enough unfair advantages for one day, Jazz? First you manage to cheat us of our share in our family home and the family savings. If you think that after that charming little caper we'd agree to let you put your boyfriend in as special administrator—think twice.''

"What do you think he'd do?" Jazz said hotly. "Pad the feed bills? Rustle the cattle? Steal the silverware?"

"All of that, and a hundred other things you haven't mentioned. Between the two of you, the place would be stripped clean.''

"We saw you make your big play for Casey Nelson at the Fiesta,'' Fernanda said with a delicately prudish sniff of her little nose. "You must think we're pretty stupid.''

"Actually, no. I think Valerie's *incredibly* stupid and you're incredibly jealous. And shouldn't you both be packing?''

Jazz paced back and forth in Red's living room as she recounted the story of her day.

"And then," she said, still sputtering indignantly, "that chinless freak, Valerie, accused me of fucking Casey!''

"She came right out and said that?"

"I didn't think Valerie even knew that word. Can you imagine anything so outrageous?''

"It's just shocking. I wonder how she knew?''

"You too! Jesus!''

"You mean . . .''

"Never! Not that *they* would have believed me.''

"Gee, Jazz, what's stopping you?''

Lydia Henry Stack Kilkullen was not even faintly surprised when Jimmy Rosemont invited her to have lunch alone with him. One day had passed since the reading of Mike Kilkullen's will, and she knew that with his declared interest in buying the ranch, he would be anxious to extract as much news from her as possible.

She would enjoy watching him fish ever so delicately for crumbs of information, she thought, as she dressed for lunch. It was always a treat to see someone as rich as Jimmy Rosemont working his heart out to get richer.

If all the people who could live brilliantly on the most infinitesimal percentage of what they already owned were to stop struggling for more, the world would be deprived of a spectacle that never failed to entertain, Liddy mused, as she surveyed her New York wardrobe with the calculating and matter-of-fact eye of a hangman looking at the neck of the next victim. There was nothing in it that she would bother to keep once she started getting the large sum she expected from the girls, she decided. Not that her clothes weren't still good, but she would not care to be reminded for an instant of the days when everything she wore had been bought on sale.

Liddy pushed a number of hangers aside before she found the right Bill Blass suit. It had a navy skirt and blouse with a red jacket, tailored with a sure-handed hardness that few designers still knew how to bring off successfully—a suit that spoke of rich women doing their spring shopping on Fifth Avenue, so classic that only she would know that the spring of which it spoke was two years past and not the spring of 1991.

Rosemont had asked her to meet him at the Stanhope Hotel on Fifth Avenue. Liddy approved of the choice. The restaurant of the exceptionally well run hotel was expensive and elegant, yet its location, opposite the Metropolitan Museum, was much too far uptown to attract the fashionable, gossiping crowds that lunched together in packs some twenty blocks farther south. It was the most discreet place to lunch in this indiscreet city.

She arrived at the restaurant a calculated fifteen minutes late, knowing that he would be precisely on time. It wasn't often that one could afford these little pleasures of ego, but today Liddy knew that nothing was beyond her grasp. The phone call yesterday from Valerie and Fernanda had wiped away every failure, every shortfall, every regret of her life. She knew that the victory she felt made her look twenty years younger, and she breezed through Jimmy Rosemont's greeting without a hint of apology, no longer a petitioner.

After he had admired her, after he had ordered, Liddy waited smilingly, composing herself for the small talk that must be indulged in before he began a cautious line of questioning. In her experience, people rarely came to the point until the main course had been removed from the table.

"Georgina and I were so sorry to read that your daughters had lost their father," he said.

"That's very kind of you," Liddy replied. She couldn't have put it better herself, she thought. Not a word too much, not a word too little.

"Now, shall you and I get down to business?"

"Business?"

"Liddy, we don't know each other as well as we should. That's a loss we'll have to recoup. But meanwhile, time is of the essence."

"Is it?" Liddy asked, as blankly as possible. She had underestimated this man.

"The Kilkullen Ranch will be sold, as we both know. The only question is to whom. I represent a group that is prepared to pay the highest price Valerie and Fernanda can get anywhere. Other groups will be interested in the property. The more people who get involved in bidding for it, the longer it will take to sell. The process could take a long time. I want to make a preemptive bid to ensure that my people get the ranch."

"You don't waste words," she said dryly.

"With someone less intelligent, I might have to."

"I didn't inherit the ranch, Jimmy, my daughters did. More precisely, two-thirds of it."

"I know that, Liddy. Fernanda phoned Georgina yesterday."

"I see," she said, frowning.

"I also know how much influence you have on your daughters. They know that if it hadn't been for you, they might well not be heiresses today."

"That's quite true," Liddy said, mollified.

"May I be direct?"

"Isn't this a little late to ask?" Liddy began to smile. She had *gravely* underestimated this man.

"Extremely direct?"

"By all means."

"If you use your influence with your daughters to assist my partners in securing the ranch, they will insist on showing you their gratitude."

"Can't you be more direct than that?" She laughed, and he laughed with her.

"There would be a finder's fee, as soon as the deal is closed."

"How much of a finder's fee?"

"One-half of one percent of the selling price."

"And roughly what would that come to?" Liddy asked.

"Roughly, somewhere around fifteen million dollars. Possibly more."

"Hmm. Interesting. Tell me, Jimmy, how much do you know about Orange County?"

"Enough, Liddy."

"Forgive me, but I doubt it. I've been following the rise in land values in Orange County week by week for the past thirty years. Nothing has happened there in real estate that I don't know about. I can foresee every problem your group of would-be buyers will face. First they have to satisfy the permanent administrator, who will be appointed by the court, that they are the proper buyers. Then they face problems from various state and local agencies."

"My people are aware that it won't be easy to develop the land. They expect to have to be patient."

"It can be made easier. But not for one-half of one percent."

"Oh?"

"I have one great friend in this world. A faithful friend for over thirty-five years. A friend who will do anything that I ask."

"Oh?"

"The Governor of the State of California. Deems White. He has the power to force through the permanent administrator of his choice. He has the power to make problems from state and local agencies . . . disappear.''

"I had no idea." Jimmy Rosemont spoke respectfully. "Of course, that changes things. Shall we say that it doubles them?"

"I rather think it triples them," Liddy said.

"That seems fair."

"Then we understand each other. The details can wait until the time comes."

"It can't come soon enough, Liddy."

"I quite agree."

Jimmy Rosemont raised his glass to her. He had indeed underestimated this woman. But on the other hand, she had underestimated the value of her influence. If she had demanded a hundred million dollars to ensure that this deal happened, he would have agreed happily to her price. It was going to be the ultimate deal of his life. One hundred million would have been a most reasonable price to pay for a hundred square miles of the most valuable land in the United States.

17

"**W**hat kind of cooperation are the Soviets going to give you on the shoot in Kiev?" Jazz asked Sam Butler as they spoke on the phone.

"Why are you so sure we'll have to go to Kiev?" Sam asked.

"You're playing a Ukrainian political leader, right? Last I heard, Kiev was the capital of the Ukraine. Definitely Soviet."

"What the hell, locations are Milos's problem. One of those places looks just like the other anyway. Grim, that's the big point, Jazz, the location's gotta be grim. I'm bloody excited."

"Of course you are—it's exactly what you were looking for. I still don't understand how you got out of the male-model gig."

"I convinced Guber and Peters that you can't force an artist to do something against his will. After I shaved my head, they believed me."

"You didn't!" Jazz stifled a rising giggle.

"You wanna bet?"

"Have they recast the part yet?"

"I wish you hadn't asked, but yeah." Sam Butler's bubble of ebullience was dented but not punctured.

"Tell me," Jazz demanded.

"Daniel Day-Lewis," Sam said in disgust. "Would you have believed that Daniel Day-Lewis would agree to play a male model? After getting an Oscar for *My Left Foot*?"

"It's a change of pace for him, that's all, Sam, don't be upset. Think of it as a tribute to you that Milos Forman asked you first."

"Yeah, cobber, that's right, I hadn't thought of it that way," he said, pleased by her opinion.

"Has your hair started to grow back in?" she asked, trying to sound concerned.

"Like crazy, thicker than ever, wouldn't you know?"

"When you were completely bald, did people treat you differently? Were they more friendly, less intimidated, at least while it lasted?"

"Nah. It weirded them out. Face it, Jazz, I'm stuck with my instrument. To transcend your instrument, you've gotta have a nothing face. Oh well, it may be a dirty job but somebody has to do it. I guess things could be worse."

"I hope the shoot goes brilliantly, Sam," Jazz said, thinking fervently that Daniel Day-Lewis most certainly didn't have a nothing face, and yet he transcended it with each new role.

"I'll miss you, cobber. A hell of a lot."

"I'll miss you too."

"See you when I get back?"

"Of course, Sam. Have fun."

As she hung up the phone, Jazz knew that she would never see Sam Butler again except as a friend. Distance had dissipated a never-solid enchantment; absence, far from making the heart grow fonder, had proved a definitive cure of what had not been love. Now that Milos Forman was spiriting him away for months to Kiev or some suitably grim substitute, she could forget about him in good conscience.

She glanced at the clock on the bed table of her familiar room at the hacienda. It had been a morning of unexpected phone calls, and she'd been interrupted several times as she tried to dress for an unwanted meeting with her sisters.

First there had been the conference call from the Diet Pepsi people. As soon as Jazz had decided that she was far from ready to go back to work, she'd called her new friends to regretfully resign the job.

Today, in the middle of January 1991, they'd phoned and told her that they had decided to wait for her, even if it meant a month or two. Their campaign had been tailored to her work, they told her. They considered her as irreplaceable as a great actress who would always surprise you; they never knew to what new limits she'd be able to take celebrity photography, and her new approach was too innovative to consider having another photographer copy it.

While Jazz was still thinking about the Pepsi call, Red had phoned, sounding a little more like her old self than she had since the night Mike Kilkullen had been killed, and they'd made a dinner date.

Casey had been out of the hospital for days, eating as much, under Susie's watchful eye, as any man could be expected to. Next week he planned to resume his full duties as Cow Boss, using one of the Jeeps to get around, until he was completely mended. Casey had not been surprised when Jazz gave him a delicately expurgated version of why her sisters had refused to agree to his appointment as special administrator. Joe Winter, of Wells Fargo, a sensible and likable man, had been appointed by the state to serve as special administrator. He had been delighted that Casey had agreed to continue as Cow Boss until the Kilkullen cattle, a famous "Reputation Herd," were satisfactorily sold.

Valerie and Fernanda had settled in at the Ritz-Carlton in nearby Laguna Niguel, hanging around the area as if they thought their inheritance would vanish if they weren't in the neighborhood. What could they want from her today, Jazz wondered, feeling a plunge of uneasiness add itself to the condition of grief in which she existed. Her state of mind was utterly dominated by the loss of her father, to which was added her dread of the inevitable sale of the land and an ever-growing, painful nostalgia for the life of the ranch that was about to end.

She had found herself incapable of making the only sensible move and returning to Los Angeles and her work at Dazzle. She was unwilling and unable, emotionally and physically, to separate herself for even a day from the ranch while it still existed as it had always existed, tranquil, timeless, majestically beautiful, its hundreds of rounded mesas unchanged from the days when the friendly Gabrielino Indians greeted the first Spanish soldiers as they arrived from the Royal Presidio of San Diego in 1769 on their north-ward exploration of the land that was to become California.

Every morning she saddled up Limonada and rode the lively roan in a different direction, taking her last looks. Here and there, Jazz could not ignore a Jeep track or a windmill or a reservoir that betrayed the presence of modern man, but once her horse mounted the hill behind the hacienda, the vast, glo-rious, downward sweep of the land was intact, as it curved in its roughly fanlike shape that narrowed bluntly at the top of Portola Peak and widened out to its longest boundary at the Pacific Ocean.

When Jazz urged her horse to pick its way down into an arroyo, the world of 1991 disappeared entirely. Often she would slide down from her saddle and stretch out on a bed of dried leaves, watching the sun travel overhead for hours, feeling each time as if today were the last chance she might ever have to be alone in each sweet-scented, humming pocket of shelter.

She knew she should be praying for more rain, as Casey and Joe Winter were, but the dry days that had followed the heavy rains earlier in the year seemed to be giving her a reprieve from reality. When Jazz craved company in her sadness, she spent her time out on the open pastures among the vaqueros, who were busy watching over the breed herd.

Winter was always the liveliest time of the year on the range. The bulls, who spent ten idle, lonely months of the year in the purely male company of the "Bull Battery" corral, had been put in among the cows on the first day of December, one bull to every twenty cows. On the first of February they would be "gathered up" and sent back to bull purdah, but for the moment they were roaming frisky and free, as they finished their function of impregnating the entire herd. Every cow still had a nursing calf, born last fall, by her side, and some ninety percent of them had been "bred back" and were due to calve again next fall, a cycle that ended only if the cow failed to breed during these two winter months, became dry, and had to be sent to market.

Casey and Joe Winter had quickly agreed, at their first meeting, that the best time to sell the herd would be at an auction held no sooner than late spring, after the calves were weaned and independent. The fattened cows would all have been tested to make sure that they were bearing calves. If the sale took place before the calves were weaned, the cows would be sold as a "three-in-one package," the nursing calf and the unborn calf sold with each cow, at a much less desirable price.

She'd never been sharply aware of these particular financial aspects of ranching, Jazz realized, because Mike Kilkullen had never talked about money. But as much as she would miss the sight of the cattle wandering slowly and peacefully over the immemorial curves of the mesas, it was the land that called to her. Each three-hundred-year-old oak, each blooming sprig of each sage bush, each meadowlark she heard in the morning, each owl that hooted at night, imprinted itself on her heart, another beloved reminder of her father.

The enormous Ritz-Carlton at Laguna Niguel, between Emerald Bay and Three Arch Bay, is located on a particularly tall bluff, one hundred and fifty feet above the shore. Although Jazz knew it was described as being in the Mediterranean style, she saw nothing Mediterranean about its vast marble lobbies and gigantic public rooms, decorated in French and English antiques. The whole place was staggering in its ostentation; everything about it was ten times too big, she decided angrily as she strode through one immensely long, expensively carpeted corridor after another in search of the elevator that would take her to the suite Valerie was occupying.

If someone had to build such a bloated blimp of a hotel on the coastline, why couldn't they have done it in a way that would make it seem as if it bore some relationship to its California location, instead of creating an over-scale imitation of the Crillon in Paris? Even if this hotel, like the Crillon, had been located on the Place de la Concorde, the most impressive square in France, it would still be condemned as trying too hard to be grand. As she rode up in the elevator, Jazz realized that she really didn't hate the innocent, if pretentious, hotel; she hated having to lay eyes on Valerie and Fernanda.

She had pulled herself together after her last phone call of the morning, determined to get through this unwelcome meeting as quickly as possible. She'd glanced in the mirror and suddenly viewed herself through her half sisters' critical eyes. Without makeup, her hair flapping every which way, like a flag attacked by the wind through which she rode all day, Jazz saw that she seemed almost waiflike, a rustic, sun-touched, unkempt, female Huckleberry Finn, in the worn jeans, the faded blue chambray shirt and the favorite sweater from her school days that had become her uniform during the past days on horseback.

Almost everything she owned was still back in her closets in her Santa Monica apartment, but Jazz hunted around until she found the Yves Saint Laurent pant suit in which she'd traveled back from New York on the day of her final showdown with Phoebe at Dazzle. She'd driven straight out to the ranch after that Christmas party, only a little more than three weeks ago, and hadn't returned to her apartment since.

The pant suit was one of Yves Saint Laurent's daytime tuxedos, a "smoking," as he called it, stricter, more severe, more commanding than anything a man can put on short of a military uniform, a classic design that Saint Laurent repeated in a dozen versions every year, his signature, as much as the Chanel suit was her signature. Smokings, made in black fabrics from satin to hard-surfaced wool, play directly to a woman's need to possess at least one garment that can act as an impenetrable carapace to cover and protect any inner insecurities she may feel.

Jazz took out the perfectly cut authority symbol with displeasure. She resented having to slant anything about herself with an eye to how she would appear to Valerie and Fernanda, but she knew that it was necessary in dealing with them.

She brushed her hair and forced it to lie flat on her head with mousse, binding the dark golden strands into a smooth, tight chignon, and fastened it securely with a black velvet ribbon. Then, putting on a terry robe, she started to work on her face. She used a light foundation on her apricot-hued skin and pressed white powder onto it, so that her face became a pale matte mask on which anything could be painted. She darkened to the limit the straight punctuation marks of her eyebrows; applied layers of mascara to her golden lashes until they were black; used a red lipstick she had bought but never worn because it was too dark a red to be flattering. By the time she finished, Jazz had added a decade to the face she had seen in the mirror a half hour ago, and a hundred years of hardness.

After she had put on the Saint Laurent and low-heeled, highly polished black boots, she inspected herself again. This elegant lady bouncer with the toughest shoulders in couture had never heard of Huckleberry Finn, she decided, as she finished off her outfit with a pair of massive jet-and-gold earrings and two wide, plain gold cuff bracelets, which would have to substitute for the brass knuckles she would have liked to wear but didn't possess.

The elevator stopped on the top floor of the hotel, where the most expensive accommodations were located. A young woman came forward from behind a small desk and introduced herself as the concierge. When Jazz gave Valerie's name, the concierge immediately escorted Jazz to a pair of double doors that, except for their newness, would not have looked out of place in the Petit Trianon. At the touch of a bell the doors swung open on the largest sitting room Jazz had seen in any hotel in the world. At the far end of the room, four arched windows looked out at the panorama of the sky and the sea in the distance, but Jazz focused on the group of people who sat around a table in the middle of the room: Valerie, Fernanda and two men she had never seen before.

She paused, frowning, as the strange men rose. Valerie had said nothing about them, and Jazz was immediately glad she had taken the trouble to get herself up in an image that betrayed none of the desperate hurting in her heart, or the feeling of intense vulnerability she could not shake off. She stood just inside the room, stubbornly immovable, aware that if she did not advance toward them, they would be forced to come to her.

After a tiny pause, Valerie stood up and led the two men to Jazz to make the introductions.

"Hello, Jazz," she said, in as friendly a manner as she ever felt obliged to display to anyone. "You're looking wonderfully well."

"Thank you," Jazz said coldly. To her astonishment, Valerie leaned over and kissed her on the cheek in a breezy, casual way, as if she had totally forgotten their last encounter.

"This is Jimmy Rosemont," Valerie said, "and this is Sir John Maddox. My sister, Jazz Kilkullen."

"How do you do," Jazz said, offering her hand

to the men as briefly as was consistent with a minimum of politeness.

"Come on in, Jazz," Valerie said, taking her arm and leading her over to where Fernanda was sitting with a welcoming smile in her brilliant turquoise eyes. Everything about her looked, Jazz thought, as if a fairy godmother had been overly generous.

"No, thank you," Jazz said, waving away the offer of coffee and greeting Fernanda in the same economical gesture. She sat down on the only chair that wasn't deep and puffy, placing herself on the seat as precisely as any Victorian lady come to pay a ten-minute courtesy call, sitting stiffly upright, her back not touching the chair.

A mahogany cart laden with trays of tea sandwiches, small pastries and pots of tea and coffee stood next to Fernanda's chair.

"Something to eat, Jazz? These little éclairs are awfully good," Fernanda asked, with one of her most fetching looks.

"Nothing, thank you." Did her smoking make her look so masculine that Fernanda thought she'd had a sex change, Jazz wondered. That was the look she reserved for anything in pants, all right, but not a dame.

"How is everything at the ranch?" Valerie asked.

"No different from the way it was when Mr. Rosemont flew over it in a helicopter on an inspection tour a few months ago," Jazz said evenly.

"So you heard about that, did you?" Jimmy Rosemont didn't sound surprised, but faintly amused. Jazz didn't like his devilish, jovial, too-well-groomed looks any more than Mike Kilkullen had.

As for Sir John Maddox, he had the perfect relaxation of surface that only the British seem able to achieve. He was a man in his late sixties whose thinning gray hair was just exactly the trifle too long that indicated that he didn't worry about his haircut; his double-breasted, rather formal gray suit was immaculate, yet old enough to seem as if it were a member of his family; his handsome head had a dignity of prominent bone structure that was more than sufficient to show that he was accustomed to the exercise of power.

"I thought the best way to get an overview of the ranch was by air," Jimmy Rosemont added, unabashed. "Have you ever done that? Amazing experience, shows you things you could never dream of from the ground."

Jimmy Rosemont's voice and manner could undoubtedly be considered charming, Jazz thought, if you were in the market for a sharp, foxy, tricky charm, which she was not. She didn't bother to answer him, but waited silently, her chin lifted, one trousered knee over the other, her arms folded across her breasts, staring into the neutral middle distance. Her body language was calculated. She might be outnumbered, but she knew that she looked as if she were reviewing her troops. Eventually, one of them would get around to explaining the point of this meeting.

"Jazz," Valerie said, "as you're aware, when Jimmy first came out here and saw Father, he was interested in buying the ranch. Since Jimmy and his wife, Lady Georgina, are both good friends of Fernanda's and mine, after Mr. White explained to us that the ranch had to be sold, we both thought of him first, before any stranger."

"I can understand that, Valerie. What I don't understand is the reason for this rush. According to Mr. White, nothing at all can be sold until the court appoints a permanent administrator, and that may take months. It's only been a few weeks since Father died."

"What you say is quite true, Miss Kilkullen." Sir John Maddox entered the conversation smoothly, with an inclination of his head, a pause and a glance that managed simultaneously to convey a wordless homage to Mike Kilkullen, an acknowledgment of Jazz's loss, and the need to pass on to matters of business.

"However," Sir John continued, "there is an important advantage to be gained if the three of you should be able to come to an agreement about the future of the ranch without any waste of time."

"Is there?"

What was it about a certain kind of British voice that inspired confidence, Jazz asked herself. This distinguished man had the kind of aristocratic benignity radiated by Sir John Gielgud or Sir Ralph Richardson. Two consummate actors.

"You see, Miss Kilkullen, during the period of the special administrator, you still control the destiny of the ranch." Sir John leaned slightly forward and addressed himself entirely to Jazz.

"You three sisters, acting together, can petition the court to set aside the special administrator. You can then decide to sell the ranch to a buyer whom you have personally chosen, someone in whom you all have confidence. However, once a permanent administrator is appointed, none of you will be able to rid yourselves of him except, as the law puts it, 'for cause,' and that would be excessively difficult and highly unlikely. In other words, no matter what the permanent administrator chooses to do, or how long it takes him to do it, you will be entirely in his hands, at his mercy as it were."

"Are you a lawyer, Sir John?" Jazz asked.

"Yes indeed, a barrister, but I no longer appear in court." He smiled a graceful, self-effacing smile.

"Sir John was the governor of the Crown Colony of Hong Kong for many years," Jimmy Rosemont said. "During that time he presided over the Executive Council of the colony and was president of the Legislative Council of Hong Kong. Since he resigned those responsibilities, he has become an internationally recognized expert on land use and development."

"Is that why you're here, Sir John? To advise us all on land use?" Jazz asked. An actor killed Lincoln, she reminded herself.

"Not entirely, Miss Kilkullen, but in part, yes. I am also here on behalf of a group of men I have known for well over fifteen years. They form a consortium of the owners of the largest banks in Hong Kong."

"You're acting for a bunch of Hong Kong Chinese bankers?"

"Precisely, Miss Kilkullen."

"And these . . . clients . . . of yours want to buy the ranch?"

"Indeed they do, Miss Kilkullen. In fact, one could say without fear of contradiction that they want it more than any other buyers in the world. You see, my banker friends *must* get their money out of Hong Kong before it is returned to Communist China. Six years from this coming June, the agreement by which Hong Kong was leased by Britain will expire. My friends live in fear that the Communists may not be willing to wait till 1997. They're running out of time, as you can understand, and that's why they'll pay *more* than the market value."

"Forgive me if I seem confused, Sir John," Jazz said, "but as I understand it, only months ago Mr. Rosemont tried to buy the ranch himself. Now here you are, with Mr. Rosemont, only you're representing Hong Kong bankers who want the same piece of land. Exactly what's going on?"

"Oh, come on, Jazz," Valerie said, "don't get your fur ruffled over nothing. Jimmy's been advising the Chinese from the beginning. Sir John is another one of their most trusted advisers. Jimmy never told Father about the gentlemen from Hong Kong because he couldn't manage to get that far before the conversation was terminated. You know how abrupt Father could be when he didn't want to listen."

And she knew what an excruciating pain Jazz was going to be, Valerie thought. She'd warned them all about her, but nobody except her mother had been ready to believe that such an absolutely wonderful opportunity could be held up temporarily by one pig-headed girl. Every time their mother had telephoned to discuss the situation, she'd reminded them that Jazz had spent years worming her way into their father's heart, and had told them not to discount the nuisance she would make of herself. God knew, she and Fernie had to admit that they owed their position in their father's will to their mother's insistence that they put in their duty time at the ranch. When their mother had told them that selling to the Chinese was the best thing they could do, and that they should put their trust in Jimmy, she was unquestionably right, as she had been for the last thirty years.

Valerie lifted her chin and presented her celebrated profile to Jazz as if it were a guarantee of her right to mediate between Jazz and Jimmy. Fernie wouldn't be of any help.

"Mrs. Malvern is right," Sir John said. "When a sophisticated group of bankers attempt to move their money from one country to another, they are forced to depend on a number of different specialists. I daresay Jimmy has been doing business with them almost as long as I have. We're both working with our Hong Kong friends, trying to find a solution to their problem that will benefit you and your sisters as well."

"John," Jimmy Rosemont spoke hastily, as he watched Jazz's face close up and reject the Englishman's words, "before we start talking details, why don't you let me give Miss Kilkullen an idea of the way in which the ranch would be developed? Obviously she'd want to know that before she began to make any sort of judgment about the buyers."

"Of course, Jimmy."

"You see, Miss Kilkullen, your ranch isn't just another piece of real estate, and it would never be treated as if it were ordinary, garden-variety, undeveloped land. The concept is to turn it into the most spectacular, splendid residential and recreational complex anywhere in the world. The name would never be changed, it would always be the Kilkullen Ranch, or Rancho Kilkullen, or whatever name you and your sisters liked best, but the idea—well, the idea is nothing short of magnificent."

"Is it?" How long could she endure the sulfurous smell of snake oil, Jazz wondered. Long enough to find out exactly what this salesman had in mind, she decided grimly, no matter how noncommittal or even enthusiastic she had to seem to get it out of him.

"Bear with me, Miss Kilkullen. We all know that large parts of Orange County have been covered with houses that are lined up side by side, one looking just like the other, to the point that they might just as well be tract houses anywhere. They're very comfortable little places, I don't deny that, but they wouldn't do justice to the Kilkullen Ranch. They are exactly the opposite of what we've been thinking about."

"I see." So it was "we," was it? No one could accuse her sisters of being slow on the draw. While she'd been lost in her brooding around the ranch, taking her long, melancholy leave of it, they'd gathered together this pair of selfless experts and brought them out to California to tell her what her best interests were.

"Now picture this, if you will. The entire ranch forming one single unified community of pure luxury, one single, *flawless* community, a jewel that would stand out in the same way that Monte Carlo stands out from the rest of the Côte d'Azur—except that it would be in a thousand ways more spacious and gracious than Monte Carlo, which, to my way of thinking, is decidedly over-built. What I visualize is a community in which not one single house would be worth less than ten million dollars—most of them would be worth a great deal more—and each one would be surrounded by such lush landscaping so that there'd be privacy for everyone."

"Pure luxury, you say?" Jazz spoke with interest. She wouldn't buy a pair of Lakers playoff tickets from this man, not even if they were in Row A at center court.

"Luxury beyond anything you can imagine. And, even more important, *security,* so that the residents would be free to revel in their life-styles. Now here I'd like to take a lead from Monte Carlo itself, because there would be a security system similar—only better in every way—to the one that makes Monte Carlo such a pleasure to spend time in. We would employ security police by the tens of dozens, discreet but always dependable. The women in Monte Carlo think nothing of wearing their great jewels whenever they like—they can walk down any street in the principality wearing jewels, because they know that they are safe in their own community at all times. How many places in the world can you do that today, Miss Kilkullen?''

"I have no idea, Mr. Rosemont." Somehow, Jazz thought, she had the feeling that she could count on him to tell her.

"None! Absolutely none. Not in Beverly Hills, not in Bel Air, certainly not in any cosmopolitan city in the world. The Kilkullen Ranch would be more closely guarded than the Crown Jewels of England. No one could enter a single one of its gates without passing the inspection of several armed guards and without verbal permission from the person they've come to see. It would be the ultimate gated community, a Shangri-la, a total refuge against the ever-increasing dangers of modern life.''

"Who would actually . . . live . . . there?" Jazz asked.

"Ah—the most important point of all! The superrich from all over the world. It's as simple as that. Such people would flock from everywhere to buy homes here, not just because of the extraordinary safety factor but because of all the other advantages enjoyed by this area. We have the best weather in the world during the winter months; on the shore of the Kilkullen Ranch there is a natural harbor more than wide enough for a marina that could accommodate dozens of oceangoing yachts as well as smaller boats by the hundreds; there's plenty of space to build an airport so that the residents could arrive in their jets; the community would support a fleet of small planes and helicopters so that they could whisk off to Costa Mesa or San Diego or L.A. whenever they wanted to go shopping or to the theater, to a restaurant or to catch a plane if they don't already own one. *Transportation*, Miss Kilkullen—instant, easy transportation— is something the very rich *have* to have, or what's the point in serious money?''

"I've often asked myself that very question. Do these people *have* to have children as well as transportation?"

Jimmy Rosemont laughed. "We've thought of that. We'd establish a school here just for that reason, from kindergarten through high school, a private school system comparable to the finest anywhere. For the residents' children only, of course."

"Wouldn't the residents have to have servants?"

"Indeed they would. Servants are equally as important as transportation. There will be accommodations for servants, in the residences, if desired, or in a special servants' village that we'll build at a suitable distance. Of course, the servants' backgrounds will be subject to a thorough check by the security system of the community. We'll take no chances."

"Urine testing on a daily basis?"

"You're having a good time making fun of me, Miss Kilkullen, but let me tell you, that's not at all a bad idea."

"Why, thank you, Mr. Rosemont."

"What we envision for the Kilkullen Ranch planned community is, quite simply, *the very, very best of everything!*" Jimmy Rosemont stood up and began to pace back and forth in excitement. "Of course there would be several championship golf courses, created by the leading designers in the field, of course there would be a racetrack and equestrian facilities for riders, again they would be state-of-the-art in every detail; the same lavishness and style would apply to the tennis club, the country club and the beach club. The Sporting Club at Monte Carlo would instantly seem down-at-the-heels in comparison. These clubs would be the centers of galas and parties that would attract guests from every capital and every resort in the world."

"Guests? Friends of the homeowners. Family? Poor relations?"

"Even poor relations." Jimmy Rosemont's pointed, graying eyebrows peaked in appreciation. "But when I said guests, I was speaking of the inter-

national travelers who would turn the Kilkullen Ranch
into a fabulous vacation resort as well as a planned
community, very special, very fussy people who have
been spoiled for anything less than the most magnificent of accommodations. And once they've discovered what we'll have to offer, they won't want to
leave."

"What magnificent accommodations?" Jazz
picked the important words out of his smooth flow of
words and fastened on them.

"The hotels, Miss Kilkullen, the many splendid
hotels that will be built along the beachfront. They'll
make this hotel look shabby, I promise you. Nothing
will be lacking to attract the cream of travelers except
a casino, but every afternoon jets will leave for Las
Vegas and return whenever needed, so no one will
notice the lack of on-site gambling."

"How foresighted."

"Yes, I think we can honestly say that we've tried
to think of everything. The hotels, even the largest of
them, will be designed and integrated into the shoreline, so that we can use as much of the available beach
as possible. The condominiums will be built only on
Portola Peak, where they will rise from the base, each
one high enough above the others so that the views
will be unobstructed. Our aim here is to maximize land
use by eliminating all wasteful space, such as grazing
land, and creating new space in areas such as Portola
Peak, which has never been put to use before."

"Tell me more about the condos," Jazz asked.
Condos! Mike Kilkullen's least favorite word.

"Not one of them will be under twelve rooms.
Comparatively, they'll be priced in the same range as
the residences and offer less upkeep. I can't be entirely certain yet, but my rough estimate is that we'll
be able to build perhaps two dozen condominium com-
plexes, with the usual swimming pools, health clubs
and all those essential amenities."

"This won't be cheap." In her voice, a reflective
note blended into a slight timbre of temptation.

"Indeed not, Miss Kilkullen." Sir John Maddox

rejoined the discussion. "No question about that. The advantage of having my Chinese friends behind it lies precisely in the enormous expense involved. You see, the Chinese take a long view, a historical overview, if you will. They don't expect immediate results from their investments. They're willing to wait patiently for construction to take place. Once assured that they own the land, they will be content to wait for the returns on their investment. In addition, they can write checks for the purchase price without having to go to banks to borrow, because they *are* the banks. My friends have more than just their own money to get out of Hong Kong. They have the fortunes of their depositors, every one of whom is as worried about the future as they are. Once you make the decision, should you choose to, you won't have to wait for your money."

"Interesting," Jazz said. "Very interesting."

"Jazz, what do you think?" Fernanda asked eagerly. "Isn't it the most exciting idea you've ever heard of? I'd want to have a place here myself, and I never felt that way about California before."

"Jazz, you realize that the hacienda would continue to be entirely separate, that it would be respected, isn't that so, Jimmy?" Valerie reminded him.

She didn't like the fact that Jazz hadn't moved from her Little Napoleon pose since she'd sat down. She hated to admit it even to herself, but she almost had to admire the way Jazz had forced Jimmy to sing for his supper. His descriptions of his plans had gone into far more detail than they ever had before, and the way in which he talked about throwing giant sums of money around reminded her vividly of the very people she most disliked in New York. Yet she mustn't get all holy-Philadelphia about it, she reminded herself sharply.

"Clearly, Val," Jimmy Rosemont answered her. "Miss Kilkullen's own property would never be overlooked by another house—the condos would be too far away to bother her. In fact, we'd be delighted to set aside a belt of land for you above and beyond the land that was included in your father's will, to ensure your privacy. If you couldn't live here, because of your work, we'd undertake to keep up, in perpetuity, the Hacienda Valencia and the grounds in perfect condition as a living museum of ranching life, so that the spirit of the great old days would never be forgotten.''

''Hmm.'' Jazz tapped her booted foot.

''Come on, Jazz, don't you think it's the chance of a lifetime?'' Fernanda demanded.

''I couldn't say that, Fernanda. No. But then how can I judge, in my condition? I have a violent need to throw up all over this very expensive carpet.''

Jazz walked to the door quickly, turned and spoke to all of them. ''Before we meet again, I think I'll have a word with my lawyer.''

Two days later, Jazz found herself in the offices of Johnson, O'Hara, Klein, Bancroft and Johnson, in the Arco Building in downtown Los Angeles, the heart of the serious business district. She had come to consult with the senior partner, Stephen Johnson, who had been recommended to her by Gregory Nelson.

''He's one of the best, if not *the* best, probate litigator in the country,'' Mr. Nelson had assured her when he received Jazz's panicky phone call. ''These guys are a tight little fraternity, you know. They've all worked with each other a dozen times, no matter what city they're in, and Steve Johnson is the man I'd choose for myself. He'll tell it to you straight, whatever you want to know and a lot you don't.''

''It sounds perfectly legitimate to me,'' Steve Johnson said thoughtfully, after a pause while he considered everything Jazz had just told him about the meeting at the Ritz.

''I know Sir John, and he's a good man, well connected and honest,'' Johnson assured her, his round face earnest behind his dark-rimmed glasses. ''As for the Chinese, it would be their single largest American purchase, but there's no reason to doubt that they have the money. They've been active in Canada for a long time—they've bought so much of the country that they're just about wearing out their welcome in Vancouver, as a matter of fact.''

"Why did I feel as if I were being railroaded?"

"Because you were. The normal way to go about selling the ranch would be to wait until the permanent administrator is appointed. His basic job is simply to get the best price available. That means surveying the land, ascertaining its value, hiring brokers, putting the property on the open market and entertaining bids. Obviously, if they can talk you into making a deal now, they won't have to go through that process.''

"Why their passion for the Chinese?"

"Rosemont and Maddox will get a big piece of that action for putting the deal to bed. I'm sure Rosemont will have some of his own money invested in the purchase as well.''

"Oh.''

"Listen, Jazz, you're not supposed to know all that, but I am. First of all, if the permanent administrator comes in, they have the Japanese to worry about. I have no doubt that they'd want the ranch badly. They can make damn near anything, but they can't make land. Then there are huge American consortiums to deal with, major Swiss money, major, major German money, literally dozens of prospective suitors . . . but the Chinese would probably be willing to top the highest bid, pay more than market value, and end up with the land. They're highly motivated, as Sir John explained.''

"Then why was everyone pushing me so hard?"

"*Time.* It's a matter of time. There's a good reason why lawyers tend to think that time is of the essence. Before the administrator could be satisfied that he'd settled on the top price, years could go by. Just arguing over who would be the proper brokers could take forever. And every year that passes means a great deal of money permanently lost to all parties.''

"Could you give me a concrete example?" Jazz said in a tight voice.

"Sure. Let's say your share of the ranch comes

to about a billion dollars. You pay your taxes and you're left with half a billion.''

"Right. Half a billion dollars,'' Jazz said expressionlessly.

"O.K. You put your money into tax-free municipals, the safest ones you can find, paying—and this is a deliberately low-ball figure—six percent a year. Now your unearned income becomes thirty million dollars a year, and you can spend every dime of it. If the ranch isn't sold, that's how much you'd be out of pocket for every year that the sale of the land drags on.''

"I'd be losing thirty million a year that I hadn't earned,'' Jazz said, so incredulously that her voice was utterly flat. Even her eyebrows didn't lift.

"Exactly.''

"My God.''

"Damn right. You couldn't spend it, unless you started collecting art, in which case, depending on your tastes, you might even have to go into principal. But normally you'd reinvest some of it and your income would just get bigger and bigger.''

"So that's how the rich get richer.''

"It is indeed.''

"Now I know why everyone said I needed a lawyer.''

"Greg Nelson said you didn't have one. Frankly, I couldn't believe it.''

"I can't either, now that I've talked to you. Listen, Steve, what if, just for instance, I wasn't in a hurry to have thirty million dollars a year to spend. What if I didn't need it, didn't want it. What if I really liked earning my own living? No, don't look at me like that—I just said 'for instance.' What if I were like my father and I didn't want to sell the ranch?''

"You could stall and stall and stall. You could bring up a number of roadblocks that couldn't be ignored. You could get injunction after injunction. The permanent administrator would have to listen to all your arguments, you'd run up millions—and I mean *millions*—of dollars in lawyers' fees. You'd have

teams of guys like me working full time for you, as
hard as we could, and in the end you'd still have to
sell. If you dragged your feet long enough, the court
would *force* you to sell in order to be fair to your
sisters.''

"Right. O.K., Steve, let me ask you another
dumb question. What if I decided to be sensible and
sell fast, but I didn't want to turn the ranch into a
state-within-a-state for the richest people in the world,
an armed fortress bristling with police, a kind of max-
imum-security prison with everything but gunboats
out in the harbor and machine guns on the roofs to
keep the world safe for billionaires; what if I had another idea about the way the land should be used?''

"Whoever buys the land can do whatever they
want to with it. Your ideas won't matter. If they decide to turn it into a parking lot or a drive-in movie,
the law doesn't change. It goes to the highest bidder
and it becomes his property. No whorehouses, no ca-
sinos, but otherwise the sky's the limit.''

"Are you telling me to agree with Valerie and
Fernanda and sell the land to the Chinese bankers?''

"I think you'll end up doing just that. Your sisters
own two-thirds of the land, you own one-third. You'll
be forced to come to an agreement with them sooner
or later, no matter what, and they seem enthralled
with the Chinese purchase. So if you hate the Monte
Carlo concept, Jazz, unless you can come up with
another buyer who'll pay more, I'm afraid that's the
bad news.''

"What's the good news?''

"You're going to be very rich, whether you want
to be or not.''

"But if I don't?'' Jazz spoke with dogged persistence in spite of the small, sympathetic but ironic
smile Steve Johnson couldn't hide.

"You can always give it away as fast as it comes
in. In my experience, that doesn't often happen.
Money—well, let's just say that most people get used
to having it faster than they think they will.''

Resolutely, Jazz tried to put the conference she'd just had with Steve Johnson out of her head as she negotiated the drive out to Venice by way of the Harbor Freeway and the Santa Monica Freeway. It was a speedy, unfamiliar route that snaked cleverly from one end of the city to the other, complicated but not bewildering enough to keep her mind off the probate expert's words. The inadmissible concept of being forced to sell repeated itself over and over in her mind, becoming more and more intolerable, drowning out everything else Steve Johnson had told her, and Jazz wished fervently that she'd had her car radio repaired so that she could tune in to one of the radio shrinks and listen to someone else's problems.

Jazz arrived at the parking lot with a huge exhalation of relief. As she walked up the street to Dazzle, she felt her preoccupation fading away for the moment, soothed by the bizarre ambience of a world that had remained bohemian and predictably outlandish. Here, at least, nothing could turn topsy-turvy in the blink of an eye; Venice had survived every kind of ruin, fire, and devastation, constantly rebuilt and reborn for the last eighty-five years, without losing its loopy holiday charm. The day of the ten-cent camel ride and the Big Dipper roller coaster might be gone, but its spirit lived on in the looks of expectation and pleasure on everyone's face as they hurried past her toward the boardwalk.

Jazz walked around Dazzle the wrong way to Pete's studio to avoid being seen from inside the double glass doors. She was in no mood to cope with Sandy, the receptionist, or any of the other people who worked at Dazzle, except Mel and Pete, whom she'd planned to meet for lunch today.

Soon after Mike Kilkullen's death, when Jazz had realized that she didn't know when she'd start working again, she'd given all her studio staff an openended, fully paid leave of absence. The expense was well worth the security blanket of knowing that she'd still have Sis Levy, Toby and Melissa with her when she started shooting again.

As Jazz peered into the car photographer's studio, she saw Pete and Mel, deep in conversation while they started to set a table with the lunch from the Purple Tostada Grande that they'd promised to order for her. A sharp pang of desire for stuffed quesadilla, for burritos, for guacamole, made Jazz realize how long it had been since breakfast.

"Could we eat first and talk later?" she called from the door. Mel and Pete both dropped the covered cardboard cartons on the table and rushed toward her in an exuberance of welcome.

"Just in time!" Pete exclaimed as he crushed her ribs and lifted her off her feet.

"If you hadn't come today, we'd have come down to get you," Mel told her fervently as he kissed her.

"You can tell me how much you've missed me later," Jazz informed them, in a rush of deep affection for her two friends, "but first, feed me!"

She watched, her mouth watering, as the men slapped plates and paper napkins on the table and carefully opened the steaming cartons, her teeth so set for Mexican food that it took her a half-minute to realize that she was looking at a magnificent spread of hot dishes that had not been inspired by any place south of the border.

"Fried rice?" she faltered, disbelievingly. "Lemon chicken . . . sweet-and-sour pork? *Chinese!* Oh, no . . . no, say it isn't so."

"It was the best we could do at the last minute," Mel said plaintively.

"I knew Phoebe was an evil, misbegotten bitch," Pete exploded, "but how anyone could sink this low is beyond me!"

"But you love Chinese, don't you, Jazz?" Mel asked anxiously.

"Normally, Mel darling, normally. But not today. Don't ask why. What happened to the Tostada you promised me?"

Both men turned and looked at her incredulously.

"Didn't you see?" Pete demanded.

"How could you miss what she did?" Mel asked.

"I came in from the other side . . . what happened?"

"It's the last fucking straw! Phoebe tore down the Tostada over the weekend when we weren't here," Pete told her furiously.

"It's gone, bulldozed into splinters, razed to the ground," Mel mourned.

"But she promised to keep it just the way it was when she bought it!" Jazz said disbelievingly. "We all depend on the Tostada take-out, and she knew it."

"That's what I told her," Pete said, enraged, "but Phoebe reminded me that she'd never made any guarantees, just given us a chance to go in on it with her, and none of us wanted to. And, unfortunately, she's right. In fact, she even had it written in the minutes of that meeting."

"What's she going to do with the space?" Jazz demanded fiercely.

"I asked her that," Mel said, "and she informed me that she hadn't decided yet, but whatever kind of fine restaurant it became, it would never be so utterly 'in' that there wouldn't be a table for me, provided I remembered to let her know before four in the afternoon. She's lucky I'm so controlled. I almost bit her."

"After the way she screwed Jazz about Magic's party, I've been at war with the bitch," Pete said vengefully, "not that I ever was at peace with her, but the sight of no Tostada across from Dazzle—she's finally gone too far."

"Pete, are we going to let her get away with this?" Mel's normal quality of calm repose had entirely deserted him. His smoothly barbered head seemed to have grown spikes, his Buddha-like composure was laid aside.

"No, Mel, we are not. We are going to fire Phoebe, give her the boot," Pete announced, with the satisfied and decisive tone of a man who has seen the light and is about to act on it. "No woman capable of such a heartless, selfish, hostile action can be trusted to be my rep."

"I agree entirely," Mel said solemnly. He and Pete shook hands over a carton of snow peas and mushrooms. "Pete, tell her that whatever you say goes double for me."

"Me? Why should I tell her?" Pete asked. "You're firing her too."

"I can't stand confrontations," Mel complained smugly. "Everybody knows that about me."

"That doesn't mean you don't have to take some responsibility," Pete said, outraged.

"You can do it for the both of us."

"No, I can't. Phoebe has ways . . . you know her ways . . . she'll manage to fuck my mind somehow, unless you're there to back me up."

"Guys," Jazz interrupted. "Are you both *absolutely* sure you want to change reps? I mean, without a shadow of a doubt? And without it having anything to do with me and Magic? Only for your own reasons?"

"Absolutely," they said in unison.

"Who would rep you instead of Phoebe?" she asked.

They looked at each other blankly. "We haven't got that far, Jazz," Pete admitted. "You have any advice?"

"I haven't done anything about a new rep, myself," Jazz said. "But when I do, I'm calling Trish Burlingham. She's super-smart, she's effective as hell, but on top of it, she's nice, really nice. Or for a male rep, with a bigger organization, you couldn't do better than Daniel Roebuck of Onyx."

"We'll call them both, check it out, right, Mel?"

"Right. But first you have to fire Phoebe," Mel reminded Pete.

"Hold it, Mel," Jazz said. "First we have to decide about Dazzle. Dazzle the studio, not Dazzle the organization. Do we want to keep on owning this place with Phoebe, or do we want to buy her out?"

"She probably won't sell," Pete said, "but, Christ, I wish she would."

"Me too. I'd buy her out in a second if I could," Mel said.

"Ah, but we can force her to sell," Jazz said sweetly. "When we bought it together, one of the rules was that if any three of the partners unanimously wanted to buy out the fourth, it would be done at fair market value, to be established by three independent appraisers."

"You sound just like a lawyer," Pete said in admiration.

"I've been sitting at the feet of members of the profession, but I have a way to go before I pass the bar," Jazz said airily.

"So, it's settled," Mel said in relief. "Pete tells her she's history, I hold his hand while he does it, and then we'll get the appraisers in. Now can we eat?"

"No," Jazz said. "Nobody eats with unfinished business on the table."

"Ah, have a heart, Jazz. I don't want to tell her when I'm hungry," Pete pleaded. "A mission like that can't be done on an empty stomach."

"Look, I know you two cuties are capable of handling this yourself," Jazz said, "but if you'd like, I don't mind being your spokesperson with Phoebe. Her cunning little ways don't work with me."

"It wouldn't be asking too much?" Pete beamed.

"I'll hold your hand too," Mel offered.

"Follow me, guys," Jazz said, and led the way to Phoebe's office, where the rep was eating her favorite lunch: fake cheddar cheese made from tofu, and melba toast.

"Well, well, what brings you here, Jazz?" Phoebe asked, looking up in feigned surprise. She'd known that Jazz would come crawling back as soon as the memory of the shots of Magic's great party had dimmed. She'd made up her mind to be gracious but firm. From now on, Jazz would have to cut down on her editorial work and spend at least two-thirds of her time shooting ads. At her fee of twenty-five thousand dollars a day plus expenses for commercial work, Jazz couldn't continue to blow her time on portraits that would only end up in yet another seventy-five-dollar coffee-table book. Her choice of work was costing Phoebe a fortune in commissions.

"I'm here on business, not pleasure. I'm representing Mel and Pete," Jazz said, standing in front of Phoebe's desk and looking down at her. "They have empowered me to dismiss you as their representative, starting immediately. In addition, the three of us are exercising our contractual right to buy out your share in Dazzle. Your unfeeling destruction of the Purple Tostada Grande has proven that you don't have our best interests at heart. We will choose three independent appraisers of our own; you pick three others. That's three more than the contract calls for, so we don't have to haggle over which appraisers to use. When the appraisals come in, we'll average them out and arrive at a fair price for your one-quarter share of this building. Unless you have a better way of establishing the proper value, I suggest that we begin the process this afternoon. Time is of the essence. We need your space as soon as possible."

Jazz's gaze was mild, her voice neutral, her manner dry and matter-of-fact.

"My space!" Phoebe sprang up, her split ends flying. *"My space?"*

"For the new Tostada," Jazz said, as she turned and led the way out of Phoebe's office.

"That went fairly well," Jazz said as they regained Pete's studio and she had accepted the men's dazed, delighted compliments.

"Jesus, Jazz! What's happened to you?" Pete exclaimed. "You're beginning to scare me. Our problems are all solved and the food's still hot!"

"Ah, Pete, honey bun, I've just been hanging out with some wrongos . . . picked up a few moves. Listen, I forgot all about Gabe. What are we going to do about his space?"

"Don't worry, he'll be long gone. He left for Russia on a big assignment, won't be back for months. Where did he say he was going, Mel?"

"Who knows exactly? He went rushing off with his pockets stuffed with ten rolls of gaffer's tape, muttering something about covering the impact of a major capitalist venture on the government of the Ukraine, something about staying with it till the bitter end, even if it took till summer. I wasn't listening to the details. Wait! Now I remember—he's going to Kiev, where the chicken comes from."

"Was it . . . with Milos Forman?" Jazz asked, beginning to quiver all over with rising mirth, thinking of Sam and Gabe, each one with his unique instrument, dividing the available female filmmaking and local talent during the long Russian winter.

"Right! That's exactly what he said, come to think of it . . . hey—why'd you ask, if you knew already?"

"Because . . . I . . . wasn't . . . exactly . . . sure."

"Jazz, stop laughing so hard—for God's sake, you're going to choke on the fried rice."

"How was your trip to the big city?" Casey asked the next day, as Jazz came wandering in after lunch.

"Illuminating. I liked Steve Johnson."

"Dad knew you would. Was the news good, bad or indifferent?"

"Sort of. I can become a major contributor to a lot of worthy causes, or I can spend the next two decades in litigation and make major contributions to members of the American Bar Association. I'm considering my options."

"Something tells me that you don't want to talk about it right now."

"I just want it all to go away and leave me alone."

"How about coming riding with me?"

"Who said you could ride yet?" Jazz asked suspiciously.

"The doctor. I saw him this morning, and he said I was as good as new."

"How could he tell?"

"Oh, knock it off, smartass, and take off those

city clothes. I want to get out there while there's still plenty of light.''

As Jazz and Casey reached the rim of the natural hollow in the upland mesa where the Fiesta was held each year, he slowed his horse to a walk and finally a halt, while he looked around.

"Remember?" he asked Jazz.

"The Fiesta? Of course."

"Not just the Fiesta. This spot, this exact spot."

"What about it?"

"This is where we met. This is where I deliberately, with malicious intent, threw a plate of greasy chili at you, this is where you first called me 'dickhead,' which, in some ways, I prefer to 'fascist pig.' "

"Hey, don't get all sentimental, all of a sudden."

"I will if I want to," Casey said stubbornly. "I'll never forget that night."

"No," Jazz said, suddenly serious, "neither will I . . . I didn't know it was going to be the last Fiesta . . . I'm so glad I couldn't see into the future."

"I wish I could have," Casey said with a fierce intensity, in a voice that held some strong, repressed emotion. He kicked his horse into a slow canter and took off, his horse climbing steadily sideways across the bowl toward its upper rim. She followed, watching him carefully, for in spite of his assurances that the doctor had told him he could ride, she was worried that Casey might not yet be fit. He sat in the saddle easily, with no trace of favoring the side that the bullet had entered. However, Jazz decided that on this first day back on a horse, he shouldn't ride too long without a break.

"Follow me," Jazz called, as she caught up with him at the rim and led the way across a wide, gentle plateau to the edge of an arroyo where she had discovered a gradual track to the bottom, one on which the horses couldn't possibly slip. "Down here," she said, showing him the easily overlooked natural trail. Leading, she let her horse pick its way into the deep fold between the mesas, where a cluster of majestic oaks and sycamores grew in a thicket that made a gray-green, sun-splotched parasol overhead.

"Let's rest for a minute," Jazz suggested, and jumped down onto the ground, where thousands of years of drifting sycamore leaves had left a soft surface. Casey joined her and they both sat down, leaning against a tree trunk.

"Now," Jazz demanded, turning toward him, "I want a full explanation of that last remark. Why do you want to see into the future? What's the good of it? Isn't it better not to know?"

Casey looked at her silently, as if he were trying, rebelliously but unable to help himself, to memorize her. The sun fell in shafts of diffuse brightness on her head, so that he could see even the tiniest hairs that separated themselves from the others, some brown-gold, some red-gold, some beige-gold, rippling wavelets of hair whose color he had never been able to name satisfactorily, even to himself. His eyes traced the straight, mysteriously satisfying lines of her brows, which were elevated in curiosity, the artless, independent impudence of her nose, the delicate, precise line of her upper lip that made such a fascinating contrast to the frank, all-but-outrageous fullness of her lower lip. Although he knew that skin couldn't be gold, hers was, and her eyes were gold too, he thought, and she was a perfect little golden idol from some primitive past who had been set on earth to torment him, to punish him for crimes he would never dream of committing, to drive him around the bend, he who had always been sane and proud of it. She had been designed by the fates to teach him bitter lessons, to cure him of being cocky, to change the luck of the Irish, to let him know that he wasn't in charge here, to inform him that he had never been appreciative enough of a past life in which he had had the incredible luck not to become acquainted with one Juanita Isabella Kilkullen.

"Stop looking at me like that," Jazz commanded nervously. "And answer my question."

"If I could have seen into the future, I would

never have written your father and asked him for a job," Casey said slowly.

"I didn't know it had been as bad as all that," Jazz said, stunned and hurt by his words. "You seemed content . . . or at least you gave a pretty good imitation . . . of a man who liked what he was doing. You certainly had me fooled."

"This is *exactly* what I mean! The perfect example! Every time I say something to you, it's the wrong thing to say, I use the wrong words and you take everything the wrong way, every time I do anything to you it's the wrong thing to do, if I dare to kiss you it's wrong, if I try to seduce you it's wrong, if I don't try to seduce you, it's wrong, if I even *stand* near you, I ruin your great-grandmother's shawl! Oh, what's the use?"

"You mean that you wish you'd never come here just *because of me?*"

"There it is again! You're twisting my words, as usual. You listen but you don't hear. Or if you hear, you don't understand. I'm not saying that anything is your fault, Jazz, I'm saying I wish I'd done the right things to . . . capture your attention. And I know you won't believe me, but I've never had this problem before. Not with anyone, male, female or in between. It's something about you—no strike that!—it's something about *me,* I don't know what, but I'm fatally clumsy around you, I make all the wrong moves, send out the wrong signals . . ."

"Let's try to get this straight. You want to capture my attention, is that correct?"

"Yes," Casey said miserably.

"You want to make the right moves?"

"Yes again."

"You want to send the right signals?"

"Yes, guilty as charged."

"Why?"

"Don't be so damn dense," he said gruffly, hanging his dark red head in frustration and embarrassment at the relentless interrogation, which made him sound even more like an idiot as she repeated his words.

"You're saying the wrong thing again," she warned, her voice saturated with well-hidden delight as she saw the pitiful state into which she had reduced him.

"I know. I'm . . . damn it, Jazz, I'm so fucking shy! You make me shy, it *is* all your fault that you're so totally . . . whatever it is you are . . . oh, hell, I love you, O.K.? I'm crazy about you, madly in love, O.K.? I want to live with you for the rest of my life, I never want to let you go, I never want you to look at another man, I know I can't have you but I'm stuck with it for life, loving you and needing you even though I know it's hopeless, so go ahead and gloat, chalk up another victim."

"O.K.," she whispered.

"O.K.? Is that all you can say? Not even a gratified sneer?"

"I love you too, O.K.?" Her voice shook with glad, long-deferred release, and Jazz fought laughter as well as tears. He had been so gloriously oblivious of what any other man must surely have seen a long time ago. Of course, she had been as stubborn and elusive and frivolous and tantalizing as she knew how to be, but only because she didn't want to make it too easy for him, didn't want to fall at his feet, didn't want to scare him off by premature surrender, and anyway, weren't men supposed to make the first move, didn't the laws of human nature still hold true?

While she spoke the few uncomplex words, Casey's downcast glance was on her hands, and he watched them unfolding toward him as if they were accepting a gift or giving a gift, it didn't matter which. She wasn't making fun of him, he realized, looking up into her startled, revealing eyes in which a great alchemy had transformed mockery into a clear, unflinching declaration even he couldn't fail to understand. The world turned over and righted itself, time stopped and started again.

"Will you marry me, too?" He spoke hastily, as if he were afraid she'd change her mind.

"I'll marry you *also*," Jazz assured him as he

grabbed her, not clumsily but triumphantly, and pulled her toward him so that her upturned face lay just under his chin. "We'd better get a dictionary. Let's not try to talk. Oh, darling, just kiss me. It's the one thing we never get wrong."

18

Jazz struggled reluctantly out of a deep sleep, completely disoriented. She didn't know what day it was, she didn't know what time it was, she didn't even know *where* she was. The only thing she was entirely sure of was that it was finally raining, a downpour that beat so heavily on the roof and windows that it had roused her from the most satisfying sleep, a sleep she tried vainly to reenter for a few seconds until she became aware of the fact that Casey Nelson was in bed with her, not her bed but his. Once she had registered the warm, steadily breathing, solid and permanent substance of Casey, everything else rushed back into her mind and she closed her eyes the better to savor the completeness of her happiness.

It was so clear and strong, this happiness, so free of ambiguity, of overtones, of questions. It didn't just "feel" right, it *was* right, an element of nature that must always have existed, waiting for her to stumble into it. Well, it had taken them long enough to get it straight, she thought, months and months when it should have been hours—or minutes—but of course they were too civilized for that, too blinded to the games people played, the disguises people wore, the suspicions people had, to simply look at each other and know—for they *must have known* right from the beginning—and admit to each other that they knew.

She might be the only woman of her age group who had agreed to marry a man who had done nothing more than kiss her, but since yesterday they had more than made up for it. Casey was . . . she searched her mind for the right word and finally found it with a private shiver . . . a *virtuoso*. He made her wish she'd never known another man, but if she hadn't, how would she know he was a virtuoso, Jazz asked herself virtuously, muffling herself under the covers so that she could inhale the smell of his body. Was it wrong for a man to smell so good? In so many different places? She should really wake him up, for his own good, because he was wasting his smell while he slept when he could be awake and making love to her again.

Trying to decide if it was too early to decently rouse Casey, Jazz looked at the clock and discovered that it was almost noon. Either that or it was almost midnight. They had still been awake last midnight and they couldn't have slept for twenty-four hours. So it must be noon, and an exceptionally dark and wet one. Fortunately it was Sunday, when Susie didn't come in, otherwise she might have checked the hacienda for hungry people, discovered them in bed together and been shocked. Jazz giggled softly at the thought of Susie, so worldly-wise that the only thing that might genuinely shock her would be their innocence.

A drop of water struck Jazz's forehead. She jerked her face out of the nest of blankets and looked indignantly at the ceiling. More drops followed, becoming a trickle and then, as Jazz shook Casey briskly, a miniature waterfall.

"What . . . darling, darling . . ." he mumbled.

"The roof's leaking!"

"Damn . . . I'll move . . . the bed . . ."

"Wake up, city boy!"

"No, you promised never to insult me again . . . come here . . ."

"Casey, darling, please! It hasn't rained for weeks—it's an old roof, there could be leaks all over the place, we've got to go check out the house . . ."

"Do we have to?"

"We don't have a choice."

"Let's find another bed and let my bed drown. Oh, my God, the fax will drown too!" His drowsiness vanished.

"Casey!"

"All right, all right, but you'll have to make it up to me."

"My pleasure," Jazz promised fervently, trying to find her clothes, while Casey unplugged his fax and put it on a high table in the living room.

Rapidly they raced around the veranda, checking the many rooms of the hacienda, and found no more leaks, but Jazz was uneasy. She had a peculiar impression that rain was coming in somewhere, and not just in Casey's room.

"The archive room," she remembered. "How could I have forgotten? Where's your key?"

As they unlocked the door to the archive room, they heard the unmistakable sound of water where there should be no water. Jazz held her breath in guilt as Casey switched on the lights. The archive room held the only irreplaceable things in the hacienda; it should have been the first room they checked. Relief crept slowly over her as the source of the leak was apparent. It came from the corner opposite the shelves of portfolios, where a stream of rainwater had already formed a large pool on the uneven floor, but the far wall behind the portfolios themselves showed no damp spots.

"Thank goodness, they're safe," she said with a sigh of relief.

"That leak's going to spread," Casey warned, "and new ones might start. We'd better move the portfolios someplace where we can keep our eyes on them and still stay warm."

"Move them? The two of us? There are hundreds of them!"

"We're strong enough," he grinned.

"I used to be," Jazz muttered, resigned, "before you started messing with me."

"We still have time to mess around a little more before the roof falls in."

"You climb that library ladder and hand them down to me," Jazz answered. "When this is all finished, I'll make lunch. Then we'll see."

Two hours later, weary but with a sense of a job well done, Casey and Jazz had moved all the portfolios to the living room of the hacienda, where they put them on the floor in the order in which they had been removed from their shelves. Jazz had separated the little brown portfolio that belonged to her great-grandmother, and placed it on the desk in her room. She'd remembered the charmingly frilly old valentines it held, and had formed a secret plan to recycle them, for surely Amilia wouldn't mind and Valentine's Day was coming next month.

It was late on Sunday night. After the rescue, she and Casey had celebrated their heroics by the fire with food and love and wine, remembering from time to time to rush around and empty buckets of rainwater from his bedroom and the archive room. It had been an exhausting day, and Casey was asleep again, this time in her bed. Jazz watched him in puzzlement. Was there some fundamental difference in the sexes that permitted a man to fall asleep instantly after making love on and off all during a rainy, constantly watchful and interrupted day, while a woman stayed awake, listening to the diminishing rain, feeling as overtired as a child after the excitement of Christmas, wishing she could sleep too, but unable to stop thinking about all the new marvels in her life? She felt she'd be up all night.

Maybe a dull book? She looked around the room and saw many books, not one of which had been bought because it promised boredom. She'd already

had a lulling bath; she'd tried counting down from a
hundred, she'd tried imagining that she was descending in an elevator while visualizing the numbers of the
floors, she'd tried imagining that she was on a giant
ferris wheel going slowly backwards, but none of the
familiar tricks worked.

Jazz slipped out of bed, picked up Amilia's portfolio, and crept back under the down quilt. She remembered the letter from her great-great-grandmother
and decided that an attempt to use her rusty high-
school Spanish to make a translation into English,
from a document written in elaborate handwriting, had
to be the final answer to her insomnia. Her brain
would shut down from the sheer tediousness of the
endeavor, and she'd slip into the unconsciousness that
all her senses craved.

Less than an hour later her eyes were half closed
and her notes all but unintelligible. The letter had
started out as a warm but conventionally formal welcome to the prospective new bride, Amilia Moncada
y Rivera, from her future mother-in-law, Juanita Isabella Valencia Kilkullen. Apparently the two women
were second cousins, a fact Jazz had never known.
Jazz, her brain increasingly weary, had translated
more and more roughly, and the next-to-last paragraph had been so difficult to translate that when she
had it down on paper she gave up the task, rereading
what she had just scrawled.

> *Now that you are about to something
> something your family and become a
> Kilkullen wife, you will learn of something
> covenant(?) that my family, the Valencias,
> made at the place of (?)with the holy
> something Fathers many (?)ago. I feel
> something something that you will be as
> proud as I (?) to discover that the
> Kilkullens, something something not
> Spanish, are as God (?) as something
> Valencias. They (?) agreed to the covenant
> when my something husband something my*

father's ranch and they respect it with the
same something of the Valencias.

"Something something question mark, something
something question mark," Jazz muttered, turning out
the light and pushing the yellow pad aside, with the
letter folded into it. She was asleep before the pad
slipped off the bed to the floor.

Her saleslady at Bergdorf's was a tactful creature,
Liddy Kilkullen reflected, but her tact had not been
equal to the task of concealing her surprise when a
customer who had never bought anything that wasn't
on sale headed straight toward the new resort clothes
that had just come into the store, and asked to have
them brought to her in the dressing room. The saleswoman had actually told her, *warned* her, no less, that
these clothes were new and wouldn't be marked down
for months.

Of course she'd been kind to the foolish, flustered
creature, Liddy thought, as she stretched out on her
chaise longue in Fernanda's guest room and sipped a
cup of tea. She'd passed over the gaffe, pretending not
to notice, said something vague about her ship coming
in, and gone on to buy and buy and buy. She hadn't
bothered to glance at a single price tag. If something
was becoming, she bought it; clothes for morning and
afternoon and evening; ten times more clothes than
she'd ever bought at one time before; the resort
clothes that were always so much more experimental
than the ordinary summer line, the clothes that she'd
need when she flew to California to supervise her
daughters.

Actually, Liddy admitted to herself, she didn't
actually *need* these new clothes right now. California
in winter didn't have resort weather, but something in
between, weather that called for a suit and blouse with
a warm coat for the evenings. She was perfectly aware
that she'd used her trip as an excuse for a shopping
binge with the only clothes in the city that weren't on
sale after Christmas, and she didn't give a damn.

It was the only way she knew to celebrate her fortune, and she had to celebrate or bust. If she were a chocolate-eating woman, she'd have consumed enough chocolates to bring on a liver attack; if she were a drinker, she'd have spent the time in an alcoholic haze; if she' were an eater, she'd be twenty pounds heavier than she had been when she'd struck her deal with Jimmy Rosemont. But the discipline of a lifetime had long ago caused her to lose whatever craving she might ever have had for food or drinks or sweets, and she wasn't going to buy jewels yet, not until she had completed her new wardrobe.

Some women chose their clothes to show off their jewels, others selected jewels to complement their clothes, and she was of neither group, Liddy saw in a sudden burst of pleasurable insight. She was one of the very few whose clothes and jewels, no matter how brilliant, would always form a perfect background against which she herself would be the only object of attention.

So this was what real money could do. It could make her realize her potential in a way that had always been obscured by having to plot and plan how best to spend what little money she had. She'd constantly been fascinated by her rich friends, always wondered what it felt like, *really and truly felt like,* to be them, but she'd always known that there was no way to imagine or to understand something so central to a person's inner core of self unless you had it yourself, unless you controlled it yourself, in a way that depended on no one else in the world.

She wondered what their money would do to Fernanda and Valerie. They would change, of course, but in what way? Unforeseen ways. Perhaps unfortunate ways, precipitate, unbecoming, unwelcome to her. It was that realization that had prompted her to decide to join them in California. The telephone wasn't a satisfactory way to communicate with her daughters, and now that they had finally become the heiresses she had planned for them to be for so long, they needed her counsel and advice more than ever. For the last three decades she had watched and observed the kind of life they were going to lead now, and she knew the traps that lay thick on the ground.

Yes, Liddy mused, if there was one thing she was an authority on, it was the way of life of the very rich. No one could be as objective about it as someone who had not been forced to be a—why not use the harshest word she could think of, since it no longer had the power to wound?—a hanger-on. True, she had been one who paid for her place in the world of the very rich, paid on a daily basis, with her accounts always neatly balanced, but a hanger-on nevertheless, not truly entitled.

But just as the legendary English tailor was never supposed to dun a rich man for his overdue bill, she would never have to balance her accounts again. Never again the charming, prompt thank-you notes, never again the flowers sent the day after a party, never again the wondering if she owed someone an invitation—from now on people would feel as if they *owed* her. Like a great beauty, a great star, or a great talent, a very rich woman could live carelessly, pleasing only when and if it pleased her to do so.

Startled, Liddy realized that she would never go back to Marbella. As if she had been making a conscious decision and had arrived at it carefully, she suddenly knew where she had chosen to live: San Clemente.

How funny, how wonderfully funny that now that she could live in style anywhere in the world, she would make a full circle and go back to a small town in California. But so long as Deems White was Governor of the state, so long as he and Nora kept a second home in San Clemente, she would be near him.

Would she ever learn to be absolutely honest with herself, Liddy wondered, smiling like a girl, as she slowly put the teacup down. Trying on clothes in the dressing room today, she had considered nothing but whether they would appeal to Deems. All those excellent reasons that explained how she could be essential to her daughters had very little to do with them and everything to do with Deems. They could manage nicely for themselves, but her love needed her, and at last she was free to go to him.

Who, she wondered, was the top real-estate agent in San Clemente? The one who handled the very finest properties?

"I thought I'd never find a way to lure you away from Valerie," Lady Georgina Rosemont said to Fernanda.

"I thought you liked her," Fernanda answered, as the two women drove back to the Ritz. Georgina had bought her way solidly through the intriguing collection of antiques at Gep Durenburger's shop in San Juan Capistrano, leaving the charming place quite stripped of its best objects and furniture.

"I do," Georgina replied, "but somehow nothing's quite as much fun when she's along as when it's just the two of us. I feel a hundred years younger than Val, don't you? Thank goodness the old dear decided that she didn't want to take a busman's holiday. Wait till my precious assistants see that huge crate that they're going to ship to New York from Durenburger's —they'll have to start showing a tad more respect for me."

"Oh, Georgie, they adore you," Fernanda protested. She looked at the petite, auburn-haired Englishwoman in ever-renewed amazement. The casualness with which she wore her unfathomable beauty never changed, she didn't have a self-conscious bone in her body, and her attitude toward herself was one of constant mild amusement.

"I'm just being honest, Fernie. You know as well as I do that I'm not the genuine article, not a real decorator . . . Jimmy just wants to be sure I have something jolly to do. When it stops being jolly, I'll stop and find something else. Perhaps a perfect little flower shop. I could bring back nosegays singlehandedly. Whatever they are."

"Why not a tearoom?"

"Oh, splendid! I'll toast the muffins and split the crumpets and you can preside over the teapot. Would you like that? We could go into business together. Seriously, Fernie, it would be fun to work together, wouldn't it? You've got to have something to do, you know, you can't just sit around and count your money."

"I've never done anything. Why do I have to start now, just because I'm going to be filthy rich?"

"It looks better if you make an effort, pitch in, show the flag, all that nonsense—you don't want to have to be on all those frightful charity committees, do you? Selling tickets to balls, buying tickets for balls, and then actually going to the balls, with never an end in sight? It'll give us the perfect excuse— 'Sorry, ladies, we can't possibly come out to lunch, we have to bake the scones and then there's the washing up.' "

"I thought you liked those parties and balls . . . you do them all so well." Fernanda gave the car to a valet parker and the two women started for the elevator at the Ritz, where the Rosemonts had their suite on the same floor as Fernanda's and Valerie's.

"Oh, most of that is for Jimmy. I suppose I don't mind, or at least I didn't last year, when it was still fresh and a bit of a novelty. Now I'm beginning to find it all just too much—boring, useless and exhausting. I'd far rather just send them the money and not go. Come on in, sweet, and we'll order some tea and we can see if they serve it as well here as we're going to serve it in our own little shop."

"Where's Jimmy?"

"Off to San Francisco for the day. He won't be back till after dinner. Meetings and more meetings . . . you know Jimmy."

The two women drank their tea and ate their thin sandwiches in relative silence. Georgina seemed plunged in contemplation of the crazy new tea-shop idea, Fernanda thought, and she was content just to look at her and admire her. Georgina was twenty-nine, ten years younger than she, Fernanda realized with surprise, yet they always felt so comfortable together that it was hard to believe they weren't the same age. Either there was something very grown-up about Georgina, or else, she, Fernanda, was childish. Probably both.

While the tea tray was removed, Georgina went into her room. "Do come in and chat, Fernie. I just want to stretch out for a minute. I think I overdid the antiquing."

"I'll go to my room. Maybe you can take a nap."

"No, honestly, I'm not sleepy, just footsore. And I don't want Valerie to know you're back."

Definitely childish, Fernanda thought. She felt the same way. They were both like kids hiding from a strict governess. Ever since Georgina had arrived to join her husband at the Ritz, a few days after Jimmy Rosemont and Sir John had held the meeting with Jazz, she and Georgina had been trying to find time to spend together as they did during their frequent lunches in New York, but Valerie had made them into a threesome.

Fernanda knew that the sale of the ranch was going to take place in a manner organized by wiser business heads than hers. She was content to let Jimmy and Sir John proceed on their own. Just getting away from New York had lightened her heart and Georgina's presence made her feel as if she were on vacation.

She didn't want Valerie to know they were back from their antiquing expedition either, Fernanda thought, she didn't want Valerie to know in the worst way. She didn't want to . . . *share* Georgina, she realized. There was a thrilling feeling of exclusivity when she was alone with Georgina that was ruined when Valerie, sensible, organized, capable Valerie, joined them, as she had done often in the last days. That must be the way girls felt about their best friends, she thought. She'd never had that kind of high-school best friend, the kind you whispered to about other girls, told secrets to, felt jealous of, as if she were a boy. She'd always been too occupied with her own inner cravings to look around for a friend, there hadn't been any other girls like her to talk to, or if there had been, they were as solitary and secretive as she.

She followed Georgina into the elaborate bedroom of the two-bedroom suite. Georgina had explained that she and her husband never shared a bedroom because he was so often up at odd hours of the late night and early morning, telephoning business partners all over the world.

"Come over here and sit down, sweet," Georgina said, patting the bed. "I simply must put my feet up."

"You don't look tired."

"I'm not really. I feel comfy, now that we're here. I told the maid to keep the curtains drawn so there'd be some refuge here that was decently dim. All that sunlight . . . it's a shock to my system after yesterday's rain. At least, most of the time, New York is decently gray in winter."

"Do you miss London?"

"A little. Or at least I did, until I met you. You're such great fun, Fernie, such a mad rascal, such a flamboyant, heartless flirt, a wild child all done up like the most gorgeous fraud of a cowgirl. You remind me of someone I adored . . . of course, she didn't look anything like you, but she was even more wicked."

"Who was she?" Fernanda asked, feeling a sharp pluck of jealousy at the longingly reminiscent tone in Georgina's voice.

"A girl at boarding school . . . Claire. She was older than I was . . . she must have been fifteen and I was only twelve . . . but we became great friends in spite of the difference in ages. I'll never forget Claire."

"Do you still see her?"

"I doubt if I'd recognize her today. I hear she's turned into the perfect suburban hostess and the perfectly stuffy mother of four perfectly stuffy children . . . do promise me you'll never do that, Fernie."

"I couldn't if I wanted to. I'm fundamentally imperfect."

"When Claire was at school, she was different.

We were in the same house. I had the most agonizing crush on her . . . I used to watch her during choir practice and forget to sing. I never took my eyes off her at meals, I spied on her whenever I had a chance, I know I've never been so blindly in love."

"In love?"

"Of course, Fernie, in love. Pure love, first love, the most painful kind, the kind you never forget."

"And then she graduated and you never saw her again?"

"Oh, no . . . that would have been too cruel. No, one night, after I was in bed, Claire came to my room —the big girls could do all sorts of things that the little girls couldn't do, like stay up late—and she shut the door and she came over to me and sat on the bed, just the way you're sitting there, and she leaned over and kissed me on the forehead."

"Did she say anything?"

"She said she'd noticed me watching her and she wanted to know why. Of course she was just teasing me, she knew why perfectly well. I was too utterly tongue-tied to say anything, and then she kissed me on the lips . . . it was the first time anyone had ever kissed me on the lips . . . oh, she kissed me and kissed me, over and over again . . . she knew what she was doing." Georgina's voice was low, lulled, as if she spoke out of a trance of memory.

"She had the sweetest lips, Fernie, and after I dared to start to kiss her back, oh, a long time after, she pulled down my nightie and she started to kiss my breasts . . . I was just growing them and they were so tender and small, I used to feel them every morning when I woke up to see if they'd gotten any bigger overnight . . . and she kept on kissing my breasts, and playing with them until they felt as if they were swelling, and then she got under the covers with me and I could feel her hands reaching down between my legs and then she started to play with me there . . . so gently, so wonderfully, Fernie, no one had ever touched me there except . . . well, I did, all the time . . . but I didn't know how different it would feel when it was somebody else . . . it was . . . oh, it's hard to explain, but nothing had ever felt so . . . so terribly *important* . . . it was as if I'd never understood why I was alive, not really, until Claire touched me between my legs until . . . she didn't stop, Fernie, not even when I started to . . . well, you know, I don't have to explain. I didn't have any idea what to do to show her how wonderful it was, so she showed me what to do to her, to make her happy. That was my first time. After that, Claire came to my room every time she had a chance, and I learned . . . I learned so many different things . . . I was a good pupil.'' Georgina gave a low laugh. ''Her star pupil.''

''What happened when—Claire left school?'' Fernanda's voice sounded strange to her, as if it came from a distance.

''At first I didn't know what to do. I thought about her all the time, I did it to myself, of course, but it wasn't the same . . . I needed it so much by then . . . I was thirteen—it was all I thought about, I could barely concentrate on my books enough to get by— and then I noticed a girl in my own form, a girl who watched me the way I'd watched Claire—and one night I went to her room . . .''

''Yes?'' Fernanda asked hoarsely.

''And I made love to her, the way Claire had shown me. There's always been some girl, ever since, until I left England, but there was never anyone who could take the place of Claire, no one who fascinated me so completely, no one I wanted as much, no one I had such a frightfully real crush on . . . until I met you.'' Georgina's low voice trembled, but she didn't move from her recumbent position on the bed, didn't make a gesture toward Fernanda.

''I didn't . . . I had no idea . . . I've never . . .'' Fernanda's words stumbled and she didn't dare to look at her friend. She was thrown into utter confusion by the surprise of what she had just learned, shock combined with an unwilling but irresistible excitement. Sitting in a chair in this shadowed bedroom, listening to Georgina's dreaming, beautiful voice as she pictured the scene between the two girls, she had become frantically aroused. But how was it possible? She'd never been attracted to another woman . . . naturally the thought had crossed her mind, many times, only to be immediately supplanted by another thought that told her it was only intellectual curiosity, everybody had such notions all the time, they didn't mean anything.

"I know you had 'no idea,' you darling goose. Why do you think I told you about Claire? You don't think I'd tell anyone else but you that story, do you? Fernie, you've never found the right man, have you? People think that you find men, use them up and go on to the next, but I know that you've never been made love to properly. Isn't that so?"

"I . . . yes . . . but I think it's . . . me . . . something wrong."

"That's impossible. Oh, my sweet, nothing could be wrong with you. See here, I know I've probably horrified you, telling you about how I feel about girls, and I know you're nervous and uptight and have all sorts of theories against it, but what harm could it do to try . . . with me? Just as an experiment . . . just once? If you don't enjoy it, we'll never do anything again, we'll forget it happened and we'll still be best friends, I promise, because I love being with you so much. Let me just show you. You don't have to do anything at all, you don't have to move a muscle, and if you ask me to stop, I'll stop . . . I'll give you a beginner's lesson the way I used to do, at school."

As if she could refuse, Fernanda thought, as if she could possibly get up and walk out of this room, when she was having trouble with simple breathing.

"Lock the door," Fernanda managed to say. While Georgina did so, she wondered if she should lie down on the bed, but she was too befuddled to move from her chair. She didn't know how to do this, she thought wildly, and then Georgina came back, stood behind the chair and started to stroke her hair back from her forehead with a touch so reassuringly tender that Fernanda gradually felt the tension in her shoulders relax.

"Yes, yes, that's better. Oh, I've wanted to touch your hair for so long," Georgina whispered, and cradled Fernanda's head to her bosom. "I used to look at you at lunch and wonder how it would feel—so soft, so fragrant, softer than I dreamed. Come over to the bed, darling, that's right, just lie back and let me look at you."

She put one arm under Fernanda's head and kissed her on the forehead. Fernanda shuddered with anticipation, remembering how Claire had begun her lesson, and she leaned her head back on the pillow, closed her eyes and allowed her mouth to receive Georgina's kisses. That exquisite mouth, she thought, that marvelously shaped mouth that was never covered with lipstick, that warm mouth, that small, pointed tongue darting in such timidly inquisitive forays between her lips, not like a man's blundering tongue that was often too big or too demanding.

She was aware that Georgina had stopped kissing her long enough to take off her clothes, and she began to unbutton her own shirt when she felt Georgina's hand on hers.

"Don't, let me do that. I want to be your slave."

"*What?*"

"Your slave, darling. I want to wait on you, do everything for you, whatever you want, there's no rush, we have all the time in the world. The longer it takes to make you happy, the better it will be. Oh, I like it to take a long, long time. *I like to be told what to do.*"

"Was that what Claire said to you?" she muttered.

"No, I didn't find out I wanted that until much later . . . may I be your slave?"

"Yes . . . oh, yes . . ."

"May I unbutton your blouse?"

"Yes."

As Georgina slowly unbuttoned each button, Fernanda could hear her breathing come more quickly, but when Fernanda's arrogantly splendid breasts were freed from the confinement of the silk, Georgina waited to touch them until Fernanda gave her permission. Only then did she caress them with the tips of her fingers that knew exactly how much pressure brought the optimum amount of pleasure, experienced, supple fingers that knew exactly how to draw a line of lovely promise across Fernanda's breasts, closer, ever closer to the nipples, but holding back from actually touching them, so that Fernanda felt her nipples aching with tightness for a touch that did not come and that would not come if she did not demand it.

She lay tensed under the exquisite torture, arching her back and her neck and willing herself to wait until Georgina asked for permission. Georgina, her slave. But although she could feel Georgina's warm breath on her breasts as she bent to her task, she asked for nothing, and Fernanda finally understood that a slave could ask only for certain things and that other intimacies were for Fernanda herself to demand. She licked one finger and briefly touched it to a nipple, in a signal of command, and Georgina's open mouth immediately descended, fastening on the nipple with an adept but diffident suction that took infinite care not to suck her to the point of pain, as so many men did in their frenzy.

"We have all the time . . . the longer the better . . ." Georgina murmured, and Fernanda sighed in ecstasy. She had always wanted her nipples sucked for much longer than any man was willing to, and sucked like this, the sucking an end in itself, and not merely a way to stimulate her so that she'd allow them to enter her. She turned on her side, so that her breasts would fall forward in all their fullness, and abandoned herself to Georgina's swollen lips and licking tongue and barely nipping teeth, thinking nothing of her slave but only of herself and her pleasure, for here was no man with an urgent need, with a goal he had to reach, but only a beautiful, adoring slave she was allowing to please her.

Much time, luxurious, concentrated, sighing time, time without a preordained ending, went by before Fernanda motioned to the waistband of her trousers and Georgina obediently unfastened the one button, opened the zipper and tugged off Fernanda's trousers. Fernanda was wearing bikini panties which she perversely left on, to test Georgina's willpower. She had not touched Georgina's naked body, but she gazed at it in wonder through half-closed eyes. She had never met another woman who had a better body than she, but petite as Georgina was, she had much larger, firmer breasts, a more dimpled, plump behind, a slimmer waist, and wider, fuller hips. No wonder she always looked too rounded in clothes. Naked, she was a goddess.

Now Georgina, who had not received permission to take off Fernanda's panties, was directed by a pointing finger to put her mouth on Fernanda's silk-clad crotch. Fernanda knew that the silk was wet through, and she wanted Georgina to feel the moisture with her lips, to tongue her through the cloth, to give her that sensation she longed for, yet not give it to her fully, on her naked mound. Not yet. Georgina put her mouth on the spot Fernanda had indicated, but just pressed her unassertive lips to the silk, the top of her smooth head bowed in submission. "Use your tongue, slave," Fernanda whispered harshly.

Fernanda lay back, trying to hold still, as she felt the little tongue lapping warmly on the material that covered her lower lips, but soon she knew that she had to have more. She pulled off her panties in a quick movement and spread her legs apart, breathing shallowly, holding herself open with her fingers so that Georgina had complete access to her clitoris. "More," Fernanda commanded, "more, don't dare to stop . . . put it in as far as you can." She felt the small tongue push forward with surprising strength, entering

her and circling knowingly around a few marvelously
sensitive inches, and then draw back while Georgina
released and exposed Fernanda's clitoris with her fingers, curling her tongue around the fattening flesh and
sucking with her whole inner mouth. Over and over,
with groans of ever-renewed hunger, she repeated the
two acts, first invading as far as she could, then withdrawing and sucking again, and each time she did so,
Fernanda felt herself growing bigger and bigger, as if
her clitoris had turned into the swelling tip of a small,
firm penis. She lost herself in growing passion, a passion only possible because there was no invasion of
her body, a passion only possible because Georgina
knew so precisely what to do to her, because Georgina
had a woman's body and a woman's mind and knew
how to give another woman exactly what she needed.

Slowly, from far away, she felt a climax building,
but she gave no indication of it because she was absolutely secure in the knowledge that her slave would
not stop until she allowed her to stop, that her slave
wanted this act to last as long as possible, that her
slave demanded nothing, that her slave could last forever. No rush, there was no rush, Fernanda thought,
drowned in sensations she had never had before, how
wonderful to know that there was no rush.

Slowly the tugging and licking of Georgina's
mouth, the thrusting of Georgina's tongue, began to
become too exciting to endure in silence, soon Fernanda was unable to stop herself from making noises
she'd never made with any man, sounds that didn't
make Georgina falter in her rhythmic plunder. Nothing would make her stop too soon, nothing would
make her take her lovely tongue away and substitute
a hard, determined penis, an unwanted, unnecessary
penis. Fernanda arched higher and put her hands
behind Georgina's smooth head and ground her
distended, engorged, open mound into Georgina's
greedily obedient mouth, urgently, madly, as the climax that had started far away came closer and closer
until it was upon her, until it could be held back no

longer, until she gave herself up to it, finally feeling the power, bigger than she was, take her in its grip and make her scream with joy.

"Everything . . . everything's different now," Fernanda said, when she could finally speak.

"I love you, Fernie."

"All these years . . . oh, Georgie . . . never never knowing what it could be . . . you were so . . . I can't tell you . . ."

"Don't say anything, just let's cuddle, just let me hold you quietly, my beautiful darling." She took Fernanda in her arms and rocked her gently, holding her firmly but without any sensual intention, yet Fernanda, who had just had the first real orgasm of her life, now freed of her preoccupation with her own body and its unsatisfied needs, suddenly found herself acutely conscious of the pungent fragrance of Georgina's naked body.

Her curiosity awoke, and the wonder with which she had looked at Georgina's ripe nakedness quickly turned into something other than wonder. That lush, opulent young fullness, that white skin with its sensuous pink shadows, those light brown nipples riding those large, luxuriously heavy breasts, those delectable light red curls that hid Georgina's rounded mound, were all unexplored, untasted, all tantalizingly unknown, and all incredibly tempting. Without thinking about what she was doing, she started to fondle Georgina whose eyes were filled with laughing submission, Georgina whose whole face was rosy and open and joyful, Georgina whom she loved. Fernanda felt a flame of unaccustomed, violent lust, a newborn, foreign desire that no man had ever caused, begin to rise from her deepest center, and without a word, without asking the slightest permission, she drew herself up on the bed and pinned Georgina's arms to the mattress as she straddled the magnificent body that lay sprawled under her, that still-mysterious body that belonged to her now. She could feel herself swelling heavily, aggressively, needily. Again, oh yes, *again*.

"You don't have to . . ." Georgina whispered. "It was just to make you happy . . ."

"Be quiet and lie still. I'm going to fuck you."

"Susie, did you ever hear much about my great-grand-mother Amilia?" Jazz asked, as she sat at the kitchen table watching the tiny cook work with her usual busy efficiency.

"How could I have, Jazz? I didn't start to work here till 1961. We're not going to fight about my age again, are we?" Susie squinted at Jazz through knowing eyes. Her girl had been up to something, that was for sure, and on a rainy Sunday, what else could it have been but what she'd been expecting for a long time now? It hadn't made her ugly, that was for sure. High time too. Mike Kilkullen would have wanted Casey and Jazz to find out that they loved each other, no matter how miserable they were about him.

"You speak Spanish at home, don't you, Susie?" Jazz asked.

"That depends. My boys speak both, my husband feels happier speaking Spanish, my mother only speaks Spanish, my grandchildren don't know much Spanish but the swear words."

"Can you read traditional Spanish?"

"Juanita Isabella, can you read English?" Susie sniffed. "What do you think I had to study for four years in high school?"

"Sit down, for heaven's sake, and look at this." Jazz thrust the yellow pad and the letter at Susie.

"Oh, been doing homework, have you?"

"Not exactly."

"That's the way your homework used to look. What a mess! But not as bad as Casey's room and the archive room. I've got the roofers working up there already, before it rains again."

"Please, Susie, give me some help. This is a letter I found from my great-great-grandmother to my great-grandmother Amilia. I can't translate this paragraph —it doesn't make much sense to me." Jazz showed her the part of the letter that she had attempted to translate the night before, and Susie took out her glasses and puzzled over the faded brown ink of the elaborate baroque handwriting.

"I've got the gist of it," she said at last. "Do you want it word for word?"

"The gist."

"Well, as far as I can tell, it seems that when the Valencias sold the ranch to the Kilkullens, there was some sort of strict covenant on the ranch that one of the Valencias had made a very, very long time ago with the local Franciscan friars, the priests at the Mission probably, when they were still there. Anyway, the Kilkullens were just as good Catholics as the Valencias, and they agreed to respect this sacred covenant. Basically, Amilia was being reassured that the Kilkullens were as God-fearing as the Valencias and that she should be proud to marry into the family."

"How could that be? I've never heard of any covenant," Jazz protested.

"Maybe it wasn't called a covenant. Maybe it had something to do with the story about the Mission that my mother used to tell me. She heard it from her grandmother, who probably heard it from her mother, so it goes back really far. They called it the story of the 'Promise of the Mountain.'"

"You never told it to me."

"While you were little enough for bedtime stories, you had your mother . . . and then . . . you had Rosie taking care of you, and your father to tell you stories—you weren't sitting around the kitchen bothering me, and anyway I had work to do, cooking for everybody in the house."

"Tell it to me now!"

"Oh, it's a lovely tale about the building of the Mission in San Juan Capistrano. It took nine long years to build the Great Stone Church. It wasn't finished until 1806. The bell tower of the church was taller than any other building that had ever been built in California. It was the wonder of the land. Year after year, men and women and every child who was old enough, helped to build the church. Some of them carried stones by hand, some of them brought them in wooden carts, they found sycamore wood on the Trabuco mesa, sandstone and limestone were quarried miles away, even stones from Valencia Point were carried to the church. When the Great Stone Church was finished, people flocked here from ranchos everywhere in California, soldiers and dignitaries and hundreds of Indian converts, all the people dressed in their finest clothes, so proud and so happy. Afterwards there was the greatest fiesta anybody can remember, and the people celebrated for days on end. They prayed and paraded and danced and sang. To give thanks for the completion of the Great Stone Church, old Teodosio Valencia and a group of Franciscans climbed up Portola Peak—only they called it the Mountain of the Moon then, of course—and they say Teodosio found a holy place all the way up on the mountain where he made a solemn promise to the holy fathers who had made the pilgrimage. He took a vow that the hand of man would never change anything on his land, not for as far as the eye could see from the Mountain of the Moon.''

"That was the 'promise of the mountain'?''

"Yes, the story always ended with those words, 'for as far as the eye can see.' Now, Jazz, you know about those old stories. There's supposed to have been an old mission in San Juan too, one that's still older than the Mission, but nobody's ever been able to find out where it was—the Mission Viejo—and there's probably no holy place, no shrine, or whatever on Portola Peak either.''

"But that story lasted almost two hundred years!''

"All good stories do, and a lot longer than that— I could tell you dozens of them, each one with a miracle in it. I'll start with the parting of the Red Sea.''

"Susie, you're a cynic.''

"I'm a realist, honey. Working for the Kilkullens has overloaded my sense of romance.''

19

When Jazz brought herself to tell Casey of the discouraging discussion she had had with Steve Johnson, the deep vein of business acumen that underlay his other activities forced him to agree with the verdict of the probate litigator: Jazz might delay the development of the land, but she could never stop it.

She added what she knew of Susie's tale of the promise of the mountain and Amilia's perplexing, unclear letter about a covenant.

"Don't they sound as if they must mean something important?" Jazz asked hopefully.

"Look, darling, the Monte Carlo idea is appalling," Casey replied, "but we can't fight it with anything but hard facts. There's got to be someone who might make a connection between the story and the letter, otherwise we're dealing with phantoms, clutching at straws. Who, besides Susie, is a repository of local yarns?"

"Maybe . . . maybe Mr. White, the man who read us the will, although he's about a hundred years too young. Still, his family has done business with my family forever.''

"Let's make an appointment with him. He may not be an Indian medicine man, but he's the only game in town.''

As they climbed the flight of stairs to Henry White's office in San Clemente, Jazz stopped halfway up. "Maybe it's not even a straw I'm clutching at, maybe I'll be wasting his time.''

"Nonsense," he said, propelling her up the stairs, "how often does he get to enjoy looking at a girl like you?''

Henry White received them with his usual graciousness, less startled by Jazz's introduction of Casey as "my fiancé" than was Jazz, who had never used those words before, but felt that there was no other way to present Casey properly to such a dignified figure as the retired banker.

After she'd shown him Amilia's letter and told him Susie's story, he leaned back in his chair and shook his head wistfully.

"That's a pretty bit of a romantic jigsaw puzzle you've found, my dear Jazz, but I've never heard this particular story before, and the letter could mean anything or nothing.''

"I know, but . . . Teodosio Valencia was granted the land by the Crown of Spain in 1788 . . .''

"My dear, if we're going to get involved with Spanish land grants, we're going to waste our time. There were only between twenty and thirty original Spanish land grants made—experts disagree on the number—and no documentation of them, to my knowledge, exists today. Perhaps there is an actual grant in the bottom of a trunk somewhere, but the odds are that they have all been lost or destroyed. Nobody I've heard of has ever seen one. The Dead Sea Scrolls aren't as mysterious.''

"Still, the covenant has to mean *something*," Jazz said stubbornly, "or Juanita Isabella wouldn't have written about it in a letter that was so important to Amilia that she put it in her portfolio with her most precious souvenirs, her love letters and her photographs of her husband.''

"If there were something really important in the form of a covenant with the Franciscans, it would have been mentioned elsewhere than in a wife's private hoard of sentimental bits of paper," Henry White said. "No, my dear, it would have been documented and registered and had legal authority behind it, somewhere, somehow.''

"What kind of documentation?" Casey asked.

"Ha! What kind indeed! You've jumped straight into the middle of the godawful morass of California history, a pitiful story of injustice piled on injustice, a veritable sinkhole of complications and confusion. Ha! Not from around here, are you, Mr. Nelson?''

"No sir, New York.''

"Well, it wouldn't make any difference if you'd been born here. Nobody even studies the history of the United States any more, much less California.'' Mr. White smiled at them both, looking like a man who had been waiting for years for two fools like them to come asking him things he knew and they didn't, Jazz decided through her impatience to know whatever he knew.

"Mr. White," she said, meltingly, "could you try to fill us in?''

"Ha! Fill you in, indeed! There's no way to do it except to start at the beginning, in 1769, when the Spanish viceroy established a Royal Presidio in San Diego. He sent an expedition up the coast to look for Monterey Bay, sixty-three men and two priests, led by Don Gaspar de Portola. They walked their way up the coast, baptizing every child they could get their hands on, I wouldn't wonder. Eventually the Franciscan priest Fra Junípero Serra established twenty-one missions from San Diego north. Most of the surrounding land was claimed by those missions, but some land grants were made to individuals, primarily old soldiers who had served well.''

Jazz ventured a tiny glance at Casey. Even if he

hadn't learned this in school, she most certainly had. The Junípero Serra saga was impossible for even a casual tourist to ignore, unless he never set foot outside of Disneyland.

"Now we get to the sticky part. Ha! In 1821, Spain lost California to Mexico. The local settlers, the Californios, who were a mixture of Spanish and Mexican, demanded that the mission lands be secularized, and gradually they took away the power of the Franciscans. Between 1833 and 1840 you had a land grab of major proportions. It was every man for himself, believe me. If you already owned land, like the Valencias, you had to petition to reaffirm your right to ownership by appearing in court before the Mexican governor, by petitioning the governor, by proving that you had at least two thousand head of cattle and a house, by giving every possible justification for continuation of the original grant. Believe it or not, in each case this process took an average of *thirty years* of hearings and testimony, and what was the result? Disgraceful! Most of the old owners lost their land and their money before it was over, while hundreds of new owners, many of them with political connections, took over with newly issued Mexican land grants."

"But the Valencias held on to their land," Jazz cried, "or they couldn't have sold it to the Kilkullens."

"Quite so, my dear, they were among the lucky and persistent few. Their file, the *expediente*, would have contained the petition to the governor, a crude topographical map called a *diseño*, and a copy, which they called the *borrador*. The whole *expediente* should have been kept in the Provincial Archives. All official, and as tidy as they got at that time."

"Where would that *expediente* be now?" Casey asked.

"I can't imagine, my dear young man. I haven't got a clue," he said blandly. "Anyway, it didn't do much good to have that *expediente*, because no sooner did the Valencias think they finally owned their land fair and square when along came the United States and declared war on Mexico in 1846. Not much of a war—the Californios surrendered the whole state in January of 1847, just before the Gold Rush in 1848— amazingly poor timing, I've always thought. Or amazingly good, depending on your citizenship. Ha!''

"If the Californios surrendered the whole state, how did the Valencias hold on to their land?'' Casey asked evenly. Mr. White showed a relish, as he described the horrors of the landowning process, that seemed unfeeling, almost as if he enjoyed dashing their naive quest.

"They had to go back to court *again* to satisfy Congressman Gwin's Act of 1851, which provided three commissioners to settle land claims. Within two years every single grant, some eight hundred of them, had to be submitted to this commission—believe it or not, the claims covered about twelve *million* acres. Confusion! Total confusion, my dear Jazz. I can imagine it all too well.''

Henry White stopped talking and sat shaking his head, as if he were heartily glad to have missed that episode in California history.

"But, Mr. White, the Valencias sold to the Kilkullens in 1865,'' Casey insisted. "They *must* have had a valid deed.''

"Oh, I don't question that. No, the first of the Kilkullens wouldn't have paid up without a deed . . . too smart a fellow for that, I'm sure. To satisfy the confirmation hearing of the United States government, the Valencias would have had to affirm the Mexican grant with another petition, another more complete *diseño* that was approved by the Surveyor General, as well as every bit of paper they might have supporting their claim. When it was approved, all the documentation would have formed yet another *expediente*. It was copied on tracing paper, and an officer of the Surveyor General would have authenticated the original.''

"I have a feeling that I'm not going to like the answer to this question, but where would that second *expediente* be found?" Jazz asked, trying to read the answer in his expression.

"I really hate to tell you this, my dear, but most of the affirmations would have been registered in the General Land Office in—alas—San Francisco."

"*Before* the earthquake." Jazz's voice blended recognition with incredulity.

"Before the earthquake and, worst of all, before the fire. It would have been destroyed in the fire, I'm afraid."

"But this is like a paper chase with no paper!" Jazz burst out indignantly. "It's so unfair!"

"That's probably why they don't teach California history," Casey said, taking her hands in his. "It's too heartbreaking."

"Obviously, when the land changed hands," Mr. White added, as an afterthought, "the title, the deed to the ranch, would have been deposited in the County Recorder's office in Santa Ana."

"*What!*"

"Oh, I assumed you must know that, or I would have mentioned it earlier. Yes, yes indeed, the purchase of the Rancho Montaña de la Luna by Michael Kilkullen would have had to go to the County Recorder, to be enforceable, you know, to be legal. Ha! All those original documents we've been talking about are nonessential, irrelevant . . . quite irrelevant . . ."

Then why didn't he say so in the first place, Jazz thought furiously. Why did he have to put us through all the nonessentials instead of just sending us off to Santa Ana? But Henry White hadn't finished talking, and Casey had a firm hand on her arm so that she couldn't jump up and rush out to the car and drive off.

"On the other hand," Henry White mused, taking off his glasses and looking at the ceiling, "titles, deeds, maps—they're often not the only pieces of the puzzle, are they? That's why we have historians and librarians and curators, not just real-estate lawyers. Ha! Yes, you could always try the Bancroft Library, up at Berkeley, you know, or the Archives of the San

Diego Historical Society, or the Department of Manuscripts at the Huntington in Pasadena, the Orange County Historical Society or even the San Juan Capistrano Historical Society . . . never know what you'll turn up. They have all sorts of bits and pieces . . . old papers . . . bits and pieces . . ."

"Thank you, Mr. White," Casey said firmly. "You've been extremely helpful. Jazz and I are very grateful."

"Anytime, Mr. Nelson, anytime. It's always a pleasure to give young people a little history lesson. I can't think when I've had such a pleasant morning."

"Oh, there you are, I've been looking all over for you two," Valerie said in irritation as she discovered Fernanda and Georgina having lunch out by one of the two swimming pools of the Ritz. "You might have left a message for me, Fernie. I'm starving and I didn't want to eat alone."

"Sorry, Val. I thought you were off to Los Angeles with Jimmy."

"So did I, but it turned out that he and John had a meeting about some other business deal. Nothing to do with us. I hate it when everyone goes off in different directions without telling me!"

Valerie spoke with more indignation than the subject deserved, but she was still angered by her conversation with her husband earlier in the day. Billy simply did not seem to have factored her new position as an heiress into his consciousness. He treated her the way he had always treated her, as good old Valerie, that taken-for-granted spouse of many years, who happened to make a little handy money of her own.

William Malvern Jr. had had nothing but complaints. The cook was leaving, a maid had quit, the fridge wasn't working properly and the ice cubes were half water, each one of their three daughters had a different problem she expected him to solve, he was sick and tired of being an extra man at parties, Valerie had been hanging about in California far too long, one petty bit of foolishness after another, as if Valerie were still the person she had been before her father's death.

Go live in a hotel, she'd wanted to scream at him, eat at your clubs, tell the girls to stop being idiots, and, for God's sake, stop nagging! But she'd held her tongue and tried to smooth things over, without actually promising to come back to New York that very day, as he had wanted her to.

A plan had been forming in the back of Valerie's mind, but she wasn't ready to act on it yet, and until she was, she wasn't about to confront her husband, for almost twenty-two years of marriage had disciplined her to appreciate the high value of possessing an attractive, agreeable man, irritating or not.

Her plan involved burning bridges, burning every God damned bridge that linked the disgusting, filthy, overcrowded island of Manhattan to the rest of the United States, and burning them so thoroughly that unless Billy Malvern decided to follow her to the far side of the bridges, she would never see him again. She wasn't at all sure that she was ready; she didn't know yet if she had the courage to take a step that would possibly end in having to leave behind her marriage and everything else she had thought was important.

But, oh, how tempted she was, how deeply, almost atavistically tempted she was to throw away everything she had striven for, and retreat—for retreat it would unquestionably seem to everyone she knew—to Philadelphia and a life of different pleasures, of milder habits and reduced reference points, a life in which it was impossible to buy status.

Ah, but could she, who had earned her solid credentials in the toughest town of them all, could she, Valerie Malvern, who was counted as one of the most durable figures of the New York establishment, be content to turn into a Main Line lady? After so many years at the white-hot center of fashion and glamour, at the American equivalent of Versailles at the peak of the reign of Louis XVI, would life on the sidelines be a terrible letdown? What if her feelings about Philadelphia were romanticized because she didn't live there and know the reality of daily life, as opposed to occasional visits? Perhaps New York was more addictive than she realized and Philadelphia would prove as tedious, as flat, as country chateau life had appeared to the French aristocrats who, exiled from Versailles, pined away quickly.

Once you'd abandoned New York, you were quickly forgotten. There were women as rich as she would soon be in other cities all over the United States —but no one had ever heard of them in New York, no one photographed them or wrote about them except in their local society pages. Their one brief and unimportant moment in the sun, as far as New York was concerned, came when *Town and Country* decided to devote an issue to their city, and included them. If such women visited New York, their arrival barely made a ripple, they had to depend on New York friends to entertain for them, and when they left, they disappeared immediately from the New York consciousness.

Valerie sat down at the table with Georgina and Fernanda, ordered a shrimp salad and began to eat it without attempting to join in their conversation, which seemed, of all things, to be devoted to a discussion of the merits of different jams and jellies.

Valerie tried to take stock of her new position in the city where the last decade had been a constant strain to seem to be as rich as people had assumed she was.

Now she was about to possess endless resources. Her family background was as good as that of any other woman's in the city . . . no, *better* actually, now that she thought about it seriously. Her style had never been questioned. Money, family, style. She had everything to make her queen of New York without her lifting a finger to bring it about.

But, Christ, how competitive it had become! All those other people, jammed together in a constantly photographed pack, dressing competitively, giving to charity competitively, buying art competitively, entertaining competitively, vacationing competitively—did she truly want to be queen of those people?

Billy Malvern would enjoy every second of it, she couldn't doubt that. He'd never see it as clearly as she did. Would Billy agree to move? Could he be uprooted?

"Valerie, why so silent? Don't you approve of our tearoom plans?" Georgina asked.

"What tearoom?"

"The one Fernie and I are thinking of opening," Georgina said, shaking her head incredulously. "That's all we've been talking about, ever since you sat down."

"I'm sorry, I wasn't paying attention. I have phone calls to make." Valerie got up hastily. She would not endure silly, silly people like Georgina with her silly decorating business, or Fernie with her silly husband problems, no, not for another minute. It was too much to expect her to listen to some utterly silly scheme for opening a tearoom. "I'll see you two later," she said savagely.

"Was it something I said?" Georgina asked Fernie. "If so, remind me to say it again."

"Val gets that way sometimes. Her husband phoned her this morning and she's been in a snit ever since."

"Husbands . . ." Georgina said, on a thoughtful note of reserved judgment.

"Why did you marry Jimmy?"

"Fernie, darling, what a question!"

"Well . . . I just thought that knowing how you felt about men so early in your life . . . you might have, oh, I don't know, not bothered?"

"You mean that since I didn't need a man for my love life, I didn't need a man at all? Fernie, you're such a child! First of all, Jimmy's rather a pet, and since it's far more convenient to marry than not, he was a good choice. The money was frightfully important . . . my papa is not one of the rich earls, rather the contrary, and there are a lot of us children to see settled. So my parents were terribly pleased when I

accepted Jimmy. Nobody would ever have understood it if I hadn't married. Worse yet, they might
have begun to wonder about me, even, eventually, to
suspect. A husband's the most convincing camouflage
of all. And, who knows, eventually I might want children, just like every other woman.''

Georgina's lips curved gently, tenderly at the idea
of children. One day, why not, after all? She had the
best of all possible worlds.

''And then,'' she continued, ''there's always that
inescapable escort problem. Mobs of men always
wanted to take me out, take me to parties, be at my
beck and call as it were, but naturally each one of
them thought that after a while he deserved more than
a good-night peck on the cheek. So I'd have to drop
him. It became too predictably dreary for words. I got
a reputation as a heartless flirt—we couldn't have
that, could we?''

''And Jimmy? Does he get more than a good-night
peck?'' Fernanda asked, deeply curious. She needed
to know the answer, but she dreaded it.

Georgina's eyes dropped to the tablecloth and a
curious hardness, fleeting but unmistakable, transformed her face, making her look far older than she
was. She bit her lips and didn't answer at first, as if
she were trying to make up her mind to fend Fern off
with her usual tranquil, self-mocking humor. Finally
she shook her head in the unmistakable manner of
someone determined to tell the truth, but she spoke
with lowered eyelids.

''When I said Jimmy was rather a pet, just now, I
meant that he was unfailingly sweet to me. But bed
. . . that's the price I have to pay, and, oh, God, how
I hate it! I suppose I shouldn't complain, any man
would expect the same thing, but Jimmy . . . well,
you can't imagine what it's like. It's not as if he abuses
me, darling—don't think that—he's never hurt me,
but he's so . . . voracious. So revoltingly, sickeningly
voracious, so avid, so tireless. Oh, I don't know, Fernie, maybe they're all that way, I've never slept with
another man so I can't compare, but he never seems

to be satisfied. Do you think that's normal?" Georgina
dared to look Fernanda in the eyes as she asked the
faltering question.

"Normal? There's no such thing as normal," Fernanda said violently. "Not where men are concerned.
You've only been married less than two years; he's
certain to become less demanding sooner or later, I
can promise you that much." Fernanda thought of the
afternoon she'd spent with Jimmy Rosemont, and if
she had been able to kill him on the spot, she would
have done so with joy.

"Oh, that's exactly what I'm praying for! For one
thing, everyone knows perfectly well what a cheat he
is. Even on our honeymoon he had other women,
thank heaven. The more women he goes after, the less
pressure I'm under. And when he's involved in the
last stages of putting a deal together, like these last
few weeks, he almost leaves me alone. Of course,
when it's concluded, he'll want to . . . celebrate."
Georgina shuddered. "And, Fernie, the weird thing is
that he's convinced that I'm frigid, and it simply
doesn't make any difference to him. Wouldn't you
think it should? How can a man force himself on a
woman who doesn't want him? But no, if anything, he
somehow *likes* the idea. If he can't make me—well,
you know—then no one else can either. He considers
my frigidity an invisible chastity belt. An asset in a
wife. Oh, let's never talk about him again, promise
me, my darling? He has nothing to do with us . . . he's
a necessary evil in that department."

Georgina's smile as she looked Fernanda in the
eye was devouring, dangerously alluring, filled with
memory and worship and acceptance of her right to
all her emotions, all her impulses.

"God! When you say that 'well, you know,' like
a prudish spinster, I almost . . . well, you know,"
Fernanda said, lowering her voice.

"Oh, my darling, let's get the check and go back
to the suite," Georgina said urgently. "I'm so horribly
jealous of you already that I can't stand it."

"Jealous! You don't think I'll let another man

touch me! I'm getting a divorce the instant I get back to New York, no matter what it costs.''

"It's not men I'm jealous of. Now that you're . . . aware . . . now that you know exactly what you need . . . there'll be women everywhere, women who you never dreamed preferred women, trying to get you to go to bed with them. And the older you get, the more of them there'll be, swarming around you. Women like us don't reach our most desirable age until we're forty.''

"Oh, that's crazy! That's the opposite of real life!'' Fernanda protested.

"Wait and see, Fernie darling. So many women are looking for mother figures, and who can begin to qualify under forty? But don't go and gain weight—that would make you even more irresistible.''

"Why?'' Fernanda demanded, fascinated.

"You'd look more womanly. Women who prefer women adore the female body, and you're still much too slim, too pert, too much of an ingenue for some tastes.''

"Good Lord, how strange,'' Fernanda said, almost indifferently. She'd never had so much good news in one time in her life, but she certainly wasn't going to take advantage of it. Not for years and years.

"Barbra would really appreciate this place,'' Jazz said to Casey.

"Who?''

"Streisand. When I went to her place in Malibu to photograph her for *Vogue*, the security was just as good as it is here.'' She waved around the reception room of the Huntington Museum's manuscript collection.

She didn't have to entertain him, Casey thought, looking at her unnecessarily beautiful face, in which only the rueful eyes betrayed her woebegone state of mind. When they had hightailed it off to the Santa Ana County Recorder's office, and eventually located the title record of the sale of the Rancho Montaña de la Luna, property of Don Antonio Pablo Valencia, to

Michael Kilkullen, they had excitedly pored over the one-page legal description of the land, dated 1865 and signed with the names of the grantee and the grantor, and found nothing, absolutely nothing, that related to any covenant.

"I think it ends here, darling," Casey had said.

"It *can't* end here!" Jazz had blazed. "I won't let it!"

Casey had told the temporary Cow Boss, a seasoned vaquero who had replaced him while he was in the hospital, to carry on his duties, and he and Jazz had spent all the next day in San Diego, at the Historical Society, trying to find one of Mr. White's "bits and pieces." The day after that, they had turned the San Juan Historical Society upside down, with just as little success, and spent another fruitless, frustrating, dusty day at the Orange County Historical Society. Next, Jazz had become possessed of an idea that the Bancroft Library, up at Berkeley, should have been the first place for them to look, for she reasoned that during the San Francisco fire, someone had probably had the presence of mind to save files from the General Land Office. They had flown to San Francisco in the morning and returned the same night, not just empty-handed but hungry, for in that mecca of good food they hadn't been able to spare the time to go to Chez Panisse for a meal.

They had seen more "bits and pieces" of California history than Casey would have imagined still existed, but nothing that related to the particular sixty-four thousand acres between the mountain and the sea that had become the Kilkullen Ranch.

Now they were down to the last destination Mr. White had mentioned, the Huntington, in the San Marino section of Pasadena, known to most people as the museum that owned the *Blue Boy*.

Of course, they could spend weeks and weeks in California, going through the files of minor historical societies in each and every old town, but the curators who had witnessed their disappointment had told them pointedly that they shouldn't expect to find anything of serious interest outside of the larger, better-known collections.

Nobody had used the words "wild-goose chase," but you could see them thinking it, Casey thought mordantly. When they had explained that they were looking for a covenant, the mere word sounded so improbably otherworldly, as if it were a pact with the devil, that the people they'd talked to had probably pigeonholed them in the nut file anyway, Casey decided. Not that they hadn't been helpful, they'd been entirely professional, but they certainly hadn't been surprised by the nonexistence of a covenant with the Franciscans.

The day after their doleful, weary return from San Francisco, Jazz had telephoned the Huntington and made an appointment with William P. Frank, the Associate Curator of Western manuscripts.

Today, after being checked out twice by uniformed men on the sweeping drive that mounted through the magnificently landscaped gardens and lawns that had once been the park of the Huntington Mansion, they had parked, located the modern building that housed the library, and climbed a staircase past a bewildering series of doors to this perfectly appointed room in which they were the only people waiting.

Casey could wish that Jazz had never found her great-grandmother's letter, wish that she had not tried to translate it, wish that Jimmy Rosemont had a clear-cut victory in hand, so that Jazz could turn her attention away from her furious obsession about the sale of the ranch and begin to think about their future together.

Since the day she had agreed to marry him, they had spoken of nothing, it seemed to Casey, but that letter, that legend, that covenant. Jazz was a creature utterly possessed by her need to keep the land out of the hands of the Hong Kong bankers and their Monte Carlo plans. All of her concerns in life had been put on the back burner. Love, no sooner admitted, and marriage, no sooner envisioned, had both immediately taken second place—a far second—to the mysterious promise of the mountain.

Was chasing the promise of the mountain Jazz's way of not letting herself be happy with him, Casey wondered. Did she feel, on a deep level she wasn't aware of, that she had no right to happiness so soon after her father's murder? Deeply worried, Casey knew that the quicker this fantasy faded, the quicker this last chance failed to pan out, the faster she'd come back to the real world, and to him.

"Darling," Casey said, "when Mr. Frank asks you what we're looking for, why don't you not say 'a covenant,' but call it 'a private land agreement'? I haven't been able to feel comfortable asking a stranger to help us find a covenant that's over two hundred years old."

"It sounds perfectly reasonable to me," Jazz objected.

"Could we compromise and try it my way? This time?"

"Compromise," Jazz said darkly. "That's what Red told me. Marriage was all about compromise."

"But when we told her, she was so delighted—"

"Of course she was, but later, when I was alone with her, she started talking about how I'd have to learn to compromise. *Shit,* I hate that word! It's so incredibly dreary and dull, just when the most wonderful, exciting thing you could ever imagine happens to you, everyone jumps down your throat with compromise, compromise, like a bunch of bush-league Dear Abbys, even Susie cackled that I'd better start to expect to compromise, and she's always on your side anyway. Why didn't Susie ask when we were going to get married, why didn't Red ask me what I was going to wear, why didn't anyone get all carried away with surprise and Mumsie-like?"

The only satisfactory response had been Pete's, Jazz thought. He'd shouted that she couldn't possibly get married until she'd given him a chance to fuck her brains out and change her mind, an offer she decided not to pass along to Casey.

"I'll make a deal with you. *I'll* compromise," Casey said.

"I thought it took two."

"Only one, if he's a mind reader, bewilderingly crafty, and a monumentally classy guy."

"I'm lookin' at him." Jazz laughed, and for a moment they both forgot where they were and why.

They jumped when Bill Frank came into the room. The curator was young, tall, with dark sandy hair and a friendly expression. In exasperation, after San Francisco, Jazz had decided that all curators had friendly expressions in direct proportion to how little they had to show you. Now, in order to get practice with compromise, she let Casey do the talking.

"A private land agreement between the Franciscans and the Valencias? Hmmm? The Franciscans had no power after 1833, but still, who knows? There aren't too many places to look. Let me go and see what I can find," Bill Frank said, as he ushered them into a larger room, furnished with a long table and a number of chairs. He unlocked the door to the manuscript room with a key he fished out of his pocket, and disappeared into his treasure troves. Jazz looked with longing at the fortunate researchers who shared the room with them, all of them bent intently over old manuscripts.

It seemed forever before Bill Frank came back, carrying a brown portfolio that was at least two feet square. He put it down on the table and sat opposite them.

"Sorry to have kept you waiting, but there was quite a lot to eliminate first. I didn't find anything that looked promising except this portfolio, and it's only a long shot," he said, opening it. "Here we have sets of tracings of documentation relating to various land holdings, all of them made by the Land Commission *after* the Treaty of Guadalupe Hidalgo in 1848, which ended the war between Mexico and the United States. There probably won't be anything here that goes back as far as the Franciscans, but I thought I'd go through it with you, anyway. I'm curious myself."

There were seven pink-jacketed files, each bound into a sort of pamphlet by a ribbon. "These are copies of seven *expedientes* that were destroyed at the General Land Office in the San Francisco earthquake," the curator said. "In other words, they'd be United States reaffirmations of Mexican land grants, which might possibly, but only rarely, be reaffirmations of Spanish land grants. Living history."

"We've already been to San Francisco," Jazz told him. "We didn't find anything useful there!"

"Documents have a strange way of getting lost and turning up elsewhere, in fact, just about anywhere except where they should be." Bill Frank meticulously untied one of the pink pamphlets and carefully looked through pages of thin paper, bound together, crackling and brittle and yellow with age. The *diseño* was a separate document, a rough map on a folded sheet of paper, with a compass drawn at the top, place names written here and there, and a river clearly indicated. He showed them the petition and the succeeding pages that contained the Spanish testimony of various witnesses to the legitimacy of the Mexican land grant. He looked at it and shook his head. "This land is up north." He looked through several more of the pink pamphlets and found nothing helpful.

The fifth pamphlet looked like all the others, but when Jazz and Casey saw the fanlike shape of the land drawn on the unfolded map with the wavy lines that indicated the ocean they both shouted, "Wait!"

"Look! *Diseño del Rancho Montaña de la Luna* —it's written on the top! That's it!" Jazz was so electrified that her voice filled the room. The researchers looked up, startled, and Bill Frank quickly picked up the large folder, closed it and took all its contents into his office. He took out the *expediente* they had looked for so stubbornly and held it open, beginning to translate from the archaic Spanish into a contemporary English version.

"Here, on the first page, is the petition, dated 1851. It's from Don Antonio Pablo Valencia, a native-born citizen of California to the Land Commission of the United States. He's asking the commission to confirm the Mexican land grant that was made in 1839. He informs them that he's the sole legitimate son of Don Bernardo Valencia. Don Bernardo, his father, was also an only son. His father—the first Valencia in California—was Teodosio María Valencia and it was Teodosio who received the original Spanish land grant in 1788—apparently he had retired from the company of the Presidio of San Diego and received the land from the Spanish governor, Pedro Fages, for his honorable services to the Crown of Spain.''

Bill Frank looked up at Jazz. ''That's an unusually straight line of inheritance for that period—the Valencias didn't run to multiple sons, did they? That explains why they didn't have to divide up the land. Now let's see what else this says. Apparently Teodosio, the former soldier, lived on the rancho until his death in 1816 at the age of seventy-three. He built a large adobe house, stocked the land with cattle, about twenty-five hundred head, and two herds of horses as well as much other livestock—the details are all here, down to the last unbroken mule. He also planted vineyards and orchards, properly fenced in wood. Don Antonio claims that his father, Don Bernardo, improved the house and built other buildings as well—a school, a buttery, a tannery and so forth. *Hmmm*—this is interesting. Don Bernardo seems to have been a highly successful man, he employed a large number of people, including a schoolmaster, a winemaker, trained carpenters, gardeners . . . it goes on and on—a big establishment—and he faithfully maintained the herds and oversaw the fruitful cultivation of the land—''

Bill Frank read to himself, quickly, and put down the petition. ''These are far more extensive and elaborate claims than most, but basically they're similar to claims made in all petitions, except for the fact that they go back so clearly to the original Spanish grant.''

''Oh, keep reading!'' Jazz begged fervently, luminescent with expectation. Bill Frank set the map to one side. As quickly as possible he skimmed the remaining pages. "All of this is the normal testimony from solid citizens of the region, establishing the fact that the Valencias had occupied the Rancho Montaña de la Luna as long as they or their fathers or grandfathers could remember."

Jazz's head slumped forward, her vision blurred by this final deception. Afraid that a tear might fall on the map, she moved it from its place on the desk.

"I'll take one more look at the map, if you don't mind," Bill Frank said. "There's something unusual about the writing down here at the bottom. Probably it's a more detailed description of the boundaries, the 'Metes and Bounds' as we call them, although it appears to be far longer than any I've seen before."

He studied the old map for several minutes. "Hmm. Well . . . here's an addition to the map unlike anything I've ever run across before. Just listen to this:

> " *'In the name of the Holy Trinity, Father Son and the Holy Ghost, three distinct persons and one true God, Amen: I, Bernardo Valencia, say to all who may read this, that in full enjoyment of my reason, I wish to repeat and renew the sacred Promise made verbally by my beloved father, Teodosio María Valencia, on the occasion of the Completion and Dedication of the Mission of San Juan Capistrano, the Queen of Missions. On the fifteenth day of September, in the year 1806, my father, in his sixty-third year, made a pilgrimage to the heights of the Mountain of the Moon and there, in the presence of the six Holy Fathers of the Order of Saint Francis who had undertaken this pilgrimage with him, he gave his solemn oath to leave forever unchanged by the hand of man, all of his land that can be seen from the Place of the Three Sentinel Rocks on the Mountain of the Moon. This land extends as far as the eye can see, from one extremity to the other extremity,*

> *unto the Sands of the Sea in the westerly direction and unto the Heights of the Mountain in the easterly direction, unto the Rock shaped like a Turtle in the northerly direction and unto the Twin Pointed Rock in the southerly direction. I, Bernardo Valencia, repeat and renew this solemn vow made by my father, Teodosio María Valencia to the Fathers of the Order of Saint Francis before the witnesses Rámon Martínez and Leandro Serrano and the two Holy Fathers, Fra José López and Fra Juan Orozco, whose names are hereto signed.' "*

Bill Frank looked up with a huge grin. "The signature is that of Bernardo Valencia and it's dated January 9, 1820. The Franciscans were still in power then. If this can't be called a private land agreement I don't know what could be. The entire *expediente* of which this map is a part, was accepted and approved by the Gwin Commission and a copy of the final grant to Don Antonio Valencia, Don Bernardo's son, is right here on this last page, signed and sealed by both the recorder of the General Land Office and by the then President of the United States, Millard Fillmore, in 1853."

"The promise of the mountain," Jazz whispered in awe.

"I think you could properly call it a covenant," Casey said quietly.

" 'Three rocks,' " Jazz gasped, " 'three rocks,' wouldn't you have thought Bernardo could have been more specific?" She sat down abruptly on a large stone, streaming with sweat, afraid that she might never get up again.

"It must have seemed enough at the time," Casey responded, trying to catch his breath. "Anyway they're 'sentinel' rocks, not just 'rock' rocks."

"Oh, Casey, 'rocks are rocks, trees are trees,

shoot it in Griffith Park'—what movie producer said
that?''

"Either Spielberg or Lucas, I'm not sure exactly.''

Jazz fought to hold tight to the leaping impression
of certainty that she had felt in the Huntington Library, when it seemed that the last piece of the puzzle
had fallen into place. For it had not been the last piece
in the puzzle, but, as Bill Frank had pointed out in his
precise vocabulary, the 'penultimate piece,' for unless
they found the Place of the Three Sentinel Rocks, they
would have no way of knowing what part of the ranch
the covenant covered.

Portola Peak resisted climbing. Now, Jazz
thought, as she used a damp bandana as a towel, now
she knew exactly why the family mountain had never
been a picnic site for the Kilkullen family, why a jug
of wine or a shaker of martinis wasn't occasionally
carried up at sundown to be enjoyed with the view.
The mountain that looked so deceptively climbable
from the hacienda was, on close inspection, an ideal
location for a perfectly hideous Outward Bound experience, the kind of experience she had avoided scrupulously ever since her photojournalist days.

Jazz and Casey had left on horseback while the
morning air was still chill. Jazz, on a last-minute impulse, had gone to the archive room and supplied them
with two of the sturdy walking sticks that Hugh Kilkullen had collected, which were still kept in an um-
brella stand by the door. Susie had provided a package
of sandwiches and a flask of water, and Jazz had taken
a camera in a bag she strapped around her waist. What
they had really needed, she realized in retrospect, was
an armored tank, or at least a couple of machetes, but
it was too late to mention this to Casey.

It must be well over two hours since they had
been forced to tie their horses to a small tree and take
to their feet. Above the highest upland pastures of the
ranch, the lower slopes of Portola Peak rose steeply
until the spur of the mountain itself was reached. It

was there that the vicious underbrush, a combination of prickly pear, mesquite and chaparral, became too tangled and dangerous for the horses.

Ah, but human beings, Jazz thought, as she blinked the sweat out of her eyes, could go where horses could not. Man could spelunk and spend months in wet, dark, nasty caves under the surface of the earth, hanging out with stalactites and stalagmites; man could snorkel and frisk and flirt with stinging jellyfish and hungry octopi; man could reach the North and South Poles and talk to the animals, and man could get to the moon and schlepp around, turning somersaults and planting flags; so it stood to reason that this man and this woman, protected by the denim they wore, could most certainly claw their way up through this fiendish mass, using the walking sticks, held in front of them in both hands, to bend the underbrush back far enough so that they could force a passage.

When they'd started out, it seemed obvious that there was only one direction to take, for the spur of the mountain was so narrow that it was the only way up. But as they climbed, the spur grew wider and wider until the mountain offered vistas of a wilderness of dry, sage-scented, bloodthirsty brush rising in every direction, brush that deceptively masked the brutal steepness of the pitch of the land over which they had been struggling.

"If you were a Franciscan friar, which way would you go?" Jazz asked Casey.

"If I were a Franciscan friar, I'd be wearing a long robe and sandals and I wouldn't be here, no how, no way, my lady."

"It's nice that you can stay optimistic in the face of adversity," Jazz observed.

"Oh, I'm optimistic. Those Sentinel Rocks are here somewhere. I'm merely glad we're wearing boots."

"Rattlesnakes?" Jazz asked. She could face mountain lions, but rattlesnakes?

"Rattlesnakes and tarantulas. But they can't bite

through leather. Also coyote, quail and some very un-friendly cacti.''

"I keep looking for something like a trail, a path worn by pilgrim feet,'' Jazz said plaintively. "Anyone would think we were the first people to climb Por-tola.''

"We know for sure that Teodosio and six friars climbed it in 1806, but since then? This is not exactly what's known as a walk in the park.''

"Ah, come on, Casey, they must have made other pilgrimages up here. And I remember that when I was a kid, my father told me that his grandfather, old Hugh, had climbed Portola . . . maybe a hundred years ago, now that I think of it. You're right, that wouldn't leave much of a trail.''

"Still . . .'' Casey wearily tapped something ly-ing on the ground with his walking stick. "Look at this . . . clear evidence of recent civilized visitation.''

"It can't be,'' Jazz said slowly as she focused on the can of Diet Pepsi that lay, all but concealed from view, under a layer of dirt. "It just *cannot* be.''

"I didn't bring it up with me.''

"But who . . . ?''

"It could only have been someone who strayed from the regular hiking trails. After all, we're sur-rounded by national parks. Believe me, whoever left it behind strayed down, not up.''

"I've got to get a shot of that. Larry Bush will never believe this.''

"Who's he?''

"One of my friends at Pepsi—public-relations chief.'' Jazz got down very low, brushed some of the dirt off the can and took several shots of the Pepsi can lying in the foreground, with the majestic view of the dominion of ranch and ocean in the background. "He'll get a kick out of this. They've probably got cans flying around the earth in orbit too. What is the universal definition of mankind? Litterbugs!''

"If you have the strength to shoot film, you have the strength to keep looking for the rocks. Upwards!''

With Casey in the lead, as before, they continued

to labor slowly up through the wilderness, stopping
every once in a while to scan the surroundings. There
were rocks aplenty, but none that were distinctive.
Each time they stopped, Jazz looked backward, in the
direction of the hacienda. It had become smaller and
smaller until it was invisible in its cluster of trees and
garden, and now its site was blocked entirely by a
bulging bump of stone covered with strands of mesquite.

Jazz heard Casey humming snatches of a tune as
he scrambled, and realized that she too was hearing a
melody in her head. She put words to it and gave a
wry smile. "How are things in Glocca Mora?" were
the words that ran endlessly in her head. Glocca
Mora, the village in *Brigadoon* that appeared only
once every hundred years, and then disappeared again
into the Irish mists. Or was Brigadoon the village in
Finian's Rainbow that disappeared into the Scottish
mists? Never mind. It was too hot to figure out. It
didn't make any sense.

But the Sentinel Rocks were no village, they were
a place specifically mentioned in the handwriting of
Bernardo Valencia on a map. Bernardo Valencia had
been the grandfather of Juanita Isabella Valencia Kilkullen, making him at least Jazz's great-great-great-
grandfather, she thought fuzzily, and if you can't trust
a great-great-great-grandfather, who can you trust?
Not only that, but Millard Fillmore had put his signature on that map. For some reason this fact gave Jazz
a powerful feeling of hope. There was something
about that particular name, destined by reason of pho-
netics to be the butt of jokes, that sounded decidedly
presidential.

"Casey, what are you humming?"

"The theme music from *The African Queen*. I
can't get it out of my mind."

"Casey, can we stop for lunch?"

"You starving?"

"Gotta eat."

"O.K., but only for a few minutes. We have to

find the rocks and get back down again before sunset, and it'll be dark in four hours.''

"What if we don't find them?"

"We'll come back tomorrow. We'll keep looking until we do.''

"My leader, my inspiration, what did I do before I knew you?" Jazz asked as she found another rock to sit on. The air was cooler here, although the sun was high overhead. She took off her jacket and pulled her wet cotton shirt out of her jeans. Her bandana was so soaked that she spread it out on a small rock and allowed the breeze to dry her face and neck and hair.

"I often wonder what exactly you did. Not a wasted life, I'll bet," Casey answered.

"Not wasted, definitely not wasted," Jazz assured him, as she handed him a sandwich. "But definitely not fulfilled.''

How could she be so much in love, she wondered, looking at Casey, sprawled on another rock. How was it possible to be so much in love with somebody you *liked* so much? Gabe—she'd been overwhelmed by him, passionately in love with him, marked for life by him, but had she ever really liked him? No, somehow *like* was not a word she could ever apply to Gabe. Sam —she'd liked Sam . . . who wouldn't . . . but his actor's ego amused her too much for her ever to love him. And the others—not one of them had ever even come close.

Even if they never found the rocks, climbing this bitch of a mountain with Casey was a profound pleasure, Jazz decided, for amid all the hot, scrambling discomfort and itchy effort, they were together and she liked him, loved him and trusted him. She'd found the man of her life. The one and only.

Jazz and Casey sipped some water from the flask, careful not to drink it all up, and, refreshed, continued upward. The brush became thinner underfoot, and easier to walk around than through, but the number of big pebbles multiplied, so that they often found themselves slipping and sliding. Jazz used Hugh Kilkullen's indispensable walking stick in her right hand, and finally she had to grasp Casey's left hand with her own left hand for safety's sake, although it made progress slower. She couldn't see much through the sweat rolling down her forehead into her eyes. They should have brought a rope to tie themselves together like mountain climbers, she thought, and left their hands free.

Blisters were forming under Jazz's western riding boots, but she vowed not to think about them, using all her imagination to see herself as a sturdy, indestructible Englishwoman of a certain age, wearing what were always known as a pair of "stout boots," an Englishwoman who wouldn't break into a sweat under any circumstances, a hearty woman on a walking tour of the Lake District of England, strolling along easily, stick in hand, amid a rolling landscape of wide, mysterious lakes, abundant greenery, and graceful trees, with clumps of spring flowers springing up here and there along the gentle, well-marked track where hundreds of thousands had walked before, all the way back, no doubt, to the Druids. Or were the Druids Welsh? Well, they were witches and prophets and sorcerers, that she knew for sure, Jazz thought dizzily, and tripped and fell.

Casey was jerked abruptly backwards and narrowly avoided falling himself.

"Jazz, did you hurt yourself?" he asked in concern.

"No," Jazz said, sitting on the ground, "I don't think so. I was just going along blindly, and suddenly . . ." Curious, and glad to remain sitting down, she poked around, looking for the object on which she had tripped. Whatever it was, it was covered by a low pile of stones that Casey had stepped over but she had blundered straight into.

"Help me," Jazz said in sudden excitement. Quickly she and Casey lifted a few concealing stones. Under them lay a cross made of two branches of wood that had once been a living tree, the pieces of wood tied together with a leather thong, flecked here and there with white paint.

"It fell, it must have been stuck into that pile of stones and then it fell and got covered up by stones moving in the winter storms," Jazz said in a stunned voice.

"But what's it doing here?"

"I don't know." Jazz looked at the cross in excited puzzlement. "The legend said that there had been a shrine on the mountain, but the description on the map said nothing about a cross." Casey sat down next to her and inspected the rough cross, as if it would yield up an answer.

"Look around," Jazz said, pointing with her right hand. "Does that rock look something like a turtle to you?"

"Maybe—a little—from the ground. When I was walking, I didn't notice it."

"What about over there?" She gestured with her other hand.

"Twin points! At least I think so."

"But where are the three Sentinel Rocks?" Jazz beseeched him, looking behind her at a particularly steep upward slope, bare of all but small stones. It was impossible to see what stood above the slope.

"Get up. We've got to climb higher!"

With pounding hearts they mounted the steep slope, traversing it level by level as they would have traversed a dangerous ski slope, until they reached the top, where a small, sandy plateau spread before them.

Toward the middle of the plateau, too far back to be seen from below, stood three tall, thin rocks, not one of them more than eight feet tall, sticking up from the sandy surface so that they formed a triangle, three rocks that might indeed be standing sentinel over the panorama that spread below the plateau.

"Oh!" Jazz cried out, realizing only now how much she had hoped, how much she had doubted. The plateau was quiet, isolated, yet it seemed to her that it reverberated with a great thunder, she thought she heard a swooping of wings, she thought she felt a singing vibration that came from the heart of the mountain itself. She reached out and pressed tightly to Casey, needing the reassurance of the presence of another human being, in the face of the three rocks that had mounted guard over this land for millions of years.

For minutes they stood silently, leaning together as they greeted the Sentinel Rocks and were greeted in turn, until they felt that they had been accepted on the plateau, that they were welcome in this place. Only then did they turn to look outward, standing on the edge of the plateau with the rocks behind them. From that vantage point the Turtle Rock looked clearly like a turtle and the points of the Twin Pointed Rock were sharply defined.

" 'Unto the Sands of the Sea,' " Jazz said, looking toward the west. Far away, on the horizon, the sea and the sky melted together in a passion of blue. Closer, the natural harbor and Valencia Point were clearly visible, as was the untouched beach running the entire length of the boundary of the ranch, forming a pure break between the seaside constructions on either side.

Jazz turned and looked up behind the Sentinel Rocks, where the mile-high bare top of Portola Peak, still distant, sparkled as sunlight glanced off bits of mica. Behind it, the snow-capped peaks of the Santa Ana Range floated off in the distance.

"Look north—the view takes in half of Orange County—Bernardo may have overreached a bit there," Casey said.

"But, Casey, he was only pledging his own land, remember? Look, south, after the Turtle Rock there's a long, flat gully, and the land drops away steeply— you can't see far beyond the Turtle Rock. From where we're standing, we can see a good two-thirds of the whole ranch. Oh, Casey, Casey, nobody's ever going to be able to change it—not with the hand of man!"

Jazz and Casey stood, hand in hand, listening to a whisper in the wind, a whisper of a promise made on a mountain that could never truly be the property of any man, not even of the man who had made the promise, for the nature of a mountain is to limit man to his proper size. Before them lay California, a marriage of land and water, westward-facing, that could not exist anywhere else on earth.

Suddenly remembering her camera, Jazz started shooting, moving around to take in everything that lay in a circle from where she stood. Then she stood just behind the Sentinel Rocks and shot in such a way that the photographs would reveal the rocks in the foreground and the view they overlooked. Then she took shots from above of the cross lying on the ground where they had unearthed it, the cross that had led them to the Promise of the Mountain.

"We've got to start down, Jazz. It's getting late," Casey warned her suddenly.

"All right. I'm out of film anyway. There's just one little favor . . . I wonder if . . ."

"Anything," Casey promised, "anything."

"Oh, darling, I knew you'd say yes!" Jazz collapsed gratefully into his arms. "Carry me down!"

20

"Everything hurts," Jazz said joyously, as she lay in a tub of steaming water with her freshly shampooed hair pulled up into a damp top-knot. "The roots of my hair ache, my toenails are killing me, my knees won't work, I can't lift my arms, my sunblock didn't block, I may not live till morning."

"Jane Goodall you're not," Casey agreed. He'd just finished a long shower and sat companionably on the edge of the tub, wrapped in a terry cloth robe. "But you got up there and you got back."

"No thanks to you. You said you'd do anything I asked, and then you reneged. Getting down was worse than climbing up."

"Would you like me to scrub your back?" he offered.

"It's not that easy to worm yourself back into my good graces." She gave him an intimate look of reversible pique. "May I have a drop, please?"

Jazz held out the glass for more of the vodka they'd been drinking in celebration of their finding the

Sentinel Rocks. When they'd finally ridden back to the hacienda, an hour after dark, as exhausted as they were excited, they'd told Susie to go home early, and now they had the place to themselves. After the heat of the struggle up the mountain in the sun, the winter temperature had plunged abruptly just as they'd reached their horses and they'd galloped back in a chill wind. Casey had the forethought to light the fire in the living room before they went to soak away the day's fatigue.

Neither of them felt hungry, although they had eaten nothing but sandwiches all day. They were too alight with the glory of their achievement to do anything as mundane as eating, but vodka chilled in the freezer suited the triumphant moment.

"When are you getting out of that tub?" Casey asked. "You've been in for a half hour."

"When I get the strength and not a second before." Jazz was imperious.

"Want me to help?"

"Ha, as Mr. White would say. Ha! You wouldn't carry me down a mountain, but now you want to help me out of a tub. I suspect your motives, Casey Nelson. You want to sneak a peek. Turn your back and hand me that bath towel."

"I'll hold it for you."

"I'm too modest and too ladylike to reveal myself to you without garments. Turn your back and hold it out."

"But we're going to get married," Casey objected. "Why can't I sneak a peek?"

"And close your eyes too. You might see me in the mirror. I intend to maintain my mystery. From now on we make love in the dark."

"Not even a candle?"

"Not so much as a match."

Casey reached into the tub and lifted Jazz out, squeaking and giggling. He clasped her to his chest while she kicked indignantly. "It's not that I can't carry you," he said. "It's just not a good idea going downhill. From now on I'll carry you all night."

"Let me go!"

He took a big towel and, seating her on his knee, dried her off thoroughly, as he fended off her efforts to get away. When she was dry he bundled her in another terry robe and carried her into the warm living room, deposited her in front of the fire, lay down next to her, and held her tightly.

"You're going nowhere," he informed her.

"That's exactly where I want to be. More vodka?"

"Sure. Hungry yet?"

"No, I'm too thrilled. Oh, Casey, it's very hard to be in love with a guy like you. You make me feel unworthy. I know I'm a bit of a shit, but you're so good to me. You take care of me, you don't pay any attention to me when I'm rotten, you know what I really want before I do. How can I ever be a good enough person to deserve such a wonderful man?"

"It won't be easy," Casey grinned.

"Especially when you remind me so much of . . ."

"Of who?"

"It's not exactly a person . . . but there was this Airedale once . . ."

"A dog?"

"All Airedales are dogs," Jazz said reasonably, drinking more vodka, "such a darling dog, just like you. He was without fear, he had very long legs, a dense coat, almost the color of yours, he had a good disposition, he was loyal, keen-eyed, capable, clownish, strong, and he had a mug, such a cute little mug with sort of drooping whiskers and his ears stood up so beautifully. A prize terrier, that's what he was, a bit of a hound, but *all* dog, a *real* dog, the kind you used to have when you were a kid."

"Gee, I never had a dog like that."

"Neither did I. That's why I feel so unworthy of having you. I'm not used to owning such a good dog."

"Marriage isn't the same as owning a dog."

"Oh yeah? So what is it?"

"I'm still not sure. Maybe you're right. My first

marriage was sort of like owning a bad dog and my second marriage was like owning a rare bird, and my third marriage, come to think of it, was like owning a racehorse."

"You've been married before!"

"Three times."

"Why didn't you tell me!"

"You never asked."

"It's a lie!"

"Maybe . . . maybe not."

"Well, I don't care. You could have three other wives right now, this minute, and I'd still marry you."

"I can't scare you off?"

"Never."

"Jazz," he said urgently, "*when* do you—"

"Casey," Jazz interrupted hastily, as she unpinned her topknot and let down her wet hair, "I haven't got a towel. Can I rub my hair dry on your robe?"

"You're welcome to try," he said, as he realized that she'd interrupted him once more, the way she invariably interrupted him whenever he started to make specific plans for their marriage. There was probably a particular note in his voice that warned her of his intention to get down to a serious discussion that set off Jazz's interruptive reflex, because not once, not one single time since she'd agreed to marry him, had they discussed the future in any serious way. It was as if, having agreed to marry, she'd condemned him to play house indefinitely.

Jazz was as expansive as she was elusive; she'd tell him that she'd marry him if he had three other wives, but she wouldn't tell him if it would be this week, this year or this decade. Was it, as he'd wondered, Mike's death? Or was she merely afraid of taking that final step, of setting the date? This best of all women—or was she a child?—had managed to stay single for thirty years. Clearly she was gunshy. She still flickered out of his fingers, as uncapturable as a rare tropical fish in a big aquarium, and they had not made a single, down-to-earth plan for their future.

They both knew—*she must know*—that they couldn't keep on living in the hacienda forever. Maybe it was the word *when* that tipped Jazz off, Casey reflected. He'd try it another way, spring it on her without preamble.

He waited passively as Jazz used the bottom of his robe to towel her hair, a ticklish business and not an easy operation for him to endure, as she well knew. Then he pounced, holding her head between his hands.

"Question. Wedding. *When?*"

"*Oh, darling, not now!* My mind's literally whirling with ideas! I have so much to think about, I just can't concentrate on the future of two people when I'm thinking about thousands and thousands of people," she said with a laugh that promised nothing.

"How many thousands exactly?" Casey turned away from her with a flinty look that she ignored. "And why?"

"Well," Jazz said, dreamily lying back against him, "I've been thinking . . . you have no idea how much I've been thinking, ever since we started to look for the Sentinel Rocks. I decided to make two plans: Plan A, what to do if we never found them, and Plan B, what to do if we did."

"What if we'd never found them?" Against his will, Casey found himself lured into going along with her, for the potent magic of her voice was too compelling for him to resist.

"I couldn't even focus on Plan A because it was unthinkable. You know how sometimes you just block out something because it's too awful? It was like that. So I concentrated on Plan B. First I thought about what my father would want to do if he were alive, and I discovered something."

Jazz sat up and looked into the fire. "He was only half-right. He wanted to keep the land just the way it is forever, and that's not possible for one family in this day and age. In his time . . . maybe . . . but not anymore. The Kilkullen family can't own over sixty thousand acres of land all for ourselves unless it's somewhere so remote that no one else wants to live there. But in California, where so many people want to live, it's not fair. We should share it . . . but in the right way.''

"I never thought I'd hear you say you wanted to share the land.''

"I never seriously imagined it before. But now . . . I think that the part of the land that can be developed, the part that lies to the south of the rock with the twin points . . . there's about twenty-five thousand acres there, and you could take, oh, let's say eight thousand or ten thousand acres of it, and build a new town where about sixty or seventy thousand people could live and still be surrounded by open country on all sides.''

"My sweetheart, the urban planner.''

"You don't have to be an urban planner to know that—all you have to do is read the papers. It's the new ideas that count, the ideas that would restore what's been left out of most developments.''

"Like what?'' Casey was interested in Jazz's take on a subject that had been in the back of his mind.

"Community.''

"How do you restore community? Always assuming that you are building a town for seventy thousand people, and it's not that solid platinum parking lot for Rolls-Royces that Valerie and Fernanda want.''

"Without the beach they haven't got a chance, and the whole beach and the harbor were excluded by the map. Listen, Casey, this is how you get a community. *You leave out malls and you put in main streets!* In one stroke you've got a community again! Each neighborhood will have a main street, a real, honest-to-God, old-time main street, with soda fountains and Bijou movie theaters and bakeries and grocery stores with real, live butchers and hardware stores and bowling alleys and dance studios and hamburger joints and dry cleaners and delis and barbershops and beauty parlors and bookstores and drugstores and pool halls and lots and lots of cafés, outdoor sidewalk cafés, and shops of all kinds and places to loiter and gossip and bike racks everywhere because that's how people get from the different neighborhoods to the main streets, unless they walk or ride a horse.''

"What different neighborhoods?" Casey asked.

Jazz was pacing around the living room, so carried away by her vision that she had left the warm spot by the fire, the warm spot where she had been so close to him, and Casey felt that the only way he could keep in touch with her was to ask her questions.

"People won't live in streets with houses you can't tell apart; they'll have neighborhoods, like there used to be, like some New England towns, or even San Juan Capistrano, places where some people have houses and some have apartments and some have one-room studios, and some pay a whole lot less rent than others, and some own their own houses and some are young and some are old and some are somewhere in between, with children of all ages . . . but, Casey, they have porches and verandas and window boxes and courtyards and patios and backyard gardens and attics—I have the feeling that attics are very important, although I don't know why—and all the houses are near enough together so that people have neighbors and they can sit out on their porches and say hello to each other, and everything is on a human scale, a pedestrian scale, and there'll be places to picnic and play chess, and horses to rent everywhere, and baseball diamonds and playgrounds just for the little kids, and basketball hoops all over the place!"

"What about the ranch, the herds?"

"But, Casey, don't you see? We'll still ranch, with a few less cows, but the idea is to have the ranch and the town *coexisting,* so that everyone who lives in the town can see cattle grazing when they look out of their windows. They'll be able to ride horses everywhere, right down the middle of Main Street, but we'll discourage them from holding their own roundups.''

"How are you going to run this town?"

"With town meetings and a city government in the town hall on the town square—did I mention the town square?" Jazz waved the question of running the town away. "There'll be a big public library and a bandstand with live music on the weekends so everybody gets to know everybody else, and lots of fountains, so that there's always the sound of running water, and more cafés, and art galleries and arcades with columns so people can walk anywhere and be sheltered from the sun and everybody can walk or bike or ride down to the beach and swim or surf or sit and listen to the waves and look at the sunset but they can't change it, *not ever,* or—"

"Schools?"

"Naturally," Jazz said, "naturally schools, churches, synagogues, and light, clean industry and businesses so that people can work near their homes. City planners are thinking along these same lines all over. I kept reading about it, but I never paid attention till Phoebe tore down the Purple Tostada Grande. . . ." She paused by the window and shook her head at the memory.

"Come over here and sit down. What did that have to do with it?"

"She took away a part of Dazzle's neighborhood. Overnight, just like that! Venice is a real neighborhood, one of the last, and Phoebe destroyed a piece of it, something that we all took for granted, the way people used to take their main streets for granted. So when I saw that we had the chance to build a new town, I knew that it had to have neighborhoods and main streets . . . and from there it's easy, all you have to do is remember what it used to be like twenty-five years ago . . . twenty-five years ago . . . that's about how long ago it was before it all started to change . . ."

Jazz sounded as if she were in a trance, Casey thought. She hadn't worked out any of the formidable problems of actually building such a town, either financially or in any other practical way, nor had she asked herself for one minute how she was to become appointed the master planner of this new, utopian town, given the existence of her non-utopian-minded sisters.

"Jazz," he asked, "do you know what infrastructure is?"

"Vaguely," Jazz said, deep in her vision.

But she'll find out, Casey thought. It won't take her long before she's a mistress of infrastructure. She may be dreaming out loud and a little drunk, but she's not talking about anything impossible. She makes sense. Damn good sense. He knew a thousand times as much as she did about land development, and he knew her ideas were the wave of the future. Oh, she'd get caught up in this new town, she was so enthralled with it already that she'd forgotten a life's career as a photographer; she was so involved that she didn't even know he was in the room except as a listener; she hadn't wondered if he'd participate in the new town, or even asked if he was interested. She was no more concerned about his nonexistent three ex-wives than she was about his role in this newly born project, as if being Cow Boss were the limit of his ambitions. Jazz will keep not having time for getting married, or even talking about it, and pretty soon the real city planners and architects and builders will move into her life, and then what? Was this the moment to mention his own feelings? Was this the moment to bring her down to earth, when she was in such a state of rapture? No, he couldn't do it. Was it the selflessness of love, or was it fear of what she might say? Maybe the answer to that was something so awful that he should block it out, the way Jazz had blocked Plan A. All he needed now, Casey told himself harshly, were stronger powers of denial, as strong as hers.

They won't like this, Jazz gloated, as she arranged a pile of papers and photographs on the bare top of the desk in her father's office. They won't like it at all, but they can't refute it. It's official, with all the power of the United States government behind it, no folktale this, no straw grasped at in desperation. Nothing was missing but the photographs of the Pepsi can.

In a few minutes, Jazz was expecting the visit of Jimmy Rosemont and Sir John Maddox. She had sum-

moned them—no other word than *summoned* was
equal to the manner in which she had informed them
that she had matters to discuss with them—as soon as
her documentation was complete, six days after finding the Sentinel Rocks.

At first, Jazz had thought of offering them tea and
showing them the evidence of the covenant afterwards, but she had rejected this idea almost as soon
as it came to her mind. No tea, no coffee, not so much
as a glass of water unless they asked for one. This was
business, as downright inhospitable as any business
that she could imagine, and she didn't intend to give it
a veneer of false feminine graciousness.

She was dressed to do business, as much like a
man as possible, like a rancher, a proprietor. She wore
straight, dark brown leather trousers tucked into fine
lizard Western boots and a man-tailored shirt of heavy
white cotton with a string tie of black leather. On her
head she wore an old Western hat that a vaquero had
given her for her eighteenth birthday. It had been a
joke to him, but on Jazz's head it had a terrifying
panache, a hat like a battle flag. The simple pieces of
Jazz's clothing came together to form a martial look
as unmistakable in its own way as a bullfighter's suit
of lights.

Today, Jazz walked with none of the feminine,
long-legged grace she normally possessed; the boots
ensured a steady, authoritative tread. Her insouciance, that light, carefree balance of a tightrope walker,
was countermanded by the unexpected severity of her
hat, set straight above her eyebrows. She could almost
have passed for a young man, for she had done away
with her hair, braiding it and tucking the braid out of
sight at the back of her neck.

She had weighed the idea of asking Casey to be
present at this interview, but had decided that since
he had no formal connection to the land, it would be
out of place. She hadn't asked her sisters to come,
since Jimmy Rosemont and Sir John clearly acted for
them, and they would only be a distraction from what
she planned to say. Jazz stood behind her father's

desk and tapped the heel of one of her boots impatiently. In two minutes they would be late.

Jazz heard a car drive up, heard Susie open the front door, heard the footsteps of two men approaching the office. At last! She stood her ground, not advancing from behind the desk, unsmiling, letting them come to her to shake hands.

"Make yourselves comfortable, gentlemen," Jazz commanded. She sat down in her father's chair and tilted it backwards so that her booted feet, crossed at the ankle, could rest on the desk. She looked around the room, at the walls hung frame-to-frame with photographs taken over the last hundred years, with bills of sale for prize bulls, and cherished letters from various Democratic leaders, and felt herself surrounded by the presence of Mike Kilkullen.

"When we first met," she said, looking calmly from one to the other, "the two of you unfolded a plan for the disposition of the Kilkullen Ranch, or, as it was called in the early days of California, the Rancho Montaña de la Luna. Do you know why it was called that, Mr. Rosemont?"

"No, Miss Kilkullen."

"It means Mountain of the Moon. For as long as men have lived on this land, and it's been a longer time than we know, they've seen the moon rise directly behind the mountain, the one we call Portola Peak, and no doubt some of them, in their ignorance, thought that the mountain gave birth to the moon. But you, Mr. Rosemont, and you, Sir John, are intelligent men, too modern to deal in such ancient fancies. When you see a mountain, you see an *opportunity* for it to give birth. To condos."

"Touché, Miss Kilkullen. But times change," Jimmy Rosemont said, "and mountains change with them."

"Not as much as you imagine, Mr. Rosemont. I loathed your idea—"

"So we noticed," Sir John said dryly.

"And I still do. But I didn't know then what I

could do to prevent it from happening. I undertook a search to find out just how much legality there might be in my father's homemade will, and I discovered something very interesting indeed. He left land to his daughters that he had no right to give us."

"You don't say." Jimmy Rosemont had a small smile, a condescending, bantering smile.

"Land," Jazz continued steadily, "to which he did not have a clear title, land on which there lies a covenant that prohibits him from leaving it to anyone without including the facts of the covenant."

"What sort of nonsense is this?" Sir John's voice was unconcerned, genial.

"Not nonsense, Sir John." Jazz stood up. "I have a number of items to show you both. First, a letter from my great-great-grandmother, Juanita Isabella Valencia Kilkullen, to her future daughter-in-law."

Slowly Jazz read the translation of the letter, a translation that had been prepared by a professor of Spanish at UC Irvine and then notarized. Rapidly but precisely she took them step by step through the history of California land grants, and she explained the significance of the enlarged black-and-white reproduction of the document she and Casey had found at the Huntington Library, translating the vow Bernardo Valencia had made, and the signatures of the four witnesses. Again, it had all been notarized. She showed them the presidential seal that finally validated the claim to the land, as well as a photocopy of the title deed signed by Antonio Valencia and Michael Kilkullen. She displayed the photographs taken from the Sentinel Rocks, enlarged to ten-by-twelve. Finally, using a modern topographical map of the present land, she showed them the outline, traced in red, of the area of the land that must remain "unchanged by the hand of man," the covenant that had been respected by the Kilkullens as closely as it had been by the Valencias.

She finished her presentation and stood behind the desk, trying to repress a cocky grin. Jimmy Rosemont and Sir John Maddox exchanged a glance, the meaning of which Jazz couldn't read. The first person to break the silence was Sir John.

"This is indeed fascinating, Miss Kilkullen, I congratulate you on your detective work." His manner was as mellow as ever.

"Clever and neat," Jimmy Rosemont agreed. "You can have a job working for me anytime."

"A most interesting curiosity of history," Sir John added, "and a charming one at that, romantic, generous and certainly, one may safely say, deeply pious. I'm grateful to you for allowing me to hear all this."

"Sir John, don't you realize *yet* what it means?" Jazz had been prepared for anything but complacency. She knew these men would not be good losers. Why weren't they more upset? A snake of fear wriggled into Jazz's heart.

"*Could mean*, my dear Miss Kilkullen, could mean, if it were not for this." Sir John Maddox leaned forward and fished out a piece of paper from the pile. "This title deed to the ranch, registered at the County Recorder's office in Santa Ana, is the only *enforceable* item on this desk."

"What are you talking about?" Jazz's voice rose. "The Mexican land grant is enforceable, for God's sake, *it's the key*! It's the culmination of years and years of proof that the ranch belonged to the Valencias from 1788 until they sold it to the Kilkullens. Don't try to tell me that it's not *enforceable!*"

"That's exactly what we're telling you," Jimmy Rosemont said, his entire well-groomed face, from his jowls to his hairline, carelessly affable. "That piece of old paper has no legal validity. *It was never recorded in Santa Ana*. Now if it had been—we'd be bound by it—but that's speculation, mere speculation. Fact is, it wasn't."

"You're crazy! It can't be possible! That's just a technicality, and I won't—"

"Miss Kilkullen, I appreciate your distress, I sympathize fully." Sir John leaned forward to emphasize his words. "There is no way to stop the sale of this land because of a purely *verbal* agreement that may have been made between two men, Antonio Valencia and Michael Kilkullen, both long dead, to respect the wishes of Teodosio María Valencia, long dead, and reported in a letter from one woman to another, again both long dead. Even the seal of Millard Fillmore is utterly irrelevant."

"Sir John's right," Jimmy Rosemont said, almost lazily. "Your father had a perfect right to leave all the land, free and clear, to you and your sisters. Nothing in the Recorder's Office says otherwise, and that's the only thing we have to be concerned with."

"That can't be possible." Even as she fought them, the snake of fear grew into a serpent that tightened its grip around Jazz's heart. She felt cold all over as she began to comprehend the flaw, the hideously unjust flaw in the documents.

"We don't expect you to take it on faith," Jimmy Rosemont interrupted, clearly impatient now. "We're wasting time arguing about something only your own lawyers can convince you of. Call them and ask them if we're right or not."

"I will, Mr. Rosemont, don't worry about that! One thing they did tell me was that there are dozens of different ways I can drag my heels and keep this land from being sold, even if it turns out that the covenant isn't enforceable, which I don't believe for one minute."

"Now there you're quite right," Sir John said. "I estimate that with clever lawyers you could drag this thing out for twenty or thirty years. But you'd lose in the end, you know. You'd have wasted your life in a hopeless battle. And how would you pay your lawyers for such a long fight?"

"That's my problem!" Jazz shrugged the question off as her panic mounted until it felt as if her chest would explode.

"Indeed it would be a problem, Miss Kilkullen, even for a very rich woman. My Hong Kong friends, however, have inexhaustible resources, they can litigate forever, they will never give up, for they take a long view of history, as I explained when we first met, but your life . . . well, I should hate to see such a charming young lady ruin her life.''

''I'll mortgage my share of the land to pay,'' Jazz said defiantly. ''God knows, it's worth plenty.''

''Then you won't just lose the fight,'' Jimmy Rosemont said scornfully, ''you'll lose your inheritance too.''

''Don't think you only have me to deal with,'' Jazz cried ferociously. ''California's full of well-organized groups who'll fight you into the ground; environmentalists, no-growth, slow-growth, wetlands conservation, wildlife conservation—''

''We'll deal with them,'' Sir John said, with the serene confidence that came from knowing that Liddy Kilkullen had the Governor in her back pocket. How wise Jimmy had been to make that arrangement. ''And when necessary, we'll give them something. A few hundred acres here, a few hundred acres there. You'd be amazed how they—'tree huggers,' I believe you call them—will listen to reason when they get even a small slice of the pie.''

And no help, Sir John thought smugly, from the government of a state that had already, in another administration, reduced the once-powerful Coastal Commission to relative toothlessness.

''We'd better get back, John, I'm expecting a phone call.'' The two men got up to leave. With one glance at Jazz's face, contorted with intractable determination, they wordlessly agreed not to try to shake hands with her. They turned and walked toward the front door.

Stunned, Jazz sagged back in the desk chair. There was a ripping in her heart, a feeling of things being torn apart by a force she couldn't control, vital parts being severed one from the other and the juices squeezed out of them. Seized by a last, desperate idea, she jumped up and ran to the front door.

''Sir John! When the Chinese hear about the covenant, what will they think? I know that they're incredibly superstitious. It would be the worst possible kind of bad luck to build on the land that's protected by that covenant.''

"Nice try," Jimmy Rosemont said, in a voice between a laugh and a sneer.

"You're right, Miss Kilkullen," Sir John said courteously. "But my friends are more superstitious about losing their fortunes than they are about bad luck. They'll be willing to risk it, oh, yes, more than willing—delighted. There's no cure for superstitions as effective as a billion and a half Communists pushing in your front door."

21

"For the tenth time, Fernie," Valerie said as she drove toward the Hacienda Valencia, "I don't know why Jazz wants us to come today, but I didn't see how we could refuse when she insisted that it was important. Jimmy said there's no question that she's going to have to sell, but he also said she could hold things up if she wanted to be difficult."

"I suppose you're right," Fernanda grumbled, "but why couldn't you have asked her to come to the hotel at our convenience, instead of agreeing to go see her? Georgina and I were planning to drive up to Beverly Hills today and do some shopping."

"Don't you two ever do anything but shop?"

"What else is there to do around here?" Fernanda murmured.

Thank heaven for shopping. No one would ever suspect, when two women set off to do some shopping, that they had a room reserved at a hotel where they could be together all afternoon long. And no one would ever be the wiser, even if they didn't come back laden with packages. She was so rich now that it would surprise no one if she shopped for weeks and never found anything that was fine enough to buy. It was going to be fun, being so difficult to please that nothing would ever be quite good enough.

Once they all got back to New York, after Jimmy had the sale in hand to his satisfaction, she and Georgina could be together as often as they wished. They would buy a small apartment in an impersonal, modern building without elevator men, midway between their two places, where they could meet in perfect freedom, without ever having to worry about servants or husbands or phone calls.

Fernanda's whole body shivered as she thought of how perfectly she and Georgina were mated.

"Are you catching cold?" Valerie asked.

"There must be pollen in the air."

"Hmmm." Valerie neither agreed nor disagreed nor listened to her sister's answer. She felt so agreeably smoothed out inside, as if some chronic, low-level, irritating physical problem had disappeared.

This enforced stay in Southern California, tedious though it was, had been the slow stretching and final snapping of a frayed cord. New York life, she thought, seen from a distance, was like riding an enormous carousel, a gaudy, brilliantly painted carousel with garish, larger-than-life horses, flaunting spangled headdresses of multi-colored plumes and draped in yards of glittering tinsel. The carousel spun so quickly that she hadn't seen the spectators except as a blur; her world had been reduced to the other riders, rising and falling on the poles that held their horses, laughing and waving to each other in savage glee.

Then it had stopped for her, she had stepped off. Valerie felt astonished by the depth of her feeling of release. Although she still heard the shrieks of the riders above the cheap, intoxicating calliope music, each day the carousel receded further, each day the brassy music grew fainter, the riders had turned into a band of strangers.

She had finally understood that she had only to

raise the tip of one finger and the carousel would stop
again for her. She could climb back on anytime she
wanted to. But did she? Was it a ride worth taking?
Being very, very rich, aside from what it could buy,
allowed you not to give a damn about anybody else,
it allowed you never to wonder what anyone thought,
because you knew everybody was too busy envying
you to judge you. Perhaps that was the ultimate luxury.

"Did Mother call you today?" Fernanda asked.

"Just to say hello. She was going out looking for
a house with a real-estate lady and didn't expect to be
back till much later. Thank heaven she's staying with
the Whites in San Clemente. If she were at the hotel,
I'd strangle her."

"You'd think we were absolute children," Fernanda agreed, "the way she keeps telling us to tie up
the sale of the ranch before the permanent administrator is appointed. Does she imagine that it's not on our
minds? It reminds me of nothing so much as how she
used to nag me to stand up straight when I was a little
girl. She'd appear out of the woodwork and catch me
slumping, or reading with round shoulders, and she'd
snap, 'Posture, Fernanda, posture.' "

"Has she said anything to you about Father?"
Valerie asked.

"Not a single word. You'd think that with Father
murdered and the beasts who did it caught and waiting
for trial, Mother might at least have said something
about it, even though she couldn't stand him."

"She's still too bitter. She'll always be too bitter," Valerie said reflectively. "It shows you to what
point she must have hated him. I've been wondering
what it would have been like if they'd stayed mini-
mally friendly after the divorce . . . been like for us, I
mean."

"I think he must have loved us," Fernanda said
slowly, "in his own way. I always had a feeling that
he just *had* to, in that bossy, demanding, gruff manner
of his. How could a man not love his children? But
we'd have felt . . . oh, *easier* around him . . . less

. . . frozen. We could have tried to get closer to him without being disloyal to Mother.''

"Even when I resented him the most," Valerie said, "I always had to admit that he was a . . . force. You knew he was there. It seemed he would always be there. But Mother made him seem so unkind, so inaccessible . . . she made us afraid of him.''

"That wasn't fair of her.'' Fernanda's voice was astonished.

"Don't try to tell her that," Valerie said dryly.

"What point would there be? It's too late now, so why look for trouble?''

"Precisely," Valerie agreed, thinking that this was the first time she and Fernie had talked about their father since he'd been killed. There had been the shock of the news and the confusion of the funeral, followed so quickly by the news of the will and the arrival of the Rosemonts and Sir John, that they had rarely been alone together long enough to have any sort of conversation. They hadn't had any real time to mourn. And how could you not mourn your father? It felt good to exchange opinions with Fernie again. She'd missed the familiar way in which they understood each other with so few words. Fernie might be dizzy, but no one could say she was stupid.

Valerie turned the car into the driveway of the Hacienda Valencia and drove slowly through the splendid welcome of the giant trees. As she pulled up to the entrance to the hacienda, Jazz ran out to greet them, covering the awkwardness they all felt on entering the family home that now belonged to her. She offered them a variety of things to eat and drink.

"No, thanks, we've just finished lunch," Valerie said. "What is it you wanted to talk to us about?'' She was deliberately abrupt.

"Actually, it's more show-and-tell than a formal talk.''

"What's that supposed to mean?'' Fernanda was immediately suspicious. She would put nothing past Jazz, she thought, remembering how she had waltzed off with Casey Nelson, waltzed off with the hacienda. Although Fernanda couldn't lay claim to the man nor the house, she didn't like having them snatched away from her.

"Here's my proposition," Jazz said. "You both come riding with me and listen to what I have to tell you, and then, if it doesn't mean anything to you, I'll sign everything that you want me to sign and everybody can go home. Your riding stuff is still here, in your old rooms."

"Riding! Jazz, what kind of crazy ploy is this?" Valerie asked severely. She was wary of Jazz when she looked reckless and brave, as she did now, in spite of the fatigue betrayed by her eyes.

"Nothing more than what I said. A ride, and a show-and-tell. Look, I'm in a position where I have to go along with the two of you. I have no real choice, you know that. Just do me this one favor and I won't ask for another."

Valerie thought rapidly. Jimmy Rosemont had assured her that nothing important had been said when he and Sir John had seen Jazz a few days ago, a mere "blip on the radar screen," he'd called it. But somehow she felt that there might be something to be gained by humoring Jazz in this typically off-the-wall scheme of hers. They were, after all, in this sale together. And she could use some exercise. It wasn't safe to ride in Central Park anymore, it hadn't been for years.

"All right, Jazz. Come on, Fernie, let's go change."

While they put on their jeans and boots, Jazz paced nervously around the fountain in the middle of the patio. The sky was a deep, pure turquoise, utterly clear after the downpour of the last few days; drops of rain that still trembled, here and there, on the vividly red Yale geraniums, became miniature prisms when the sun touched them; the air was electric in its freshness; the last roses, which she hadn't yet had the heart to have pruned, scattered stray pink and white petals, and the trunks of the old trees on the cypress walks were almost black with moisture.

The past week had been grim. Steve Johnson and his battery of real-estate lawyers had studied all the documents and come to the same conclusion as Rosemont and Maddox. She could devote the best part of the rest of her life to struggling, but the covenant was ultimately unenforceable.

The unanswerable decisions of her own lawyers had made Jazz withdraw entirely into herself. She had soared so high with her triumph that now she felt a thousand times a dupe and a fool for having been so cocksure that she had won. She was profoundly angry at the outcome of events, and yet so unutterably sad that she found herself unable to deal with her tattered and tangled feelings. She refused to talk about them even with Casey. All during these endless, weary days of heavy rain she'd wandered silently around the hacienda like a shamed and defeated prisoner while Casey and Joe Winter had attended to the business of the ranch from the office they shared.

Jazz felt profoundly alienated from Casey. He had taken the news of their defeat stoically, almost as if he'd expected it. He had put it behind him, accepted it as the luck of the draw. Naturally, she thought, naturally he wasn't capable of really giving a damn, not in his heart of hearts. He'd just been humoring her, ever since she'd translated the letter. There was no reason why he should care deeply. This was just an episode in his life. The hacienda had never been his home, Mike Kilkullen hadn't been his father. his life wasn't intertwined with this beloved land. Why had she trusted him?

There was an invisible wall between them now, a high wall, a thick wall, a wall of unexpressed feelings and unasked questions and unmentioned sorrows and unspoken reassurance. Jazz lacked the desire even to think about it now. Marriage to Casey Nelson seemed as improbable as it would have on the night she'd met him, but she simply didn't have the emotional energy to deal with the problem now. She put him off with abrupt coldness whenever he tried to approach her, showing her bitter, unspoken resentment, her indifference. She couldn't, in all justice, lump him in with her enemies, but his love—or rather what he claimed was his love—seemed no more than a memory.

Yesterday, at noon, the rains had stopped and it had turned breezy and warm enough so that Jazz had decided to take out a sailboat, looking for solace from the rhythm of the sea. But each time the wind had taken her in the direction of land, she had been confronted by the majesty of Portola Peak, and her heart had shriveled as she imagined the Sentinel Rocks being flattened by a bulldozer as the mountain was mangled and reduced to rubbish, becoming a convenient rising surface that would provide views for two dozen condos.

She'd returned from her sail, sunburned, tousled, but determined to make one last appeal to Fernanda and Valerie, face to face. She had no fantasy that she could make them change their minds, but at least when she thought about Portola Peak in the future, she wouldn't feel that she hadn't made one final effort to save it.

Before Fernanda and Valerie arrived, Jazz had asked one of the vaqueros to saddle up three horses on the chance that her sisters would agree to go riding. Now they ambled out of the house toward the stables, in jeans and windbreakers, walking easily in the old boots they hadn't bothered to take with them when they'd packed after the funeral.

"Where are we going?" Fernanda asked.

"Way up beyond the bowl, to the higher land."

"That figures," Valerie said, settling herself on her bay horse. "Playing the landscape card, is that it, Jazz?"

"More or less. Follow me." Jazz took off on Limonada, Valerie and Fernanda trotting after her. Once they passed the steep rim of the bowl, she urged the strawberry roan into a smooth canter. If she and her sisters shared anything at all, it was the ability to ride vaquero-style, she thought as the strong mare forged ahead.

Jazz's destination was a solitary sycamore on a height about eight miles away, far up and to the south, from which, by reason of the topography of the land, there was a particularly broad view that gave an idea of the grandeur of the hundred square miles of the ranch. It was far enough away from Portola so that you could see the mountain in a way that was impossible when you stood too close to it. The ancient sycamore was probably the closest thing to a central point that you could find on the fan-shaped piece of land that formed the ranch on which Jazz could ride all day and never come to a boundary.

As they rode across miles and miles of high, newly green hills, skirting groups of grazing cows and waving greetings to the vaqueros they passed, Jazz looked behind her from time to time. Her sisters were strung out behind her, Valerie first and Fernanda bringing up the rear, their hair blowing wildly, at ease in their saddles, different beings than they were indoors. She had never ridden with them like this before, not once in all these years, she realized with a pang.

"All right, Jazz, now what?" Valerie asked, once they'd arrived at the solitary sycamore. The fields that fell away from them on all sides were empty, new grass just beginning to grow on mesas that were the burnt copper of a lion's mane. Above, a few wisps of clouds seemed pinned to the purple heights of Portola Peak. They could see the lines of waves beating against Valencia Point, but they were too far away to hear. In the silence of the vast, tranquil, blue-gold spaces of these uplands, the world was very far away.

Jazz unrolled a blanket and spread it on the damp grass. "We might as well sit down and get comfortable."

"Curiouser and curiouser," Fernanda muttered, but she flopped down on the blanket.

"Just don't ask me to take a deep, cleansing breath, Jazz, I assume that this isn't a Lamaze class," Valerie said, as she sat down in a dignified way.

"I wanted to bring you here because it's the best place to show you what the covenant includes and doesn't include, without trying to climb up to the Sentinel Rocks." Jazz's statement carried the matter-of-fact truthfulness of someone with nothing left to lose.

"Covenant?" inquired Valerie.

"*What* kind of rocks?" Fernanda's question was automatic.

"*My God, you don't know! They didn't tell you!* They had no right, *no right*—I can't believe they kept it from you!"

"Jazz, did you tell Sir John and Jimmy something they didn't report to us?" Valerie's voice was sharp.

"Damn right I did. It's not enforceable, not legally binding, but how could they dare not even mention it! You're both just as affected as I am, you both have exactly the same heritage as I do!"

"Wait a minute," Fernanda spoke up suddenly. "Maybe it was that thing Georgina mentioned. She said that Jimmy said you'd come up with some bizarre story, 'a folkloric diversion,' he called it, but it wasn't important and Jimmy wanted to be careful not to make it seem more important than it deserved."

"That insufferable bastard! That arrogant, dishonest scum! It's impossible that he took it upon himself not to tell you!"

Furiously, Jazz went to get the bundle of papers she'd attached to her saddle earlier, just in case Valerie and Fernanda expressed enough curiosity to ask to see the actual documents. Her hands were shaking with rage as she spread the copy of the *diseño* on the blanket and started to arrange the other papers and photographs around it.

"Jesus Christ, he didn't even tell you about the letter from our great-great-great-grandmother! 'Folkloric diversion,' my ass!"

Valerie's ancestor interest was immediately

aroused, particularly since Jazz had already said that nothing was legally binding.

"Jazz, start from the beginning. Stop shuffling all those papers around and tell us what this is all about," she commanded.

"Only if you promise not to interrupt." Suddenly Jazz saw a patch of hope appear on the gray screen of her mind. Her father had told her the history of the Valencias little by little when they sat keeping each other company in the archive room, but there was no reason to assume her sisters had necessarily heard anything more than just a sketchy account. Mike Kilkullen had never been one to glory in tales of old families, even his own.

She began to relate the story of her search, starting at the very beginning and taking them through the discovery of the map at the Huntington Manuscript collection and the translation of the covenant made by Bernardo Valencia, in which he had renewed the promise made by Teodosio Valencia in 1808.

"Michael Kilkullen," Jazz said as she showed them the tracing of the map, "our great-great-grandfather, respected this covenant and his son respected the covenant. The letter's proof of that. There's a powerful reason why the ranch has never been sold, why it's been handed intact from one head of the family to the other. Father used to say that even when he was a child, his grandfather made him promise never to sell even an acre of land."

"I remember him saying that . . . but it isn't anything more than an outmoded point of view," Valerie insisted.

"Oh, Val, don't be so literal, it's family history," Fernanda protested.

"You're both interrupting," Jazz said, and proceeded to tell them about the search for the Sentinel Rocks, right up to the day she had confronted Rosemont and Sir John with her evidence and learned that it was worthless in a court of law.

"Since you believed that we'd been told about

this already, Jazz, why did you bring us here today?''
Valerie asked, wariness clear in her voice. ''What's
your point? To make us feel that we're doing something wrong? Breaking faith with the past? My God,
that old covenant was made practically two hundred
years ago—at a time when it cost Bernardo Valencia
absolutely nothing to make such a promise—you
know as well as I do that no one would ever do it
today, not in the modern world.''

''Val, I never had a plan to accuse you of guilt. I
wanted you to *feel* something and I knew that the only
place you could feel it was here, right here, with the
ranch spread around us, not in a hotel suite. Valerie!
Fernanda!'' Jazz's voice rose in intensity. ''Has it
ever really sunk into your heads that once this land is
sold it can *never be replaced*? One of the most precious real properties on the planet will disappear forever under millions of square feet of concrete and
stone and marble. Think of all the people who buy
expensive objects: antiques, old masters, Chinese Im-
port dinner services and Aubusson carpets. Then they
stuff their new houses with them to show everyone
how rich they are. They buy castles, they buy islands,
they buy vineyards. But not one of them, not one of
those men in the *Forbes* list of the richest men in
America, could buy our ranch without putting up his
entire fortune and more. Look around you! This land
is our birthright, and once it's gone, no power on earth
can replace it. If we don't sell it, we'll be rich beyond
imagination.''

''You can't spend imagination,'' Valerie said
flatly.

''Jazz, this land is worth too much money to
keep. We can't afford to hold on to it.'' Fernanda was
almost plaintive, but positive.

''Wait a minute! Don't get me wrong. I'm not
suggesting that we keep every last acre of the land for
ourselves. Of course that's out of the question. But I
am asking you to consider an alternative.''

Jazz pointed south, beyond the area protected by
the Twin Pointed Rock, where miles of mesas lay.

"Way over there, near the ocean, but not on it, the three of us could develop an entirely new town, a sort of urban village, planned for tens of thousands of inhabitants. Eventually as many as eighty thousand people could live together surrounded on all sides by unchanged countryside. It would generate a vast income in the future, it could only become more valuable every year, and you could be proud of it in a way you could never be of the development plan that Jimmy Rosemont told me about that day at the Ritz."

"Just what is wrong with that plan, may I ask?" Valerie asked defensively.

"Oh, Valerie, Valerie, I may not know you as well as Fernanda does, but I'm absolutely sure of one thing—you wouldn't be caught dead in that place! You wouldn't even be *sick* there."

"It's clearly not designed to appeal to me." Valerie tossed her head in vexation. "What does that have to do with its commercial value?"

"The houses and condos would sell, I don't doubt that. The kind of high-tech security it would offer would appeal to every international arms dealer, every major junk-bond salesman—the ones who are still out of jail—every big-time money launderer, every oil-rich foreign billionaire—it would turn into an enclave of frightened rich people from all over the world, huddled together, busily outspending each other. Can you even begin to imagine what Father would have thought of turning the ranch he loved so much into a place like that? You can't deny it, Valerie, the plan calls for the creation of a citadel to protect people with nothing in common but the most pretentious and ostentatious way of life—it's simply not *you,* Valerie."

"I never said I wanted to have a place there," Valerie snapped, biting her lips. "My individual preferences have nothing to do with it."

"Ah! But our name would be on it. 'Rancho Kilkullen,' as that bastard Rosemont called it. And even if we gave it another name, do you think everyone won't know that the Kilkullen sisters have sold out their family's Spanish land grant, a piece of American history that goes back *eight generations,* to Hong Kong bankers? It would be a hell of a story all over the world. One thing we'd have to face would be publicity—all of it *vile,* you can count on that—which would follow us for the rest of our lives, and follow your children too. You *must* know it would spoil them rotten. As for us, we'd be sitting ducks for the press, three present-day, ready-made little Barbara Huttons or Christina Onassises. The three sisters who got a billion dollars each for their land. The media will cover every step we take, for God's sake! That's one reason why the old rich in this country—in every civilized country, for that matter—stay so carefully out of the public eye. How much publicity do you see about the Mellons or the Goelets or Betsy Whitney or the Browns of Providence or the Biddles or the Mathers or the Pennocks?"

"Oh, shit," Valerie said, flinching at the validity of Jazz's words.

"Jazz, you're so horrible!" Fernanda wailed.

"Oh, I know, Fern, there's something almost . . . almost irresistible about so much money. It's hideously tempting. It's practically impossible to turn away from it. Or rather from the *idea* of having it. The reality would make freaks out of us. Father loved us all too much to allow that to happen to us . . . but he made an absolutely awful will, his love didn't protect him from that."

"But I thought that . . . *more* . . . would mean something wonderful!" Fernanda wailed.

"Like what?"

"Oh, damn it, Jazz, I haven't been sitting around planning how to spend it. I just think it's so thrilling and glamorous to finally really be an heiress, and now you're trying to take that all away from me."

"No, no! I'm not. We *are* heiresses . . . we're the only Kilkullens left. Nothing can change that, Fernie. In his will, Father said he believed that we'd know what to do with our inheritance. He must have had faith in our wisdom—even though that will certainly didn't make it easy for us."

Jazz looked from one of her sisters to the other, forcing them to make eye contact with her, to hear her words and know the truth of them.

"When I think of how anxious he always was to tempt you to come out here to visit, when I think of how much he missed both of you while you were growing up, so far away, and how sad he was when you had to leave each time, it breaks my heart. The only time he ever felt justified in insisting that you come out was for the Fiesta. Otherwise he could never beg; he was too proud to show you how he really felt, and it was exactly that same stubbornness that made him refuse to sell a single acre. Because of Dad's particular character, difficult as he could be at times, we've inherited a big, beautiful stretch of California . . . a part of the country that has become valuable beyond belief, simply because of its location. What matters . . . desperately . . . is how we decide to use it, what we do with it."

"Jazz, you're making a speech," Valerie said, almost sighing, "and I hate having speeches made at me."

"I can't help that, Val. I have to say my piece now because there'll never be another chance. Listen to me a little bit longer. Remember, I said that if it didn't mean anything to you, I'd sign any papers you wanted. O.K.?"

"I don't seem to have a choice."

"We can be greedy and selfish and act without any respect for our heritage and what we know Dad would have wanted, and sell out to the highest bidder," Jazz continued. "In a few months the bulldozers will get to work and we'll be three *unnecessarily* rich women. Each one of us will have so much more money than we can ever find ways of spending that we'll be *ruled* by it—an ultimately meaningless glut of money making more money until it ceases to have the slightest relation to any human life or any human desire. That's one option."

Jazz stood up and threw her arms wide as if she were trying to gather in the sky and the ocean and the mountain and the newly green mesas in one enveloping sweep and present them to her sisters in all their primeval beauty.

"We can tell the world that our heritage isn't for sale," she cried. "We can decide that we don't have to exploit it to the maximum to have enough. We don't have to sell to anybody, we can exercise the power we possess right now to protect this land that has protected seven generations of our family. We can use it wisely and well. Don't you both see it? Can't you both feel it?"

"Look, Jazz," Valerie said reluctantly, "I can't maintain that when you get on your soapbox you don't make a certain amount of sense—but we don't know anything concrete about those things you mentioned, new towns or urban villages. You're no city planner, we aren't either, none of us has experience in these areas. You're just an idealistic dreamer who talks a good game."

"Valerie, Fernanda, both of you, stand up and tell me if you can see that huge boulder way off to the south?" Jazz pointed to an enormous rock that a glacier had left behind, too large to be removed by man, clearly visible five miles to the south, a rock that lay much closer to the ocean than the sycamore under which they sat.

Fernanda and Valerie both stood, peered toward the rock and nodded.

"From that rock," Jazz said, "there are mesas out of your field of vision that are exceptionally large and well wooded. They roll toward the ocean and form a generous, gentle slope, perhaps ten thousand acres all told. That's where the new town could be built, from the big rock down and out in every direction except north."

"But, Jazz, that's way off in the middle of nowhere!" Fernanda exclaimed. "You'd never even know it was there."

"It just seems that way, Fernie. At the far end of the slope, you're almost on the Pacific Coast Highway, and yet it's protected from the road by a wide band of oaks and brush. I've been riding this ranch for years, and I haven't gone that far more than a few dozen times. Even if it was all built up, we'd still conserve over fifty thousand acres for ranching.''

"What kind of income would we get from a town down there?'' Valerie's question was unvarnishedly practical.

"Right away, nothing. But eventually, many, many millions a year. As more housing is built, as more commercial buildings go up, our income will grow steadily. The people who live there won't have to spend hours every day on the highway getting to work—there'd be enough jobs for everybody who wants one.''

"It sounds sort of . . . ordinary, if you ask me,'' Fernanda said in disappointment. "You said something about an urban village, and you come up with something typically Orange County; suburbs and business buildings.''

"It's Orange County, unquestionably,'' Jazz said. "But typical—no, Fern, not typical at all.''

"Not typical in what way?'' Valerie inquired, unable to restrain herself.

"I'm glad you asked. Even if you hadn't, I was going to tell you.'' Jazz's laughter rang exultantly. It had been harder to get that question out of Valerie than it had been to get a belly laugh out of Woody Allen, but now that she'd opened that door . . .

Jazz spoke rapidly, the words crisp and positive. She talked with the bold strokes of a master draftsman, with a concise grasp of the essentials, and a choice of the precisely vivid detail. After Jazz had finished telling her sisters about her ideas for the new town, they fell into an obdurate silence that seemed to hum with the working of their minds. They were lost n the rush of images she had conjured up, bewildered by an utterly unexpected excitement; they didn't even exchange glances. At last, Valerie spoke.

"I can tell you one thing, Jazz, you haven't thought this thing through the way I would. For instance, it's impossible not to plan gift shops, with so many people living there—any decent gift shop would be a gold mine, particularly with all the babies that will be born sooner or later. And you need a few good cheese stores and gourmet stores and some decent florists, for heaven's sake. People like to celebrate, you know, and entertain. And did you ever stop to think that not everybody wears tennis shoes? If you don't have a reliable shoe-repair place, you're going to have people walking around with run-down heels and flapping soles.''

"Oh, Valerie, you're absolutely right!" Jazz threw her arms around her sister and hugged her tightly. "We could never do it without you!"

"You didn't mention a single tea shop, just all those cafés and espresso bars," Fernanda sniffed. Jazz was smart, but she certainly hadn't thought of everything. "There's nothing like a good cup of tea when you need it. And I insist that there absolutely has to be a marina, for all the people who love to get away from the land. I don't care what you say about leaving the beach untouched . . . we simply can't build homes with a gorgeous view of the ocean and not expect everybody to want to get out there and sail.''

"No, Fernie, we couldn't possibly do that, could we?" Jazz hugged the two of them, squeezing them to her and jumping up and down in joy, and all three of them laughed and laughed and then wept a little together, partly in excitement and partly because, for the first time in their lives, they felt like sisters.

"Who's going to break the news to Mother?" Fernanda asked, as they drove out of the gates of the hacienda.

"I nominate you," Valerie said, laughing. "You're always in trouble with her anyway. A little more won't make any difference."

"The hell I will! You're older. You should take the responsibility."

"We'd better do it together. Or we could just write her a little note and leave the country for a month," Valerie said, giddy with an interesting combination of fizzing emotions she hadn't begun to analyze.

"Or a year."

"Shit, I'm not afraid of Mother, even if you are. I'll do it," Valerie announced.

"I'm not either! I'm going to do it." Fernanda blew the hair out of her eyes defiantly.

"Good. I'll watch."

"Oh, you bitch. You trapped me." Fernanda leaned over and kissed Valerie on the cheek. "I should have remembered how you always used to do that."

"It's my secret and you'll never figure it out. But listen, Fernie, seriously, we're going to have to give her some kind of allowance. We always knew she expected it when we inherited."

"But we're not going to turn a penny's profit for years and years," Fernanda objected.

"Still, we'll have to do something for her now. A little something."

"A very, very tiny something. A token. Anyway, she loves Marbella and she's had that villa forever, it's not as if she needs a lot of money. The notion of moving to San Clemente must have been some sort of aberration."

"You're right," Valerie agreed. "Of course, it means that she'll still have to come to New York to shop at the sales. Only she'll be forced to stay with you."

"What do you mean, 'forced to'?"

"I won't be there. I'll be in Philadelphia."

"Valerie! That's a dream right out of never-never land, a fantasy you like to trot out whenever you get fed up with New York. You can't possibly mean it!"

"*Oh, but I do*. I do, Fernie, with all my heart. I finally realized that I truly wanted to go when I knew I could move to Philadelphia without—oh, without . . . losing face in New York, I guess you'd have to call it, disgusting as that sounds. But that fear of losing face has vanished along with the Hong Kong billions.

It was something I imposed on myself. It's sort of a contagion. You get it out of the air in New York. Or maybe it's in the water.''

''You know who else said 'I'd rather be in Philly,' don't you?''

''No, but whoever it was, I agree totally.''

''W.C. Fields. On his tombstone,'' Fernanda giggled.

''Fernie, the poor man probably didn't have family and nice friends there,'' Valerie said with a serene and happy smile that transformed her into a lovely woman.

''But I'll miss you, damn it! What'll I do without you?''

''We can telephone all the time, just as often as ever, and you can come to visit, and I can come to spend a few days . . . it's only an hour and a half away, remember.''

''It's a million miles in attitude.''

''That's exactly why I'm moving. Oh, it's going to be heaven to relax in Philadelphia. It's so divinely *cozy*. As soon as the apartment in New York is sold, I'll take the money, find a *perfect* house—I know just what I want it to look like—put my feet up, let down my hair, and see all my old friends again, before I even start to redecorate. Or maybe I'll never redecorate, just re-slipcover. That would be more Philadelphia. Bliss!''

''Aren't you forgetting about Billy?''

''He's just going to have to accept it. I've done it his way long enough. He can change if he has to, and if Billy wants to stay married to me, he does. If he doesn't—I'll live without him and manage very well. Who needs a man who won't move out of that sinister, *toxic* city?''

''Right on!''

''Actually, Billy's been telephoning twice a day. The poor creature is helpless without me, and he knows it. I don't think he'll give me a problem once he realizes that I'm totally serious. I'm feeling very sure of myself, Fernie. Isn't it amazing how the fact that we're going to be so much richer someday, even though it's way down the road, makes it seem as if we're rich now? Rich and powerful?''

"Attitude again. It's all in your attitude," Fernanda said thoughtfully.

She realized, listening to Valerie, that there was nothing in the world she wanted that she didn't have already. She'd been desperate to be immensely rich only because she'd been terrified of growing older without capturing an elusive satisfaction. How could she ever have believed that a young man could provide it? Or any kind of man? Georgina. Her Georgina . . . she wished she could tell Val, but she knew she couldn't. At least not yet, not for years, possibly never.

"I'll announce the news to Jimmy and Sir John," Fernanda volunteered, out of her sudden silence.

"Ah, no—I'm not going to miss out on that! We're going to tell them together. I can't wait to confront Jimmy with his lies and deceptions. I wonder how big his cut of the pie must have been to make him so anxious about this deal? The worst part is that he almost got away with it. When I think about his plan —Fernie, I'll admit it to you, and no one else, I always disapproved of his version of Monte Carlo, but I let him talk me into it. We were so gullible—it's unforgivable.''

"Of him or of us?"

"Both," Valerie answered wholeheartedly.

"Hmmm." Fernanda's mischief-loving, pussycat smile appeared at the corners of her mouth. Jimmy Rosemont was so infinitely, incurably detestable! She couldn't wait to see his face when they told him that they'd all decided not to sell, that they'd agreed to petition the court immediately to dismiss the temporary administrator and turn the ranch over to the three of them. Georgina had always hinted that she thought Jimmy's plan was . . . vulgar . . . at best. She'd be thrilled that they'd decided against it, and the massive disappointment of their news should dull even Jimmy's libido for a few months.

"Val, would you think I was crazy if I told you that . . . oh, never mind.''

"What, since you're going to tell me anyway.''

"I've changed the way I used to feel about Jazz. I . . . I like her. I like her a lot.''

"So do I. You *have* to like someone who can persuade you that you should turn your back on a quick billion and make you feel good about doing it,'' Valerie said, tartness mixed with an amused warmth.

"Not a *whole* billion,'' Fernanda said comfortingly, "not after taxes.''

"Why quibble? I intend to get all the credit for having the taste and wisdom to turn down a billion, not a penny less.''

"Valerie Kilkullen Malvern, Our Lady of Ecological Balance, Preservation of Traditional Values and Slow Growth; Blue-Blooded Queen of Conservationism, New Heroine of Land Use.''

"Bravo, Fernie. I couldn't put it better myself. About Jazz . . . I never honestly knew her before today. I'm proud that she's my sister, I'm thrilled that we'll all be building a new urban village together . . . you and I have been acting like children, still thinking about her as an enemy, a rival—thanks to Mother again. Don't you feel bad about how we used to tease her? God, we were mean. Remember calling her an 'orphink'? . . . What a pair of little bitches we were.''

"You're only saying that because now we're orphinks too,'' Fernanda said sadly.

"Isn't that enough of a reason?''

"Shouldn't we tell her—let her know exactly how we feel? Tell her we're sorry or something?''

"Oh, Fernie, couldn't you see? I mean, for heaven's sake, didn't you realize? Jazz knows it already.''

"Oh, you're right, but still . . . well, someday I want to say something. I'll find the right moment. Oh, Val, isn't it wonderful news about Jazz and Casey? I knew it all along, of course—you could tell, right from the beginning, that she'd never let him get away. But you know what it means, don't you? We're going to have to turn around and fly back here for the wedding just a few weeks after we finally get home.''

"Fernie, for heaven's sake, stop complaining. It'll be wonderful. I have a weird sentimental thing about weddings, and after all, don't forget, we're the only family she has.''

22

As soon as Valerie's car left the hacienda, Jazz went looking for Casey. Joe Winter told her that he'd driven up to Los Angeles on business while she was out riding, and wasn't expected back until after dinner.

"Don't you know where I could try to reach him?" Jazz pleaded, bursting with her miraculous news.

"Not a clue. He could be anywhere."

Ferociously frustrated, not wanting to say anything to Joe before she told Casey, Jazz returned to the hacienda and telephoned Red. She'd neglected her friend as badly as she'd neglected everyone else in her life, but Red let Jazz talk her into meeting her for an early dinner in Newport Beach.

Jazz poured out the whole story, so exultant that all Red could do was sit back and eat while she listened, nodding and gasping, gasping and nodding at all the appropriate places. As they reached the end of dinner, Jazz's talking jag ground slowly to a halt.

"Tell me what you've been up to, Red," she asked, at last.

"Who, me? Little old me?"

"You must have been doing something while I was busy ignoring my best friend."

"I've been reading books I've always meant to read, thinking more or less noble thoughts, taking long walks, going religiously to exercise class, listening to music, potting up pansies, putting up pickles—"

"I don't believe you."

"It's all true except the pickles. I've been slowly getting used to being without Mike. It's not as if I have a choice, is it? Life has to go on. I've been all right, Jazz, not great, but not helplessly miserable, and it's getting a little bit easier week by week. Sometimes I go out for dinner with friends, sometimes I invite them over—I had a nice lunch with Gregory this week when he was here . . ."

"Gregory who?"

"Oh, Jazz, you're certifiable. Gregory Nelson, your future father-in-law."

"Casey's father was out here this week?"

"Jazz, where have you been?"

"I . . . I . . . honestly don't know. On a quest, I guess. I feel like one of those medieval knights who goes tearing off after some Grail or other, and when he comes home at last, a hundred years later, everybody he ever knew has disappeared, and nobody even remembers him or why he went away."

"It's only been a month or so. And believe me, you haven't been forgotten," Red said teasingly.

"But I never even knew Casey's father was here!"

"He flew out on business for a day or so, and he happened to call."

"Just exactly how did he know your number?"

"I assume Casey must have told him. Jazz, it was merely a friendly lunch. We have you and Casey in common, after all."

"*Lunch*. Why is it that lunch sounds so much

more meaningful than dinner?'' Jazz was deeply interested.

"Just don't start," Red warned her.

"Forget what I said! It's much too soon to even be thinking that way."

"Much," Red agreed severely.

"I don't know what came over me."

"I accept your apology."

"Where'd he take you? What'd you talk about? Is he as nice as I think? Are you going to see him again?"

"Jazz!"

"Just curious—I don't know him yet, I've only met him once. Anyway, Red, why would there be anything wrong in your making a new friend? You said it yourself, life goes on . . ."

"Go home before I give you a good pinch."

"Right. Right! I'm on my way."

Jazz returned to the hacienda at nine in the evening. She darted immediately into the kitchen, to find only one light on over the stove, and a pot of chili with a brief, pointed note from Susie saying that she'd left it there, just in case, before leaving for the night, although no one seemed to eat at home anymore. There was no message from Casey, no sound of life came from any room of the great, rambling adobe; no vases of flowers, no fire brightened the dark living room, where the massive Spanish furniture brooded in the gloom. She opened a door to the veranda, and even the night with its secret sounds, the sighing of leaves, the cathedral of the starry sky, seemed remote, not unfriendly, but as if it had no connection to her.

Jazz sat down in a kitchen chair and considered a constellation of suddenly ominous facts. Casey's father had been here, right here in California, and Casey hadn't said a word to her about it. Casey had been away all day on business in Los Angeles several times in the last week, and she hadn't noticed it until now. Today he had disappeared without leaving any explanation without saying good-bye. He'd been sleeping in one of the guest rooms for a number of nights, how many she wasn't sure. She hadn't cared.

Casey. He'd been with her every step of the way in the search for the map and the Sentinel Rocks. His reward was that she'd trampled all over him. She'd taken out her impotent fury at her lawyers' verdict on Casey. She'd behaved toward him as if, in some obscure but unmistakable way, it was *his* fault that she didn't have a case. She hadn't shared her defeat with him, only her triumph. Casey must have known that you can celebrate a victory with anyone, even a stranger, but when you lose, you turn only to someone who loves you.

Why had she cut Casey out of her life when she needed him the most? Jazz sat in the dim kitchen, abrupt tears running down her face, and tried to understand herself. Slowly, with much hesitation, with much denial, with much unwillingness and pain, she realized that she was, in spite of being grown up, still terrified of letting herself go and trusting anyone as much as she needed to trust Casey. He hadn't disappointed her—not yet—but what if she was wrong? What if Casey ultimately abandoned her? Others had. Wouldn't it be safer to drive him away before it happened?

But, Jazz asked herself, could she survive if she withheld her complete trust from everyone, now that her father was gone? Wasn't it better to take a chance —even if she lost—than to face a life in which she dared to count only on herself? Was she going to allow the possibility of abandonment to rule her future as it had shadowed her past?

Jazz stood up resolutely. She'd asked herself a lot of questions and she'd glimpsed some necessary answers, but she was finished with soul-searching for tonight. There was only one immediate answer available to one vitally important matter. Where was Casey's fax?

An hour later, when Casey finally walked in the front door, the only light in the hacienda came from the bright kitchen. He went in and found Jazz at the stove, stirring a pot.

"What do you think you're doing?" he asked, startled.

"Heating up this chili. I thought you might want some when you got in."

"I had dinner hours ago," he replied automatically.

"Aren't you always hungry before you go to bed? I am."

Jazz whirled quickly away from the stove, a maddening figure of concentrated, bewitchingly distilled romance in her finely pleated, long, white dress. Dozens of yards of chiffon swirled swiftly about her as if she were dancing; one bare, polished shoulder gleamed, and from the other a wide panel of the airborne fabric fluttered like the wing of a hovering angel.

"What the hell . . . ?"

Jazz's golden eyes widened at his surprise, and she shook the tawny treasure of her hair so reprovingly that it rippled from her scalp to its burnished tips.

"It's my dress from Madame Grès, can't you tell? The one you almost ruined. It's perfect again. I had to send it to Paris after the Fiesta, because there are only four people left alive in the world who know how to clean a dress like this, and they all live there. It took them months of careful work, not on a par with restoring the Mona Lisa, but still . . ."

"Am I supposed to understand why you're wearing it for cooking?"

"You could hazard a guess. No? Oh, all right, then I'll have to tell you. When you spill chili all over it again, as you will, *as you won't be able to avoid doing,* I'm going to smile graciously, the way a lady should, and I'm going to say, 'Oh, it's nothing at all, darling, don't give it another thought, it's not as if it were a new dress.' " She turned back to the pot and busily continued stirring.

Casey moved in a streak across the kitchen, and grabbed her shoulders in his big hands.

"Put . . . down . . . that . . . spoon," he commanded, "and do it very carefully."

As soon as Jazz had obeyed, he turned her around and walked backwards, never relaxing his firm grip until they stood far from the stove.

"All right, what's this all about?" he asked gently. She'd cracked under the strain, he thought wildly, he should never have left her alone, how had he not seen this coming?

"I decided that the only way to get things straight with you was to start out all over again, from the very beginning," Jazz said in a perfectly rational tone of voice, although her eyes betrayed her nervousness. "And there was all that good chili going to waste, and a priceless dress I hardly ever wear, so I thought, 'Why not show Casey that I'm truly a better person than he thinks I am?' Actions speak louder than words, I said to myself, and when he spills the chili, or even throws it at me, the way he did the first time we met, to capture my attention, I'll rise above it— and you don't have to look at me as if I've gone mad, I'm perfectly sane."

"I didn't throw it at you!"

"Oh, I believe you. Rather I believe that *you* believe it, which amounts to the same thing. Let's just say that there will always be two versions of that one particular episode, both of which are true."

"Please, God, don't let this woman drive me out of my mind," Casey pleaded, addressing the ceiling.

"But, darling, I have to do something special to make you believe that I'm a better person," Jazz insisted stubbornly.

"I don't want a better person, a better person would be different, I want the old, unimproved version, the impossible one."

"But you *do* want me, you're absolutely sure? I haven't made you wonder if it wouldn't be wiser to change your mind, the way I've been acting? Oh, Casey, I know how horrible I've been to you, how cold, how unfair, how indifferent—I was terrified that I might have driven you away. If I hadn't found your fax still plugged in, I would have been sure that you'd had enough of all my blowing hot and blowing cold, and had gone away." All of Jazz's fears were in her voice.

Casey shook his head in bewilderment. She really was a fruitcake. He hoped it wasn't catching. One in a family was enough.

"Jazz, remember back to when we got engaged?" he said, as patiently as someone talking to a small child. "That wasn't so long ago, now was it? Say 'No, Casey, it wasn't.' "

"No, Casey, it wasn't," Jazz repeated with a sense of overwhelming relief that made her voice tremble.

"Good girl. Now, didn't I tell you I wanted to live with you for the rest of my life? Didn't I say that I never wanted to let you go? If you think that when you get abstracted and distant it's going to make a difference to how much I love you, well, think again and again. It never will."

" 'It never will.' " Jazz clutched him around the neck, heedless of hundreds of crumpled chiffon pleats that no one in California knew how to press. She could stay this way for hours, she thought, with all of her weight completely entrusted to the support of his body. So safe . . . so safe.

"That's even better," he said.

"That's even better."

"You can stop doing that now."

"What if I don't want to?" She spoke with delight, seeing new ways to torment him.

"Don't even consider it." There was a resolute undertone of serious warning in his voice.

"You're the boss," Jazz assured him hastily, and pulled herself away, remembering the fire under the pot of chili. He really did love her, she reflected as she turned off the burner, but she was getting the distinct impression that he had her number.

"I'm going to get a fire going in this dark house, and you're coming with me," Casey said, "and you're not getting away until you demonstrate whatever complicated system releases you from that dress.'' Gingerly he propelled her into the living room, placed her firmly on a chair, and bent to light the fire.

''First tell me where you were all day,'' Jazz demanded.

''Jesus! You're such a pain in the neck that I forgot the most important thing! There's only one way left to keep from selling the ranch, and that's to buy out your sisters, remove the threat of the Hong Kong deal. I've been working on a plan all week. My father came out from New York, we've been in nonstop communication with our bankers here and back East, and it's definitely feasible.''

''Buy out my sisters,'' Jazz said blankly.

''Sure, and build the new town. Dad and I and one of our business partners would put up a third in cash, the banks are ready to lend us another third, and the last third is yours anyway—''

''But your father's in the tugboat business,'' Jazz said numbly, trying to deal with the astonishing development one step at a time.

''The tugboats are only a small part of what he does. He's ready for a change. He likes the long-range potential out here, and anyway, he's lonely in New York—he's even thinking of moving to California.'' Casey adjusted a large log so that the fire burned more brightly.

''But, Casey, what about you? You've always wanted to own a huge ranch,'' Jazz said in confusion. ''In serious ranching terms, this is just a small one.''

''I've always wanted to be in ranching, but now, after being Cow Boss, I've lived it thoroughly enough to see I'd never make a full-time rancher—I'm not happy without a fax on my saddle.'' Casey turned around and grinned, satisfied with the jangled flames of his firemaking. ''And there's something else . . . something very important. I love this land, this particular piece of land. It's all connected with how much I love you and how I feel about your father, how we used to talk together about its history, and how you and I went off to try to rescue it together. I can't imagine ever leaving it now for someplace else."

"But, darling, Casey, I—"

"Jazz, remember that night when you were dreaming out loud about a new town, the night we found the Sentinel Rocks? That idea of yours came to life in my mind the way nothing else ever has! I'm invested in a dozen different big businesses, but this is the only one I've ever wanted to get involved in personally. Listen, Jazz, don't think I could possibly do this to make you happy. No businessman would commit that kind of money—and that much of his own time—to a project unless he had great faith in its future."

"And you and your father have that kind of money—to buy out a third?"

"With a little assistance from another guy who wants to get in on it . . . yeah."

"I never knew . . . I mean, you never said . . . *that* rich?"

"Sort of—we've done pretty well."

"What if you didn't have to buy out anybody? What if you could just go ahead and build the new town without buying the land?"

"As an investment it would be the best of all possible worlds . . . the less you have to borrow . . . but why torture yourself with questions like that?"

"Well . . ." Jazz's eyes brimmed over with fun. "Well . . ."

" 'Well'? I've never heard you say it in quite that tone . . . like a chicken the size of an elephant about to lay a diamond egg . . ." He scrutinized her ravishingly victorious face suspiciously.

"I had a nice little chat with Val and Fernie today. They're not going to sell to anyone. They want to build the new town too."

"Say that again!"

"You heard me the first time."

"But how . . . *how on earth?*"

"It's complicated. I sort of explained it to them

better. It went something like, 'Hey, kids, let's put on a show.' ''

''Witchcraft!''

''That's as good a word as any,'' Jazz said, delighted with herself.

''But what did you say when they asked about the financial partners in joint-venture agreements, about building a pipeline thirty-five miles from Yorba Linda for the water supply, about the ratio of office space to free-standing industrial buildings, about an internal transportation corridor . . .''

''Details,'' Jazz said airily, waving them aside. ''We discussed concepts, not details.''

''None of you three know fuck-all about building a town!''

''Of course not,'' Jazz said majestically. ''It may be my idea, more or less, but that doesn't mean I ever had an intention of getting bogged down in the problem of cubic feet of sewer construction. Infrastructure —if that's the right word—is what men are for. You're so good at it. Not that women couldn't be, if we chose to be, but some of us have more interesting things to do. In fact, I may even have given Val and Fernie the impression that you were going to be in charge of infrastructure.''

''Don't you mean, 'in fact,' that's exactly what you told them?''

''They were reassured to know that they'd be in your safe hands.''

''Wait a minute, Jazz. You told them that *before* I told you I didn't intend to buy a big ranch.''

''I guess it must have been an attack of wishful thinking,'' she said plaintively, but respectfully. Goodness, she thought, Casey had a scary way of keeping track of every last little word she said. She'd have to remember that.

''It was a con, an out-and-out con.''

''Not in retrospect,'' Jazz cried indignantly.

''And then you would have talked me out of buying a ranch and persuaded me to stay here,'' he said thoughtfully, ignoring her words.

"I would have tried—after all, my own work is
basically here, not in Montana or Texas or wherever
the big ranches are—but if you'd still had your heart
set on buying a big ranch, of course I'd have gone
along, kicking and screaming a little, but I'd *never*
have let you go without me. I can work as a photographer whenever I want to, wherever I want to. That's
why they invented airplanes."

"Hmmm." Casey considered everything he knew
of Jazz, that staunch, tricky, complex, determined,
earthy, ariel, impetuous, bewilderingly self-confident
and bewilderingly insecure creature he'd captured
when he'd all but given up hope.

"Don't you believe that I'd have gone anywhere
with you?"

"As a matter of fact—I do."

"Like Marlene Dietrich," Jazz murmured dreamily, as she unfastened row upon row of tiny, hidden
hooks that Casey's fingers would be too large to handle.

"Dietrich?" he asked, watching her closely.

"In *Morocco*, when she leaves behind a dozen
men who adore her in spite of her wicked, wicked
ways, and falls in love with Gary Cooper. He marches
away with the Foreign Legion, so she kicks off her
high heels and follows him, barefoot across the hot
sands . . . you know."

"Every time I saw it, I used to get one tiny tear
in my eye," Casey said, "but don't tell anybody."

Jazz sighed with the felicity of boundless harmony. "It's so wonderful—you're as big a sap as I
am," she murmured.

Her eyelids were almost closed when she saw
Casey abruptly leave the room without an explanation. Astonished, she waited, with her dress still clinging to her in a dozen tiny, cunning, hard-to-discover
ways, until he came back, carrying a pile of blankets.
He threw them on the floor in front of the fire.

"Now," he ordered, "get undressed and be quick
about it. When you're stark naked, not one stitch on,
I want you to wrap yourself in one of those blankets

and sit right here and wait patiently, no moving, no complaining, and absolutely *no* backtalk.''

"Yes, sir."

"I just remembered that chili. I'm hungry, after all. I'm going into the kitchen to help myself to a heaping plateful, and I'm going to bring it right here and eat it, and if anything unforeseen happens, the only thing that will be ruined will be an old blanket. Do I make myself clear?''

"Yes, sir. Please sir, may I have some chili too?" Jazz asked pathetically. No, decidedly, she could never have married an unromantic man, she thought. She wondered if she should remind Casey to make sure the chili was still hot, but decided against it. He'd said no backtalk. And she had the strangest, most unexpectedly rewarding certainty that he meant exactly what he said.

ABOUT THE AUTHOR

JUDITH KRANTZ lives in Bel Air, California, with her husband, movie and television producer Steve Krantz. They have two sons, Nicholas and Tony. Born and raised in Manhattan, she graduated from Wellesley College and began her career as a fashion editor and magazine article writer. Her first novel, *Scruples,* became number one on the best-seller lists, as did each of her four other novels, *Princess Daisy, Mistral's Daughter, I'll Take Manhattan,* and *Till We Meet Again.* All five books have been made into major television miniseries. Judith Krantz is currently at work on her seventh novel.

Dear Reader,

When I finished writing my first novel, Scruples, *back in 1977, I never dreamed that one day, fourteen years later, I would write a sequel. (But neither did I dream that I'd write five more novels, among them* Princess Daisy *and* I'll Take Manhattan, *in the interim, which goes to prove that it's impossible to anticipate!)*

The characters from Scruples *refused to fade from my mind. Billy Ikehorn, Spider Elliott, and Valentine O'Neill all remained vibrantly alive, until I finally understood that I wanted to continue their story.* Scruples Two *begins on the day after* Scruples *ended in April 1978, and continues for another five years. Many delightful and fascinating new characters have joined the story. I'm delighted to introduce the most important of them in this part of the first chapter of my new novel,* Scruples Two. *I hope you'll enjoy this small taste of a long book.*

With my very best wishes,

Judith Krantz

In the momentary wait before the presentation of the Oscar for Best Picture, that pause during which Oscar fever reaches its height, while the presenters walk out of the wings and downstage to read the list of nominations, Vito Orsini began to sweat. What if Maggie MacGregor's information had been wrong? What if Mirrors hadn't won Best Picture? Jesus—he'd have to buy the rights to The WASP come what may, according to the terms of his bet with Curt Arvey. But what the hell. He shrugged his shoulders and smiled. Right or wrong he had to have that book. It had been written for him to produce. He knew it.

Billy Orsini, squeezing his hand tightly, had no such last-minute panic. Dolly Moon had called her first thing that morning, unable to hold back the good news. But Billy hadn't wanted to tell Vito because she suspected he might feel that in some way it diminished the Oscar he was about to get if he knew the secret of the envelope had been revealed before the actual presentation. Nor would she tell him that she was pregnant until tomorrow, when the glory of this night was less fresh. The news, for bambino-loving but childless Vito, would upstage whatever industry recognition he could ever be given. And as she felt Vito's hand tense more firmly than ever over her own, she told herself to be honest. She, Wilhelmina Hunnenwell Winthrop Ikehorn Orsini, did not have the faintest intention of sharing the particular spotlight of glorious maternity with any little gold-plated statuette that the Academy of Motion Picture Arts and Sciences, in its infinite wisdom, might ever bestow.

Billy woke reluctantly from a dream of such happiness that she tried to cling to it as long as possible. She was running in the dream, running effortlessly up a circular flight of steps that led to a platform at the top of a tower from which, she knew even as she ran, she would see a radiant springtime woodland leading to the adventure of a beckoning turquoise sea. She opened her eyes with a sigh and waited for the emotion of the dream to fade, but all the joy stayed with her.

Blissfully disoriented, confused even as to the date and place, she dreamily consulted the high ceiling until memory floated back. She was in her own bed in her own house in California. It was 1978. Last night Vito had won the Oscar for Best Picture and Dolly Moon, her dearest friend, had won for Best Supporting Actress. Four hours later Dolly had, with dispatch and composure, given birth to a magnificent baby girl. She and Vito, with Lester Weinstock, Dolly's publicist, had skipped the post-Oscar party and waited at the hospital together. Then they had all returned here, to celebrate with scrambled eggs, English muffins, and champagne. Billy remembered cooking the eggs and she had a clear vision of Vito opening champagne, but after that everything blurred into a haze of toasts and laughter. Perhaps both men were in bed with her? A quick peek revealed that she was alone and on Vito's side of the bed the covers were thrown back.

Yawning, stretching, groaning with pleasure, Billy eased herself cautiously upright. Her bedside clock told her that it was past noon, but she didn't feel at all guilty. If a woman couldn't sleep late after enduring the many nervous tensions of yesterday, when could she? Especially in her condition, her incredible condition, her excessively interesting, newly discovered condition that was still a secret. But now the time had come to make her announcement. She heard Vito's voice on the phone in the sitting room next to their bedroom. Good, that meant she could throw some water on her face and brush her teeth before he realized that she was awake. As Billy brushed her hair, dismissing as always the bugle call of her insistent beauty, even she couldn't fail to notice the fresh color of her skin, the brightness of her smoky eyes, the electricity of her deep-brown hair. She looked ten years younger than her thirty-five years. It must be hormones, she thought, up to their notorious tricks.

When she emerged from the bathroom Vito was still on the phone, so Billy was inspired to take a quick shower. From the instant she told Vito about this baby, he'd be so excited, so thrilled, so blind to distraction that everything else would be put on hold for hours of talking and planning, so she might as well grab this opportunity. A few minutes later, still damp from her hurried shower, barefoot and dancing in eagerness, Billy threw on a peignoir made of almost-transparent crepe de chine and flung open the door to the sitting room.

In quick, reflex confusion, she stepped back into the bedroom. What the devil was Vito's secretary, Janet Miller, doing sitting on Billy's favorite chair in her very own, very private and off-limits sitting room, murmuring discreetly into Billy's private phone whose cord Janet had dragged over from Billy's desk? Neither Vito nor Janet had noticed her, so absorbed were they in their separate conversations. Billy shrugged out of her indiscreet peignoir and put on slippers and a robe made of heavy toweling, feeling her waking mood dim just slightly around the edges.

"Good morning," she said to Janet and Vito. Janet made an apologetic grimace and continued talking. Vito looked up quickly, waved, smiled, blew her an abstracted kiss, and continued listening intently.

"Yes, Mr. Arvey, Mr. Orsini will take your call as soon as he gets off the other phone," Billy heard Janet say. "Yes, I know how long you've been waiting; would you rather he called you back? No, I can't say exactly when, that's the problem. We don't have a switchboard here, and the phone hasn't stopped ringing all morning. Mr. Orsini hasn't even had time to dress to go to his office. It shouldn't be long now, Mr. Arvey, but this phone doesn't have a hold button. Yes, I know that's ridiculous but I'm on Mrs. Orsini's private phone."

Billy scribbled a question mark on a piece of memo paper and thrust it at Vito. He shook his head at her and pointed toward Janet.

"Who's he talking to?" Billy asked.

"Lew Wasserman, about *The WASP*," Janet answered, putting her hand over the mouthpiece of the phone. The two women looked at each other in mutual congratulation. The combination of the most important and powerful man in Hollywood and Vito's cherished new project in which he hoped to star Robert Redford and Jack Nicholson explained everything about Vito's intensity.

"Great," Vito said, "that's great, Lew. Yeah . . . yeah . . . uh-huh . . . I understand your point . . . Right. Listen, Lew, thanks again for the advice. Breakfast tomorrow morning? You're on. Seven-thirty? No problem. Good-bye, Lew." He hung up and gave Billy a quick, violent hug and a brief, hard kiss, triumph and victory making him move twice as quickly as usual. "Sleep okay, darling? No time to talk, I absolutely have to take the other phone and talk to Curt Arvey. That miserable sucker should never have bet me that *Mirrors* wouldn't win. Now he's going to shell out the million and a half for the rights to *The WASP*, so it's the least I can do. I want to make sure he's closed the deal with that New York literary agent—if ever there was a hot property . . ." He had picked up Billy's private phone and was deep in conversation with Arvey while Janet jumped to answer the other phone, which had started ringing the minute Vito put it down.

Billy looked at the two of them and realized that they had forgotten her. Well, her news would wait, she told herself, and she was starving. She all but waltzed down the staircase and corridors of her Tudor mansion, through the great double living rooms and the music room, smiling brilliantly at her three maids as she crossed their busy paths. Two of them had their arms filled with flower arrangements that had just arrived and the third clutched sheaves of telegrams.

In the kitchen Billy's chef concealed his surprise at the appearance of his employer who normally contacted him on the house intercom. Twice a week they would confer together about menus, but he had never seen Mrs. Orsini in a bathrobe before. He had never seen her in his kitchen before, as far as that went. Billy asked him to send Vito and Janet a platter of club sandwiches and make her a dish she saved for very special moments: three slices of white toast covered thickly with Tiptree's Little Scarlet strawberry jam and topped by carefully layered slices of very crisp bacon. The combination tasted like sweet and sour Chinese food for infants and was a masterpiece of empty calories.

Sugar, salt, white flour, and animal fat. Billy gloated while she waited in the breakfast room for the bacon to be browned almost to the point of burning. This would be her last hurrah before she began her pregnancy diet, a bravura farewell gesture that could be appreciated only by a woman as compulsive as she was, a woman who knew the value of every calorie she had ingested since the age of eighteen, when she had lost a lifetime accumulation of fat and determined successfully to stay thin forever.

Nothing but melon, broiled tomatoes, and steamed fish tonight, Billy thought, without regret, as she sipped orange juice and considered the scene in her sitting room. This phone marathon couldn't go on much longer. Presumably it had started hours ago since Vito, an early riser under all circumstances, still hadn't had time to shave or dress. Soon the calls would taper off, most people would be out to lunch, Janet and Vito would go to his office to handle things more efficiently. Of course there'd be more calls to the house and more flowers and telegrams, but this post-Oscar frenzy couldn't last more than a few hours. After all, the world had a million really important things to focus on no matter how important this big win was to both of them.

She'd finished her sinful meal without tasting it, Billy realized as she hurried back upstairs to the private part of the house, hoping to hear Vito busy in his own dressing room, expecting to find her sitting room empty. But both Vito and Janet were exactly where she'd left them. "What the hell?" Billy wrote and shoved the paper under Janet's nose. Janet grimaced in semidesperation and wrote, "He's talking to Redford—I'm keeping *Nicholson* waiting."

"Good lord!" Billy said to the air, in a mixture of mystification and exasperation. My God, those actors had perfectly good agents. Why was Vito talking to them directly? Or had they called him? That must be it. *The WASP* had been on the top of the best-seller list for seven months, it was the hit book of the decade, everyone wanted to be involved in it; but such a breakdown in Hollywood protocol was something she'd never heard of before. She'd settled down to listen when Janet waved another note at her.

"Maggie's on her way here now with a camera crew . . . a special day-after-Oscar roundup show for tonight's news. Shouldn't you dress?"

Billy's jaw dropped. This was a goddamned invasion of privacy. She'd turned over her house to Vito and his band of workers without a second thought for six weeks of postproduction when it had been a question of getting *Mirrors* edited and mixed without the studio's interference. She'd worked eighteen hours a day as a script girl; she'd never complained at the damage her splendid house had sustained during the entire mad and feverish process, but Maggie MacGregor and her gonzo camera crew were something else again. She didn't give a shit for the fact that Maggie's weekly television show from Hollywood was, week in and week out, one of the five most widely viewed programs in America. Nor did she care that Maggie had tipped Vito off about winning the Oscar. Maggie was Vito's friend, not hers, never hers. She and Maggie never met without reinforcing their cordial mistrust. They couldn't afford to allow themselves to become enemies—the town and the business were too small for that—but they'd never truly trust each other. Her house wasn't a soundstage, for Christ's sake, she didn't want strangers inside it, she'd never allowed a single magazine to photograph it, and Maggie damn well knew that.

For the past three years, from the time she had bought her Holmby Hills estate, on the coveted south side of Sunset Boulevard just beyond Beverly Hills, Billy's property had been discreetly patroled twenty-four hours a day by armed men with Dobermans; barbed wire fences were concealed in every foot of the thick perimeter hedges of her eleven acres; the entrance to her gatehouse was guarded by two uniformed men who waved away anyone who stopped a car to rubberneck up the driveway. All that security went with being one of the richest women in the world, as sensible and necessary as it was to any boss in organized crime, and now Maggie MacGregor, without so much as a by-your-leave, was thrusting her way in with a camera crew. Why couldn't Maggie interview Vito in his office?

Still unwilling to disturb Vito, Billy scribbled the question and plunked it down in front of Janet. Janet stopped flirting with Jack Nicholson for a second and murmured, "Human interest, she's shooting everyone at home."

Billy retreated to the absolute quiet of her vast dressing room and the cozy window seat on which she'd huddled yesterday when she realized that she was three months pregnant, when hours of soul-searching had revealed to her stubbornly disbelieving mind that she had wanted all along to have a baby without consciously realizing it.

It was two in the afternoon, more than twenty-four hours later, and she still hadn't told Vito. *Nobody* knew. She was quivering, bursting, palpitating with her great news and Vito couldn't be pried away from the phone so that she could tell him first, before anyone else, as was right and proper. Until he knew, she had to stay silent. It was getting a little hard to hold on tight to that otherworldly happiness she'd carried intact from her dream into her life, Billy realized, and then she brightened. She would go and spend the next few hours at Scruples. If she didn't actually have to see the camera crew invade her house, it would be as if they'd never been there.

Billy dressed rapidly and managed to leave without causing Vito or Janet to look up from their phones. During the eight-minute drive from her house to her sumptuous boutique in Beverly Hills, Billy realized that the splendid early spring weather was the perfect match for her mood. Oscar weather like Rose Bowl weather was uncannily dependable. No one in the worldwide television audience had ever seen less than perfect weather in California on those two particular days. No one had ever seen the gloom of those endlessly foggy June mornings when the sun doesn't fight through the clouds until afternoon; no one had ever seen the dark chill and frightening floods of the January rains or, far worse, the glare of the dangerous sunlight in the late-summer forest fire season . . . no, Hollywood always primped itself silly and presented its best face when the world was watching. Typical, thought Billy, typical. She was still enough of a Bostonian to be able to sneer slightly at a city that managed reliably to fool the public.

She drove down Rodeo Drive and turned into the underground parking lot at Scruples, feeling the familiar, proudly swelling warmth of ownership. Scruples was the extravagant fantasy she had brought to life four years earlier, the most opulent and successful specialty store that had ever existed. Last night, during the Oscar ceremonies, Billy had decided to open new branches of Scruples all over the world, in the great capital cities where those rich women lived whose lives revolved around shopping and entertaining, that tiny but endlessly greedy consuming class born to become Scruples customers.

She'd made a resolution, Billy reminded herself, not to jump too quickly into building the new branches, not to make a single important move without the advice of Spider Elliott and Valentine O'Neill. She intended to make them her partners in the new Scruples company that Josh Hillman, her lawyer, would set up. Spider, the former fashion photographer who now managed Scruples, had been the one to supply the key inspiration that had set the right, lighthearted tone for the store's success, and, God knows, she couldn't operate without Paris-bred Valentine, her head buyer and designer of the brilliant custom-made clothes that gave Scruples much of its cachet. She couldn't wait to tell them her plans, Billy thought, as the elevator mounted to the third floor, where the executive offices were located.

Strangely, neither Spider nor Valentine was to be found. Spider's secretary ventured that he and Valentine had gone shopping. Of all the bizarre ideas, Billy thought; gone shopping *where,* she'd like to know, when Scruples was the shopper's chief mecca in the world? Frustrated once more but clinging doggedly to her good temper—probably they'd gone to buy Vito a victory present, something you couldn't find in a woman's store—Billy decided to tour her domain, as she often did, pretending that she was an out-of-town visitor seeing it for the first time. But no sooner had she begun to drift as inconspicuously as possible through the ground floor of Scruples, conjuring up the mind-set of a tourist from Pittsburgh, than she was besieged by a dozen women, some of them acquaintances, some total strangers. Each one of them wanted to share vicariously in Vito's Oscar by congratulating her, by being able to go home and say to as many friends as possible, "I told Billy Orsini how thrilled I was for her and Vito today." Instinctively, with polite smiles scattered in every direction, Billy fled to her own office and locked the door behind her.

Billy sat at her desk and considered the situation. She couldn't possibly go home for hours; she didn't feel like doing a Joan Didion and taking her classic Bentley on a long freeway drive to nowhere, so clearly she had to remain sequestered in here simply because she couldn't face the barrage of women downstairs. Wouldn't another woman, on a similar winning day, have stayed to bask in the generous, largely well-meant babble of goodwill from which she had just run away?

Damn it to hell, would she *ever* stop being shy, Billy asked herself, finally admitting why she was unable to enjoy compliments and congratulations without painful self-consciousness. She'd had good reason to be shy while she'd been growing up, a chubby, embarrassingly dressed, motherless poor relation of all the aristocratic and financially secure Winthrops of Boston, exposed to a score of happily adjusted cousins who, at their kindest, ignored her. She'd had more than good reason to be shy when she'd been sent off to Emery Academy, an exclusive boarding school for future debutantes, where she had spent six unendingly cruel, searingly lonely years as the designated outsider and freak of the class, a girl of five feet ten inches who weighed two hundred and eighteen pounds.

But then she had spent a magical year in Paris and returned, thin and finally grown into possession of her dark and dominating beauty, returned to go to New York and work as a secretary for Ellis Ikehorn, the mysterious multimillionaire whose Ikehorn Enterprises owned businesses all over the world. She had made the very first friend of her life, Jessica Thorpe, with whom she shared an apartment. Jessica lived in New York now, but Billy still spoke twice weekly on the phone to one of her only two real women friends in the world. Dolly Moon was the other.

Two close women friends, Billy mused, not much for thirty-five years. When she was twenty-one she had married Ellis Ikehorn, and from that day until his stroke seven years later, she and Ellis had led a life of international travel during which Billy, with her staggering sense of style and princely jewels, had become a fixture on the Best Dressed List. When they weren't roving on business they settled for pleasure at their villa at Cap Ferrat, they visited their ranch in Brazil, they stayed weeks at a time in London in their suite at Claridges, then flew off to their seaside house in Barbados or the manor house of their vineyard in the Napa Valley. Their New York headquarters were in their Sherry Netherland tower apartment; their photographs appeared constantly in scores of magazines, they were among the few who had entree into the Olympian level of society around the globe, it would seem that they had dozens of friends. However, no one but Ellis and Billy ever penetrated to the truth behind the screen of the stardust of privilege that radiated across their life to its single important reality: the closeness of their relationship was the only thing that mattered to them. Entertaining and being entertained, they never made a single new friendship that really mattered, for no one really caught their attention but each other. The magic circle they created of their life, as surely as it protected them, kept other people severely out.

When Ellis had the stroke that incapacitated him in 1970, Billy had just turned twenty-eight. For the next five years, until his death, she had lived almost as a recluse in a Bel Air fortress where all life gravitated around the paralyzed man. Her contacts with other women were limited to the members of her exercise class, women whose poorly concealed curiosity about her had warned her off any possibility of a deeper friendship. Yet, Billy thought, naturally they had been curious, for had she not still been a freak? A supremely well-dressed, thin, and beautiful freak whose wealth actually created her freakishness?

Face it, she just didn't fit into any of the groups that formed among the women of this one-industry town. She was too preoccupied with her dying husband to join in their gossipy, dressy luncheons, which were often based on the excuse of planning a charity ball. She didn't belong with the set formed by the wives of studio executives in which each woman's position was totally determined by her husband's power in the film business, a fierce Hollywood version of Washington, D.C.'s, political wives pecking order. She wasn't remotely a member of the guerilla wives, the early-thirtyish, firmly fleshed, desperately calculating beauties who had married for money, who had signed prenuptial contracts that eliminated a division of community property, whose chief interest in life was collecting jewelry for resale in case their already-twice-divorced husbands dumped them. And she would never make a friend among the handful of women writers, producers, and stars of the film business who respected only their working peers and had no time for civilians.

She might have discovered potential friends in Hancock Park or Pasadena, Billy thought, where the quietly elegant, old-money set lived, rarely deigning to cross to the "Westside," where all the movie money settled; but even without knowing them she was sure they'd be California versions of those conservative, predictable Winthrop cousins who had made her childhood so miserable.

When Ellis had died and she had been released from her solitude, rather than accepting the role of the new widow and extra woman, she had thrown herself obsessively into making a success of Scruples, until, two years later, she had married Vito and been immediately caught up in the whirl of making *Mirrors*. She hadn't been shy with Dolly Moon when they met, because Dolly had no idea of who she was and didn't let it make a difference when she found out.

Dolly and Jessica. Two true, eternal women friends out of a lifetime. Perhaps that wasn't really such a low number. Perhaps it was about average, perhaps most women fooled themselves about how staunch their good friends were? Billy put her feet on her desk and hugged her knees. She was just feeling like a misfit because this day, which was to have started with her telling Vito about their baby, had gone so abruptly and immediately off course. She was a fool to remember the ghosts of so many lost and lonely years, to allow them to intrude on the wonder of her new life. Her aunt Cornelia would have told her to pull up her socks, Billy reflected, as she swung her feet back to the floor and bent over her desk, where there was more than enough work to keep her busy until the coast was clear back home. She was glad to have the work to distract her a little from feeling the growing feverish ache to be with Vito, to have his full attention, to lie in his arms and tell him her news and watch the happiness on his face, to get him off the fucking phone!

As she drove up to the gatehouse at five-thirty, one of the gatemen assured Billy that the television people had just left. But some other visitors had arrived, he added, people Mr. Orsini had told them to admit.

Who in holy hell could they be, Billy asked herself in a wave of disappointment and irritation. It was evening, she had been gone for more than four hours, the business day was finished even for Oscar winners. Visitors! She'd throw the pack of them out, whoever they were, double quick! She didn't care if it was Wasserman, Nicholson, Redford, and the ghosts of Louis B. Mayer, Irving Thalberg, and Jean Hersholt, with Harry Cohn and the brothers Warner thrown in for good measure. She'd have them out of her house!

Billy glared incredulously at two dozen cars parked in front of the house, threw open the front door, and stood riveted at the sight and sound of at least forty people talking and laughing at the top of their voices, beginning to fill up the two living rooms. She refused to believe what she was seeing. A roaring party, what promised to be a hurricane of a party, was taking place and Vito was the center of it. From the mob she spotted Fifi Hill, the director of *Mirrors,* the stars, the editors, the composer, and a score of others who'd been involved in the making of the movie from the beginning. And behind her, pushing their way through the door, came more people, all crew and cast members, every one of whom kissed and hugged her quickly before rushing over to Vito.

Billy pushed through the crowd until she reached her husband.

"How . . . why . . . Vito, what the hell . . . ?"

"Darling! About time! I wondered what happened to you. We're having the wrap party for the picture—remember the first one was cut short, so I had an inspiration and decided to have it over again. Everybody's still high as kites. Don't worry about the food, Janet called Chasen's and told them to send over everything. Isn't this a great idea? Listen, I've got to find Fifi, I still haven't congratulated him on getting Best Director."

"You do that," Billy said to the spot where Vito had been standing. Had Alexander the Great ever been as blazingly exuberant, as triumphant, as consumed with energy and excitement after any of his victories, she wondered, following her bold, bronzed Caesar of a husband with her eyes as he dashed into the throng. She had married Vito out of passionate love, hardly knowing him. Only after their marriage had she realized how much of his own passion was reserved for his work, how obsessed he was by filmmaking. Now, after a difficult year of compromise and adjustment, Billy thought she had come to terms with it. Yes, she certainly *had* come to terms with it, she assured herself as she slipped through dozens of people to reach the staircase; she accepted him exactly as he was, and tonight was as it should be, a blaring, riotous celebration of a unique achievement no one but Vito had believed possible for a low-budget movie.

As Billy threaded her way across her sitting room she noticed teetering piles of unopened telegrams tossed between the baskets of flowers that covered every surface, including the floor. Tomorrow they'd all be sent to Vito's office and opened, she determined, tomorrow they'd open all the cards on the flowers. But right now she'd put on something festive and join the party. Sooner or later the guests would have to leave and she'd be alone with Vito and the only other news that could possibly matter on this day of jubilation and rejoicing.

Vito and Billy were wearily saying good-bye to their last guests when one of the gatemen called the house to say that another person had arrived, asking for Mr. Orsini.

"Tell whoever it is I'm sorry but it's too late, Joe, the party's over," Vito said. "*What*? What? You're sure? No, it's all right, let the car through."

"Totally impossible," Billy muttered, "even the catering crew on the picture was here tonight. Vito, make an excuse, don't dare let anyone in. If I can find the strength to climb the stairs I'm going to bed, I'm beat."

"Go on, darling, I'll handle it."

Ten minutes later, after Billy had stripped off her clothes, put on a robe, and was starting to take off her makeup, Vito entered her dressing room and closed the door behind him.

"Who on earth was it?" Billy asked, drooping with exhaustion in front of the mirror.

"It's . . . a long story."

There was a note of utter disbelief and shock in Vito's voice that told her this had nothing to do with a guest who was too late for the wrap party.

She spun around and looked at him searchingly. "It's bad news, isn't it?"

"Don't look so frightened, Billy. This isn't about us, this isn't about you."

"Then it's about you! Vito, *what's wrong*?"

"Oh, Jesus," he said, dropping onto a chair and looking past her, his eyes seeming to focus on the wall. "I've never told you so many things about me . . . it's unforgivable. From the second we got married I've been so fucking preoccupied with the picture, not a minute to spare, I kept promising myself that as soon as all this craziness was over I'd tell you the whole story, the minute we had some peaceful time together. . . . I should have told you the day we met but it was the last thing on my mind, it didn't seem to matter then because I didn't know we were going to get married . . . the only thing that I could think of was the present, the past was the past, and then everything happened between us so quickly. . . ."

"Vito, if you don't get to the point—"

"My daughter's here."

"You can't have a daughter," Billy said flatly.

"I can. I do. I was married before. It lasted just over a year. We were divorced and she's lived with her mother ever since."

The shock of his words kept Billy's voice almost even. She struggled so hard to keep from shouting that she almost whispered.

"A child. I wouldn't care if you'd had ten other wives, but a child, Vito? In the year that we've been married, are you trying to make me believe that there was never, *ever* a single minute when you could have told me this, for Christ's sake? My God, so what if you've been divorced, but a child! You must be insane. We've had hours and hours, you could have told me during any one of hundreds of meals, before we went to bed, when we got up in the morning . . . don't give me that shit about never having peaceful time!"

"I was always going to tell you, it just didn't happen," he mumbled.

"No way, Vito, give me a fucking break. You let it go too long and then you didn't want to rock the boat. You should have told me before we got married, it wouldn't have made any difference; but now, springing it on me now? I just can't believe this is happening. What's her name?"

"Gigi."

"Why did she come here tonight?" Billy asked, fighting the desire to scream. She had to remain calm because Vito looked as if he were going to faint. "Because of the Oscar?"

"Her mother . . . her mother died. . . . She was buried . . . yesterday. In New York. Gigi sent me a telegram. It must be with all the others. When she didn't hear anything from me she got on a plane and just . . . came."

"Where is she now?"

"In the kitchen. I gave her a glass of milk and some cake and told her to wait until I'd talked to you."

"How old is she?"

"Sixteen."

"Sixteen," Billy screeched. "Sixteen! My God, Vito, that's not a child, that's a teenager! Practically a woman. Don't you know anything about sixteen-year-olds? Vito, get me a brandy, a large brandy. Never mind, just bring the bottle." Billy scrubbed off the cream that was still on her face and hurried toward the door.

"Billy . . ."

"What?"

"Shouldn't we talk more before you meet Gigi?"

"About what, Vito?" Billy said furiously. "She wouldn't be here if she had another place to go, would she? She hasn't seen you in at least a year because I'd know if she had, so if she flew all the way across the country without even hearing a word from you, you've got to be her only refuge, wouldn't you say?"

"Oh, Christ! Billy, you're not giving me any credit for anything, this is an old story, it was over fifteen years ago and you're being as judgmental as if it had just happened."

"I'm being realistic," Billy said viciously. "It *has* just happened—to me." Billy turned and quickly made her way down to the big kitchen. She hesitated only a second before pushing open the double doors, hearing Vito still on the staircase.

A small figure was sitting very still on a high stool behind the big butcher block table. In front of her were an empty glass and an empty plate. When Billy walked in Gigi looked up and slid off the stool, standing wordlessly, without moving. Billy's first thought was that Vito must be wrong, she didn't look old enough to be a teenager. And she didn't look like Vito. What was visible of her face through a mess of plain brown hair was delicate, oddball, somehow immediately and indefinably elfin. In the several baggy, rather ragged sweaters she wore layered indiscriminately over her jeans she seemed to be a waif, a scrap, a sprite, blown into this grand, bright kitchen by a teasing gust of wind.

Gigi remained still and speechless for a long minute, enduring Billy's inspection. In her straightforward stance, poised squarely on her cowboy boots, standing as straight and tall as she could. There was nothing of apology nor of defiance yet somehow, tiny and nondescript as she was, she had presence, immediate, undeniable presence. She was tired and very sad but not pathetic, she was alone but not needy. Something about her was deeply interesting. Gigi's eyes met Billy's, Gigi smiled—and a piece of Billy's heart she didn't know she possessed fell in love.

**To be continued
in Judith Krantz's SCRUPLES TWO,
to be published in
hardcover in Summer 1992.**